Lawrence Sanders

THREE

COMPLETE

NOVELS

Lawrence Sanders

THREE

COMPLETE

NOVELS

McNally's Caper

McNally's Trial

McNally's Puzzle

G. P. PUTNAM'S SONS | New York

G. P. Putnam's Sons
Publishers Since 1838
a member of
Penguin Putnam Inc.
375 Hudson Street
New York, NY 10014

LIBRARY OF CONGRESS CATALOGING-IN-PUBLICATION DATA

Sanders, Lawrence, date.
[Novels. Selections]
Three complete novels / Lawrence Sanders.
p.   cm.
Contents: McNally's caper—McNally's trial—McNally's puzzle.
ISBN 0-399-14435-8
1. McNally, Archy (Fictitious character)—Fiction. 2. Private investigators
—Florida—Palm Beach—Fiction. 3. Detective and mystery stories, American.
4. Palm Beach (Fla.)—Fiction.
I. Title.
PS3569.A5125A6   1998   98-14551 CIP
813´.54—dc21

Printed in the United States of America

10 9 8 7 6 5 4 3 2 1

This book is printed on acid-free paper. ∞

Book design by Patrice Sheridan

Contents

Lawrence Sanders

THREE

COMPLETE

NOVELS

McNally's Caper

1

After a great deal of heavy reflection I have come to the conclusion that everyone is nuts. And I mean *everyone,* not just a sprinkling of ding-a-lings.

You think me a misanthrope? Listen to this . . .

I am the chief (and sole member) of the Discreet Inquiries Department of McNally & Son, Attorney-at-Law. (My father is the Attorney, I am the Son.) We represent some very prestigious clients—and a scurvy few—in the Town of Palm Beach. Occasionally they request the services of a private and prudent investigator rather than take their problems to the police and risk seeing their tribulations luridly described in a supermarket tabloid, alongside a story headlined "Elvis Lands in UFO!"

One of our commercial clients is a sinfully luxe jewelry store on Worth Avenue. They had recently been plagued by a shoplifter who was boosting a choice selection of merchandise. Not their most costly baubles, of course; those were locked away in vaults and shown only in private. But they were losing a number of less expensive items—brooches, rings, bracelets, necklaces—that were on public display.

Their concealed video camera soon revealed the miscreant. They were shocked, *shocked* to recognize one of their best customers, a wealthy widow who dropped at least a hundred grand annually in legitimate purchases. I shall not reveal her name because you would immediately recognize it. Not wishing to prosecute such a valued patron, the jewelry store brought its distressing predicament to McNally & Son, and I was given the task of ending the lady's pilfering without enraging her to the extent that she would purchase her diamond tiaras elsewhere, perhaps at Wal-Mart or Home Depot.

It was a nice piece of work and I started by learning all I could about the kleptomaniacal matron. I consulted Consuela Garcia first. Connie is employed as social secretary to Lady Cynthia Horowitz, possibly the wealthiest of our chatelaines. Connie is my inamorata and au courant with all the latest Palm Beach rumors, scandals, and skeletons that have not yet emerged from the closet.

I also phoned Lolly Spindrift, the gossip columnist on one of our local rags. He has an encyclopedic knowledge of the peccadilloes, kinks, and outré personal habits of even our most august residents.

From these two fonts of impropriety, if not of wisdom, I learned that the shoplifter in her younger years (several decades ago) had been an actress. Not a first-magnitude star, but a second-echelon player who had never quite made it to the top. I mean that in films she always lost the hero to the leading lady and in TV sitcoms she invariably played the wisecracking but sympathetic roommate. She did very well financially, I'm sure, but I doubt if sophomores ever Scotch-taped her photo to dormitory walls.

Then, her career in decline, she had the great good sense to marry a moneyed business executive whose corporation reaped satisfying profits by producing plastic place mats imprinted with classic scenes such as the Parthenon and Las Vegas at night. Upon his retirement the childless but apparently happy couple moved to Palm Beach. He died five years later on the tennis court while playing a third set in 104° heat, and his widow inherited a bundle.

Having learned all I needed to know about the lady in question, I had a videocassette made of all the snippets of tape taken by the jewelry store's hidden TV cameras. The subject was easily recognizable and clearly shown slipping glittering items into her capacious handbag. She did it so deftly, so nonchalantly, I could only conclude she had long practiced the craft.

I decided my best strategy was a "cold call," descending upon her suddenly without making an appointment and giving her the opportunity to prepare a defense. And so on a warmish evening in mid-September I tootled my flag-red Miata down the coast to the Via

Palma. The lady's home turned out to be a faux Spanish hacienda with the most spectacular landscaping I had ever seen.

The door was opened by a uniformed maid who accepted my business card and advised me to wait—outside. In a few moments the door was reopened and the matron herself stood before me, clad in hostess pajamas of ginger-colored silk.

"Yes, Mr. McNally," she said, pleasantly enough, "what's this all about?"

I mentioned the name of the client represented by my law firm and told her I wished to discuss a personal matter of some importance. She hesitated briefly, then asked me in. She led the way to a small sitting room where a television set was playing. And there, on the screen, was the lady herself, thirty years younger. I wondered if that was how she spent her evenings: watching reruns of ancient sitcoms in which she had performed.

She was a striking woman with a proud posture and complete self-possession. Her features had the tight, glacial look that bespoke a face-lift, and her figure was so trim and youthful that I imagined breast implants, a tummy tuck, and a rump elevation had been included in a package deal.

She switched off the TV and, without asking me to be seated, looked at me inquiringly. There was no way I could pussyfoot, but as gently as I could I explained that her favorite jewelry store was well aware of her shoplifting. If she doubted that, I said, I had brought along a video-cassette that showed her in action.

I didn't know what to expect: furious denial, tears, hysteria, perhaps even a physical assault on yrs. truly. What I received was a welcome surprise: a really brilliant smile.

"Hidden TV cameras, I suppose," she said.

I nodded.

"That's not fair," she said with a charming pout. "Would you care for a drink, Mr. McNally?"

"I would indeed, thank you, ma'am."

Five minutes later we were seated on a mauve velvet couch, sipping excellent kit royales, and discussing her criminal career like civilized people. I was immensely relieved.

"I suppose you think me a kleptomaniac," she said easily.

"The thought had occurred to me," I acknowledged.

She shook her head and artfully coiffed white curls bobbed about. "Not so," she said. "I did not have a deprived childhood. I never lacked for a loving mate in my life. I have no feeling of insecurity nor do I desire to seek revenge against a cruel, unfeeling world."

"Then *why?*" I asked, truly perplexed.

"Boredom," she said promptly. "Shoplifting gives me a thrill. It's such a naughty thing to do, you see. And at my age I must battle ennui as vigorously as I do arthritis. Can you understand that?"

I laughed. I *loved* this splendid woman. "Of course I understand," I said. "But I'm afraid your motive, no matter how reasonable it may seem to you and me, would not constitute a convincing legal defense."

"What is it the jewelry store wants?"

"Payment for or return of the items you have stolen. I presume you still have them?"

"I do."

"What they *don't* want," I went on, "what they emphatically do not wish is to lose you as a customer. They value your patronage."

"As well they should," she said. "I spend a mint there. But they are very agreeable people, very eager to please. I should hate to go elsewhere for my trinkets."

We looked at each other.

"You strike me as a very clever young man, Mr. McNally," she said. "Can you suggest a solution?"

"Yes, I can," I said without hesitation. "Continue shopping there. At the same time resume the depredations that relieve your boredom. But grant permission to the store to bill you monthly for the merchandise you steal."

She laughed delightedly. "A wonderful solution!" she cried.

"It won't spoil it for you to know that your thefts are being observed and you will be charged for them?"

She lifted her chin. "I am an actress," she said with great dignity. "I know how to pretend."

"Excellent," I said, finishing my drink and rising. "I am sure our client will be delighted with the arrangement."

She escorted me to the door and we clasped hands.

"Do come see me again," she said.

"Thank you," I said. "I certainly shall. It's been a delightful visit."

"Hasn't it?" she said and leaned forward to kiss my cheek.

I drove home in a sportive mood. I was more convinced than ever that goofiness was engulfing the world, but I also admitted that if everyone acted in a sensible, logical fashion there would be little gainful employment for your humble correspondent.

I arrived at the McNally manse at about ten o'clock. I pulled into our three-car garage between my father's black Lexus and mother's antique wood-bodied Ford station wagon. The lights in mon père's study were still ablaze, and when I entered the house through the back door I saw the oak portal to his sanctum was ajar. It was his signal that he deigned to receive visitors. That evening, I knew, he was awaiting a report on my confrontation with the piratical widow.

He was seated behind his magisterial desk and, as usual, there was a glass of port at his elbow. And, as usual, he was smoking one of his silver-banded James Upshall pipes. And, as usual, he was reading one of his leather-bound volumes of Dickens. I admired his perseverance. He was determined to plow his way through that author's entire oeuvre, and I could only hope he survived long enough to succeed.

He looked up when I entered and put his book aside. He invited me to pour myself a glass of port. I respectfully declined, not daring to tell him that I thought the last case he had bought was on the musty side. But I did relax in one of his club chairs and delivered an abbreviated account of my meeting with the bored shoplifter.

He did not laugh aloud but one of his hirsute eyebrows rose a good half-inch and he stroked his guardsman's mustache with a knuckle, a sure sign that he was mightily amused.

"A win-win outcome, Archy," he commented. "Well done."

"Thank you, sir."

Then he was silent and I knew he had slipped into his pondering mode. I have mentioned several times in previous tales that my father is a worldclass muller, always meditating before making any meaningful pronouncement or taking any significant action. After all, he is an attorney and knows the dangers of hasty words and decisions. But is it absolutely necessary to ruminate for three minutes before resolving to add a drop of Tabasco to one's deviled egg?

"Archy," he said finally, "are you acquainted with Griswold Forsythe the Second?"

"Yes, sir, I am," I replied. "The all-time champion bore of Palm Beach."

"And his son, Griswold Forsythe the Third?"

"I know him also. A chip off the old blockhead."

Father grimaced. He did not like me to jest about the clients of Mc-Nally & Son. He felt that since their fees paid for our steak au poivre we should accord them at least a modicum of respect.

"The senior Forsythe came to the office this afternoon," mein papa continued. "His problem is somewhat akin to the case you have just concluded."

I groaned. "He's so antiquated he remembers the two-pants suit. Don't tell me the old gaffer has become a shoplifter."

"No, he is not a thief but he suspects someone in his home may be. He claims several items of value have disappeared."

"Such as?"

"A first edition Edgar Allan Poe. A large, unset cushion-cut emerald belonging to his wife. A Georgian silver soup ladle. A small Benin bronze. An original Picasso lithograph. And other things."

"The thief has expensive tastes," I observed.

"Yes," father agreed, "and Forsythe is convinced he or she is a family member or one of the household staff, all live-in servants who have been with him for years."

"But the thefts are a recent development?"

My liege nodded. "Naturally Forsythe doesn't wish to take the matter to the authorities. He would much prefer a discreet investigation."

This time I moaned. "That means I will have to spend a great deal of time prowling about the Forsythe castle, that ugly heap of granite north of Lady Horowitz's estate. How does Mr. Forsythe propose to account for my presence? Does he intend to tell family and staff what I'm up to?"

"Oh no, definitely not. He will be the only one who knows your true purpose. As you may be aware, he has a rather extensive private library. He suggests that he tell the others you have been employed to prepare a catalog of his books."

I considered that a moment. "It might work," I admitted. "But is he absolutely certain the thief is not an outsider? A deliveryman perhaps. The guy who trims his shrubbery."

"I asked him that, but he believes it would be impossible. When workers are allowed inside they are always accompanied by the housekeeper. And some of the missing items were hidden. The Benin bronze, for instance, was not on display but placed far back on a closet shelf in Forsythe's study. And the unset emerald was in a suede pouch tucked into the bottom drawer of his wife's dresser. Family members and staff may have been aware of their existence and site, but strangers could not know and had no opportunity to search. Mr. Forsythe is expecting you tomorrow morning at nine o'clock."

"Nine?" I said indignantly. "Father, I'm not fully awake by then."

"Try," His Majesty said and picked up his Dickens.

I climbed the creaking stairs to my mini-suite on the third floor. It was hardly lavish—small sitting room, bedroom, bathroom—but I had no complaints; it was my cave and I prized it. The rent was particularly attractive. Zip.

I poured myself a wee marc from my liquor supply stored within a battered sea chest at the foot of my bed. Then I lighted an English Oval (only my third of the day) and plopped down behind the ramshackle desk in my sitting room. I donned reading glasses, for although I will not be thirty-seven years old until March of next year, my peepers are about sixty-five and require specs for close-up work.

I keep a journal of my discreet inquiries, jotting down things I have learned, heard, assumed, or imagined. The scribblings, added to almost daily when I am working on a case, serve as a reminder of matters important and matters trivial.

That night I wrote finis to the story of the shoplifting widow and started a fresh page with my latest assignment: discovering who in the ménage of Griswold Forsythe II was swiping all that swell stuff. I thought the inquiry would be as much of a drag as the victim and his tiresome son. I reckoned the chances were good that the allegedly purloined items had simply been misplaced. For instance, I still haven't found my Mickey Mouse beach towel although I am fairly certain it hasn't been stolen.

I went to bed that night still musing on the looniness of the human condition. My investigation of the Forsythe thieveries was to prove how right I was. But the craziness I uncovered turned out to be no ha-ha matter. It was scary and before it was finished I began to believe the entire world was one enormous acorn academy—with no doctors in attendance.

2

"I was a dirty old man at the age of nine," Griswold Forsythe II pronounced in his churchy voice and waited for my laugh.

I obliged, fighting valiantly against an urge to nod off.

"I see these young girls in their short skirts," he droned on. "Tanned legs that start under their chin and go on forever. And I feel a great sadness. Not because I shall never have them but because I know their beauty will wither. Age insists on taking its inevitable toll."

"Mr. Forsythe," I said, "about your missing treasures . . ."

"But then," he continued to preach, "age does have its compensations. I'll tell you something about death, Archy: one grows into it. I don't mean you begin to die the day you're born; everyone knows that. But as the years dwindle down you gradually come to terms with your own mortality. And, in my case, begin to look forward to dissolution with curiosity and, I must admit, a certain degree of relish."

"How long, O Lord, how long?" I prayed silently. And you know, the odd thing about this garrulous fogy was that he was not all that ancient. Not much older than my father, I reckoned; I knew his son was about my age. Yet the two Forsythes, II and III, had brought codgerism to new heights—or depths. I shall not attempt to reproduce their speech exactly on these pages; the plummy turgidities would give you a sudden attack of the Z's.

And not only in their speech, but both father and son affected a grave and stately demeanor. No sudden bursts of laughter from those two melancholics, no public manifestations of delight, surprise, or almost any other human emotion. I often wondered what might happen if their rusty clockwork slipped a gear.

"Mr. Forsythe," I tried again, desperately this time, "about the stolen items . . ."

"Ah, yes," he said. "Distressing. And we can't let it continue, can we?"

"No, sir."

"Distressing," he repeated. "Most distressing."

We were seated in his library, a gloomy chamber lined with floor-to-ceiling oak cases of books, most of them in matching sets. There was a handsome ladder on wheels that enabled one to reach the upper shelves, but I couldn't believe he or anyone else in his ménage had read even a fraction of those thousands of volumes.

"I suggest you make this room your headquarters," he instructed. "Your combat center, so to speak. Feel free to come and go as you please. Speak to anyone you wish: family members and staff."

"They are not aware of my assignment?"

"They are not," he said firmly. "Not even my wife. So I expect you to conduct your investigation with a high degree of circumspection."

"Naturally," I said, reflecting that I had been called many things in my lifetime but circumspect was not one of them. "Mr. Forsythe, could you give me a brief rundown on your household."

He looked at me, puzzled. "The people, you mean?" he asked.

Did he think I meant the number of salad forks? "Yes, sir," I said. "The persons in residence."

"Myself and my wife Constance, of course. Our unmarried daughter Geraldine. Our son, whom I believe you know, and his wife Sylvia and their young daughter Lucy. The staff consists of Mrs. Nora Bledsoe, our housekeeper and majordomo, so to speak. Her son, Anthony, serves as butler and houseman. Two maids, Sheila and Fern. The chef's name is Zeke Grenough. We also employ a full-time gardener, Rufino Diaz, but he doesn't dwell on the premises."

"Quite an establishment," I commented.

"Is it?" he said, mildly surprised that everyone didn't live so well-attended. "When my parents were alive we had a live-in staff of twelve. But of course they did a great deal of entertaining. I rarely entertain. Dislike it, in fact. Too much chatter."

I was tempted to ask, "You mean you can't get a word in edgewise?" But I didn't, of course.

"I'm sure I'll get them all sorted out," I told him.

"And when may I expect results?"

"No way of telling, Mr. Forsythe. But I'm as eager as you to bring this matter to a speedy conclusion. And now, with your permission, I'd like to take a look around the grounds."

"Of course," he said. "Learn the lay of the land, so to speak, eh?"

I could have made a coarse rejoinder to that but restrained myself.

Griswold Forsythe II led me to a back door that allowed exit to the rear acres of the estate.

"When you have completed your inspection," he said, "I suggest you request Mrs. Bledsoe to give you a tour of the house. There are many hallways, many rooms, many nooks and crannies. We don't want you getting lost, do we?"

"We surely don't," I said, repressing a terrible desire to kick his shins. Because, you see, I suspected he didn't want me strolling unescorted through his home. Which made me wonder what it was he wished to keep hidden.

The Forsythe estate wasn't quite Central Park but it was lavish even by Palm Beach standards. The landscaping was somewhat formal for my taste but I could not deny it was attractive and well-groomed. There was a mini-orchard of orange, grapefruit and lime trees. Birdhouses were everywhere, some seemingly designed to mimic the Forsythe mansion in miniature. I thought that a bit much but apparently the birds approved.

I was examining a curious lichen growing on the trunk of an oak so venerable it was decrepit when a young miss popped out from behind a nearby palm and shouted, "Boo!"

I was not at all startled. "Boo, yourself," I replied. "What is the meaning of this unseemly behavior—leaping out at innocent visitors and yelping, 'Boo!'?"

She giggled.

I am not expert at estimating the age of children. They are all kids to me until they become youngsters. This particular specimen appeared to be about eight years old, with a possible error of plus or minus three. She was an uncommonly fetching child with flaxen hair that tumbled to her shoulders. Heavy braces encircled her upper teeth but she had the self-assurance of a woman quintuple her age.

"What's your name?" she demanded.

"My name is Archibald McNally," I replied. "But it would give me great pleasure if you called me Archy."

Silence. "Don't you want to know my name?" she finally asked.

"I can guess," I said. "You are Lucy Forsythe and you live here."

"How did you know that?"

"I know everything," I told her.

"No, you don't," she said. "Do you want to hear a dirty word?"

I sighed. "All right."

"Mud," she said and laughed like a maniac. I did, too.

"You're very pretty," she said.

"Thank you," I said. "Not as pretty as you."

"Do you have a girlfriend?"

"Sort of," I answered. "Do you have a boyfriend?"

"Sort of."

"Why aren't you in school today, Lucy?"

"I'm sick," she said and giggled again.

"Nothing catching I hope."

"Well, I'm not really sick but I said I was because I didn't feel like going to school today. You won't tell anyone, will you?"

"Not me," I said. "I know how to keep a secret."

"Hey," she said, "want to see my secret place?"

"I'd like that very much."

She was wearing a pink two-piece playsuit and a matching hair ribbon. She was a gangly child with a lovely apricot suntan and a deliciously gawky way of moving, flinging arms and legs about as if she had not yet mastered the art of controlling those elongated appendages.

She took my hand and tugged me along. We stepped off the bricked walk and slipped into a treed area so thickly planted that sunlight cast a dappled pattern onto ground cover sprinkled with small white flowers I could not identify. Then we came into a small open area hardly larger than a bathmat but carpeted with bright green moss.

"This belongs to me," Lucy said proudly. "It's my secret place. Isn't it nice?"

"It is indeed," I agreed. "What do you do here?"

"Mostly I just sit and think. Sometimes I eat a sandwich."

"Do you invite many guests?"

She looked at me shyly. "You're the first."

"I'm honored," I said. "When you come here to think, what do you think about?"

I wasn't trying to pump the child, you know; just making conversation I hoped would interest her. I know she interested me. I thought her alert and knowledgeable beyond her years.

She considered my question. "Well, sometimes I come here when things get noisy at home."

"Noisy?"

She looked away. "They start shouting. That scares me. I'm afraid they'll kill each other."

"I don't think so, Lucy. Grown-ups have different opinions and occasionally they begin arguing and their voices get louder."

"Then they send me out of the room," she said. "They always say, 'Little pitchers have big ears.' I don't think my ears are so big, do you?"

"Of course not. You have beautiful ears. It's just a saying, like 'Children should be seen and not heard.' I bet you've been told that one, too."

She stared at me in astonishment. "How did you know?"

"I told you I know everything. Lucy, I've enjoyed your company and I thank you for showing me your secret place. But I've got to get back to the house and go to work."

"What kind of work?"

"I'm preparing a catalog of your grandfather's library."

"What's a catalog?"

"A list of all the books he owns."

"There's an awful lot of them."

"There certainly are. That's why I've got to begin. Would you like to come back with me?"

"No," she said. "I'll just sit here and think."

I nodded and started away.

"Archy," she called, and I turned back. "Will you be my friend?" she asked.

I said, "That would make me very happy."

"What we could do sometime," she said, suddenly excited, "is have a little picnic here. Zeke will make us some sandwiches."

"That sounds like fun," I said. "Let's do it."

I left her then. Curious child. Lonely child.

I emerged from the wooded area and stood a moment on the back lawn, examining the Forsythe mansion. I had been correct in describing it to my father as a castle. I have never seen such an excess of turrets, battlements, parapets, and embrasures. All that hideous pile of stone lacked was a moat and drawbridge. The whole thing looked as if the architect had expected the Visigoths to descend on the Town of Palm Beach at any moment.

The rear entrance to the Forsythes' granite shack consisted of double doors. The inner was solidly planked and fitted with a stout lock. That portal was wide open. The exterior door, closed, was merely a screen in an aluminum frame.

Although Mr. Forsythe had granted me permission to come and go as I pleased, I thought it best to announce my arrival and so I rapped lightly on the jamb of the screen. No response. I thought that odd since I could hear a muted conversation within. I knocked more vigorously. Still no answer, but I became aware that the volume of the dialogue was rising.

Eavesdropping is one of my minor vices, and I moved closer to the screen in an effort to hear what was being expressed so forcibly. But I could make out no words, only angry voices. One, male, seemed to be supplicating. The other was female, furious and scornful. I recalled what Lucy had just told me of being frightened by the loud arguments of grown-ups.

Then I heard what had to be a violent slap: someone's palm smacked against another's face. This was followed by a woman's gasp and wail. I delayed no longer but opened the screen door and shouted, "Hallo, hallo! Anyone home?"

Silence. And then, a moment later, a woman approached from what appeared to be a tiled corridor. She was sturdily constructed, wide through shoulders, bosom and hips. I could not get a good look at her features for she was holding a hand to her right cheek.

"Good morning!" I said cheerily. "My name is Archibald McNally. I hope Mr. Forsythe informed you that I'll be to-ing and fro-ing while I catalog his library."

She nodded. "Yes, sir," she said in what I can only describe as a strangled voice, "he told us. I am Mrs. Nora Bledsoe, the Forsythes' housekeeper."

"Pleased to make your acquaintance, ma'am," I said and held out my right hand, knowing that to shake it she would have to uncover her face. She hesitated an instant then did what I had hoped. I saw at once that she had been the slapee, for her right cheek was reddened.

"I've been taking a look at your bully greenery," I said breezily. "Mr. Forsythe suggested you would be willing to give me a tour of the interior."

It took her half a mo to regain her composure. I could understand that; she had just taken a good clop to the jaw and it had rattled her.

"Yes, of course," she said finally. She tried a brave smile but it didn't work. "If you'll follow me, Mr. McNally, I'll show you everything."

I doubted that but I willingly trailed after her. She was remarkably light on her feet for such a heavy woman. She was wearing a flowered shirtwaist dress and I noted her thick, jetty hair was drawn back and held with a silver filigreed pin.

"That's a handsome barrette, Mrs. Bledsoe," I said. "Is it an antique?"

She turned and I could see she was pleased. She reached back to touch it. "Oh yes," she said, "it's Victorian. Mr. and Mrs. Forsythe gave it to me as a birthday gift. I do like nice things."

"Don't we all," I said, and we both laughed. She ceased leading and we walked alongside each other, shoulders touching occasionally in the narrow hallways.

"I think we'll start at the top," she said, "and work our way down. From attic to dungeon."

"Dungeon?"

"That's what we call the basement area. Very dark and damp. Nothing but cobwebs and our wine racks."

"Cellars are rare in South Florida," I commented.

"Ours is supposed to be haunted," she said. "By the ghost of Mr. Forsythe's grandmother."

"Oh?" I said.

"She committed suicide."

"Ah," I said.

3

What a mazy mansion that was! As we traipsed from floor to floor, room to room, I became convinced that the architect had been totally deranged. Regal corridors led to naught but cramped window seats; artfully carved walnut doors opened to reveal a shallow linen press; some of the bedchambers were ballrooms and some were walk-in closets.

I had welcomed this inspection as an opportunity to spot a hidey-hole where the purloined works of art might be stashed. But it was hopeless; there were simply too many "nooks and crannies," as Mr. Forsythe had warned. It would take a regiment of snoops a month of Sundays to search that hodgepodge—and even then a cleverly concealed cache could remain hidden.

"An astounding home," I remarked to Mrs. Bledsoe.

"Well, it is a little unusual," she admitted. "I've been with the family for many years, and it took me two to learn where everything was and how to get about. Just last month I discovered a cupboard I didn't know existed. It was behind draperies in one of the guest bedrooms."

"And what was in it?" I asked eagerly.

"Old copies of *Liberty* magazine," she said.

We were on the third floor, or it might have been the second, when I heard harpsichord music coming from behind a closed door. I stopped to listen. I thought it might be Scarlatti or perhaps Jelly Roll Morton.

"That's Mrs. Sylvia playing," my guide explained. "The younger Mr. Forsythe's wife. She's very good."

"Would she mind if we intruded?"

"I'm sure she wouldn't."

She knocked once, pushed the door open, and we entered. It was a mid-sized chamber completely naked of any furnishings except for the bleached pine harpsichord and the bench before it. The seated woman stopped playing and looked up inquiringly.

"Mrs. Sylvia," the housekeeper said, "this gentleman is Archibald McNally who is preparing a catalog of Mr. Forsythe's library."

"Of course," the young lady said, rose and came sweeping forward, if one may sweep while wearing tight blue jeans and a snug T-shirt inscribed with Gothic lettering: *Amor vincit omnia*. Right on, Sylvia! She had the same flaxen hair as Lucy; the two could have been sisters instead of mother and daughter.

"Mr. McNally," she said, giving me a warm hand and an elfin smile, "welcome to the catacombs."

"A bit overwhelming," I confessed. "Please forgive this interruption."

"Not at all," she said. "I needed a break. Vivaldi is *so* difficult."

So much for Scarlatti and Jelly Roll Morton.

"I had the pleasure of meeting your daughter earlier this morning," I told her. "An entrancing child. We had a nice chat."

Her smile faded to be replaced—by what? I could not decipher that expression but I imagined I saw something cold and stony.

"You mustn't believe everything Lucy says," and her laugh was as tinny as the harpsichord. "She's quite imaginative."

"Children usually are," I agreed. "How long have you been playing?"

"Years," she said and turned to look at her instrument. "I made it."

"You didn't!"

"I did," she said, nodding. "Didn't I, Nora? It came in a kit but I put it together. It took ages."

"Good for you," I said. "I play tenor kazoo with a pickup jazz combo at my club but that's the extent of my musical talent."

She looked at me thoughtfully. "I'm sure you underestimate your talents, Mr. McNally. Do stop by again. Whenever you like."

"Thank you," I said. "I shall."

Mrs. Bledsoe and I continued our tour. But I was wearying. In truth, it was a dreary dwelling, a fitting abode for the Addams Family. I could understand why Lucy yearned for a sunlit place all her own.

I was given a brief peek into the haunted dungeon and then we returned to the kitchen, large enough to feed the 1st Marine Division. The entire staff had gathered, preparing for lunch. I was introduced to all, tried to remember names and faces, and failed miserably. They were pleasant enough except for Anthony, Mrs. Bledsoe's son, who seemed somewhat surly. And Fern, one of the maids, was apparently afflicted with a nonstop giggle.

The chef, Zeke Grenough, a diminutive man who wore a wire-rimmed pince-nez, was stirring a caldron of what smelled aromatically like squid stew. I hoped I might be invited to share their noontime repast, for I am hopelessly enamored of calamari in any form whatsoever. But no one urged me to remain and so I bid that lucky crew a polite adieu and departed.

I tooled the Miata south on Ocean Boulevard, my salivary glands working overtime as I reflected there was probably red wine in that stew and it would possibly be served over saffron rice. It was enough to make me whimper.

I pulled into the driveway of the lavish estate belonging to Lady Cynthia Horowitz and drove around to the rear. I entered the main house through the unlocked back door and went directly to the office of Consuela Garcia, social secretary and the lady with whom I am intimate and to whom, regrettably, I am inevitably unfaithful.

Connie, as usual, was on the phone but raised her face for a cheek kiss. I was happy to oblige. Then I flopped into the only visitor's chair available and listened with delight as my leman tore the hide off a florist whose last delivery of arrangements to the Horowitz home had wilted and shed petals not in days but within hours.

"In hours!" Connie shouted wrathfully. "Do you understand what I'm saying? Those flowers had rigor mortis when they arrived. Where did you find them—on graves?"

She listened a moment and seemed mollified. "I should think you would," she barked into the phone. "Get the replacements here by three o'clock or we cancel our account—is that clear? And go easy on the daisies. We're paying orchid prices for daisies?"

She slammed down the receiver and grinned at me. "I love to read the riot act to these banditos," she said. "They think that just because Lady C. has zillions she's a patsy. No way! How are you, hon?"

"Tip-top," I said. "Lunch?"

She shook her head. "No can do. We're planning a benefit dinner and I've got to get cracking on it."

"Benefit for what? Or whom?"

"Unwed mothers."

"Don't look at me like that, Connie," I said. "I'm not guilty."

"I wish I could be sure," she said. "Is that why you popped by—to ask me to lunch?"

"That and some information."

"It figures. Who is it this time?"

"The Griswold Forsythes."

"Dull, dull, dull," she said promptly. "Except Sylvia, the daughter-in-law. She's a live one. The others are lumps."

"What about Geraldine, the unmarried daughter?"

Connie thought a moment. "Strange," she said finally. "Bookish. Travels a lot. And brainy—except when it comes to men. A few years ago she had a thing going with a polo player who turned out to be a slime. Not only did he dump her but, according to the gossip, he took her for heavy bucks."

I nodded. It never ceases to amaze me how many seemingly intelligent women grant their favors to absolute rotters. (I myself have been the lucky beneficiary of that phenomenon.)

"But I guess the Forsythes could afford it," Connie went on. "It's old money, isn't it, Archy?"

"So old it goes back to beaver pelts and canal boats," I told her. "All neatly tied up in a trust fund. I don't think the Griswolds Two and Three have done a lick of work in their lifetimes. They keep a small office on Royal Palm Way not far from the McNally Building and they employ a male secretary one year younger than God. A few months ago I had to deliver some documents and the three of them were playing tiddledywinks."

She howled. "You're making that up!"

"Scout's honor. What else have they got to do except clip bond coupons? Well, luv, if you can't have lunch I better toddle along and see what the Chez McNally has to offer. Thanks for the info."

"Call me tonight?" she asked.

"Don't I always?"

"No," she said. "Kissy-kissy?"

So we kissed. Very enjoyable. Almost as good as squid stew.

I arrived home to discover the only inhabitant present was our taciturn houseman, Jamie Olson. He and his wife, our cook and housekeeper Ursi, are the McNallys' live-in staff and manage our home with Scandinavian efficiency and an Italianate delight in good food. They are an elderly couple and a blessing, both of them.

Jamie is also a great source of backstairs gossip currently making the rounds amongst the domestics serving the nabobs of Palm Beach. Butlers, maids, and valets know or can guess who's doing what to whom, and more than once I have depended on Jamie Olson to fill me in on the high and low jinks of our uppercrust citizens.

My mother and Ursi having departed on a shopping expedition, Jamie was preparing a luncheon that consisted of four varieties of herring with warm German potato salad, plus buttered black bread. I saw nothing to object to and the two of us sat at the kitchen table and scarfed contentedly.

"Jamie," I said, "do you know Mrs. Nora Bledsoe, the keeper of the keys for the Griswold Forsythes?"

"Uh-huh," he said.

"Married, divorced—or what?"

"Her mister took off a long time ago."

"Oh?" I said. "Present whereabouts unknown, I suppose."

"Yep."

"So she went to work for the Forsythes. What about her son, Anthony? Butler and houseman, I understand. Do you have any scoop on him?"

"Mean."

"By 'mean' I presume you wish to imply he's a bit on the nasty side."

He nodded.

Jamie really does know things but getting him to divulge them requires infinite patience.

"Anything else you can reveal about the Forsythes' staff—for or against? What about the chef, Zeke Grenough?"

"He's straight."

"And the maids, Sheila and Fern?"

Jamie gave me a gap-toothed grin. He had, I realized, neglected to insert his bridge that morning. "Those two like to party," he reported. "There was some talk that Forsythe junior was making up to Sheila—she's the pretty one—but the old man soon put a stop to that."

"I'll bet he did," I said. "And what about the mistress of the castle, Constance Forsythe. Anything on her?"

"Horsey."

"You mean she looks like a horse?"

"Boards 'em. Got a farm out near Wellington."

"That's interesting. Racehorses? Polo ponies?"

"Show horses. Jumpers."

And that's all he could tell me about the Forsythes. I finished lunch and handed him a tenner. The Olsons drew a generous salary, of course, but I never considered Jamie's confidential assistance was included in their monthly stipend so I always slipped him a pourboire for extra services rendered. My father would be furious if he ever learned of it.

Before I returned to the Forsythe manse I went up to my digs and loaded a Mark Cross attaché case with yellow legal pads, file cards, a small magnifying glass, and a roll of gummed labels. Since I was going to be on stage I figured a few props would help authenticate my role as an earnest cataloger of libraries. I also took along my reading glasses, although I hate to wear them in public. They make me look like a demented owl.

The Forsythes' front door seemed stout enough to withstand a battering ram but was fitted with a rather prissy brass knob in an acanthus design. I pulled it and heard chimes sound within. A moment later the heavy portal was swung open and I was greeted by Sheila, the pretty and nongiggling maid.

"Me again," I said, giving her my 100-watt Supercharmer smile. (I decided to hold the 150-watt Jumbocharmer for a more propitious time.)

"Oh sure," she said, stepping back to allow entrance. "You know your way to the library?"

"If I get lost I'll scream for help," I said. "What's your last name, Sheila?"

"Hayworth," she said. "And no, I'm not related to Rita."

Saucy, this one.

"You could have fooled me," I said. "The resemblance is striking."

We both laughed because she was a shortish blonde on the zoftig side and looked more like *Klondike Annie* than *The Lady from Shanghai*. She waggled fingers at me and sashayed away. She was, I noted, wearing high heels, which I thought rather odd for the maidservant of a genteel and apparently hidebound family.

After two wrong turnings in those lugubrious corridors I finally located the library. The door was ajar and I blithely strolled into my designated "combat center." Then I stopped, entranced. A woman, perched high on the wheeled ladder, was reaching up to select a volume from the top shelf. She was wearing an extremely short denim skirt.

Her position in that literary setting *forced* me to recall Browning's apt observation: "Ah, but a man's reach should exceed his grasp, or what's a heaven for?"

4

She heard me enter and turned to look down at me coolly. "You must be Archibald McNally," she stated.

I confessed I was.

"I am Geraldine Forsythe. I understand you are to compile a catalog of father's books."

"That is correct, Miss Forsythe, but please don't let me disturb you.

I intend to work as quietly as possible with no interruption of the family's daily routine. Your father suggested I make this room my headquarters, but whenever my presence is inconvenient for you, do let me know."

"No," she said, "it'll be no problem."

She began to step down from the ladder and I hastened forward to assist her.

"I can manage," she snapped at me. "I've been doing it for years and haven't fallen yet."

So I stood aside and waited until she was standing on the parquet floor facing me. And we were almost eye-to-eye, for she was quite tall, rangy, with wide shoulders and a proud posture. I guessed her age at forty-plus. She had a coffin-shaped face with remarkable eyes, as astringent as an iced dry martini.

I noted the novel she had selected: *Mansfield Park*.

"You admire Jane Austen?" I asked.

"Not particularly," she said curtly. "But I no longer read books written by men. They don't address my concerns."

That seemed to me an uncommonly harsh judgment. "Have you tried the Bible?" I asked as pleasantly as I could, but she glared at me.

"Are you a trained librarian?" she demanded.

"Unfortunately I am not," I replied, "but I don't believe this project requires philological expertise. It's really just a matter of taking inventory, isn't it?"

"Like a grocery clerk," she said, and there was no mistaking the sneer in her voice.

"Exactly," I said equably. "The only problem I anticipate is locating books borrowed by family members and staffers and not returned to the library."

I was thinking of that missing first edition of Edgar Allan Poe.

I thought Geraldine blushed slightly but I wasn't certain.

"I assure you," she said stiffly, "I shall immediately return all the books I have borrowed and finished reading. And I'll leave you a note of those still in my possession."

"Thank you for your kind cooperation," I said politely.

She stared at me, looking for sarcasm and not finding it. Little did she know that she was facing the King of Dissemblers. She started to move away, then turned back to stare again.

"I have a feeling I've seen you before," she said, and it was almost an accusation.

"That's possible," I replied. "I've lived in Palm Beach most of my adult life, and the town isn't all that big."

"Are you a member of the Pelican Club?" she asked suddenly.

I admitted I was.

"That's where I saw you," she decided. "I went there once. No, twice. It's a dreadful place. So vulgar."

I smiled. "We prefer to think of it as unpretentious, Miss Forsythe."

"Vulgar," she insisted, paused, then said, "If you'd care to invite me there some evening I'd like to confirm my first impressions."

Shocked? My flabber was gasted. I mean we had been clawing at each other's throat for the past several minutes—in a civilized manner, of course—and now the lady was asking for a date. Connie had been right; Geraldine was a strange one.

"It would be a pleasure," I said gravely. "This evening?"

She gave that a moment's serious thought as if she had other social engagements that required her presence.

"Very well," she said finally, "but not for dinner. Later, and only for a drink or two."

"Excellent," I said. "Suppose I stop by around nine o'clock."

"That will be satisfactory," she said in a schoolmarmish fashion. "I assume informal dress will be suitable?"

"Perfectly," I assured her.

She gave me a chilly nod and stalked from the room. She left me, I must admit, shaken and bewildered. I couldn't even begin to fathom her mercurial temperament nor understand her motives for wanting to revisit a saloon she had decried as vulgar. One possibility, I mournfully concluded, was that Geraldine Forsythe's elevator didn't go to the top floor. More evidence of the basic nuttiness of human behavior.

I actually worked as a cataloger for more than an hour. I started separate pages for each of the north, east, south, and west walls of the library. I then counted the number of bookshelves on each wall and made a note of that. I assigned a key number to each shelf—N-1, E-2, S-3, W-4, and so on—and began counting the number of volumes on each shelf.

I was busily engaged in this donkeywork when my labors were interrupted by the entrance of a stocky woman clad in twill jodhpurs and a khaki riding jacket. She was carrying a crop and brought with her the easily identifiable scent of a stable, but not so strong as to be offensive. I rose to my feet and shook the strong hand she offered.

"Constance Forsythe," she said. "The older Mrs. Forsythe, as I'm sure you've guessed. And you're Archibald McNally?"

"Yes, ma'am. I'm pleased to make your acquaintance. I hope my presence here won't be an inconvenience."

"Not to me," she said with a short laugh. "I'm out at the barn almost every day. Do you ride?"

"No, ma'am, I do not. Horses and I have an agreement: I don't ride them and they don't bite me."

"That's smart," she said. "They can give you a nasty chew if you're not careful. Listing my husband's books, are you?"

She said "my husband's books" not "our books."

"Yes, I'm preparing a catalog," I told her. "I've just started."

"I don't know why Griswold wants a catalog," she said. "Insurance, I suppose, or estate planning. Something like that. Your father is our attorney, is he not?"

"That's correct. Prescott McNally."

"I met him years ago. A gentleman of the old school, as I recall."

"He is that," I agreed.

She wandered about the library flicking her riding crop at the shelves of leather-bound volumes. "I've read damned few of these," she commented. "Not very spicy, are they? Geraldine is the reader of the family. Have you met my daughter, Mr. McNally?"

"Yes, I had that pleasure about an hour ago."

She snorted and it sounded amazingly like a whinny. "I'm glad you found it a pleasure. Most young men are put off by Gerry. She has a tendency to speak her mind. Gets it from me, I imagine." She turned suddenly. "Are you married, Mr. McNally?"

"No, ma'am, I am not."

She nodded. "Who was it that said every woman should marry—and no man?"

"I believe it was Disraeli."

"He was right, you know. If I had been a man I would never, never have married."

I smiled, amused by this forthright woman. She was bulky and had a mastiff face, ruddy and somewhat ravaged. I wondered if she was a

heavy drinker as horsewomen frequently are. But there was no denying her brusque honesty. I thought of her as the leviathan of the
Forsythe Family with all these little sloops bobbing about her.

"You've met everyone in the house?" she asked me.

"I believe so. Of course I already knew your husband and son. Do
they ride, Mrs. Forsythe?"

I heard the whinny again. "Not those two," she said. "Unless the
horse is wood and bolted to a merry-go-round. I'm the only nag nut in
the family. Well, that's not exactly true. Sylvia comes out to the farm
occasionally when she gets bored with her harpsichord. She rides very
well indeed."

"And your grandchild, Lucy?"

"That darling! I'm going to get her up on a pony if it's the last thing
I do."

"Mrs. Forsythe," I said, "perhaps you can answer a question that's
been puzzling me for years. Why do so many young women—I'm
speaking mostly of teenagers—become enamored of horses?"

She gave me a mocking grin. "That's easy," she said. "Because
horses are big, strong, handsome, affectionate, and loyal. Everything
the lads they know are not."

I laughed. "Now it *does* make sense."

"Usually young girls grow out of it," she continued. "After they realize they can't go to bed with a horse. Then they settle for a man."

"We all must compromise in this life," I said jokingly.

But suddenly Mrs. Forsythe was serious. "I wish Geraldine had
learned that." She looked at me speculatively. "Perhaps you can teach
her," she added.

Then, apparently feeling she had said enough, she left the library
abruptly, leaving a slight odor of eau de equine in her wake.

I sat down again at the desk. But I didn't immediately return to my
work. There was no mistaking Mrs. Forsythe's intention, and I spent
a few moments recalling all the instances when anxious mommies had
attempted to interest me in their unmarried daughters. I am not claiming to be a great catch, mind you, but neither am I an impecunious
werewolf, and so I am fair game.

I do not condemn the mothers for trying desperately to ensure their
little girls' futures. Nor do I blame the daughters, for they are frequently unaware of mommy's machinations and would be horrified if

they did know. Nor do I feel any guilt in slinking away from maternal schemings with as much speed and dignity as I can muster.

I spent an additional hour listing books in the Griswold Forsythe library and meticulously recording title, author, publisher, and copyright. This was all camouflage, you understand—a subterfuge to convince everyone (including the thief) that I was engaged in a legitimate pursuit. My labors were as exciting as tracing the genealogy of the royal family of Ruritania.

Finally I revolted against the tedious task and made preparations to depart. I carefully left my preliminary notes atop the desk where they could easily be examined by any interloper. But first I plucked two sun-bleached hairs from my scalp (when the job demands it, your hero will endure any agony) and placed them on pages 5 and 10 of my manuscript. It was, I thought, an artful method of determining if anyone was interested in inspecting my work.

I then left without encountering any of the residents, although I heard raucous laughter coming from the kitchen area. But when I approached my fiery Miata, parked on the bricked driveway in front of the Forsythe mansion, I found Anthony Bledsoe eyeballing the car. He was clad in a uniform of sedate gray alpaca, but his hands were thrust deep into his trouser pockets—bad form for a properly sniffish butler.

The surliness I had noted early that morning had apparently dissipated, for he greeted me with a small smile. "Nice wheels," he remarked.

"Thank you," I said. "Hardly a Corniche but it suits me."

"Fast?" he inquired.

"Enough," I replied.

He walked slowly around my chariot and I thought I saw longing. "What do you drive?" I asked him.

"My mother's car," he said dolefully. "An Oldsmobile. Six years old and ready for a trade-in."

"I don't think she'll go for a two-seater like this," I observed.

"No," he said, "but I would."

He gave the car a final admiring glance and turned away. "Anthony," I called, and he looked back. "What time do Mr. Forsythe and his son customarily return from their office?"

"Four o'clock," he said. "Exactly. Every day. You can set your watch by those two characters."

It was not an appropriate demonstration of respect for his employers. I didn't expect him to tug his forelock in their presence, you understand, but he might have spoken of them without scorn. I am somewhat of a traditionalist, y'see. I mean I always remove my hat when a funeral cortege passes by and, at the start of baseball games, I have been known to hum the national anthem.

I drove home reflecting that although Connie Garcia had labeled the Forsythes as "dull, dull, dull," I was finding them a fascinating and perplexing family of crotchety individuals. Eccentrics, I reckoned, and one of them had recently adopted stealing as a hobby. But for what reason this deponent, at the time, kneweth not.

I changed to swimming trunks (in a modest tie-dyed pattern) and went for my daily swim in the Atlantic, one mile north and return in a gently rolling sea as warm as madrilene. I returned to my rookery to shower and dress. Since I was to meet Geraldine Forsythe later that evening I selected my rags with care: a jacket of cranberry silk over slacks of olive drab. The polo shirt was Sea Island mauve and my loafers were a pinkish suede.

I thought the final effect was eye-catching without being garish, but at our preprandial cocktail hour my father took one look at my costume and exclaimed, "Good God!" But you must realize his sartorial preferences include balbriggan underwear and wingtip shoes.

Dinner that evening was a delicious feast. Ursi Olson had located a rack of out-of-season venison somewhere and, after marinating, served it roasted with a cherry sauce spiked with cognac and a frosting of slivered almonds. What a dish that was! It made one believe that human existence does have a Divine Purpose.

Before my father retired to his port, pipe, and Dickens I asked if he would provide me with a copy of the list of items Griswold Forsythe II had reported as missing. He promised to supply it and asked what progress I had made in my investigation.

"None," I reported cheerfully, and his only reaction was the arching of one eyebrow, a shtick I've never been able to master.

I trotted upstairs to the second-floor sitting room, where mother was watching a rerun of *Singin' in the Rain* on television. I was terribly tempted to forget about my date and stay so that once more I could see Gene Kelly perform that exhilarating dance in a downpour. But duty commanded and so I kissed the mater goodnight and bounded downstairs to the garage.

Ursi and Jamie Olson were still in the kitchen cleaning up, and I popped in long enough to filch a single cherry from the leftovers of the venison roast. Then I was on my way, thinking life is indeed just a bowl of cherries—if enough good brandy is added.

5

Geraldine Forsythe had asked if she might dress informally, and certainly my own raiment would not be unsuitable for Bozo the Clown, but when I saw her awaiting me outside the Forsythe front door I thought I should have donned dinner jacket and cummerbund. She was wearing a black satin slip dress, obviously sans bra, held aloft by spaghetti straps. Draped loosely about her neck was a white silk scarf so gossamer it seemed ready to waft away on the next vagrant breeze.

"You call this casual dress?" I asked her.

She shrugged. "I felt like gussying up," she said.

"Well, you look splendid," I assured her, and that was the truth. Her broad, tanned shoulders were revealed and although she was no sylph, apparently having inherited her mother's stockiness, she definitely had a waist, and her long, bare, rather muscular legs were of centerfold caliber.

She was much amused by my little red runabout and it took her a moment to solve the problem of how to swing into the bucket seat without popping a seam. But she was soon safely ensconced, belt buckled, and we set off for the Pelican Club.

This private eating and drinking establishment is located on the mainland in a freestanding building not far from the airport. It is easy to describe what it is *not:* the Pelican Club is not elegant, austere, hushed nor dignified. It is, in fact, rather raffish and the favorite watering hole of young male and female roisterers in the Palm Beach area. I am proud to be one of the founding members and it was my idea to place over the door, in lieu of a neon sign, a bronze plaque inscribed with Merritt's famous limerick anent the capacity of the pelican.

It was Friday night and the joint was noisy, smoky, and beginning to crank up to the riotous behavior for which it was justly infamous. I secured two adjoining stools at the crowded bar, and Geraldine

Forsythe looked about with an interested glance that belied her condemnation of the Club as dreadful and vulgar.

"You said you've been here before, Miss Forsythe?" I inquired.

"Yes, Mr. McNally," she answered. "Twice. And it hasn't changed."

I didn't pursue the topic but asked if she would be offended if we became Gerry and Archy in place of Miss Forsythe and Mr. McNally. She readily agreed and I used the diminutive to introduce her to Mr. Simon Pettibone, an elderly gentleman of color who is the Club's manager and bartender. We ordered vodka gimlets that were served on cocktail napkins bearing the Club's crest, a pelican rampant on a field of dead mullet, and our motto: *Non illegitimi carborundum.*

Because of the high decibel rating we found it necessary to lean close to converse. I found that a pleasurable experience. She was wearing "Passion." She was certainly not a great beauty—I thought her jaw too aggressive and, as I have stated, her eyes were flinty—but she was no gorgon, and that evening her frostiness had thawed. She seemed to be making a determined effort to be agreeable and succeeded admirably.

We chatted awhile about her travels (extensive) and mine (limited). We concurred that London was more enjoyable than Paris and the best food in Europe was to be found in the Provence. We also decided that Edith Piaf and Aznavour were marvelous balladeers but couldn't compare with Billie Holiday and Sinatra. In fact, there was so little disagreement between us that our conversation began to flag and I ordered another round of gimlets.

But before they arrived Gerry leaned even closer and put a warm hand on my arm. "Archy," she said, "you're a lawyer, aren't you?"

"No," I said, "regrettably I am not. My father is an attorney; I am a sort of para-paralegal."

She stared into my eyes, all seriousness now. "I've asked around about you," she said, "and I understand you do private investigations."

"Occasionally," I admitted. "Discreet inquiries when requested by our clients."

"Well, the Forsythes are clients, are we not?"

"True enough," I said, wondering what was coming.

We didn't speak while our drinks were being served. Gerry sipped her fresh gimlet and leaned close once again.

"Could you make an investigation for me, Archy? A very confidential investigation?"

Then I understood the reason for her softened attitude; she wanted something from me. And I had fancied her affability was the result of the McNally charm. Are there no limits to the male ego?

I took a gulp of my drink. "Tell me about it," I suggested.

She had removed the silk scarf and held it folded on her lap. Now, as she pressed closer, one of those spaghetti straps slipped off a smooth shoulder and dangled. I replaced it as delicately as I could, fearing that if I did not the lady might lose something she could ill afford.

"Well," she said, almost breathlessly, "lately I've been missing things. Personal things."

"Missing?"

"They've just disappeared. Jewelry mostly. A pearl choker from Tiffany. A cameo brooch I bought in Florence. A silver and turquoise bracelet. And most recently a miniature portrait painted on ivory I inherited from my grandmother. Archy, they are all beautiful things and I loved them. Now they are gone and I'm convinced someone in our house has taken them."

"No possibility of their being misplaced?"

"None whatsoever," she said decisively. "They've been stolen."

"Did all the items disappear at once?"

"No. One at a time, I think. Over a period of several weeks."

"Gerry, have you told your parents about this?"

She shook her head. "They'd immediately think it was someone on the staff, and father would want to call in the police and there'd be a big brouhaha. I want to avoid that if I possibly can. I was hoping that while you're cataloging daddy's books you might poke around, or do whatever investigators do, and see if you can discover who's stealing all my things."

"No sign of a forced entry? I mean it couldn't be an outsider, could it?"

"Not a chance," she said. "We have a very expensive security system. It has to be someone who lives in the house."

"Do you suspect one of the staff?"

"I just hate to. They've all been with us for years and we trust them. Nothing like this has ever happened before. It's so depressing."

"Gerry, I really think you should tell your father."

"No," she said gloomily. "He'd fire everyone. I think the best way is to handle it quietly without anyone knowing you're making—what did you call it?—a discreet inquiry. Will you help me, Archy?"

I sighed. "All right, I'll look into it. With the proviso that if I don't come up with something in, say, a few weeks or a month at most, you'll tell your father about the thefts and let him handle it as he sees fit. Is that satisfactory?"

She nodded. "You'll do your best, won't you?"

"It's a promise."

"You're a sweetheart," she said. "I think we better leave now. The place is getting awfully wild."

I didn't think so; just the normal Friday night insanity. But I signed the tab and we departed, leaving the revelry behind us, which saddened me exceedingly.

We drove directly back to Ocean Boulevard and I pulled into the Forsythe driveway.

"Don't bother getting out," Gerry said. "I'll just pop inside. Archy, thank you so much for the drinks and for listening to my problem. You will help, won't you?"

"I'll do what I can, Gerry. No guarantees."

"Of course. I understand that. But I can't tell you how much better I feel knowing you're going to try."

She twisted awkwardly to kiss me. I held her a brief moment. Her strong body felt slithery under the black satin.

I waited until the front door closed behind her, then I headed homeward. I was in a thoughtful mood, asking a number of questions to which I had no answers, to wit:

Why did she select the Pelican Club as a setting in which to tell me of her missing jewelry? We could have had the same conversation in the privacy of the Forsythe Library.

With whom had she previously visited the Club—her ex-beau, the polo player who allegedly dumped her—but not before clipping her for "heavy bucks"?

Why had she thought it necessary to dress as she had—to help persuade yrs. truly to come to the aid of a damsel in distress?

Why did she believe her father would immediately call in the police if she told him of her stolen gems when he refused to inform the authorities when his own property was snatched?

I fell asleep that night still wrestling with those conundrums. (Naturally I neglected to phone Connie Garcia.) And when I awoke on a rainy Saturday morning I had not solved a blessed one. I began to wonder if Geraldine Forsythe might be a Baroness von Munchhausen with a penchant for spinning wild and improbable tales.

I could understand that. I like to spin them myself.

Usually my father spent Saturdays at his golf club, playing eighteen holes with the same foursome for the past century or two. But that morning was so wet and blowy there was no hope of getting in a game and so he had retired to his study with a copy of *Barron's*—to check the current value of his Treasury bonds no doubt.

Griswold Forsythe II belonged to father's club, an organization with a male membership so long in the tooth it was said you could not hope to be admitted unless you could prove prostate problems. A canard, of course.

I reckoned the same wretched weather keeping Sir McNally indoors was also forcing Mr. Forsythe to remain at home. I felt I needed more information from him regarding his missing geegaws: insured value, location of the items before they disappeared, who amongst family and staff knew where they were kept, and so forth. I phoned the Forsythe home and, after identifying myself, asked to speak to the lord of the manor.

When he came on the line it was obvious he was extremely agitated. "Archy," he said, "can you come over at once?"

"Is anything wrong?" I asked.

"Something dreadful has happened."

"Be right there," I promised.

I pulled on a yellow oilskin and, not wanting to waste time putting the lid on my barouche, I asked mother if I might borrow her ancient Ford station wagon. Within moments I was driving northward along the shore through a squall so violent it threatened to blow me off the road. If I had been in the Miata I suspect I would have ended up in Tampa.

And when I arrived at the Forsythe castle I found the atmosphere as chaotic inside as out. It took me awhile to learn the cause of the disturbance, for everyone insisted on speaking at once and there was a great wringing of hands, tears from the women and curses from the men. Disorder reigned supreme.

I was finally able to extract a semicoherent account of what had occurred. Apparently, during the wee hours of the morning, someone had entered the bedroom of Mrs. Sylvia Forsythe III and attempted to strangle her. She and her husband occupied separate bedchambers, she never locked her door, and the assault was not discovered until she failed to appear at breakfast.

The giggling maid, Fern, was sent to ask if Mrs. Sylvia wanted something brought up, and it was she who found the victim lying unconscious on the floor, nightclothes in disarray. Fern's screams brought the others running and when the young woman could not be roused the family physician was called.

He arrived within a half-hour and was able to revive Mrs. Sylvia. She was presently in bed and according to the doctor, had not suffered any life-threatening injury. She was able to speak in a croaky voice but could not identify her assailant. She had been sedated and was in no condition to be questioned further.

Mr. Griswold Forsythe II pulled me into the library and closed the door.

"GD it," he said angrily, and it was, I imagined, the strongest oath he was capable of uttering. "I don't understand what's happening around here. First thievery and now attempted murder. What on earth is going on?"

"Mr. Forsythe," I said as gently as I could, "this matter must be reported to the police."

"No, no!" he shouted. "Absolutely not! The newspapers, television, the tabloids—all that. Can't have it. *Won't* have it."

"Sir," I said with the solemnity the moment required, "you *must* report it. Attempted homicide is a serious crime, and not making a police report might possibly result in your becoming the subject of an official investigation. I strongly urge you to phone the authorities at once. I suggest you speak to Sergeant Al Rogoff. He and I have worked together several times in the past, and I can vouch for his intelligence, competence and, most of all, his discretion."

He gnawed on that a moment, then drew a deep breath. "Yes," he said finally, "you're probably right. I'll call."

He picked up the phone and I left the library. I met a tearful Fern in the corridor and she directed me to Mrs. Sylvia's bedroom on the second floor. I found Griswold Forsythe III standing guard outside his wife's door. He was wearing a three-piece suit of mud-colored cheviot, almost identical to his father's. I wondered if the male Forsythes patronized the same tailor and ordered two of everything.

"How is she, Griswold?" I asked.

"Dozing," he said distractedly. "The doctor is with her now. He says her respiration and heartbeat are normal and she should make a complete recovery. But I'm worried."

"Of course you are," I said. "Have you any idea who might have committed such a horrible act?"

He stared at me and his eyes seemed slightly out of focus as if his thoughts were elsewhere. "What?" he said. "Oh. No, I have no idea. It has to be someone in the house. That's what makes it so awful. I simply cannot believe this happened."

I was saved from replying when the bedroom door opened and the paunchy doctor came out carrying his black satchel.

"You may go in now, Mr. Forsythe," he said. "But stay only a few minutes and try not to disturb the patient."

Griswold nodded, stepped inside, and closed the door behind him.

"How is Mrs. Forsythe doing, sir?" I asked the physician.

He looked at me. "I am Dr. Cedric P. Pursglove," he said haughtily, and I wondered if that middle P. stood for Popinjay. "And who might you be?" he demanded.

I was tempted to answer that I might be Peter the Great but, sadly, I was not. "Archibald McNally," I told him. "My law firm represents the Forsythes."

Of course he immediately assumed I was an attorney and I didn't disabuse him. I mean there was no point in confessing I was merely a scullion in the McNally & Son kitchen.

"From a legal point of view," he said in such a pompous manner that I had a terrible urge to goose him, just to see him leap, dignity shattered, "—from a legal point of view this distressing matter should be reported at once to the proper authorities."

"I so advised the senior Mr. Forsythe," I informed him.

"Wise counsel," he said as if pronouncing a benediction. "I further recommend a police physician be called to examine the patient and perhaps take photographs."

I was startled. "Why should that be necessary, sir?"

"The contusions caused by the attempted strangulation are obvious on the neck of the intended victim. But there are other wounds of a superficial nature that might prove significant."

He spoke of his patient as if she were a laboratory specimen. This doctor, I decided, had all the bedside manner of Jack the Ripper.

"What kind of wounds?" I asked him.

"Deep scratches and a few small, open cuts on the neck."

"Have you any idea what caused them?"

"I am not a forensic pathologist," he said crossly, "but it is my firm opinion that they were made by long fingernails."

I stared at him, shocked. "Dr. Pursglove, are you implying that Mrs. Forsythe's assailant was a woman?"

"It is, I think, a reasonable assumption," he said at his pontifical best—or worst. "And there is contributing evidence. It is no simple task to strangle a human being, particularly one as young and vigorous as the patient. It would require considerable physical strength."

"And that is an added indication her attacker was a woman—she was rendered unconscious but not killed?"

He nodded with grim assurance. "It is my belief that if the strangler had been a man Mrs. Forsythe would now be deceased."

6

I reclaimed my yellow slicker and left the Forsythe home without speaking further to any of the inhabitants. Although my name is Archy, let me be frank: I departed in unseemly haste because I did not wish to be on the premises when Sgt. Al Rogoff arrived. His accusations, I well knew, would come later. And better later than sooner.

I arrived home to find my father and mother, Madelaine, in the living room moodily inspecting an inconsequential puddle on the parquet floor. It had been caused by the fierce rain leaking in under French doors to our small flagstoned terrace. My parents were tsk-tsking in unison.

I told them what had occurred at the Forsythes', and they were both stunned.

"How dreadful," mother said, putting a trembling knuckle to her lips. "Prescott, is there anything we can do?"

"Have the police been notified?" father asked me.

"Yes, sir," I said. "After I persuaded the senior Mr. Forsythe. I do think you should be there during the police investigation and questioning."

"You're quite right, Archy," he said. "I'll go at once. Maddie, where did I leave my umbrella?"

I waited until he had been adequately outfitted in raincoat, rain hat, and rubbers, and equipped with a bumbershoot large enough to shelter four close friends. He departed in his Lexus and I moved into his study to use the phone. I called Connie Garcia.

"Thank you for phoning last night," she said coldly, "as you so sincerely promised."

"Sorry about that, dear," I said. "We had a tremendous flood in the living room—the rain was gushing in under the French doors to the terrace—and I was busy with mop and bucket for hours. Listen, how about lunch at the Pelican?"

"Today?" she said. "Are you mad? It's still pouring and I've just washed my hair and have no intention of taking a step outside."

"Ah, what a disappointment," I said. "Oh, by the way, Connie, you mentioned that Geraldine Forsythe had been blindsided by an unscrupulous polo player. You don't happen to recall his name, do you?"

She was silent a moment. "Sorry," she said finally, "I just can't remember it—if I ever knew."

"Oh, well, it's not important," I lied. "I'll buzz you tomorrow and if the weather has cleared by then perhaps we can have a nosh."

"Sounds good to me, Archy. I could do with a bowl of chili to chase my chilly."

We chatted a few more minutes about this and that, and she was in a sparky mood when we rang off. Connie does have her snits but usually they are not of long duration. Unfortunately while they last they sometimes result in physical assaults on the McNally carcass. But infidelity, like all delights, has its price.

I then tried my favorite chronicler of Palm Beach turpitude. I knew Lolly Spindrift worked on Saturdays preparing his gossip column for the Sunday edition of his paper. Naturally he would demand a newsworthy disclosure in return for the information I wanted but I thought I could finesse that.

"Hi, darling," he said chirpily. "Don't tell me you called to remark that it's great weather for ducks. If I hear that once more today I'll scream."

"Actually, Lol," I said, "I phoned to invite you to lunch. How about Bice? We'll have a nice salad with a side order of quid pro quo."

"Oh-ho," he said, "it's tattle time, is it? I'd love to, doll, but I just can't. I'm chained to this sadistic word processor and it won't turn me loose until my copy is complete. What have you got for me? I hope it's something juicy. I need a final item that'll cause a splash or my devoted readers will think old Lolly is losing his edge."

"This will cause a splash," I promised, "but you'll have to write it as a question because I don't know the answer."

"All right, all right," he said impatiently. "Half my scoops are phrased as questions. It's a great way to avoid libel suits. Let's have it."

"Quote: 'What were the police doing at the Griswold Forsythe mansion early Saturday morning? Rumor hath it that there have been dark doings in that haunted castle.' Unquote. How does that sound, Lol?"

"A doozy," he said immediately. "A smash finish for the column. But is it for real?"

"Have I ever stiffed you?"

"No, you've been true-blue, sweetie. But why do I have the feeling you're not telling me everything you know?"

"It's everything, Lol," I assured him. "If I learn more you'll be the first to hear about it."

"I better," he warned, "or you'll go on my S-list. You do know what that is, don't you?"

"I can guess," I said. "Now here's what I need: A few years ago Geraldine Forsythe, the unmarried daughter, reportedly had a thing going with a polo player. Apparently he treated her in a most ungentlemanly manner including nicking her for a sizable sum. Question: Do you know the name of the knave?"

Lolly laughed. "I don't even have to consult my private file. It so happens I hoped to start a thing with that hulk myself but it came to naught. It wasn't that he was unwilling to swing, but he was suffering from a severe case of the shorts and was looking for a fatter bankroll than mine. I heard later that he had latched onto Geraldine. His name is Timothy Cussack."

"Cussack?" I said and smote my brow with an open palm. "I should have guessed. He was cashiered from the Pelican Club a year ago for nonpayment of his bar tabs. Is he still playing polo?"

"Heavens, no! He fell off a horse and broke a bone. His fetlock or pastern or something silly like that."

"And what's he doing now, Lol—do you know?"

"The last I heard he was working as a trainer at a horse farm out near Wellington."

"Uh-huh," I said. "Interesting—but not very. Thanks for the poop, Lol, and keep defending the public's inalienable right to know."

"Up yours as well, Priapus," he said, and I hung up laughing. Outrageous man!

My next move might have been to learn the name of Mrs. Constance Forsythe's horse farm out near Wellington and determine if she was employing the man who had betrayed her daughter. But I thought additional research was required first.

I donned my oilskin again and set out for the Pelican Club in mother's station wagon. The rain had not lessened but at least the wind had lost its intensity and I was able to navigate the flooded roads successfully. The vehicle I was driving, I suddenly realized, was older than I, and I hoped when I was its age I might be as stalwart and dependable.

As I suspected it would be, the Pelican Club was deserted on such an indecent day. Only the staff was present, with Mr. Simon Pettibone behind the bar watching a rerun of "Dynasty" on his little TV set. He looked up with amazement when I entered.

"Mr. McNally," he said, "you braved the elements to honor us with your presence?"

"Thirst will drive a man to desperate measures," I replied, swinging aboard a barstool. "What do you recommend to banish the blues, Mr. Pettibone? I plan to have only one so I suggest it be muscular."

"A negroni will provide needed warmth and nourishment. But only one," he warned. "For it is a potion to be respected."

"As well I know," I said, "from sad experience. Very well, one negroni, Mr. Pettibone. And if I insist on a second I advise you to summon the gendarmes."

I took one sip of the ambrosial concoction he set before me and suddenly the rain ceased, the sun shone, and Joan Blondell and I planned a weekend at Biarritz. Not literally, of course, but that's the effect a ne-groni can have on an impressionable youth.

"Mr. Pettibone," I said, "do you recall an ex-member named Timothy Cussack?"

"I do indeed," he said promptly. "A welsher."

"Exactly," I said. "I don't believe I ever met him. What kind of a chap was he?"

"Oozy."

"And what precisely did he ooze?"

"Personality," Mr. Pettibone said. "Charm. Too much, and so it oozed."

"Ah," I said, "a trenchant observation. I've heard him described as a hulk. Large, is he?"

"Oh yes. And handsome in a meanish kind of way, as if he might enjoy kicking a dog."

"Doesn't sound like a sterling character."

"No, that he is not."

"A scoundrel?"

Mr. Pettibone considered a moment. "I do believe he's working up to it," he said. "Or down."

"What do you suppose drives him?" I asked.

"Mr. McNally, some people just have a natural talent for meanness. I think that may be true of Timothy Cussack. And also, of course, he was perpetually short of funds."

I nodded. "As Shaw once remarked, 'The lack of money is the root of all evil.' "

"I never had the pleasure of meeting Mr. Shaw," Pettibone said solemnly, "but obviously he was a man of wisdom."

I thanked him for his assistance and finished my drink. (Take note: only one.) I then drove home in a negroni-bemused mood. I was accumulating additional bits and pieces of information but to what purpose I could not have said. The Forsythe saga was beginning to resemble one of those children's puzzles in which numbered dots are connected in sequence to form a picture. But in this case most of the dots were unnumbered—or missing.

At dinner that evening my father commented that the police questioning of the Forsythe family and staff had been brief and inconclusive. Everyone had eagerly cooperated but nothing new had been learned. Sgt. Rogoff had stated that his investigation would continue. I could believe that; tenacity is his middle name. (Not really, of course; it's Irving.)

Later that night I was upstairs making desultory scribblings in my journal when the sergeant phoned, as I knew he inevitably would.

"You know," he started, "I'm beginning to see us as Laurel and Hardy. I'm the fat one who always says, 'Here's another fine mess you've got me into.' "

"Al," I said, "I swear I had nothing to do with it except recommend that the police be notified."

"But you told Griswold Forsythe to hand me the squeal, didn't you?"

"Well, yes," I admitted. "But only because I knew he demanded discretion."

"Discretion?" He honked a bitter laugh. "It's hard to be discreet, sonny boy, when someone's tried to choke a woman to death."

"I know you'll try to keep a lid on it," I said soothingly. "How did you make out at the Kingdom of Oz?"

"The Forsythe place? Hey, that's a creepy joint, isn't it? As damp inside as it is out. It's a wonder they all don't have webs between their toes. Archy, it's another NKN case—nobody knows nothing. And don't tell me that's a double negative; I still like it."

"Did you talk to the family physician, Dr. Pursglove?"

"Oh yeah," Al said. "He's Mr. Congeniality, isn't he? I called in Tom Bunion from the ME's office. He was delighted to come out in this monsoon, as you can well imagine. Anyway, he more or less confirms what Pursglove says: the attacker was probably a woman. So where does that leave us?"

"Well, it certainly narrows the list of suspects to the women who were in the house at the time, doesn't it?"

"Not necessarily," Rogoff argued. "It could have been an outsider."

"Al, they're supposed to have a state-of-the-art security system."

"Doesn't mean a thing," he said. "It can be switched off, can't it? As it is every morning. The control box is in a pantry off the kitchen. Anyone in the place could have thrown the switch and allowed someone to come in without making the balloon go up. By the way, what were you doing there before I was called in?"

"The Forsythes are clients of McNally and Son. The senior Griswold was in a panic this morning after they found Mrs. Sylvia. My father was busy so I went over."

"Uh-huh," Rogoff said. "And what were your notes doing on the library desk? I recognized your scrawly handwriting."

"Oh *that*," I said breezily. "I'm cataloging Mr. Forsythe's books."

"You're doing *what?*"

"Cataloging the Forsythe library. I don't spend all my time nabbing villains, you know."

"Son," the sergeant said heavily, "you've got more crap than a Christmas goose. But I'll let it go—for now. You know all the people in that nuthouse?"

"I've met them all, yes."

"Excluding the injured woman and Lucy, the kid, that leaves Constance Forsythe, the daughter Geraldine, the housekeeper Mrs. Bledsoe, and the two maids, Fern and Sheila. Five females, all with fingernails long enough to make those wounds on the victim's neck. Assuming no outsider was allowed in, who's your pick?"

"Al," I said, "I just don't know and that's the truth. I can't even guess. Too many imponderables."

"I love the way you talk," he said. "You mean it's all shit—right?"

"Something like that."

He sighed. "I hate these domestic violence cases. You can dig for weeks, months, years and never get to the bottom. You know that Fern, one of the maids?"

"Sure. The one who giggles."

"Well, she wasn't giggling this morning. Boohooing as a matter of fact. But I guess that's understandable; she found the victim. Anyway, we were making a half-assed search of that loony bin and came across some bloodstained tissues in a wastebasket in Fern's bedroom. She claims she got blood on her hands when she tried to revive Mrs. Sylvia. Could be."

"Of course it could," I agreed. "And that's all you discovered?"

He laughed. "Not quite. Griswold Forsythe the Third, the uptight, upright heir to the throne, has a small but choice collection of nude photos."

"You're kidding!"

"I'm not. They aren't professional. I think he took them himself. Polaroids. Same background, same lighting. We left everything where we found it. Now is that discretion or isn't it?"

I didn't want to ask my next question but I had to. "Did you recognize any of the models?"

"Sure," Rogoff said cheerfully. "The two maids." He paused for dramatic effect. "And Griswold's sister Geraldine. Now do you know why I hate these family messes?"

"Yes," I said dully, "now I know."

We hung up after warm expressions of fealty, some of which were heartfelt. I like Al and I think—I hope—he likes me. But although we may be friends we are also, during the cases we work together, avid competitors. Nothing wrong with that, is there?

I admit I was shaken by his final revelation. Griswold Forsythe III an eager snapper of nude photos? Including his maidservants and sister? It was mind-boggling. I imagined for one brief moment that it might be just an innocent hobby, somewhat akin to collecting Indian head pennies.

Then I realized how insane that was. My fault was that I had assumed a man who wore mud-colored, three-piece cheviot suits and to whom verbosity was a way of life was incapable of passion, legitimate or illicit. It was obvious that I had underestimated Griswold Three—and probably all the other denizens of the Chez Forsythe as well.

I went to bed that night resolved to practice and exhibit more humility in my relations with others. But I knew in my heart of hearts that this noble resolution, like so many I had made in the past, was doomed to ignominious failure.

7

The rain had stopped by Sunday morning but the sky still had the color and texture of a Pittsburgh sidewalk. I confess I am somewhat phobic about the weather; when the sun doesn't shine I don't either. But my spirits were boosted when I breakfasted with my parents in the dining room. Ursi Olson served us small smoked ham steaks with little yam cubes in a dark molasses sauce. I could almost feel the McNally corpuscles perk up and move onto the dance floor for a merry gavotte.

Mother and father departed for church, and I phoned Connie Garcia. She was in a laid-back Sunday morning mood and didn't seem inclined to make a definite date for lunch or dinner.

"Did you see the paper, Archy?" she asked.

"Not yet."

"Lolly Spindrift says something is going on at the Forsythe home. He says the police were called."

"Good heavens," I said. "I wonder what it could be."

"I thought you might know," she said. "You've been asking a lot of questions about that family lately."

"Well, they *are* our clients, you know. Perhaps I'll take a run up there and see if they require assistance. I'll call you this afternoon, Connie, and maybe we can meet later."

"Sounds good," she said. "I'll try to get my act together by then. Archy, if you learn anything spicy at the Forsythes', will you tell me?"

"Don't I always?"

"No," she said.

We hung up and I meditated, not for the first time, on my romance with that dishy young woman. I had a great affection for her, no doubt about it, but my tender attachment did not prevent my being unfaithful when an opportunity occurred. I could only conclude that infidelity was part of my genetic code, like snoring, and I must learn to live with it. I could only hope that Connie would as well.

I donned a blue nylon jacket, clapped on a white leather cap, and ventured out into a muggy world. I spun the Miata northward along Ocean Boulevard and en route I spotted, coming in the opposite direction, the big, boxy Rolls-Royce belonging to Griswold Forsythe II. I don't know what model it was, but it was aged and seemed high enough to allow a formally attired gentleman to enter without removing his topper.

It was proceeding at a sedate pace and I was able to note that Griswold III, the famous nude photo fiend, was driving while his mother, father, and sister occupied the rear. The family was on its way to church, I reckoned, which gave me the chance of chatting up the stay-at-homes without interference.

I encountered, on the front lawn of the Forsythe estate, a blocky servitor clad in faded overalls and sporting a magnificent walrus mustache. He was raking the grounds of palm fronds and other arboreal debris blown down by the previous day's gusty winds. Assisting him in his labors was my new friend, Lucy, who was striving mightily but futilely to stuff a very large pine branch into a very small plastic garbage bag.

"Hi, Lucy," I called.

"Hi, Archy," she sang out. "Look what the storm did."

"I know," I said. "But everything will dry out eventually."

The gardener glanced at me and tipped his feed-lot cap.

"Good morning," I said to him. "My name is Archibald McNally, a friend of the Forsythes. You're Rufino Diaz?"

"Thass right," he said, surprised I knew his name. "I take care of the outside."

"Much damage?"

"Not too bad," he said. "We lost some ficus, and two new orchid trees I had just planted got blown over. But I stuck them back in, tied them up, and I think they'll take. The ground got a good soaking and thass important."

I nodded and turned back to the little girl. "How is your mother, Lucy?"

"She got hurt."

"I know. Is she feeling better now?"

"I guess. She's got a bandage around her neck."

"Perhaps I'll see if she's able to receive visitors."

I started away but Lucy came running after me. She clutched my arm and pulled me down to her level.

"You remember?" she whispered.

"About what?"

"My secret place. You promised you'd come to a picnic there."

"Of course I will—after it dries out."

"And we're still friends?"

"Absolutely," I told her. "Stick with me, kid, and you'll be wearing diamonds."

She sniggered and scampered back to her work. I went to the half-open front door and found Mrs. Bledsoe peering out.

"Good morning, Mr. McNally," she said. "I'm keeping an eye on Lucy. I don't want her to get too wet."

"She's doing fine. How are you, Mrs. Bledsoe, after yesterday's unpleasantness?"

"Bearing up," she said. "This too shall pass."

"I'm sure it shall," I said, not at all certain. "And how is Mrs. Sylvia?"

"Much better, thank you. She is wide-awake and alert and had two poached eggs and a cup of tea for breakfast. No toast because her throat is still sore, you know."

"I can imagine," I said. "Do you think she's in any mood for company?"

"I can ask."

I followed her down the hallway and up the staircase, seeing again what a robust woman she was. Curious, but she and Constance Forsythe were the same physical type: square and resolute. I thought of them both as no-nonsense women who managed that rather giddy household with an iron hand in an iron glove. But I may have been moonbeaming.

I waited outside Mrs. Sylvia's door while Nora Bledsoe went in to confer with the patient. She came out a moment later.

"Yes," she said, "she'll be happy to have company. The doctor has ordered her to stay in bed and rest for another day, and she's bored. Wants to get back to her harpsichord, I expect."

"That's understandable," I said. "Mrs. Bledsoe, do you have any idea who might have done this awful thing?"

"None whatsoever," she said grimly and marched away.

I entered the bedroom and found Sylvia Forsythe lying under a canopy as fanciful as a Persian tent. She was wearing a white gown, her head on two lace-trimmed pillows. A silk sheet was pulled up and tucked beneath her arms. There was a gauze wrapping about her throat, and atop the flowered counterpane was an opened musical score. She smiled brightly as I approached.

"Mr. McNally," she said, "how very nice of you to visit."

Her voice was husky and unexpectedly come-hitherish.

"My pleasure," I said. "I do hope you're feeling better."

"Much," she said. "I want to be up and about but I promised Dr. Pursglove to stay in bed another day. Pull up a chair."

I moved a chintzy number to her bedside and sat down. She reached a hand to me, I clasped it and she did not release my paw.

"I'm delighted to see you looking so well," I told her. "And Mrs. Bledsoe says you had not one but two eggs for breakfast."

She laughed. "And I'm famished. I've been promised pasta alfredo for lunch and I can't wait."

I nodded toward the score. "And meanwhile you're studying Vi-valdi."

"Scarlatti," she said, and we smiled at each other.

She was an enormously attractive invalid. Her wheaten hair was splayed out on the pillows in a filmy cloud and her paleness gave her features a translucency revealing an inner glow. And she held my hand in a warm grip. This woman is married, I sternly reminded myself. And she is recovering from a grievous injury. But the McNally id could not be restrained.

She noted me staring and turned her head away. "I feel so help-less," she said in her husky, stirring voice.

How was I to interpret that comment? I didn't even try.

"Mrs. Forsythe," I started, but she looked at me again and shook her head.

"Sylvia will do," she said. "And may I call you Archy?"

"Honored," I said, and gently disengaged my hand from hers. It was a noble act but a moment later I wanted to grab it up again and nib-ble her knuckles.

"Sylvia," I said, "do you have any idea who attacked you?"

She sighed. "So many people have asked me that: the doctor, that police sergeant, my husband, father-in-law—just everyone. I've told them all the same thing but I'm not sure they believe me. The last thing I remember is being awakened from a sound sleep and becoming aware that someone was choking me. After that I have no memory at all. It's just a total blank. Dr. Pursglove says that sometimes happens: the mind wipes out a painful, traumatic experience to aid healing. Self-protective, you know. But he expects the recollection will slowly re-turn."

She looked at me wide-eyed and I did not believe a word she had said. But "You're lying!" is not something one shouts at a convalescent young female—or at a healthy young male either. I was convinced Sylvia Forsythe knew the identity of her assailant. Why she chose not to reveal it was another unnumbered dot in that picture puzzle I was trying to draw.

It seemed useless to pursue the matter and so I continued my de-tecting by switching to another subject. "Your mother-in-law tells me you're an expert rider," I remarked.

"Not expert," she said, "but I do enjoy it. I'm proud to say I've been thrown only once."

"I understand Mrs. Forsythe operates a horse farm and trains jumpers," I went on. "Do you ever compete?"

"Oh no," she said, "I'm not that good. I just like to ride around and gallop occasionally. That's exciting."

"What is the farm called?" I asked casually. "It sounds like an interesting place."

"Oh, it is. You really should see it, Archy. It's called the Trojan Stables. Isn't that a wonderful name?"

"It surely is."

"It costs a fortune to run. Do you know the price of hay?"

"No," I said, "I haven't been eating much lately."

She grinned at me. "Well, I suspect the function of Trojan Stables is to train jumpers and serve as a tax loss. I hope this conversation is confidential, Archy."

"Of course it is," I assured her. "I'm a loyal employee, and even if the IRS uses thumbscrews I won't talk. I may blubber but I won't talk."

She laughed and took up my hand again. "I like you, Archy," she said. "You're fun and there's not much of that around here. Perhaps we might go out to Wellington together and I'll show you around the Trojan."

"I'd enjoy that," I said, and wondered what Griswold Forsythe III might think of my squiring Sylvia. But then, I recalled, when Sgt. Rogoff had listed the models in Griswold's nude photos he hadn't mentioned the man's wife.

Then we were silent, but it was a reflective quiet. I imagine most of you ladies and gents have known such a moment—a briefness of balance, a shall-I or shall-I-not choice when you question not if you have the desire (that's a given) but if you have the energy, psychic or physical or both.

And always, of course, there is the problem of logistics. If the union contemplated is to be consummated, then where, when, and how? Sometimes craving remains just that only because to scratch the itch would require planning as complex as that for D-Day.

And so Sylvia Forsythe and I gazed at each other tenderly while all we were thinking remained unspoken. Finally she released my hand and I assumed that was a signal of dismissal. I rose and expressed hope for her quick recovery.

"I'll be fine," she said with a radiant smile. "And thank you again for stopping by. How is your cataloging job coming along?"

"Slowly," I said.

"Good," she said and left it to me to figure out what she meant.

I was retreating down one of those gloomy corridors when suddenly Fern stepped from an alcove and clamped my arm. "What did she tell you, Mr. McNally?" she demanded, sharp face hard with anger.

I was tempted to make a tart reply—"None of your business!"—but thought better of it. "Mrs. Sylvia?" I said softly. "Only that she was feeling better and hoped to be up and about in a day or so."

The maid released my arm and began to gnaw on a thumbnail. "She thinks I did it," she said fiercely, "but I didn't. I couldn't do something like that. I hate and detest violence in any way, shape, or form."

Then I was thoroughly convinced I had blundered into a haunt of boobies.

"I don't believe Mrs. Sylvia believes you did it," I said. "She remembers almost nothing about the attack and can't identify the perpetrator."

"Well, I didn't do it," she repeated, still chewing at her thumb. "And anyone who says I did is a double-damned liar."

"Fern," I said, hoping to calm her, "I must confess I don't know your last name. You know mine but I don't know yours. That's not fair."

"Fern Bancroft," she said glumly, and I thought how odd it was that both maids had the surnames of movie stars. But then my own name is similar to that of a famous mapmaker and during my undergraduate days I was known as Randy McNally.

"Well, you mustn't worry about this unfortunate incident," I told her. "To my knowledge no one has accused you of anything. Try to put it from your mind."

"You know I'm innocent, don't you?"

What a question! She was referring to the attempted strangling of Mrs. Sylvia, of course, but it was difficult to attest to the complete innocence of a young woman who had posed for nude Polaroids.

"I believe you," I said simply, thinking that might suffice.

"I just don't know what's happening around here," she wailed. "Everything is so mixed up."

"It will all settle down," I said soothingly.

"I don't think so," she said and leaned closer, still munching on her thumbnail. "There are things going on," she added in direful tones.

I began to get a new take on Fern Bancroft. When we had first been introduced I had thought her something of a linthead, only because of her chronic giggle. But now I suspected that habit might have a neurasthenic origin. She was not giggling because she found life amusing but because she found it close to unendurable, and a constant laugh was her guard against hysteria.

Thank you, Dr. McNally.

"Fern," I said, "what exactly is going on that upsets you so?"

"Things," she said and darted away. I was left in a state of utter confusion and a lesser lad might have been staggered by it. But I have learned to live with muddle—e.g.: my relations with the feminine gender—and so I was more fascinated than daunted by the hugger-mugger in the Forsythe household. It merely confirmed my belief, previously propounded, that the world is a nuthouse run by the inmates.

I hoped to make a quiet and unobserved departure but I was doomed to another slice of fruitcake that Sunday morning. Sheila Hayworth, maid No. 2, was in the entrance hall busily wielding a feather duster with no apparent purpose or effect.

"Hi, Mr. McNally," she said cheerily. "Aren't you glad the rain stopped?"

"Delighted," I said. "People always say the farmers need it, but truthfully I don't much care what the farmers need—do you?"

"Not me," she said forthrightly. "I grew up on a farm and never want to see another one as long as I live."

"A farmer's daughter," I marveled. "I wouldn't have guessed."

"Now don't tell me you're a traveling salesman," she said coquettishly. "I've heard all those old jokes."

What a flirt she was!

"I may travel occasionally," I said, "but I have nothing to sell."

She gave me a bold glance. "I wouldn't say that. Tuesday is my day off."

Her impudence was impressive. "I'll keep that in mind," I told her.

"You do that," she said. "You can always leave a message for me with Rufino."

"The gardener?"

"Uh-huh," she said, staring at me. "He has a cute little apartment in West Palm."

Her brazenness was amazing and, I must admit, engendered a slight weakening of the joints between femur and tibia. I mean I'm as eager for a romantic lark as the next johnny but I like to play a role in its creation. But in this drama (comedy? farce?) Ms. Hayworth seemed to be playwright, director, set designer, and female star. It was a trifle humbling to be reduced to a walk-on.

Naturally I didn't wish to offend the lady by a brusque rejection, but neither did I wish to flop upon the floor and wait to have my tummy scratched.

"It's something to think about," I said, a spineless remark if ever I heard one.

She gave me a mocking glance. "Do you require references?" she inquired archly.

I realized I had met my match with this one and a hasty escape would be prudent. But then she added, "I could provide them, you know. From men whose opinion I'm sure you trust."

I was aware that my smile was glassy as I fled without saying another word. Rufino Diaz was still raking the lawn and gave me a half-wave of farewell as I drove away. I headed homeward, thoughts jangled, trying to guess the identities of those men whose opinions I would trust.

I had to conclude she was referring obliquely to the Griswold Forsythes, II and III. And perhaps Anthony Bledsoe, the butler. And perhaps Zeke Grenough, the chef. And perhaps Count Dracula and Friar Tuck.

I realized I was now making no sense whatsoever. I blamed the fogging of my keen, cool, and lucid mind on a morning spent at the Forsythe asylum. I seemed to have been contaminated by whatever was afflicting the residents. I decided a good dose of normalcy was needed as an antidote. And so the moment I arrived home I built myself a vodka gimlet.

Purely for medicinal purposes, you understand.

8

The remainder of that Sunday was blessedly uneventful. I stayed inside all afternoon and the quiet ordinariness of the McNally household was a comfort. We had a fine rack of lamb for dinner, I took a nap, worked on my journal, ate cold corned beef and cheese sausage as a late supper, and forgot to phone Connie Garcia. Everything seemed refreshingly sane and orderly.

Of course Ms. Garcia called me later that night to read me the riot act for neglecting her. It required twenty minutes to beg forgiveness and squirm my way back into her graces. But even my performance was a relief because I had done it so many times before and routine was welcome after that confused morning at the Forsythes'.

Monday brought genuine sunshine and a concurrent return of the McNally brio. My father supplied me with a list of the items of value reported as missing by Griswold Forsythe II, and to that I added the articles of jewelry Geraldine Forsythe told me she had lost. It made an impressive inventory. Obviously someone was looting the family manse—but for what purpose? Was the thief fencing the swag or merely assembling his or her own collection of objets d'art?

By the time I arrived at my miniature office in the McNally Building I had decided I needed to know more about the finances of that seemingly dysfunctional Forsythe clan. I phoned Mrs. Trelawney, my father's private secretary, and asked if His Majesty might spare me a few moments.

"Fat chance," she scoffed.

"Try," I urged. "The fate of the civilized world hangs in the balance."

"That's a good one," she said. "You've never used that before. Okay, I'll give it a go."

She came back on the line a moment later and announced I would be granted an audience of ten minutes if I arrived instanter. I went charging up the back stairs to the boss's sanctum, not wanting to wait for our lazy automatic elevator. I found the padrone standing before his antique rolltop desk. He did not appear to be overjoyed by my visit.

"Yes, yes, Archy," he said testily, "what is it now?"

"The Forsythe investigation," I said. "Father, it would help if I knew a little more about the family's finances. To be specific, who controls the exchequer?"

Of course he immediately lapsed into his mulling mode, trying to determine how much information he might ethically reveal. Finally he decided to trust his bubbleheaded sprout—to a limited degree.

"There is a grantor trust in existence," he said briefly. "The elder Forsythe is the trustee."

"Wife and children have no independent income?"

"They are given rather meager allowances for their personal expenses."

"Meager, sir?" I said. "As in skimpy, paltry, and stingy?"

"That is correct," he said with a wintry smile. "But he is also responsible for the taxes and upkeep of the Forsythe properties, including salaries of staff. It is not an inconsiderable sum, I assure you."

I persisted. "In other words, spouse and children are totally dependent upon Mr. Forsythe's largesse."

"Yes," he said irritably, "if you wish to put it that way."

"And in the event of the trustee's demise?"

"The estate is then distributed to the named beneficiaries. After payment of taxes, of course."

"And wife, son, and daughter are the named beneficiaries?"

He nodded. "The granddaughter's legacy will be held in trust by her father until she comes of age. There are additional bequests to members of the domestic staff."

"I don't suppose you'd care to reveal the value of the individual bequests."

"You don't suppose correctly," he said frostily.

"Considerable?" I suggested.

"Yes," he said, "I think that's a fair assumption."

I knew I'd get nothing more, thanked him for his assistance, and returned to my office. What had I learned? Little more than I had already guessed. The one mild surprise was that Mrs. Constance Forsythe was not independently wealthy. In Palm Beach, as elsewhere in the world, money usually marries money—which is why the rich get richer and the poor get bupkes.

I spent the next several minutes consulting telephone directories—more valuable to the amateur sleuth than a deerstalker cap and meerschaum pipe. I looked up the address and phone number of Rufino Diaz, the Forsythes' gardener. My purpose? No purpose. But during an investigation I am an inveterate collector of facts. Most of them inevitably turn out to be the drossiest of dross—but one never knows, do one? I also found the address and phone number of the Trojan Stables in Wellington.

I scrawled notes on both locations and tucked them into my wallet. I then bounced downstairs to our underground garage, boarded the Miata, and set out to explore.

On that morning, I recall, I was wearing an awning-striped sport jacket with fawny slacks, pinkish mocs (no socks, naturally), and my favorite fedora of white straw. The sun was beaming, the humidity mercifully low, and I felt it quite possible that I might live forever. The denouement of the Forsythe affair was to demolish that illusion.

I found the home of Rufino Diaz with little trouble. I was not amazed to discover he lived in a motel—many South Florida motels are happy to have year-round tenants—but I was surprised by the prosperous appearance of the place. I don't wish to imply it was the Taj Mahal, but it did seem to be more elegant and expensive than one might expect of the residence of a man who raked lawns for a living. I realized that Sheila Hayworth had probably spoken the truth when she said Rufino had a "cute little apartment." With Jacuzzi and ceiling mirrors, no doubt.

The Trojan Stables required a more lengthy search but was well worth the effort. It was a handsome spread—twenty acres at least, I estimated—with a smallish office building and a barn that looked large enough to accommodate twenty horses. The grounds were well groomed, with a practice ring, bridle paths, hurdles, and a water jump. The entire layout was encircled by a picket fence of weathered barn wood. Very attractive.

I cruised slowly, eyeballing the site. I thought I spotted Constance Forsythe standing firmly planted, hands on hips, observing a rider putting a young bay over the hurdles. But I did not stop to say howdy. Instead I drove back to the beach, pausing en route at a small deli in a strip mall to scarf a roast beef on white (mayo) and bologna on rye (mustard) with a bottle of Whitbread ale. I make no apology for this prodigal consumption of calories. After all, I'm a growing boy—and especially around the midriff.

I arrived at the Forsythe mansion and was admitted by Sheila Hayworth. She blinked twice when she saw my attire but made no comment, pro or con. Occasionally I am forced to endure the sneers of philistines who believe wrongfully that my flamboyant dress indicates color blindness or a sad lack of taste. I point out to them that I am merely following the laws of natural selection. All biologists know that the peacock with the most extravagant tail wins the peahen.

I used the phone on the library desk to call the Trojan Stables. A man answered and I asked to speak to Mr. Timothy Cussack. I was informed that Cussack did not work Mondays but was expected on the morrow. I hung up having confirmed that the former polo player who had treated Geraldine Forsythe so shabbily was now employed by her mother. A curious situation, wouldn't you say?

I then leafed through the stack of notes I had left atop the desk. The hairs I had carefully placed on pages 5 and 10 had disappeared. But that, I admitted ruefully, did not prove a family or staff member had been prying; it might have happened during Sgt. Al Rogoff's search. My dilemma reminded me of President Truman's anguished plea for a one-armed economist, someone incapable of saying, "On the other hand . . ."

I went looking for Mrs. Nora Bledsoe and found her seated at a small desk in the pantry, a room larger than the McNally kitchen. She was wearing horn-rimmed specs and appeared to be working on household accounts, entering bills and invoices into a ledger. She gave me a smile of welcome, a very nice smile that softened her somewhat imperious features.

"May I help you, Mr. McNally?" she asked.

"I hope you can," I said. "Mrs. Bledsoe, I notice that in a few of Mr. Forsythe's matched sets of leather-bound books a single volume is missing. It may have been borrowed by a member of the family or staff and I intend to ask everyone to provide a list of books temporarily removed from the library. My concern is that outsiders may have had access to the shelves. Is that possible? For instance, who handles the dusting chores?"

"My son and I and the two maids do the day-to-day straightening up," she replied. "And once a week we have a commercial cleaning service that takes care of vacuuming, washing windows, waxing the paneling and things like that. But they are never left alone. Never! We accompany them wherever they go. In addition, I make certain no bags or packages are taken from the house. I'm not saying it's utterly impossible for one of the cleaning crew to steal something small, slip it into his pocket, and walk out with it. We don't search them, you know. But we've been using the same company for years and to my knowledge we've never lost a thing. As for removing one or more of Mr. Forsythe's books, I'd say that was highly unlikely."

"Thank you, Mrs. Bledsoe," I said. "You've been very helpful. By the way, is your son around?"

"Not today. Anthony is off on Mondays."

"Well, I'll catch him another time. Perhaps he's borrowed a book or two."

"I doubt that," she said dourly. "Very much."

I started out but she called, "Mr. McNally," and I turned back.

"I have a book in my bedroom from Mr. Forsythe's library," she said with a weak laugh.

"Oh?" I said. "Could you tell me the title, please. I'll make a note of it."

"*The Love Song of J. Alfred Prufrock,*" she said, blushing slightly.

"Excellent choice," I told her and left. I returned to the library, musing on the vagaries of us all. I mean, who could have guessed the formidable housekeeper read Eliot? But then who would guess I enjoy listening to barbershop quartets?

I went back to my drudgery for the nonce, having nothing better to do. You know, the surprising thing was that most of the books showed evidence of having been read. The pages were cut, some were dog-eared, and a few bore lightly penciled comments in the margins—such profound judgments as "Well put!" and "Rubbish!"

I simply could not believe the Griswold Forsythes II and III had read all that much. But most of the volumes had been published at least a century ago, and I could only conclude the dog-earing and notations had been made by Forsythe forebears, perhaps including the lady who had committed suicide and whose ghost was said to haunt the dungeon.

I was laboring at my cataloging chores when the library door was opened. Geraldine Forsythe entered, and I rose to receive her.

"Good afternoon, Archy," she said.

"Good afternoon, Gerry. You're looking perky today."

"I feel perky," she said. "It's the sunshine I suppose. I brought you a list of books I've borrowed from the library."

"Thank you," I said, wondering how much longer I'd have to continue this masquerade. "It will be a big help."

She lowered herself into the leather armchair alongside the desk. She was wearing a poet's shirt, tails dangling over rather scanty white twill shorts. She lolled back and hooked one long, tanned leg over the arm of the chair. I am not an expert on body language but even an amateur might rightfully term that pose provocative.

"How is your sister-in-law feeling?" I inquired.

"Sylvia? Oh, she's up and about. Playing that stupid piano of hers, I expect."

"Harpsichord," I said gently.

"Is that what it is?" she said indifferently. "Well, she's recovered. You haven't seen her?"

"Today? No, I have not."

"That's a surprise," she said. "Our Sylvia is not a shy one."

I didn't quite know how to interpret that and made no reply. The sandaled foot hanging over the chair arm began bobbing up and down which indicated, I reckoned, a certain amount of emotional perturbation.

"Archy," she said, "do you know a man named Timothy Cussack?"

I frowned with concentration. "Cussack?" I repeated. "Sounds familiar but I don't believe I've ever met him."

"He once belonged to the Pelican Club."

"Perhaps that's where I heard the name. But he's not currently a member?"

"No," she said. "He was booted out for bouncing checks."

"Ah," I said, eager to hear what might be coming.

"Well," she said, not looking at me, "he was a polo player until he got hurt. I had a thing going with him for a while but then it ended."

I said nothing, waiting to hear how much more she would reveal.

"The reason I bring up his name," she continued, "is that I think he may have something to do with the disappearance of my jewelry. I'm not accusing him, you understand, but Tim was always hurting for money. I just thought you might want to check up on him."

I was silent a moment, thinking how best to handle this. "Gerry," I said, finally, "I'll certainly look into it, but where can I find this Cussack fellow?"

Then she turned to stare at me. "He's working at mother's stables. That's a laugh, isn't it?"

Her stare was at once defiant and challenging, and I knew she expected a reply—or at least a remark.

"Gerry," I said softly, "is your mother aware of your previous relationship with this man?"

"Of course," she said crossly. "Mother likes to come on tough but she's such a softy. She gave the skunk a job because she felt sorry for him. I guess he's a good trainer, but I was furious when I heard about it."

"And now you feel he may be involved in the theft of your jewelry? But would he have the opportunity? Has he ever been a guest in the house? Is he a frequent visitor?"

"No," she said, "not since we broke up. But I'm not accusing him of stealing the stuff himself. I think someone else may be taking it and giving it to Tim."

Was I dumbfounded? You betcha. "Giving it to him?" I said. "As a gift?"

Her short laugh was ugly. "More like a payoff," she said.

It took me half a mo to understand what she was implying.

"Are you suggesting blackmail?" I asked her.

She shrugged. "Could be. I'm just guessing, you understand. I have no evidence."

"Supposing, just supposing, your suspicions are correct, who is the victim of the blackmail and committing the actual theft?"

She leaned forward to scratch a bare ankle. Her head was lowered and I couldn't see her face. "My sister-in-law," she said in a tight voice. "Sylvia goes out to the farm to ride once or twice a week. I think she and Tim have something going and she's paying him off with my jewelry to keep his mouth shut—or maybe just in return for favors granted."

"Gerry," I said, "that's a very, *very* serious accusation."

Then she raised her head and showed me a face twisted with hurt. "It's not an accusation. I told you I have no evidence. But it's what I think is happening. I know Tim Cussack and I know Sylvia, and believe me it's possible. They're not nice people."

"It's a bloomin' soap opera!" I burst out.

"Of course it is," she readily agreed. "That's what life is, isn't it—a soap opera?"

"Sometimes," I said, and then with more prescience than I knew I possessed, I added, "Until it becomes a tragedy."

"There's nothing tragic about this," she said decisively. "It's just a tawdry sitcom and I want it ended. I couldn't care less if Sylvia wants to cheat on my brother. It's their problem, not mine. But I don't want to finance my sister-in-law's fling. You understand?"

I nodded.

"And you'll help me, Archy?"

"I'll do what I can."

She smiled and it made her look ten years younger. She stood up suddenly and before I had time to rise she was at my swivel chair and had slipped a warm arm about my shoulders. She leaned down, lips close to my ear.

"Oh, you're a sweetie," she said. "A sweet, sweet sweetie. Help me, Archy, and I'll make it worth your while. Really I will."

She pressed close and kissed me. Then she straightened and winked—yes, she actually winked!—and strode from the library, tanned legs flashing.

I sat behind the desk a few moments longer, reflecting that two hours spent in the Forsythe home were equivalent to a frontal lobotomy. I felt I was being reduced to their level of craziness. These were people Connie Garcia had called "dull, dull, dull," and they were all turning out to be actors in an amateur production of *Animal Crackers*.

The hell with it. I packed up and went home. The sea was too choppy for my usual afternoon swim, so I trudged upstairs to my lair. I lighted what I hoped was my first cigarette of the day (but wasn't sure) and poured myself a small marc. Then I donned reading glasses and set to work on my journal. I had much to record since the last entry.

After almost an hour of scribbling I read my disjointed notes, observations, and conjectures. Then I read them again. And you know, I realized I had learned something that day that might prove to be extremely significant.

Surely you can guess what it was.

9

I awoke late on Tuesday morning after having enjoyed a good night's sleep and a dream so lubricious I cannot recount it here lest I earn the censor's wrath—and the envy of my No. 1 pal, Binky Watrous, who complains constantly and bitterly that he can dream only of forklift trucks. I think the poor lad needs professional help.

I bounced downstairs to a deserted kitchen and fixed my own breakfast: a glass of chilled Clamato, duck pâté on a toasted bagel, and two cups of black instant. That may sound rather unusual to you but I see nothing bizarre about it. I once ate a whole baked flounder for breakfast—but that's another story.

The weather was splendid, an instant replay of the previous day, and as I headed up the coast in my sparky chariot I felt such a surge of joie de vivre that I broke into song. I wished for an audience so many could enjoy my rendition of "Bill Bailey, Won't You Please Come Home?"

When I pulled up to the front entrance of the Forsythe manse I saw an elegant trio lounging beneath the portico. The Griswold Forsythes, senior and junior, were wearing brass-buttoned navy blazers over white flannel slacks. And between father-in-law and husband stood Mrs. Sylvia Forsythe, obviously dressed for riding: jodhpurs and boots, an open calf-skin vest over a white turtleneck sweater.

Those three moneyed people looked so well scrubbed, so insouciant and faintly bored, that I had a sudden onslaught of nostalgia for a time I never knew. I could see them posed negligently for a Pierce-Arrow ad or perhaps debating whether or not to drop in at one of Gatsby's parties. Sleek was the word for them, the men with their hair slicked back and the woman with a cool glow. They made me feel like a lumpen.

I alighted from the Miata and Griswold III came ambling over to offer me an anodyne smile and a languid hand to shake.

"Hullo, Archy," he said. "Ready for another go at father's books? Making progress, are you?"

"Coming along," I answered. "And where are you off to? Not the office surely."

"Not today," he said. "Father and I are going out on some fellow's yacht."

"Sounds like fun," I observed.

The word seemed to offend him. "It's business," he said with such an air of self-importance that I wanted to feed him a knuckle sandwich. "This fellow hopes to sell us his boat. We're considering it. Ah, here's our wagon."

The big Rolls-Royce, driven by Anthony Bledsoe, came purring from the back of the mansion where the five-car garage was located. The houseman parked, hopped out, and held the door open.

"See you around, Archy," Griswold the Lesser said with a casual wave. "You and I must have a proper lunch one of these days."

"Yes," I said, "we must." I was horribly tempted to add, "So we can discuss the proper lighting of nude photos."

He climbed behind the wheel of the Rolls, his father joined him up front, and the tank pulled slowly away. Tony Bledsoe trotted back to the garage again and I joined Sylvia Forsythe.

"Hi, Archy," she said, putting a light hand on my shoulder. "Listen, you don't really want to spend such a scrumptious morning in that depressing library, do you?"

"Not really," I confessed.

"Why don't you follow me out to the stables and I'll show you around."

"Splendid idea," I said.

Bledsoe brought Sylvia's car around. It was a silver-gray Saturn, a very jazzy vehicle. He got out and held the door for her.

"Tailgate," she called to me. "I don't want you getting lost."

I nodded and headed for my roadster.

"Have a good time," Tony said, and I heard the longing in his voice.

Sylvia headed south to take the Flagler Bridge across Lake Worth to the mainland. I must tell you that woman drove as if pursued by Old Nick. I mean we *flew* and I nervously anticipated being stopped by the polizia and dragged off to durance vile.

But we arrived at the Trojan Stables without incident. By the time I dismounted from the Miata, Sylvia was standing near the office building chatting with Mrs. Constance Forsythe, who looked a mite blowsy with stained riding pants and a bush jacket that had spent too much time in the bush. I joined the ladies.

"Mrs. Forsythe," I said, addressing the elder, "I must tell you that your daughter-in-law drives like a maniac."

"I know she does," she agreed. "She'll break her lovely neck one of these days. If she rode my horses like she drives her car I'd have her gizzard."

Sylvia laughed and touched the other woman's cheek. "Horses are different, darling," she said. "Is Tim busy?"

"Out with a student right now."

"I want to show Archy around. Okay?"

"Of course. See if you can persuade him to muck out a few of the stalls."

"Not me," I protested. "When it comes to pitchforks I'm a complete klutz."

"You might learn to enjoy it," Constance said with a throaty laugh. "All that *Parfum d'Manure.*"

I wanted to say, "That's offal," but it's a written not a spoken pun.

Sylvia and I strolled about the horse farm and there is little I can add to what I have already described. The only surprise was the main barn, which had only half the stalls I had estimated. But the building included a tack room and living quarters for the stable boys—something like a dormitory.

"No drinking or drugs allowed," Sylvia said. "Caught once and out you go."

"Very admirable," I said, thankful I wasn't a stable boy. "Handsome horses," I commented although I know absolutely nothing about horseflesh except that when I place a bet it causes them to run slower.

"Constance doesn't own them. She boards them and feeds them, takes care of their ailments, and provides instruction in riding, jumping, and dressage—things like that. For a hefty fee, of course."

"It's a pricey hobby," I guessed.

"Horse people are nuts," Sylvia said flatly. "Hey, there's Timothy. Tim!" she called, waving. "Over here!"

We were standing on the tanbark outside the barn. The young man turned, waved back, and came sauntering toward us. Something insolent in that gait, I thought.

"Archy," Sylvia said, "meet Timothy Cussack. Tim, this is Archy McNally."

We shook hands, smiling like villains at each other. He was a hunk, no doubt about it. But not heavy or clumpy. More like a fencer or diver: tall and whiplike. Face suntanned almost to cordovan, which made his choppers startlingly white. Pale eyes and a wide mouth with faint laugh lines. I could see what had seduced Geraldine Forsythe.

"I've been giving Archy the fifty-cent tour," Sylvia said.

"Yeah?" he said. "You ride?" he asked me.

"Wheels," I said. "Not legs."

He laughed and I heard another clue to his charm. It was a hearty up-from-the-chest laugh and infectious. It was difficult to doubt his sincerity—but I managed.

"Sylvia will convert you," he advised me. "She's becoming one of our best exercise boys—girls, persons, whatever."

"What do I get today?" she asked him.

"How about Lady Macbeth?" he suggested.

"Tim!" she cried. "That's like riding a desk."

"She needs a run. Her owner is still up north and the poor beast hasn't been able to sniff the clover. Give her a break."

"Okay then," Sylvia said. "Lady Macbeth it is."

She went back into the barn; Timothy Cussack and I were left together.

"I keep thinking I've seen you before," I told him. "It couldn't have been the Pelican Club, could it?"

"Might have been," he said peaceably. "I drop by there occasionally. Not often. Dull place."

"It can be," I said, not yet ready to condemn him for this minor fabrication.

"What do you do?" he asked idly.

"I'm a flunky at my father's law firm, McNally and Son."

"Sounds like you got it made," he said.

I thought that was an extraordinary thing to say, expressing contempt and envy simultaneously.

"Well, I don't have a law degree," I informed him. "I just do odd jobs. Investigations and such."

Perhaps I had said more than I should have, because up to then he had been placidly pleasant, not displaying any great interest in our chatter. But suddenly his expression and manner became more animated.

"Investigations?" he said. "Like what?"

I was saved from answering by the reappearance of Sylvia, leading a saddled white mare, undeniably plump.

"We've only had her a few weeks," Cussack explained to me. "She does need thinning down. Right now I doubt if she could step up a curb, let alone take a low hurdle."

I must admit I admired the man, admired the way he talked and the way he carried himself. He leaked self-assurance, but nothing pushy, you understand; just cool confidence and an amused way of looking at things. I thought it possible he was totally amoral.

Sylvia brought Lady Macbeth alongside us. I took a small step backward. That horse looked enormous.

"Timmy," she said, "give me a leg up."

He linked his fingers, she stepped in the cup his hands formed, and he tossed her onto the English saddle. The whole movement was so smooth it was almost balletic. Sylvia waited, erect, while he adjusted the stirrups. Then she walked the horse away.

"No more than a canter," Cussack called after her, then turned back to me. "Want to try a ride?" he asked. It wasn't quite a jeer but it came close.

"I think not," I said. "But thank you for the offer."

"Listen," he said, serious now, "you mentioned you do investigations. Free-lance?"

"Nope," I said promptly. "Only for clients of McNally and Son. You're in need of a shamus?"

He looked at me a long moment and I saw wariness in those fallow eyes. then he turned to watch Sylvia Forsythe, who was now trotting Lady Macbeth along one of the bridle paths.

"Maybe," Cussack said. "It depends."

I was dying to ask, "On what?" but decided not to pin him. "Happy to have met you, Tim," I said, departing.

"Likewise," he said absently.

I decided to stop at the Pelican Club on my journey back to the beach and accumulate some nourishment. All that time spent in the bracing air of the Great Outdoors had given me an appetite—and a thirst.

The bar was crowded with the lunchtime mob and I glanced into the dining room. There, seated at our favorite table, was my light-o'-love, Connie Garcia. I scuttled to her side and she looked up.

"May I join you?" I asked.

"Sorry," she said, "I'm waiting for Humphrey Bogart."

"He's been dead for some time," I pointed out.

"So have you," she said. "You don't call, you don't write, you don't fax. What's *with* you?"

"My dear child," I said loftily, sliding onto the chair opposite her, "you must realize that I toil for a living, and frequently at jobs that require long hours and the utmost concentration on the business at hand."

"Which is usually monkey business," she added. "Are you going to feed me or not?"

"You haven't ordered yet?"

"Just got here before you arrived."

I waved at Priscilla Pettibone and she came sashaying to our table.

"Oh my," she said, "how nice it is to see Romeo and Juliet back together again. Or is it Julio and Romiet?"

"We didn't come here for a side order of sass," I told her. "We want food and drink, in reverse order. What's the special today?"

"Me," she said. "But if that doesn't suit you, Leroy is pushing crabmeat salad. Real crab, not that rubbery stuff you get in plastic packages."

"Sounds great," Connie said. "I'll have the crabmeat salad and a glass of chardonnay."

"Double it," I said. "And the sooner the better."

She winked at us and went into the bar area. Connie and I helped ourselves to kosher dill spears placed in Mason jars on each table along with a basket of peppered focaccia wedges.

"All kidding aside," Connie said, "what *have* you been doing?"

"All kidding aside," I answered, "I can't tell you. Client confidentiality and all that rot."

"But it has to do with the Forsythes, doesn't it?"

"Why do you say that?"

"Because you asked me about them and then there was that item in Lolly Spindrift's column."

"Clever lady," I said.

"So your job *does* involve the Forsythes?"

"Wild horses—and I met a few this morning—couldn't drag that information from me."

"Too bad," Connie said, "because just yesterday I heard some hot gossip about the Forsythes."

I'm not sure how one's ears perk up but I think mine did. "That's interesting," I said. "What did you hear?"

But then Priscilla served our wine and salads, and there was a cessation of talk as we began stuffing. An observer might think we had both been on oat bran diets for several weeks.

"So," I said after my hunger pangs had diminished slightly, "what gossip did you hear yesterday?"

She stopped excavating her salad bowl and looked up. "What will you give me?" she demanded.

"Connie," I said, "what you have just asked leaves me totally aghast. I mean I am saddened that after our many years together—intimate years I might add—you should require payment before divulging rumors that might possibly be of assistance and further my career. This is extortion, nothing less than rank extortion, and I refuse to be a party to it."

"How about a dinner at Cafe L'Europe?"

"You've got it," I said eagerly. "What did you hear?"

"Well, I heard it through a friend of a friend of a friend. The original friend was having lunch in the back room of Ta-boo and at a nearby table were the Forsythes, father and son. They weren't exactly shouting at each other, you understand, but there was a king-sized argument going on: red faces, raised voices, some pounding on the table. Very nasty it was, the informant reports."

"And did the informant overhear the subject of the fracas?"

"Afraid not. But apparently it was a first-class squabble. Archy, is that a clue?"

I almost choked on a chunk of crabmeat. "A clue to *what?*"

Connie shrugged. "Whatever it is you're doing."

"Darling, I appreciate your help. Really I do. But I'm not certain of the importance of the Forsythes' brannigan. Perhaps they were arguing about the best way to iron one's shoelaces. They're quite capable of that. But thank you for the report."

"And our dinner is still on?"

"Of course. Give you a call tomorrow."

"No," she said firmly. "I'll call you tonight."

We had lemon sorbet and cappuccino for dessert. Then I signed the tab and we went out to our cars.

"Thanks for the grub, luv," Connie said. "Do I get a goodbye kiss?"

"With mucho pleasure," I said, and so we kissed in the sunbaked parking lot: a delightful kiss tasting faintly of garlic. Connie looked smashing that day—but then she always looks first-class. She is short-ish and plumpish but has a glowing suntan that doesn't end, a mane of long, glossy black hair, and burning eyes. All admirable physical at-tributes, to be sure, but her greatest attractions are her wit and super-charged esprit. What bounce she has! Kissing her is akin to sticking your tongue in a light bulb socket. Then she turns on the switch.

After that fervent parting I drove to the Forsythe estate wondering what might have been the cause of the altercation that made both men, *père et fils,* become red-faced and pound the table. I could not believe it was anything serious simply because I did not take either of them se-riously. I thought they were both bloodless prigs. What a mistake that turned out to be!

Anthony Bledsoe opened the front door for me. I had the weirdest feeling that he had been awaiting my return.

"Have a good time?" he asked.

"Very enjoyable," I replied. "Although I'm not all that keen about horses. Do you ride?"

"Occasionally," he said. "I like it. Sometimes, on my day off, I go out to Mrs. Forsythe's farm and she lets me exercise one of the nags."

"Oh?" I said. "Do you know Timothy Cussack?"

"Tim? Sure, I know him. Nice guy."

"Seems to be," I said. "I met him for the first time today. Was he a good polo player?"

Bledsoe laughed. "When he wasn't hung over. Our Timmy likes the sauce."

"Don't we all," I said, tempted to add that bordelaise was my fa-vorite. "Is Lucy home?" I asked him.

"Oh yeah," he said. "The school van dropped her off about fifteen minutes ago. She's out back somewhere."

I nodded and went into the library, thinking I really should do a spot of cataloging. But the dreary chamber depressed me and I fled. I went hunting for Lucy, that lorn child who seemed like an outsider in the disordered Forsythe household.

10

I finally found her in the secret place. She was sitting on the ground, a small pad on her lap. She was chewing the stub of a pencil and her face was twisted with concentration.

"Hi, sweetheart," I said.

She started, then looked up and smiled. Sunlight glinted off the bands on her teeth.

"Am I really your sweetheart?" she asked.

"Of course you are," I told her. "I have several but you are definitely Numero Uno. What are you doing?"

"I'm writing a poem," she said timidly.

"Good for you," I said. "Will you read it to me?"

"It's not finished yet."

"Well, when it's finished may I read it?"

"I don't know," she said doubtfully. "It's very private."

"I thought we were friends, Lucy. Friends can show each other their private poems."

"They can? Do you have any private poems?"

"Many," I assured her.

"Tell me one."

I thought she was a bit immature for "There was a young man from Nantucket," so I recited "I never saw a purple cow." It was an immediate success; she laughed and clapped her hands.

"That's a nice poem," she said. "I like it when they rhyme. My poem rhymes."

"Grand," I said. "Did you go to school today?"

"Uh-huh."

"And what did you teach the teacher?"

She laughed again. "You're silly," she said. "The teacher teaches us. Everyone knows that. Today we learned about George Washington."

"Splendid chap. Never lied."

"Yes, he did," she corrected me. "But only when he had to. He didn't like to lie. Some people do, you know."

Her wisdom was breathtaking.

"I can't believe anyone lies to you, Lucy."

"Oh, yes they do," she said sadly. "My mother, my father—lots of people. They're supposed to love me but they really don't. Leastwise they never say they do and so they're lying, aren't they?"

This was becoming murky and I didn't quite know how to handle it. "I'm sure your parents love you, Lucy," I said, "but sometimes people find it hard to express their love. They just assume you know it."

"Well, if they both love me," she said with the illogic of the very young, "then why are they always fighting?"

"Darling," I said, "perhaps it has nothing to do with you. They may disagree about other things but I'm certain they agree about their love for you."

"I don't know," she said gloomily. "I heard mom say to dad, 'If it wasn't for Lucy I'd be out of here tomorrow.' And he said, 'Don't let the kid stop you.' That doesn't sound like they love me, does it?"

I felt like weeping. She was disclosing things I really didn't want to know. I was acutely uncomfortable listening to these distressing revelations. Most of all I was anguished by the intensity of her unhappiness. No child should be a shuttlecock between gaming parents and, even worse, be aware of it.

"Lucy," I said, "I love you," and the moment I said it I knew it was true. I leaned down to stroke her silken hair. "So don't ever believe no one loves you. Many people do, I'm sure, and I'm one of them."

"That's okay," she said bravely. "I'm not going to cry. I decided I'm never going to cry again."

I had to leave her; I just couldn't take more.

"Listen, dear," I said, "I hope you haven't forgotten about that picnic you and I are going to have."

"Oh no," she said, eyes wide. "I remember."

"Good. Let's make it real soon."

"I love you, too," she said suddenly.

Then I left and stumbled my way back to the main house, sad and shaken. I was ready to return as quickly as possible to the McNally digs and have a wallop to restore my belief in this, the best of all possible worlds. But it was not to be.

As I proceeded down the main hallway to the front door, the Griswold Forsythes, II and III, were just entering in their blazers and flannel bags. We stopped to chat.

"Good voyage?" I asked them.

"Nice cruise," the younger replied. "Fine lunch with bubbly. But I don't think we want to buy that particular yacht, do we, father?"

"We don't want to buy *any* yacht," the older said sharply. "Archy, may I see you in the library for a moment."

Griswold III departed, his crest somewhat droopy, and I followed the II into the library. He took the swivel behind the desk and I sat in the armchair alongside. I imagined, with dread, he was about to report another item of value was missing. It turned out to be worse than that.

"My wife and I occupy separate bedrooms," he said stonily. "Last night I retired shortly before midnight and found this note placed on my pillow."

He reached into his jacket pocket and then handed me a square of paper. It had two straight and two ragged edges as if it had been torn from the corner of a larger sheet of white foolscap.

Written on it in large block letters were two words: YOUR NEXT. The printing was quavery, as if it had been done with the left hand of a right-handed person, or vice versa. There was no way of knowing if it had been inscribed by man or woman.

I studied those two words a moment and naturally, because I have rather pedantic leanings, I immediately noted the absence of an apostrophe. If the first word was intended to be a contraction of YOU ARE, the writer was obviously a dolt. But perhaps the message was meant to be an abbreviated warning that another of Mr. Forsythe's possessions would soon disappear: YOUR (something) NEXT.

I explained this to our client. He listened impatiently and didn't seem impressed.

"I guessed all that myself," he said irritably. "I am not an idiot, you know. I believe it is a misspelled threat against my person—YOU ARE NEXT, without the apostrophe. Do you agree?"

"Yes, sir," I said. "I think that's the correct assumption. And after

what happened to Mrs. Sylvia I urge you to report this to Sergeant Rogoff as soon as possible."

He looked at me queerly. "It's a shock," he said, "to realize that
someone in your home plans to do you harm. Strangle you, perhaps."

"You have every right to feel that way, Mr. Forsythe. It's a terrible
thing. Who has access to your bedroom, sir?"

"Everyone in the house. The door is never locked."

"All the more reason to call in the police. Would you like me to
phone Sergeant Rogoff now?"

He paused a moment. "No," he said, "not yet. I want to make a few
inquiries myself this evening."

"Please, Mr. Forsythe," I urged, "don't postpone it. I take this note
very seriously. Your life may be in danger."

"I am well aware of that, young man," he said almost angrily. "And
this evening I shall lock my bedroom door and prop a chair under the
inside knob. I'll survive the night, I assure you." He pondered, pulling
at his lower lip. Then: "I suggest you, Sergeant Rogoff, and I meet at
my office tomorrow. You know where it is?"

"Yes, sir."

"My son has an appointment with his periodontist at noon. Our
clerk"—(he pronounced it 'clark')—"customarily leaves for lunch at
twelve fifteen. If you and the sergeant arrive at twelve thirty I believe
we'll be able to have a private discussion about this unpleasant matter
without interruption. Is that satisfactory?"

"I would prefer the police be notified immediately, Mr. Forsythe, but
if that is your wish we'll meet with you tomorrow. You don't want to
discuss it here?"

"No," he said shortly. "Not in this house."

"During our talk with Sergeant Rogoff do you intend to inform him
about your missing property?"

"No."

"Have I your permission to tell him?"

"No."

The Abominable No-Man.

I sighed. "Very well, sir, we'll do it your way—against my better
judgment I might add. May I keep the note?"

"Keep the damned thing," he said roughly. "The writer has made his
point."

"Or hers," I said.

He stared at me a sec. "You may be right," he said.

I stuffed the note into my pocket and rose to depart.

"Archy," Griswold Forsythe II said formally, "I wish to thank you for your efforts on my behalf."

It was a gentlemanly thing to say and also, considering the circumstances, rather gallant and touching. He was not lacking in courage. Foolhardy perhaps, but not a craven.

I drove home at a carefully disciplined speed because if I surrendered to my baser instincts I would have broken all local and state laws dealing with the reckless operation of a vehicle. But once inside the Mc-Nally kitchen I mixed a vodka and water with such haste that Ursi Olson, preparing our dinner, looked at me with surprise.

"Thirsty?" she asked.

"Parched," I told her.

I took my plasma into father's study and used his phone to call Sgt. Rogoff at his office. He wasn't in, but the desk sergeant who knew me said he was on a forty-eight. I had Al's home phone number and called him there. After seven rings he answered and I knew at once I had wakened him.

" 'Lo," he said sleepily.

"Aw," I said, "I interrupted your nappy-poo. Sorry about that, chum."

"I'll bet," he said. "What's on your mind—if I may exaggerate?"

"You and I have a date tomorrow," I said.

"Oh goody," he said. "How shall I dress? Long gown?"

"Just shut up," I said. "Al, this is serious."

I told him about the note Mr. Forsythe had found lying on his pillow.

"Son of a bitch," Rogoff said bitterly. "Something screwy is going on in that joint. I hate these family cases; they always turn out to be a mess. Give me a straight, cut-and-dried mugging any day. Who's got the note now?"

I said I did and would deliver it to him when we met at the Forsythes' office at twelve thirty on Wednesday to discuss the situation with Griswold II.

"Why there?" Al asked.

"Because he refused to meet at his home. Perhaps he's afraid the

place is bugged. I'm beginning to believe the entire family are para-
noids."

"Or maybe just plain wacky. Well, I'm supposed to be off duty tomorrow but I'll be there. Thanks so much for dumping this slumgul-
lion on my plate."

"That's what friends are for," I said and hung up.

I went into the living room and then out onto our little terrace that
afforded a good view of the ocean. I saw a lot of whitecaps and decided
a swim would be dicey. So I climbed upstairs to my dorm and worked
on my journal until it was time for the McNally cocktail hour.

We dined on vichyssoise that night, followed by crab cakes with a
salsa that had a zing. Dessert was an almond torte with a white chocolate frosting, which meant that the waistbands of my slacks would
continue to shrink.

I huffed and puffed to my lair and continued bringing my professional diary up-to-date. When my phone rang around nine o'clock I
was certain it would be Connie Garcia calling to set a time for our dinner date Wednesday night. So I answered with a warm "Hi!"

My caller laughed. "This is Sylvia Forsythe," she said. "Do you customarily answer your phone by shouting, 'Hi!'?"

"Hardly," I said. "But I was expecting a call from my grandfather
in Spokane and he's a bit hard-of-hearing."

"What a faker you are!" she marveled. "Archy, I was disappointed
you had left when I returned from my ride this morning. I was hoping
we might have lunch."

"Sorry about that," I said. "But I didn't know how long you'd be
gone. We'll make it another time."

"I'm going to hold you to that," she said. "You and I have a lot to
talk about, don't we?"

That was a poser. But it would have been boorish to ask, "About
what?" So I said nothing.

There was a pause requiring a pregnancy test; apparently the lady
was awaiting a reply. Finally, when there was none, she said, "What
did you think of Tim Cussack?"

"Seems like a solid fellow," I answered, lying valiantly. "Very handsome."

"Isn't he?" she said with some enthusiasm. "All the women go gaga
over him."

"You too?" I asked boldly.

"Me too," she admitted. "But the competition is fierce."

She talked in riddles and I was lost. I decided to switch to less intimate topics.

"Still playing your harpsichord?"

"Oh yes. I'd go mad without my music."

"And riding."

"And riding," she agreed. "And other things," she added throatily.

The sexual innuendo again.

"As long as you're happy," I said lamely.

"I wouldn't go that far," she said, laughing again. "But I'm working at it. Archy, the next time you're in-residence I insist you give me a few minutes. I may be plinking away at Vivaldi or I may be in my bedroom. In any event, do look me up. Okay?"

"Of course."

"Bye-bye," she cooed and hung up.

I took a deep breath and exhaled noisily. She had just succeeded in putting the kibosh on Geraldine Forsythe's dizzy scenario: Sylvia Forsythe was making nice-nice with Timothy Cussack, her sister-in-law's former lover. But that plot now wilted. If she and the matinee idol were having an affair, why on earth was she coming on to me so blatantly? A puzzlement.

I continued scribbling in my journal and it couldn't have been more than five minutes later when my phone jangled again. This time I was certain it was Connie Garcia. "Hi!" I said ardently.

There was a short silence, and then the caller, a woman, asked, "Is this Archy McNally?"

"It is," I confessed.

"This is Geraldine Forsythe. Do you usually answer the phone by saying 'Hi!'?"

"A slight mistake," I said. "I was expecting a call from my dear old grandmother who's in the hospital with a severe case of shinsplints resulting from her run in the Boston Marathon. How are you, Gerry?"

"Very well, thank you. Archy, I was wondering if you've managed to meet Timothy Cussack."

"As a matter of fact I have, just this morning."

"And what is your take on him?"

"Seems to have a great deal of charm," I said cautiously.

Her laugh was flimsy. "Oh yes," she said, "charm is Tim's stock-in-trade. You're going to follow up on it, aren't you?"

"You're referring to your suspicions?"

"They're more than suspicions, Archy. Believe me, I know I'm right. But I need evidence and I'm depending on you to provide it. You will try, won't you?"

"Of course."

"This is very important to me, Archy. I'm sure you realize that."

"I do."

"Good. I won't be able to pay you with money but I think you'll be happy with your reward. Nighty-night, darling!"

She hung up, leaving me to reflect that Al Rogoff had been correct: the Forsythes were a clan of wackos.

To make a long story short (if it's not too late) when my phone rang fifteen minutes later I was careful to answer formally, "Archibald McNally." And of course it was Connie Garcia. We made a date for the following evening at the Cafe L'Europe at seven thirty. Our conversation was brief because Connie was watching a Bugs Bunny Festival on cable TV.

"Bugs reminds me of you, Archy," she said before she hung up.

After reviewing my three phone calls I didn't feel like Bugs Bunny; I saw myself more like Pepe Le Pew. It made me wonder if since taking on the Forsythe case I had been living in a cartoonish world. I longed for the day I could stutter, "Th-th-that's all, folks!"

Wednesday morning brought reality and I dressed with less than my usual panache, preparing for the meeting with Griswold Forsythe II at twelve thirty. I breakfasted with my parents in the dining room and mother remarked how "spiffy" I looked in my black suit, white shirt, maroon tie.

"Is it graduation day?" father asked with heavy good humor, but I could see he was pleased that for once I wasn't attired like Carmen Miranda.

He drove to work in his black Lexus and I followed in my jauntier surrey. I went directly to my tiny oubliette and began working on my monthly expense account, a fictional masterpiece that might be entitled "Great Expectations." I smoked one cigarette that morning and made one phone call—to the Cafe L'Europe, reserving a table for two that evening.

Shortly after twelve o'clock I left the McNally Building and strolled westward on Royal Palm Way to the structure housing the Forsythes' office. It was a rather grungy three-story edifice of indeterminate age and something of an eyesore. In fact, local newspapers occasionally published indignant Letters to the Editor demanding that the damned thing be demolished in favor of a more attractive building suitable for that prestigious avenue.

It was a warren of small offices, occupied mainly by attorneys and real estate and insurance agents. The Forsythes' cubby, I recalled, was on the top floor, reached by a creaky automatic elevator. I remembered their suite as being a smallish reception room, hardly large enough for the clerk's desk, and a larger office in the rear that held a handsome oak partners' desk, used by father Griswold and son Griswold.

I waited across the street in the shade of a plump bottle palm. At about twelve-twenty I spotted Sgt. Al Rogoff's pickup cruising slowly along while he scanned building numbers. I waved, he saw me, waved back. He turned the corner and apparently parked, for a few minutes later he appeared on foot, trundling along like a fire hydrant on wheels. He was wearing a loose-fitting khaki safari suit and if he was armed, as I assumed he was, it was not noticeable.

"You look like you're going to a funeral," he said, eyeing my duds. "You bring the note?"

I took it from my jacket pocket and handed it over. Al studied it a moment.

"No apostrophe," he commented. "How do you figure that?"

"I figure the writer was not a Rhodes Scholar," I said.

"Brilliant, Mr. Holmes," Al said. "Let's go get this over with. I've got a heavy pinochle game planned for this afternoon."

That elevator was scarcely larger than a coffin and it made alarming thumps and groans as it carried us slowly to the third floor.

"We'd have made better time walking up the stairs," Rogoff groused.

The door to the office had an upper half of frosted glass and bore the inscription GRISWOLD FORSYTHE II and below that GRISWOLD FORSYTHE III, both names in a painted script that had flaked away in spots.

I pushed the door open and we entered the empty reception room.

"Mr. Forsythe," I called. "Archy McNally. We're here."

No answer.

The sergeant and I looked at each other.

"Are you sure he said twelve-thirty?" Al asked.

"Yes, I'm sure," I said peevishly and called again, "Mr. Forsythe!"

No answer.

Rogoff tried the knob on the door to the inner office. It turned easily, the portal swung open, we stepped in.

Griswold Forsythe II was lying supine on the worn Persian rug behind the partners' desk. His arms were spread wide and his open eyes stared sightlessly upward.

Al went down quickly on one knee alongside him, leaned close, peered, touched his neck.

"A mackerel," he said.

I took a deep breath. "There goes your pinochle game," I said.

11

Al commanded me to wait outside in the tiled corridor and I obeyed. I paced up and down, smoked two English Ovals, and watched as the investigation got under way. I heard sirens, uniformed and plainclothes officers appeared. Then Tom Bunion, the ME's man, showed up, gave me a cool nod, and disappeared inside. He was followed by a crew of ambulance attendants wearing whites and carrying a body bag and folding stretcher.

Finally, more than a half-hour later, Sgt. Rogoff came out of the Forsythes' office, juicing up one of his fat cigars.

"Heart attack?" I asked him.

"Don't I wish," he said. "Strangled."

"Oh lordy," I said. "Did he have scratches and cuts on his neck similar to the wounds Mrs. Sylvia received?"

"Nope," Al said. "Where's the son?"

"The late Mr. Forsythe told me he had a twelve o'clock appointment with his periodontist."

"And the clerk?"

"Apparently he went out to lunch every day at twelve fifteen."

The sergeant nodded. "Then eventually they'll both show up—I hope. Forsythe told you about the note yesterday?"

"That's correct."

"Why didn't you call me immediately?"

"I tried to persuade him, Al, but he wouldn't have it. He said he wanted to make some inquiries himself last night."

"Maybe he did. And maybe it got him aced."

"You think it was someone from his house or someone he knew?"

Rogoff flipped a palm back and forth. "Could be. But he's got no wallet on him."

"You mean it could have been a stranger, a villain casing the building for a soft touch and stumbling on Forsythe alone in an unlocked office?"

"I doubt it," Al said. "He had a gold pocket watch in his vest with a gold chain heavy enough to moor the QE-Two. It wasn't touched. A grab-and-run scumbag would have lifted that. No, I think all the killer wanted was the wallet—if Forsythe carried one and he probably did. The son or wife will know. Go home, Archy. There's nothing more you can do here."

I nodded. "Keep me up to speed, will you?"

"Sure," he said. "That flock of loonies aren't a laugh anymore, are they?"

"No," I said. "Not funny at all. Just one more thing, Al: when was he killed?"

"Maybe a half-hour ago, give or take."

We stared at each other.

"You mean," I said, almost choking, "the strangler might have been bouncing down the stairs while we were coming up in the elevator?"

"It's possible," the sergeant said grimly. "How does that grab you, sonny boy?"

I started back to the McNally Building, then detoured to the nearest pub for a shot of single-malt Scotch. I was spooked, no doubt about it. As Al had said, the crazy doings at the Forsythe castle were no longer amusing. The wall between comedy and tragedy had come tumbling down.

I found I had no appetite at all (surprised?), returned to my office, and phoned Mrs. Trelawney. She said my father was lunching at his desk and couldn't be disturbed. I knew what that meant: he was having his customary roast beef on whole wheat bread (hold the mayo) and a glass of iced tea. Woe betide anyone who interrupted that sumptuous feast. Mrs. T. promised to call me when he had finished his dessert—a Tums.

I spent the next twenty minutes at my desk, smoking up a storm and recalling those meandering comments Mr. Forsythe had made about death during our first interview. He had claimed he looked forward to dissolution with curiosity and a certain degree of relish.

I didn't believe a word of it. Knowing the man, I was positive he had died outraged that anyone would *dare* usher him so unceremoniously into the hereafter.

My summons finally arrived and I climbed the back stairway to father's office. I found him seated at his rolltop desk, reviewing a stack of blue-bound legal documents.

"Yes, Archy," he said pleasantly enough, "what is it now?"

"Bad news, sir," I said.

I told him of the death of Griswold Forsythe II and how Sgt. Rogoff and I happened on the scene so soon after the murder had been committed. I related the few details Al had revealed and assured father I had done my best to persuade Mr. Forsythe to call the police immediately after I had learned of the threatening note.

The guv listened to my recital in silence. I thought I saw sadness in his eyes but perhaps I was imagining. Then he swung halfway around in his swivel chair so I could not see his face. I wondered if there might be tears aborning.

"I knew that man for forty years," he said, his voice steady. "One of my first clients. I cannot say that I particularly liked him but I respected him. He was an honorable man. Testy occasionally and something of a bore, but honorable. Archy, do you feel his murder has any connection at all with the thefts of his property?"

"It's only a guess, father, but I'd say yes, the two are somehow connected."

"I concur," he said stonily. "I want you to continue your investigation. Is that understood?"

"Yes, sir."

"Has the family been notified?"

"I don't know. I doubt it. It happened only a few hours ago."

He stood up and when he turned to me he was in character again: the conscientious, reliable family solicitor. "I'll call Sergeant Rogoff at once. There is much to be done. I suggest you not visit the Forsythe home for a day or two. Leave them alone with their grief. Unless your presence is requested, of course."

"I'd like to attend the funeral, sir."

"All the McNallys will attend," he said firmly, "if it is not limited to the immediate family."

And on that somber note we parted. I returned to my office, and what I did next may strike you as rather crass and unfeeling. But I considered my actions as deposits (of information) that might possibly earn a profit (of information) in the future. And so I phoned Lolly Spindrift.

"Hi, hon," he said breezily. "What luscious tidbit of gossip are you in need of today?"

"None," I said. "But I have something for you. About two hours ago Griswold Forsythe the Second was murdered, strangled, in his office on Royal Palm Way."

I heard him gasp. "For real?" he asked.

"Absolutely, Lol. I saw the body—but for God's sake keep me out of it."

"So I shall, sweetie," he said. "I'm going to hang up now and dash over to the news desk. Thanks, luv. I owe you one."

My second call was to Connie Garcia. I told her what had happened. Her reaction was unexpected.

"Shit!" she said furiously. "Is there no end to this madness? Archy, what's happening to our world? When does the killing stop?"

"Never," I said.

"Don't say that!" she cried. "I don't want to hear it."

"I'll call if I learn more," I said. "And if you hear anything about the Forsythe family please let me know. I'll meet you tonight at seven thirty at Cafe L'Europe."

I hung up before she could reply. I didn't feel my two phone calls had been unethical. The murder, I was certain, would be featured on the evening newscasts of local radio and TV stations, so I was revealing no secrets. And by briefing my informants in advance I was convincing them that providing me with inside info was not a one-way street.

People occasionally accuse me of being devious. They may be right.

But now I had an immediate problem. Father had instructed me to continue my investigation but had warned me to stay away from the Forsythe home for a day or two until their mourning had lessened. Unless my presence was requested, he had added. But I thought that an unlikely possibility. How then was I to spend my working hours for two days? The fiddling of my expense account would take only a fraction of that time; I am a rapid fictioneer.

I decided I might profitably use the time to investigate the past and present activities of Timothy Cussack. That dashing lad seemed to be intimately involved with the three Forsythe women—Constance, Geraldine and Sylvia—and I needed to know more about him. If the truth be known (and I would prefer it not be) I was a trifle envious. He was everything I was not—maddeningly slender, catnip to the female gender, and with an aloof self-confidence I could never hope to equal. He seemed a good target for my discreet inquiries—the swine!

I planned the usual credit check with the agencies McNally & Son uses. And there was a new national service to which we had recently subscribed. It had computerized all cases of fraud in insurance and medical claims, including names and addresses of claimants, Social Security numbers, aliases, and disposition of their cases. It really is becoming more difficult to be a successful swindler. Just thought I'd let you know.

But computers, as any street cop will tell you, are no substitute for pounding the pavement and knocking on doors. But before I started traipsing about I looked up the address of T. Cussack in the West Palm telephone directory. I found it. Was I bowled over? A perfect strike! Apparently he lived in the same luxe motel as Rufino Diaz, the Forsythes' gardener.

Remember my telling you the Forsythe ragout resembled one of those kids' puzzles in which numbered dots are connected to form a completed picture? Only in this case, I remarked, all the dots were unnumbered. After discovering where Timothy Cussack lived I realized I had just added another dot.

A less adroit chap might be tempted to phone Timothy Cussack at the Trojan Stables and ask straight out, "I say, old boy, do you and Rufino Diaz occupy the same apartment at that jolly motel?"

To which his reply was likely to be one of the following:

1. "Why do you want to know that?"

2. "Are you investigating me?"

3. "Go dance around the maypole, chum."

Motels are organized more like hotels than condominiums. I mean they usually have a central switchboard through which all phone calls are routed. I tried Cussack's number and was rewarded by a chilly female voice declaring, "The Michelangelo Motel."

I was awfully tempted to say, "The Sistine Chapel, please." But instead I said, "May I speak to Mr. Timothy Cussack, please. I'm afraid I don't know what room he's in."

"We do not have rooms," she stated severely. "All our accommodations are suites. Mr. Cussack occupies Suite 309, but he won't be in until this evening."

"I'll try him then," I said. "Thank you so much for your kind assistance."

That softened her. She replied cheerily, "You're quite welcome, sir."

My next call was to Mrs. Trelawney, pop's ancient private secretary. "How would you like to play detective, Mrs. T.?" I asked.

"Do I get to frisk a suspect?" she asked eagerly.

"Not quite," I said, laughing, "but you'll earn my undying affection. Here's what I'd like you to do . . ."

I gave her the phone number of the Michelangelo Motel and told her to ask for Rufino Diaz. It was almost certain he would not be home but that was fine; all I wanted was the number of the suite he occupied.

Mrs. Trelawney called me back in less than five minutes.

"Rufino Diaz has Suite 309," she reported.

"Loverly," I said. "Thanks so much, sweet."

"Archy, what's this all about?"

"I'm setting up a bordello staffed by studs for the convenience of bored and/or lonely ladies."

"You will send me a menu, won't you?"

"For you," I promised, "everything's on the house."

She made a coarse rejoinder to that and I hung up laughing again. Mrs. T. is a glorious antique, wears a wig of wiry gray hair, and may be the raunchiest lady I know. She has served my father for aeons and he still believes her to be the soul of propriety. The governor is tremendously wise, you understand, but in some things he is not too swift. When it comes to street smarts, for instance, he may even be a bit retarded.

You may feel all the foregoing was a roundabout way of determining whether or not Cussack and Diaz shared the same digs. But I did it that way because I did not want either lad to become aware that the famous bloodhound, A. McNally, was sniffing along his spoor. And if I had made a personal visit to the Michelangelo Motel, I might have been remembered and described by the desk clerk. You see how indefatigably sneaky we sherlocks must be?

It was then getting on toward my ocean swim time, and despite the wrenching events of that day I was resolved to maintain my routine. I returned home and, still lunchless, did my two-mile wallow. I then showered and dressed for the family cocktail hour and my dinner with Connie Garcia.

But routine was shattered when mon père did not appear to mix the traditional pitcher of martinis. I did the honors while my saddened mother explained that he was at the Forsythe home, offering what solace he could.

"Mother," I said, "I refuse to have you dining alone. I'll postpone my date with Connie, and you and I shall console each other."

"No, no, Archy," she protested. "Father promised to be home for dinner and you know he always keeps his word. No, you go ahead. Oh dear, I feel so sorry for the Forsythes. I must call tomorrow and ask if there is anything I can do to help."

"Father said we'll all go to the funeral unless it's limited to the immediate family. In any case we must send flowers."

"Of course," she said determinedly. "I'll take care of it."

I moved to her, hugged her shoulder, kissed her velvety cheek. Isn't it odd how death prompts an immediate display of love? I suppose it's realization of human fragility and a desire to hang on to something lasting.

I admit that when I drove to Worth Avenue to meet Connie Garcia I was not in the sprightliest of moods. But I could not allow my megrims to affect our dinner. I decided I would play my usual bubble-headed self, ready with a silly jape and the sort of surreal nonsense that made Connie laugh uncontrollably. I fancied myself a sufficiently skilled farceur to make the evening a success.

Actually it was Connie who turned the trick. She was at her frisky best, and during that splendid feast she kept our banter light and frivolous. It was not until we had espresso and shared an apple tart that our conversation became weightier and we spoke of the death of Griswold Forsythe the 2nd.

"You know," Connie said, "after you phoned this afternoon I went into the sitting room where Lady Cynthia was playing solitaire. Cheating, of course; she always does. I told her of the murder and she just grunted. Didn't even look up from her cards."

"Typical reaction," I commented.

"Yes, but then when I started to leave the room she said, 'I had a brief fling with that man once. Very brief.' That's what she said, Archy."

I smiled. "I imagine Lady Horowitz has had a brief fling with most of the male population of Palm Beach."

"I suppose. But then she repeated his name, Griswold Forsythe, and said, 'We used to call him Grisly Forsythe. What a lump he was. It was hard to believe the gossip about him.' Well, you asked me to tell you if I heard anything about the Forsythes so naturally I said, 'What gossip was that?' And she said—still laying out the cards—'Oh, it happened years and years ago. Before you were born, Connie.' Then she said, 'Don't you have any work to do?' And I knew it would do no good to question her again and I left."

I was intrigued. "She said it was gossip years and years ago about Griswold Forsythe?"

"That's right."

"Gossip Lady Horowitz found it hard to believe?"

"Uh-huh."

"Flimsy," I said. "Definitely flimsy. But I'll try to pin it down."

"Oh golly," Connie said. "Don't ask Lady Cynthia about it. If she finds out I told you what she said she'll break my face."

"Of course I won't ask her. She'd just tell me to get lost, as you well know."

Connie finished her espresso. She said, "It's funny, isn't it, Archy?"

"What's funny?"

"That years and years ago, before you and I were born, people were misbehaving."

I laughed. "Did you think you and I invented sex?"

She looked at me wide-eyed with mock solemnity. "Didn't we?" she asked.

We left the Cafe L'Europe and reclaimed our cars. I followed Connie home to her condo on the east shore of Lake Worth. I accompanied her upstairs to her trig little apartment. And we invented sex—again.

I departed shortly after midnight and drove home to the darkened McNally manse. I made certain the back door was relocked after I entered, and then I trod as quietly as I could up to my miniature penthouse on the third floor. I undressed and pulled on a robe of black silk—a fitting garment, I mournfully reflected.

I poured myself a very small marc but did not light a cigarette after recalling I had gone through half a pack during that tumultuous day. I sat at my desk, bare feet up, and thought about the curious allusion Lady Cynthia Horowitz had made to long-ago gossip about the murdered man.

I knew it would be hopeless to ask her to tell me more. I liked Lady C. and I think she liked me, but as an aged friend of hers (now deceased) once remarked, "Archy, if you can't be mean, nasty, and cranky, what's the point of growing old?" The lady was a living confirmation of that philosophy. She would refuse to reveal a secret the moment she discovered it might be of value to someone else. She had a net worth of zillions and she didn't amass her wealth by being Lady Bountiful.

And that led me to wonder if every human being is a sanctuary of secrets. We all know things—about ourselves and about others—we will take to the grave—not so? I admit there are several things I know that are better left unwritten and unspoken. You, too.

After a few moments of this dreary pondering I put on earphones and listened to a tape of Ethel Merman singing Cole Porter's "Down in the Depths."

It suited my mood perfectly.

12

Thursday brought so-so weather but I was not discouraged. I awoke molto vivace, ready to challenge fate with a smile on my lips and a song in my heart. And my solitary breakfast—bagel, cream cheese, lox and onion—reinforced my confidence. I was certain that before night crashed I would solve all the Forsythe puzzles that bedeviled me—and possibly discover what happened to Jimmy Hoffa.

I took my second cup of instant black into father's study to search the Yellow Pages for addresses of local pawnbrokers. What a jolt that was! There were almost fifty in the West Palm Beach area, and that made me wonder how our stretch of shore had earned the sobriquet of Gold Coast since so many citizens were apparently in hock.

I am not totally allergic to routine labor, mind you, but it struck me that visiting fifty pawnbrokers scattered over many square miles of South Florida was not the most creative way of spending my time. I compromised by making a list of a dozen hockshops closest to the Town of Palm Beach. Then, carrying my catalog of items purportedly stolen from the late Griswold Forsythe II and his daughter, I sallied forth to play the dogged flic undaunted by the enormity of his task.

It was about three in the afternoon when I stopped at a pawnshop on Dixie Highway in West Palm. Surprisingly, it seemed to be an up-scale joint with an attractive window display of estate jewelry. But what caught my attention was a small, sturdy sculpture, the bust of a young African woman, her neck encircled with yards of necklaces.

I entered the shop, a bell jangled, the proprietor came shuffling from a back room. I estimated his age at 342 but his eyes were clear, sparkling and knowing. He used a cane with the carved head of a fox as a handle. An apt touch.

"Yes, sir," he said brightly, "what can I do for you today?" His voice was firm and vigorous. I hoped that when I was as venerable I would be as fortunate.

"That statue in your window, sir," I said. "Is that a Benin bronze?"

His sly smile was charming. "You have a good eye, sir," he said. "That's exactly what it is—a Benin bronze. Lovely—no? You are a collector?"

"Amateur, sir," I told him. "Is the piece for sale?"

"Not at the moment, sir," he said. "It is still in pawn. But I suspect it may be offered to the public about a week from now."

I knew it would be useless to ask the name of the pawner. He would never reveal that information (except to the police) and the question could destroy our rapport.

"Sir," I said, "if I leave you my business card would you be so kind as to inform me if the bust becomes available?"

"My dear sir," he said, "that would be my very great pleasure."

I gave him my card, he gave me his, we parted with expressions of mutual esteem. A very pleasant encounter.

I sat in the Miata a moment before heading back to the beach. I had no precise description of the statue stolen from Griswold Forsythe II, but how many Benin bronzes could one expect to find in the West Palm Beach area? And a pawnshop seemed the likeliest place for the thief to derive some cash from the loot, even though it would be much less than the actual value.

Driving eastward I reflected it was not the smartest thing for the go-niff to do. He or she should have known that pawnshops would be the first places police would check after the theft had been reported. From which I could only conclude I was dealing with an extremely stupid crook or that he or she was confident the disappearance of those pricey items would not be reported to the police. A perplexity, wouldn't you say?

I returned home looking forward to an afternoon swim in a warm, gently rolling sea, but it never happened. As I entered through the back door, Ursi Olson, aproned, came from the pantry to inform me that Griswold Forsythe III had phoned and was quite insistent that I return his call as soon as possible. I used the kitchen phone and eventually got through to the Forsythe heir.

"Archy," he said, "I must see you at once." There was no entreaty in his voice but rather a tone of command—something new for Junior.

"Of course," I said equably. "Where and when?"

"Now," he said, "and not here. You're at home?"

"I am."

"I'll come over. Twenty minutes." And he hung up.

I used the interval to build and drink a vodka-rocks with a splash of aqua. It was my first alcoholic libation of the day and I had an uneasy feeling I would need more before that lucky old sun dipped beyond yon far horizon. So vodka makes me poetic. Sue me.

The Forsythes' Rolls-Royce came purring into our driveway in less than twenty minutes and Griswold III alighted. I wondered how long it would be before he traded in the family's armored personnel carrier for something a little racier.

We shook hands and I expressed the condolences of the McNallys on the death of his father. He nodded, thanked me in a distracted way, and then asked where we could talk without fear of interruption or being overheard.

"We might take a stroll on the beach," I said giddily. I confess it was a somewhat derisive suggestion, for he was dressed in a three-piece suit of heavy wool and wearing black wingtip brogues.

He missed the irony completely. "Good idea," he said. "Let's go."

So we crossed Ocean Boulevard and descended the rickety wooden stairway. It was a cloudy afternoon and sultry. I figured the temperature hovered around 80° and I had a wild vision of him swooning of heat exhaustion in his cumbrous costume. Then I'd be forced to hoist him aloft in a fireman's carry and lug him back to air conditioning.

But he seemed oblivious to the heat. We went down close to the water where the sand was firmer and began to plod northward.

"Have funeral arrangements been completed, Griswold?" I asked.

"What?" he said, his thoughts obviously elsewhere. "Oh. No, the police haven't yet released the body. In any event it will be a private interment. Just the family and staff."

"I can understand that," I told him. "But it seems a shame that friends and neighbors won't have an opportunity to pay their respects."

"You think so?" he said, and I think he was genuinely surprised by my comment. "Well, I suppose we can always have a memorial service later, can't we?"

I didn't reply but glanced sideways at him. I could see he was beginning to perspire as we trudged along and it did my heart good.

"So much to do," he said fretfully. "I'm having lunch with your father tomorrow. The will and all that. Settling the estate. I'm not certain I understand it."

"I'm sure my father will explain."

"I guess we'll be coming into a bundle. Mother, Geraldine, and me, I mean. With a trust fund for Lucy and something for the servants. Dad handled all those things." He turned his head to give me a toothy grin. "Making money is the most fun you can have without taking your clothes off."

Ordinarily I might have considered that a mildly amusing remark. But under the circumstances I thought it crude. This twit seemed positively gleeful a day after his father had expired and I found it offensive. But possibly the death of his papa had lifted his spirits by freeing him from the domination of an imperious paterfamilias. Meanwhile I was happy to note the Forsythe scion was sweating bullets.

"But that's not what I wanted to discuss with you," he went on. "I mean talking about money is vulgar, don't you think?"

"Only if you have plenty," I said, and he had the grace to laugh. One short, feeble laugh.

"What happened was this . . ." he continued. "On Tuesday night, after dinner, father went prowling around asking questions of the family and staff."

"Did he? What sort of questions?"

"All I know is what he asked me. Very personal questions. Was I happy with my wife? Was she happy with me? How much money did we have in our bank accounts? Very odd. And apparently he was asking everyone in the house similar things about their private lives. Got the staff quite upset, I can tell you that."

"I can imagine."

"Well, after he finished making all those inquiries I went into the library, where he was sitting behind his desk, just staring into space. To tell you the truth, Archy, he looked like someone had sandbagged him. I asked him what was going on. Then he told me."

"Griswold," I said, "I think we've walked far enough. Shall we go back now?"

He was beginning to look a bit puffy about the gills and I feared my wild vision of him collapsing might well become a reality. I was happy when he acquiesced and we turned around to retrace our steps.

"Your father told you what?" I asked him.

"That several valuable things had disappeared from the house and he was sure someone in the family or on the staff was stealing them. What a shock it was to hear that! But that was why father had been asking all those questions—to try to discover if anyone was desperately in need of money."

"I see."

"Also," Griswold said, almost panting as he spoke, "he told me he had employed you to investigate and try to identify the thief. Is that right?"

I thought half a mo and decided the truth wouldn't hurt—a dreadful mistake. "Yes," I said, "that's correct."

"Well, father said he had determined to his satisfaction who was doing the stealing and he had made certain it would not continue. He was very firm about that. In fact, he said he intended to tell you to end your investigation. That's what I wanted to relay to you, Archy: you can stop snooping around because there won't be any more stuff disappearing. Dad said so."

"Uh-huh," I said. "And did your father tell you who the thief was?"

He turned his head to look out over the ocean. "No," he said, "he wouldn't reveal it."

He was a very unskilled liar. If he had stopped there I might have been inclined to believe him, but he continued to embellish his yarn.

"I begged him to tell me who it was," he went on, "but he refused. He just kept repeating the robberies would end and you could stop your search. Of course I expect McNally and Son to bill us for the time you've put in."

"Of course," I said.

By the time we climbed that stairway to Ocean Boulevard, Griswold III was tottering. He finally made it to the Rolls in the McNally driveway and grabbed a door handle for support. Oh, how I enjoyed his discomfort!

"So you'll wind up your investigation, Archy?" he asked anxiously.

I nodded and didn't even murmur, "When shrimp fly."

"Good," he said, whipping out a handkerchief to swab his dripping face. "But I do want you to continue cataloging the library. After the estate is settled I plan to sell off all those moldy books. Maybe turn the library into a billiard room. That would be jolly, don't you think?"

"Oh yes," I said. "Jolly."

He gave me a damp hand to shake and then he drove away. I stood there a few moments considering what he had told me.

I did not believe it was wholly a falsehood. I thought Griswold II had actually made those inquiries the night before he was murdered (he had told me he intended to), and I reckoned his son had talked to him later as he had claimed. How else could Griswold III learn I had been employed to investigate the thefts?

But I definitely did not trust him when he said his father refused to identify the thief. Why did he lie about that? The natural assumption would be that he lied because he himself was the crook. But I found that difficult to accept. I thought him a twit but not a larcenist. Which left only one other possibility: he was lying to protect someone else. But whom?

That puzzle continued to excite the McNally neurons during the cocktail hour, dinner, and after I ascended to my belfry to bring my journal up-to-date. My labors were interrupted by a phone call. Sgt. Al Rogoff was abrupt.

"You got anything?" he demanded.

"*Nada,*" I said. "You?"

"Zilch. The alibis of the son and clerk hold up. Griswold Three was at his dentist and the clerk was eating a tuna salad at Ta-boo. No one in the building saw the proverbial stranger lurking about. I figure it was family, servants, or friends who did the dirty deed."

"I agree. Or their accomplices. What about the missing wallet?"

"Oh yeah, he had one. Black calfskin with gold corners. He usually carried a couple of hundred cash and his credit cards."

"Where do you go from here, Al?"

"Out to the Forsythe place tomorrow for a day of talking to the screwballs. I'm looking forward to that. I also look forward to root canal work. I wish you'd come up with a lead, old buddy."

"So do I," I said. "But do not fear; McNally is here."

"Stuff it," he said and hung up.

I sat at my desk in a broody mood. But I was not thinking of the skimpy information Al Rogoff had just revealed; I was reviewing my afternoon meeting with Griswold the Third and wondering why I had an antsy feeling that I was missing something.

It took a small marc to identify the reason for my unease. The son apparently had an intimate conversation with his father on Tuesday night. But he made no mention that daddy had said anything about the threatening note he had received. Which meant the senior hadn't told the junior, or he had and Griswold III was deliberately concealing his knowledge.

I was in the midst of these gloomy musings when I received my second phone call. Sylvia Forsythe. I repeated the McNallys' condolences on the death of her father-in-law.

"Thanks, Archy," she said. "I really liked the old fart."

I did not feel that expressed sincere grief but I said nothing.

"Listen, boy," she said, "you promised me a feed. Hubby dearest is lunching with your father tomorrow, so how about it?"

I was more dismayed than shocked. "Surely the family is in mourning," I said.

"The family may be," she said, "but I'm not. Where can we meet?"

Ticklish. Definitely ticklish. I didn't wish to offend hubby dearest but neither did I want to reject overtures from one of the personae of this drama—comedy—farce—tragedy—soap opera—whatever.

"The Pelican Club," I suggested, and gave her instructions on how to find it. "Twelve thirty? How does that suit you?"

"It suits, it suits!" she cried merrily. "See you there, darling!"

I hung up somewhat shaken. It is not that I object to or am frightened by forthright women—Connie Garcia is a paradigm of unambiguity—but let's face it: this eager and apparently randy lady was the wife of a client of McNally & Son and possibly a suspect in an investigation of both robbery and homicide. A man would be a fool to become involved with a woman like that.

I'm a fool.

13

On Friday morning I yawned my way to work fashionably late (about ten thirty), having overslept and then pigged out on a breakfast of eggs scrambled with shallots and more buttered scones than I care to mention. I collapsed at my desk and decided to complete my larcenous expense account if only to delay wrestling with the puzzle of connecting all those unnumbered dots.

Shortly before noon I dropped my magnum opus on the desk of Ray Gelding, treasurer of McNally & Son. He inspected the total.

"You jest," he said.

"You are fortunate," I said loftily, "that I did not bill the company for job-related mental and emotional stress."

"Mental I can believe," he said. "You are obviously suffering."

I withered him with a glance and went on my merry way.

I arrived at the Pelican Club in time to order refreshment at the bar before the arrival of Mrs. Sylvia Forsythe.

"Tonic with a twist, please, Mr. Pettibone," I said.

He stared at me in astonishment. "Have you changed your religion, Mr. McNally?"

"*Mens sana in corpore sano*," I told him. "Which freely translated means I do not wish to get tanked before the lady shows up."

"Very wise," he nodded approvingly, and served that noxious concoction.

Sylvia was only twenty minutes late and well worth the wait. She came floating into the club clad in a filmy jacket and Bermuda shorts of honey-colored silk. She had a presence. She had an attitude. And sixty years ago observers would have said she had *It*.

I introduced her to Mr. Pettibone and she asked for a grasshopper, a drink I thought suited her nature famously. I drained my tonic and ordered a vodka-rocks which I suppose suited my nature as well.

"Have any trouble finding the place?" I asked her.

"Oh no," she said. "I've been here before. A year ago, or perhaps it was more than that, Griswold and I had dinner with Geraldine and Tim Cussack, and we stopped here for a nightcap."

"Tim Cussack?" I said, feigning surprise. (I'm a topnotch feigner.) "He and Geraldine were dating?"

"For a while," she said. "Hot and heavy. Then he dumped her or she dumped him; I never did get it straight. I thought you knew."

I was saved from replying when our drinks were set before us and we both sipped.

"Yummy," Sylvia said. "Fattening, I expect, but who cares?"

"Surely you don't have a weight problem."

"Not me," she said. "I can eat anything."

It was the kind of comment that invited a ribald response but I resisted. "Tell me," I said, "how is your daughter reacting to her grandfather's death?"

"All right, I guess. Lucy lives in a world all her own. Sometimes it's hard to know what she's thinking or what she's feeling."

"A deep child," I observed. "Charming and deep."

"I suppose," she said and took another gulp of her syrup. "She was an unplanned child, you know, and perhaps she senses it."

That was not a revelation I cared to hear. "Why don't we go into the dining room," I suggested. "In another half-hour it may be mobbed."

It was already crowded, but Priscilla found us a table for two. Not the one, I was gratified to note, that was favored by Connie Garcia.

Sylvia and I decided on a salad of Florida lobster, which unfortunately have no claws, the poor dears. We also ordered a basket of garlic bread and a bottle of sauvignon blanc.

"On a diet?" Priscilla inquired.

"You know me, Pris," I said, "lean and mean."

She giggled. "Honey," she said to Sylvia, "keep your eye on this cat. When he's in his cups he'll proposition the Goodyear blimp."

She bopped away laughing and my companion said, "I gather you two are pals."

"Long-standing," I assured her.

"Keep it that way," she advised. "Standing."

I thought that a thigh-slapper and told her so.

"I do have a brain, you know," she said. "But I don't get much chance to use it."

"Oh?" I said idly. "Why is that?"

"I'm sure you know what my husband is like," she said. Then she paused and apparently decided not to detail his failings. "I just feel stifled," she concluded.

"Where are you from, Sylvia? Not Florida, I presume."

"You presume correctly. Milwaukee. I left because I wanted to see what the sun looked like."

"And how did you meet Griswold?"

She smiled. "He picked me up. In the bar at an airline terminal. And they lived happily ever after. Only they didn't."

I was spared further disclosures by the serving of our salads and wine.

"I've got to get out," she said, stabbing at her clawless lobster as if it were her own malignant fate.

"Out of where?" I asked her. "And into what?"

"Out of the Forsythe crypt," she said. "And into someplace open and airy and free."

"Divorce?" I asked, not looking at her.

"Whatever it takes," she said determinedly, exhibiting a steel spine in a velvet back. "Life is short, isn't it?"

"Someone once said we must strive to die young at a very old age."

She brightened. "That's exactly right," she said. "That's how I feel and what I intend to do. This salad is scrumptious and I'd like another glass of wine, please."

I poured. "Your husband is now a very wealthy man," I mentioned casually.

"Yes," she agreed, "and it does change things, doesn't it? Before the old man died we were on a mingy allowance. But now hubby dearest is loaded in his own name, and I've got to plan."

"What about Lucy?"

"She'll have her own trust fund."

"You'd be willing to give her up?"

"Yes, I would," she said defiantly, staring at me. "It's my life and I want to live it."

"It may not prove to be more satisfying than what you have now."

"I'm willing to risk it," she said boldly. "Risk doesn't scare me. Never has, never will."

I had thought her an airhead but now I was getting a glimpse at the demons that drove her. It was True Confessions time and I wanted to hear more, but she put an end to it.

"Enough of this whining," she said, pushing back her naked salad bowl. "Never complain and never explain—isn't that the First Commandment?"

"For the haut monde."

"That's me. Now let's talk about what we're going to do this afternoon."

I looked at her. "I assumed you'd want to return home. The funeral arrangements and all that."

"Is that what you assumed?" she said. "Wrong!"

It wasn't difficult to infer what she meant. And because mama didn't raise her son to be an idiot, I could guess where we were heading. That prospect didn't spook me. What I found worrisome was that Ms. Garcia would indubitably learn of my lunch with this attractive lady (Connie's snitches were everywhere) and I didn't wish to imagine her reaction. Violent, I had no doubt.

I signed l'addition, we left the Pelican Club and, as expected, Sylvia Forsythe said, "Why don't you follow me?"

"To Timbuktu?" I asked.

"Not quite that far. To a fun place. You like fun places, don't you?"

I'm sure my grin was glassy. "Be lost without them," I assured her.

It was the Michelangelo Motel, as anticipated. I had already decided the Cussack-Diaz suite in that elegant bagnio served as a trysting place for most of the Forsythe family and staff. A sort of home away from home. I could now understand how the mustachioed gardener could afford such costly digs. He was paying a monthly rental and in turn was collecting a daily rental—or at least a generous pourboire. A win-win arrangement.

There was absolutely no problem when we arrived. We sailed past the desk with scarcely a glance from the clerk on duty. Sylvia had a key to Suite 309, and I had a mad vision of that key hanging from a hook in the Forsythe pantry, available to any member of family or staff who suddenly fell victim to his or her carnal appetites and needed a cozy auditorium for an afternoon of giggles.

The two-bedroom apartment wasn't quite as garish as I had imagined, but I would hardly call the decoration in subdued good taste. There were several colored prints of Florida beach scenes complete with palm trees and bikinied sun-freaks.

I spotted evidence of Timothy Cussack's occupancy: polo mallets and boots tossed into a corner. But I saw no signs of Rufino Diaz's presence; apparently he was more discreet. The suite boasted an enormous TV set equipped with a VCR. I suspected a library of porn videos might be available on request. I did not request.

"Who owns this place?" I asked Sylvia.

"A friend," she said evenly, and then, "A glass of vino?" she inquired pleasantly as if she were welcoming a guest to her own home.

"That will do me fine," I said.

She looked at me thoughtfully. "No," she said, "I think brandy would be better."

She marched into the kitchen, obviously familiar with the layout, and returned a few moments later with small snifters. She handed me one and I took a cautious sip.

"Calvados," I pronounced.

"Close," she said. "It's an American applejack."

"Vintage of last Tuesday?"

"Probably," she said, shrugging. "But who cares?"

"That's the second or third time you've said that," I observed. "You keep repeating, 'Who cares?' Don't you really care?"

"Nope," she said, "I really don't. And if you're trying to lay a guilt trip on me, forget it. I'm immune."

"Not me," I protested. "It's your life."

"You bet your sweet patootie it is. Now can we stop this chatter and get down to business?"

She took me by the hand and led me into one of the bedrooms. Perhaps boudoir would be a better word. Lace, chintz, and ruffles everywhere. No mirrors on the ceiling but definitely an intimate chamber designed for lovemaking. The coverlet on the king-sized bed had been turned down and I could see the fresh sheets were peach-colored satin.

"I guess I better take off my shoes," I said.

She laughed, punched my arm, and began to undress.

"Matinees turn me on," she said.

How can I describe that charged afternoon and stay within the bounds of decorousness? I'll try.

She was a sprite, a mindless sprite, and absolutely delightful. Her long hair was the color of butterscotch, her skin ivory and untouched by Ol' Sol. There was a wispiness in all her gestures. In all her caresses. More fey than feh! I feared I might break her but she was too pliant for that. And compliant.

I was convinced it wasn't the two glasses of wine and sip of applejack, but she seemed inebriated on—what? On her passions, I reckoned, and her dreams. She was dwelling on her own planet, wherever that was, and I was merely a visiting astronaut.

"More," she kept breathing. "More."

I must admit that for one brief moment during our vigorous session I had the most awful feeling that I was abusing a child.

I was freed from that notion when, depleted and apart, she sighed, smiled at me, and said, "That was a smasheroo!" Then I definitely knew I was dealing with a willful and experienced woman. I wondered how many sets of horns Griswold III was wearing.

Our parting was totally without the awkwardness that usually attends first affairs. We finished our applejack, dressed, exchanged a chaste kiss and parted, all in great good humor with no vows, promises, or entreaties. Two civilized people sharing their jollies. Quite bloodless.

I suppose I should have been in a triumphant mood when I drove home, or at least plumped with peace and satisfaction. Instead I found myself in a melancholic mood. Sylvia Forsythe's unhappiness had been palpable that afternoon. And although she had seduced me, I had the nags that rather than help alleviate her miseries I had contributed to them. It bothered me. I make no claim to nobility, you understand, but neither do I delight in jostling the blind. All actions involve moral choice, do they not?

When I arrived at the McNally spread I sought out my mother and found her in our little greenhouse, chatting up her begonias. She lifted her cheek for my kiss.

"Mrs. McN.," I said, "you are a very wise woman."

"Oh Archy," she said, "are you broke again? I can't lend you very much."

"No, no," I said hastily. "Nothing like that. I just need a word of advice. When a wife cheats on her husband, what might her motive be?"

"Unhappiness," she said promptly.

"I know that, dear. I'm asking the reason for the woman's unhappiness. Lack of affection from her spouse? Silly dreams that can never be realized? Or finding another, more attractive mate?"

Momsy went on watering her plants for a moment before she replied.

"It could be any of those things, Archy," she said finally. "A wife can become unhappy for so many reasons. Those you mentioned and more. But do you know what I think it is in many cases?"

I waited.

"Boredom," she said firmly. "They can't find enough to keep them occupied. Oh, they may have clubs and charities and hobbies and sports, but those are just surface things. In their personal lives, their deep emotional lives, they are just bored. 'Is this all there is?' they keep asking."

I thought about that awhile. "Yes, mother," I said, "I believe you are right. As usual. Thank you for your help."

"That's what mothers are for," she said brightly.

It was a reflective swimmer who braved the ocean's wimpy ripples that afternoon. As I plowed along I thought of what mother had said of wives who stray from the fold. She was right, you know. Sylvia's flapdoodle about seeking someplace open and airy and free was simply a cloak for her basic motive: the woman was bored out of her skull.

During the cocktail hour and dinner my parents and I were unable to avoid discussing the brutal murder of Griswold Forsythe II, for it had become a cause célèbre in the Town of Palm Beach and was featured in all our local newspapers and TV newscasts. Many theories as to the identity of the killer had been suggested, but scanty information had been released. "Several promising leads are being investigated" usually means the police are stymied.

I retired to my cupola to record in my journal the events of that day. As I scribbled a brief (and discreet) account of my tumble with Sylvia Forsythe I fell to wondering how many other men she had granted a "smasheroo" and who they might be. Timothy Cussack? Anthony Bledsoe? Rufino Diaz? Zeke Grenough? Groucho Marx? Ben Turpin? I stopped, fearing I was verging on madness.

I welcomed the interruption of a phone call, hoping it would bring me back to reality. It did—with a jolt.

"Who was she?" Consuela Garcia demanded.

"Who was who?" I asked. "Or who was whom—whichever is grammatically correct."

"Screw grammar," she said wrathfully. "That dolly you had lunch with today at the Pelican Club. Who was she?"

"The lady happened to be Mrs. Griswold Forsythe the Third," I replied stiffly. "I was merely attempting to console her on the death of her father-in-law."

"I'll bet you consoled her right into bed."

"Connie, I am aghast, utterly aghast. What a frightful accusation."

"Keep talking, buster; you're just making it worse."

"Would I lie to you?"

"Constantly," she said bitterly. "And sometimes when you don't have to—just to keep in practice."

"It's the absolute truth. If you don't believe me, ask Simon Pettibone. I introduced Mrs. Forsythe to him."

"Why did you have lunch with her?"

"Because the Forsythes are valued clients of McNally and Son, and it was the first opportunity I had to express our sympathy."

"And what did you do after lunch?"

"Why, we each returned to our respective homes. She had her car."

"I can just see your nose getting longer and longer."

"Connie," I said earnestly, "do you really think me the sort of bloke who would take advantage of a young woman devastated by the murder of her beloved father-in-law and consumed by sorrow?"

"Yes," she said and hung up.

It hadn't been as bad as I had feared. I was confident I could eventually smooth things over, nurture that shrunken belief she had in my devotion. I *want* to be faithful to Connie, really I do, but fate conspires against me; I am constantly offered opportunities to betray her trust and I do not have a resolve strong enough to resist.

It is positively amazing that Connie has endured my infidelities as long as she has. What is even more amazing is that her forbearance increases my affection for her.

Diversity makes the heart grow fonder—ask any philanderer.

14

During that weekend I played the blade-about-town. Tennis. Golf. A poker game with a quartet of felonious cronies. And a riotous bachelor party for one pal who had decided to desert his wild, dissolute life and seek marital somnolence. I must admit I felt a wee twinge of envy.

The only happening during those two days that concerned the Forsythe case occurred on Saturday afternoon when I met with Sgt. Al Rogoff, at his request. He came to our home in his pickup and we sat in the cab while he smoked a cigar and, in self-defense, I inhaled more cigarettes than I should have.

"Anything new?" he asked.

"Nothing of any consequence," I said. "You?"

"I've practically been living at the Forsythe place," he complained, "and it gets nuttier by the hour. You know Rufino Diaz?"

"The gardener? The chap with the jungly mustache?"

"That's the guy."

"Yes, I've met him."

"I checked him out. He used to be a cop in Havana. That's interesting, isn't it?"

"I guess," I said. "But what does it mean?"

"Not much," Al admitted. "But he lives in a swanky motel in West Palm. And meanwhile he's mowing lawns. I can't figure that, can you?"

"Nope," I said.

He turned to look at me. "Why do I have this itchy feeling that you're holding out on me?"

"Al, would I do that?"

"Sure you would."

"Nothing that would impede a homicide investigation and you know it."

"Maybe," he said grudgingly. "I'm going to keep digging at Rufino. And also on Fern Bancroft."

"The maid? The one who found Mrs. Sylvia half-strangled?"

"Yep. She's got a ticket. An old sheet with no convictions. But she was racked up twice for committing a public nuisance."

"Such as?"

"Archy, you're not going to believe this."

"Try me."

"For taking her clothes off in public places. Once in a supermarket, once in a movie theater."

"You were right," I said. "I don't believe it. You think the Forsythes were aware of her record when they hired her?"

"That I doubt."

"Al, did it ever occur to you that craziness is engulfing the world?"

"Occasionally I have that thought at three in the morning when I can't sleep."

"Tell me something," I said. "Did you check the whereabouts of the Forsythe clan at the time Griswold the Two shuffled off this mortal coil?"

"I love the way you talk," Rogoff said. "You mean when the old guy got iced? Of course I checked their alibis. What do you think I am—a potted palm? They all claim they were at home, with two exceptions. Sylvia Forsythe says she was out at the family's horse farm in Wellington. Anthony Bledsoe—the butler or houseman or whatever—says he had driven the Rolls into town to fill the tank and get the car washed. I'm still trying to pin down their statements."

We were silent awhile. The sergeant relighted his cold cigar and I started another English Oval. The atmosphere in that truck cab was so noisome I suspected both of us might soon require CPR.

"Al," I said, "I know your investigation has hardly started, but if you had to choose the villain right now who would you select?"

"John Dillinger," he said.

I laughed. "He died sixty years ago."

"I know," Al said gloomily. "But maybe he came back from the grave. That makes as much sense as everything else in this mishmash. Have you talked to the kid?"

"Lucy? Yes, we've spoken."

"I can't get a thing out of her," he fretted. "She just clams up. I have a feeling she knows something but just won't spill. And I can't lean on her because she's practically an infant."

"Not quite," I said.

"Well, see what you can do with her, will you, Archy? Maybe she saw something or heard something."

"I'll try," I promised. "You still figure it was someone in the family or one of the servants?"

"What the hell else can I figure?" he demanded. "It wasn't a coked-up intruder who throttled the old man. I'm practically certain of that. You agree?"

"Yes, I think that's a reasonable assumption."

"Thanks a bunch," he said bitterly. "And a Happy New Year to you."

We were both grumpy when we parted. Neither of us enjoyed insoluble puzzles. They were an affront to our talent and intelligence. Which implies we shared a healthy dose of chutzpah: as if all the problems of the world can be solved by talent and intelligence. Rubbish, of course. Still, we were being challenged—by the killer—and no one likes to be snookered.

I wasn't in the greatest good humor when I arose Monday morning. To tell the truth (a rarity) I felt totally unraveled. I simply could not concentrate and feared I might be a victim of premature senescence. But then I realized my befuddlement was caused by the Forsythe investigation: all those unconnected and unnumbered dots.

The weather didn't help: unseasonably warm, humid, overcast. Definitely not the sort of day to inspire one to shout a hosanna or dance a flamenco. But with gritted bicuspids I pulled myself together, showered, shaved, dressed, breakfasted, and drove to the Forsythe abode.

Mrs. Nora Bledsoe opened the door for me. I was startled; the woman looked destroyed: drawn features, soiled bags under the orbs, slumped shoulders, a general air of hopelessness and despair. I had an immediate and probably base impression that her grief was excessive.

I mean she had served the deceased for many years, and sorrow for her employer's death was understandable. But she seemed totally overwhelmed.

"A sad time, Mrs. Bledsoe," I said.

"It is that, Mr. McNally," she said in a choked voice, and I feared she might begin weeping.

"Mr. Forsythe," I began and then added hastily, "—the younger—has asked that I continue cataloging the books."

She nodded and led the way down that crepuscular corridor to the library. I noted that all the strength had disappeared from her formerly stalwart figure; she seemed shrunken and defeated.

"Mrs. Bledsoe," I said, "is Lucy at school?"

"Not today," she said dully. "Because of what's happened—the funeral and all—her parents thought it best to keep her home for a few days. I think she's out back somewhere."

That library was even gloomier than before. I suppose it's a fanciful notion but the death of the owner made all the leather-bound volumes seem equally defunct, fit for no place but an auction house. A nutty feeling, I admit, but I thought the books had died when the owner expired and could only regain a second life from the love and respect of a new owner.

I shuffled listlessly through my cataloging notes and then tossed them aside. When I thought Mrs. Bledsoe and the others might be safely out of sight I went looking for Lucy. I knew where to find her—in the Secret Place, and I now capitalize it because I was certain she did in her own mind.

Sure enough, I found her seated on the greensward in her minuscule amphitheater. She was not reading a book, there was no pad or pencil in evidence. Clad in a wrinkled romper, she was simply staring into space with a wooden expression that alarmed me. Her eyes were reddened and puffy. But when she became aware of my presence she looked up with a timid smile that warmed the old cockles.

"Hi, darling," I said. "How's by you?"

Her smile grew. "Hello, Archy," she said. "Gee, I'm glad to see you. Did you hear what happened to granddad? He's dead."

"I know," I said, flopping down beside her. "It's awful and I feel very bad about it. Don't you?"

"Oh yes," she said sadly. "He was very nice to me. Sort of like very cool, you know, but nice."

"Sure he was," I said. "A nice man. You know what I think you should do, Lucy?"

"What?"

"Write a poem about him."

She brightened. "Hey," she said, "that's a good idea. What kind of a poem?"

"That's up to you," I told her. "How you felt about him and how sorry you are that he's gone."

She nodded. "I'll do it," she said determinedly. "I'll write it tomorrow or maybe even tonight before I go to bed. Archy, do you know more keen poems?"

"Of course I do," I said. "How about this one?"

I recited the verse beginning "As I was going up the stair/I met a man who wasn't there."

When I finished she hugged her ribs and rocked with merriment. "That's neat," she said. "I love it."

"So do we all," I said and took her little hand in my paw. "Lucy, about your grandpop, try not to cry too much or too long."

"I didn't," she said, lying bravely. "I don't cry anymore. I told you that."

"You did but I'm not sure it's right *never* to cry. Sometimes it's best. Then you feel better afterward."

She looked at me dubiously. "Are you sure?"

"Absolutely."

"Do you ever cry?"

"Not often," I said, "but occasionally. It does help."

She considered that a moment. Then: "I guess," she said, sighing. "I know grown-ups cry. I saw Nora and she couldn't stop. But it wasn't about my grandfather dying. She was having a fight with Tony. They're always fighting."

I was dreadfully tempted to ask her about what but I refrained. I must emphasize again that never did I attempt to pump this child. I have, now and then, acted ignobly in my life but I draw the line at interrogating an innocent as young as Lucy.

"I don't know what it's about," she said, answering my unspoken question. "They're always fighting. I hate it when people fight, don't you?"

"I certainly do."

"Everyone in our house is always fighting," she went on. "Like Fern and Sheila. And my mother and my aunt. Fighting all the time. I wish they'd stop. It scares me."

"Lucy, you and I will never fight, will we?"

"Well, I should hope not," she burst out indignantly. "Because we're friends and friends never fight, do they?"

"Never," I assured her. "They may argue but they don't fight."

"Of course not," she said. "That would be silly because then they wouldn't be friends anymore."

What a wise child she was! I released her hand and rose to my feet. Is it a sign of aging when rising becomes much more of an effort than sitting? I reckon gravity is the final victor.

"Lucy," I said, "I've enjoyed talking to you, and when you finish your poem about your grandfather I hope you'll let me read it."

"Okay," she said cheerfully. "I love you, Archy."

So artless it made the old ticker skip a beat.

"And I love you, sweetheart," I vowed and meant it.

I wandered back to the main house, doing some heavy cogitating on what Lucy had said. All those fights. Mrs. Nora Bledsoe and son Anthony. Fern and Sheila: maid versus maid. And Sylvia against Geraldine. Of course it was possible that what Lucy, in youthful trepidation, described as "fights" were merely noisy and brief disagreements, soon forgotten. But I didn't think so. I was beginning to believe the Forsythe household was riven and the fault lines ran deep.

I used the phone in the library to call Sgt. Rogoff. He was as grouchy as he had been the last time we conversed.

"Will you do me a favor, Al?" I asked.

"Why the hell should I?" he demanded. "No one does me any—including you."

"I'm doing you one now," I said. "Run a trace on a lad named Timothy Cussack. Two s's in the last name. He works on a horse farm owned by the Forsythes out in Wellington. He used to be a polo player and now he trains jumpers."

"Interesting—but not very. Why should I check up on this guy?"

"Because he lives in the same apartment Rufino Diaz occupies at the Michelangelo Motel."

I waited patiently until Al's silence came to an end. "Now that *is* interesting," he said finally. "All right, I'll sniff him out. Local, national, or worldwide?"

"Local," I said. "For starters. You'll let me know?"

"Don't I always?"

"No," I said, and he was laughing when we hung up. That was a plus.

I was feeling better too and I didn't know why; I hadn't really learned anything meaningful that morning except that cornflakes with milk and sliced bananas followed by a filet of pickled herring with onions does not constitute the most felicitous breakfast combo. But I seemed to be recovering and went out to my car whistling, the McNally juices once again at tsunami strength.

I found Anthony Bledsoe wiping the hood of my Miata with a shammy.

"Hey," I said, "you don't have to do that. I appreciate the attention but the baby just had a bath."

"I can see," he said. "But while you were inside a gull hit the target."

"In that case," I said, "keep swabbing. Do you mind if I call you Tony?"

"Why should I mind?" he said, that note of surliness creeping back into his voice. "Everyone else does."

"Just to make us even," I told him, "everyone calls me Archy. Is it a deal?"

"I guess," he said.

I was trying to charm the fellow and obviously making little progress. He seemed in a constant state of resentment and I hadn't a clue to the reason. Envy, I supposed, or jealousy—or both. Whatever was gnawing at him appeared perpetual; I had never seen him lighthearted or flashing a "What, me worry?" grin. Condemned to the doldrums, this chap.

I thought him reasonably handsome. Not a young Clark Gable, you understand, but with a brooding intensity I imagined would be attractive to women. The odd thing was that his rather heavy, squarish features reminded me of someone and I could not think of whom. Not a movie star, not a public figure, but someone with whom I was familiar. I gave up trying to identify the resemblance.

"A bad week, Tony?" I suggested.

He finished polishing and stood back to examine his handiwork. "Bad enough," he said. "The old man was king around here, and now with the prince taking over no one knows what's going to happen. Like today is supposed to be my day off but the new boss said No. Everything is all screwed up."

His words were innocent enough but there was venom in his voice.

"Surely your job is secure," I said.

"Maybe," he said. "Maybe not. I don't give a damn. Believe me, I'm not going to be a gofer all my life."

"Tony," I said gently, "I think you're more than a gofer for the Forsythe family."

His laugh was sarcastic: a contemptuous laugh. But whether the contempt was for me, his employers, or himself, I could not tell.

"If you leave the Forsythes," I said, "what will you do?"

He stared at me. "I'll live," he said, and trudged back to the house.

"Thank you for the cleaning job," I called after him, and he gave me a casual wave of his hand without turning around.

A very troubled young man, I reckoned, beginning to believe everyone in that wealthy and idiosyncratic household was troubled.

I was granted added evidence of that a moment later. I started to pull out of the driveway and then stopped to allow entrance of a new Ford Taurus Wagon, pearly blue. It halted and Mrs. Constance Forsythe emerged. She slammed the door and the Taurus backed onto Ocean Boulevard, but not before I recognized the driver—Timothy Cussack.

Mrs. Forsythe came over to my Miata and I climbed out. We shook hands.

"I'd like to express the sympathy of—" I started, but she waved my sympathy aside.

"Understood," she said, "and appreciated. It's a downer, I admit, but I'm not about to do the sackcloth-and-ashes bit. No one will do it for me when I croak."

I tried not to be but I was amused by her sangfroid.

"What the hell," she continued, "life goes on. At least mine does, thank God. Hey, want to come back in the house for an early pick-thee-up?"

"Thank you," I said, "but I'll take a raincheck. I have a heavy lunch date awaiting."

She looked at me speculatively, head to toe and back again. "Yes," she said with a roguish smile, "I can imagine. Like the girlies, do you, Archy?"

"I enjoy feminine companionship," I admitted.

"And I'll bet they enjoy yours," she said. "And why not? What other pleasures does life have to offer—except horses, of course."

This feisty woman never ceased to amaze and I wondered how she had ever brought herself to marry such a hidebound man as Griswold Forsythe II. But maybe she had developed her forthright persona *after* marriage—perhaps as a reaction to finding herself wedded to a stick. There will be no extra charge for that Jungian analysis.

She was wearing jodhpurs and the badly stained bush jacket. Her face was free of makeup and she seemed to flaunt her wrinkles. Her hair was a mess and I guessed she had her last manicure shortly after the Korean War.

"Was that Tim Cussack driving the Taurus?" I asked.

"Sure it was," she said. "My right-hand man. I don't know what I'd do without him. Timmy makes me feel young again. He's such a scamp I've just got to love him."

I thought her praise somewhat effusive and, coming from a new widow, in questionable taste. But I knew better than to expect tender feelings from this bumptious lady. I don't know why, but every time I saw her I thought of Teddy Roosevelt waving a saber and shouting, "Charge!"

I was about to make my farewell when she stepped closer to me and clamped a heavy hand on my arm.

"My son tells me you're to continue cataloging the library."

"Those were my instructions."

"It makes sense," she said. "We'll probably sell off all those old books. Did Griswold tell you anything else?"

She spoke very intently, her uninhibited brashness suddenly gone. I found the abrupt change startling. And her question posed a kind of Hobson's choice. Griswold III had told me to scratch my investigation into the thefts, but I didn't know if he had revealed that to his mother. I wanted to respect his confidence, but if Mrs. Forsythe *was* aware of it, I didn't wish to appear a barefaced liar. And so, as usual, I temporized.

"Griswold said merely that I was to confine my activities to cataloging the library."

There was no mistaking her relief. Her grip on my arm fell away, her smile was huge, and her hearty manner was reborn.

"And so you shall!" she cried, clapping me on the shoulder. "Why, you've practically become a member of the family."

Mother of pearl! I prayed. Save me from that!

She gave me a final blow on the clavicle and strode to the house. I watched her go, convinced now that she knew I had been assigned to investigate the disappearance of Forsythe valuables and was delighted to learn my inquiry had come to an end.

I believe it was at that precise moment that I began to get a glimmer of what was going on in the Forsythe booby hatch. And Connie Garcia had called these people dull! Au contraire, dear Connie. They made the Jukes Family look like saints.

It was all ludicrous, of course, except that a woman had been half-strangled and a man totally. I found it difficult to snicker.

15

Did you ever see one of those old movie melodramas about life on a daily newspaper? The star reporter was usually played by Lee Tracy, and he'd come rushing into the newsroom, press pass tucked into the band of his fedora, and scream, "Stop the presses! I've got a yarn that's going to tear this town wide open!"

I now have a similarly dramatic announcement to make: On that particular Monday I skipped lunch. Yes, I did. The continued shrinkage of the waistbands of my slacks alarmed me and I was determined to regain the Apollo-like physique that had formerly been the envy of my compadres and had elicited whistles from female construction workers.

So upon arriving home I marched resolutely past the kitchen and went directly to my quarters, manfully ignoring the excruciating pangs of hunger. It was my intention to work on my journal for as long as it took to bring my record of the Forsythe case up-to-the-minute.

Instead, I found myself seated behind my desk, feet up, staring blankly into space while I pondered an oddity that puzzled me. I had already established the fact that Anthony Bledsoe and Timothy Cussack were pals. And I had noted—as I am sure you did too—that both lads took Monday as their day off. I had decided to look into that coincidence to determine if the two spent the day together and, if so, what their activities might include.

But on that Monday Tony Bledsoe was working, apparently at the command of Griswold III. That was understandable; the new lord of the manor wished to assert his authority immediately. But Tim Cussack was also working on that Monday. At least he was chauffeuring Mrs. Constance, and she had been dressed as if she had just come from the Trojan Stables.

It was a minor mystery, I admit, but I found it perplexing. I could think of a dozen innocent explanations for Cussack being busy on a Monday, driving his employer hither and yon. But I could devise a dozen other scenarios not quite as innocent.

Obviously I had insufficient information at the moment to come to any reasonable conclusion, so I put that riddle aside for the nonce and ruminated on another enigma that had been stirring in that bowl of tapioca I call my brain. It concerned what Connie Garcia had told me was related to her by Lady Cynthia Horowitz; to wit, years and years ago Griswold Forsythe II had been the subject of Palm Beach gossip that Lady C. found difficult to believe.

It was a very small nugget indeed, and even if I was able to assay it I had no insane hope it would prove to be the "smoking gun" that would solve all the Forsythe mysteries in one swell foop. But it would certainly do no harm to attempt to learn more, and so I phoned Lady Horowitz.

Her housekeeper, Mrs. Agnes Marsden, answered and I identified myself.

"Mr. McNally!" she said. "How nice to hear from you again."

We chatted a few moments about this and that, for we were old friends, and then I asked if I might speak to Lady Horowitz.

"I don't know," she said doubtfully. "She's out at the pool having a pedicure and hates to be disturbed when she's having her tootsies treated."

"It's really not necessary that I speak to her," I said hastily. "Would you be kind enough to act on my behalf and ask if I may visit? At her convenience of course. It's a matter of some importance."

"I'll try," she said. "You hang on now and don't get impatient. This might take some time."

"I'll wait," I promised.

It was almost six minutes by my Mickey Mouse watch (an original, not a reproduction) before Mrs. Marsden came back on the line.

"Mr. McNally?"

"I'm still here."

"Lady Horowitz says that if you come over at one o'clock she'll be glad to see you."

"Splendid."

"But she wants you to bring a bottle of gin. We're running low and won't get a delivery until tomorrow."

I laughed. Lady Quid Pro Quo was at it again.

"I'll be happy to," I said. "Will Beefeater gin be okay?"

Mrs. Marsden humphed. "I think bathtub gin would be okay," she said.

I had about twenty minutes to get to the Horowitz estate. But that was no problem; it was a short drive up the coast and I knew we had a case of Beefeater in our utility room, a sufficient supply for many family cocktail hours to come. So I freshened up, bopped downstairs, and filched a liter, slipping it into a blue Tiffany shopping bag.

The Horowitz spread is only slightly smaller than the State of Delaware and is surrounded by a high wall of coral blocks topped with razor wire. Within is a Tara-like mansion that lacks only Spanish moss dripping from cypress trees. The large patio area is at the rear and has been the scene of many a memorable bash, usually ending with guests leaping fully clothed into the enormous swimming pool.

Loyal readers need no introduction to Lady Cynthia Horowitz, but for the benefit of newcomers I should explain that Lady C. is one of the wealthiest matrons of Palm Beach, as well she should be since she's had six moneyed ex-husbands. She is about seventy years old, give or take, and in her youth had been a famous nude model for painters and photographers. Happily, age has not withered her physical beauty from the neck down. It would be ungentlemanly to comment on the neck up.

I found her at poolside, lounging on a chaise in the shade of an umbrella table. As usual she was protected from the semitropical sun by a wide-brimmed panama hat, a long flannel robe, white socks, and long white gloves. And, as usual, she was sipping her customary gin-and-bitters.

"Hallo, lad," she sang out. "You've been neglecting me."

"Shamefully, m'lady," I agreed and proffered the Tiffany shopping bag. "Perhaps this will make amends."

She peered at the contents. "God bless," she said. "Would you care for a belt?"

"Not at the moment, thank you, but could we chat for a few moments?"

"First you must tell me what mischief you've been up to."

"Regrettably little," I said, pulling a webbed patio chair close so I could share the umbrella's shade. "I've been involved in investigating the death of Griswold Forsythe."

"Have you?" she said indifferently. "What's your interest?"

"Ma'am, he was a valued client of McNally and Son."

"That's nonsense," she said. "Leave it to the cops, lad. It's their migraine."

"Well, yes," I admitted. "But we would like to provide as much cooperation as we can."

She stared at me over the rim of her glass. "Who's handling the case?" she asked.

"Sergeant Al Rogoff."

"That animal!" she said wrathfully. "Why, he smokes cigars."

"I know, but he's a very capable detective."

"Cowpats! If he's in charge the murder will never be solved."

"I'm not so sure of that," I said. "He came across something he wants me to ask you about."

My reason for lying, of course, was to protect Connie Garcia, my source.

"Why doesn't Rogoff ask me himself?" she demanded.

"Perhaps he knows how you feel about him."

She laughed. "And he's right, lad; I wouldn't give him the time of day. What does he want to know?"

"He heard a rumor that years ago the victim was the subject of some hot gossip, but Rogoff can't pin it down. Because you've lived in Palm Beach such a long time he hoped you might remember what it was all about."

She opened the bottle of Beefeater I had brought and poured a generous dollop into her crystal tumbler. She drank without a grimace. I am not a devotee of warm gin. Are you?

"No," she said finally, "I think not."

"Ma'am, don't you want to help investigate a heinous murder?"

She shrugged. "It makes no nevermind to me."

"I find that hard to believe," I said boldly. "Forsythe was a man of your generation. Palm Beach is a small town; surely you must have known him."

"Of course I knew him. What a stiff he was—even before he died. And when you speak of my generation you make me sound like an antique."

"That was not my intention, I assure you."

She looked at me thoughtfully. "Your father is also of my generation," she said. "And he knew Griswold better than I did. Why don't you ask him about the gossip?"

I sighed. "Because my father is a self-righteous fuddy-duddy, as you well know, and would never even consider repeating an unsubstantiated rumor."

"You've got that right, lad," she said, laughing. "But I hate to talk about the past. Nostalgia can be addictive, you know. Once you start down that path your life becomes a constant 'Remember when . . .' and your brain turns to mush. Retreat into the past and you're lost. You've got to keep facing up to the present and the future."

"Is that what keeps you so young?" I asked.

She laughed again. "What a clever, devious lad you are! Have you ever considered the understanding companionship of an older woman?"

"Frequently."

"Put me first on your list," she urged. "We could play fun games. Like the prince and the shepherdess."

It was my turn to laugh. "More like Catherine the Great and a serf," I said. "I thank you for your kind offer but I must respectfully decline. After all, you are a client of McNally and Son, and we do have ethical standards."

"Since when?" she said.

It was apparent to me that this conversation had strayed from the main track and wandered into byways I had little wish to explore. I was wondering how I might get back to the purpose of my visit when the mercurial Lady Horowitz solved the problem.

"So what you want from me," she said, "is a tidbit of foolish gossip that must be almost thirty years old."

"Yes," I said eagerly, "that's exactly what I want."

"It's important to you?"

"It is," I said. "Very."

She stretched inside her voluminous robe and gave me a tantalizing glance. "You may be a clever, devious lad," she said, "but you have a lot to learn about negotiation. To be specific, what's in it for me?"

"The satisfaction of knowing you have assisted in solving a homicide."

The tantalizing look turned to mockery. "Not a very solid reward. Try again."

I thought a moment. "A case of Bols?" I suggested.

She came alive. "Genever!" she cried. "Oh lordy, I haven't had a sip of that stuff since my third husband kicked the bucket. Flavored with caraway, isn't it?"

I nodded. "Not for cocktails," I admonished. "Cold and neat."

"You've got a deal," she said. "But if you tell anyone I told you I'll cut out your heart."

"My job is discreet inquiries, m'lady," I reminded her. "With emphasis on the discreet."

"Well, it's an impossible story and I really didn't believe it when I heard it. We used to call him Grisly, you know. Anyway, there was talk that Griswold Forsythe the Second was having a mad, passionate love affair with a married woman who worked in a West Palm bakery. Grisly mad? Grisly passionate? It was not to be imagined! But the rumors persisted and after a while it became common knowledge, so to speak."

"Forsythe was married at the time, of course."

"Of course."

"I'm disappointed," I said. "I'm as surprised as you must have been to learn that such an unadventurous man could have an extramarital liaison. But it's the territorial disease of Palm Beach. I can't see how it might affect the investigation of his murder."

"Wait a minute," she said, and took another sip of her warm gin. "There's more to the story. Apparently they were careless and the woman got preggy."

"Uh-oh," I said.

"About the same time the woman's husband disappeared. Just vamoosed. I guess he knew what had been going on and figured it wasn't his kid. He took off for parts unknown, deserting his pregnant wife. Grisly did the honorable thing and took care of her and their infant son."

That was the moment I decided I had been a fool for rejecting my hostess's invitation to share her gin.

"Are you going to tell me," I said hoarsely, "that the woman in question is now the Forsythes' housekeeper, Mrs. Nora Bledsoe, and her son Anthony is the illegitimate offspring of Griswold Forsythe the Two?"

"You've got it," Lady Horowitz said cheerfully. "The boy is Grisly's bastard. Or so the gossip has it. Satisfied?"

"Stunned," I said, and I was.

"I told you I don't believe a word of it," she went on. "But where there's smoke there's fire."

"Yes," I agreed. "One never knows, do one?"

I arose, somewhat shakily, and made a farewell oration: "I thank you, ma'am, for your kind cooperation. And I promise that what you have told me shall remain entre nous."

"And don't forget the Bols," she called gaily as I departed.

I drove directly to the McNally Building. I was not looking forward to bearding daddy-o in his den but I consoled myself with the thought that it was the only way I could verify what Lady Horowitz had just told me—providing father would relax his cast-iron rectitude sufficiently to breach a client's confidentiality.

I phoned Mrs. Trelawney the moment I arrived in my office. "Listen, dear," I said, "I must see hizzoner at once for about ten minutes or so."

"No can do," she said firmly. "He's reviewing briefs and doesn't want to be disturbed."

"Try," I urged. "Tell him it concerns the murder of Griswold Forsythe. That should persuade him to put aside his briefs—even if they're his own."

She giggled. "I'll give it a go," she promised.

She came back on the line a few moments later to say I had been granted a ten-minute audience. I galloped up the backstairs and found the don seated at his desk. He swung around in his walnut swivel chair when I entered.

"Yes, Archy," he said irritably, "what is it now?"

"Sir," I said, "in my investigation of the thefts at the Forsythe home I've come across a story that needs verification. I hope you may be able and willing to provide it."

I repeated what Lady Horowitz had told me of Griswold Forsythe's dalliance years ago with the married lady from the West Palm bakery and how she was now ensconced as the Forsythes' housekeeper while Griswold's illegitimate son served as butler-houseman.

Father was silent when I finished and I could see he had slipped into his mulling mode. I had expected it and waited patiently. You cannot hurry a man capable of pondering three minutes whether or not to put piccalilli on his cold roast beef. Finally the oracle spoke.

"I don't know from whom you heard that story," he said in rather testy tones, "and I don't wish to know. Essentially the story is correct."

"Father, if you had told me from the start it might have aided my investigation."

"I could not tell you," he said sharply. "The client was alive when this thing began and I had to respect his confidence. But now that he is deceased I believe I may ethically reveal details of the matter. I said the story is true and it is, with one glaring inaccuracy. Mrs. Nora Bledsoe's husband had deserted her *before* Mr. Forsythe and she began their affair. Her child was his responsibility—there was no doubt of that in his mind—and he was willing to provide for her future and for her son's. I told you he was an honorable man."

"Perhaps," I said. "Honor is an elastic word, is it not?"

"Just what are you getting at, Archy?"

"For instance," I said, "do you think his relationship with Mrs. Bledsoe continued after she entered his employ and his home?"

He looked at me stonily. "I have no way of knowing that," he said. "Forsythe never volunteered the information and naturally I never asked."

"Would you care to hazard a guess, sir?"

"No, I would not."

I went at him from another angle. "Father, when you spoke to me of the disposition of Mr. Forsythe's estate you mentioned nothing of a specific legacy to Mrs. Nora Bledsoe or to Anthony Bledsoe. Had he made such provisions in his will?"

He drew a deep breath. "He had. Amply, I might add."

"Do you think the Bledsoes were aware of his bequests?"

"I have no idea. In any event the matter is now moot."

"No, sir," I said. "I beg to disagree."

He stared at me a long moment in silence. Then: "Are you implying Mrs. Nora Bledsoe and/or her son Anthony may be implicated in the murder of Griswold Forsythe?"

"It is certainly a possibility, is it not?"

He shook his head sadly. "Perhaps," he said. "Archy, are you continuing your investigation of the thefts?"

"Yes, sir."

"And working with Sergeant Rogoff on the homicide?"

I nodded.

"Good," he said. "I want you to keep at it until this nasty business is cleared up. I hope to see both the thief and the killer brought to justice."

"Father," I said softly, "it may be the same person."

"So it may," he agreed. "Now I suggest you return to your job and allow me to return to mine."

But I felt I had toiled in the vineyards sufficiently for one day. I stopped at a local liquor emporium and, paying with plastic, had a case of Bols sent to Lady Horowitz. I then returned home, donned my fuchsia Speedo trunks and Daffy Duck cover-up, and went down to the ocean for a two-mile swim. The family cocktail hour and dinner followed in due course and during all that time I resolutely restrained myself from brooding about the Forsythe tangle.

But when I went upstairs to resume scribbling in my journal I was faced once again with the puzzle of those unconnected dots. I did not despair of eventually finding the solution, mind you, but at the moment I felt I was sans paddle and up the famous creek.

But the travails of that confusing day had not ended. I received a phone call around nine thirty.

"This is Geraldine Forsythe," she said crisply. "I must see you at once."

16

She came for me in an oldish Buick sedan I presumed was her personal car. It was, in fact, so old that it had a bench seat up front with an armrest that could be lowered from the middle of the back to form two quasi bucket seats. When I climbed into the passenger side Geraldine flipped up the armrest so there was no divider between us. It was, well, um, uh, cozy.

We exchanged brief greetings and without another word she headed out of the McNally driveway and turned south on Ocean Boulevard. She made no mention of our destination.

"Miami?" I inquired pleasantly.

"Anywhere," she said. "I have to talk to you privately and this seemed the best way. Have you done anything about my missing jewelry?"

"No significant progress," I reported. "Your father's death has complicated things. I am sure you and everyone else in your household has been questioned by the police."

"Endlessly," she said gloomily.

"Of course. Which temporarily puts your personal problem on the back burner."

"But you're not forgetting about it, are you, Archy?" She sounded desperate.

"No way," I assured her. "I promised you I'd do what I can and so I shall."

"Good," she said. "Because another of my lovely things has been stolen. A necklace of gold rose petals. I wanted to wear it last night and it was gone."

"Expensive?" I asked.

"About five thousand. But it meant a great deal more than that to me. It was a birthday gift from my father years and years ago, and now it's gone."

"What a shame," I said. "Where was it kept?"

"In its original velvet case hidden under lingerie in the top drawer of my dresser. The case was still there but it was empty."

"Not a very secure place to keep a five-thousand-dollar necklace," I remarked.

"What do you expect me to do?" she said angrily. "Put all my jewelry in a safe deposit box?"

I swung sideways to look at her. She was wearing a black silk jumpsuit, zippered to the chin, and she appeared to be under considerable tension. She was gripping the wheel tightly, leaning forward, her formidable jaw clenched. If she was gritting her teeth I wouldn't have been a bit surprised.

We drove in silence until we were south of Manalapan. Traffic was light, the night cloudy. A hard onshore wind was kicking up whitecaps on the sea, and far out I could see the twinkling lights of fishing boats and the blaze of a cruise ship. Nothing seriously amiss with that scene but I would have much preferred being home, enjoying a small marc and listing to Sarah Vaughan singing "Lost in the Stars."

Gerry abruptly made a wild and totally unexpected U-turn, pulled into a parking space on the corniche, and braked so violently that I was thrown forward against my seat belt.

"Hey," I said in mild protest.

She killed the engine and snapped off the lights. Then she grabbed my arm. "It's my sister-in-law," she said fiercely. "I know it is. You believe me, don't you, Archy? She's giving that bum all my lovely jewelry."

"Timothy Cussack?"

She nodded.

"Gerry," I said as gently as I could, "you may be correct but you have no real evidence, do you?"

"But I know how to get it," she said eagerly. "I'll bet if you search his apartment you'll find my things. Maybe not all of them because he's probably sold some by now. But I'm sure you'll find enough to prove what I'm saying is true."

"And how do you suggest I search his apartment? Break into the place? I don't even know where he lives."

"Suite 309 at the Michelangelo Motel in West Palm," she said rapidly. "And you won't have to break in because I have the key."

She dug in the pocket of her jumpsuit and handed me a key slipped onto a large paper clip.

"How do you happen to have this?" I asked.

"From when Tim and I were going together. Then we broke up but I never gave back the key. Will you do it for me, Archy? You'll find my things, I know you will."

"And if I do? What will you do then?"

"Go to the police," she said promptly. "Report what's been happening and have them arrest Sylvia and Tim for stealing."

It was, I reflected mournfully, Looney Tunes time and I had a starring role.

"You will do it for me, won't you, Archy?" she repeated in a breathy voice and pressed closer, lifting her face.

I don't know what it's termed in these hyperkinetic days but it used to be called smooching or necking, and I hadn't indulged in such amorous and ultimately frustrating behavior since I was a lustful and frantic teenager. And limped home simultaneously exhilarated and disappointed. Ah, the joys and pains of youth!

Our juvenile grappling became so de trop that I had to interrupt a soulful kiss long enough to giggle.

"Why are you laughing?" Gerry demanded.

"Because I'm so happy," I lied valiantly, and she accepted that.

Eventually she apparently felt she had bestowed a sufficient reward for suborning a criminal act (breaking and entering) and pulled away from me, raising her zipper to its original position.

"Wasn't that nice?" she whispered.

"Sublime," I said, thinking my granddaddy, Ready Freddy McNally, a famous second banana on the old Minsky burlesque circuit, would have been proud of me.

Having accomplished what she had set out to do, she drove me home and dumped me—just like that. I felt like Passion's Plaything.

"I expect you to do what you promised," she said firmly before departing.

"Of course," I said and watched her drive away, more convinced than ever that the entire world had gone bonkers—including, I am sure you will not be shocked to learn, me. Because I had every intention of doing exactly what Geraldine Forsythe had requested: entering Timothy Cussack's apartment and searching for items Gerry had told me were stolen.

It would be illegal and I am ordinarily a law-abiding cuss, except when circumstances dictate otherwise. But later that night, snug in my chambers, a tot of marc in my fist and a tape of the Divine Sarah playing softly, I stared at the key to the Cussack-Diaz motel apartment lying on my desk blotter and realized a surreptitious break-in represented a risk I need not take.

There was a way of gaining entry to Suite 309 at the Michelangelo that held little danger of my being nabbed for committing a felony. I must tell you from the start that the caper I planned was not honorable, chivalrous, or estimable in any way, shape, or form. But my motive, I assure you, was irreproachable: I wanted justice to triumph. And if, in the process, I profited personally—well, that was just honey on the croissant, was it not?

I retired to my trundle trying to recall who it was who said morality is merely a matter of time and geography. I swear it wasn't me.

I might still be sleeping to this day, a mod Rip Van Winkle, if I hadn't been awakened by a phone call on Tuesday morning. I glanced bleary-eyed at my bedside clock and saw it was close to nine thirty.

"What's *with* you?" Sgt. Al Rogoff groused. "Don't you ever get up?"

"Actually," I said, yawning, "I've been awake for hours, just lying in the sack quietly contemplating."

"Uh-huh," Al said. "And I've been sitting in my squad car doing macramé. Are you conscious now?"

"Of course I'm conscious," I said indignantly. "What's up?"

"Not you," he said. "That's for sure. About that guy you wanted me to trace—Timothy Cussack . . ."

"He has a record?" I asked eagerly.

"A sheet as long as a piano roll. The thing that grabs me is that it starts out with penny-ante things like shoplifting and committing a public nuisance."

"Such as?"

"Peeing in the middle of Worth Avenue. Then he graduates to slightly heavier stuff like writing bad checks and attempted fraud. And finally to robbery and felonious assault."

"Has he ever done time?"

"Not a day. Made restitution, paid fines, or drew short-term probation. Two things that get me: One, his cons show a steady progression from minor to major. And two, he's got a lot of pals in high places who wrote letters to the court saying he's just a naughty, high-spirited lad and please go easy on him. That's understandable if he was a good polo player running with the richniks."

"Al, did you find anything that ties him to the Forsythes?"

"Nope. Except that, like you said, he shares a motel apartment with the Forsythes' gardener."

"*As* you said," I admonished him. "Not 'like you said.' "

"Thank you, professor. It's a treat having my grammar corrected so early in the morning. Have you got more on Cussack?"

"Nothing conclusive," I said, "but I'm working on it."

"I'll just bet you are. And if you dig up something juicy I'll be the first to know—right?"

"You can count on it," I told him.

His reply is unprintable.

I rose and moved somnambulistically through my morning routine.

Cussack's record of illegal activities seemed to confirm Geraldine Forsythe's accusations—but then things are not always what they seem, are they? All of which lent added importance to the caper I had devised.

After a lone and Spartan breakfast (OJ, toast, black coffee) I pointed the Miata northward to the Forsythe manse, beginning to have a few quivers of doubt if the action I planned would be as easy and rewarding as anticipated. But then I remembered Admiral Farragut's famed command and the McNally chutzpah revived.

Sheila Hayworth opened the door for me and she looked uncommonly attractive. I thought she was wearing a trifle too much makeup for a servant in a house of mourning but, on occasion, I can be as blimpish as mein papa.

"Hi!" she said brightly. "Back on the job again?"

"You betcha," I said. "Life goes on."

"I hope so," she said, looking at me with a smile I can only describe as inviting. "I could use a little life."

"I'm sure you could, after the events of the past week. Sheila, you haven't borrowed any books from the library, have you?"

"Not me," she said. "I don't read much except the tabs. Mostly I watch TV. But that can be a drag too."

Again she smiled and now it was positively lubricious. At another time I would have been tempted to continue this suggestive chatter and discover where it might lead. But at the moment I had other devilry in mind.

"Must get to work," I said briskly. "By the way, is Mrs. Sylvia at home? I must ask her about borrowed books."

"Yeah, she's here, playing her harpischord."

"Harpsichord," I corrected, thinking I was rapidly becoming a fusspot—and at such a tender age.

"Whatever," Sheila said indifferently. "You know where her studio is?"

"I can find it. Thank you for your help. I hope to see more of you."

"That's up to you," she said saucily, and I was glad to escape. I recalled those nude photos Griswold III had snapped, and I also recalled hearing that he once had eyes for Sheila until his father lowered the boom. I was beginning to believe that all the rumors about the Forsythes weren't gossip, they were incontrovertible facts. It was just your average all-American, Norman Rockwell family. And I am Ethelred the Unready.

But I was ready enough when I paused outside the door of Sylvia's studio. I could hear her plinking away on the harpsichord. It sounded like bored noodling to me and I hoped it was. I knocked and won a shouted, "Come in!"

I entered and received a sizzling welcome.

"Archy!" she yelped, leaped from the bench, and rushed forward to embrace me. "Where have you been? I thought you had forgotten all about me."

"Not a chance," I said, beginning to recite the playscript I had, in my own mind, entitled "Seductio Ad Absurdum." "But because of Mr. Forsythe's death I thought it better to stay out of the way for a while."

"Oh pooh," she said. "That's ancient history."

And so it was; the poor man had been deceased for almost a week.

"Sylvia, I stopped by hoping you might be able to join me for lunch."

"Frabjous!" she cried. "And I want to eat in a diner. You know, one of those places made of shiny aluminum that looks like a railroad car."

"I know exactly what you mean. I practically lived in diners during my undergraduate days."

"Well, this morning when I woke up," she rattled on, "the first thing I thought was that I simply *must* have meat loaf with mashed potatoes and gravy."

"And peas."

"Or pale string beans. And you got two slices of white Wonder bread with one small pat of soft butter."

"Memories, memories," I said. "And if you didn't want the meat loaf there was always fried liver with bacon and onions, or corned beef and cabbage."

"And a choice of desserts. Vanilla or chocolate ice cream, or lemon Jell-O."

"Formica-topped tables," I reminded her.

"With a paper lace doily under your plate."

"And cutlery stamped U.S. Army," I added, and we both burst out laughing. "Sylvia, every diner from New York to L.A. must have had the same menu. But where can we get food like that today?"

"A new diner opened up on Dixie Highway about a month ago.

Lolly Spindrift wrote that it's the new *in* place, a perfect replica of a vintage diner. Archy, can we have meat loaf for lunch?"

"Only if they have a crusty bottle of ketchup on every table."

"You wait right here," she said breathlessly. "I'll go change and be right back."

She hurried away leaving me to question why she would want to change; she had looked fetching in a linen shift in a yummy molasses shade. I wondered if she intended to dress in true diner fashion: a felt dirndl skirt decorated with a large appliqued poodle (complete with chain) and a pink cardigan sweater set.

Sylvia came scampering back still wearing the molasses shift and I could only fantasize about the "changes" she had made. She asked that we drive in my Miata and I readily agreed. We left by the front door and found Anthony Bledsoe and Rufino Diaz standing in the driveway engaged in what appeared to be a very intent conversation.

They stopped speaking as we approached. Diaz tipped his baseball cap respectfully to Sylvia but I earned a dark glower from Tony, as if my presence offended him. After what I had learned about his antecedents I could sympathize with his perpetual ill-will. It must be awful to be in a constant state of biliousness that no antacid can cure.

The joint on Dixie Highway turned out to be a paradigm of diners, and the owner's efforts to duplicate the glories of yore even included an antique Wurlitzer jukebox with those glorious neon tubes. It was loaded with music of the Diner Dynasty: e.g., "The Yellow Rose of Texas" and "Sam's Song." Surely you're not too young to recall those monumental melodies.

The meat loaf turned out to be just as I remembered it: wonderful and completely tasteless. The gluey gravy was ladled on abundantly and, sure enough, we both received two slices of spongy white bread with one small square of melting butter. That lunch was a time warp and I must admit I enjoyed every morsel of it.

"Dessert?" I asked.

"Of course," Sylvia said, giving me a tender glance. "But not here."

"If not here," I said, "then where?"

"You know," she said, and so I did, much encouraged that the scenario I had planned was progressing so smoothly.

Of course we ended up in Suite 309 of the Michelangelo Motel. I refuse to apologize further for my actions.

Our second sexual rapprochement exceeded the pleasure of the first. She was, as she had claimed, a free spirit seeking only to satisfy her whims. I would never claim she found me impossible to resist. Let's just say I was handy, and I wondered how many other men had played the same role of temporary consort.

We concluded our barbaric coupling and lay depleted, panting like greyhounds that had caught the rabbit. It was time, I reflected muzzily, to engineer the second part of my caper: I had to separate myself from my companion long enough to search the second bedroom, used by the apartment's residents.

I hadn't envisioned how it might easily be accomplished but had consoled myself with the thought that if I failed on the first attempt, a second or even third try might be necessary. I assure you it was not a prospect that daunted me.

But fate sometimes favors the undeserving, as it did in this case.

"I've got to go to the john," Sylvia said.

"I also," I said immediately.

"Use the one in the other bedroom," she advised, the darling, and whisked out of bed.

And as soon as she was out of sight I whisked into the adjoining bedroom. Twin beds in there with matching chests of drawers, two lamps on two bedside tables. There was enough careless masculine disarray to convince me it was the sleeping chamber of Timothy Cussack and Rufino Diaz.

The first dresser I opened obviously belonged to the latter, for the top drawer contained a baseball cap, several copies of Spanish language newspapers, and three folded denim coveralls. I switched to the second chest and found a jumbled collection of memorabilia of the former polo player: programs of games, reviews, photos, invitations to parties of years past. I searched as swiftly as I could, anxious to finish before Sylvia began to wonder at my absence.

The bottom three drawers of the bureau were jammed with a tangle of shirts, socks, bikini briefs, and the oddments of a horseman. I delved into this disorder frantically but found none of the jewelry Geraldine Forsythe claimed had been stolen from her. But in the bottom drawer, far in the back, I discovered a tissue-wrapped package. I drew it out carefully.

It was a worn and stained first edition of Edgar Allan Poe's *Tamer-*

lane. Staring at it, stunned, I realized it was one of the items the murdered Griswold Forsythe II had listed as having been looted from his home.

Zounds!

17

We drove slowly back to the beach sorry that our meat loaf matinee had ended. At least *I* was and, glancing sideways at Sylvia, I hoped she felt as radiant as she appeared. Her cornsilk hair flickered in the breeze and I had never seen her look so vibrant, so zestful. I knew she was a woman who lived for excess, who welcomed it, and I admired her foolish courage.

"Thank you for a marvelous afternoon," I said politely.

"And will you love me always?" she asked with mischievous solemnity.

I smiled, not so much at her mockery as at the recollection of what my buddy Binky Watrous had once said. He insisted the Irving Berlin lyric should be sung, "I'll be loving you all ways." Good, but not as good as George S. Kaufman's comment that it should be "I'll be loving you Thursdays."

"Sylvia," I said, "I've never asked you who inhabits that motel suite we use. It's none of my business but I *am* curious."

"I thought you knew," she said. "Timmy Cussack and Rufino Diaz, our gardener, live there. They're very good about letting friends use it. For an occasional tenner or a bottle of booze, of course."

"And you have a key?"

"I borrowed it from Rufino this morning when I left you alone in the music room."

Then I understood why Tony Bledsoe had shot me such a venomous glance on the Forsythe driveway before we departed. He knew very well we were planning fun and games in Suite 309. But why should that infuriate him? Unless . . .

"Tell me something else, Sylvia: does Cussack have a steady?"

She laughed immoderately. "Half a hundred steadies. Our Timmy is quite a playboy."

"I can imagine; he has the charm. Where does he hang out—do you know? I'd like to look him up and slip him something for the use of his digs."

"You don't have to do that, Archy. Tim is very well taken care of, I assure you."

"It wouldn't do any harm to buy him a drink or two."

She laughed again. "He'd like that. Tim is not an alcoholic, mind you, but he's never learned how to say 'When!' Connie told me he favors the Sea Turtle off Worth Avenue. Do you know the place?"

I had a brief instant of cardiac arrest because I thought she was referring to Consuela Garcia, my one-and-almost-only.

"Connie?" I said hoarsely.

"Constance," Sylvia said, puzzled by the terror in my voice. "My mother-in-law."

"Oh," I said, much relieved. "Yes, I know the Sea Turtle. Not exactly my cup of oolong. In fact, I consider it somewhat unsavory."

"It is," she agreed. "Hopeful young chicks and old men with fat wallets and skinny buns. But Timothy seems to like it."

"I'll look him up one of these days," I said casually and let it go at that.

I delivered her to the portal of the Forsythe fortress and we exchanged a firm handclasp and a complicit grin. Sylvia ran inside and I drove home through the waning afternoon sunlight thinking I should be ecstatic because my caper had succeeded beyond expectations. But I was definitely not gruntled. My guileful plot had resulted in more questions than answers.

I had returned the first edition Poe to its original place in the bottom drawer of Timothy Cussack's bureau. But his possession of that valuable volume was a puzzlement. How on earth had he managed to filch it? There was one obvious explanation, of course. Geraldine Forsythe had been correct and Cussack was having a lunatic affair with Sylvia. To keep him supplied with walking-around money she was swiping her sister-in-law's jewelry. But in addition she was also stealing those items the late Griswold Forsythe II had said were disappearing.

It was a neat solution to all the thefts but I could not buy it. Too simple. Sgt. Al Rogoff is continually complaining that I have a taste for complexity and he may be right. But in this case I thought my doubts were justified. Geraldine's accusations, if verified, could account for the thefts. But they provided no solution to the cruel murder of the senior Forsythe.

We had a splendid skirt steak for dinner that evening. Father was in an uncharacteristically jolly mood and contributed an excellent bottle of a vintage merlot from his sequestered stock. The reason for his good humor became apparent when he remarked that McNally & Son had just signed on a new client: a chain of prestigious funeral homes in the South Florida area. I drank to that.

I retired to my upstairs sweatshop in a mellow mood. I made entries in my journal, pondered the events of the day and what significance they might have, if any, and then exchanged my duds for a costume more suitable for a foray to the Sea Turtle, Timothy Cussack's hangout. I wore a shrieking plaid sport jacket, mauve Izod, and slacks that looked as if they had been dipped in Welch's grape juice.

I must tell you now that the name "Sea Turtle" is fraudulent. If I used the actual name of the nightclub I might find myself a defendant in a libel action. The place has been the scene of several mini and a few gross Palm Beach scandals. It is a popular pickup joint for the in-season crowd but most year-round residents shun it. It really is awfully infra dig. I mean how can you, with a clear conscience, patronize a bar willing to serve drinks topped with little paper parasols?

It was late September but the snowbirds had already started to flutter down and the Sea Turtle was cranking when I arrived. The scene was as expected: women in tight leather miniskirts; men with gold medallions; the air swirling with smoke smelling of pot; and laughter too loud and too harsh.

Most of the roisterers were seated at tables or squirming on the dance floor and I had no trouble finding a place at the bar. I was waited upon by a lissome maid wearing black net hose, short shorts, and a Spandex halter top refuting the notion that Less is More. The young lady was living proof that More is More.

"What's your pleasure, sir?" she asked.

"If I told you," I said, "you'd be shocked. But right now I'd like a Sterling on the rocks."

"Fruit?" she said, and for a half sec I feared it was an accusation.

"No, no," I said hastily. "Just the vodka with a splash of water."

She built my drink swiftly and expertly, placed it before me and, leaning elbows on the bar, cupped her face in her palms.

"I'll bet you're visiting from up north," she said.

"Not me," I protested. "I live here."

"In Palm Beach?" she said, astonished.

I nodded.

"Then how come I've never seen you before?" she demanded. "Everyone in Palm Beach comes here."

"I dropped by—oh, it must have been a year ago. You weren't here then."

"I started about six months ago. I love it. It's a real fun place. My name is Gladdie. For Gladys, you know. What's yours?"

"Archy. For Archy, you know." We both laughed and shook hands.

"Looking for someone special, Archy?" she asked, giving me a knowing grin.

"Right," I said. "But not the girl of my dreams. I'm looking for Timothy Cussack so I can buy him a drink. You know him?"

Her expression changed. "Sure," she said. "Everyone knows Timmy."

"And likes him?"

"Mostly," she said cautiously. "He's sure to come in tonight. He practically lives here. You just hang around and he'll show up."

She moved away to serve another customer. I sipped my drink slowly, observing the frenzy on the dance floor. Few of the gyrating couples had any talent. They were trying but it was all ersatz boogie. I rarely attempt to dance to rock, but if you ever saw me glide about to "Ole Buttermilk Sky" you'd swoon with delight.

I beckoned Gladdie, pointing at my empty glass. She brought me a refill.

"Thank you, nurse," I said.

She laughed. "You're cute," she said.

"Not as cute as you," I told her.

"I get off at two," she said in a low voice.

"I'll be unconscious by then. Another time. If you get a chance, slip me your phone number."

"No problem," she said happily. "Oh—hey! There's Tim Cussack. He just came in."

I turned to look. He was standing in the doorway surveying the action. He was clad totally in black: leather jacket, turtleneck pullover, denim jeans, mocs. I think he meant his half-smile to be sardonic; I thought it smarmy. But I could not deny he was lean, self-assured, and mucho macho—three things I am not. And so, naturally, I detested him.

I left the bar and approached him before he found other companions.

"Hello, Cussack," I said genially. "Buy you a drink?"

It took him a mo to recognize me. "McNally," he said finally. "The lawyer fella."

"You've got it," I said. "How about that belt?"

"Sure," he said. "First of the night. And if you believe that, I've got a rhinestone mine I'd like to sell you."

We moved back to the bar. He was drinking Jack Daniel's Black Label, a potent potable. He took it straight with a water chaser he never touched. If I tried that I'd have to change my address to Intensive Care.

"What's the occasion?" he asked idly. Very bored, very affected.

"I just wanted to thank you for the use of your dorm."

"Yeah," he said indifferently, "Rufino told me we had guests this afternoon. Had a few laughs, did you?"

"A few," I acknowledged.

"That's the name of the game, isn't it?" he said. But even as he spoke his head was on a swivel, gaze floating everywhere. It was obvious he was casing the joint looking for—what? Opportunities, I supposed. Female opportunities.

It had been my intention to ask him about his work at the Trojan Stables and gradually, ever so subtly, inquire about his relations with the Forsythe women: Constance, Geraldine, and Sylvia. But it was not to be; this stud simply wasn't much interested in my company. I wasn't wearing a skirt.

He slugged his sour mash, slid off the barstool, and squared his shoulders. "Thanks for the refreshment," he said. "I see someone I want to—"

At that moment a bulky chap stalked up and confronted him. The guy was in his middle forties, I guessed, but well put-together: barrel chest, no paunch, aggressive thrust of head. There was no doubt he was steaming.

"I told you to keep away from her," he said to Cussack in a gritty voice. "Don't you listen to me?"

Timmy looked at him coldly. "No, I don't listen to you," he said. "I listen to the lady. Why don't you?"

Their voices had become louder during this taut exchange and I stood and prudently moved out of the range of a flying fist. There was a sudden quiet at our end of the bar. Gladdie started toward us but a beefy bartender shouldered her aside and leaned toward the two antagonists.

"Take it easy, gents," he said softly. "We don't want no trouble here."

"Stuff it," Cussack advised him.

"You need a lesson," the interloper said to Tim. "Let's go outside."

"Suits me," Cussack said. "Come on, schmuck."

By this time their altercation had attracted fascinated attention from bar patrons and a few couples at nearby tables. When the two moved outside, a small crowd of perhaps a dozen would-be spectators followed, including me. I had no desire to get involved in this fracas but I wanted to witness how Timothy Cussack handled it.

We all marched out to the small parking area, the accuser leading the way. His back was toward Cussack, which proved to be a mistake. Before he had a chance to turn around and face his foe, Cussack swooped, grabbed one of the man's ankles, and pulled sharply backward and upward. Naturally the hapless fellow went thudding facedown on the blacktop.

Cussack straddled his fallen opponent, clutched his hair to raise his head and then smashed it down. There was a sickening crunch that brought a gasp from all of us, and I had no doubt that a nose had just been splintered.

The former polo player released his grip on his adversary's hair and turned to the spectators with an ugly grin.

"The show's over, folks," he said. "Keep those cards and letters coming. Now let's go have a drink."

He reentered the Sea Turtle. I followed him, leaving a few kind souls to minister to the injured man. He was still lying prone and groaning. There was blood. I was shaken by the speed and viciousness of Cussack's attack. He had struck swiftly, callously, with no mercy whatsoever.

I saw him move casually to a table of two middle-aged ladies and begin to chat them up. I went to the bar and asked Gladdie for my bill.

"What did Tim do to him?" she asked anxiously.

"Not nice," I said. "Did anyone call the police?"

She nodded.

"Then I must be on my way," I said, leaving her a generous tip. "The only enjoyable thing about this evening was meeting you."

"Likewise," she said and handed me a slip of paper. "My phone number. If a man answers it'll be my father. You may have to shout because he's hard-of-hearing."

"I'll shout," I promised and got out of there before the guardians of the law arrived. The victim was sitting up on the parking lot, holding his face. One woman, a matron, was bending over him, rubbing his neck and speaking to him solicitously. I boarded my Miata and departed, hearing the sound of an approaching siren.

That night I made sure every door to the McNally sanctuary was securely locked and bolted. That is my father's task and I was certain he had not neglected his duty. But I needed to check. Witnessing senseless violence was the reason for my irrational behavior of course.

I climbed the stairs to my personal refuge and then ran up the last flight when I realized my phone was ringing. I grabbed it thinking it might be Timothy Cussack asking if I could provide bail.

"Hello?" I said breathlessly.

"What were you doing at the Sea Turtle?" Connie Garcia demanded.

"How do you know?" I cried despairingly. "How *do* you know?"

"My spies are everywhere, laddie," she said. "And don't you ever forget it. Well? I'm waiting. What were you doing there?"

"Having one drink with an old pal—a classmate at Yale. He's passing through Palm Beach on his way to Key West and wanted to renew acquaintance."

"And you didn't make a play for any of the available tootsies?"

"Connie, I swear the only woman I spoke to was the barmaid, and she's eighty-three and has a glass eye."

"And you're going to have a black one if I find out you've been doing what I think you've been doing. When are you going to buy me a feast?"

"As soon as humanly possible," I vowed.

"Liar, liar, pants on fire," she said and hung up.

What a bodacious woman!

I emptied my pockets before putting my duds away. I found Glad-die's phone number and tucked it into my wallet hoping she might be able to provide eyewitness accounts of Cussack's previous she-nanigans. Then I poured myself a marc to put lead in the McNally Faber #2.

I am not a stranger to violence, you understand, but it always trou-bles me. I keep hoping for a mannerly world and instead of civility I find only throttled clients and former polo players gallivanting about mashing noses on parking lots. It's very discouraging. Perhaps my sen-sibility is too fragile for a career as an investigator. I might be happier teaching the tango at nursing homes.

I mean people like Tim Cussack (and Sylvia Forsythe) scare me. They never seem to consider the consequences of their actions but sim-ply plunge ahead, whistling, as they follow their fancies. I imagine Alexander the Great was like that—and so was Charles Manson.

In my opinion their temerity springs from a dark, abiding hopeless-ness. They feel they have nothing to lose and so they are doubly dan-gerous.

This analysis comes to you through the generosity of Dr. Sigmund McNally at no additional cost.

18

Wednesday began auspiciously. A client of McNally & Son, vacation-ing in Oregon, had sent us a package of smoked steelhead trout. I had a goodly portion with a few rings of red onion for breakfast and almost howled with bliss. That's what I want to be when I grow up: a smoked steelhead trout.

I had the day's activities planned but, as usual, fate dealt me a cruel blow as it always does when I attempt to organize my untidy life. But "There's a divinity that shapes our ends . . ." I think Gypsy Rose Lee said that but I may be wrong.

I stopped at the McNally Building on the off chance I might have re-ceived an answer from the credit agency I had asked to investigate the financial condition of Timothy Cussack. Mirabile dictu, their reply was on my desk and revealed the poor chap was suffering from a bad case of plastic dehydration. In other words, loss of liquidity; his credit card debts were enormous and the interest charges positively enfeebling. If I had been in his position I might ponder escape via Chapter 7. Not of this tome but Chapter 7 of the Bankruptcy Code.

Even more intriguing than the report on Cussack's lack of lucre was a message asking me to return a phone call from a person named Simeon Gravlax. I had a short-term memory loss and then recalled he was the superannuated pawnbroker who had taken in hock the Benin bronze stolen from Griswold Forsythe. I dug out his business card, called instanter, and identified myself.

"Good morning, my dear sir," he said cheerily. "I trust you are in good health."

"Tip-top," I said. "And you, sir?"

"I am in working order," he said. "Which, for a man of my age, may be the ninth wonder of the world."

"Oh?" I said. "And what is the eighth?"

"That I am still alive," he said with a throaty chuckle. "Mr. Mc-Nally, you asked me to inform you when the Benin bronze you admired had not been reclaimed and was available for sale. That has happened. Are you still interested?"

I didn't give him a direct answer—another of my nasty habits. "May I visit you this morning, Mr. Gravlax?" I inquired.

"I shall be overjoyed to see you, sir," he said and disconnected.

I had intended my first order of business that day would be a drive to the Trojan Stables to determine if Tim Cussack had been arrested by the cops for his nose-bashing spree. But a stop at the pawnshop would not require much of a detour and so I set out in the Miata on a blindingly brilliant morning with a dazzling sun and pure sky.

I found Simeon Gravlax in a chipper mood, leaning heavily on his cane and regarding the world with some bemusement. The Benin bronze was still on display in his window and after an exchange of pleasantries I asked the price.

"Twenty-five thousand," he said softly. Then, apparently noting my shock, he added, "It is a museum piece, my dear sir."

"I have no doubt of that whatsoever, sir," I said. "But it's a little rich for my blood. Actually, I am more interested in the person who pawned this work of art. I realize you cannot legally or ethically reveal that information."

"That is true," he said, nodding.

"And I would never attempt to bribe you, sir," I told him.

It was his turn to be startled. "You are not familiar with the ancient wisdom?" he asked. "Never trust a man you cannot bribe."

I thought a moment. "In that case, sir," I said, "I am prepared to make you an offer. I shall describe the person I believe pawned the bronze. I ask only that you tell me if I am correct or wrong. I shall not ask you to name the pawner."

"In that case," he said somewhat ironically, "I am prepared to accept your offer."

I handed over fifty dollars and then, smugly, I described Timothy Cussack to a T: a tall, well-built young man, willowy, probably in his early or mid-thirties, deep suntan, very white teeth, with a sardonic smile.

Mr. Gravlax slowly folded my fifty-dollar bill and tucked it into a waistcoat pocket. "My dear sir," he said sorrowfully, "I must inform you that you are totally and completely incorrect. The pawner had absolutely no resemblance to the person you describe."

I gulped. "Thank you for your kind cooperation, sir," I said, giving him a glassy smile, and departed with as much aplomb as I could muster, which wasn't much.

I drove away, heading for the Trojan Stables, so piqued I could have kneed myself in the groin if that were humanly possible. I believe Mr. Gravlax had told me the truth; he had no reason to lie. It meant my theory that Tim Cussack was the thief was seriously if not fatally flawed. But if not him, then whom?

I was in a splenetic temper when I drove into the grounds of the Forsythes' horse farm. I enjoy a challenging riddle as much as any tot but when it turns out to be as difficult as the *London Times* crossword one can only feel frustration and fury at being such a lamebrain.

No one greeted me but I spotted Mrs. Constance Forsythe, foot up on the lowest rung of a rail fence, watching a helmeted young lady—12? 14?—taking a bay mare over low hurdles. I strolled toward her and was almost at her side before she became aware of my presence and turned.

"Hullo, Archy," she said with a broad grin. "Slumming, are you?"

"Hardly," I said. "It's such a splendid day I wanted a taste of the Great Outdoors. What better place than here?"

That plucked a chord. "Yes," she said, gazing out over the green acres, "it *is* nice, isn't it? I think of it as my home rather than that pile of stones on the beach."

"The Forsythe mansion is impressive," I offered.

"It's a dungeon," she said flatly. "From cellar to roof. A prison. Out here I can breathe. I love this place. It was part of Griswold's estate, you know, and now it's mine. My son and daughter can have the castle. I'll build a home out here, a small ranch house." She laughed. "No one around but me and the horses. Who needs people?"

She was trying to keep it light but I could guess the intensity of her dream. I am not an outdoorsy person myself but I could understand how she felt about this open spread. It was sweet freedom: sleek horses, eager riders, a rolling turf, and the glory of hot sun and limitless sky. I happened to prefer the smoky bar at the Pelican Club on a rainy night. But different strokes for different folks.

"I really stopped by to see Timothy Cussack," I told her. "Is he about?"

"Not today," she said shortly, turning back to the practicing horse and rider. "One of our customers is thinking of buying a jumper at auction and asked our advice. Tim went over to take a look."

"I'll catch him another time," I said. "Have a great day."

"How can I miss?" she said.

I paused at my chariot and looked back. She was still at the fence, one foot up, and looked planted there. I wondered a lot of things: Did she know Tony Bledsoe had been fathered by her husband, now deceased? Was she aware of all the thefts from the Forsythe household? And why on earth was she employing a harum-scarum chap who had treated her daughter so shabbily?

I seemed to be drowning in questions and, hoping to find water wings, I headed for what Mrs. Constance had called that pile of stones on the beach. I was convinced that if answers were to be found they lurked in the murky corridors of the Forsythe home, which could well be pictured on the cover of a Gothic paperback novel (with one window alight high in a turret). And within, bodices were probably being ripped.

I was admitted by Fern Bancroft. To refresh your muzzy memory she was the twitchy maid who had discovered the half-strangled Sylvia Forsythe and was convinced she was being blamed for the assault. She had also posed for Griswold the Third's eager Polaroid. Do try to pay attention; I hope no more reminders will be necessary.

But Fern was hardly in an agitated state that day. Instead she was all beams and softness, said she was delighted to see me again, and inquired as to the condition of my health. A transformation had taken place and I could only hope it would not prove temporary.

"You're looking very well, Fern," I told her and it was the truth; she had a glow.

"Thank you, sir," she said, coming dangerously close to simpering. "I'm as happy as a pig in the mud."

I laughed. "Where did you learn that expression?"

She thought a moment. "From Tony, I guess," she said finally. "Why? Is it gross?"

"Not at all," I assured her. "Very picturesque."

I went along to the library thinking that if, for the want of a nail, a kingdom was lost, then it followed that with the addition of a nail a kingdom might be won. And I had the curious feeling that my brief and casual exchange with Fern had provided such a nail. But at the moment I was incapable of hammering it home. I will readily admit to cool competence but prescient I am not.

I wandered about that gloomy chamber looking dolefully at the stuffed shelves and questioning if Griswold III actually thought I would ever complete my assigned task. I mean how eager can you get by contemplating a leather-bound set of Trollope that seemed to stretch for miles.

I was just beginning to take up my cataloging chores once again when the clown prince himself came barging in. I was not so much surprised by his entrance as by his appearance. The pupa had emerged from the cocoon and the imago was now complete. And what a butterfly it was!

Heliotrope slacks. A rugby shirt with mauve stripes. A jacket of inflammatory madras. Pink mocs with vermilion socks. A sight? You wouldn't believe! I favor jazzy colors in my dress but this dolt was a rainbow on amphetamines.

"Hallo, hallo, hallo!" he caroled with a disgusting excess of good-fellowship. "Poking about my books, are you?"

"Something like that," I said dourly. I mean the man was a walking toothache. Now they were "*my* books." This heir was more than apparent.

He stalked up and down, a preening fop inspecting his domain. I really can't explain why I held him in such contempt. I guess it was a case of hate at first sight; he was *such* a yuck. And then, of course, there was his hobby of snapping nude photos of his sister and female employees. Even granting their willing cooperation it was not the avocation of a gentleman.

"Listen, Archy," he said, and I detected a note of anxiety, "that business we talked about—your investigating the thefts. There's been no further action—right?"

"Right," I agreed, soothing him with a half-truth. "No further action."

"Good-oh," he said, obviously relieved. "As I told you, the matter's been cleared up. No more thefts, I promise you that."

"Glad to hear it."

"Oh yes," he said, "one more thing . . ." And he snapped his fingers as if it were a matter of little importance he had suddenly recalled. It was the phoniest display of casualness I've ever witnessed. "Gerry tells me you're a member of the Pelican Club."

"That's correct."

His short cough of laughter was pure sham. "How do I go about joining?" he asked. "Naturally I belong to my father's club. And your father's too."

I nodded.

"Nice club," he said. "But a bit stodgy, wouldn't you say?"

"I'd say so."

"So I've been thinking about joining a younger club. Something jazzier, if you catch my meaning. Not so frumpy."

"Well, yes," I admitted. "The Pelican *is* looser. But you realize it has no golf course, pool, or tennis courts. It's really just an eating and drinking establishment. Emphasis on the latter."

"Just what I'm looking for!" he cried enthusiastically. "A place to let down one's hair, so to speak. How do I get a card?"

"I'd be happy to propose your name to the membership committee," I told him. I refrained from adding that I chaired that committee, there was a long list of would-be Pelicanites ahead of him, and I'd do my damndest to keep his name at the bottom.

"Good man!" he almost shouted. "I knew I could depend on you. I'm looking forward to spending a lot of time there. Let me know when I'm elected."

He gave me a hand flap and sauntered out, leaving me to reflect on how the death of the papa had wrought such a radical change in the son. But we all know, do we not, that where there's a will there's a way. I am, of course, referring to the will of the deceased Griswold Forsythe II.

Feeling I had done enough cataloging for one morning (zilch) and beginning to feel the stirrings of lunchtime hunger, I decided to return home and explore the McNally larder. I was almost at the front door when my escape was interrupted by the bouncy appearance of Sheila Hayworth. She seemed in an even more exuberant mood than Fern Bancroft, and I wondered if the Forsythes' chef was sprinkling hashish in the squid stew.

"Hi!" she said brightly. "I was hoping to see you so I could say goodbye before I leave."

"Leave?" I said. "You're going to Disney World? Say hello to Mickey for me."

"No, no," she said, laughing. "I'm leaving the Forsythes."

"Are you indeed? I'm sorry to hear that, Sheila."

"I'm not sorry," she said forthrightly. "I wasn't cut out to be a maid. I'm just too independent. I don't like waiting on other people."

"That's understandable," I told her and meant it. What a surly (and oafish) butler I'd make! "What do you plan to do?"

"Well, I'm taking a small condo in West Palm for starters. It's just a little studio apartment but it'll be all mine. And I've saved up some money, and if I can get a bank loan I want to open a boutique that sells lingerie. Like Victoria's Secret, you know. Do you think that's a good idea?"

"An excellent idea," I assured her, forbearing to mention that her chances of getting a bank loan to open a shop that sold thong bikinis ranged from anorexic to impossible.

"Well, that's what I want to do," she said determinedly. "Anyway I just wanted to say so long, wish you the best, and hope I see you again sometime."

She held out her hand. I took it to shake and noticed she was wearing a tennis bracelet. The diamonds weren't large—quarter-or half-carat I estimated—but it was an attractive trinket.

"That's a lovely hunk of jewelry," I said. "New?"

"Brand-new," she said joyously, holding up her wrist and turning it this way and that, admiring the glitter of the stones.

"A gift from an admirer, no doubt."

"Yep," she said and grinned. "Me! I'm so happy about leaving this draggy place I had to buy myself a going-away present."

"Good for you," I said, not believing a word she said.

She gave me an air kiss before we parted and I had twinges of regret at never having accepted her earlier come-ons. Whittier wrote: "For all sad words of tongue or pen/The saddest are these: 'It might have been'!" I don't think so. To me the saddest words of tongue or pen are these: "Who ate all the turkey bologna?"

On the drive home I had my first epiphanic moment of the day. After reviewing the conversations of that morning with Constance Forsythe, Fern Bancroft, Griswold III, and Sheila Hayworth, I realized the slaying of the senior Griswold had popped the cork from a jeroboam of champagne and everyone in the Forsythe ménage seemed in a giggly mood. It was cruel to impute their good spirits to the old man's demise but so it appeared.

Which suggested they all had a motive for doing him in. Which also meant yrs. truly was still out in left field, gloved and ready, vainly searching the sky for a ball that might come his way.

My luncheon was delayed and that was a shame because Ursi Olson had prepared a cold seafood salad with endive and watercress bedding chunks of shrimp, crabmeat, and Florida lobster. Ursi likes to add a tablespoonful of Dijon mustard to the dressing.

But there was a message from Sgt. Al Rogoff asking me to call him. So I postponed my noontime banquet, went into my father's study, and used his phone.

"I'm eating an anchovy pizza," Al said. "What are you having?"

"A liverwurst sandwich," I said, not wishing to upstage him.

"Rather you than me," he said. "You got anything?"

I thought it a propitious time to give him a tidbit. Al and I are competitors, in a sense, but our investigations are also cooperative ventures. If we don't share *all* the information uncovered by each of us it's understood we trade salient discoveries.

So I told Rogoff about my recent chat with Sheila Hayworth: she was leaving the Forsythe household to take her own place in West Palm and hoped to open a lingerie boutique if she could secure a bank loan.

"And I am Queen Marie of Romania," the sergeant said. "How do you figure?"

"Well, she was wearing a diamond-studded tennis bracelet she claims she bought for herself."

"Ho-ho-ho," Al said. "Who do you guess was the donor?"

"Griswold the Third," I said. "He had a thing going with Sheila until his father broke it up. But now that daddy's gone I think he's yielding to his baser instincts. I reckon he bought her the bracelet, is picking up the tab on her new apartment, and will probably finance her boutique. It's all glands, Al."

"What else?" he said. "Sex and money. If it wasn't for that cops wouldn't have a thing to do."

"What have you got for me?" I asked him.

"Not much," he admitted. "We found the calfskin wallet that had been lifted from the victim. It was in the bushes behind the building. The cash was gone but everything else was there, including credit cards. So it wasn't your ordinary, run-of-the-mill creep who offed Forsythe. He'd have taken the plastic."

"Did you dust the wallet?"

"What do you think?" he said indignantly. "We're not mutts, you know. The wonks picked up a fuzzy partial that didn't belong to the owner. It's not something you can take to court but it's a teaser."

"Any ID?"

"No, but they're working on it. By the way, your pal Timothy Cussack was involved in a barroom brawl last night. The other guy got his nose smashed and wants to bring charges of assault. He hasn't got a chance; witnesses say he was the one who started it. Anyway, just for the fun of it, I went out to the Forsythe horse farm this morning, picked up Cussack, and brought him in for questioning. Son, that lad is one cool customer. He knew we couldn't hold him and we didn't. He waltzed out in a couple of hours. That bum goes bad-assing his way through life and never draws more than a wrist slap."

I thought about what he had just told me. "Al, when you went out to the stables to pick up Cussack, what time was it?"

"Time? Early. Around nine thirty I'd say. Why?"

"Was Mrs. Constance Forsythe there when you took him in?"

"Sure she was."

"And she knew why you were taking him—for questioning about the barroom brawl?"

"Of course she knew. And gave us a lot of mouth about it. That's one tough cookie. But what's your point?"

"Al, I went out there about an hour or so later, looking for Cussack, and she told me he had left to inspect a horse a client was thinking of buying. I was just wondering why she thought it necessary to lie to me."

We were both silent a long time. I was the first to speak.

"Toto," I said, "I have a feeling we're not in Kansas anymore."

"Yeah, Dorothy," Rogoff said. "I think you're right."

19

I returned to the Forsythe manor after lunch. I assure you I did not anticipate proving or disproving a grand theory that explained all the goings-on in that household. I had no such theory. I was not yet certain of *anything* concerning the Forsythes but I was curious—nay, obsessed!—about the passions that were riving the family. I have mentioned in previous narratives my unquenchable nosiness, and now I found myself plunged into the middle of a living, breathing soap opera. It was heaven!

But perhaps, regarding my lack of a theory, I am being too modest—a fault of which I am rarely accused. I did have some vague notions of what had happened and was happening—and I am certain you do too. Human behavior is endlessly fascinating, is it not? I began this magnum opus with a few well-chosen remarks on the craziness of human primates, and my involvement with the Forsythes had only reinforced that opinion. They were loons! And if you mutter it takes one to know one, you may be correct.

I had no specific program planned for the afternoon. After Ursi Olson's seafood salad (with a glass of chilled pinot grigio) I was in a benevolent mood and willing to accept whatever fate shoveled my way. I did hope I'd have a chance to exchange a few giggles with Lucy, that lorn child. It seemed to me she was the only true victim in this tragicomedy. The others were riddles.

Mrs. Nora Bledsoe opened the door for me. Unlike the other residents I had met that morning, she seemed subdued. There were two little vertical lines of worry between her heavy brows.

"I trust you are in good health, Mrs. Bledsoe," I said. "I'm sure it's been a troublesome week."

"I'm surviving, sir," she said with a sad smile. "I'm good at that."

"Of course. I presume you and the rest of the staff will continue as before."

"I don't know what's going to happen," she said fretfully. "Things are so mixed up since Mr. Forsythe passed. Sheila Hayworth is leaving and Zeke Grenough threatens to quit because the younger Mr. Forsythe told him the short ribs we had last night weren't spicy enough. And Miss Gerry is moping and has hardly come out of her room since her father died. I just wish things would settle down and get back to normal."

"I'm sure they will," I comforted her.

"I don't know," she said gloomily. "Everything seems to be breaking up." She was silent a moment as if debating a decision. Then: "And I have a personal problem that's bothering me. I wonder if I might speak to you about it, Mr. McNally, and ask your advice. I trust your judgment, sir."

That was flattering and completely mistaken. I mean I'm the guy who said rock would never replace bebop and who voted for the loser in every Presidential election since I came of age.

"Of course, Mrs. Bledsoe," I said. "I'll be happy to offer what help I can. Why don't we move into the library."

We did, and the housekeeper sat in the armchair alongside the desk while I occupied the giant swivel, tapped fingertips together, and prepared to listen with solemn mien. Meanwhile I reflected that asking me for advice in a personal problem was akin to requesting Godzilla's aid on protecting the environment.

"It's Tony," Mrs. Bledsoe started. "My son. He'll be coming into some money soon. Mr. Forsythe's will, you know. He was very generous. I was hoping Tony would go to college and get a good education, but he wants to open a bar in Palm Beach."

"A bar?" I said, thinking that was just what we needed: another bar.

"A sort of nightclub," she said. "Dancing and all. He has a friend named Timothy Cussack. Do you know him?"

"We've met," I said cautiously. "I can't say I really know him."

"Well, I think he's a lowlife. I've told my son not to associate with him but Tony won't listen to me."

Oh-ho. I wondered if that was the cause of the slap, son to mother, I overheard during my first visit to the Forsyth home.

"Anyway," she continued, "he's convinced Tony they could make a lot of money if they opened this—this *saloon* for rich young people. I guess Cussack knows a lot of them. And that's how my son wants to use the money he'll get from Mr. Forsythe's estate. I've tried to talk him out of it but he won't listen to me and it's keeping me awake nights. I just don't know what to do."

"Mrs. Bledsoe," I said gently, "there are some things we can't change no matter how strongly we feel or how right we might be. Tony is an adult and can do whatever he pleases with money that is legally his. If you can't persuade him to invest it wisely, I don't believe you have any choice but to let him live his own life, make his own decisions, wish him well, and hope for the best."

"I don't trust that Timothy Cussack," she said angrily. "I think he's a conniver and he's going to cheat Tony."

"You may be correct, Mrs. Bledsoe, but I doubt if your telling Tony so will change his mind. There's a point you haven't considered: it will take months, perhaps a year, before Mr. Forsythe's estate is settled and your son receives his bequest. What I'm suggesting is that this is not an immediate problem. A lot can happen during the next year. Perhaps Tony and Cussack will have a falling out. Perhaps your son will find a more attractive opportunity to invest his legacy. I don't have to tell you the future is unpredictable. That's why I think you are worrying unnecessarily about something that may never come to pass."

I was gratified to see her brighten after listening to my Solomonic discourse.

"Of course," she said. "You're right, Mr. McNally. Things can change, can't they?"

"They always do," I assured her, refraining from quoting "*Plus ça change,* etc."

"Yes," she said, "and I must think positively. That's very important."

"It is indeed."

She rose and reached across the desk to shake my hand. "Thank you so much for your help," she said earnestly. "Since Griswold died I've had no one I can talk to."

Then, realizing she had used her former employer's given name and implied an intimacy she had kept hidden for so many years, she blushed and fled. She left me feeling proud of the way I handled a rather delicate situation and at the same time realizing I now had another motive for the murder of Griswold II. The only person I could confidently absolve from complicity in that violence was little Lucy, and I went looking for her.

But I was told by Anthony Bledsoe—in a definitely surly manner, I might add—that Lucy would be late returning that day since she was rehearsing a school play in which she was acting the part of a tangelo. I thought it a fitting role for such a sweet child.

But what I could not comprehend was Tony's enmity toward me. It went beyond his quite understandable rancor at not having been legally fathered: a sullen railing against fate. He obviously had an antipathy toward me personally. I was not aware of ever having offended him yet he treated me with a mixture of dislike, envy, and scorn. It was offputting and another part of the Forsythe puzzle.

Searching about wildly for any activity to delay my cataloging chores, I traipsed up to the music room and put my ear to the door. I heard no jingling of the harpsichord. Just to make certain Sylvia was not present I knocked but received no answer. She was apparently busy elsewhere. Possibly Suite 309 of the Michelangelo Motel, I acknowledged.

I then sought Mrs. Bledsoe and asked directions for finding the private chambers of Geraldine Forsythe. Finally, after a few wrong turnings in those labyrinthine hallways, I found the correct door and rapped softly.

"Who is it?" she called.

"Archy McNally."

After a moment I heard the sounds of a bolt being withdrawn and a chain unlatched. Superfluous security for the daughter of the house, I thought, but perhaps the attack on her sister-in-law had spooked her.

She opened the door and stood blocking the entrance.

"Yes?" she said.

It was not what one might call a warm, enthusiastic welcome.

"Just wanted to say hello, Gerry," I said as breezily as I could. "And give you a progress report on the investigation—or lack of progress I should say."

"Oh," she said, thawing, "that. I want to talk to you about it. Do come in."

I entered and she bolted and chained the door behind me. She had a small suite: sitting room, bedroom, bath. But the ceilings seemed at least twelve feet high and there were enormous windows facing northward. It was heavily furnished with velvet drapes and overstuffed furniture, everything in maroons and lifeless blues. There was a depressing dinginess about her quarters and I looked in vain for some evidence of lightheartedness. Zip. A fun place it was not.

She led the way into the bedroom. It was in disarray, with two large suitcases and one small, all on the floor, opened and half-filled.

"I'm packing," she said unnecessarily.

"So I see. Where are you off to, Gerry?"

"First to London. I have friends there and I'll stay with them a few days while I make up my mind where I want to go next. Vienna perhaps. I love strudel. I'm glad you stopped by, Archy. I was going to give you a call before I left. I want you to end your investigation of my missing jewelry."

"Oh?" I said. "Why is that?"

"I changed my mind."

I stared at her. "You have every right to do that of course, but I'm curious as to why."

"I just decided it wasn't important."

When some people lie they first lick their lips to lubricate their falsehood.

"You seemed to think so when you asked me to undertake the inquiry."

"That was then," she said. "This is now. I want you to drop the whole thing. Okay? They were just things. I can always buy more things."

"I thought they had considerable sentimental value."

She shrugged. "I can live with their loss. You'll stop looking into it?"

"If you say so."

"I do. Let's just forget about the whole thing. I really don't care if my sister-in-law is having a fling with Timothy Cussack. It's all a bloody bore."

I was silent, trying to evaluate this switcheroo and link it to the recent orders I had received from Griswold Forsythe III to cease investigating the theft of his late father's property. I was certain there was a link but what it might be I could not at the moment conceive.

Those north windows filled the room with a dullish afternoon light that had the hue of sullied brass. A desultory breeze billowed lace curtains. I was struck by the dead quiet of stodgy rooms enclosed in thick stone. I wondered if that was the reason for the Forsythes' behavior: everyone was trying to break out—dig tunnels, smash walls, fly, whatever it took.

"Listen, Archy," she said, "I don't know if I'll have a chance to see you again before I leave. I keep a bottle of Jack Daniel's Black up here to help when I can't sleep. Could we have a goodbye drink?"

"I'd like that."

"I don't have any ice."

"No problem," I said.

She went back into the sitting room while I reflected that Jack Daniel's Black was Timothy Cussack's choice and wondered what significance that had—if any.

She returned with two reasonably clean tumblers, each holding what I estimated to be about two ounces of 90-proof plasma.

I raised my glass. "Bon voyage," I said.

I sipped, she gulped. It seemed to have no effect on her but I was aware of a sudden jolt to the red corpuscles and looked at her with altered and slightly concupiscent interest.

She was wearing cutoff denim shorts with frazzled cuffs and a white T-shirt that bore no printed legend or image. A blank white T-shirt makes a statement, does it not? In her case it did; I mentioned before she was a robust woman. I imagined her capable of lofting me into the bleachers or perhaps out of the park. I jest, of course, but I was willing to accept the challenge.

She must have seen libidinous thoughts reflected in my expression because she smiled and said, "I always keep my promises, Archy."

"I wasn't aware you had made any."

"Oh yes," she insisted. "I asked you to do a job for me and promised a reward. The fact that I've ended the job doesn't relieve me of my obligation. It's payday, Archy."

I refuse to apologize for my conduct. I was less seducer than seducee—and if there isn't such a word there should be. Suffice to say that I allowed myself, heartily, to join in her desire to pay what she apparently felt was a debt. I considered her complaisance more than adequate compensation for my labors on her behalf and would gladly accept more employment at a similar salary.

What a stalwart woman! And what a vigorous lover. All firm muscle and glossy skin. My one objection to her behavior during our frantic joust was that she was so vocal—yelps, bleats, and yowls. Thank God for thick walls!

In all honesty I must confess I might have been guilty of a yodel or two.

Away we flew and a pleasant time was had by all. So pleasant, in fact, that after we had completed our escape and returned, perforce, to harsh reality, Gerry turned to me and said, "If you ask me to, Archy, I'll unpack."

"No," I said promptly, "don't do that."

She accepted it calmly as if she had long ago recognized that rejection by men was her destiny. I could have given her a lot of blather about my own personal obligations and how a closer relationship would prove awkward if not catastrophic. But I thought it best to make our parting short and sweet. Cowardice of course. Another go-around with Gerry and I reckoned I'd be using a walker.

Our farewell turned out to be happily casual with no recriminations and, I hope, no regrets.

"Send me a postcard from Vienna," I said lightly.

"I may even send you a strudel," she said.

We both laughed, kissed, and parted.

I had accumulated enough experiences that day to keep me scribbling in my journal for hours. I returned home and decided to forsake my two-mile ocean swim. I was in such a frail condition that even wading up to my ankles might have caused collapse. But collapse I did, in my bed, for an hour's nap that was more resuscitation than sleep.

The family cocktail hour and a splendid dinner of broiled wahoo helped restore my vigor and confidence. But before I set to work that evening recording the day's events in my professional journal I phoned Connie Garcia. I always do that after I have been unfaithful. Guilt, naturally.

"Hi, hon," I said. "How are you?"

"You're alive?" she said. "Good heavens, I was sure you had passed away ages ago."

I snickered, a mite falsely I must admit. "I've been chasing my tail," I told her. "Busy, busy, busy."

"As long as you're not chasing someone else's tail. What are you up to?"

"All sorts of things, most of them gruesome. Dinner tomorrow night?"

"Can't make it. Lady C. is having a sit-down for a passel of politicos. Black tie. It's about local taxes."

"Which she thinks are too high."

"You've got it," Connie said. "But I can grab a quick lunch."

"Sounds dandy to me," I said. "Tomorrow at the Pelican Club. Let's make it at noon. I haven't seen you in years."

"And whose fault is that?" she demanded before she hung up.

I wish I could understand my attachment to that lady. I want her and I need her. I think she wants me and needs me. But we can never make a final commitment. It's not a love-hate relationship; it's more like a yep-nope. Nothing endures but the struggle—which ain't bad.

I settled down to my bookkeeping entries. And as I jotted rapidly in my scrawly script I came across something I found intriguing. Both Griswold III and Gerry Forsythe had instructed me to end my investigations into the thefts. Their orders had come after the murder of their father. But I could not see how his death could possibly influence their decisions.

Then, flipping back through my journal, I found something interesting and possibly meaningful. On the afternoon before the day he was slain Mr. Forsythe had told me about the pernicious note he had received: YOUR NEXT. He had forbidden me to report the matter to the police because, he said, he intended to make inquiries himself that evening in an attempt to discover the author of the threat.

It occurred to me that perhaps, as his son claimed, he had succeeded and in the process had learned the identity of the person or persons responsible for the disappearance of his artworks and his daughter's jewelry. If so, he had paid dearly for his success.

And what the king of the hill had uncovered had led to his son and daughter commanding me to cease and desist from any further inquiry into the thefts. It all made a crazy kind of sense. I began to draw tentative lines between those unnumbered dots. It might result in a recognizable picture but it was not a pretty one.

I yearned to spend the remainder of that evening ruminating on the complexities of the Forsythe affair while tasting a marc and listening to a tape of Leadbelly singing "Goodnight, Irene." But my peace was disturbed by a phone call from—guess whom? Timothy Cussack himself.

"I hear you were looking for me this morning," he said bluntly.

"Well, yes," I admitted. "I wanted to ask how you made out after your imbroglio at the Sea Turtle last night."

"Imbroglio?"

"The fight."

"Shit," he said, "that was no fight. The guy asked for it. The cops pulled me in but they had no case and they knew it. I walked out. Listen, I'm calling from the Sea Turtle right now and—"

"How did you get my personal phone number?" I interrupted.

"It's in the book."

"No, it isn't."

"You gave me your card."

"No, I didn't."

"Hey," he said, "don't make a federal case out of it. I got your number from someone—okay? Like I was saying, I'm calling from the Sea Turtle and I want to talk to you. How about joining me and we'll hoist a few."

"Sure," I said. "Give me twenty minutes or so."

It was not a prospect I welcomed, but when duty calls, A. McNally stands to attention and salutes.

20

Cussack was clad in his ninja costume of black jeans, black turtleneck, black leather jacket. What's even worse was that he was wearing a musky cologne I loathed; it called to mind an ox that had neglected to shower for several days.

We sat at a corner of the bar and were served by Gladdie, who gave me a nervous smile and, when Cussack wasn't looking, rolled her eyes to express—what? Nervousness or perhaps fear, I reckoned. But Timothy seemed in an equable mood, sipping his sour mash peaceably and paying no attention to the frenetic action on the dance floor behind us.

"Nice of you to join me," he said. "How's it going?"

I had no idea what he meant. Just a casual inquiry about life in general I supposed.

"The madness rolls on," I answered.

"Yeah," he said, "doesn't it. Listen, the reason I wanted to talk to you may be nothing but it may be something."

I turned sideways to look at him. The man had a profile as grim as an Easter Island statue. I took a sip of my vodka gimlet. Gladdie had missed on that one: too puckery by far.

Since Tim was silent and seemed to be awaiting a reply to his inexplicable opener, I said, "What's it all about?"

He may have been a lowlife as Mrs. Nora Bledsoe had claimed but he was a dynamite salesman: manner serious and intent, eyes steady, voice lowered to give the impression he was revealing a valuable confidence. "You know Tony Bledsoe?" he asked.

I nodded.

"Tony and I are close," he said earnestly. "We party around together. He's a lively one, Tony is, when he gets out of that Forsythe zoo. He's an okay pal but he's got one fault: he's a bad drunk. Gets mean and wants to take on the whole world. Confidential?"

"Of course," I said.

"Well, the reason I'm telling you this," Cussack went on, "is that Tony's got a grudge against you."

"He does?" I said. "I can't think why. I've never offended him."

He signaled Gladdie for a refill—for himself, not for both of us. It was just as well; I wanted to keep the McNally brain (both halves) clear and undulled by strong drink. I had the distinct impression that I was being manipulated but for what purpose I could not guess.

Cussack took a gulp of his fresh jolt. "It's Sylvia Forsythe," he said, leaning toward me and lowering his voice even more. "Tony has eyes for her but she won't give him a tumble. I told him why: Sylvia can't stand men who try to put the make on her. She doesn't want to be hustled. But treat her like you couldn't care less and she's a pushover." He paused to laugh shortly. It was not a pleasant sound. "Ask me," he added. "I know."

I said nothing. I detest men who brag about their conquests. Definitely not pukka.

"That's why Tony hates your guts," Cussack continued. "He knows you're making it with Sylvia and it's driving him right up the wall. I've tried to calm him down, tell him she's just a chippy."

"I don't think she's a chippy," I said.

"No?" he said. "Well, whatever. Here's the problem: Tony is dead serious. I mean the poor guy is truly, madly in love with her and told her so. That turned her off. Some women are like that, you know."

"I suppose," I said. I thought he might possibly be correct in his analysis of Sylvia Forsythe. He was a man eager to exploit the weaknesses in women but utterly incapable of recognizing their strengths.

"Sure," he said. "I mean what does Tony have to offer? He's a fucking servant—right? Good for a roll in the sack if she feels like it. But now he's driving her nuts and talking about them taking off together. And all the time she's married to a rich cat so why should she even listen to this idiot? That's the way things were when you appeared on the scene. You've been spending a lot of time at the Forsythes' lately—am I correct?"

"Yes, I've been given the job of cataloging the books in their library."

"Uh-huh," Cussack said. "But all Bledsoe can see is that you and Sylvia are having fun and games. And like I said, he's stewing. The reason I'm telling you all this is to warn you how he feels. As much as I like the guy I know he has a ferocious temper and I really think he might go off the deep end. I've seen him completely unwired after a night of boozing. What you do about it is your problem; I'm not going to make any suggestions. But you've always treated me fair and square, and I just thought you should know about the situation."

"Thank you for your concern," I said, trying hard to keep any trace of irony out of my voice. "I'll certainly think about my best course of action."

"You do that," Cussack said. "The guy can be a killer if you push him too far. And I do mean *killer.*" He swung about and began casing the crowded nightclub, sizing up the possibilities (unescorted women) no doubt. "There's someone I've got to see," he said abruptly and drained his glass. "Thanks for the shots."

I wasn't aware I had offered to pay for his drinks; he had invited me. But there wasn't much I could do about it, was there?

Gladdie took my money with a sympathetic smile. "He's a card, isn't he?" she said.

I agreed. But whether Timothy Cussack was a joker or a knave I did not yet know.

I drove home in a legal fashion utterly flummoxed by Cussack's reasons for requesting that brief meeting. He may have been completely honest and sincere, of course, wanting only to warn me of Tony Bledsoe's enmity toward me and his potential for violence. But I suspected Cussack had more cunning motives. I thought him a deep man—deep in the sense that while his actions might seem logical to him, they were obscure to others.

Mrs. Nora Bledsoe had also called him a conniver. I was beginning to respect the wisdom of that lady.

I had the small marc I had promised myself, listened to "Goodnight, Irene" through earphones, and lapsed into a Scarlett O'Hara mode: "I'll think about it tomorrow."

I was true to my resolve, for when I awoke on Thursday morning I sat on the edge of my bed a few moments, still dopey with sleep, and thought again about that weird conversation with Timothy Cussack. He had casually mentioned he had enjoyed the favors of Sylvia Forsythe. If that was mere braggadocio, and I suspected it was, it helped solve part of the puzzle that had been bedeviling me. Now, if I did not see a blinding light at the end of the tunnel, I did glimpse a flickering candle flame.

Cussack had spoken of the "Forsythe zoo." A more apt metaphor, I decided, was that all the denizens of that cobwebby manse were playing the kids' game of Snap the Whip. Griswold Forsythe II had been on the tag end—and he had been spun off.

I went through my usual morning routine and, remembering my noontime lunch with Connie Garcia, I dug out my puce beret, which always puts her in a felicitous mood—after her hysterical laughter has calmed. Then I clattered downstairs to a late breakfast with Jamie Olson, who was kind enough to scramble me a brace of eggs with sliced shallots sautéed in butter. O cholesterol, where is thy sting?

It was over our coffee refills that I asked if he was aware Sheila Hayworth was leaving the Forsythes' employ.

"Yep," he said. "I heard."

That didn't surprise me. In the Palm Beach milieu the servants know what is going to happen before it does.

"Taking a condo in West Palm," I said. "Thinking of opening a lingerie shop." Frequently, while conversing with Jamie, I found myself mimicking his elliptical speech pattern.

"Uh-huh," he said.

"Costs money to open a shop," I observed.

He looked at me. "The boy," he said. "They took up again after the old man passed."

It was gratifying but a mite depressing to have my suspicion confirmed. "What about the other maid?" I asked. "She seems happy enough to stay."

"Loopy, that one," he remarked. "Ursi says her brassiere size is larger than her IQ."

I laughed. "That's cruel," I said.

"Yep," he agreed. "Since she's flat-chested."

"Why do you suppose she's staying on with the Forsythes? Needs the job?"

"Thought you knew," he said, chewing on his pipe stem. "Talk is she's in heat over that young butler."

"Tony Bledsoe?"

He nodded.

"Thank you," I said and slipped him a sawbuck.

I returned to my barrack and began scribbling furiously in my journal. There was much to be recorded for I had been neglecting my journalistic chores. As I jotted down all the tidbits I had recently collected, the pattern of what had happened and was happening in the Forsythe menagerie began to take shape. When I clapped on the puce beret and set out for my luncheon date I had a theory that put numbers on most of those dots. And what a nasty picture they formed.

I was seated at the bar of the Pelican Club, enjoying a vodka gimlet and chatting idly with Mr. Simon Pettibone when Connie came sailing in. Her glossy black hair swung free and she was wearing a slip dress of some shimmery stuff in a soft butterscotch color. Be still, my heart!

She waltzed over, gave me a peck, and looked accusingly at my empty glass.

"You started without me," she protested.

"My dear," I said loftily, "I assumed you were aware that the universe is composed of five elements: earth, air, fire, water, and vodka."

"I thought vodka *was* firewater," she said.

"Not a bad joke as jokes go," I told her. "And as jokes go, it went. What'll you have?"

"Food," she said. "And lots of it. I'm famished."

"Mr. Pettibone," I said, "I regret I must leave you now. I am faced with the problem of a famished lady."

"Such is the way of the world," he said philosophically.

Priscilla seated us at our favorite corner table in the dining area. She seemed in a churlish mood.

"Pris," Connie said, "is anything wrong?"

"My guy-of-the-month," Ms. Pettibone said grumpily. "He's turning out to be a first-class louse."

"Welcome to the club," Connie said, looking at me. "I know exactly how you feel."

"Food!" I cried heartily. "Pris, we're in dire need of nourishment. Starving, in fact. What's Leroy pushing today?"

"Humongous club sandwiches on whole wheat buns. With grilled chicken breast, Swiss, bacon, lettuce, tomato, and mayo."

"That's for me," Connie said happily. "With a glass of chardonnay."

"I'll go along," I said to her, "but only if you promise not to look at me while I'm eating. It's going to be messy."

"Try not to dribble," she urged.

The sandwiches were as good as described and I didn't dribble too much. It's a bit twee to eat a club sandwich with fork and knife— don't you think? We were halfway through our lunch, gossiping of this and that, when I said, "Listen, dear, there's something I'd like you to do for me."

She stopped nibbling on a curl of bacon to stare at me. "Oh?" she said. "And what is that?"

"Well, you know I'm involved in the investigation of the murder of Griswold Forsythe. Not officially of course; just trying to lend what assistance I can to Sergeant Al Rogoff, who's a good cop but a little lost when it comes to Palm Beach anthropology. I mean he's just not plugged in. Anyway, when this whole foofaraw started you mentioned that the daughter, Geraldine Forsythe, had been taken over the jumps by a former polo player."

Connie said nothing.

"You were right," I went on. "His name is Timothy Cussack and your tip may prove to be significant. Now what I need to know is exactly why they split up. Do you think you could find out?"

"Why are you so interested in Geraldine Forsythe?" she asked suspiciously. "Is there hanky-panky going on between you two?"

I laughed merrily. "Perhaps a soupçon of hanky," I said, "but definitely no panky. How about it? Will you try to find out?"

"Maybe," my dearest one said. "What's in it for me?"

I sighed. "Connie, I do believe you've contracted the quid pro quo syndrome from Lady Horowitz. Very well, what do you want in return—assuming you can obtain the information I seek?"

"A weekend in Freeport," she said.

"Done," I said promptly. "Get me what I need and we'll be off for two days of unbridled delight. Plus bowls of that marvelous conch chowder."

"Okay," she said happily. "I'll try."

We finished our lunch, I signed the tab, and we moved outside to the sunbaked parking lot. I donned my puce beret and, as expected, Connie collapsed with guffaws.

"It's *you!*" she screamed. "Oh lordy, is that hat ever *you!*"

We exchanged a smeary kiss and, still giggling, she drove away in her new green Camry. That woman changes cars more frequently than I change my unmentionables. I stood there a moment after she departed, pondering my next move. I had a grand theory about the Forsythe affair and sooner or later I'd have to put it to the test. But that scared me; if I flunked I'd be up sc without a p.

But buoyed by my vodka gimlet, chardonnay, and calorie-stuffed lunch I decided to go for broke. So I headed for the pawnshop of the urbane Mr. Simeon Gravlax. I found him in good health, his sly smile intact—the soul of amused curiosity as if the world had been created for his enjoyment.

"Sir," I said, "several days ago we had a small transaction during which I paid to ask you to approve or reject my description of the person who pawned the Benin bronze. I lost."

"I remember, sir," he said, nodding vigorously. "A most interesting negotiation. And profitable, I might add."

I withdrew a fifty-dollar bill from my wallet. "May I try again?" I asked.

A claw reached out and snatched the half-yard from my grasp. "Delighted," he said.

I then delineated in great detail the person I now believed had pawned the work of art stolen from Griswold Forsythe II. Mr. Gravlax listened to my recital closely.

When I had finished he smiled and reached up to pat my shoulder. "My dear sir," he said, "you are absolutely correct."

What a rush that was! I wanted to do a small entrechat but controlled myself. "Thank you, sir," I said huskily. "You have made me a very happy man."

"As you have me," he said. "It was a dull day until you arrived. Dealing with poverty as I do is not the most exhilarating of professions. Even if your business with me is concluded I hope you may stop by occasionally if only to schmooze for a few moments."

"An honor, sir," I said.

"A pleasure, sir," he said.

I drove back to the beach singing another of my favorite songs—"It's Only a Paper Moon." They don't write songs like that anymore. I wonder why?

It was almost four o'clock when I arrived at the Forsythe mansion which, in my own mind, I now labeled the Hôtel des Kooks. I drove around to the back and parked close to their mammoth garage. Then I headed into the greenery, hoping to find Lucy Forsythe in her Secret Place.

The young miss was there, seated on the lawn with a notebook open on her lap and pencil stub in hand. Her head was lowered, wings of silky hair hiding her face.

She looked up as I approached. "Hi, Archy," she said. "Gee, I'm glad to see you. I thought you had forgotten all about me."

"Nah," I said, plumping down beside her, "not a chance. How are you, darling?"

"Okay," she said. "Sort of. I'm writing that poem about my granddad but I'm not going to show it to you until it's finished."

"That's best," I assured her. "I know it's going to be fine because you're very creative."

"Creative? What does that mean?"

"You're very good at making things up."

"I guess," she said and stared at the thick shrubbery surrounding her miniature amphitheater. It occurred to me that she hadn't yet smiled. "Archy, may I ask you something?"

"Of course."

"Can I come and live with you?"

How do you handle something like that?

"Lucy," I said, "this is your home, right here with your family."

"I know," she said, "but I don't like living here. Besides, I don't think I'm going to have a family. I heard my mother and father yelling at each other and what I think is that they're going to get a divorce. I know what that is. A lot of the kids at school, their parents got a divorce."

"It happens," I said. "But the kids are still living with their mother or father, aren't they?"

"Most of them. Except for Emma Bradbury; she's living with her grandmother. But what if neither my mother or father wants me?"

I swallowed. "I don't think that's possible, honey."

She turned to look at me, eyes brimming. "But what if it *is?* It worries me. That's why I'd like to come and live with you. Do you have a house?"

"Yes, I live with my parents."

"Well, couldn't I come and stay? I'd just need a little room and I promise I wouldn't cry or get sick or anything like that."

I had been right: she was the main victim. The adults went their selfish, screwball ways and this child was hurting.

"Tell you what, Lucy," I said. "If no one wants you, I promise you can come and stay at my home. I don't think that's going to happen because even if your parents got a divorce, one of them will want you and the other will want to visit and take you on trips and things like that. Please try not to worry about it. You're never going to be left alone."

That seemed to brighten her a bit. She finally gave me a smile, a small, frail thing. Hope is hard to kill in kids.

"You promise, Archy?" she said.

"Positively," I said with more confidence than I felt. I climbed to my feet. "Now you finish your poem. And don't forget that you and I are going to have a picnic right here. But you must let me bring the lunch."

That quickened her; the shy smile turned to a grin. "You know what I'd like?" she said, excited now.

"What?"

"A pizza."

"Good choice," I said. "With lots of cheese."

"And maybe those funny little pieces of meat that look like coins. I like those."

"Pepperoni," I said. "You're so right; they're good. That's what we'll have."

"Thank you," she said gratefully. "I love you, Archy."

It came close to being a mawkish moment but her innocence saved it.

"And I love you, Lucy," I mumbled and stumbled out of there.

21

I had time for my ocean swim, a melancholy wallow I must admit because I could not sluice away my memory of Lucy's misery. Adults are supposed to be able to cope with troubles but we want kids' lives to be a constant joy—and they so rarely are.

No family cocktail hour that evening because my parents were leaving early to have drinks and dinner at the home of septuagenarian friends. It would be followed by a ferocious contest of high-stakes bridge. The victorious couple might win as much as forty cents.

And so I dressed casually, planning to dine in the kitchen with the Olsons. To my delight, Ursi had prepared a rabbit stew made Italian-style with, amongst other goodies, salt pork, garlic, and red wine. Served with small roast potatoes. Also a round of pepper focaccio. Luscious.

I was in the pantry uncorking a bottle of the Chianti Classico we keep on hand in case of an impending nuclear catastrophe when the phone rang and I picked it up in the kitchen. Sgt. Al Rogoff was calling.

"Interrupting your dinner?" he said gruffly.

"Not yet. What's happening?"

He didn't answer that. "Can you and I get together tonight?" he asked.

"Easiest thing in the world," I told him. "My parents are out this evening and I'm going to scarf with Ursi and Jamie in the kitchen. Come join us."

"Oh, I couldn't do that," he said. "We'll meet later."

"It's rabbit stew and roast potatoes."

"Be right there," he said and hung up.

"Ursi," I said, "Sergeant Rogoff will be joining us for dinner. Is that all right?"

"Of course," she said. "There is plenty."

Al showed up bearing our dessert: a chocolate cake layered with raspberry mousse, and my diet immediately became a dim remembrance. What a merry feast we had! Good food, good wine, good talk. Like all cops Al had an inexhaustible store of amazing and amusing true tales to relate. My favorite was of a well-known investment banker of Palm Beach who was arrested pedaling his ten-speed bicycle along Worth Avenue at midnight while wearing his wife's lingerie. How many times must I tell you that madness is engulfing the world?

Rogoff and I retired to my father's study after dinner. I broke out a bottle of the pater's Rémy Martin and poured us ponies of cognac. We sat in facing club chairs and simultaneously sighed with content.

"Great dinner," Al said.

"Great dessert," I said. "No-cal, of course."

"Of course. Would your old man object if I smoked a cigar? He'll smell it."

"Go ahead," I urged. "I'll tell him we had a conference on the Forsythe investigation."

"That's the truth." He lighted up one of his Louisville Sluggers and I had an English Oval, wondering how many I had had that day. Two, three, four or more—I couldn't recall. And I was in such a replete mood I didn't much care.

"How are you coming along on the Forsythe homicide?" I asked lazily, for to tell you the truth I really didn't want to think about it. That raspberry mousse cake was stupendous! And guess who had two slices.

"I'm not coming along," the sergeant said grumpily. "No hits, no runs, just errors. I can't get this thing off the ground. That's why I'm here. You got anything? Anything at all?"

I hesitated half a mo. I had a lot I could tell him but it was all suspicions, conjectures, presumptions. Still, I reckoned it was time to reveal *some* of it. At least I could give him a few bones to gnaw, and he had the resources and official heft to find answers to the questions troubling me.

"As I recall," I said, "you told me Sylvia Forsythe and Anthony Bledsoe were not at home when the murder occurred. Did you check out their alibis?"

He nodded. "She's clean. She was having a pedicure and a massage at the time Forsythe was offed, just like she claimed. Bledsoe is a little more iffy. He drove the Forsythes' Rolls in for a wash and wax, as he said, but he didn't hang around while the work was being done. Says he just wandered around window-shopping and then had a hamburger. Maybe. We haven't pinned it down."

I took a deep breath. "Al," I said, "Tony Bledsoe is the illegitimate son of the recently deceased Griswold Forsythe the Second."

He looked at me, blasted. Suddenly he chomped down on his cigar and bit off the tip. He made a grimace of disgust and deposited the severed smoke in a nearby ashtray.

"Is that for real?" he demanded.

"It is," I said. "Reported to me as gossip and then confirmed by an unimpeachable source."

"Why didn't you tell me before this?" he said harshly.

"Because I only learned of it a few days ago and I thought it of little significance. A footnote, so to speak. But then I heard that Bledsoe has a propensity for violence, especially after he's had a few drinks."

"Propensity for violence," the sergeant repeated. "Love the way you talk. Couldn't you just say the guy's a hothead?"

"All right," I said. "Anthony Bledsoe is reputed to be a hothead."

"And you have a propensity for prolixity," said Al who, as you may have guessed, is no fool. He looks as if he was hacked from a side of beef by a careless butcher but he is an extremely astute and conscientious detective. He also happens to be a closet balletomane—but that's neither here nor there.

"Okay," he said, "so Tony is the dead man's bastard. What does that get us?"

"Motive?" I suggested. "Resentment and anger. He was a servant in his father's home. That couldn't have been easy to endure."

"Who's his mother?"

"Mrs. Nora Bledsoe, the Forsythes' housekeeper."

Rogoff shook his meaty head in wonderment. "That place is a zoo," he said.

"You're the second person who's said that."

"Who was the first?"

"Timothy Cussack."

"Oh-ho. And have you any secrets about that bum you'd care to reveal?"

"I'm leery about him," I admitted, not answering his question directly. "But I can't imagine what his motive might be for strangling Mr. Forsythe. Surely not for the few hundred dollars in his wallet."

The sergeant hunched forward. "But you figure he's a possible?"

I nodded.

"And Bledsoe is another?"

"Or the two of them in cahoots. Al, they're close friends, drinking buddies. They may have cooked up the whole thing together. Bledsoe gets a nice bequest after his father dies. The two of them, Bledsoe and Cussack, want to open a saloon or nightclub or whatever. Maybe they got impatient and decided the old man was worth more dead than alive."

That wasn't *quite* the way I saw it, but I knew the suggestion would be sufficient to start Al digging deeper into the whereabouts of the two suspects at the time of the murder.

The sergeant sat back, finished his brandy, and began to juice up a fresh cigar. "You know," he remarked, "the only reason I put up with you is that you're one of the beach people. They'll talk to you and tell you things they'd never tell me because I'm just a lousy cop."

"You know," I said, "the only reason I put up with you is that you can flash your potsy and get the street people to tell you things they'd never tell me because I'm just a lousy civilian."

We glowered at each other, then burst out laughing.

"Not a bad team," Rogoff said.

"Not bad at all," I agreed.

He rose to depart without lighting up his new cigar, for which I was thankful. I walked him out to his pickup truck. It was a splendid night, cool and clear.

"Thanks for the feed," Al said. "And for the leads. I'll take a closer look at Bledsoe."

"And Cussack," I said. "Don't forget him."

"I won't," he promised. "And if you learn anything new don't be bashful. Support your local police."

"Don't I always?"

"Sometimes," he said. "After a delay. But better late than never."

"What a brilliant expression," I told him. "I wish I'd said that."

"Go to hell," he said cheerfully and drove away.

I went back inside and cleaned up father's study, taking brandy snifters and ashtray into the kitchen to rinse. I asked Ursi to give me a wakeup call on Friday morning. Eight o'clock, no later.

"Make sure I'm out of the hay," I urged.

"I'll make sure, Mr. Archy," she said, smiling. "If necessary I'll have Jamie play his concertina in your bedroom."

"That'll do it," I acknowledged and climbed the stairs to *my* Secret Place. I undressed and pulled on a Japanese kimono imprinted with a scene of a samurai battling dragons. Fitting?

I worked on my journal awhile and then surrendered. I treated myself to a marc, lighted a cigarette, and put on a tape of Tony Bennett singing cabaret songs. What a balladeer he is! Did you ever catch his "Night and Day"? Magic.

While I sipped, smoked, and listened I reflected on my conversation with Sgt. Al Rogoff. I was satisfied with the way it had gone, confident I had spurred him to do the donkeywork needed to add flesh to the bones of my theory of what had happened. I was not absolutely sure of it, you understand, but there is little I am totally certain of—except that a stock will rise in price the day after I sell it.

I finished my drink, cigarette, and Tony Bennett's tape. His last song was "I'll Be Seeing You." It was beautifully done but had no relation to the discreet inquiry that concerned me. A more apt selection might have been "The Lady Is a Tramp."

Ursi was true to her word and pounded on my door at eight A.M. Friday morning and continued pounding until she heard my strangled shout, "I'm up, I'm up!" I cannot claim I bounced out of bed at that ungodly hour full of p & v. But I did manage to drag myself through the morning's ablutions, shaving, dressing, and arriving downstairs in time to breakfast with my parents in the dining room.

It was not a festive repast. As usual, father kept his nose buried in *The Wall Street Journal,* checking the current status of his Treasury bonds, and I was in no mood for brilliant chatter, aching for at least another hour of slumber. Poor mother had to provide what conversation there was, relating a droll tale of a woman in her garden club whose springer spaniel apparently had an insatiable appetite for her impatiens.

After breakfast we all separated. Father drove his Lexus to the office, mother retired to the greenhouse to wake her begonias, and I set out in the Miata on my morning program, planning to visit the Trojan

Stables. Horse people, whether engaged in the activities of farm or racetrack, are notoriously early risers, sometimes (ugh!) before dawn. So I expected Mrs. Constance Forsythe would be present when I arrived.

And so she was, supervising a morning exercise of all the horses entrusted to her keeping. The riders were mostly her stable boys, plus a few owners, plus Timothy Cussack atop a handsome chestnut mare. I was glad to see him so occupied; I had no desire to have an immediate encounter with that scalawag.

Mrs. Constance was all beams. "Hiya, Archy," she said genially. "You awake so early?"

"Barely," I said.

She was looking a bit puffy about the gills that morning, as if on the previous night she had enjoyed a pajama party with a regiment of dragoons. I had noted her ruddy and ravaged face on our first meeting, and wondered if she might be a heavy drinker. Now I was convinced of it. The outdoor life was not the cause; hers was an 80-proof complexion.

"Ma'am," I said, "I don't know whether or not you are aware of it but I have been working with the authorities in the investigation of your husband's murder."

She looked at me sharply. "Are you now?" she said. "And why on earth would you be doing that?"

"Griswold Forsythe was an old and valued client of McNally and Son. Naturally we want to provide the police with whatever assistance we can."

"Uh-huh," she said, turning to look at the cantering horses. "I hope that doesn't include revealing any confidential information."

"Of course not," I said stiffly. "As I'm sure you know, my father is a very principled man."

She wheeled around to stare at me again. "I believe he is," she said. "I'm not so sure about you."

"You can trust my discretion," I assured her.

"I don't have much choice, do I?" she said with a hard laugh.

"Mrs. Forsythe, I would think you'd be eager to aid in solving this brutal crime."

"Of course I am," she said peevishly. "But the cops ask such stupid questions. I don't think that clunky sergeant—what's his name?"

"Al Rogoff."

"Yes, well, I don't think he's got a clue."

"Don't underestimate him," I advised her. "He may move slowly but he's very determined."

"So what?" she said sardonically. "I've seen thoroughbreds who move slowly but are very determined. They finish twelve lengths back."

I didn't feel like smiling but I did. "Actually," I said, "I'm here more or less on Sergeant Rogoff's behalf. He is so occupied analyzing the physical evidence he has had little opportunity to interrogate the people who may or may not be personally involved. That is why he has deputized me—not officially of course—to ask questions and try to provide him with profiles of relatives, employees, friends, and acquaintances of the victim."

It was a long, rambling speech, pure fudge, and I wasn't sure she'd buy it. But she did.

"All right," she said, tightening the belt on that scrofulous riding jacket she wore, "what do you want to know?"

"Anthony Bledsoe," I said. "What can you tell me about him?"

"A barrel of laughs he ain't," she said with that whinny of hers. "A sullen kid. Oh, he does his job; no complaints there. But he's got a grudge against the world."

"Any evidence of violence?"

"Occasionally."

"Against whom?"

"His mother, for one. There seems to be a constant squabble going on between those two. I've never asked about it. None of my business. If they do their jobs that's all I ask."

"Does Tony drink?"

"Don't we all?" That whinny again.

"Do you think he'd be capable of assaults against others while under the influence?"

She considered that a brief moment. "I think probably he would. He's got a ferocious temper. To tell you the truth, Archy, I'm not sure he's got both oars in the water."

"Is he having an affair with Fern Bancroft?" This was a supposition on my part but evidence pointed to it and I reckoned it was time for verification.

Constance Forsythe gave me a crooked grin. "You do get around, don't you?" she said. "Well, she's as nutty as he is and it wouldn't surprise me a bit if they had a thing going. Listen, why are you asking all these questions about Tony Bledsoe? Is he a suspect in my husband's murder?"

"There are several," I replied. "He's one of them."

She nodded. "I can understand that. I'd hate to believe it but he's hyper and strong enough to have done it, especially if he was in one of his wicked moods."

"What would be his motive?" I asked her.

"Money," she said promptly. "What else? Tony has dreams he'd never realize on what Griswold was paying him. Maybe he went to the office that day, asked for a raise, got turned down and blew his stack."

"That's possible," I said. "Thank you for your help, Mrs. Forsythe. I'm sure it will aid the investigation."

"You'll report to Sergeant Rogoff what I've just told you?"

"Unless you have any objections."

"No," she said. "No objections."

She walked away from me abruptly to meet the returning riders. I headed for the Miata but stopped when I saw Sylvia Forsythe's silver-gray Saturn come gliding into the parking area. It stopped and she hopped out, wearing white jeans and an aqua tank top. No matter what her costume, it had a dégagé look, as if she had grabbed the first things in her closet that came to hand. The result was elegant insouciance.

She came bopping over to me with a sassy smile. "And a jolly good morning to you, Archy," she said. "Sorry, luv, but I can't have lunch with you today."

I laughed. "I don't recall inviting you."

"However," she said, drawling the word and looking at me speculatively, "I should be free by three o'clock. The Michelangelo Motel. Okay?"

"Why not?" I said hoarsely, hating myself for the weak-kneed craven I am.

"That's what I like in a man," she said saucily. "Uncontrollable passion." She tossed me an air kiss and scampered over to Mrs. Constance and the sweated horses.

Stay tuned.

22

I pointed the Miata toward West Palm, singing mightily and revising the lyrics of that old spiritual to "Swing high, sweet chariot." For I was in a frolicsome mood. That verbal fencing with Constance Forsythe had added confirmation to my ramshackle theory. I began to glimpse the end of the Forsythe affair and could imagine the whole story being condensed in *Soap Opera Digest*.

It was then about eleven o'clock or so. I stopped at the first public telephone kiosk I could find and dug into my wallet for Gladdie's number. Surely you remember Gladdie—the barmaid at the Sea Turtle. I reasoned that because of the hours she worked it was possible she was now astir and ready for breakfast.

"Yeah?" a man answered in a croaky voice.

"May I speak to Gladdie, please."

"Who?" he said. "What?"

Then I remembered her warning about a hard-of-hearing father. "Gladdie!" I shouted. "Your daughter!"

He grumbled but in a few moments she came on the line, sleep in her voice.

" 'Lo," she said. "Who's this?"

"Archy," I said, then added modestly, "I don't suppose you remember me."

"Archy!" she said. "Of course I remember you. You're that cute redheaded boy with the funny little goatee."

Somewhat discomfiting. "Not quite," I said. "I'm the cute boy who was drinking with Timothy Cussack."

"Of course," she said. "Now I remember. You're a vodka gimlet."

"You've got it," I said gratefully. "That's exactly what I am. Gladdie, I realize I probably woke you up and I apologize. But I was hoping I might treat you to breakfast."

"Hey," she said, "that sounds utter. I usually go to our local IHOP. I love their pancakes—don't you?"

"Divine," I said.

Which explains why, thirty minutes later, I was seated across the table from her, watching with fascination while she attacked plates of pancakes, a T-bone, eggs, potatoes, toast, a pint of OJ, and enough heavily creamed coffee to float the USS *Wisconsin*. I had already enjoyed an abstemious breakfast of a single English muffin (admittedly slathered with Rose's lime marmalade) and I could not believe this young miss was gobbling a meal that would have staggered Lucullus.

"Archy," she said, "you don't think all this is fattening, do you?" Oh yes, she was quite serious.

"I'm not a doctor," I told her, "but I play one on TV. In my judgment your breakfast is not fattening providing you get sufficient physical exercise."

She gave me a bright smile. "I try," she said.

She really was a *nice* woman, destined, I was sure, to marry a handsome rake who would starve her shamefully, not recognizing what a treasure he had won.

I took a sip of my black coffee. "Gladdie," I said, "I must be honest with you. I need some information from you for which I am willing to pay."

She stopped gorging long enough to ask, "Information? About what?"

"You have a drop of maple syrup on your chin," I mentioned. "It's about Timothy Cussack. Two questions, and if you don't wish to answer them, that's your prerogative and I'll understand completely."

"What are they, the questions?"

"What kind of a car does he drive, and do you know of any particular woman with whom he has been closely associated. Recently, that is."

She wiped her chin. "This won't get me in any trouble, will it? Timmy is a meanie when he's riled. You saw that."

"Our conversation is confidential, Gladdie. I promise you he'll never hear about it."

"Okay. How much?"

"Fifty."

"Works for me," she said blithely, starting on her dessert: a bowl of chocolate ice cream. "Tim used to drive an old beatup Pontiac, a real clunker. Then, a couple of months ago, he showed up in a new Taurus wagon, pearl blue. A real beauty. Okay?"

"Fine," I said. "And his favorite woman—if he has one."

"There I can't help much," she said. "The guy's a real Don Juan." (She pronounced it Don Joo-ann.) "But I've noticed he's got a thing for older women. Not ancient, you know, but older than him. Does that help?"

"Immeasurably," I said and watched, disbelieving, as she stole the salt and pepper shakers and glass ashtray, slipping her loot unconcernedly into her shoulderbag. The only thing I've ever lifted was a stein from McSorley's Old Ale House in Manhattan.

I paid for our breakfast and in the parking area outside the IHOP I passed a fifty to Gladdie.

"Thank you, sir," she said pertly.

"My pleasure," I said.

"When will I see you again?" she asked eagerly.

"Soon," I promised. But I didn't think so.

It was nudging one o'clock when I finished that bacchanalia with Gladdie but I was in no mood for lunch. Watching her gourmandize had somehow robbed me of an appetite. I mean, who puts catsup on scrambled eggs? That qualifies for the icky category, wouldn't you say?

So I had two hours to slay before my rendezvous with Sylvia at the Michelangelo Motel and, despite the travel involved, I resolved to make a quick trip back to the beach and do a spot of discreet inquiry. My flaccid theory was beginning to sit up and bay at the moon. I was convinced a few more bits of info would prove me the most brilliant detective since Nancy Drew.

Arriving at the Forsythe Bedlam, I drove around to the back, intending to enter through the rear door. But the man I sought was standing outside, smoking a twisted cigar that looked like two entwined pieces of rope that had been soaked in tar. Zeke Grenough was wearing chef's whites, his wire-rimmed pincenez clamped to the bridge of his nose.

His greeting was affable enough and we exchanged news about the most recent of the season's hurricanes, which was now apparently weakening and would exhaust its remaining fury in the North Atlantic.

"Mr. Grenough," I said, "I heard a distressing rumor that you may be leaving the Forsythes' employ. Surely that can't be true."

"Oh no," the little man said calmly. "No, no. I admit there was a minor disagreement right after Mr. Forsythe was killed. But things were so upset, you know. Now we've all calmed down. No, I'm staying and young Mr. Griswold has promised me a new microwave."

"Glad to hear it," I said. "I know how much the family depends on you." (McNally's Law: If you wish to seduce by flattery, pile it on.)

"I try," he said modestly. "When I arrived they were strictly beef and potatoes people. Gradually I have been introducing them to more subtle dishes. For instance, this evening we are having veal medallions and scallops sautéed with sundried tomatoes and fresh basil."

"With a good white wine," I gurgled, my appetite suddenly returning in full force.

"Of course. Perhaps a chablis or sauvignon blanc."

"The Forsythes have a good wine cellar?"

"I am gradually creating it," he said complacently. "When I started I was horrified to find most of their bottles had screw tops and handles."

"Incredible," I said, shaking my head. "So in addition to increasing their fondness for haute cuisine you are also teaching them the glories of good vintages."

"Oh yes," he said, apparently happy to discuss what was not only his job but his passion. "As they say, life is too short for cheap wine. Mrs. Constance has been especially supportive of my efforts."

"And what about Anthony Bledsoe?" I asked lightly. "I hear he enjoys a glass or two."

He stared at me through those crazy specs. "Tony?" he said. "Oh no, you have been misinformed. Tony has no interest in wine—or any other spirits as far as I know. He drinks Diet Pepsi with my *chef d'oeuvre:* poached salmon with pears. That offends me."

"I should think it would," I said.

We chatted a few moments on vital topics, such as which is the best sauce for tournedos, béarnaise or bourguignonne. We came to no agreement but parted firm friends, each recognizing in the other a fervor for tasty vittles. I hopped back into the Miata having determined, in my opinion, exactly what I had hoped.

I sped back to the Michelangelo Motel in a mood more depressive than manic. It was gratifying, of course, to have added confirmation that my analysis was correct but it gave me no joy. Instead I was saddened by human perfidy. I am no saint, mind you, but my sins were small spuds compared to the evils committed by the miscreants who had conspired to murder Griswold Forsythe II.

My visit to the doldrums was mercifully short. By the time I arrived at the Michelangelo the McNally spirits were once again bubbling like an uncorked magnum of Bollinger. I espied Sylvia's silver Saturn in the parking area and found her already in Suite 309, nibbling on a small beaker of applejack. She was wearing a grin of luxurious content. And nothing else.

I realized we had enjoyed only two passionate scrums but sometimes brief encounters are more meaningful than a lifetime of intimacy, are they not? In any event this flighty woman still had the magic to entice me. It was, I decided, a clear case of déjà voodoo.

She was in no mood to waste time, nor was I. In the blink of a gnat's eye we were jousting on sea-foam-colored satin sheets and howling (pianissimo) with delight. What a madcap she was! She gave new meaning to the phrase "fancy-free." But I was not so insensible with passion that I did not recall Ms. Browning's words: "How do I love thee? Let me count the ways." Before that afternoon ended I was up to fourteen.

Finally, dizzy with rapture and exhaustion, we lay panting as if we had just set a record in the high hurdles, which I believe we had. I staggered from the track and stumbled to the kitchen where, with trembling hands, I prepared transfusions of applejack on ice. Lots and lots of ice.

"Bless you, my child," Sylvia murmured when I delivered her glass. "That was quite a go, was it not?"

"The only trouble," I said, "was that it went."

"Tomorrow's another day," she said blithely and sat up, pressing the icy glass to her swollen bosom.

I sat on the edge of the bed, hunched over, lacking the strength to straighten my spine. "Sylvia," I said, trying very hard to keep my voice from becoming a weak croak, "what's happening between you and Griswold? The last time we spoke you implied you were thinking of leaving him."

"Not now," she said cheerfully. "We've come to an understanding. Soon after we married I realized my husband was a victim of the seven-week itch. That's how long it took him to stray. And guess who he picked."

"I have no idea," I said, one of my easier falsehoods since she could have had no idea of how much prying I had done.

"Sheila Hayworth!" she cried. "Can you believe it? Our maid! I do believe El Jerko is hooked. But that's okay; it's his problem. Anyway we've come to an arrangement. We're going to stay married. He'll go his way and I'll go mine. Naturally we'll have a financial agreement."

"Naturally," I said.

"It's best for everyone," she said, and I thought she was trying to convince herself as much as me. "Lucy will still have a momma and a poppa, and Griswold and I will have complete freedom to live the way we want to live. Don't you think that makes sense?"

"It does," I said, trying not to reveal my doubts.

She began stroking my bare back with drink-chilled fingers. *Then* my spine straightened. The woman *dabbled* with me. I can think of no other word that better describes her actions. I had the insane notion that she saw me as a human harpsichord and was playing me. Vivaldi? It felt more like Scott Joplin.

"Sylvia," I said hoarsely while this noodling was going on, "I'd like to ask you a personal question and if you wish to tell me to go to blazes you'll be entirely within your right."

"Okay," she said. "What's the question?"

"Did you ever make it with Tony Bledsoe?"

"Once," she said ruefully. "It was a rainy afternoon and I was bored. But then he got serious and I can't stand that. He had this crazy idea of our running away together. Rubbish! You probably think me a fluffhead but I do have a keen instinct for the bottom line. I mean what did he have to offer? Love? You can't pay your Neiman-Marcus charge with that."

"Indeed you can't," I agreed. "And is Tony still lovesick?"

She shrugged. "I suppose. He keeps giving me these moony looks. He'll get over it."

I wasn't so sure. A lark on a rainy afternoon for her might well have been an epiphany for poor Tony. He had caught a glimpse of how glorious life could be. I suspected it had given focus to all his inchoate longings. Now, suddenly, he knew what he wanted: he wanted *her.*

"It was Fern Bancroft, wasn't it?" I asked.

"What?" she said sharply.

"It was Fern Bancroft, the other maid, who tried to throttle you."

She looked at me, first puzzled then wry. "You're a busy busybody, aren't you? How did you guess that?"

"Elementary, as Mr. Holmes said to Mr. Watson. I put two and two together and came up with five. Fern is slightly off the wall and not a lady to be trifled with. She has hot eyes for Tony Bledsoe, he is enamored of you, and she attempted to remove the competition. Is that the way you see it?"

She nodded.

"Sylvia, why didn't you report her to the police?"

"Give me a break, Archy! I didn't want to put that silly girl behind bars. I had a long talk with her and convinced her that Tony is all hers; I have absolutely no interest in him."

"You're very forgiving," I said admiringly. "She could have done you in."

That earned a laugh. "But she didn't, did she? It's all water under the bridge or over the dam or whatever. Now come here."

I rolled back onto the bed and we nuzzled a moment. Why do so many nice things begin with an "n"? Nuzzling, nestling, nibbling, necking. Even noshing.

"Now that you're in a confessional mood," I said, "tell me about Timothy Cussack."

"You mean am I bedding him? No. Have I ever? No. You asked me that before, Archy."

"So I did. But I've since learned what a lecher he is."

"I suppose," she acknowledged. "I admit I was willing but I'm just not Tim's type. Too young."

"And not enough money?"

"That too," she agreed. "I don't always make a grand slam, you know."

"It didn't bother you?"

"His turning me down? Of course not. Why should it? There's no shortage of studs. You, for instance," she added, giggling. "You know what I'd like to do now?"

"Yes," I said.

I was right. We parted an hour later, having showered *(à deux),* dressed, and pledged to each other mock declarations of undying love. We both snickered. She was not a serious woman but then I am not a serious man. I suppose that's why we hit it off so splendidly.

"Sylvia," I said before we went our separate ways, "'I want you to know that everything we talked about today, everything you told me, is strictly confidential." What a whopper! Connie Garcia is right: my nose gets longer by the minute.

"I don't care," she said carelessly. "You can't hurt me. No one can hurt me."

I thought that was a very brave and very foolish thing to say.

It was too late for an ocean swim even if I had the energy for it, which I didn't. Instead, before sprucing up for the family cocktail hour, I phoned Sgt. Al Rogoff and found him at his office. He was in a spleeny mood.

"Now what?" he demanded irritably.

"What did you have for lunch?" I asked him.

"Tortillas with onions and peppers. With black coffee."

"Ah," I said, "the surly-bird special. Listen, Al, I'd like to get together with you tomorrow."

"You've found a new disco? I don't enjoy dancing with you, Archy; you always want to lead."

"Oh, shut up. There have been developments in the Forsythe case you should know about."

He was silent for a tick or two. "Something good?" he said.

"I think so. I'll spell it all out for you."

"*All?*" he repeated. "Including the homicide?"

"Yes," I said firmly. "The whole shebang."

"You wouldn't be diddling me, would you, old buddy?"

"Not me. But it's going to take some work on your part to prove it out."

He sighed. "Hell, I'm still stuck in square one so I might as well listen to you. I really have no choice."

"That's right, Al. As the French say, when there's no alternative a man must sleep with his wife."

He laughed and we agreed to meet at ten o'clock on Saturday morning. "Come over here," I urged. "We can talk in the kitchen while you have your fourth cup of black coffee."

"I'll be there," he promised. "This better be good."

"It is," I said and rapped knuckles on my noodle for luck.

Ursi served saltimbocca that evening: a hearty dish of veal, ham, and cheese in a wine sauce. It was just what I needed after that exhausting day. I had intended to spend several hours working on my journal but when I retired to my chambers and undressed I saw the bed inviting me with fresh linen and plumped pillows.

This will shock you, I know, but despite my sybaritic tendencies—a fondness for good food, good wine, good love—I truly believe one of life's greatest pleasures is a good night's sleep.

"Go for it, McNally," I said aloud and slid gratefully between the sheets.

23

Rogoff was latish but I had no objections; before he arrived my father had departed for his Saturday golf game, mother and the Olsons had taken the station wagon into town for a spot of weekend shopping, and I had the McNally wickiup to myself.

I also had time to phone Connie Garcia. She wasn't at home so I took a chance and called her office.

"Lady Cynthia Horowitz's residence," she recited.

"Working on a Saturday?" I said. "You must really love your job."

"Bite your tongue," she said tartly. "I was planning to have a relaxed day, just futzing around my apartment, doing laundry, washing my hair. Then Lady C. decided she wanted to go over budgets and accounts today, so here I am. Hey, Archy, when are we going to the Bahamas?"

"Next weekend."

"You promise?"

"Of course. I'll provide an affidavit if you insist. Connie, how are you coming along on that matter I asked you to investigate?"

"I've got an answer for you. Actually, I've got half an answer."

"Better than none at all. Can you have dinner with me tonight?"

"Can I ever!" she cried. "Listen, Archibald, I'm going to be stuck here till late and won't have time to go home to change. I'm wearing scruffy jeans and a T, so I think we better meet at the Pelican Club. Okay?"

"Fine. Sevenish?"

"Around there. I warn you, after spending eight hours crunching numbers with the Lady, I'll be in need of a powerful transfusion. One, at least."

"Only one?"

"I'm driving and the roads are full of troopers. But we can always go back to my place and continue the festivities."

"What a marvelous idea," I said. "Shall I bring my tarot cards?"

"That's not exactly what I have in mind," quoth she, and disconnected.

Just in time, for through the kitchen window I saw Al Rogoff drive his pickup into our turnaround, and I went out to greet him. He was wearing khaki slacks and a Hawaiian shirt President Truman would have admired.

"Al," I said, "you shouldn't have dressed so formally."

"Go to hell," he said amiably. "It's Saturday, I'm off duty, and my dinner jacket is at the cleaners. Sue me."

Ursi had left a pot of coffee; all I had to do was heat it up and put out cups and saucers. I also piled a platter with her homemade chocolate chip cookies. They're chewy and rich enough to tempt a chocoholic to overdose.

We sipped our steaming java, wolfed down calories, and I began my recital. I started by advising Al to F & F (File and Forget) the attempted strangling of Sylvia Forsythe. I explained the circumstances: the assault was committed by Fern Bancroft, Ms. Non Compos Mentis herself, in an effort to kill the woman she feared had stolen the heart of the man Fern coveted. Namely, Anthony Bledsoe.

"Beautiful," the sergeant said. "I love it. I also love 'Tillie's Punctured Romance.' Do you think Sylvia wants to bring charges against the Bancroft dame?"

"Nope."

"Will she sign a statement attesting to the identity of her assailant?"

"I doubt that very much."

"Good," Rogoff said happily. "I'll deep-six the whole schmear. Now what about the homicide."

"Here's where the wicket gets sticky," I said.

I explained what I thought had happened. I was careful to differentiate between hard evidence—of which there was precious little—and my own suppositions and blue-sky guesses. I told him of the theft of property from Griswold Forsythe II, but I made no mention of the disappearance of Geraldine Forsythe's jewelry.

I finished my discourse. Rogoff's expression had not changed one bit during the telling. But in the brief silence that followed he rose to fetch the coffeepot and refill our cups.

"You know," he said finally, "sometimes you act like a mental dumpling. And sometimes I think you've got more than matzo balls between your ears."

"Thank you," I said humbly.

"Why didn't you tell me about the theft before this?"

"Because our client would not allow it. That's why I was assigned to make discreet inquiries. Forsythe wouldn't even go to the police immediately after receiving that threatening note. Al, the rich are firmly convinced they're more intelligent than poorer folks."

"I know," he said mournfully, "but you could have told me after the guy was chilled."

"I didn't realize how closely the thefts were connected to the homicide until last Thursday. Then little bits and pieces of evidence accumulated until I had enough to fill a sporran."

He looked at me. "What in God's name is a sporran?"

"A Scotch fanny pack but worn in front of the kilt."

"You have more useless information than anyone I know."

"True enough," I agreed.

"Let's get back to business. Where do we go from here on the Forsythe kill, assuming your theory is on target?"

"Here's what I suggest," I said and detailed the things I could do and the things he might do. "It may turn out to be a blind alley," I admitted. "No guarantees."

"I realize that, Archy, but I like it. You know why?"

"Sure. You've got nothing better."

"I've got nothing, period. There's not much I can do today or tomorrow but I'll get cracking on Monday. With any luck we should have this thing wrapped up by midweek."

"We better," I said. "I'm planning a jaunt to Freeport next weekend."

"Alone, of course."

"Of course."

He laughed. "When pigs whistle. Thanks for the coffee and cookies. Hit the spot. I'll be in touch."

He left and I cleaned up the kitchen. Then I debated what my next move should be. I decided it was time I made good on at least one of the promises I scattered about so freely. I phoned.

"The Forsythe residence." A young woman's voice.

"This is Archy McNally. May I speak to Miss Lucy Forsythe, please."

She giggled and I knew it was Fern Bancroft. "Just a moment, sir," she said.

I waited patiently and eventually I heard a piping voice: "This is Lucy Forsythe. To whom am I speaking?"

What a grammatical treasure the child was!

"Lucy, this is Archy."

"Hi!"

"Hi! Listen, dear, it looks like a lovely day and I was hoping we could have that picnic we talked about."

"Oh yes!" she said, suddenly excited. "I was afraid you'd forgotten all about it."

"No chance. Now I'm going to bring our lunch; you don't have to do a thing but be there. Suppose we meet at your Secret Place at noon."

"Okay," she said happily. "This is the first date I've ever had."

"You'll have plenty more," I assured her.

"Archy, I've finished my poem."

"Wonderful! I can't wait to hear it."

After we hung up I went back upstairs to don a costume suitable for a picnic. Actually, all I did was change to black denim jeans, hoping they wouldn't show grass stains. I knew where I'd be sitting.

I returned to our utility room and rummaged a moment before I found what I sought: a small insulated tote bag designed to keep things hot or cold.

I breezed over to West Palm to a takeout joint I had patronized in the past. Not great but fast. I bought a large pizza, half-cheese and half-pepperoni; four cold cans of Coke; a pint of Pistachio ice cream; paper napkins and plastic spoons. I had the pizza tightly wrapped in aluminum foil. The cola and ice cream went into my insulated tote. I can be practical when the occasion demands.

By the time I arrived at Lucy's Secret Place she was already seated on the grass and clapped her hands when I uncovered all the goodies I had brought. I flopped down beside her and we started our picnic, trying to eat delicately and making an enjoyable mess of it.

As we gobbled, she chattered—if one can chatter with a mouthful of cheese and sausage—about activities at school, what the teacher had said, a project being planned that would require Lucy and her schoolmates to write personal letters to the world's leaders. Listening to her jabber, I realized this child was telling me things she should rightfully be relating to her parents. I could only conclude they lacked the interest to listen, and Lucy knew it.

We had begun working on our ice cream when she said, shyly, "Would you like me to read my poem now?"

"I surely would."

She dug a much-creased sheet of notepaper from the pocket of her cotton pinafore, unfolded it, and began reading.

" 'To my Grandfather,' " she said, then looked up. "That's the title."

I nodded and she continued reading.

I wish with all my heart I could tell you it was a wonderful poem: simple, heartfelt, and touching. In all honesty I cannot. I wasn't expecting Alfred, Lord Tennyson, you understand, but it was an awful poem. Just awful. Wasn't it Oscar who said, "When it comes to sincerity, style is everything"? Well, someone said it.

She finished and looked at me expectantly.

"Lucy," I said warmly, "it's a marvelous poem. Absolutely marvelous."

She ignited with happiness. "You really think so?"

"I certainly do."

"I read it to Mrs. Bledsoe, and she said it was a beautiful poem, and then she started crying. Why did she do that?"

I could guess but didn't answer. "Did you show it to your mother and father, Lucy?"

"No," she said shortly, and we finished our ice cream in silence. I could see my mention of of her parents had saddened her. She sat slumped over, cob-webby hair hiding her face. Finally she said, "I can't come live with you, Archy."

"Oh?" I said. "Why is that?"

"Mom and dad aren't going to make a divorce. They're going to stay married and we're going to stay here. They told me so."

"I'm happy to hear it. That's good news."

"I guess," she said forlornly. "But I can come visit you, can't I?"

"Of course. Whenever you wish."

"Do you have a Secret Place, Archy?"

"Sort of. I have my own apartment at the top of our house."

"Gee," she said, "I wish I had like an apartment. I've just got this one little bitty room."

I was beginning to be infected by her mournfulness and determined to wrench us out of it. "Would you like to hear another funny poem, Lucy?"

She brightened. "Oh yes!"

I recited, " 'Twas brillig and the slithy toves/Did gyre and gimble in the wabe . . ." By the time I finished she was rocking with merriment, her face alight, and I reminded God to give me a Merit Badge for good intentions.

I gathered up the refuse from our picnic, shoved all the trash into my tote, and rose to depart.

"Be happy, darling," I said to her. "Will you try?"

"Okay," she said with a smile as sweet as halvah.

What I planned next shriveled my heart. But I had promised Sgt. Al Rogoff I would attempt it, and I admit my incurable nosiness overcame my misgivings. Still, I knew it was going to be a touch-and-go confrontation, and I've never been much good at playing the inquisitor.

I found Mrs. Nora Bledsoe in the Forsythe pantry, working on her accounts. She looked up when I entered and gave me a wan smile. "I can't believe you're going to spend a lovely Saturday afternoon cataloging books, Mr. McNally."

"Not quite," I said. "May I speak to you in private, Mrs. Bledsoe? I suggest we adjourn to the library."

Her expression of alarm was fleeting—or perhaps I merely imagined it. "If you wish," she said warily.

She rose and preceded me through that maze of hallways. I finally decided why Mr. Forsythe's grandmother had committed suicide: the poor dear was lost and couldn't find her way out.

I closed the library door carefully and ushered Mrs. Bledsoe to the leather armchair alongside the desk. I took the swivel chair but wheeled it out so we were facing each other closely, no barrier of clunky furniture between us. I hoped it might help create a mood of intimacy. I didn't intend to browbeat the woman.

"Mrs. Bledsoe," I started, "as you're probably aware I have been assisting the police in their investigation of Mr. Forsythe's murder. He was an old and valued client of McNally and Son, and we want to do everything we can to help solve this horrible crime."

She nodded. She sat upright, face set, hands clutched tightly on her lap. I knew she feared what was coming—almost as much as I did.

"The police have a number of suspects," I continued. "I must tell you that your son is one of them. They've been unable to pinpoint his exact whereabouts at the time of Mr. Forsythe's death."

If she was shocked her expression didn't reveal it. I think she had been expecting to hear her son accused.

"Tony is innocent, Mr. McNally," she said, her voice low but steady.

"I hope he is," I said. "But apparently the authorities are basing their suspicion on rumors that he is a heavy drinker."

"That's rubbish!" she said, flaring. "My son has a single glass of wine or one beer at the most. He is not a boozer. I can testify to that, and so can everyone else in this house."

"Glad to hear it," I said, leaning toward her. "But it's also been reported he is prone to violence, has an ungovernable temper. Is that also false?"

That shook her, I could see. She bit her lower lip, twisted her linked fingers.

"Tony does get angry at times," she finally admitted. "But it never lasts long. He says things he doesn't really mean and sometimes he does things he's sorry for later. But my son is a good boy, Mr. McNally."

That last was a plea. She wouldn't be, I reflected, the first mother who didn't know her own son and whose opinion was in direct conflict with the judgment of others. You may think me a wimp, for instance, but my mother believes me to be an admirable combination of Tom Swift, Robert E. Lee, and Noel Coward.

The first portion of my interrogation was finished and I was convinced Mrs. Bledsoe had answered my questions honestly; nothing she had said was irreconcilable with what I had already learned. But the most difficult part of my discreet inquiry remained.

"Mrs. Bledsoe," I said softly, "I must also tell you the police are aware of your relationship with Griswold Forsythe. Your past relationship. Need I say more?"

Then she began weeping. Not noisily, not sobbing, but quietly and steadily, tears wet on her cheeks. I was not proud of what I was doing, you understand, but it was necessary. And I had more pain to administer.

"I'm not surprised," she said, her voice suddenly thick. "After Griswold died I knew it would all come out eventually. Yes, it's true. Tony is Mr. Forsythe's son. But I won't hear a word said against the father. He saved me—*saved* me!—when I thought there was no future for me but walking into the sea. He was the dearest, sweetest, most gentle and most understanding man who ever lived."

I found that hard to believe. I've made it plain I thought Griswold Forsythe II had been a stuffed shirt, a long-winded bore, a skinflint, and a man so convinced of his own omniscience I'm sure he would offer advice to the surgeon about to perform a quadruple bypass on him.

But then who of us is one and complete? I mean we all present different faces to different people, do we not? And they react accordingly. A woman might be a saint to her lover and a devil to her husband, or vice versa. So it was not too surprising that Mrs. Bledsoe saw qualities in the father of her son to which I was totally blind.

"One more question, Mrs. Bledsoe," I said. "I would not dare ask if it were not so important. You may find it offensive and a gross invasion of your privacy, but I *must* ask it."

"What do you want to know, Mr. McNally?"

"Did you continue your intimacy with Griswold Forsythe after you came to work for him and lived in his home?"

She lifted her chin. Eyes blazed. She was no longer the defeated woman she had been moments before.

"Yes!" she said defiantly.

I rose and thanked her for speaking so frankly. We shook hands and I resisted a desire to kiss her cheek. We separated in the hallway. I returned to the Miata, schlepping my tote bag containing debris from the picnic with Lucy. I don't wish to get fancy-schmancy about this but it seemed to me I was also carrying the detritus of an entire family: all their sins and wicked secrets.

On the drive home, to dispel my melancholy, I sang, "Toot, Toot, Tootsie!"

It helped.

24

What a joy it was to see Connie Garcia that evening! After the Sturm and Drang of the Forsythe household, Connie came on vibrant, bubbly, and full of hope. As warned, she was clad in tight jeans and a snugger T-shirt. More importantly, she wore an elfin grin. My spirits ballooned.

The Pelican Club was filling rapidly with frenetic Saturday night merrymakers, so we hustled into the dining room to grab our favorite corner table. Priscilla told us the special that night was barbecued pork ribs with a Cajun sauce. Oh yes, we went for that, with garlicked shoestring potatoes and a Mt. Everest of coleslaw.

We nattered nonstop as we gluttonized, exchanging gossip about friends and acquaintances, and who was doing what to whom—and why. Connie told me an amusing story about my pal Ferdy Attenborough. It was rumored that he had been arrested, while somewhat in his cups, for attempting to create an obscene sand sculpture on the beach, complete with a turret shell planted in an upright position.

"Somewhere a mother's heart is breaking," I said sorrowfully.

While we dawdled over our sublime dessert—chunks of pineapple soaked in Captain Morgan's Coconut Rum—I asked Connie what she had learned about the breakup between Geraldine Forsythe and Timothy Cussack.

"As I told you, Archy, I was able to learn only half the answer. Everyone agrees he dumped her for another woman. But no one seems to know who the other woman was—or is. Sorry I couldn't do better."

"You did just fine," I assured her. "It's exactly what I need. You're becoming a real female shamus—called a shamusette."

"You made that up," she accused.

"I did indeed," I admitted. "May we leave now and have a quiet, thoughtful evening in your digs while we discuss Heisenberg's discovery of the uncertainty principle?"

"Is that really what you want to do?" she asked.

"Not quite," I said.

Less than an hour later we were lolling in her snug little condo on the shore of Lake Worth and there was no uncertainty about our actions. We discussed, while recuperating, our coming jaunt to Freeport on the following weekend. We both asserted, vowed, swore we would gamble a limit of a hundred dollars each in the casinos. Absolutely. No more than a hundred. Then we almost strangled with laughter, acknowledging what liars we were.

I departed, regretfully, shortly after midnight and wheeled home in a mellow mood. I did not sing during the drive, as was my wont, but questioned for the umpteenth time what my life might be like were I to be married to Consuela Garcia, that estimable woman.

Not idyllic; I was not such a dolt as to imagine that. Our wedlock would have its pluses and minuses I had no doubt. But the bottom line, I reckoned, would not be written in red ink. Still, there was that damnable cowardice of mine which I blamed on a faulty gene that caused me to break out in a rash at the thought of being shackled by the holy bonds of matrimony.

And if that were not enough, my discreet inquiry into the affairs of the Forsythe clan had given me fresh insight into the perils of conjugality. They had made unholy messes of their marriages. And even though I knew they were probably in the minority, their shocking example was enough to give second, third, and fourth thoughts to any young bachelor contemplating a lifetime commitment.

My mind is a Dumpster of remembered tunes; old films; ancient jokes; actors, poets, singers, and clowns long gone. That night before sleep whisked me away, I was still mulling the pros and cons of hubbyhood. I recalled a line from an Andy Hardy movie I had caught at a grungy rerun cinema. The son (Mickey Rooney) is asked by the judge (Lewis Stone), "Don't you ever intend to wed?" The reply: "Why should I marry and make one woman miserable when I can stay single and make so many women happy?"

Ah, yes.

I awoke the next morning with no firm determination of how I wished to spend the day. I peeked out the window and it looked okay: hazy sun, pallid sky, a few cumulus clouds that didn't seem to be going anywhere. One of the problems of living in South Florida is that you expect every day to be perfect. They aren't, of course, but even the ones categorized as "not half-bad" can be enjoyable. That Sunday appeared to be one of those.

By the time I arrived downstairs my parents had gone to their church and the Olsons had gone to theirs. I inspected the fridge for breakfast possibilities. After the pizza and barbecued ribs of the previous day I decided a little abstention might be in order so I limited my intake to a glass of cranberry juice, a toasted English muffin coated with Dundee grapefruit marmalade, and two cups of black decaf. I felt very virtuous. And very hungry.

Ordinarily I am a socialbe bloke but occasionally I like to spend a few hours of selfish solitude, regarding my navel and reflecting on the absurdities of human existence. Actually, my activities on that quiet Sabbath were not quite so highfalutin.

I changed to cerise Speedo swimming trunks, pulled on a purple velour coverup, and shod myself in raffia flip-flops. I gathered up my Yogi Bear beach towel and returned to the kitchen. I mixed a thermos of vodka gimlets and constructed two sandwiches: turkey on wheat (mayo) and liverwurst on sour rye (mustard). I also added an apple to my tote. Then I went down to the beach, coated exposed hide with SPF 15, and reclined in the partial shade of a royal palm.

Time passed. What more can I tell you other than I drowsed, nibbled sandwiches, sipped gimlets, took an occasional dip in the warm sea, stretched my bones, and craftily kept my mind totally blank for five hours—although my father would assure you it required little effort on my part. I returned home to shower and dress for the cocktail hour and dinner. Then I retired to my mini-suite for a long evening of scribbling notes in my journal on everything that had happened since the last entry.

About ten o'clock I received a phone call: my first personal contact that day with the Forsythe hullabaloo.

"Archy?" she said. "This is Gerry."

"Hey!" I said. "I've been meaning to call. When are you leaving?"

"Wednesday afternoon. I just phoned to say good-bye."

That alarmed me; I wasn't certain Al Rogoff and I would have the package gift-wrapped and tied with a gold bow by Wednesday. And Gerry's presence was essential if justice was to triumph.

"Perhaps I'll have a chance to see you before you leave," I suggested.

"I doubt it," she said bluntly. "I have a million things to do; a lot of running around."

"I can imagine," I said and then, lying through my molars, I added, "I hope we can get together when you return."

"That would be nice," she said with all the effervescence of flat beer.

"Have a good trip, Gerry."

"I intend to," she said and hung up.

Not bloody likely, I thought, and mused on the role I imagined Geraldine Forsythe had played in the meshugass now drawing to its close. I could not forgive her for what I surmised she had done. But it seemed to me her transgressions had been more sleazy than cardinal. And probably more venal than either.

I did not believe her a corrupt woman. I theorized that all her offenses had stemmed from loneliness, weakness of will, and a crippled ego. There I go again, playing Dr. Sigmund F. What the hell do I know? Get too involved in psychoanalysis and you'll hesitate to eat a banana.

If my Sunday was unplanned, my schedule for Monday was rigidly structured—and of course it started to fall apart almost immediately.

I began by oversleeping shamefully. I had a solitary breakfast, dashed out to the Miata, and my pride and joy refused to start. A moment's inspection revealed the reason: the fuel indicator signaled an exhausted tank. I gave thanks to Vishnu for allowing me to make it home Saturday night before being stranded on a deserted road.

I went back into the house, phoned the West Palm garage I use, and explained my predicament to Susan, my favorite mechanic.

She laughed. "You're losing it, Archy," she said. "I'll get someone out there this morning to give your baby a bottle—enough to get you to a pump."

"When?" I insisted. "Soon?"

"Before noon is the best I can promise."

I moaned, went outside again, and found mother chatting to her begonias in the greenhouse. I reported my problem and she readily agreed to lend me her old wood-bodied Ford station wagon. And that was the vehicle I drove to the Trojan Stables.

I must admit that despite the minor annoyances and delays, I was enthralled by that splendid morning. God was not in His heaven; He was in South Florida, and we had the lucent sky, beaming sun, and balmy breeze to prove it. What a perfect day to solve a murder!

I found Mrs. Constance Forsythe at the fence in what was apparently her customary posture: one foot up on the bottom rung as she leaned on the top rail. She was watching a horse galloping on the track. The rider, a woman, wore a helmet, but the fluttering fringe of flaxen hair convinced me it was Sylvia Forsythe.

"Hallo, Archy," Mrs. Constance said genially as I approached. "Come to visit us again, have you?"

"A pleasure," I said. "What a lovely morning."

"Just perfect," she said in a dreamy voice. She gazed out over the neatly trimmed acres of her farm, everything trig and glowing in early light. "I can never get enough of this place, Archy. I've been thinking of changing the name to Paradise Stables. I mean the combination of Trojan and horses might imply deceit to some people—don't you think?"

"It might," I agreed, "and it has another connotation as well."

She laughed. "What a naughty boy you are!" She turned away to observe the galloping horse and rider.

"Is that Sylvia up?" I asked her.

She nodded. "She's becoming quite good. I may start her on dressage soon. She's a natural."

"Talking about naturals," I said casually, "is Timothy Cussack about?"

"Nope. It's his day off. Sundays and Mondays."

"Oh damn!" I said, snapping my fingers. "I knew that but forgot. Don't know how I can get in touch with him, do you?"

She took her foot from the rail and turned to face me. "Haven't the slightest," she said. "On his days off Timmy is here, there, and everywhere. Why do you want to find him—something important?"

"It may be," I said. "To him. Look, I trust your discretion, and if you hear from him you might relay this: I've been working with the police on the investigation of your husband's murder. They've narrowed the list of suspects to a half dozen names. Cussack is one of them. I like Tim—we've hoisted a few together—and I thought I should alert him. He's liable to be picked up for questioning."

Her expression didn't change. I told you from the start she had the face of a mastiff, heavy and somewhat droopy. But there was rugged strength. Mastiffs are great protectors. I reckoned she qualified.

"Why on earth would the cops suspect Timmy?" she inquired, mildly enough. "He had nothing to gain from Griswold's death."

"Exactly," I said. "What could possibly be his motive—the theft of a couple of hundred bucks? I think that's a crock, but you know what the police are like. In this case I believe they're simply floundering. Just between you, me, and the lamppost, they have precious little hard evidence and so they're casting a wide net. I thought I'd mention it to Cussack so it won't come as a rude shock if he gets pulled in for interrogation."

She looked at me thoughtfully. "That's very decent of you, Archy. But Timmy has had run-ins with the law before; he knows how to handle himself."

"Glad to hear it," I said. "I'm sure the whole thing will just dissolve into thin air. But if you hear from Cussack today you might repeat what I've told you."

"I will," she said. "Thanks, Archy. You're true-blue."

I wasn't; I was just being my usual devious self. But she didn't know that, and I was pleased. I genuinely liked the woman. She was so strong, you see, so determined, with the resolve of a sergeant major. I wished I had half her assurance. I have trouble deciding whether or not argyle socks can tastefully be worn with a seersucker suit. Important choices like that stump me.

"Enjoy your paradise, Mrs. Constance," I said, giving her my 100-watt smile (the Supercharmer), and then I departed.

I tooled the station wagon back to the McNally Building, hoping to finagle an audience with m'lord. I felt it was time to brief the executor of the Forsythe estate on what had happened, was happening, and what I anticipated would happen. It would not, I knew, inspire him to leap exuberantly into the air and click his heels with glee.

I went directly to my office—a cubicle small enough to serve as a loo for pygmies—and found on my desk a message to phone Sgt. Al Rogoff as soon as possible. I did and found him in a fractious mood. He wasted no time on idle prattle.

"Did you get out to the horse farm?" he demanded.

"Just got back."

"Were they there?"

"Yep. Both women."

"Did you go into your song and dance?"

"A magnificent performance," I assured him.

"Uh-huh. Well, things are moving right along on this end. It's beginning to look good. We got a search warrant from a friendly judge and I'm leaving now."

"I'll be home all night. Will you phone me and bring me up to speed?"

"Sure, I'll call."

"Guaranteed?"

"I told you I'd call," he said aggrievedly. Al hates to be goosed—as who does not?

He hung up abruptly, leaving me to reflect on what an ass I'd be if my suspicions turned out to be just that—suspicions. But faint heart never condemned fair lady, and so I lighted and smoked an English Oval slowly (first of the day) before I phoned Mrs. Trelawney and asked if *Il Papa* might consent to grant his only son a brief hearing.

She put me on hold and then came back a few moments later to inform me I had been given the gift of fifteen minutes if I arrived at once. And so, hoping my flowered sport jacket (peonies) would not doom the interview from the start, I headed upstairs to my father's sanctum sanctorum dreading what his reaction might be to the news I was bringing. Why did I suddenly recall the ancient custom of killing the messenger with bad tidings?

But to my relief I found him in a benevolent mood. Not exactly cheery, you understand—he hated to have his daily routine interrupted—but not spleenish either. We sat at opposite ends of his bottle-green leather chesterfield, and I launched into my speech.

I told him the whole schmear: what I knew, intuited, and presumed. My report took longer than the allotted fifteen minutes but not once did he interrupt. As I spoke, his features became increasingly stern, darkened with an ineffable sadness. We sat in silence after I finished. I awaited his reaction with some trepidation.

Finally he stirred, shifted position on the couch, and crossed his legs, being careful not to crush the crease in his trousers. "If what you say proves to be correct, Archy," he said in his precise courtroom voice, "I cannot represent any family member in this affair. It would constitute an obvious conflict of interest. If they ask me to recommend competent counsel to represent them, I believe I could do that."

"Yes, sir."

He fell silent again. I have commented several times in these chronicles on what a champion muller my father is. But at that moment, from his expression and manner, I deduced he was not mulling but he was brooding. There is a difference, you know. One may mull over whether to request a two-minute or a three-minute boiled egg. But one broods on the existential meaning of boiled eggs.

"How fragile life is," he eventually observed, and I knew I was in for a short lecture in Philosophy 101. "We all know accidents happen, illnesses appear without warning, chance defeats us all. But the greatest danger surely must be human passions and follies. We look for reasons and meaning in human behavior and they simply don't exist. We are left with only awe or despair or foolish hope."

"Yes, father," I said, longing to be gone.

He must have sensed my impatience from the tone of my voice for he looked at me sharply. "Assuming your suppositions are substantiated, how long do you estimate it will take to resolve this mess?"

"By tomorrow," I said boldly. "If it hasn't unraveled by then, I'll be proved totally wrong and we'll start all over again."

He sighed. "Archy," he said somberly, "everyone knows death is inevitable. But that realization is not much consolation when a man's or woman's life is ended violently before its time. That is why I desire very strongly that the murderer of Griswold Forsythe be apprehended, convicted, and punished. I appreciate your efforts to make that desire a reality."

He was thanking me! My old man was thanking me! What a delightful surprise. And he hadn't even lifted a hairy eyebrow at my peony-patterned sport jacket. I left his office feeling like one of Hannibal's elephants. Having crossed the frozen Alps I had debouched into sunny Italy. It felt so *good!*

I trundled the station wagon home and switched to the Miata. Jamie Olson informed me it had been given a high-octane IV, as Susan had promised. I slid into the leather bucket with a groan of content and sped off to West Palm where I had the tank filled and the windshield washed free of mashed bugs—a constant South Florida vexation.

And then, being in the neighborhood so to speak, I headed for the Pelican Club. After that exhausting morning I was in dire need of refreshment, liquid and solid. What awaited me that afternoon, I knew, required that I be in tiptop physical and emotional condition, ready for a spot of derring-do. And so I had a double cheeseburger with chips and coleslaw at the bar, the cholesterol helped on its way by two bottles of Heineken.

Before I departed I used the public phone in the rear of the bar area and called the Forsythe home. Fern Bancroft answered.

"Fern," I said, "is Anthony Bledsoe there?"

"Sure," she said, "Tony's here. You want to talk to him?"

"No, no," I said hastily. "I just wanted to confirm his presence. I'll drive out and speak to him *mano a mano.*"

"What?" she said.

I hung up and went back to the bar to pay my bill. "Mr. Pettibone," I said to our wise majordomo, "why do so many women fall in love with absolute rotters?"

He looked at me with mild astonishment. "Why does a chicken cross the road?" he asked—quite reasonably I thought.

25

Fern had evidently informed him of my impending arrival for when I scrunched to a stop on the Forsythes' driveway, the front door jerked open and Anthony Bledsoe stood glowering at me, completely lacking in the hospitable welcome department.

"Good afternoon, Tony," I said.

"You want to talk to me?" he said truculently.

I decided it would be wise to establish the tone of our interview immediately. After all, I came not as a supplicant but as a succor. And I had had quite enough of his petulance.

"Yes, I want to talk to you," I said stiffly. "But not if you persist in acting like a wounded child. There's already one in this house. If you feel you can converse like a thinking adult, then we'll talk. If not, I want nothing more to do with you."

He backed off at once. "Well, yeah, okay," he said grudgingly. "Come on in."

We went into the library. This time I took the swivel chair and kept the wide desk between us. It gave me the superior position, you see: the magistrate deciding the fate of the accused in the dock. He was not comfortable in the armchair and I was happy to see it.

"Let's get to it," I said briskly. "First of all, my relationship with Mrs. Sylvia Forsythe is none of your damned business."

"It's got nothing to do with me," he said sullenly.

"It shouldn't," I said, "but apparently it does. Mrs. Sylvia is a free spirit, utterly independent. She selects her friends and will continue to do so as her whims dictate. I have been fortunate. You have not. Do I make myself clear?"

"Yeah," he said, "I know where you're coming from."

"Tony," I said, softening my voice, "give up this impossible dream. Or endure endless misery."

He was silent, head bowed.

"And besides," I added, "you have a young lady madly in love with you."

He raised his eyes to look at me. "Who?" he said.

"Fern Bancroft."

"She's a fruitcake," he said scornfully.

"She may or may not be," I said, "but don't take her love lightly. She thinks you a man of value."

His laugh was a snort. "Oh sure," he said, "after she heard I'm going to get a bundle from Forsythe's will."

It angered me. "That's a lie," I said hotly, "and you know it. Fern had a yen for you long before Mr. Forsythe was killed. That's why she tried to strangle Mrs. Sylvia. She wanted to remove her rival."

His eyes widened. "How do you know all this?" he asked, and I found his awe gratifying.

"I see all and I know all," I said—a slight exaggeration. "But please, try to forget your infatuation with Mrs. Sylvia—it can only lead to tragedy—and try to make a new life. With or without Fern Bancroft. The choice is yours, and I wouldn't have the temerity to advise you."

"Without," he said. "I have plans and she's not part of them."

"I think that's regrettable," I told him, "but it's your decision to make. Which leads me into the second topic I want to discuss. Your mother said you and Timothy Cussack are planning to open a restaurant-bar, a disco kind of place."

He stared at me, startled. "She shouldn't have told you that," he said wrathfully.

"Why not, Tony? Your mother's main concern—perhaps her only concern—is your welfare. She doesn't want to see you risking your bequest with a man whose reputation is somewhat flimsy, to say the least. He does have a police record, you know. All I'm asking is that you consider very, very carefully before investing all your legacy in an enterprise with a man of doubtful probity who apparently doesn't have a nickel to his name."

That lit the fuse. He lurched to his feet and leaned far over the desk, face twisted with fury. For one awful moment I feared he might launch himself at me with designs on my jugular. I arose hastily to my feet and retreated a step.

"You don't know a thing about it, you lousy snoop," he said, voice crackling. "For your information, we're going in as equal partners. I'm putting up half the money and Tim is putting up the other half. So don't tell me he's tapped out. And don't try to scare me with that police record stuff. Sure, he's been picked up for some piddling little things but he's never done time. You make him sound like a master criminal."

"No," I said, "he's not that." But my irony was wasted.

He straightened up and drew a deep breath. His rage was fading but there was cold venom in his stare. "Just butt out of my life," he said harshly. "I don't need you giving me advice—or my mother or anyone else. Now I don't have to answer to anyone."

"I wish you the best of luck, Tony," I said and I meant it, knowing he was doomed. It was presumptuous of me, I know, but I had him pegged as a loser.

"Yeah," he said, whirled around, and stalked out.

It had been a ticklish confrontation but it had served its purpose: I had connected another pair of those unnumbered dots. The final picture was almost complete. Not obscene but nasty, definitely nasty.

I drove home wondering how many more times I'd be required to visit the Forsythe fun house. Once, I reckoned, or perhaps twice. Then I intended never again to set foot in that mausoleum. If I wanted to see Lucy—and I hoped our friendship would not languish—I could always find her in the Secret Place. I now appreciated what a refuge that was for the poor lass.

I skipped an ocean swim and went directly to my aerie, thinking Sgt. Al Rogoff might phone. He didn't and I had no wish to bug him; I was certain he was carrying out his part of our scheme. I could have worked on my journal but postponed that chore, praying my next entry would be the last in the Forsythe epic.

Instead I sat at my battered desk and neither smoked nor imbibed strong drink. Proud of me? I was. But I did ruminate heavily, reviewing all the tangles of greed and passion that were finally being unraveled and the role I had played in their unsnarling.

I make no claims to being a Great Brain, mind you. Ask me what a quark is, for instance, and I'll probably reply it's the quack of a ruptured duck. No, it was not sharp intelligence, reason, and logic that enabled me to discover what the Dotty Forsythes were up to.

If the truth be told—and I *must* tell it—the only reason I have achieved a modicum of success in my discreet inquiries is that I am just as loopy as the miscreants I investigate. There's an affinity, no doubt about it. I think, feel, and act as they do. And so I'm one step ahead of the gendarmes who have studied human behavior in such scholarly tomes as *Practical Homicide Scene Procedure.*

What I'm trying to say is that I'm just as guilty of daffiness as the Forsythes or any other crackpots. Are not my emotional entanglements, outré dress, and my inordinate fondness for frog legs meunière proof of that? But who's complaining? Not I, since my outlandish conduct may well be an essential aid in the profession to which I have been relegated.

The cream of the jest: I began this narrative with a few snide comments on how goofiness is engulfing the world. I end with the rueful realization that I suffer from the same disorder. Oh well, you told me it takes one to know one.

I was dressing for the family cocktail hour when finally my phone rang and I grabbed it up immediately.

Rogoff was exultant. "It worked!" he shouted. "He's running!"

"Banzai!" I cried. "Running where?"

"South. Right now he's on I-95. I've got an unmarked car on his tail. Two good men. They won't lose him."

"Where do you figure he's heading?"

"Who the hell knows? Maybe the Keys eventually. It's easy to hole up down there. Anyway we've alerted Broward and Dade. I don't think he'll keep going all night. He's driving a pearly blue Taurus wagon, easy to spot."

"What set him off, Al?"

"As soon as we got the warrant we tossed Suite 309 at the Michelangelo Motel. What a lush layout that place is! We found the book right where you said it'd be. What's the name?"

"Poe's *Tamerlane,*" I said.

"Yeah. Listen, Archy, can we prove it was stolen from Forsythe?"

"It was on the list of missing property he gave my father. If we can't locate the original list I'm sure pops will testify Griswold Forsythe told him the book had been taken."

"Good enough. We checked the partial prints on Forsythe's wallet against the guy's file. The match is a good possibility but not enough to convict."

"Al, the man has so much at stake, why would he lift the wallet for a measly couple of hundred dollars and endanger himself?"

"Because he's a cheap crook, that's why. Probably figured that since he was croaking Forsythe he might as well glom on to a few easy bucks. Stupid, stupid, stupid!"

"All right, you found the book in his bedroom and grabbed it. When did he start running?"

"We made certain we left the place looking like it had been searched. And besides, I'm sure the desk clerk told him we had been there. Naturally I put a stakeout on the motel. He showed up about three o'clock in a helluva hurry. Went inside and the stakeout alerted me. I scrambled over there in time to see him come out with luggage: a duffel bag, valise, and what looked like a rifle or shotgun case."

"Oh-oh," I said.

"Yeah," Rogoff said. "My exact words. Anyway, he took off like the proverbial bat outta hell with my tail car right behind him. I'm back in the palace now, listening to radio reports, marking his progress on a map, and trying to figure when and where we can take him."

"Do you have an arrest warrant?"

"Come on, Archy, talk sense. We've got probable cause coming out our ears."

"Did you have a chance to check the pawnbroker?"

"Yep," he said happily. "The pawner was just who you figured. Tomorrow we'll start covering all the local hockshops. Maybe we can find the other loot. Something I need to know: will the three Forsythe women be available tomorrow?"

"As far as I know. Geraldine is leaving for Europe on Wednesday, but the other two haven't mentioned anything about getting out of town. Al, I'm going to be in all night. Will you phone me when you catch up with the fugitive? I don't care what hour it is. Wake me up if you have to."

"My pleasure," Sgt. Rogoff said and hung up.

I was late getting to the cocktail hour and father raised an eyebrow but made no comment. Mother was in a bubbly mood because one of her begonias had just won second prize at a garden show, and she had the framed certificate to prove it. We congratulated her and the family went down to a fine dinner of broiled red snapper.

After coffee and dessert (pecan pie with coconut ice cream) I started upstairs but was stopped in the hallway by my father.

"Developments?" he asked tersely.

"Yes, sir," I said and gave him an abbreviated account of what I had just learned from Al Rogoff. The news seemed to depress him.

"It appears your presumptions were correct, Archy," he said sadly.

I didn't reply.

"Keep me informed," was all he added, went into his study and closed the door. He would, I guessed, have a glass of port, smoke a pipe, and resume doughtily working his way through the six zillion words of Charles Dickens. I wished him well. I often thought he read those plump volumes not so much for enjoyment as from a sense of duty. One of these days I'm going to introduce him to Thorne Smith.

I continued upstairs, and since I did not expect an uninterrupted night's slumber I decided a short nap would be in order. I kicked off my loafers and lay down atop the coverlet. It had scarcely been a half-hour since dinner, and I know doctors advise against sleeping on a full stomach. So I slept on my back.

I had intended it to be a brief doze but when the phone shrilled, I roused, glanced at the bedside clock, and was shocked to see it was almost one A.M.

"I hope I woke you up," Rogoff said.

"You did," I admitted.

"Good," he said. "Our pigeon's gone to roost. Went east at Deerfield. Got onto A1A and turned south along the beach. Checked into a sleazebag motel across the Hillsboro Inlet. I'm on my way, phoning from Boca. When I get there I'm going to call in the locals for backup. I figure we'll take him around four or five in the morning. He should be smoggy with sleep by then."

"What's the address of the motel?" I asked.

"Archy!" he said sharply. "Stay home. This is cops' work."

I uttered a rude expletive. "Al, he's *my* pigeon. I did most of the work; I want to be in on the kill."

"Well, yeah," he said gruffly, "I guess you rate. Just keep out of the way. Agreed?"

"Positively," I said, and he gave me the address.

I looked out the window and it seemed to me a fine mist was falling. I pulled on a black nylon jacket and stepped downstairs as softly as I could. But not quietly enough. The door of my parents' bedroom opened and my father accosted me. He was wearing Irish linen pajamas but no matter what that man wore it looked like a three-piece suit.

"Where are you going?" he asked in a low voice.

"Father, they've got him cornered. In a motel south of Hillsboro."

He stared at me a long moment. I knew he wanted to say, "Be careful," but he didn't—which is why I love him. He just nodded and went back into the bedroom.

I was right about that mist; it wasn't heavy but it was persistent—and warm. I had a plaid golf cap stuffed in the pocket of my jacket. I donned that but it wasn't long before it was soaked through and flopped down on my ears.

The road south was slick and the infrequent street lamps were dimmed and haloed by the mist. I drove cautiously, having no desire to skid off the corniche onto the beach. Traffic at that hour was mercifully light, but it still took almost two hours to drive through the Hillsboro Mile and across the inlet.

I slowed, trying to glimpse numbers on motels and stores in the strip malls. I finally found the address Rogoff had given me: just your average single-level motel of perhaps twenty units. It looked like a hot-pillow joint to me, and I reckoned the neon sign outside showed VA-CANCY since the place opened.

I saw no evidence of police presence, but about a half mile down A1A toward Pompano Beach I came upon a parked collection of official vehicles that looked like a cops' convention. There were squads from Pompano, Broward County, an ambulance, a red fire rescue truck, and two cars from Palm Beach. I pulled up near this jumble and got out of the Miata slowly and warily. My approach had been noted and immediately three uniformed heavies moved toward me, hands on their holsters.

I was happy when Sgt. Al hustled up and waved them away. He was as soaked as I but grinned when he saw the sodden cap plastered to my skull.

"You look like you're wearing an unbaked pizza," he said.

"Al, I passed the motel but I didn't see any police cars. I'd have thought you'd have the place boxed in."

"And spook him?" he demanded indignantly. "You think we're nuts? We pull up a fleet of cars, and the guy's liable to hear the traffic and come out blasting with a rifle or shotgun or whatever he's got in that violin case of his. Why take the chance? He's not going anywhere; we've got guys on foot covering the front and back."

"Well, what are you waiting for?"

"Tear gas grenades and launchers," he said. "It turned out no one's equipped so we sent for them. They should be here any minute now. Probably won't need them but as you like to say, one never knows, do one?"

Rogoff and I joined a group of cops, all smoking and chatting casually about the won-lost record of the Marlins, Florida's new baseball team. Most of the officers, I noted, were wearing bulky bulletproof vests, either under their shirts or over. Al wasn't and I wasn't either. Not a comforting thought.

Finally a van from the Broward County sheriff's office arrived. Launchers, tear gas, and stun grenades were unloaded. Rogoff left me to confer with COs from other jurisdictions. All the officers present watched and waited. Then Al turned toward them, lifted his right fist and pumped it up and down twice.

The parade got under way, moving slowly, no sirens. I followed the last car. As we approached the target the units separated, apparently following a prearranged plan. The main road, A1A, was blocked north and south of the motel. The remaining cars coasted into the lighted parking area, forming a semicircular barrier around the front door.

Sgt. Rogoff got out, followed by two officers from the Palm Beach tail car. And after them came three Pompano Beach cops. No doors were slammed. The six men formed a wedge, Al leading. I watched from the misty distance, standing beside the Miata. I wondered if I had the courage to do what those men had to do. I decided I did not.

It seemed to me a well-planned operation, and it was. But who can prepare for the unpredictable? And that's what happened. As I watched, the motel's front door slammed open. Timothy Cussack strode out. He was holding a long double-barreled shotgun against his hip, muzzles pointed at the approaching men.

He fired. In that misted gloom it sounded like a cannon's roar. All six men crumpled as if an anarchist's bomb had been rolled into their midst. I didn't know—no one knew—if they were dead, wounded, or had hit the ground hoping to escape a blast from the second barrel.

There was a moment of shocked silence. Then I began running toward the motel entrance.

I insist it was not an act of heroism; it was an act of sheer idiocy. But the sight of Al Rogoff lying prone on wet concrete maddened me. At that moment I was irrational; I admit it.

An officer, guessing my intent, moved swiftly to block my way. "He's got a shotgun," he yelled. "What have you got?"

"The gift of gab," I yelled back, pushed him away, continued on.

I slowed as I walked into the lighted area, my arms raised high, palms frontward. I heard someone scream, "Hold your fire! Hold your fire!"

Cussack swung to face me, the shotgun still held against his hip. I am not an expert but I thought it a gun ordinarily used for trapshooting or potting doves. I am neither skeet nor dove, but I had no doubt that weapon could cause me grievous injury—if not instant quietus.

"You!" Cussack said. "I knew you were bad news the first time I met you. Just too damned slick."

I kept moving slowly toward him, arms still hoisted, until I was less than a yard away.

"Tim," I said quietly, "give it up. There's an army here. You can see that, can't you? You're an intelligent man. Take your chances with the law."

I didn't think him intelligent, of course. I thought him a thug—and a dangerous thug. He had expectations he could never gratify.

"My chances with the law?" he repeated scornfully. "Like the chair, you mean?"

He kept glancing at those six officers still lying quiescent. I don't believe he realized how close I had come to him.

"But what about the woman?" I pleaded. "You still have the power to get her a reduced sentence."

"Screw her!" he said furiously. "She's the one who got me into—"

That's when I made my move. You may think I have the muscle tone of linguine, but my sinews are not as flabby as you might expect.

I stepped in, chopped down, slapped the long-barreled gun aside, and grappled. I knew at once he was stronger than I—but then who isn't? We stood swaying a moment, locked in a lovers' embrace.

He finally flung me aside and, still holding the shotgun, swung the muzzles to point at my brisket.

I saw his eyes go vacant and thought sadly that my riotous weekend with Connie Garcia in the Bahamas was about to be put on hold—perhaps eternally.

It was at that moment that Sgt. Al Rogoff, still lying facedown, propped himself up on his elbows and, sighting his service revolver steadily in both hands, put four shots into Timothy Cussack's chest, firing rapidly. (Later it was discovered the four bullet holes were so close they could have been covered by a small saucer.)

Cussack was smashed back. I stepped in swiftly to snatch the shotgun from his grasp. He went down slowly. I leaned over him. He looked up at me with a dimming stare. I think he wanted to say something but it was too late.

Al Rogoff climbed shakily to his feet. I was expecting thanks for my intervention. But he glared at me.

"Moron!" he shouted.

26

Cleaning up that mess seemed to take forever. Three cops had been hit by the initial shotgun blast, two with minor wounds, one seriously. He was treated by paramedics and then taken away in the ambulance. The other two were given first aid before being assisted to a squad car for the trip to a hospital. The corpse of Timothy Cussack remained temporarily sprawled in a bloodied puddle.

While all this was going on, crime scene tape was strung and police photographers moved in to record everything. Rogoff and four other officers went into the motel to search Cussack's room. I remained outside, pacing up and down, smoking furiously and waiting for my flood of adrenaline to subside.

The sergeant finally returned. He was in a snarly mood.

"If you had done what you promised and stayed out of it, they'd have made Swiss cheese out of the guy. He was standing in a lighted area and there were plenty of shooters out there, including a couple of snipers."

"Al, I—"

"But, oh no, you had to interfere and almost got blown away. What in God's name were you thinking of?"

"Al, I—"

"How could I ever explain to your father why his son got iced during a police shoot-out? Let alone what the newspapers and TV clowns would say. Did you stop to—"

"Oh, shut up," I said. "I admit I acted like an imbecile but at the moment it seemed the right thing to do. It turned out okay, didn't it?"

"No, it didn't," he said. "I was hoping to take the bozo alive. I figured he'd plea-bargain and implicate the woman. Too late now."

"Did you find anything in his room that could help?"

"Maybe. We found almost five thousand in cash. Fifty-dollar bills."

I was astonished. "Where do you suppose he got that?"

Al gave me his cynical cops' grin. "Down payment," he said. He paused a moment, then drew a deep breath. It was hard for him to say it but he did. "Thanks, Archy," he muttered.

"You're welcome," I said. "How long are you going to be tied up here?"

"Hours," he said. "Why don't you hang around and we'll grab breakfast somewhere. On me."

"Sounds good," I said.

It did take hours. It was past eight o'clock Tuesday morning before Al could break free. We breakfasted in a joint that looked like a Ptomaine Palace, but the food turned out to be excellent: fresh and flavorful. We were both famished and gorged on OJ, ham steaks, grits, home fries, toasted bagels, and enough black coffee to float the Staten Island ferry—if he's still around.

We finished that feast and Al picked up the tab, as promised. We went out to our cars.

"Look," the sergeant said, "you had a nice few hours' sleep. I didn't but I can keep going awhile. What say we pick her up before she learns about what happened to Cussack."

"Suits me," I said. "Just the two of us?"

"Sure. I really don't think we'll need a SWAT team, do you?"

As we drove northward the sun burned off a morning fog, and by the time we arrived at the Trojan Stables the sky was so clear you could glimpse a pale crescent moon in the west. The horse farm was bustling with several riders trying the low hurdles. I spotted Sylvia Forsythe, sans helmet, trying to coax an enormous gray nag to walk with a mincing gait. I was happy to see she had exchanged her harpsichord for a stallion.

Mrs. Constance Forsythe was nowhere to be seen. A stable lad was walking by lugging an English saddle and Rogoff stopped him.

"Is the owner around?" he asked.

The boy eyeballed Al's uniform with some alarm. "In the barn, sir," he said, jerking a thumb over his shoulder.

We headed there.

"Let me take it first," the sergeant said. "I want to shake her. Then you start with your charm routine."

"Bad cop-good cop," I observed.

"Something like that," he agreed.

Mrs. Constance was supervising the mucking out of several stalls. The air was choked with dust and the odor was pungent—to say the least. I know there are people who relish the scent of manure. There are also people who enjoy boiled cabbage. Include me out.

She was wearing jodhpurs and her usual stained riding jacket. But her white T-shirt was fresh, and I thought she had recently had her hair done. It appeared groomed and burnished in the speckled sunlight streaming through skylights. And she carried a crop as if it were a scepter.

She turned as we approached. "Well, well," she said, inspecting us, "two nonpaying visitors. I'm underwhelmed."

Rogoff wasted no time. "Mrs. Forsythe," he said stonily, "about five hours ago Timothy Cussack was shot to death while attempting to escape arrest for the murder of your husband."

If he intended that bald statement to shake her, he failed miserably; she was unshakable. I've told you she was a strong woman. Her only visible reaction was a tightening of the jaw, teeth clenched, a muscle ticking under her chin. She recovered quickly.

"Hard to believe," she said. "But Timmy was always a wild one."

"He was," Al said. "We also have evidence that you were implicated in the crime. That it was committed at your instigation, your urging, and that you, in fact, paid Cussack to murder your husband."

She picked up immediately on the key word. "Evidence?" she said sharply. "What evidence?"

"That you sold and pawned items of property removed from your home without the knowledge or permission of your late husband. That you used those funds to lure Timothy Cussack into joining your conspiracy. That he bought a new car with money you supplied. And that, finally, you gave him five thousand dollars as a down payment for the homicide. A withdrawal from your personal checking account attests to that."

Most of what Rogoff said was b.s., of course. He had not yet proved she had paid for Cussack's Taurus wagon nor had he uncovered a withdrawal from her checking account of five thousand dollars. He was running a bluff, and it didn't work.

"Are you wired?" she asked.

"Am I what, ma'am?" Al asked, startled.

"I watch TV crime shows," she said impatiently. "Are you equipped with a tape recorder?"

"No, I am not. Do you wish to search me?"

"No, thanks," she said. "I'll take your word for it. Now take my word. It is true I removed property from our home because I needed the money to keep the Trojan Stables operating. Expenses are horrendous, and I simply didn't want Griswold to know how much I was spending. Surely you don't expect to convict me of the theft of property owned by a married couple; it was as much mine as his. And it's true I paid Timmy Cussack extra from time to time because he was our most valuable instructor. The clients, mostly women and young girls, just loved him. But as for hiring him to kill my husband, that's garbage! Complete garbage!"

Rogoff sighed. "Will you be willing to accompany me to headquarters, Mrs. Forsythe, and sign a statement of what you have told us?"

"Is this an arrest?" she demanded.

"No, it is not," he said. "Just a voluntary action on your part to help us clear up this matter. You may have an attorney present if you wish."

"I don't need a lawyer," she said. "What I've told you is the truth, and I'm willing to swear to it. Now would you mind leaving me alone with Archy for a few moments? I'd like to speak to him privately."

The sergeant hesitated a moment, then nodded. "I'll wait outside for you," he said. "I have a car."

He glanced at me, turned, and marched out of the barn, leaving me to face that redoubtable woman. She watched him go.

"Stupid man," she said.

I made no reply.

She moved closer to me. "I don't suppose your father would like to represent me," she said. It was more of a statement than a question.

"It's not what he'd *like* to do," I said tactfully. "It's a problem of conflict of interest. After all, he is the executor of your late husband's estate. But I'm sure if you have need of a reputable attorney, he could recommend someone."

"Yes," she said, staring at me thoughtfully, "ask him to do that, will you? In spite of what I told that odious cop, I may want to have a smart lawyer on my side."

The odor of manure in that vaulted space was so acrid that my eyes began to water. She noticed my discomfort and grinned. "The stink getting to you?" she inquired maliciously.

"Somewhat," I acknowledged.

"I happen to like it," she said. "Earthy. Primitive. God, what a stiff he was!"

At first I thought she was referring to Sgt. Al Rogoff. Then, to my horror, I realized she was speaking of Griswold Forsythe II, recently deceased.

"A stiff!" she repeated. "A mean, stingy old man. No juice in him."

I was offended. *De mortuis nil nisi bonum.*

"Others may think differently," I said.

She tried to appear amused but couldn't quite hide her hurt. "Nora Bledsoe, you mean?" she said. "He was screwing her from the day he moved her in. She could have him, with my blessings. He was a lousy lover."

I tried to be crafty. "Surely divorce would have been preferable to murder."

She laughed. "You *are* devious, aren't you? Archy, I'm not admitting a thing, to you or anyone else. Don't take it so hard. With Cussack's death, the cops can close out the case. Now my kids can live the way they want to, the Trojan Stables belongs to me, and everyone will live happily ever after."

"Not everyone," I said in a low voice. I don't believe she heard me.

We walked outside together. Al Rogoff was waiting. But before we joined him, she paused a moment to survey her domain: acres of greenery, jumping horses, the excited cries of young riders—all sunspangled and glowing.

"Not bad, is it?" she said.

"No," I had to agree, "not bad at all."

"Paradise," she breathed.

She and Rogoff moved toward his car. I waited because Sylvia Forsythe was heading for the barn, on foot and leading her huge gray horse.

"Hiya, Archy," she said brightly. "Did you see me trying to make this monster behave?"

"I saw," I told her. "Have fun?"

"Loads," she said. "Busy this afternoon?"

"Afraid so," I said. "Besides, I suspect Suite 309 is closed down for the nonce. The police will want to conduct a more thorough search."

I told her what had happened to Timothy Cussack. She didn't seem shocked—or even interested. She shrugged.

"I knew he was a negative from the start," she said. "But you and I—we're positives, aren't we?"

"I'd like to think so," I said.

She gave me a flip of her hand. "We'll make it another time," she said lightly and continued leading her mount to the barn.

Not bloody likely, I thought. To be excruciatingly honest, she was just too frothy for me. I vaulted into the saddle of my mount and pointed the Miata eastward.

You know what I was wondering as I drove, don't you? Of course you do. You are questioning, as I was, whether or not Mrs. Constance Forsythe had an affair with Timothy Cussack, in addition to their conspiracy to murder her husband. Well, you know as much about their characters and motives as I do, and the choice is yours.

As for my opinion, berserk horses couldn't drag that from me—although an irascible Chihuahua might.

I arrived at the Forsythe aviary in a tempestuous mood, hoping both vultures would be present and strutting. There was really no rational reason for seeking this showdown; it would accomplish nothing. But I was stormy with resentment, determined to ruffle the feathers of those rapacious birds.

Anthony Bledsoe opened the door, and I could see he was stricken.

"Tim Cussack," he blurted. "Did you hear what happened? It was on TV."

"Yes," I said, "I heard."

"My God," he said, looking as if he might weep, "that's awful."

"Awful," I agreed. "Are Griswold and Geraldine Forsythe at home?"

"They're having lunch. Should I tell them you're here?"

"No," I said sternly. "Just direct me to where they're lunching."

I had never before entered the formal dining room. The phrase "baronial hall" immediately sprang to mind. The enormous arched chamber was complete with tasseled velvet drapes at the windows and ghastly oil portraits of forebears hanging on oak-paneled walls. The long table could easily have accommodated a platoon of guests, and there was a carved walnut sideboard with a marble top that would have caused instant hernia if anyone ever tried to lift it.

Griswold Forsythe III was seated at the head of the plank, sister Geraldine on his right. They were both wearing crisp white linen and appeared to be sharing a gigantic wooden bowl of Caesar salad. Their glasses were filled with white wine, and the bottle was placed on a coaster between them. I caught a look at the label. Dreadful plonk.

They both looked up, startled, when I came barging in.

"Archy!" Griswold said without rising. "How nice to see you again."

I doubted that.

But I had no desire to exchange pleasantries. "You've probably heard," I said in the coldest voice I could muster, "Timothy Cussack was shot dead by the police while attempting to escape arrest for the murder of your father."

"We heard," Geraldine said. "A shock!"

"The man must have been demented," the Forsythe scion said, shaking his thick head. "What could he possibly have gained? It's just terrible."

"Oh, come off it," I said angrily. "I think both of you are secretly relieved."

They stared at me. "What a rotten thing to say!" he shouted, and then he rose to his feet.

"Is it?" I said. "How is this for a scenario: on the evening before the day he was killed, your father determined to his satisfaction that it was your mother who had been removing valuable items from your home and either selling or pawning them."

"I must ask you to leave at once," Griswold said. "You are no longer welcome in this house."

"Oh, stuff it," I said. "Your father reported what he had discovered, told you about the threatening note he had received and, I suspect, said he was convinced his wife had written it. He also announced his intention of taking the whole matter to the police the following day."

"You're hallucinating," he said. "Nothing of the sort ever occurred."

"No?" I said. "And neither did the Battle of Waterloo. The first thing you did, reckoning how you might profit from this state of affairs, was to run to mommy dearest and tell her what your father planned. That triggered his murder the following day before he could report his suspicions to the police."

"You're insane!" Geraldine cried. "Totally mad!"

I turned to her. "And you," I said, "what a dandy you turned out to be. I guessed almost from the start that the jewelry you claimed had disappeared had never been stolen; those were baubles you had *given* to Timothy Cussack to win his fidelity when you were having a thing with him. But he dumped you, and you suspected unjustly that he had taken up with your sister-in-law. And so you resolved to prove them thieves and asked me to provide proof. Then, when your brother eventually told you of your mother's involvement, you instructed me to end my investigation."

She gave me a scathing glare. "Louse!" she said.

I felt no contrition at all. "Congreve was right," I said. " 'Hell hath no fury . . .' And after you discovered it was your mother rather than Sylvia who supplanted you, you saw, like your brother, the profit that might result from that."

"Griswold!" she screamed. "Get this maniac out of here!"

I turned back to him. "Just as you called off my search for the stolen family property when you learned Constance was probably guilty. Neither of you acted from any filial loyalty. The two of you were not part of the murder conspiracy, I admit, but yours were sins of omission. You were hoping for your father's demise—visions of sugarplums were dancing in the shape of those grand bequests you'd receive—and so you did nothing to prevent your father's murder."

"Tony!" Griswold shouted at the top of his lungs. "Tony! Come here at once!"

"No need to have me forcibly ejected from the premises," I told him. "I'm leaving, happy to have had the opportunity to inform you that I and others are fully aware of your treachery."

I stalked to the door, then turned back to face them. "By the way," I said casually, "I forgot to mention that your mother is presently in police custody and is being questioned. Ta-ta."

I didn't tell them she had denied everything and was probably going to walk away scot-free.

Let them sweat.

27

My furies somewhat ameliorated, I drove back to the McNally Building on Royal Palm Way. I was eager for hours of dreamless slumber, but there was one more chore I had to perform: my father needed to be informed of what had transpired since I last reported.

I didn't have to phone for an appointment for as I pulled into our underground garage I saw him alight from his black Lexus and walk toward the elevator. I parked hurriedly, hopped out, and scurried to his side.

"Do you have a few minutes, sir?" I asked.

He frowned. "Very few. A client is arriving shortly. What is it, Archy?"

I told him what had happened to Timothy Cussack, omitting any mention of the part I had played in that sanguinary climax. Then I related a detailed account of Sgt. Rogoff's and my confrontation with Mrs. Constance Forsythe at the Trojan Stables. I concluded with a description of my most recent encounter with Griswold the Three and Geraldine.

The squire began to pace rapidly up and down the concrete floor of the garage. I had to hustle to keep at his side.

"Mrs. Forsythe admitted nothing?" he asked.

"Nothing," I replied. "She stonewalled. Seemed very sure of herself although she did ask that you recommend an attorney she might retain."

"Do the police have any evidence other than what you've told me regarding her role in this affair? To wit, the pawning of property taken from her home, purchase of a car for Cussack, possible withdrawals from her bank account."

"No, sir. As far as I know that's all Rogoff has."

"Do you think it possible you or he may uncover additional evidence of her involvement?"

"Doubtful," I said. "Father, this woman may be perfidious but she is no dummy. I'm sure there were no witnesses to her plotting with Cussack, no letters written, nothing that might inculpate her."

I had never seen him so shaken. Because, I supposed, he admired Mrs. Constance as much as I did. Not, of course, for what she had done but for the woman she was, her awesome strength and resolve.

He wagged his head. "Not enough, Archy," he said. "Not nearly enough to charge her, let alone convict. The state attorney won't touch it. Prosecutors have no great love for lost causes. If she sticks to her denials she'll walk free."

I was indignant. "That's not right!" I cried. "I *know* the woman is guilty. I know it, Rogoff knows it, and *she* knows it. Whatever happened to justice?"

He gave me a tight smile. "Don't despair, Archy. Justice is a hope, not a certainty."

"Yes, sir," I said mournfully.

He stopped pacing to face me. "However," he added grimly, "I am the executor of the deceased Mr. Forsythe's estate. I don't believe you, or they, fully realize the powers of an executor. Almost unlimited. Obviously I cannot legally deny the widow and surviving children their inheritances. But there are two kinds of time, Archy: the ordinary of hours and days. And then there is legal time, measured in years and decades. There are many things I can lawfully do as an executor to delay the rewards Mrs. Constance Forsythe and her offspring so avidly anticipate."

My father is not a vindictive man, you understand, but on occasion he fancies himself God's surrogate on earth. I was confident he had the power and resolution to do what he had stated. It would not be as satisfactory as seeing Mrs. Constance tried and convicted for conspiracy in the murder of her husband, but it provided a small soother to my outrage.

Father continued on to the elevator, and I returned to my velocipede. I drove directly home and asked Mrs. Olson to wake me in time for the cocktail hour. Then I went upstairs, disrobed, and flopped into bed. Fatigued? I felt as if I had just completed a triathlon while lugging a 150-lb. anvil.

I was awakened in time to shower, dress, and present a respectable appearance at family gatherings that evening. The preprandial martinis were especially welcome. The dinner of broiled butcher's steak completed my rejuvenation. Who was it who said, "I love to eat red meat but it must come from a cow that smoked"?

I went up to my digs afterward, beginning to feel I might live to play the kazoo again. I intended to complete the Forsythe saga in my journal, but Al Rogoff phoned before I could even start scribbling.

"Did Constance say anything while the two of you were alone?" he demanded.

"Nothing, Al," I told him. "Didn't admit a thing."

"She's one tough lady," he said. "We couldn't budge her. Did you tell your father about her?"

"I did."

"And?"

"He said she'll walk."

"He's so right," Rogoff said, sighing. "The state attorney's office laughed at us. It's a no-win. Well, what the hell, we got one of them, didn't we? Fifty percent. I'll settle for that."

"I won't," I said.

"Come on, Archy. You want everything nice and neat. You want the good rewarded and the evil punished. You know life's not like that."

"I guess," I said dolefully.

"Besides," he went on, "I'm not totally without clout, you know. There are a lot of inspectors in this town and county. Electrical, sewers and sanitation, environmental, labor, building codes, fire safety—all kinds of inspectors. I figure to drop a hint here and there. Mrs. Constance Forsythe is going to have more inspectors than customers. Not as satisfying as seeing her in the clink, I admit, but I can make her life miserable if I choose—and I do choose. It's not the solution I wanted but it'll give me a charge. How about you?"

"Better than nothing," I admitted, thinking that with the vengeful plans of my father and Rogoff, the Widow Forsythe might find her dream of paradise slightly tarnished.

"I'm off on a forty-eight," Al reported. "Nothing but sleep. So long, old buddy. Stay in touch."

He hung up and I was left staring at my open journal. It was dispiriting to consider completing the history of the Forsythe case. As Rogoff had said, it was a half-victory. But the half-defeat rankled. I craved solace and so I phoned Connie Garcia.

"What are you doing?" I asked her.

"Painting my toenails and watching TV."

"I yearn for you."

"You *yearn* for me?" she repeated incredulously. "Since when?"

"Since this minute," I told her. "If I rush over with a cold bottle of bubbles will you allow me entrance to your abode?"

"I might," she said.

That was good enough for me; I rushed. I think it must have been around midnight when, emboldened by champagne, I stood naked on her little balcony overlooking Lake Worth. I stretched my arms to the heavens and did an awful imitation of James Cagney in *White Heat*.

"Top of the world, ma!" I shouted joyously.

McNally's Trial

1

It has been said that no good deed goes unpunished, and I can vouch for it. The donee of my act of charity was Binky Watrous, a close pal of mine and a complete doofus who once, deranged by strong drink, brushed his teeth with anchovy paste.

Actually, my tale begins on a coolish night in early October in the Town of Palm Beach. My name is Archy (for Archibald) McNally, and I am employed to conduct discreet inquiries for the law firm of McNally & Son. My father is the attorney, I am the son. My investigations are mainly concerned with solving the personal problems of our prestigious clients before they come to the attention of the police or those supermarket tabloids that might feature the client's tribulations between a truss ad and a story about twins borne by a ninety-eight-year-old Samoan transvestite.

I can't remember the date of the Battle of Actium, but I have almost total recall when it comes to splendid meals I have enjoyed, and dinner that evening was something special. Our live-in housekeeping staff, Ursi and Jamie Olson, had concocted a wondrous salad served in a wooden bowl large enough to hold the head of John the Baptist.

The main ingredients were chunks of smoked chubs enlivened with slices of fennel sausage, and lots of other swell stuff. My father, Prescott McNally, and I demolished a bottle of sauvignon blanc while consuming this feast, but my mother, Madelaine, insisted on her usual glass of sauterne. It was an eccentric habit that papa and I have attempted to convince her is ungodly, to no avail.

After that banquet (dessert was rum cake with a layer of maraschino) I felt so replete that, having nothing better to do, I thought I might make a run to the Pelican Club and perhaps down a post-prandial cognac while reflecting that life indeed can be beautiful.

But it was not to be. The lord of the manor stopped me as I was about to ascend to my third-floor mini-suite to change into snazzier duds.

"Archy," he said in that tone he uses when he wishes to couch a command as a request, "were you planning anything special this evening?"

"No, sir," I said, stiff-upper-lipping it. "Nothing of any importance."

"Good. A client is arriving at nine o'clock, and I'd like you to sit in on the meeting."

"Oh?" I said. "Who is he?"

"She," he replied. "Sunny Fogarty. I believe the lady is unmarried, but that's of no consequence."

"It might be," I commented. "To her."

"Yes," he said with his wintry smile. "In any event, she is an employee of the Whitcomb Funeral Homes, the most recent commercial client to be added to our roster."

I tried to raise one eyebrow and failed miserably. That's my father's shtick, and he does it effortlessly. "Is she an undertaker?" I asked.

Again that frosty smile. "I believe the current euphemism is 'grief counselor.' But no, she is not a mortician. Her official title is comptroller of the three Whitcomb Funeral Homes, in Broward, Palm Beach, and Martin counties."

"I hear it's an upscale outfit," I remarked. "Gilt coffins and all that. Someone suggested their advertising slogan should be 'The Deathstyles of the Rich and the Famous.' "

The squire was not amused. He does not appreciate jokes about clients who put osso buco on the McNally table.

"Miss Fogarty phoned this afternoon," he continued. "She sounded somewhat agitated and asked to see me as soon as possible. I said I would be happy to come to her office or she could come to mine. But she preferred to meet at a place where there was no possibility of our being seen conferring together. So I suggested she come here this evening, and she agreed. It was a brief and puzzling conversation, which left me suspecting it might be a situation that requires discreet inquiries on your part."

And that explains why, at nine o'clock on that fateful evening, I was seated in my father's study, prepared to listen to Sunny Fogarty explain the reason for her secretive visit.

At the moment, "Sunny" seemed a misnomer, for the lady was obviously uptight: brows pinched into a frown, lips tightly pressed, fingers clenched. She sat forward in a leather club chair, spine stiff, shoulders back, and she kept crossing and recrossing her ankles.

But despite her angst I thought her attractive. I guessed her age at forty, give or take, and she had the weathered look of a woman who had worked hard all her life and expected the struggle would never cease. We had been introduced, of course, and I had been surprised by the strength of her handclasp. She wore a black gabardine pantsuit with an unexpectedly frilly blouse, closed with a wide ribbon and bow of crimson rep.

Her eyes were a darkish brown with a definite glint, and I imagined they might harden if the occasion required it. Not a woman to be trifled with, I decided, and found myself admiring her sleek russet hairdo. It looked like a helmet worn by one of Hannibal's spearmen.

My father was comfortably ensconced in the swivel chair behind his magisterial desk, and he leaned back, fingers linked across his waistcoat, and asked pleasantly, "Now then, Miss Fogarty, what's this all about?"

The boss had already explained the role I played at McNally & Son and assured her of my discretion since as a flunky of the firm—in addition to being his son—I was as bound by the dictates of attorney-client confidentiality as he. She seemed to accept that, made no objection to my presence, and spoke freely.

She told us she had been employed by Whitcomb for almost ten years, starting as a receptionist in their Fort Lauderdale funeral home and working her way up as secretary, the executive assistant to Mr. Horace Whitcomb, the owner and grandson of the founder. Meanwhile she had studied accounting and business administration, and when the company opened its third mortuary in Martin County she had been appointed comptroller of the whole shebang.

"It's a good position," she said, "and I like the work. My salary is okay; I have no resentment there whatsoever. Two years ago I computerized our entire operation, and it proved so successful I received a large bonus. I'm telling you all this to prove I have no reason for anger against Whitcomb, no reason to seek revenge or anything like that. I want Whitcomb to continue to be profitable, and I want to keep my job. I am the sole support of my mother, who is in a nursing home in West Palm Beach. She suffers from Alzheimer's. The expenses are enormous, so my income is very important to me."

She paused and made an effort to compose herself. Father and I were silent, watching her. I cannot say what his reaction was—his expression revealed nothing but polite interest—but I thought her an honest and disturbed woman, caught in a conflict between her personal welfare and a need to reveal something she felt was just not right.

"Our president, Horace Whitcomb," she went on, "is almost seventy and says he never wants to retire. He's a fine gentleman. He's been very kind and generous to me, but he's that way with all his employees. We love him. He comes to work about four or five hours a day but sometimes skips a day or two for golf or fishing."

"Good for him," my father said unexpectedly.

"Yes," she said with a smile that was faint but transformed her features. I could see then why "Sunny" was not a misnomer after all. "Horace's son, Oliver Whitcomb, is our chief executive officer. He handles the day-to-day operations of all our funeral homes."

"And is he also kind and generous?" I asked.

She ignored my question. "And then we have several other department heads," she said. "In charge of such things as purchasing, maintenance, personnel, and so forth. I can provide their names if you think it's necessary."

"Miss Fogarty," father said gently, "you haven't yet told us the nature of your problem."

She took a deep breath. "About six months ago I became aware—from the weekly reports I receive—that the revenue of Whitcomb was rising dramatically, far above our income of last year. Naturally I was pleased and so were all the other executives who noticed it, including Mr. Horace. During the past six months the number of funerals we handled continued to increase at a really surprising rate."

She looked at both of us, back and forth, as if expecting exclamations of astonishment. But father and I made no comment. Instead we exchanged a swift glance and I suspected we were sharing the same thought: Could Whitcomb's improved bottom line be the sole reason for Miss Fogarty's distress? I began to wonder if this lady had both oars in the water.

"The income of all three mortuaries keep increasing," she said. "I was puzzled because I am a logical woman—and curious, I might add—and I started to question why we were having such an impressive uptick in business."

Father stirred restlessly in his swivel chair. "Surely there must be a simple explanation," he said. "Perhaps it is the result of a new advertising campaign. Or you have enjoyed an unusual number of referrals."

"Or maybe more people are kicking the bucket," I suggested cheerfully.

She shook her head decisively. "We're doing no more advertising than we did last year. Our rate of referrals remains constant. And there has been no extraordinary rise in South Florida's death rate. In addition, I have checked my contacts in the industry, and no other local funeral homes have had the revenue increase we've had. In fact, most of them show flat month-to-month income or a decrease. There is just no obvious reason for our good fortune, and it baffles me."

She stopped, took a small hanky from a capacious shoulder bag, dabbed at her lips.

"Miss Fogarty," my father said kindly, "may we offer you some refreshment? Cola? Coffee? Or would you like a glass of port wine?"

"Yes," she said. "The wine, please."

"Archy," he said, "will you do the honors?"

I rose from my ladder-back chair, went over to his marble-topped sideboard, and poured three goblets of port from his crystal decanter. I'd drink it, but I wouldn't smack my lips. I didn't have the nerve to tell the guv that the last case he bought was definitely corky.

Our visitor took a small sip and sighed appreciatively. "Thank you," she said. "That tastes good."

"Miss Fogarty," *mon père* said, "what exactly is it you wish us to do? From what you've told us it does not appear that anything unethical or illegal has occurred at Whitcomb Funeral Homes. It is merely experiencing exceptional financial success. That is hardly reason for concern."

"Something strange is going on," she stated determinedly. "I just *know* it is. But I can't endanger my own position by poking and prying. People would think me a brainless idiot. I was hoping you might ask a few casual questions—as our attorney, you know—and see if you can discover the reason for our sudden prosperity."

Father looked at me. "Archy?" he said.

I knew what he wanted. I was to express sympathy, ask a question or two, assure our visitor of our willingness to cooperate, and get her out of there as soon as possible.

"We'll certainly look into it, Miss Fogarty," I said briskly. "The situation you describe is certainly odd and may possibly justify further inquiries. Tell me, do you keep records of the cemeteries to which the deceased are, ah, delivered?"

"Of course," she said. "Unless they are cremated. And records are kept of that. We have all our dead on computer."

"Excellent," I said. "Could you provide me with a printout of all the cemeteries Whitcomb Funeral Homes has dealt with in the past six months?"

She hesitated a moment. "Yes," she said, "I could do that. I shouldn't but I shall."

"I'd appreciate it," I said. "It might give me a start for our investigation." I took a business card from my wallet and used my gold Mont Blanc to scribble on the back. "I'm giving you my personal unlisted telephone number. Please feel free to use it if you cannot reach me at our office."

"Thank you," she said, taking my card and tucking it away. She finished her wine and arose. "I can't tell you how much better I feel for having talked to you gentlemen. This thing has been worrying me so much that I've had trouble sleeping. It's nice to know it'll be looked into. I'm ready to provide all the assistance I can."

Father and I accompanied her outside to our graveled turnaround. She was driving a spanking new white Chrysler New Yorker. A lot of car, I thought, for a woman supporting a terminally ill mother. We shook hands and she thanked us for our hospitality and consideration. We watched her drive away.

"Curious," father remarked.

"Yes, sir," I said, "it is that."

"Archy, go through the motions but don't spend too much time on it. I fear the lady is unnecessarily troubled. Mayhap slightly paranoid. It's a matter of no importance."

"I concur," I said.

Lordy, were we ever wrong!

2

Father returned to his study and closed the door firmly. I knew what that meant: he was settling in for the remainder of the evening. He would have another glass or two of port, smoke a pipe or two of his specially blended tobacco ("December Morn"), and read a chapter or two of Charles Dickens. For as long as I could remember, he had been slowly slogging his way through Chuck's entire oeuvre. Lotsa luck, daddy-o.

I glanced at my Mickey Mouse wristwatch, saw it was scarcely ten o'clock and I could still enjoy that brandy if I so desired. I did so desire and dashed upstairs to change to fawn slacks, a madras sport jacket, and Loafers From Hell: acid-green suede—with tassels yet. Then I bounced downstairs, pausing briefly at our second-floor sitting room to give the mater a good-night kiss. Her velvety cheek was wet. She was watching a TV rerun of *Stella Dallas* and tears were leaking.

I was still driving my vintage Miata, a flaming red job of the first model year and still holding its saucy flair. I hopped in and headed for the Pelican Club, my favorite oasis in South Florida. It's a private watering hole and has a membership of effervescent lads and lasses from Palm Beach and environs. It's a pleasantly laid-back joint, serves high-caloric grub, and no one would object if I clambered onto a table and recited "Sheridan's Ride." "Up from the south at break of day . . ."

The place was clanging when I arrived. Roisterers were two-deep at the bar, and couples were to-ing and fro-ing from the dining area. I finally caught the attention of Mr. Simon Pettibone, an elderly gentleman of color who is our club manager and doubles as bartender.

"Rémy!" I shouted to be heard above the din and he nodded.

He was back a moment later with my wallop, handing it to me across the shoulders of club members bellying the mahogany.

"Rushed, Mr. Pettibone?" I inquired.

"Love it, Mr. McNally," he said. "Just love it. Pays the rent."

"So it does," I agreed happily. The Pelican Club, of which I had been a founding member, was a candidate for Chapter 7 until we had the great good fortune of putting our future in the hands of Mr. Pettibone and his family. His wife Jas (for Jasmine) was our housekeeper and den mother. Son Leroy was our chef, and daughter Priscilla our waitress. The energetic and hard-working Pettibones had turned our little enclave into a profitable enterprise, and we now had a waiting list of would-be Pelicanites, eager to wear the club blazer bearing our escutcheon: a pelican rampant on a field of dead mullet.

Glass in hand, I looked about for a place to park the McNally carcass. And there, in a far corner of the pub area, sitting by his lonesome at a table for two, I spotted my goofy buddy, Bunky Watrous himself. His head was bowed over a tumbler of an amber liquid. I made my way to his side.

"Binky," I said, "may I join you?"

He looked up and his loopy expression became a beam. "Archy!" he cried. "Just the man I wanted to see. Sit down, sit down, sit down!"

"Once will do nicely," I said, taking the bentwood chair opposite him. "What is that you're drinking?"

"Scotch," he said.

"With what?" I asked.

"More Scotch."

"Binky," I said, "we have been pals for a long time, but I must warn you that I shall not carry you home tonight. I am willing to call an ambulance, but that's the extent of my responsibility. Why on earth are you getting hammered?"

"I've got troubles," he said darkly.

"And pray, who does not?" I said, looking at him more closely.

Binky usually wears a look of blithe unconcern, but now I could see his chops were definitely fallen. He's a fair-haired lad with a wispy growth of blond hair on his upper lip that can be seen in a strong light. He's a bit on the shortish, plumpish side, and if you can imagine a Kewpie doll with a mustache, that's Binky.

Though he may not be physically impressive, he's a generous, good-hearted chap who'd give you the shirt off his back. But you probably wouldn't want it since it was liable to be voile with alternating stripes of heliotrope and mustard. But how can one dislike a man whose bedroom walls are plastered with photos of Lupe Velez?

"Binky," I said, "what seems to be the problem?"

He took a gulp of his drink. "It's the Duchess," he said mournfully. "She demands I get a job."

"A true cri de coeur," I commented.

"What's that, Archy?"

"Something like a kvetch," I explained. "And did the Duchess suggest any particular field of gainful employment?"

He shook his head. "She just said it's time for me to earn a living. Archy, what am I going to do since it's obvious I can't *do* anything?"

I should explain that Binky's mother and father were lost at sea while attempting to sail their sloop to Curaçao. Binky was a mere tot when the tragedy occurred, and he was raised by a wealthy maiden aunt, one of the grandest grande dames of Palm Beach.

Everyone referred to her as the Duchess. She was not a real Duchess, of course, but could play one on TV. I mean, she was imposing, haughty, and rather frightening. Her customary greeting was not "How are you?" but "You're not looking well."

But this Duke-less Duchess did provide for her brother's son and grimly endured his being expelled from Princeton for pushing a pie (chocolate cream) into the face of a banquet guest who made a biting remark about Binky wearing a tie patterned with the crest of the Irish Royal College of Surgeons. Binky was obviously not Irish, Royal, or a sawbones. The target of his pie turned out to be a visiting British VIP, and the resulting foofarah ended with Binky being booted.

Perhaps that was one of the reasons for our palship, since I had endured the same fate for a contretemps committed at Yale Law—a really minor misdeed. I had streaked naked (except for a Richard M. Nixon mask) across the stage during a performance by the New York Philharmonic.

Since his expulsion from Princeton, Binky had spent most of his time traveling, engaging in harmless mischief, enjoying several romantic dalliances, and generally living the life of a happy drone. The Duchess granted him an openhanded allowance, paid for his profligacies—including gambling debts—and had made no objections other than stiff chidings—until now.

"Archy," Binky said gloomily, taking another swallow of his plasma, "what am I to do? You know I'm a complete klutz when it comes to work. That's just a four-letter word to me."

"Haven't the slightest idea, old boy," I said, sipping my cognac and feeling my toes beginning to curl.

"You work, don't you? Investigations and all that. Like a detective."

"Of course I work. Very diligently, I might add. And yes, my specialty is discreet inquiries."

He looked at me thoughtfully—if such a thing were possible. "You know, I believe I could do that. Lurking about and asking questions."

"There's more to it than that," I assured him. "It requires unique skills, plus curiosity and a keen intelligence."

That pleased him. "Now I'm sure I qualify," he said happily. "I'm inquisitive and no one's ever doubted my brainpower."

"Or even mentioned it," I said, but he could not be stopped.

"I've read oodles of detective novels," he rattled on. "Shadowing villains, threatening suspects, getting beat up and all that. I'm sure I can do it."

"Binky," I said, fearful of what I suspected was coming, "it really is an extremely difficult profession. The tricks of the trade can be learned only by experience."

"You could teach me," he said eagerly.

"I'm not sure you have the temperament for it."

"Look, Archy," he said, trying to harden his cherubic features into an expression of stern resolve, "why don't you let me work with you on your next case. No salary, of course. Just to learn the ropes, so to speak."

"And then what?" I demanded. "The old man would never let me hire a full-time assistant."

"I realize that," he agreed, "but after I catch on how it's done I could set up my own business. Binky Watrous: Private Eye. How does that sound?"

"Loathsome," I said. "Believe me, son, you're simply not cut out to be a sherlock."

"How do you know?" he argued. "I mean, you didn't start out to be a snoop, did you? You were going to be a lawyer and then you became an investigator. And now you enjoy it, don't you?"

I had to agree.

"Give me a chance, Archy," he pleaded. "I'll just tag along, observe and listen, and then I'll get out of your hair. What do you say?"

I sighed. I knew it would be a frightful error, but I could not deny his request. The poor dweeb was really in a bind.

"Okay, Binky," I said finally. "I'll take you on as an unpaid helper. But I'll be captain of the ship—is that understood?"

"Of course!" he said gleefully. "You command and I obey—absolutely! Do you think I should buy a gun?"

I gulped more Rémy. Allowing Binky to buy a gun would be like handing the Olympic torch to an arsonist.

"No, I don't think you'll have any need for a firearm."

"A knife?"

"No."

"Brass knuckles?"

"No weapons whatsoever, Binky. You're not going into combat, you know."

"We'll just outsmart the bad guys," he said. "Right?"

"Right," I said feebly, knowing he was incapable of outsmarting a Tasmanian devil.

I finished my drink and rose. "Got to dash," I said. "I told Connie I'd phone."

"When do we start?" he asked anxiously. "I want to tell the Duchess I'm hard at work getting on-the-job training."

"Call you tomorrow," I promised.

"Great!" he said. "But not too early, Archy. I've got a golf date at noon."

Typical Binky. I believe I told you in previous annals that his main talent was doing birdcalls. His imitation of a loon was especially realistic. I should also mention a formal dinner party we both attended during which corn on the cob was served. Instead of gnawing at the buttered kernels, Binky played the entire ear like a harmonica while humming "America, the Beautiful." The other guests were convinced there was a lunatic in their midst.

But enough about Binky Watrous. I drove home in a remarkably equable mood. I felt certain that by the time the sun was over the yardarm on the following day and the effects of Binky's beaker of Scotch had worn off, my chum would have completely forgotten his determination to become a detective.

It was my second serious miscalculation on that portentous evening.

3

The McNally manse was darkened and silent by the time I returned home. I tiptoed quietly up to my digs, took off the glad rags, and donned a silk kimono I had recently purchased. It was Japanese, and embroidered on the back was a fearsome samurai wielding a long sword and cutting off the head of a dragon that bore a startling resemblance to my barber, Herman Pincus. I suppose that's why I bought the robe.

I lighted an English Oval—only my third that day—and poured myself a small marc. I keep my personal liquor supply in a battered sea chest at the foot of my bed. It holds a limited inventory of brandies and liqueurs—for medicinal purposes, you understand. Much healthier than sleeping pills. Honest.

Then I phoned Consuela Garcia, my light-o'-love. Connie and I have had a thing going for many years. She is Cuban, a Marielito, and a very, very feisty lady. Regrettably, I have been unfaithful to her on numerous occasions, but as I have previously explained, I am genetically disadvantaged and my infidelity is due to faulty DNA.

When Connie discovers my perfidiousness, which she inevitably does, her reaction is usually physical. I dimly recall an incident at The Breakers where I was wining and dining a lissome young miss, a friend of a friend of a friend. To my horror, Connie entered and spotted us. She marched over to our table, plucked a half-full bottle of Piper-Heidsieck from its ice bucket, shook it vigorously and spritzed me from brow to sternum. It was not a night to remember.

"Hiya, honey," I said when she picked up after the seventh ring. "Whatcha doing?"

"Painting my toenails."

"Hey," I protested, "that's my job. Listen, I haven't seen you in ages."

"And whose fault is that?" she asked tartly.

"All mine," I admitted. "I've been an absolute rotter."

"So you have," she readily agreed. "Now make amends."

"Dinner tomorrow night?"

"Can't do it," she said promptly. "Lady Cynthia is having a sit-down for twelve, and I've got to honcho the whole thing."

"How come I wasn't invited?"

"They're all local pols. Want to join the party?"

"No, thank you," I said hastily.

Connie is employed as social secretary to Lady Cynthia Horowitz, possibly the wealthiest of our many moneyed chatelaines. Lady C also holds the Palm Beach record for ex-husbands: six. She's a shrewd operator, a marvelous hostess and a demanding employer. I'm glad she considers me a friend. Her enemies usually end up whimpering.

"How about lunch?" I suggested. "Noon at the Pelican."

Connie considered a moment. "Yes," she said, "I think I can manage it. Wear your puce beret; that always puts me in a hysterical mood. What have you been up to, lad?"

"Nothing," I said. "Life has been bo-*riing.*"

"Not casting a covetous eye about for any available dollies?"

"Not a dolly in sight," I assured her. "I've really been behaving myself."

"You better," she said menacingly. "You know my spies are everywhere."

That was an unpleasant truth.

"See you at noon tomorrow," I said lightly, and we hung up after an exchange of telephonic kisses—energetic sounds that sometimes leave a bit of spittle on the mouthpiece.

When I told Connie there was no temptation of the female persuasion on the horizon, I did not prevaricate. But little did I know of the events that were to ensure from that doomed evening. I had been guilty of three grossly mistaken assumptions in less than two hours—a sad performance even by yrs. truly.

I overslept the next morning, as usual, and awoke to a world of damp gloom. Squalls were gusting in from the sea, and the sky appeared to be swaddled in disposable diapers. I was tempted to crawl back into the sack but stoutly resisted. There were deeds to be done, I told myself, and worlds to conquer.

By the time I clattered downstairs to the kitchen (not forgetting my puce beret), the house seemed deserted and I breakfasted alone. A search of the fridge provided a glass of cranberry juice, an English muffin sandwich containing boneless Portuguese sardines with a dab of Dijon, and two cups of instant black coffee.

Invigorated, I dashed out to our three-car garage and put the lid on my chariot. Then I started driving through a rain that was not vicious but vengeful. I mean, it was steady, resolute, and seemed likely to last forever. Even Sunny Florida has days like that. Tourists stay in their motel rooms, curse, drink beer, and watch television talk shows until their eyes glaze over.

But I was not deterred by the inclement weather, being determined to accomplish all the important tasks I had planned for that day. My first stop was at the salon ("Hair Apparent") of Herman Pincus, where I received a light trim, scissors on the side, nothing off the top. We discussed a possible cure for a limited but definite tonsure that had appeared on my occiput. The bare spot, no larger than a silver dollar, struck terror to my heart, and I had visions of street urchins yelling, "Hey, baldy!"

But Herman assured me a hot oil massage of the affected area would help. So I endured that, wondering if a very small, circular rug might be a better answer for my affliction. Something like replacing a divot, y'see.

My second stop was at a gentlemen's boutique on Worth Avenue, where I purchase most of my threads. I was looking for any new hats that might be available since I have an irrational love of headgear. To my delight I was able to purchase a visored Greek captain's cap woven of straw. It was definitely rakish, added a certain je ne sais quoi to the McNally phiz and, best of all, concealed that damnable loss of hair. I was convinced it signified the looming end of youth, romance, and perhaps even sexual prowess. (All is vanity, the Good Book saith, and I agreeith.)

It was then time to buzz out to the Pelican Club to meet Connie Garcia for lunch. I was a bit early, the place was almost empty because of the downpour, and I was able to sit at the deserted bar and discuss with Mr. Pettibone what I might have to chase my temporary melancholia. He suggested a brandy stinger, but I thought that a mite heavy for noontime refreshment. We settled for a Salty Dog, a lighter potion but rejuvenating.

The reason I have described my morning's activities in such explicit detail is to give you a reasonably accurate account of an average day in the life of a relatively young Palm Beach layabout—at least *this* layabout. I freely confess it was a life of carefree idleness. My only excuse is that at the time I did not think myself engaged in any serious discreet inquiries. In other words, I faced no energizing challenge. Before the day ended I was disabused of that notion.

When Connie appeared it was immediately obvious the miserable day had not crushed *her* spirits. She was her usual bouncy, ebullient self and danced toward me as if the sun were shining and the future unlimited. I know it may sound sexist, but I cannot refrain from describing Connie as dishy. The fact that I am continually unfaithful to her only proves that when it comes to a contest between a man's brain and his glands, hormones are the inevitable winner. It's sad but it's something males must learn to live with.

She was wearing stonewashed denim jeans and vest with a pink T-shirt blessedly free of any legend. Her long black hair swung free, and if it was rain-spangled it was all the more attractive for that. She exuded a healthy physical vigor, and her "What, me worry?" grin would have brought a smile to the face of a moody tyrannosaur.

"Hello, bubba," she caroled, giving me an air kiss.

"Bubba?!" I said, outraged. "Since when have I been a bubba?"

She giggled. "I just wanted to yank your chain. Hey, let's eat; I'm famished and don't have much time."

There was only one other couple in the dining room, so Connie and I were able to sit at our favorite corner table. Priscilla came bopping over to take our order while snapping her fingers. Pris is the only waitress I know who wears a Walkman while working.

We ordered Leroy's special hamburgers, which have no ham, of course, but are a mixture of ground beef, veal, and pork. He also adds other ingredients when inspired by his culinary muse. On that day I believe it was curry powder. Very nice. We also had a basket of thick chips and shared a platter of cherry tomatoes and sliced cukes. Coors Light for Connie and a Heineken for me. It was a delectable lunch as lunches go, and as lunches go, it went—rapidly.

Connie brought me up-to-date on the most recent excesses of Lady Cynthia, including a proposal to issue ID cards to all the bona fide residents of Palm Beach.

"Wouldn't a tattooed number be more effective?" I suggested. "Is the woman totally insane?"

"Not totally, but she's getting there. And what have you been up to, hon?"

"Zilch."

"No discreet inquiries?"

I want to be honest—well, I don't *want* to be, but I must—and I confess that since the meeting with Sunny Fogarty I hadn't given a fraction of a thought to the doings at the Whitcomb Funeral Homes. It seemed ridiculous to investigate a business simply because it was showing a handsome profit. But idly, for no other reason than to make conversation, I asked Connie:

"Ever hear of the Whitcombs?"

"The burying people?"

I nodded.

"Sure, I've heard of them," she said. "Oliver and Mitzi Whitcomb. Socially active—and I mean *very*. You might even call them swingers."

"Oh?" I said, beginning to get interested. "And where do they swing?"

"Here, there, and everywhere. They throw some wild parties."

"In Palm Beach?"

"Boca. But I understand they also have a villa on the Costa del Sola and a condo in Saint Thomas."

"Sweet," I said. "Shows what one can reap from planting people. Do Oliver and Mitzi have children?"

"Nope," Connie said. "Swingers are too busy to breed. Why this sudden interest in the Whitcombs?"

"New clients," I said casually. "I'm just trying to learn more about them."

She stared at me coldly. "I hope that's all it is. I wouldn't care to discover you've been consorting with Mitzi Whitcomb."

"My dear Consuela," I said loftily, "I keep my personal relations with clients to an absolute minimum. It's a matter of professional ethics."

"Son," she said, "you've got more crap than a Christmas goose."

"Zounds!" I exclaimed. "How quickly you've picked up the elegant idioms of your adopted country."

"Oh, stuff it," she said. "Listen, thanks for the feed, but I've got to run."

I signed the tab at the bar and we went out to the parking area. And there, standing in the drizzle, I donned my puce beret. As expected, Connie drove away laughing hysterically. It doesn't take much to make her happy.

I tooled back to the McNally Building on Royal Palm Way. It is a starkly modern edifice of glass and stainless steel. Not at all to my father's taste, I assure you, but the architect convinced him the headquarters of McNally & Son must make a "statement," so mein Vater went along with the express understanding that his private office would be paneled in oak, with leather furniture, an antique rolltop desk, and other solid (and rather gloomy) trappings that would have pleased Oliver Wendell Holmes.

I parked in our underground garage and sat there a moment, thinking of what Connie had told me about the sociable younger Whitcombs. Hardly earthshaking, I concluded, but it was a bit unsettling to learn that the CEO of funeral homes and his wife were swingers. I mean, one does expect somber decorum from people in that profession—not so?

But perhaps my moral arteries are hardening and I'm becoming a young Savonarola.

4

I rode the automatic elevator to my fourth-floor cubicle. It would be gross exaggeration to call it an office. I am not suggesting it was so cramped that you had to enter sideways, but I always thought of it as a vertical coffin and spent as little time entombed as possible. I do believe my liege consigned me to that windowless cubby to forestall accusations of nepotism. If so, he succeeded brilliantly. Fellow employees at McNally & Son referred to my sanctum as "Archy's locker."

I found on my desk a large, bulky package bearing no return address other than the messenger service that had delivered it. My first reaction was that it might be a bomb sent by an enraged husband. But I discounted that possibility although I removed the wrapping rather gingerly.

Within was a handwritten note (in an artful cursive) from Sunny

Fogarty. It stated merely that enclosed was the computer printout I had requested, naming the cemeteries to which the Whitcomb Funeral Homes had sent their "customers" for burial during the past six months. Ms. Fogarty also included her address (West Palm Beach) and phone number. She suggested it would be best, if I had further questions or wished to impart information, to contact her at home rather than her Whitcomb office. A very careful lady.

I was looking at the stack of computer bumf with some dismay when my phone rang. It was the would-be Philip Marlowe.

"Greetings, old sport," chirped Binky Watrous. "I'm ready to go to work."

"What happened to your golf game?"

"Washed out," he said. "I'm ready, willing, and able. When do we start?"

"Immediately," I said, eyeing the opened package on my desk. "Come over to my office."

"On my way," he said happily. "Half an hour at the most."

I used the time to phone Lolly Spindrift. He is a gossip columnist (the three-dot variety) at one of our local rags, and his jazzy comments on past, present, and future scandals are read and enjoyed by most of the literate haut monde and hoi polloi of Palm Beach County.

Lolly and I have a mutually beneficial working relationship, a quid pro quo that profits both of us. Occasionally I feed him exclusive items from current discreet inquiries, but nothing, I assure you, that would imperil a client's reputation. In return, the schlockenspieler serves as a database of local rumors and tittle-tattle. He simply knows everything that has gone on, is going on, and will go on in our hermetic social world.

"Hi, darling," he said in his flutey voice. "What have you got for me?"

"Come off it, Lol," I said. "After those tips I gave you on the Forsythe affair, you owe me."

"Very well," he said. "A clear case of noblesse oblige. What do you want, luv?"

"Oliver and Mitzi Whitcomb," I said. "Know anything about them?"

I could almost hear him rolling his eyes. "Do I ever! But why would you be interested in the happy grave diggers?"

"In due time, Lol," I said patiently. "In due time you'll be the first to hear. Now what have you got?"

"Wild ones," he said promptly. "Apparently inexhaustible funds. Chronic party-goers and party-givers. And some of the people they party with are, shall we say, on the demimonde side. A very curious couple. It isn't what I'd call a working marriage, sweetie. They both tomcat around like maniacs, obviously with each other's permission if not approval. I've always thought there's something dreadful and fascinating going on there, but I've never been able to nail them without fear of libel. Keep me informed, dear."

"Will do," I promised and hung up.

I lighted a cigarette while awaiting Binky's arrival. What Lolly had told me only confirmed and sharpened what Connie Garcia had revealed. Of course I had no conception of what the lifestyle of Oliver and Mitzi had to do with the unexplained profits of the Whitcomb Funeral Homes. But I suffer from a bloated curiosity, almost as enlarged as my liver, and it seemed to me further discreet inquiries about the "curious couple" were warranted.

Binky Watrous showed up in a blazer that would have been the envy of Emmett Kelly. He had seen my office before and was not shocked by my teensy-weensy professional crypt. First-time visitors are sometimes stunned speechless. My temporary man Friday flopped into the folding steel chair alongside my desk and helped himself to one of my English Ovals. He gestured toward the stack of computer printout.

"What's that?" he asked.

"That, son," I said, "is the start of a new investigation. It records the names and addresses of cemeteries to which the Whitcomb Funeral Homes have delivered their dear departed over the last six months. You and I must go through this encyclopedia of mortality and compile lists of the cemeteries involved and the number of deceased each of them accommodated."

Binky looked at me with something like horror. "You jest?" he said hopefully.

"I do not jest," I said firmly.

"Archy," he said plaintively, "don't you have anything more exciting for me to do? You know—interrogating predatory blonds, shootouts, bloodbaths—that sort of thing."

"Binky," I said at my avuncular best, "you have a totally mistaken concept of what the detective business is all about. It's ninety percent routine, old bean: dull, dull, dull routine. Now either you submit your resignation and endure the wrath of the Duchess or you get to work instanter."

He sighed. "Oh, very well," he said, "I'll do it. Under protest, you understand. Do you have a pencil? And paper?"

I supplied the needed and, after dividing the computer printout into two approximately equal piles, we both got busy. Binky worked in silence for about fifteen minutes. Occasionally he licked the point of his pencil—a despicable habit. Finally he looked up at me in total bewilderment.

"Archy," he said, "why are we doing this?"

"I thought you'd never ask," I said. "We're doing it because the Whitcomb Funeral Homes are making too much money."

He stared at me with that dopey look he always gets when confronting anything more profound than *Abbott and Costello Meet Frankenstein*.

"Oh," he said.

We continued our donkeywork and finished almost simultaneously. Binky shoved his notes across the desk to me. His handwriting was unexpectedly small, neat, and quite legible. Due to his long experience in signing bar tabs, no doubt. I compared his pages with mine and saw something interesting. I handed the two lists to my new subaltern.

"Take a look," I said. "See if you spot anything."

He studied our jottings with a worried frown. Then, to my pleased surprise, he caught it.

"Hey," he said, "a lot of these stiffs are being shipped north for burial."

"You've got it," I said approvingly. "Of course South Florida has a huge retiree population, and I suppose many of them want to be planted in family plots in their hometowns. But it appears that Whitcomb is handling an inordinate number of out-of-state shipments."

Binky took another look at our computations. "Sure," he said. "And the number is increasing every month. That's crazy."

"Let me see," I said and read over our lists again.

Binky was correct. But then I saw something else. The majority of human remains being sent out of Florida by Whitcomb were airlifted to New York, Boston, and Chicago. The computer printout I had received did not state who was receiving these gift packages at La-Guardia, Logan, and O'Hare.

Binky and I lighted cigarettes and stared at the smoke-stained ceiling tiles.

"You know, Archy," he said, "it's sad. I mean, old geezers retire and come down here to spend their last years in the sunshine. But when they croak, they want to go home. Don't you think that's sad?"

"No," I said, "I don't. Our transplanted oldsters are survivors. More power to them. And when they finally shuffle off, they want their final resting place to be Buffalo, Peoria, Walla Walla, or wherever. It's their prerogative, and who are we to deny their last wishes. That's not what bothers me; it's the enormous number of deceased Whitcomb seems to be exporting. Don't you find that intriguing?"

Binky shrugged. "I'd rather not think about it. Too depressing, old sport. Listen, I think I've done enough hard labor for one day. May I go home now?"

I glanced at my watch. "Almost two hours," I commented. "Well, I suppose I must introduce you to the work ethic slowly and gradually. Sure, take off. Do you plan to be home this evening?"

"I might," he said cautiously.

"Try," I said. "It's possible that I may phone you to continue your education as a detective."

"More of this stuff about people being buried? I'm not keen about it, Archy. Puts a damper on the Watrous spirits—you know?"

"Where do you want to be buried, Binky?"

"On the Cote d'Azur. Under three inches of sand."

And on that lighthearted note he departed. I cleaned up my corral, bundled the printout and the notes Binky and I had made into the original wrapping, and set out for home. I was pleased with my batman's performance. True, he had only slaved two hours at his chosen profession, but he had exhibited enough wit to catch that business of shipping caskets up north. That was a plus, I thought. And somewhat of a shock. Like discovering Mortimer Snerd could explain the Pythagorean theorem.

The weather was still growly, the sea churning, and so I skipped my late afternoon ocean swim. Instead, I went directly to my quarters, plunked down behind the battered desk, and opened my journal to a fresh page.

I keep a record, y'see, of all my discreet inquiries and try to make daily entries while a case is under way. It serves as a jog to my memory, and sometimes a written account of observations, conversations, and events reveals a hidden pattern I might otherwise have missed.

Also, my journal is a sourcebook for the narratives I pen and ensures accuracy. You didn't think I'm making up all this stuff, did you?

I made notes on what had transpired during the first meeting with Sunny Fogarty, what I had learned of the proclivities of Oliver and Mitzi Whitcomb, and what Binky and I had discovered: the perplexing number of defuncts that Whitcomb Funeral Homes were profitably putting aboard airliners for the final trip home.

I finished my scribbling in time to dress for the family cocktail hour, a rigorously observed daily ceremonial of the McNallys. We gather in the second-floor sitting room, father stirs a jug of gin martinis (traditional formula), and we each have one plus a dividend. Then we descend to dinner. If that sounds unbearably Waspish, let me remind you that my paternal grandfather was a burlesque comic, and we are merely obeying the American dictum: Onward and upward. Of course it was dramaturgy. And whose life is not?

After dinner, I rose from the table, returned to my digs, and phoned Sunny Fogarty.

After an exchange of greeting, I said, "I trust I'm not disturbing you."

"Not at all."

"I was hoping I might see you this evening. It concerns the material you sent to my office. Probably a minor matter but I'd like to get it cleared up. Could you spare me, say, half an hour?"

"Of course," she said.

"Thank you," I said. "Miss Fogarty, would it—"

"You can call me Sunny if you'd like," she interrupted.

"I'd like," I told her. "And I'm Archy. Sunny, would you object if I brought along my assistant, a very personable and competent chap?"

Long pause. "No," she said finally, "I have no objection."

"Excellent," I said. "We'll be at your place within an hour."

I hung up and called Binky Watrous. "What are you doing?" I asked him.

"Just finished dinner," he reported. "You know, Archy, I hate Brussels sprouts."

"Who doesn't?" I said. "Listen, lad, I want you to join me in an hour's time to continue our investigation by interviewing one of the principals."

He groaned. "That business of out-of-state burials?"

"Exactly."

"Do I really have to be there?" he said, wounded. "I rented a tape of *The Curse of the Cat People* and I was looking forward to—"

"Binky!" I said sharply. "You want to be the new Sam Spade, don't you? Now go get a piece of paper, lick a pencil, and I'll give you the address."

We synchronized watches and agreed to meet at Sunny Fogarty's home at nine-thirty.

"If you arrive before I do," I warned, "don't you dare enter before I show up."

"Wouldn't think of it," he said.

"And when we have our conversation with the lady, I want you to let me carry the ball. You say nothing unless you're asked a direct question. Is that understood?"

"Absolutely, boss," Binky said. "I shall be nothing more than a flea on the wall."

I was about to remind him that the expression was "a fly on the wall." But then I reflected he probably had it right.

5

Traffic was unexpectedly heavy that night, and by the time I got across the Royal Park Bridge to West Palm Beach I knew I was running late. Also, I had a bit of trouble finding Sunny Fogarty's home. It turned out to be a rather posh condo high-rise off Olive Avenue, almost directly across from Connie Garcia's apartment on Lake Worth. If that had any significance I didn't want to think about it.

I pulled into the guest parking area, disembarked, and looked about for Binky's heap. And there it was. My Dr. Watson drives a 1970 Mercedes Benz 280 SE Cabriolet. It had been beautifully restored when he bought it, but the lunkhead hadn't cosseted it. It was dented, rusted, had a passenger door that didn't quite latch, and generally presented an appearance of sad dilapidation. The vandalism wasn't deliberate, you understand—just an example of Binky's breezy treatment of all his possessions. He wears a gold Rolex that stopped four years ago.

What rattled my cage at the moment was that the Mercedes was unoccupied. That probably meant the idiot owner had disregarded my firm instructions and had barged in on Sunny Fogarty instead of awaiting my arrival. Uttering a mild oath, I hurried to the entrance and found an exterior security system requesting guests to dial a three-digit number listed on a directory, to speak to and be admitted by the residents.

I punched out the number for Sunny's apartment. She answered almost immediately.

"Archy McNally," I said. "May I come up?"

"Of course," she said. "Your assistant is already here."

"Sorry about that."

"No need to apologize. He's entertaining me with birdcalls."

I quailed. Rather fitting, don'cha think?

She buzzed me in, and I rode an art deco elevator to the sixth floor.

The living room of Sunny's apartment was elegant without being lavish. I had no idea of her annual salary or net worth, but she had mentioned the expense of keeping an ailing mother in a nursing home. Still, she drove a new car and apparently owned this charming condo that bespoke moneyed ease. It was enough to give one pause. If not you, then certainly me.

Señor Watrous, wearing his hellish blazer, was sprawled on a couch upholstered in bottle-green velvet. I glared at him and received a sappy grin in response. I turned to our hostess.

"Sunny," I said, "I see you've already met my aide-de-camp. Light on the aid and heavy on the camp."

She smiled. "I think Binky is very talented. May I offer you gentlemen a drink?"

"Oh, don't go to any—" I started, but Binky piped up.

"I'd like something," he said. "How about a vodka rocks? Do you have the makings?"

"I do," she said. "The same for you, Archy?"

I nodded.

"That makes three of us. It'll just take a minute."

She went out to the kitchen, and I whirled on Binky. "Behave yourself," I admonished. "And try to keep your big, fat mouth shut. You promised."

"Right," he said. "Positively. I shall provide nothing but attentive silence."

"That's wise," I said. "Unless you wish to confess to the Duchess that you have been summarily dismissed after one day of unpaid unemployment."

Sunny returned with a bamboo tray of three handsome crystal old-fashioned glasses containing our vodka rocks. She had put a wedge of fresh lime in each. Much appreciated. She served us, then sat in a facing barrel chair covered in a cheerful chintz.

"Cheers," she said, raising her glass.

Binky hoisted his. "Here's to our wives and sweethearts," he said. "May they never meet."

I could have killed him, but Ms. Fogarty laughed. I vowed to keep my anger in check until we left. Then I intended to flay the goof alive. What a cheeky rascal he was!

"Sunny," I said, "thank you for seeing us on such short notice. But after Binky and I reviewed the computer printout you provided, we found something that puzzles us."

She leaned forward, elbows on knees. "Oh?" she said. "And what is that?"

She was wearing loosely fitted jeans of white denim with leather sandals, and an oversized man's shirt appliquéd with gold stars, this gauzy fabric suggesting an impressive figure. I shall say no more on the subject lest I be accused of indelicacy.

"There seems to be an unusual number of deceased sent up north for burial," I said. "How do you account for that?"

She accepted my direct question calmly. "Archy, all the funeral homes in South Florida do the same thing. So many of the elderly retired are down here, you know. I can't recall the exact figures, but last year about four thousand dead were shipped from Fort Lauderdale alone. That's more than ten a day. And for the entire State of Florida, more than twenty-five thousand deceased are exported for burial, most of them airlifted. That amounts to almost twenty percent of Florida's total death toll."

"Remarkable," I commented.

"Downputting," Binky said. "Definitely downputting."

I ignored him. "Sunny, how many out-of-state shipments would you estimate Whitcomb Funeral Homes makes annually?"

She thought a moment. "Oh, I'd guess about three hundred a year. Perhaps a bit more."

"In other words, one a day on average would be a generous estimate. Is that correct?"

"Oh yes, very generous. I doubt if we do that much."

Binky and I looked at each other.

"Sunny," I said softly. "According to the computer records you furnished, during the past six months Whitcomb Funeral Homes have shipped out almost five hundred dead."

She gave every indication of being astonished. "I can't believe that!" she cried.

"It's true," I said, "if the information you gave us is accurate. You may check it yourself if you doubt it."

"I simply can't believe it," she repeated and took a hurried slug of her vodka.

"In addition," I went on, "the overwhelming majority of those shipments went to three cities: New York, Boston, and Chicago. Can you offer any explanation for that? It does seem odd."

She shook her head without disturbing a hair of that glossy helmet of russet. "I can't explain it," she said. "Are you suggesting that our rise in income is due to a huge increase in the number of out-of-state burials we're handling?"

"It's possible," I said.

"Incredible," she said. "I just can't believe it."

I thought the lady was lying—and amateurishly at that. It wasn't only the thrice repeated "I can't believe it" that alerted me; it was her manner, expressions, and her intense reactions to what I had told her. Too dramatic by half, and she hadn't the histrionic talent to make her passion believable.

Trust my judgment on this, since I am a consummate liar myself. I knew Ananias. Ananias was a friend of mine. And believe me, Sunny Fogarty was no Ananias.

"Archy," she said, "what do you think we should do next? I just can't understand that volume of out-of-state burials."

"Hey!" my acolyte said brightly. "I think I've got it! Maybe there's a serial killer on the loose knocking off scads of people."

"All of whom come from New York, Boston, and Chicago," I said disdainfully. "Binky, Sunny has already informed my father and me that there has been no unusual rise in Florida's mortality rate, and no other funeral homes have had the income increase that Whitcomb has enjoyed."

"Oh," he said.

I turned back to our hostess. "As for what we should do next, I'd like to get the names and addresses of the out-of-state funeral homes or cemeteries to which Whitcomb's shipments were sent."

She stared at me. "Archy, I gave you that. It was all on the computer printout."

"No, ma'am," I said gently, "it wasn't. Names and addresses of Florida cemeteries were noted, but out-of-state shipments were merely listed as being delivered to airports in New York, Boston, and Chicago."

Now she was truly bewildered; there was no falsity in her response. "That's impossible!" she burst out. Her face was suddenly contorted with an emotion I could not quite identify. It was either fury or fear— or a combination of both. "Of course that information is on our computer and it should have been on the printout I sent you."

"It wasn't," I said. "Was it, Binky?"

"Nope," he said. "Just the names of the airports."

I saw in Sunny's hardened eyes an affirmation of my initial instinct that she was not a woman to be trifled with. "I'll find out what happened," she said fiercely. "First thing tomorrow morning."

"If it's missing from the computer," I said, "is it irretrievably lost?"

"No," she said. "It can be restored from the original documents submitted by our funeral directors. A lot of work, but it can be done. I'm more concerned with discovering why it's not computerized as it should have been."

"Please keep me informed," I said. "I'd like to see the names and addresses of assignees in other states as soon as possible. One more thing . . . I think it would help if Binky and I could somehow meet the principals involved. Especially Mr. Horace Whitcomb and his son, Oliver, the chief executive officer, and Oliver's wife, Mitzi."

She looked at me curiously. "How did you know her name is Mitzi?"

"I'm sure I must have read it in the society pages of our local newspapers and magazines," I said without a qualm. "They're very active socially, are they not?"

"Yes," she said shortly. "Very. As for meeting them, that will be no problem. Mr. Horace is having a birthday party for his wife, Sarah, on Tuesday night next week. A black-tie affair. More than a hundred guests are expected. A big buffet, three bars, a band, and dancing. You'll be able to meet all the executive personnel of Whitcomb Funeral Homes. Archy, your parents have already been invited. I'll have invitations sent to both of you."

"Goody," Binky said. "I love huge parties with dancing. Perhaps I'll meet a wondrous lady who can do the turkey trot. As long as no one from Whitcomb follows me about with a tape measure."

"No," Sunny said, smiling, "I don't think that will happen."

I finished my drink, stood up, and motioned to Binky. He rose, obviously reluctantly; he would have been happy to stay for hours, drinking Sunny's booze and schmoozing. We thanked Sunny for her hospitality, and she promised to send me the information I had requested.

In the descending elevator I said to Binky, "A very attractive woman."

"A bit antique," he said. "Too old for me."

"Binky!" I said. "She can't be more than two or three years older than you."

"That's what I mean," he said.

Then my irritation at his behavior that evening faded. I mean, the man was such an utter bubblehead, but if you're going to be a friend of a bubblehead, there's not much point in getting furious because he *is* a bubblehead. That's a bit complicated, but it makes sense, doesn't it?

Outside, we stood a moment in the parking area lighting cigarettes. Mine. Binky never carries coffin nails, claiming he is determined to stop smoking. His pals pay for his firm resolve.

"We're going to that black-tie bash, aren't we?" he asked me.

"Of course."

"Glad to hear it. Things in the detective business are looking up. Archy, do you believe everything Sunny told us tonight?"

"Perhaps not everything," I said cautiously.

"Me neither," he said. "I think she was scamming us—or trying to."

For the second time that day I was shocked by his perspicacity. I wondered if there was a tiny, tiny spark of intelligence in that bowl of lemon Jell-O between his ears.

"Call you tomorrow," I said. "We've got things to do."

"Okay," he said cheerfully, "but not too early. I've got to watch the Cat People tonight so I'll probably sleep in. Make it around noon-ish—all right?"

I stood there and watched him pull away in his decaying Mercedes, black smoke spewing from the exhaust. Then I climbed into my barouche and headed home.

I slid into bed shortly after midnight, still pondering the events of that hugger-mugger day. Before waltzing with Morpheus I reviewed again everything that occurred and what little I had learned in the curious case of the lucrative funeral homes.

I had an aggravating itch that I was failing to recognize something significant that had happened. But the Z's arrived before I could pin-point exactly what it was.

6

It sometimes happens that one falls asleep with a problem and awakes with a solution. So it was for me on that Friday morning. I sat on the edge of my bed, and the puzzle that had bedeviled me the previous night suddenly became clear, if not completely resolved.

Question: Why had Sunny Fogarty sought the assistance of Mc-Nally & Son in the first place?

She had given us a rather frail excuse for not conducting an in-house investigation on her own: she said she might endanger her job by "poking and prying," and arouse the derision of other employees. After all, who would be silly enough to become concerned because their employer was suddenly making more money?

I might have accepted that if I had not pegged Comptroller Fogarty as an extremely competent executive, a computer maven who kept a sharp eye on Whitcomb's balance sheet and bottom line. I could not possibly believe she had missed the increase of out-of-state burials; it was so obvious that even a couple of computer illiterates had caught it immediately.

Assuming she was aware of what we'd discover before she sent us the printout—and I did so assume—what could be her motive in dumping the mystery into the lap of McNally & Son, her employer's attorneys of record? I could only conclude she had an urgent need for wanting us to investigate rather than the flimsy reasons she had stated.

But what that need might be, the deponent kneweth not. I did know that if something was seriously awry at Whitcomb Funeral Homes, it was doubtful if Sunny herself was involved in any wrongdoing. I mean, since when does a guilty party initiate an inquiry, discreet or otherwise, into his or her own conduct?

After breakfasting on eggs scrambled with chunks of smoked turkey sausage, I phoned Binky Watrous around ten o'clock. I endured his grumbling at being awakened at such an ungodly hour and finally had to cut him short by threatening to tell the Duchess of his distressing lack of ambition. He finally agreed to come to my office in an hour's time.

He was only fifteen minutes late, still yawning, and grasped my packet of English Ovals like an opium smoker reaching for a full pipe. He smoked and listened in silence while I outlined our program for the day.

We were to visit funeral homes in the area and conduct research on exactly how a person who has passed to the Great Beyond is shipped via airliner to the destination of his or her choice, as expressed in his or her will or dictated by close relatives.

"Yuck!" Binky said with a small shudder.

I hope you will not have the same reaction and consider our investigation somewhat macabre. Of course I do not know your attitude toward dying and death. I do know that for many years mine was abject terror.

But then one day at the funeral of a good friend I recalled Aristotle's classic dictum: "A whole is that which has beginning, middle, and end." It is true for a whole life, is it not? That realization has been a great comfort to me, and I hope it may be to you as well.

I explained to Binky that we would canvass funeral homes other than Whitcomb's. Since we were to attend Mr. Horace's party on the following Tuesday, I did not want to run the risk of being recognized by Whitcomb employees, who might question the presence of journalists at the private affair.

"Journalists?" Binky said, puzzled.

"That's what we're going to be today," I told him, "or for as long as it takes. We shall be two writers preparing an article for a national magazine on burial practices in Florida. Do you think you can play the role of a reporter?"

"Of course," he said confidently. "We're looking for a scoop—right?"

I sighed and we started out with two pages torn from the classified telephone directory listing all the local mortuaries.

At this moment I shall not detail the results of our peregrinations, but I promise you will learn them shortly. I do want to mention that although I feared our pavement-pounding might be dreary, it turned out to be unexpectedly fascinating.

We worked all day, pausing only once in mid-afternoon for lunch at a greasery that served French fries limp enough to be bent double. We then continued our labors until 4:30, when we decided we had accomplished enough for one day. We parted company, and I returned home to enjoy a delightful swim in a gently rolling sea just cool enough to give the McNally corpuscles a wake-up call.

Engraved invitations addressed to Binky and me had been delivered, requesting our presence at a celebration to be held on Tuesday evening at the home of Mr. and Mrs. Horace Whitcomb. My father raised one of his brambly eyebrows when being so informed at our family cocktail hour.

"How did you manage that, Archy?" he asked.

"Sunny Fogarty arranged it."

The thicket went up another millimeter. "I hope you intend to dress conservatively," he said.

"Archy always dresses beautifully," mother put in.

"Maddie," the lord of the manor reminded her, "beauty is in the eye of the beholder. But not *this* beholder."

After a ravishing dinner of baked scallops (with braised endives) and a dessert of bread pudding with sabayon sauce, I went upstairs and worked for an hour bringing entries in my journal up to date.

I spent the remainder of the evening planning my weekend and making umpteen phone calls. I lined up a golf game for Saturday afternoon;

dinner with Connie at Renato's on Saturday night (playing Benedick to her Beatrice); a tennis match on Sunday afternoon; and a poker joust with a quartet of rapacious cronies on Sunday night. If a whole life really does consist of beginning, middle, and end, I wanted my middle to be as pleasurable as possible. We are all hedonists, but I'm one of the few willing to admit it.

Mirabile dictu, the weekend proved to be as joyous as anticipated. I awoke Monday morning full of p&v and ready for another day of research into the arcane practices of human burial in South Florida. Actually, it was only half a day, for by one o'clock I decided Binky and I had completed the needful. We repaired to the Pelican Club to lunch on barbecued ribs while we compared notes on what we had learned.

If you wish to prepare yourself for this recital, I suggest a sip of schnapps would not be amiss.

The statistics Sunny Fogarty had quoted to us were generally correct: approximately 25,000 dead are exported from Florida each year, most of them to contiguous states but some as far afield as Malaysia and Tibet.

South Florida is especially active in this commerce, with about four thousand corpses being shipped annually from Broward County alone. The large population of the elderly retired accounts for that.

Coffins are packed in cartons, embalmed bodies air-lifted in special crates. All containers are labeled "Human Remains" and "Handle with Extreme Care." That's a comfort, isn't it?

The packaged deceased are delivered to airports in unmarked vans, not hearses. This custom demonstrates a nice sensibility. Can you imagine sitting in first class, waiting for your plane to take off, and you glance out the window and see a hearse pull up alongside? "Stewardess, I've changed my mind; I think I'll take the bus."

According to our calculations, Monsieur Watrous and I reckoned that almost every airliner departing from South Florida carried at least one corpus in the cargo bay. As Binky remarked, "That's one passenger who won't worry about a crash."

Of course there was an added expenditure for all this. Funeral homes charged a hefty sum, sometimes two thousand dollars, to prepare a loved one for shipment and delivery to the airport. Airlines billed about three hundred dollars for a domestic destination and at least five times that for one overseas.

A final note: Some religions forbid embalming. In that case, the body is placed in a metal container packed with ice before being airlifted. Remember that before you ask the flight attendant for your third Scotch on the rocks.

After discussing all this wonderful stuff, Binky and I fell silent and stared at each other.

"What does it all mean?" he asked finally.

"It means," I said, "that Whitcomb Funeral Homes is making a great deal of money by shipping an amazing number of dead out of Florida to points west, north, and east."

"Sure, Archy," he agreed. "We knew that before we started. But where are they getting all the inhabitants of those crates?"

I said, "Who knows what evil lurks in the hearts of living men?"

"Hey," Binky said, "you're not The Shadow."

"True, but I'm a reasonable facsimile thereof. Do you have any ideas, wild or otherwise?"

He shook his head. "Haven't the slightest, old boy."

"Nor do I," I admitted. "And there's no point in worrying about it until we get more information from Sunny Fogarty. Let's go home."

"Banzai!" he cried. "There's a rerun of *Invasion of the Body Snatchers* on the tube at four o'clock. I don't want to miss it."

"Very fitting," I said approvingly. "Maybe it'll yield a clue to what's going on at Whitcomb."

That evening I brooded in my den, staring at the journal notes I had jotted. The entire mishmash seemed to me *Much Ado About Nothing*. But then, I reflected, if there was chicanery afoot, it might be *As You Like It* to the perpetrator. In either case, it was a comedy, was it not?

I recalled the pater's admonition to go through the motions but not spend too much time on the Whitcomb affair. I had already disobeyed him and knew I would continue. I was hooked by the puzzle.

Sgt. Al Rogoff of the Palm Beach Police Department—my friend and sometimes collaborator—constantly complains that I overuse the adjective "intriguing." I suppose I do, but I cannot think of a better word to describe Whitcomb's increased revenue from the departed and deported.

If the truth be told—a painful necessity—I am a nosy bloke. I do like to stick my schnozz in other people's business and learn what's going on. It's a grievous sin, I admit, but more fun than Chinese checkers and also, on occasion, a good deal more dangerous.

Nothing of any great consequence occurred on Tuesday morning except that I had blueberry pancakes for breakfast. The afternoon was similarly uneventful. I did have my quadriga washed and its gullet filled. But other than that, the day was without excitement.

I finished my two-mile wallow in a placid sea and returned home to dress for the Whitcomb party. It was still warmish in South Florida and I decided on a white dinner jacket: a costume my father insists makes me look like the headwaiter at a Miami stone crab restaurant.

We all gathered for a cocktail before setting out for the bash. Hizzoner was wearing his rather rusty black tuxedo with a pleated white shirt (wing collar) and onyx studs. Of course his cummerbund and tie were black, and the bow was hand-tied. He considered pretied bows a portent of the decline of Western Civilization.

I must confess he looked rather regal in his formal attire, not at all like a mustachioed penguin. But mother was the star. She was absolutely smashing in a long brocaded gown and carried an aqua satin minaudière. Her white curls were a halo and she wore a three-strand choker of pink pearls. Momsy has a natural high color and that evening she positively glowed: a teenager ready for the prom.

We emptied the martini pitcher and trooped downstairs, laughing for no particular reason. Ursi and Jamie Olson came from the kitchen to tell us how magnificent we all looked and to wish us a wonderful evening.

Father drove his big Lexus with mother sitting alongside him. I followed in my flaming scooter, feeling like the skipper of a dinghy trailing the QE2. I think we were all stimulated by the prospect of attending a lavish and crowded revel. The social season in Palm Beach was just getting under way. This was the first big party and offered an opportunity to shed the doldrums of a too long and too hot summer.

I know I was convinced it was going to be a glorious rollick during which I would meet The Girl of My Dreams (Clara Bow) and be universally admired for my skill in executing the Charleston. I would forget about whatever nonsense was transpiring at Whitcomb Funeral Homes and spend a rompish night obeying Herrick's command: "Gather ye rosebuds while ye may." That was my firm intention.

One never knows, do one?

7

The home of Sarah and Horace, the senior Whitcombs, was a palazzo on North Lake Way. It was an aging edifice somewhat lacking in charm. The most amazing feature was the vegetation. I mean, the lot had to be almost two acres and looked like an arboretum with hedges fifteen feet high. You could hardly *see* the house until you were standing at the front door.

Valet parking had been provided; we surrendered our vehicles and stepped up to a portico topped by a wrought-iron balcony. Awaiting my arrival was Signore Binky Waltrous, the tyro Mike Hammer. I blinked when I saw his costume.

The idiot was sockless and wearing white mocs, white trousers, and a white shirt with a cascade of ruffles. Worse, his jacket, cummerbund, and bow tie were red checkered linen, looking as if they had been made from the tablecloth of a cheap Neapolitan restaurant. He should have been carrying an empty Chianti bottle wrapped in raffia with a candle stub stuck in its mouth.

"Fetching?" he asked, smoothing the hideously wide lapels.

"I wish someone would," I said. "Binky, where did you get that monstrosity?"

"I had it designed especially for me."

"By whom—the ghost of Liberace? Here is your invitation. I suggest you precede me and for the remainder of the evening let's pretend we are total strangers to each other."

"You want me to ask questions?" he said eagerly. "You know, interrogate people? The old third degree."

"By all means," I said. "If you can find anyone willing to be seen conversing with Bozo the Clown."

My parents had already entered. Binky went inside and I waited a few moments, mortified by the appearance of my henchman. He looked as if he'd be right at home on the stage of the Grand Ole Opry—playing a kazoo no doubt.

I walked through the open front door and surrendered my invitation to a uniformed flunky. I stood a moment to look about and then had to step out of the way as more guests continued to arrive. But the interior of that home was worth close inspection.

If the exterior had been charmless, the inside was something else again. Warm elegance is the only way I can describe it. High ceilings, museum-quality parquet floors, walls papered in an antique trompe l'oeil pattern, furnishings at once attractive and selected for comfort. There were some odd decorative touches that caught the eye: a marvelous model of the first motorcar (an 1886 Benz) in a glass display case; a mysterious Cycladic female figurine; a rattan fireplace screen mimicking a peacock's tail.

There were at least a dozen guests waiting to be received. I took my place at the end of the line and waited patiently. I had expected to be greeted by Sarah and Horace Whitcomb plus son Oliver and daughter-in-law Mitzi. But as the line moved slowly forward I saw that only an oldish gentleman was shaking hands and alongside him, in a wheelchair, was a lady I presumed to be his spouse. There was nothing doddery about either. They spoke animatedly, laughed frequently, and obviously were enlivened by their roles as hosts for this crowded jollification.

"Horace Whitcomb," he said, smiling and holding out a sinewy hand. "Thank you for coming."

"Thank you for having me, sir," I said, shaking that hard paw. "I'm Archy McNally, Prescott's son."

"Of course! So nice to meet you."

"The honor is mine," I said. "You have a lovely home, Mr. Whitcomb."

He gave me a wry-crisp grin. "It's really an ugly heap, isn't it? My father tore a photo from a magazine and had the architect imitate it."

"The exterior may be a bit awkward," I admitted, "but the interior is a sheer delight."

He was obviously pleased, a tall and slender man with the ramrod posture of a drill instructor. His fine hair was silvered and pale blue eyes were startling against suntanned skin. He had a scimitar nose and there was a network of laugh lines at the corners of his wide mouth. A genial patrician. And something majestic about him.

"That's very kind of you," he said. "Perhaps you and I might have a chat later."

"I'd like that, sir."

"Meanwhile I want you to meet my dear wife, Sarah, the lady responsible for the sheer delight you mentioned."

He introduced us and went back to greeting arriving guests. I leaned over the wheelchair and gently pressed the frail hand offered me.

"How good of you to come," she said in a wispy voice.

"My pleasure, ma'am," I said. "I understand it's your birthday."

She nodded. "But I'm not counting," she cautioned.

"I apologize for not bringing a gift."

"Your presence is gift enough," she said.

I suppose she had uttered that line fifty times during the evening, but I still thought it an extraordinarily gracious thing to say.

She seemed shrunken. The skin of her bare forearms was wrinkled as if she had once weighed many pounds more but the flesh had simply sloughed away. There was a waxen pallor beneath her makeup, and she wore a multicolored turban that covered her entire skull. I suspected she was undergoing chemotherapy and had lost her hair. But her spirit was undaunted.

"Are you married?" she asked me.

"No, ma'am, I am not."

"Do you want to be?"

"No, ma'am, I do not."

She laughed and reached up to pat my arm. "I don't blame you one damned bit," she said. "Well, you're a handsome devil. Now go mingle and break a few hearts."

"Before I do that," I said, "I must tell you how much I admire the decor of your home. It's just splendid."

"Yes," she said softly, "it *is* beautiful, isn't it? This home has been my passion. I wanted everything to be perfect."

"You've succeeded brilliantly," I assured her.

She looked longingly at the vast entrance hall, through the lofty archway to the living room. She seemed to be seeing things I had not yet viewed, things no one would ever see and love the way she did.

Her dim eyes glistened. "Thank you," she said huskily. "Thank you so very, very much."

I moved away to explore more of the Whitcomb mansion. There was a grand staircase leading to upper floors, but a velvet rope had been stretched to block use by the evening's guests. I strolled to the enormous living room, pausing occasionally to exchange greetings with friends and acquaintances, kissing a few ladies' hands because I was in a Continental mood. There was a bar set up along one wall, doing a brisk business.

A superb pine-paneled dining room accommodated the buffet boards presided over by the caterer and her crew. What a feast! I shall not detail the viands offered, in deference to calorie-obsessed readers. Well, just one: broiled chicken livers topped with squares of bacon and sharp cheddar.

The enormous dining table was still in place, surrounded by twenty chairs. Additional small tables and folding chairs, obviously rented, had been placed about so guests would not be forced to eat standing while balancing a full plate and a brimming glass. It was in this banquet hall I found the second of the three bars Sunny Fogarty had promised and ordered a double vodka gimlet, believing it would last me twice as long as a single. Silly boy.

Dancing space was provided in a smaller chamber that appeared to be an informal sitting and TV viewing room. Furniture and rugs had been removed, the planked floor waxed, and a trio tootled away in one corner, playing mostly show tunes and old favorites such as "Oh Johnny, Oh Johnny, Oh!" It was here I found my parents at the third bar, looking about amusedly while sipping what seemed to be Perrier with lime slices.

"Mrs. McNally," I said, bowing, "may I have the pleasure of this dance?"

"Let me look at my card," she said, then giggled.

We placed our drinks temporarily on the bar, and father smiled benignly as we went twirling away to the rhythm of "Try a Little Tenderness." Mother is hardly a sylph but remarkably light on her feet, and I think we justly believed ourselves to be the most graceful couple on the floor.

The tune ended, we rejoined the squire at the bar.

"Well done," he said as if delivering a judicial opinion. And then to mother: "The next dance is mine. Unless they play something too fast."

Like "The Surrey with the Fringe on Top"? I wanted to ask—but didn't of course.

I meandered back to the dining room, which I now thought of as Bulimia Heaven. It was beginning to fill with ravenous guests. I was about to join the famished throng at the buffet when I espied Sunny Fogarty standing alone at the bar. I observed her from afar and concluded she was a handsome woman. Not lovely, not beautiful, but *handsome*. There are fine degrees of female attractiveness, you know.

I moved to her side and she looked at me with a tight smile. "Good evening, Archy," she said. "So glad you could make it."

"Wouldn't have missed it for the world. Thank you for the invitations."

"I saw Binky," she said. "Does he always dress like that?"

"Always," I said sadly. "His sartorial sense is gravely retarded. He once wore spats over flip-flops to a beach barbecue."

She laughed—which was a relief for she had seemed tense, almost angry.

"I met Sarah and Horace," I told her. "Lovely people."

"Yes, they are."

"She's quite ill?"

Sunny nodded.

"Cancer?"

She nodded again. "They said it was in remission, but it wasn't."

"I thought her a very brave lady."

"An angel. She's an angel."

I said, "I was surprised that Oliver and his wife weren't also receiving."

Her bitterness returned. "So like them," she said. "So selfish. To be late at his mother's birthday party—that's not forgivable. They arrived just a few minutes ago."

"Perhaps they were unavoidably detained," I suggested.

She looked at me but said nothing.

She was wearing a snazzy tuxedo suit: black satin-lapeled jacket and trousers with side satin stripes. No cummerbund, but she wore a poet shirt of pale pink silk with protruding cuffs of lace. Very debonair. Her only jewelry was a choker of diamonds. They appeared to be of two-carat size at least, and if they were genuine, which I believed they were, it was a costly bauble indeed.

"Sunny," I said, "are you hungry?"

"I could eat," she admitted.

"Suppose you grab us two places at a table and I'll fetch us plates of cholesterol."

"All right," she agreed. "But please make mine finger food; I don't feel like digging into the curried lamb on rice or the beef bourguignonne. While you're gone, can I get you a drink?"

"I have a—" I started and then looked down at my empty glass. "Good Lord," I said, "I had forgotten about the high rate of evaporation in South Florida. Yes, I would appreciate a fresh something. A dry white would be nice if it's available."

Fifteen minutes later we were devouring heaps of the finger foods she had requested. There was an almost infinite variety and I recall fondly the shrimp that had been sautéed in garlic and oil and then chilled. That delight was enough to make me abjure bologna sandwiches for the rest of my life.

"Archy," she said as we nibbled, "will you do me a favor?"

"Of course. Your wish is my command."

She was not amused. "I intend to leave about eleven o'clock," she said. "You stay as long as you like, but would you mind stopping by my place before you go home?"

"No problem."

"There's something important I must discuss with you, and this is not the place to talk about it."

"It concerns the computer printout?"

"Yes," she said.

"Bad?" I asked.

"Very," she said.

8

We finished scarfing (although I could have managed seconds or even thirds) and ordered two more Frascatis at the bar. Carrying our drinks, we began a slow promenade through the crowd of celebrants.

"Sunny," I said, "if you spot Oliver and Mitzi Whitcomb, will you point them out to me, please."

"I'll point them out," she said, "but I won't introduce you."

"Oh? Why not?"

"I don't think that would be smart," she said grimly, leaving me to wonder what on earth she meant.

We looked in at the dance floor and there was Detective Binky Watrous essaying a tango with a rather flashy young woman. The trio was

playing "Jealously," and it was obvious Binky thought himself a reincarnation of Rudolph Valentino. It was an awesome sight and I began
laughing.

Sunny permitted herself one soft chuckle. "His partner"—she said—
"that's Mitzi."

I took another look. The wife of the CEO of Whitcomb Funeral
Homes was a stunner. She wore a tight sheath of silver sequins and her
black hair was long enough to sit on. For her to sit on, not you. She
was heavily made up and I didn't miss the lip gloss that appeared to be
phosphorescent.

I don't wish to be ungentlemanly but there was a flagrant looseness
in her dancing as if restraint was foreign to her nature. I confess her
sensuousness set the McNally testosterone flowing, but even as I reacted primitively to her physical advertisements I could not help wondering what Horace and Sarah, those aristocrats, thought of their
somewhat brassy daughter-in-law.

"Would you care to dance?" I asked Sunny.

"Some other time," she said shortly, and we continued our stroll.

It was in the living room, clamorous with phatic talk, that she
stopped me with a hand on my arm. "There's Oliver Whitcomb," she
said in a low voice. "At the bar. He's the one wearing a white dinner
jacket. He's talking to that heavy man. I don't know who *he* is."

I stared. Oliver was a good-looking chap, no doubt about it, wearing an outfit similar to mine except that his jacket had a shawl collar.
I judged him to be about forty, and his fresh complexion suggested he
was no stranger to facials. His thick black hair was as glossy as his
wife's but artfully coiffed into waves. I wondered who his barber was,
knowing it couldn't be Herman Pincus.

"I'll leave you now," Sunny Fogarty said. "Don't forget to stop at
my place on your way home."

Then she was gone and I made my way over to the bar. I finished my
wine and asked for a cognac. Oliver and the hefty man were close together, speaking quietly; I couldn't catch a word.

"By the way," I said loudly to the barkeep, "I'm looking for Oliver
Whitcomb. Have you seen him this evening?"

It was a crude ploy but it worked. Oliver turned to me and flashed
absolutely white teeth, so perfect they looked like scrubbed bathroom
tiles. The smile was more than cordial. Mr. Charm himself.

"I'm Oliver Whitcomb," he said.

"I've been hoping to meet you," I enthused. "I'm Archy McNally, the son part of McNally and Son, your attorneys."

His handclasp was firm enough but brief.

"Hey," he said, "this is great! You people have been doing a great job."

"We try," I said modestly. "I just wanted to thank you for a magnificent bash."

"Having fun, are you?"

"Loads," I assured him. "And it's only the shank of the evening."

He looked at me with a gaze I can only describe as speculative. "Listen," he said, "why don't you and I do lunch. I have a feeling we have a lot in common."

"Sounds good to me."

"Great!" he said, apparently his favorite adjective. "I'll give you a buzz."

"Fine," I said with what I hoped was a conspiratorial smile. I doubted if he'd ever call, but nothing ventured, nothing gained: an original phrase I just created. I wandered away, gripping my brandy snifter. He hadn't introduced me to his pudgy companion. But there could be an innocent reason for that—or no reason at all.

I had noticed several small, chastely lettered signs posted about: "If you wish to smoke, please step outside to the terrace or dock." And so, in dreadful need to inhale burning tobacco, I looked about for an exit to the terrace. I finally had to stop a passing servitor lugging a bucket of ice, and he pointed the way.

But before I had a chance to befoul the Great Outdoors I came upon a tottering Binky Watrous. His pale eyes were dazed and his checkered bow tie hung askew.

"Binky," I asked anxiously, "are you conscious?"

He gave me a sappy grin. "I'm in love," he said.

I looked at him. What a booby he was! "With Mitzi Whitcomb, no doubt," I said.

He was astonished. "How did you know?"

"A wild guess."

"She gave me her phone number," he said proudly. "She wants to see me again. Archy, I think she's got the hots for my damp white body."

I was about to warn him off, but then I reflected if he was able to form an intimate relationship with the nubile Mitzi he might possibly discover details of the younger Whitcombs' activities that would further our investigation.

"I congratulate you on your good fortune, Binky," I said solemnly. "Keep your ears open. Pillow talk and all that."

I don't believe he grasped what I implied, for he merely shouted, "Party on!" and staggered away in search of the nearest bar.

I found the wide, flagstoned terrace facing Lake Worth, but it was crowded with gabbling guests as intent as I on corroding their lungs. I lighted up and went down a side staircase of old railroad ties to the deepwater dock. I was alone there and could enjoy a brief respite from the brittle chatter.

I would have guessed Mr. Horace Whitcomb owned a fine, wood-bodied sloop or something similar. But moored to the dock was an incredible boat: a perfectly restored 1930 Chris-Craft mahogany runabout. It was a 24-footer, a treasured relic of the days when men in white flannels drank Sazeracs and women in middy blouses sipped Orange Blossoms while zipping about offshore waters.

I was admiring the sleek lines of this legendary craft when I sniffed the aroma of a good cigar and turned to find our host. He was holding a lighted cheroot and regarding me with a pleased smile.

"Like her?" he inquired.

"She's a pip!" I said. "Operational?"

"Fully. We used to go out frequently but then my wife became ill and . . ." His voice trailed away.

"Surely your son must enjoy piloting a classic like this."

He took a puff of his cigar. "I think not. My son's taste runs to hydroplanes and Jet Skis. You've met Oliver?"

"Yes, sir. Just a few moments ago."

"And what was your reaction?" he asked unexpectedly.

I was cautious. "I thought him very personable," I said.

"Oh yes, he is that." Horace tossed his half-smoked cigar into the lake, and I heard a faint sizzle. "His mother dotes on him."

I wanted to ask if he also doted on his son, but that would have been an impertinence.

"Tell me, Archy," he said, "do you admire things of the past?"

"Incurably addicted," I confessed. "I'm a nostalgia buff. Two of my favorite comics are Bert Lahr and Ed Wynn, though I never saw either of them perform live."

"I did," he said, "and they were even better than you think. But I was referring to antiques. I collect ship models, mostly sailing men-of-war. I have the *Chesapeake, Serapis, Victory, Constitution,* and several others. They were made by master craftsmen. I thought you might like to see them."

"I would indeed, Mr. Whitcomb. I enjoy reading about old naval battles. Wooden ships and iron men, eh?"

His smile was hard. "Exactly," he said. "Give me a call whenever you'd like to view my collection. And now I must get back to our guests. My wife has already retired and so I shall make the farewells."

"It was a marvelous party, sir," I called after him. "Thank you for having me."

He didn't turn but gave me a wave of his hand in acknowledgment. It seemed obvious he was saddened by his wife's illness. But I also detected an undercurrent of anger that perplexed me.

I smoked another coffin nail, pacing slowly up and down the planked dock, admiring the play of moonlight on the gently rippling surface of the lake. I had many sharp, jagged impressions of that MTV evening but was in too bemused a state to sort them out. I could do that on the morn when, hopefully, I would have slept all befuddlements away and awakened with a clear, concise revelation of the toil and trouble bubbling at Whitcomb's.

I finished my cigarette, drained the last drop of cognac, and went back inside with every intention of leaving immediately and hightailing it to the home of Sunny Fogarty. But there was a short delay.

I attempted to move through the throng of departing guests—all of whom were pausing to pick up their favors: crystal paperweights with a little replica of a Ford Model T encapsulated for gentlemen and, for ladies, a tiny sprig of edelweiss. You may scorn this as kitsch but think of how much more tasteful it was than if the owner of Whitcomb Funeral Homes had handed out miniature caskets suitable for pencils, paper clips, or condoms.

I was about to slip away (I really had no use for a paperweight) when a heavy hand clamped about my left bicep. I turned and faced the chubby gent who had been conversing with Oliver Whitcomb at the bar. He tugged me away from the crowd, his grip still tight on my arm. I finally shook him loose.

"Hey," he said. "Ollie tells me you're a lawyer. Right?"

He was a gloriously rumpled man wearing a wrinkled dinner jacket that looked as if he had been snoozing in it for a fortnight. He wasn't quite obese, but a lot of rare roast beef had gone into that protruding paunch, those meaty shoulders and bulging thighs.

"I'm not an attorney," I told him, trying to be civil, "but my father is. I assist him."

"Yeah?" he said with a wiseacre grin. "Like a gofer, huh?"

I kept my cool; give me credit for that. "No," I said, "not like a gofer. My duties are somewhat more extensive."

"Oh sure," he said. "Just kidding. You got a card? Maybe I can throw some business your way."

I took out my wallet and extracted a card, imagining what my father's reaction would be to a stranger telling him, "Maybe I can throw some business your way."

The fat one examined my card. "Archibald McNally," he said. "What kind of a moniker is that?"

"A serviceable one," I said. "And what is your alias?" He looked at me, startled. "Just kidding," I told him. "Like you were."

"Oh, yeah, sure," he said, and dug a creased business card from his jacket pocket and handed it over.

"Ernest Gorton," I read aloud. "Import-export."

"That's right. But you can call me Ernie."

"Wonderful," I said. "And you may call me Archy. What do you import and export, Ernie?"

"This and that."

"I hope this and that are profitable."

"Sometimes yes and sometimes no," he said. He had twinkly eyes set in a mournful bloodhound face.

"I see your business is located in Miami. That's your home?"

"Yep. You ever been there?"

"Many times."

"Next time you're in town, look me up."

"I certainly shall," I said, thinking never, never, never.

"Maybe you and me can do some business together," he said. "Have a few laughs, make a few bucks."

I had absolutely no idea what he meant and had no desire to find out.

"Nice meeting you, Mr. Gorton," I said.

"Ernie."

"Ah yes—Ernie. Now I've got to dash."

"Love the way you talk," he said. "Real fancy."

"Thank you," I said and fled.

9

Sunny Fogarty greeted me at the door of her condo holding a pilsner of beer. I made a rapid mental calculation of the number and variety of spirituous beverages I had consumed that evening, beginning with the family cocktail hour: gin martini, vodka gimlet, white wine, cognac. I reckoned a beer might push me beyond the point of no return, but then I took solace from the traditional collegiate dictum: "Beer, whiskey: rather risky. Whiskey, beer: have no fear."

Sunny ushered me into her living room, motioned me to an armchair, and brought me a duplicate of her glass of suds.

"It's Budweiser," she informed me. "I have nothing more exotic."

"Bud is fine," I assured her and swilled half my drink to prove it.

"Has the party ended?" she asked.

"It was breaking up as I departed."

"I think it went well, don't you?"

"It went beautifully. I saw no one upchuck, no one was fallingdown drunk, and there were no fights. Ergo, a successful bash. You planned it, didn't you, Sunny?"

She was embarrassed; her gaze slid away. "How did you know?"

"Mrs. Sarah Whitcomb is obviously in no condition to organize a celebration of that magnitude, and I don't believe Mr. Horace has the know-how. And Mitzi and Oliver haven't the talent, time, or the interest in arranging a jamboree like that."

"You're right," she said, "on all counts. You do see things, don't you? Well, I'm happy it went off so well. Did you personally enjoy it?"

"Indeed I did. A very intriguing evening. Binky Watrous has fallen in love with Mitzi Whitcomb."

She gave me a dim smile. "Men usually do."

"Not yours truly," I said stoutly. "I prefer to admire the lady from afar. A strong instinct for self-preservation, I suspect. And Mr. Horace invited me to view his collection of ship models."

She came alive. "Oh, they're incredible! You must see them, Archy."

"I intend to. And I met a curious bloke claiming to be Ernest Gorton. Does the name mean anything to you?"

She shook her head.

"He was talking to Oliver Whitcomb at the bar when you pointed Oliver out to me. They seem to be pals. He referred to Oliver as Ollie."

"Ernest Gorton?" she repeated. "No, I've never heard of him."

"He's from Miami and he's in the import-export business, whatever that may be. Seemed an odd sort to be a close friend of the CEO of funeral homes."

"Mitzi and Oliver have several odd friends," she said tartly. "Let me get you another beer."

"Just one more," I said, "and then I'll be on my way."

She made no reply—which I took for approval. And which only proves how fallible my judgment can be.

She brought my refill, then touched a cushion of the couch on which she was seated. "Sit over here, Archy," she said, and I noted how often her requests sounded like commands. "I have something to tell you, and it will be easier to talk if we don't have so much space between us."

I did as she asked. She had taken off her jacket and kicked away her satin pumps. She looked more relaxed than she had seemed at the party. Her tensity had thawed and her rather schoolmarmish manner vanished. She had softened; that's all I can say. Except that the two top buttons of her poet shirt were undone.

"The last time we spoke about the computer printout," she said, "I told you I could not understand why it did not include the names and addresses of out-of-state funeral homes and cemeteries to which Whitcomb's shipments were made. It was strange; that information is routinely entered on our computer."

"But it wasn't," I said.

She turned sideways to look at me directly. "It *was,* Archy, but it had been erased."

I took a gulp of beer. "You're certain?"

"No doubt about it. I caught it and then called in our computer consultant to verify what I had discovered. He agreed: someone had simply deleted that information from our records."

"Could anyone at Whitcomb's have done it?"

"You need to know a code to access our system. The code is known only by the top three executives—Horace, Oliver, and myself—and by the four department heads and our three chief funeral directors."

"Could a malicious hacker have invaded the system?"

"Of course. That's always a possibility and very difficult if not impossible to prevent. But why would a hacker *want* to delete only those specific items of information?"

"Haven't the slightest," I admitted. "But you did say you'd be able to reconstruct the missing information from the weekly reports of your funeral directors."

"That's correct," she said, "and I'm going to start on that tomorrow. But I wanted you to know that someone made a deliberate and seemingly successful effort to impede the investigation. Archy, I'm now even more certain that something very wrong is happening at Whitcomb's. It may be just dishonest or unethical but it may be criminal, and it's got to be stopped."

"No doubt about it," I agreed. "How soon will you be able to provide me with the missing information?"

She thought a moment. "It shouldn't take longer than two or three days. I'll phone you as soon as I have it."

"Fine. Those names and addresses will provide a good start. Tell me, Sunny, have you informed Mr. Horace of this inquiry and that the computers have been tampered with?"

"I have *not*," she said explosively, "and I don't intend to. And I forbid you or your father mentioning it to him. Is that understood?"

Overreacting again. I began to wonder if father's and my initial impression had been accurate: this was one squirrelly woman.

"Completely understood," I told her. "You may depend on our discretion."

I finished my second glass of beer (they were only eight ounces per) and started to rise.

Sunny gave me one of her rare sunny smiles. "Must you go?" she said.

Zing! Went the Strings of My Libido.

I set my empty pilsner on an end table and turned back. Then she was not in my arms, I was in hers. She smelled delightful.

"I should tell you," I said, "I don't kiss on the first date."

She cracked up. It was the first time I had seen her laugh with abandon and it was a joy to witness.

"I haven't heard that line since nursery school," she said when she ceased spluttering.

"*Nursery* school?" I said. "I am shocked, *shocked!* I hesitate to think of what went on by the time you got to junior high."

But of course we kissed. And kissed. And kissed. If she had an ulterior motive for coming on to me, and I suspected she had—to insure my loyalty?—I have sufficient male ego to believe what began as a manipulative ploy quickly became a more genuinely passionate experience than she had anticipated.

She was carried away. I was carried away. And we both were carried away right into her bedroom where we disrobed in frantic haste, muttering when buttons were fumbled or zippers snagged.

She owned a body as solid as the figurehead of a Yankee clipper. I don't mean to suggest she could have played noseguard for the Washington Redskins, but there was not an ounce of excess avoirdupois on her carcass. Believe me; I searched.

Our acrobatics became more frenzied, and my last conscious thought was of Binky Watrous attempting the tango with Mitzi Whitcomb. Sunny and I were doing the same thing horizontally rather than vertically. But with infinitely more expertise, I assure you. Then I stopped thinking.

I do recall that at one point during our exertions the bedroom seemed filled with light, really a soft glow. The only way I can account for it is the phenomenon of triboluminescence. Very rare and much to be desired.

I stayed in Sunny's bed until almost 2:00 A.M., during which time we consumed another Budweiser—and each other. What a loverly night that was—a fitting end to an evening of jollity. Such perfect occasions occur all too infrequently and must be sought and treasured. Remember that gem of McNally wisdom the next time someone offers you a beer.

I drove home slowly, hoping my eyelids would not clamp firmly shut before I arrived in the safety of the McNally garage. I made it and stumbled upstairs, undressing as I went, and flopped into bed with a wheeze of content. "Thank you, God," I murmured. A Category Five hurricane could have descended upon the coast of South Florida that night and I swear I would not have been aware of it. I slept the sleep of the undead.

I awoke the following day a sad Budweiser man. Listen, I know it's an ancient pun, but I was not in a creative mode that morning. Physically I felt fine, having had the foresight to pop a couple of Tylenols before collapsing into the sack. But mentally I was totally flummoxed. The Whitcomb case seemed to be growing steadily like some horrid fungus that just keeps getting larger and larger until it devours acres. The Blob That Ate Cleveland.

In addition, I was suffering from an attack of the guilts. My unfaithfulness to Connie Garcia, of course. I had committed a disloyal act and could not deny it. Well, I could to Connie but not to myself. Sighing, I blamed those treacherous genes of mine. I tell you a faulty DNA can really be hell.

I had slept a good eight hours, and by the time I finished my morning routine, breakfast was out of the question; luncheon loomed. Determined to do something—anything!—purposeful that day, I phoned Sgt. Al Rogoff at PBPD headquarters. I was told he was on a forty-eight. They wouldn't give me his unlisted home phone number, of course, but that was okay; I already had it.

I called and he picked up after the third ring.

"Archy McNally," I said.

"Good heavens!" he said. "I haven't heard from you in a week or so. I hope I haven't offended you."

"Oh, shut up," I said. "I hear you're on a forty-eight. Have anything planned for today?"

"Why, yes," he said. "I thought I might play a chukker of polo this afternoon or perhaps enjoy an exciting game of shuffleboard—if my heart can stand it."

"Funny," I said, "but not very. Al, why don't you have lunch with me at the Pelican?"

"Oh-oh," he said. "Every time you invite me to lunch I end up getting shot at."

"You know that's not true."

"It's half-true," he insisted, "and half is enough for me. I refuse to lunch with you at the Pelican Club or anywhere else. And that's definite."

I told him, "We'll have Leroy's special hamburgers with a basket of matchstick potatoes and perhaps a few pale ales."

"What time do you want to make it?" he asked.

Before leaving home I called Binky Watrous, hoping the Duchess wouldn't pick up the phone. She didn't but their houseman did, and he informed me Master Binky was still asleep and had hung a Do Not Disturb sign on his bedroom door. (I happened to know that sign had been flinched from the Dorchester in London.) I requested that Master Binky be asked to phone Archy McNally as soon as he reentered the world of the living.

"I don't know when that will be, Mr. McNally," the houseman said dubiously. "He just arrived home about an hour ago."

"Whenever," I said and hung up, wondering where my vassal had spent the night. Deep in mischief, no doubt. The apprentice shamus was becoming even more of a trial than I had expected.

10

I arrived at the Pelican Club in time to enjoy a Bloody Mary (with fresh horseradish) at the bar before Sgt. Rogoff showed up. The dining area was filling rapidly and I peeked in to see if Connie Garcia was present. Thankfully she was not. The horseradish had invigorated my spirits but not to the point where I was ready to face Connie's wrath if she had learned—as I was certain she would—that I had attended the season's first big social affair and did not invite her to accompany me.

Sgt. Rogoff finally came trundling in, wearing casual, off-duty duds. Al is a truculent piece of meat, built along the general lines of a steamroller. For career reasons he projects the persona of a good ol' boy, and he drives a pickup to aid his public image. But he is brainy, a very keen investigator, and also happens to be a closet balletomane. One never knows, do one?

We snagged a table for two in the dining room and, after some repartee with the sassy Priscilla, ordered the lunch that had lured the sergeant. Knowing our predilection, Pris served the Bass ales first, and we both took palate-tingling swigs.

"I'd like to be floating in a tank of this stuff," Al said. "Trying to drink the level down. Wasn't there an English lord or someone who did something like that?"

"Drowned in a vat of malmsey," I said, but then my mind went blank. "I can't remember who it was," I admitted.

Al looked at me reproachfully. "That's not like you, Archy," he chided. "You usually have instant recall of useless information."

"True," I said, "but that bowl of Cheerios I call my brain is not up to cruising speed this morning. I've got problems."

"Yeah? Like what?"

"Well, for starters I've taken on an unpaid assistant who wants to learn the discreet inquiry business, and he's driving me right up the wall. Binky Watrous. Do you know him?"

Rogoff took a gulp of his ale. "That twit? Sure, I know him. Last year he was charged with committing a public nuisance for riding a mule up Worth Avenue. He got off with a fine. Screwballs like him make me question the purpose of evolution. How come you tied up with an airhead like Watrous?"

"Well, he *is* a friend of mine," I explained lamely. "And he has to get a job or his aunt is liable to end his freeloading career."

"The Duchess!" Al said, laughing. He's not totally ignorant of the intricacies of Palm Beach society. "That lady is a fruitcake, too. Every year she sends the Palm Beach Police Department a subscription to *National Geographic*. How does that grab you?"

But then Priscilla brought our burgers and spuds along with a complimentary platter of sliced tomatoes and onions. The sergeant and I wasted little time in talking while we absorbed all those tasty calories. It was only when the plates were completely denuded and we were quaffing our second ales that Rogoff leaned back and said, "All right, let's have it."

"Have what?" I inquired innocently.

"Come on, Archy," he said, "don't jerk me around. Daddy taught me a long time ago that there's no such thing as a free lunch. What do you want?"

"Well, there is one little thing you can do for me."

"A little thing? Like immolation? Ixnay."

"Al, it's just a routine inquiry. One of our clients thinks someone is dipping into the till. He has his suspicions but doesn't want to risk a lawsuit for defamation if he goes to the police and it turns out he's wrong. So he asked McNally and Son to look into it first. It's really a very low-key investigation."

I wasn't exactly lying, you understand—just dissembling.

"Oh sure," he said. "That's how all your discreet inquiries begin. Then they end up on my desk. I always think of you as Archy the Jonah."

"That's not fair," I protested. "Some of your greatest successes were initiated by my preliminary labors."

"Granted," he said. "But do they all have to finish with some coked-up zombie coming at me with a machete? All right, what do you want?"

"Our client believes one of the villains ripping him off is a gent named Ernest Gorton. He runs an import-export business in Miami. I hoped you'd be willing to run a trace on him."

The sergeant finished his ale. "I can't do it officially. It's got nothing to do with the Department. But I could make some phone calls to a few compadres in Miami, who might be willing to take a look at this guy."

I fished Ernie Gorton's business card from my wallet, and Rogoff took out his little notebook closed with a rubber band. He copied Gorton's full name, address, and telephone number.

"Don't expect an answer tomorrow," he warned. "You'll be lucky if I hear back in a week or two."

"I understand that, Al," I said. "And thanks for your help."

"It was the sliced tomatoes and onions that did it," he said.

We waved goodbye to Priscilla, and I went to the bar to sign the tab while Rogoff departed in his pickup. Then I headed for the McNally Building, feeling I should at least stop briefly at my office to see if Binky had regained consciousness and had phoned to report on his previous night's misadventures.

But there were no messages on my desk and so I had little choice but to light an English Oval (first of the day) and ponder my next move. I decided it would be wise to take a nap. I had slept well but felt the McNally batteries could benefit from a short recharge. I had just finished my cig and settled down for a brief slumber when the phone shrilled me awake. Binky's call, I thought mournfully, and perfectly timed to disrupt my snooze.

But it was Sunny Fogarty, and she wasted no words.

"I'm at a pay phone outside the office," she said, speaking rapidly, "so I can talk. This morning I started checking the funeral directors' weekly reports covering the past six months. They're supposed to include invoices for out-of-state shipments with the assignee's name and address—the information missing from the computer printout I sent you. They're gone."

"Gone?"

"The shipping invoices—just vanished. Obviously someone went into the files and removed them. Damn! Now I'm sure something crooked is going on."

"It would appear so," I said carefully.

"Archy," she said, and I thought I detected a note of desperation, "what are we going to do now?"

I reflected a moment, and the McNally brain began to function on all two cylinders. "Sunny, when Whitcomb airlifts a deceased out of Florida, surely the airline keeps a copy of the invoice: nature and weight of the cargo shipped, number and date of flight, names and addresses of the shipper and the assignee."

I heard her sharp intake of breath. "Double damn!" she cried. "I should have thought of that but I'm so upset by finding our invoices have been stolen that I'm just not thinking straight. Of course the airlines will have copies."

"I'd volunteer to request that I be allowed to examine them," I said, "but I doubt very much if they'd cooperate with an outsider. I'm afraid you'll have to do it, Sunny—acting as Chief Financial Officer of Whitcomb Funeral Homes."

"You're right and I'll get on it at once. It's going to take time, Archy."

"I realize that. Meanwhile there's something you can do for me. I'd like the names and addresses of your four department heads and three chief funeral directors."

A short pause on her part. Then: "You think one of them may be involved?"

"One or more."

"I'll get the list to you immediately," she said. "Even before I start contacting the airlines. I can't tell you how relieved I am that you're on my side. We'll get to the bottom of this, won't we?"

"Absolutely," I said with more confidence than I felt.

"And Archy," she added, her voice suddenly soft, "thank you for last night."

"The pleasure was—" I started, but she hung up before I could finish.

I knew what I had to do next. Since there would be heavy expenses incurred, I felt it prudent to get the pater's permission before running up a humongous bill. I called his office. Mrs. Trelawney, his private secretary, was absent that day, sitting at the bedside of an extremely pregnant niece, and the honcho answered the phone himself.

"Father," I said, "may I see you for ten or fifteen minutes?"

"Now?" he said testily. "Can't it wait?"

"No, sir," I said. "Time is of the essence."

"What a brilliant expression, Archy," he said dryly. "Original, no doubt." He allowed himself a short chuff of laughter. "Very well, come on up."

A few minutes later I was in the sanctum sanctorum, seated in one corner of a chesterfield covered in bottle-green leather. His Majesty sat upright in the oak swivel chair before his antique rolltop desk.

"All right," he said, "get to it."

I told him everything that had happened regarding the goings-on at Whitcomb Funeral Homes since we had first been alerted by Sunny Fogarty. His expression didn't change as he listened without interrupting. I believe mein papa considers duplicity as natural a part of human nature as hope.

"You suspect there is criminal activity taking place at Whitcomb's?" he asked when I had finished.

"Yes, sir, I do."

"And what is Sunny Fogarty's role in all this?"

"Equivocal," I admitted. "She is very intent on finding out what's happening, but she is equally insistent that Mr. Horace Whitcomb not be informed of the investigation. Curious."

"Exceedingly," he concurred. "Do you think she has fears of his involvement in illegalities?"

"I simply don't know, father."

"And what do you propose doing next?"

"Sunny is going to provide me with the names and addresses of Whitcomb's executive personnel: four department heads and three chief funeral directors. I'd like to purchase their credit dossiers."

"Of all seven?"

"Actually, sir, of ten. I'd like to commission reports on Horace Whitcomb, Oliver Whitcomb, and Miss Fogarty as well. It will be costly, and because I have promised we shall not inform our client of the inquiry, it would be awkward if we billed him for an investigation of which he apparently is not aware and has not approved."

One hairy eyebrow went up as I anticipated, and the master began mulling. As I have described in previous tomes, this is a process of silent and deep reflection during which he slowly—oh, so slowly!—arrives at important decisions, such as whether or not to spread cheese on a fresh celery stalk.

"Very well, Archy," he said finally, "go ahead with the credit dossiers. If nothing comes of them, we'll eat the expense."

"Thank you, sir," I said gratefully, and escaped.

There was nothing more I could accomplish at the office and so I drove home in a surprisingly felicitous mood, warbling aloud another of my favorite songs: "Ac-cent-tchu-ate the Positive"—not only a frisky tune but an appealing philosophy as well. Much more meaningful than "Sam, You Made the Pants Too Long."

I took an early ocean swim, returned to my cell, and donned my latest acquisition: a luscious kimono of vermilion pongee. Then I set to work on my journal, for there was much to record about the affair I was not calling The Case of the Flying Dead.

I had to interrupt my labors to dress for the family cocktail hour, but after dinner I returned to work and finally, close to nine o'clock, had brought my professional diary up to date. I read everything I had scribbled, but it yielded no hint of what was transpiring at the Whitcomb Funeral Homes.

That was one mystery. Another and (to my way of thinking) more fascinating conundrum was the behavior of Sunny Fogarty. I was convinced the lady was sincere in wanting to uncover whatever skulduggery might be under way. But a sneaking suspicion also lurked that she was not telling me the whole truth, especially about her motives for sparking the inquiry.

I love puzzles like that. The conduct of *Homo saps* is a source of infinite wonder, glee, and gloom—don't you agree? I mean, there's no end to the complexities of human passions. A study of the way people act, particularly when tugged by wants and needs they cannot control, is immeasurably more captivating than, say, a game of spin the bottle.

I was brooding on the enigma of Sunny Fogarty when my mental gymnastics were brought to an unwelcome halt by a phone call. I picked up, expecting the worst. It was.

"Hi there, Archy!" Binky Watrous said in tones so excessively cheerful I wanted to throttle him.

11

I snidely remarked to Binky that I was gratified he had found time to report to his mentor, since it showed he was rapidly adopting the work ethic. Of course the chuckle-head took it as a compliment.

"Well, I didn't spend the whole night carousing, you know," he said righteously. "A gang of us left the party and went down to Mitzi and Oliver Whitcomb's place in Boca. We had a real riot, Archy, but I never forgot I was on duty, and I observed."

"Did you now?" I said. "And what did you observe?"

"Scads of swell stuff. Listen, suppose I pop over to your digs and fill you in. I've got some primo scoop."

That hooked me. "Sure, Binky," I said, "come ahead. Meet you outside."

I pulled on a nylon golf jacket and went downstairs to our graveled turnaround. I lighted an English Oval and paced slowly back and forth, watching the stars whirl overhead. It really was a super evening. The moon wasn't full but it was fat enough, and there was a cool ocean breeze as pleasurable as a lasting kiss.

About twenty minutes later my disciple pulled up in his dinged MB and promptly bummed a cigarette. Then we crossed Ocean Boulevard and went down the rickety wooden staircase to the beach. We walked close to the water to be on firm sand and headed south.

"What a crazy night that was," Binky started. "Mitzi invited me, so I couldn't refuse, could I, Archy?"

"Of course not."

"There must have been twenty of us, and no one feeling any pain. Mitzi and Oliver have this lush layout with a lot of lawn. I figure two mil at least. Marble floors, mirrors everywhere, and all the furniture is stainless steel, white leather, and tinted glass. Not exactly my cup of pekoe, you understand, but it shouted bucks."

"Do they have a staff?" I asked.

"I spotted two: a butler type and a Haitian maid, but they had to have more. I mean, that mansion is gigantic."

We strolled slowly in the moonlight, jumping back occasionally when an unexpectedly heavy wave came washing in. We saw the lights of a few fishing boats, but otherwise the sea was glimmering ink broken by a few vagrant whitecaps.

"Mucho drinking?" I inquired.

"Mucho mucho!" Binky replied enthusiastically. "I mean, they've got a wet bar that just doesn't end. But booze was only half of it."

"Oh?" I said, guessing what was coming. "What's the other half?"

"Joints and nose candy. Maybe there was heavier merchandise available, but grass and coke were what I saw. Archy, you know alcohol is my poison of choice. I smoked pot once and fell asleep, but I've never snorted. Anyway, supplies were plentiful and only a few of us were sticking to liquid refreshment."

"What about Mitzi and Oliver?"

"Higher than kites," he said. "But not as bad as some of the others. What a wild scene that was."

"Sounds like real whoopee."

"It was," he affirmed. "And it went on and on. When I finally staggered out of there a half dozen people were still partying and organizing a game of strip poker. Not my favorite sport, Archy."

"I should hope not. Binky, do you happen to recall if a man named Ernest Gorton was there?"

"Ernie? Sure he was. Hey, he's a lot of laughs."

"Was he doing drugs?"

Binky thought a moment. "I don't think so," he said. "Always had a glass in his fist, but maybe it was only one drink because I don't remember him getting smashed."

"Did he have a date?"

"Did he ever! A carrottop. Couldn't have been much more than twenty years old. Pretty enough, but to tell you the truth, Archy, she looked like a hooker to me. Naturally I didn't ask her."

"Naturally," I said gravely.

We paused, lighted fresh smokes, turned around, and began to walk back.

"Binky," I said, "I congratulate you on your keen eye. Are you going to see Mitzi and Oliver again?"

"You betcha!" he cried. "Especially Mitzi. She promised to call me and said we'll have a few giggles together."

"That's encouraging," I said. "No objections from her dear hubby?"

"Nope. He was standing right there when she said it and all he did was shake a finger at us and say, 'Naughty, naughty!' I think they have an understanding. You know? I saw him coming on to Ernie Gorton's redhead, and the two of them disappeared upstairs. Live and let live—right?"

"Right," I said, dismayed by his description of the younger Whitcombs' marital concordat. "Binky, who were the other guests? I mean, what kind of people were they?"

"Young swingers," he said. "*Rich* young swingers. Lots of Jags and Lexi parked outside. Everyone seemed to know everyone else. Just one big private club."

"Did you tell them who you were?"

"Oh sure," he said. "I told Ernie I was your assistant. He said that was interesting and invited me to visit him in Miami. Wasn't that nice of him?"

What a naif! "It certainly was nice," I said. "And did Oliver Whitcomb ask who you were and what you did?"

"Yep," he said brightly. "He wants to have lunch with me."

I said nothing. What was the use? We returned to the McNally driveway and I praised him again for the skillful job of detecting he had done, refraining from mentioning that he had let his tongue waggle too much to strangers.

He positively glowed when he heard my commendation and said that discreet inquiries were proving so enjoyable he was now firmly convinced he would make them his lifetime career. I concealed my shudder, gave him what few cigaretes were left in the packet, and sent him on his way. A cuckoo, I agree, but a lovable cuckoo, and I acknowledged his fumbling efforts might prove useful.

For the remaining waking hours of that night I resolutely refrained from ruminating on the tidbits of information divulged by my Sancho Panza. The mound of lasagna I call my brain was flaccid with the complexities it had absorbed that day, and so I treated myself to a wee marc and listened to a tape of Jimmy Durante rasping some wonderful tunes, including "Inka Dinka Doo."

I recall that just before I fell asleep I murmured the Schnozzola's famous sign-off: "Good night, Mrs. Calabash—wherever you are."

I awoke Thursday morning so chockablock with the Three Vs (vim, vigor, vitality) I was convinced the day would be a triumph for A. McNally, detective nonpareil and implacable righter of wrongs. This loopy attitude lasted for almost a half hour when disaster struck in the form of a phone call from Consuela Garcia. Before breakfast!

"You didn't invite me," she accused in the tone she uses that illy conceals her desire to transform me into a soprano. "To the Whitcombs' party."

"Connie," I pleaded piteously, "it was a business obligation. As I told you, the Whitcombs are clients. I attended with my parents and we departed early. A very dull affair."

"That's not what I hear."

My leman has a network of spies, informers, and snitches that would be the envy of the CIA. I mean, she has the uncanny ability to learn about my peccadilloes before the sheets cool off. Rarely—*very* rarely—have I been able to misbehave without news of my conduct eventually coming to her alert ears. It is a cross I have learned to bear.

"Connie," I said sincerely (I can do sincere when it's required), "I attended the party with my parents to fulfill a professional duty. We put in the requisite appearance and that's all there was to it."

"We shall see," she said darkly. "Reports are still coming in."

And she slammed down the phone. There went my ebullience. I breakfasted in a subdued mood that even buttermilk pancakes could not lighten. I drove to the office thinking of my totally unexpected and unplanned pas de deux with Sunny Fogarty on Tuesday night. I convinced myself that despite her espionage organization there was no possible way Connie could learn of my infidelity. I should have remembered Mr. Seneca's observation: "What fools these mortals be!"

I found on my desk a small sealed envelope that had been delivered by messenger. The single sheet of paper within, unsigned, listed the names, home addresses, and Social Security numbers of the four department heads and three chief funeral directors of Whitcomb's. Sunny Fogarty was prompt, organized, efficient—and had freckled shoulders.

Several words of explanation are now necessary. When I received permission from my father to commission credit dossiers on the individuals involved in the Whitcomb affair, you may have thought, in your innocence, we were merely seeking reports on their net worth, income, liabilities, and general creditworthiness. That may have been the limits of information available to us a few years ago, but no longer.

New agencies now exist—some legitimate, some a bit on the shady side—which are capable of supplying skinny of an incredibly personal nature: Your unlisted phone number. Your marital and medical history. Your shopping habits, including the brand of corn flakes you prefer. Your taste in collectibles. The types of investments you favor. The make, model, and cost of the car you drive. The size and value of your condominium or house. The name of your pet cat or dog, and how much you spend annually on said feline or canine. The duration and destinations of your vacations. Your annual expenditures on food, liquor, and clothing. Your preferences in entertainment: movies, video tapes, sporting events, theater, ballet. The extent of your gambling in casinos.

All that and more is available to interested inquirers—at a hefty price, of course—through the magic of computerized bank accounts, credit cards, mail order purchases, bar codes, and the energetic exchange of mailing lists. Surely you know that privacy is an antiquated concept. Recently, for the fun of it, I had ordered a complete dossier of myself. I was staggered by the intimate nature of the report I receieved—including the name of the Danbury, Conn., hatter from whom I had ordered my puce beret, the price I had paid, and the date of the purchase.

We may rail against this electronic intrusion into our private lives, but I do not believe it can be stopped. I foresee the day when anyone requesting a complete dossier on yrs. truly will be informed that on August 18, 1997, at 8:36 A.M., I trimmed my toenails.

Hello there, Big Brother!

I added the names and addresses of Horace Whitcomb, Oliver Whitcomb, and Sunny Fogarty to the list I had received and took it upstairs to the office of Mrs. Trelawney, the boss's private secretary. I requested it be faxed to the investigative agency we used with an URGENT label affixed thereto.

(You may feel that after caterwauling about the loss of privacy and the indecency of electronic prying, I was something of a hypocrite to take advantage of what I claimed to despise. You are correct, of course; I was acting shamefully, and in the very near future I fully intend to commit several kind and generous acts in atonement.)

"It'll cost," the beldame observed, examining my list. "Is your father aware of this, Archy?"

"He is," I assured her. "I made certain to obtain his permission."

"Smart boy," she said approvingly. "He's on his annual cut-the-costs campaign."

"I know, I know. I've been trying to reuse staples but it's difficult."

"That's no joke. He's composing a memo to all employees suggesting ways to limit the use of paper towels in the lavatories."

"From now on," I promised, "I'll dry my hands on my pants, and I suggest you do the same."

"Dry my hands on *your* pants?" she inquired sweetly. She really is a delightfully raunchy old lady.

I returned to my closet wondering how I might profitably spend the remainder of the day. The problem was solved when our lobby receptionist called to inform me that Mr. Horace Whitcomb had just phoned and requested I get back to him as soon as conveniently possible.

I called at once and identified myself to a male staffer who quavered, "The Whitcomb residence." Mr. Horace came on the line a moment later and we exchanged civilities.

"Archy," he said, "it's such a pleasant afternoon I simply cannot bring myself to make an appearance at the office and pretend I'm working. Would you care to lunch with us at twelve-thirty, say, and later I'll be happy to show you my collection of ship models."

"I accept," I said at once. "It sounds like a delightful prospect, and I thank you. I shan't be late."

I hung up, happy I had been asked but curious as to why the invitation had come so promptly. I mean, he had mentioned it casually at the party, but I had taken it as a generalized courtesy: "We must get together sometime."

But now, two days later, he had made it definite. Perhaps I too often look for ulterior motives, but if I didn't I really should be in another line of work.

12

The table had been set on the flagstoned terrace and since it faced westward we were in blessed shade. There was a flotilla of sails taking advantage of a splendid day and the ripply lake. Hobie cats were everywhere, plus a few trim sloops and one majestic trimaran. Mercifully there was not a cigarette boat in sight—or sound.

I was dressed informally, as usual, but my peony-patterned jacket didn't even elicit a snicker; these were very polite people. Mr. Horace wore a navy, brass-buttoned blazer with gray flannel slacks. Mrs. Sarah, her wheelchair pushed up close to the table, was clad in something gossamer and flowing that looked like a morning robe. A jaunty turban decorated with a single lavender orchid covered her pate.

We were waited upon by an aged servitor, he of the quavery voice, introduced to me as Jason. He moved slowly and carefully, apparently not wishing to disturb us with the creaking of his bones, but his hands were steady enough and his solicitude for Mrs. Whitcomb was admirable.

We started with kir royales, an excellent choice for lunching alfresco on such a brilliant day. I complimented my hostess on the success of her recent party. "A night to remember," I told her, and she brightened. I suspect she might have brightened even more if she had known how my memorable night ended.

"It *was* fun, wasn't it?" she said. "Everyone seemed to have a good time. Did you meet our son?"

"I did indeed. He suggested we might have lunch one day."

"Do it," she urged. "But you'll have to phone him. He's so forgetful—isn't he, Horace?"

"Yes," her husband said.

"Such a scamp!" Mrs. Sarah said and laughed. "Sometimes I wonder if he's ever going to grow up. He still gets into mischief just as he did when he was a little boy. Remember, Horace?"

"I remember," he said. "I still wish we had sent him to a military academy, but you couldn't see it."

"It would have crushed him," she said firmly. "He's such a free spirit."

I had the impression this contention was nothing new but had existed since Oliver was a mischievous little boy and would continue until he became a mischievous old geezer—if his parents lived to witness it.

Jason brought an ice bucket chilling a bottle of excellent South African Pinot blanc, a wine to die for—which, I reflected, the Whitcombs' customers were doing. Then came individual wooden bowls of lobster salad (endive and watercress) and a communal basket of focaccia with saucers of garlic-infused olive oil for dipping. That lunch, I may say without fear of serious contradiction, was superior to a Big Mac.

Mr. Horace and I ate heartily. Mrs. Sarah made a valiant effort but really just toyed with her food, forking out a few chunks of lobster meat but ignoring the greens and focaccia. One glass of wine.

"Horace," she said almost timidly, "I don't want to spoil your lunch, but I do think it best if I leave you men alone now. I better rest awhile."

He rose immediately to his feet, as I did.

"Of course, darling," he said. "Archy, continue your lunch. I'll be right back."

He wheeled her away. I slid back into my chair and poured myself another glass of that fragrant wine, wishing it was something stronger to dull a sudden onslaught of grief. The host returned in a few minutes, walking briskly, his Ronald Colman features revealing nothing of what he felt.

"She'll be fine," he told me, pulling up his chair and attacking his salad again. "We have a nurse's aide who'll take care of her. Sorry for the interruption."

"Sir," I said, then stopped, not knowing what to say.

"She insisted on joining us for lunch," he went on. "I feared it might be too much for her. But she keeps trying—which is important, don't you think?"

"Absolutely," I said. "A very brave woman, Mr. Whitcomb."

He nodded. "She is that."

"How long has your wife been ill?"

"Too long. It's been a dreadful ordeal. For everyone."

He shook off his despair and called, "Jason!" The ancient one appeared immediately and Mr. Horace gestured toward the ice bucket. "Supplies running low," he said, and a few moments later we were supplied with a second bottle along with goblets of lime sorbet and a plate of crisp anise cookies.

We finished all the edibles in sight. Even the sadness of the Whitcomb household could not blunt my enjoyment of that lunch; I gave it my 2-R rating (Ripping Repast).

"Shall we take a look at my ships now?" Mr. Horace suggested. "Bring your glass along and we'll finish the bottle upstairs."

"Sounds good to me," I said.

"My study used to be on the ground floor," he remarked as we entered the house. "But when my wife became ill and needed a wheelchair, we converted the den into her bedroom and I moved my junk upstairs. It's worked out very well."

He said it blithely, but I didn't believe him. (My father would be outraged at having *his* den moved.) I guessed Mr. Whitcomb's dispossession had been wrenching, but he struck me as a man who stoically endured setbacks and disappointments without grousing. I wish I could.

He carried the wine bottle, wrapped in a napkin to prevent dripping, and preceded me as we traipsed up that grand staircase to the second floor. The room we entered was androgynous. Even if he hadn't told me, I'd have known it had originally been designed as a lady's bedchamber; the walls were papered in a flowered pattern, the balloon drapes were chintz, and the plastered ceiling was painted with vignettes of rosy cherubim gamboling in golden meadows. I thought it all a trifle much.

But the furnishings were starkly masculine: desk, tables, and bookcases in burnished oak, all the chairs upholstered in maroon leather with brass studs. And an enormous pine etagere obviously custombuilt to fill one wall. The long, heavy shelves held Mr. Horace's collection of ship models.

Lordy, they were handsome. Not a bit of plastic to be seen, but all carefully crafted of oak, teak, mahogany, ebony. The sails looked to be fine linen, and I was certain the rigging was accurate down to the tiniest belaying pin and the exquisite miniature anchor chains.

We sipped our wine while Mr. Whitcomb gave me a short history of each ship, enlivened with a few details about the craftsmen who had built the models, working from original plans. Some of the reduced-scale copies were quite old, some of recent vintage, and I was delighted to learn there were still artisans capable of such devoted and painstaking work. The model of the clipper *Flying Cloud* was my favorite. What a beauty!

Then, the tour completed, we sat in facing club chairs to finish our wine. A civilized afternoon.

"A remarkable collection, sir," I said. "Any museum would love to have it."

His laugh was short and, I thought, rather bitter. "I expect one of them shall," he said. "Eventually. I'd hate to see it broken up and sold off piecemeal after I die. I've spent a great deal of time and money, but it's been a labor of love. I can't tell you how much pleasure these models have given me over the years. They've provided the perfect antidote to the somewhat depressing routine of my particular business."

"Your son doesn't share your enthusiasm?" I ventured.

"No," he said shortly, "he does not. Oliver has hobbies of his own."

I didn't dare ask what those might be, but I could imagine. I could also guess that despite his urbanity, Horace Whitcomb was a troubled man.

But his conversation remained light and pleasing. He related several anecdotes of sea battles between men-of-war, all of them interesting and some amusing. He was a skilled raconteur, but I had the impression he was merely repeating thrice-told tales and his thoughts were elsewhere. I presumed his wife's condition was distracting him.

But suddenly he broke off his account of the bloody engagement between the *Bonhomme Richard* and the British frigate *Serapis* off Flamborough Head. He fell silent and stared at me in what I can only describe as a contemplative, almost broody, manner.

"Archy," he said, "I understand you conduct private investigations for your father's firm."

I was startled and tried not to show it. I was certain poppa hadn't said a word about my duties to Mr. Whitcomb, and I couldn't recall mentioning them to him, his wife, son, or anyone else at the party. The fact that my profession is discreet inquiries is hardly a secret in Palm Beach, but it was a mite unsettling to learn my host was aware of it.

"That's true, sir," I said. "Occasionally I do quiet investigations when discretion is required, rather than take inquiries to the authorities and risk unwanted publicity."

"Quite understandable," he said. "You must have had many unusual experiences."

It was obviously an invitation to gab, and I was offended. Did he think me a babbler—or was he testing me?

"Most of what I do is exceedingly dull," I told him. "I wouldn't want to bore you—and naturally I must respect client confidentiality."

It was a mild reprimand and he accepted it.

"Naturally," he said, and we smiled at each other.

Wine finished, we walked down the long stairway to the ground level.

"I'll leave you here," he said. "I want to look in at Sarah. Jason will see you out."

"Thank you for a lovely luncheon," I said, shaking his proffered hand. "And for letting me view those incredible models. Please give my best wishes to your wife and my hopes for her speedy and complete recovery."

"We all hope for that," he said, but there was little hope in his voice. "Archy, you're good company. I look forward to seeing you again."

He left me and the archaic majordomo appeared out of nowhere bearing my snazzy pink panama with a snakeskin band.

"Thank you, Jason," I said. "It was a super luncheon."

"Thank *you*, sir," he quavered. "I am happy you enjoyed it."

I looked around that magnificent entrance hall, a shining vault that seemed to go on forever.

"What a wonderful home," I marveled.

"It was," he said in such a low voice I could hardly hear him. But that's what he said: "It was." Of course I thought he was referring to Mrs. Whitcomb's illness.

I drove slowly back to the McNally Building, pausing en route at a florist's shop to have a cheerful arrangement of mums delivered to Mrs. Sarah with a note of thanks. The Whitcombs were, I knew, people who honored traditional etiquette, mailed birthday and Christmas cards, and never failed to visit sick friends. My parents are similar types. I, regrettably, am not.

I hadn't been at my desk more than five minutes when Binky Watrous phoned.

"You'll never guess what happened to me," he burbled.

"You're enceinte?" I inquired.

"Better! Mitzi Whitcomb called and wants to see me tonight. Her lesser half is going down to Miami on business and she's all by her lonesome. Wants me to buy her a pizza and then we'll go dancing. How about that!"

"Sounds like you've made a conquest, laddie," I said. "Have fun but promise me one thing."

"What's that?"

"Not a word to Mitzi about our investigation of the Whitcomb Funeral Homes. Is that understood?"

"Of course."

"Not one single word," I warned him. "The lady may try to extract information in a friendly, offhand way, but you know nothing."

"About what?" he said.

I sighed. I had feared he would be a trial; he was rapidly becoming an inquisition. "About *anything,*" I told him. "Just chat her up and keep the conversation frothy and inconsequential. Do your birdcalls for her."

"Oh yeah!" he said happily. "I've got a new one—the yellow-bellied sapsucker."

"That should enchant her," I assured him. "And Binky, in the most casual way possible you might inquire what business is taking Oliver to Miami tonight. You understand?"

"Oh sure. I'll ask her."

"Don't *ask* her. Say something similar to 'Your husband must be a very busy man, driving to Miami at night.' And then wait for her reaction."

"I get it," he said. "You want me to be subtle."

"Yes, Binky, I want you to be subtle—right after you imitate the call of a yellow-bellied sapsucker."

"I can do it," he said eagerly. "I'll get the goods on Oliver."

"Call me tomorrow," I said, stifling a groan, "and tell me how you made out."

I hung up and put my head in my hands. He was going to commit a monumental balls-up, I just knew it. What concerned me most was not that Binky might reveal to Mitzi and Oliver Whitcomb that they were subjects of an inquiry by McNally & Son, but that my father might learn I was employing a certified bedlamite in one of my discreet inquiries.

I could easily envision his reaction: *both* tangled eyebrows twitched aloft, the bristly mustache drooping, and I'd get a stare that shared pain and incredulity: "Have I raised my only son to be an utter dunce?"

I felt it best to leave the McNally Building and seek solace in a slow ocean swim and the comfort of the family cocktail hour and dinner later. I'm sure it was an excellent feast, but I could not help but regard it as a condemned man's last meal.

I retired to my quarters and phoned Connie Garcia. You know, I do believe I half-hoped she had learned of my recent joust with Sunny Fogarty. If so, Connie would be aflame, steam spouting from her ears, and she would threaten me with physical punishments I don't wish to detail here, not wishing to offend your sensibilities.

No, I am not suicidal. In hoping my one-and-several might condemn me, vociferously and at length, I was merely seeking normality in a world suddenly gone awry.

13

But apparently my Dulcinea had not learned of the recent moral booboo I had committed, for she couldn't have been more affectionate. We chatted for almost twenty minutes, and our conversation was all bubbles. We ended by agreeing to meet for dinner on Saturday night and exchanged vows of love and fidelity everlasting before hanging up.

It was a puzzlement. I mean, I loved the woman, I really did, but my devotion obviously wasn't sufficient to restrain me from casting covetous eyes on others of the female persuasion. Are all men like that? I suspect we may be, and it's disheartening. Certain absolutes, such as courage, are expected of the male gender, but faithfulness is not one of them. What's worse, it's usually treated with cynical amusement while a woman's infidelity is roundly condemned.

I scribbled in my journal for the remainder of the evening, recording my impressions of the luncheon with Sarah and Horace Whitcomb. They were true patricians, I reckoned, whose breeding and bravery were being sorely tested. I thought they were enduring their trials with exemplary fortitude—which only proves how mistaken first impressions can be.

I awoke the next morning with the nagging suspicion it would prove to be an unproductive day. I was in a waiting mode: waiting for Sunny Fogarty to retrieve names and addresses from the airlines' shipping invoices; waiting for our credit agency to return dossiers on the individuals listed; waiting for Sgt. Al Rogoff to report on what he had learned about Ernest Gorton from his police pals in Miami. It was, I decided, going to be a vacant day. Hah!

Nota bene: The following times are approximate.

9:30 A.M.:

I had overslept, as was my custom, and finally clattered downstairs to a deserted kitchen, where I prepared a solitary breakfast. If memory serves—and mine usually doesn't—I found a cold pork chop left over from our previous night's dinner. I trimmed it carefully of fat and bone, and then inserted the round of meat between two toasted halves of an English muffin, with a dab of mayo. You might try it sometime. Chockful of goodness.

10:30 A.M.:

I arrived at the McNally Building to find on my desk a message that Mr. Ernest Gorton had phoned and asked that I return his call as soon as possible. I debated a moment, fearing he might invite me to visit him in Miami. I had no intention of doing that, of course, but I was curious as to why he should follow up a casual meeting at a crowded party with a call three days later. I assumed he had a motive of which I wot not. And so I phoned.

"Archy!" he said heartily. "How's by you?"

"Very well, thanks, Ernie," I said. "And you?"

"Seventh heaven," he proclaimed. "Listen, let me get right to the point." He didn't exactly say "pernt," but it was close. "When we met the other night at the Whitcomb's party, you hit me as a guy who likes wine. Am I correct?"

"Well, yes," I said cautiously. "I enjoy a glass of good wine now and then."

"I'll bet you do," he said with a sound halfway between a chuckle and a chortle. "You know anything about it?"

I was briefly nonplussed. "About wine, you mean? I do know a little, but I am no oenophile."

"Whatever the hell that is," he said. "Look, in my import-export business sometimes I luck on to a great deal and naturally I think of my close friends first."

"Naturally," I said, wondering when and how I had become his close friend.

"Suddenly I got this shipment of 1990 Chateau Margaux. That's a good wallop, isn't it?"

"An excellent drink," I assured him.

"I can let you have it for a hundred bucks," he said.

"Ernie," I said as gently as I could, "the 1990 Margaux is a fine wine, but I can buy a bottle for less than a hundred at my local liquor emporium."

"A bottle?" he said indignantly. "Who's talking bottles? I'm offering you a case."

Holy moly! I was stunned. A case of 1990 Chateau Margaux for a hundred dollars? Incredible. "Did it fall off the truck?" I said feebly.

"What do you care?" he demanded. "I got two cases left. If you want one you'll hafta tell me now. And you'll hafta pick it up. No delivery."

"Ah, what a shame," I said. "My car's in the shop, and there's no one I can trust to make the pickup. Ernie, I'll have to skip on this one, but I do appreciate your thinking of me. Perhaps we can get together if you have any marvelous bargains like that in the future."

He took rejection cheerfully. "All the time, Archy. For instance, right now I'm working on a deal for diamond-studded Rolex wristwatches. The real thing, not ripoffs. And the price will be right, believe me. Interested?"

"I may be," I said carefully.

"Great," he said. "I'll be in touch." And he hung up abruptly.

I sat there staring stupidly at the dead phone in my hand. What was that all about? Even if the Chateau Margaux was genuine and had been stolen, which I presumed it was and had been, a hundred dollars for a case was simply a ridiculous price, even for thieves attempting to fence their loot.

The only reason I could imagine for Gorton's call was an effort to concretize our relationship. But I still could not fathom his motive. I did know the man made me uneasy. I did not think him simpleminded. No stumblewit he. I was convinced he was sure of what he was doing—and I'm not sure of anything except that you can't put too much garlic on buttered escargot.

Then it occurred to me that maybe he had been testing my cupidity, just as Horace Whitcomb had tested my discretion. I was beginning to feel like a lab rat condemned to run a maze. I could only hope I would find the exit and the reward awaiting me: a nice wedge of ripe Brie.

11:15 A.M.:

I phoned Binky Watrous, eager to learn all the juicy details of his evening with the supercharged Mitzi Whitcomb. He sounded hoarse, as if he had spent too many hours imitating the call of a hypertensive parrot.

"Sore throat?" I inquired solicitously.

"Sore everything," he rasped. "Archy, I am unraveled, totally unraveled. All I want is a quick and merciful end to my suffering."

"What a shame," I said. "I was about to ask you to join me for a burger and a bucket of suds at the Pelican, but we'll make it another—"

"I accept," he interrupted hastily. "Give me an hour to get my bones in motion."

"I gather you had a riotous night."

"Times Square on New Year's Eve. I asked Mitzi to divorce Oliver and marry me."

"You didn't!"

"I did."

"And what did the lady reply to that?"

"She said, 'Let's practice first.' "

"See you in an hour," I said.

1:30 P.M.:

We had finished lunch and were dawdling over our second beers. Color had gradually returned to the pallid cheeks of my helot. When he arrived at the Pelican Club he had looked like something the cat dragged *out*. But a rare burger, a basket of FFs, and icy Rolling Rock had worked wonders; he was now his normal dorky self.

Unasked, he told me of his night with Mitzi Whitcomb. I shall not repeat the salacious details since I know you're not interested in that sort of thing. "What an orgy it was!" he concluded.

"Binky," I said, "can two people have an orgy? I thought it required a multitude."

"We had an orgy," he insisted. "Just the two of us. Archy, that woman scares me."

"But you want to marry her."

"That was last night. This morning I wanted to take a slow boat to Madagascar."

"And where was Mitzi's husband during this alleged debauch?"

"He called and said it was too late to drive home from Miami, so he was going to spend the night at Ernie Gorton's place."

Thick as thieves, those two, was my immediate reaction, and then I wondered if "thick" in that cliché meant intimate or stupid.

"Binky, did she toke during the evening?"

"Constantly," he said gloomily. "Had a pack of neatly rolled ganja. No filters."

"And what did you talk about?"

"A lot of nothing. She was flying, and I really shouldn't have had that fifth vodka. Archy, I've never met such a harum-scarum female. I've done a few irresponsible things in my life, as you well know, but she makes me look like Albert Schweitzer."

"Are you going to see her again?"

"Wild horses—" he started, but I halted him with a raised palm.

"Binky, I *want* you to see her again. As often as Mitzi wishes. I think she may prove to be a valuable source of information pertaining to the Whitcomb case. Your role will be that of a mole, boring from within. And I select my words carefully."

"Must I?" he cried. "Another night with her and I'll be calling 911 for the paramedics to come and take me away."

"Nah," I said. "You're in the full flower of young louthood and I'm certain you're capable of coping with the lady's demands. Meanwhile you will ever so cleverly be extracting delicious nuggets of inside skinny that may possibly solve the mystery."

"It will be the death of me," he pronounced gloomily.

"Rubbish!" I said sternly. "You're the lad who wants to become the Dick Tracy of Palm Beach. Here is an opportunity to prove your mettle."

"But Archy," he whined piteously, "she *bites!*"

"Bite back," I advised, and we drained our beers and left. I had a twinge of remorse watching him totter to his rusted heap, but I consoled myself with the thought that he would live to imitate the yellow-bellied sapsucker again.

2:30 P.M.:

I drove back to the McNally Building wondering about the inexplicable friendship between Oliver Whitcomb and Ernest Gorton. They seemed so unlike, and yet they were close enough to enjoy each other's hospitality—and share other goodies as well, including Gorton's carrot-topped lady friend.

I was musing on this riddle at my desk when Mrs. Trelawney called from m'lord's office.

"Archy," she said briskly, "your father is conferring with Horace and Oliver Whitcomb at the moment. The son wants to come down to your locker before they leave, just to say hello. Thought I'd alert you."

"Thank you, luv. I don't have many visitors. Perhaps I should change my socks."

"But it's only October," she said.

Oliver breezed in about ten minutes later. If he was shocked by the diminutiveness of my professional quarters he gave no evidence of it—from which I could only conclude he was extraordinarily polite (doubtful) or had seen even less prepossessing offices, hard as that was to believe.

"Great to see you again!" he said, shaking my hand with excessive enthusiasm. "Listen, I just stopped by for a minute. Father and I are having a powwow with your father."

"Oh?" I said. "No problems, I hope."

He laughed. "The opposite," he said. "We're planning an expansion to the west coast of Florida. The Naples—Fort Myers area."

"Sounds like business is booming."

"Couldn't be better," he said merrily. "People do insist on dying. Hey, how about that lunch?"

"Of course. What's a good time for you?"

"Next Tuesday," he said promptly. "Twelve-thirty at Renato's."

"I'll be there," I promised, impressed by his forcefulness. Another man sure of himself.

"Great!" he said and shook my hand again. Monsieur Charm in action. "I've got to go collect pops. I'm driving my Lotus Esprit today."

Then he was gone, leaving me to ponder his last unnecessary remark: "I'm driving my Lotus Esprit today." A bit on the vainglorious side, wouldn't you say? Similar to asking, "How do you like my eighteen-karat-gold Cartier Panther with a genuine alligator leather strap?" Too much.

But I had learned to deal with clients who possessed egos as inflated as the Goodyear blimp. Some people define their worth by their toys. I, of course, do not, although I take justifiable pride in my original Pepe Le Pew lunch box.

3:45 P.M.:

I closed up shop and cruised home in time to sluice my angst away with a leisurely ocean swim. Actually, I was not apprehensive or anxiety-ridden. But I must confess to a vague, indefinable premonition of disaster. Did you ever bite into a shrimp, taste, swallow, and get a slightly queasy feeling that you might soon be connected to a stomach pump at a local hospital?

That's the way I felt as I plowed through the warm waters of the Atlantic. I was convinced there was a clever plot in motion that was wreaking mischief, and I could not endure the thought of being hornswoggled.

14

7:00 P.M.:

Family cocktail hour.

8:45 P.M.:

Finished dinner (chicken piccata), anticipating a peaceful evening alone with my thoughts and Billie Holiday.

8:50 P.M.:

Father stopped me as I was about to ascend to my nest. "A moment, Archy," he said and motioned toward his study. He did not invite me to be seated or offer a postprandial brandy. I stood motionless as he paced, jacket open, hands thrust into his hip pockets. Our conversation became a rat-a-tat-tat interrogation.

"Any developments in the Whitcomb matter?" he demanded.

"No, sir. Nothing of any significance."

"Oliver stopped down to see you this afternoon?"

"For a few moments."

"What did he have to say?"

"That the Whitcombs are planning an expansion to the west coast. And he invited me to lunch next Tuesday."

"You accepted, of course."

I nodded.

"I presume you met Horace at the party."

"I met him then," I said, "and had lunch with him yesterday."

He stopped pacing to stare at me. "For any particular reason?"

"He said he wanted me to see his collection of ship models. I suspect he may have had another motive. He is aware of my investigative activities and seemed anxious to verify my discretion."

The guv resumed his pacing. "Curious family," he remarked. "During your conversations with Horace and Oliver, did you get the feeling of enmity between father and son? Well, perhaps 'enmity' is too strong a word. Did you sense a certain degree of estrangement?"

"Yes, sir, I did. In their thinking, their lifestyles. They're really not on the same wavelength."

"I'm glad to hear you say that, Archy. I have the same impression. Regarding their expansion into the Naples—Fort Myers area, Horace appeared to be very dubious about that project. But then Oliver began to talk of a nationwide chain, perhaps converting Whitcomb Funeral Homes into a franchise operation."

"McFunerals?" I suggested.

He allowed himself the smallest of smiles. "Something like that. Horace was outraged at the suggestion, and I had to play the role of peacemaker to keep father and son from shouting at each other. Their argument ended only when Oliver left to go down to your office. But I had a very distinct feeling there was more to their spleen than merely a difference of opinion on business strategy."

I said, "Perhaps it's partly generational and partly an attitudinal clash: young, energetic, ambitious son versus aging, conservative, risk-adverse father."

He stopped pacing again, and this time his look was almost a glare, as if I had been referring to *our* relationship. "Do you really believe that, Archy?"

"I do, sir, but I also believe there's more to it than that."

"Yes," he said, "I do, too."

He gave me a nod of dismissal and I started upstairs. I stopped at the second-floor sitting room where mother was seated at her florentine desk busily writing letters. In addition to talking to her begonias, one of the mater's favorite pastimes is corresponding with old friends, some of whom she hasn't seen in fifty years. There was one case of a school chum to whom she continued to pen chatty missives before discovering the woman had passed away two years previously.

"Mrs. McNally," I said, "I suggest you and I steal away tonight to a tropical isle. You will wear a muumuu and a lei, and I shall wear a breechcloth of coconut shells and strum a ukulele."

She looked up brightly. "Oh Archy," she said, "that sounds divine. But I can't leave tonight. On Wednesday I have an appointment with my chiropodist."

"Whenever you're ready," I said and swooped to kiss her downy cheek. Splendid woman.

10:15 P.M.:

Sunny Fogarty phoned.

"Archy," she said, "I know it's late and I apologize."

"No need," I said. "I hadn't planned to go beddy-bye for—oh, ten minutes at least."

Her laugh was tentative. "Could you manage to come over for a few moments?" she asked. "I know it's an imposition but I think it's important, and it's not something I want to write or tell you on the phone."

Paranoia again?

"Of course," I said. "I can be there in twenty minutes or so. Do you need anything? Vodka, beer, Snapple, ice cubes?"

"No, no," she said. "I've got everything."

I could have made a leering rejoinder to that but restrained myself. I combed my hair, slapped on some Romeo Gigli, inspected myself in the bathroom mirror and saw nothing to which anyone could possibly object. I loped downstairs and exited into an overcast night. There was a streaky sky with occasional flashes of moonlight, but mostly it was dark, dark, dark with rumbles of thunder to the west.

When I was a beardless youth my mother assured me thunder was the sound of angels bowling. Listen, if you don't have family jokes, who are you? And on that night, hearing the angels bowling, I wished them nothing but strikes.

10:45 P.M.:

I arrived at the Chez Fogarty wondering if Sunny's urgent summons was merely a ploy to lure me within grappling distance. Let's face it: I am a habitual fantasizer.

Do you remember those nonsensical romantic movies of yore in which a secretary (usually played by Betty Grable) removes her eyeglasses, and her bachelor boss gasps in amazement? He had always considered her a plain-Jane but now, seeing her sans specs, he realizes she is a Venus de Milo—with arms of course.

The reverse happened when Ms. Fogarty opened the door of her condo. She was wearing brief cutoffs and a snug tank top, but those were of peripheral interest. What caught my attention and set the McNally ventricles aflutter was that she wore eyeglasses, and those amber frames and glistening lenses somehow made her appear softer and unbearably vulnerable. You explain it; I can't.

She provided me with a vodka and tonic (weak) and led me into a smallish room obviously used as an office. It was dominated by what seemed to be a gigantic computer with monitor, keyboard, printer, modem—the works.

"Are you computer literate, Archy?" she asked.

"Not me," I said hastily. "I'm a certified technophobe. I have trouble changing a light bulb."

"Then I won't attempt to describe my setup here except to tell you it enables me to access the mainframe at Whitcomb's headquarters in West Palm. I frequently work at home in the evening and sometimes during the day when I need to get away from the hectic confusion at the office. Why are you smiling?"

"Your use of the term 'hectic confusion.' It's difficult for an outsider to visualize the activities of funeral homes in quite that way."

"But that's what it is," she said seriously. "Like any other business. Naturally we make certain our clients see none of it. We provide them with a quiet, dignified atmosphere."

"Naturally," I said.

"I'm still checking shipping invoices at the airlines, and I have nothing definite to report on the names and addresses of consignees to whom all those out-of-state shipments were made by Whitcomb. But this evening I started reviewing our records of the past six months. I was trying to discover how and by whom the information we want was deleted from the main computer."

"Any luck?"

"No," she said, and I could see the failure angered her. This was not a woman who took defeat lightly. "But I did find something so extremely odd I thought I better tell you about it. Would you like another drink?"

"Please," I said, holding out my empty glass. "A bit less tonic would be welcome."

"Sorry about that," she said, grinning at me. What a *nice* grin.

She returned with a refill that numbered my uvula. "Wow," I said, "that'll send me home whistling a merry tune. Now tell me: What did you find on your handy-dandy computer that was so extremely odd?"

"As I'm sure you're aware, we require a death certificate signed by the doctor in attendance before we prepare the deceased for burial, cremation, or shipment elsewhere. Whoever fiddled the weekly reports from our three chief funeral directors neglected to remove copies of the death certificates from the records. I scrolled through them and noticed one physician had signed an extraordinary number of death certificates for all three funeral homes."

"Remind me not to consult him," I said.

She ignored my tepid attempt at levity. "His name was on a surprising number of certificates," she went on. "We deal with a large number of doctors, of course, but none of them even came close to providing the volume of certificates this man has."

"In other words, a lot of his patients are turning up their toes? And they're all being delivered to the Whitcomb Funeral Homes?"

"It appears so. After noting that, I did some cross-checking and discovered that all the deceased whose death certificates were provided by this particular physician were being shipped out of Florida for eventual interment elsewhere."

I took a gulp of my drink. A big gulp. "Do the certificates signed by this one doctor account for all the increase in Whitcomb's out-of-state shipments?"

"Not *all*," she said. "But most. We're talking, like, ninety percent."

We stared at each other, and I drew a deep breath. "You're right," I said. "Extremely odd. May I have the name and address of Dr. Quietus."

"I wrote it out for you," she said and handed me a slip of paper. The first thing I saw was that it was written in lavender ink. I would have guessed Sunny Fogarty used jet black, but she was a woman of constant surprises.

The medico's name was Omar K. Pflug, and his office was in Broward County.

"Odd name," I commented.

"Is it?" she said offhandedly, and once again I had the impression she knew more than she was telling me. But I simply could not conceive a reason for her secretiveness.

"I shall visit Dr. Pflug," I said. "Not for professional advice, I assure you. I wouldn't care to end up on your computer."

She smiled. "Let's move into the living room, Archy. We'll be more comfortable there."

And so we were, sitting at opposite ends of that long couch, turning to face each other. It was then I decided to confront her. It wasn't a sudden resolve or surge of bravado. She had slugged my second drink; it was really her fault. (Are you familiar with Henry Ford's comment about a colleague?: "He took misfortune like a man. He blamed it on his wife.")

"Sunny," I said boldly, "I must tell you I have the feeling you're not revealing all you know about this matter. I'm not implying you're lying, only that you are deliberately holding back certain things that might possibly aid the investigation."

She slowly removed her eyeglasses and became once again the sovereign and rather bristly woman I had imaged.

"That's nonsense," she said sharply. "I've told you all you need to know."

"Why don't you let me be the judge of that?" I said. "Try telling me *everything*. I'm quite capable of separating the raisins from the rice pudding."

She turned her head away. "I want to protect my job," she said. "I told you and your father that from the start."

"So you did. It's a valid reason for your reticence, Sunny, but I don't believe it's the entire reason. You're stiffing me and I'd like to know why."

There was a silence that seemed to last for an hour, although I don't suppose it was more than a few moments. Then she sighed and faced me again.

"There are some things, Archy," she admitted. "But I swear to you they have absolutely nothing to do with your inquiry. Will you trust my judgment?"

"I'd rather trust mine."

Then she flared. "Impossible!" she almost spat at me. "If you insist on knowing, perhaps we should end this right now."

I drained the vodka bomb she had prepared. "Perhaps we should," I said, rising. "I'll inform my father that I've been unable to discover any evidence of wrongdoing at Whitcomb's and recommend we close the case."

It shook her.

"Archy," she said pleadingly and held out a hand to me. "Don't do that. Please. I admit I haven't been as forthcoming as I might have been, but I do have a good motive, believe me. And it doesn't affect the investigation; I swear it doesn't. Don't leave me in the lurch now, Archy. I don't know what I'd do without you."

What red-blooded American boy could resist an appeal like that? Not this boy.

"All right, Sunny," I said. "I'll stick around awhile and see what happens."

She gave a little yelp of relief, bounced to her feet, and rushed to give me a chaste peck on the cheek. I was glad she hadn't replaced her specs or I might have thrown myself upon her with a hoarse cry of brutal concupiscence.

But I knew there was to be no nice-nice that evening. She promised to inform me of the results of her inspection of the airlines' shipping invoices. I promised to tell her whatever I could uncover about Dr. Omar K. Pflug.

Just before I departed she donned those damnable eyeglasses again, and my final vision was of a stalwart spectacled woman wearing brief cutoffs and a snug tank top.

Midnight:

Fantasy, fantasy, all is fantasy. But what would life be like without sweet dreams?

15

It was a very virtuous Saturday. I awoke in time to breakfast with my parents. I played eighteen holes with a trio of cronies and never did I request a mulligan. I lunched at the country club, returned home for an energetic ocean swim, and dressed for my dinner date with Consuela

Garcia. And not once during those active twelve hours did I imbibe an alcoholic drink. I was so proud—and so thirsty.

Connie and I met at La Veille Maison in Boca, and because the snowbirds had not yet arrived in any great numbers we were able to snag that snug little room (one table) to the right of the entryway. We immediately ordered champagne cocktails, just to get the gastric juices flowing, and Connie studied the menu while I studied her.

As usual, she looked smashing. She was wearing a black slithery something held aloft by spaghetti straps. It wouldn't have been out of place in a boudoir. In a cozy public dining room it unnerved our waiter and added zest to my already ravenous appetite. We ordered sautéed pompano with pecan sauce but I knew, looking at my companion, that delightful dish would leave my hunger unassuaged.

Our conversation was casual and gossipy during dinner. But then, while we were lolling with espresso and tots of B&B, Connie remarked, "By the way, your pal Binky Watrous was seen dancing up a storm with Mitzi Whitcomb at a local disco. My informant reports both of them looked zonked."

"No kidding?" I said. "Old Binky is moving in fast company."

"Too fast for him," Connie said. "I know Binky. He's a sweet boy but nebbishy. Mitzi will chew him up and spit him over the left field fence."

"A barracuda, is she?"

"I don't really think so, Archy. Not from what I hear. I mean, she doesn't deliberately set out to destroy men. She just doesn't care. You know? She flits hither, thither, and yon, and thinks all her temporary partners do, too. But some of them get hurt."

"Not Binky. He's a bit of a flit himself."

"I hope you're right."

I thought I was but I began to wonder. Could my bird-calling chum have surrendered his heart to this Blue Angel? He was a mental flyweight, but I didn't want him wounded. My good deed—accepting him as an apprentice in the arcane profession of discreet inquiries—began to give me an attack of the Galloping Guilts. I decided I better attempt to cool Binky's ardor and turn him to more profitable pursuits. Tatting, for example.

We strolled out to our cars. You may think it curious that we both drove separate vehicles and met at the restaurant, rather than my calling for her at her home as a gentleman should. But Connie preferred the two-car arrangement, I suppose, because it gave her independence. It certainly served her well on those occasions when our dinner dates ended in turbulent conflicts—usually the result of her having learned of my misconduct.

"Archy," she said, "don't bother following me home. I'll be okay. And I want to get to sleep early. I've got a family thing in Miami tomorrow. One of my cousins is getting married. Sorry about that, pal."

"Sorry about the marriage?"

She laughed and punched my arm. "You know what I mean: sorry I can't ask you up for fun and games."

I was tempted to quote the remark attributed to Voltaire: "I disapprove of what you say but will defend to the death your right to say it." Instead, I just caroled, "We'll make it another time."

"Of course we will," she agreed and gave me a warm, sticky kiss before we parted.

And so I drove home alone on that virtuous Saturday. I'm sure you know what was giving me the glooms. No f&g with Sunny Fogarty on Friday night. No f&g with Connie Garcia on Saturday night. I feared the small tonsure on the crown of my noodle might be more serious than I had imagined. You'll admit two spurns in a row can be daunting to an always hopeful lothario.

But I am happy to report the day ended on an uptick. I arrived home, disrobed, and phoned Connie to make certain she was safe, sound, and behind a bolted and chained door. She was.

"Oh Archy," she wailed. "I made such a horrible mistake tonight."

"You didn't order a second B and B?"

"No, silly. I didn't insist you come home with me. Stupid, stupid, stupid! I wish you were here right now."

"Another time," I said grandly. "I've just undressed and am deep in volume three of *The Decline and Fall of the Roman Empire*. Exciting stuff. Otherwise I'd be happy to pop over. But another night awaits us."

"Promise?"

"Of course," I assured her.

We had no sooner hung up when my phone jangled. I thought it might be Ms. Garcia demanding to know the exact date of that promised night, but it was Sunny Fogarty.

"Archy," she said, "I want to apologize."

"Whatever for?"

"Last night. I acted very foolishly and knew it the moment you walked out. I should have asked you to stay. Am I forgiven?"

"Of course," I said grandly. Magnanimous me!

"I suppose it's too late to invite you over now. Isn't it?"

" 'Fraid so," I said. "I'm unclad and engrossed in the seventh volume of *The Original Journals of the Lewis and Clark Expedition*. Fascinating stuff. But there will be other nights."

"Promise?"

"Absolutely," I assured her.

And then grinning, I drank a marc, smoked an English Oval, and listened to the original cast recording of *My Fair Lady*. I went to bed with my self-esteem healed and intact.

Continuing my righteous weekend, I accompanied my parents to church on Sunday morning. I was rewarded by the sight of an awesome contralto in the choir and immediately lost my senses. She was quite tall, broad-shouldered, with hair cut so short it might have been razored by a Parris Island barber. Fascinating woman, and I kept staring at her while listening to a sermon exhorting us to seek the beauty of God's work on earth and be comforted thereby. Oh, how true, how indubitably true!

I thought I might audition for the choir the next time they had a casting call, but then I realized my chances were nil. I mean, my singing voice is serviceable for barroom ballads, but when it comes to such tunes as "Lead, Kindly Light," you want a tenor with a better instinct for pitch—and more religious fervor than possessed by your humble scribe.

I arrived home still pondering how I might wangle an introduction to that impressive contralto. Ursi Olson told me Mrs. Sarah Whitcomb had phoned and asked I return her call. Father had retired to his study to begin excavating the national edition of *The New York Times*, and so I trudged upstairs to take off my Sunday go-to-meeting costume and call Mrs. Whitcomb.

"Archy," she said, "I do hope I'm not disturbing you."

"Not at all, ma'am. I just returned from church."

"Oh? Do you attend regularly?"

"No," I said.

She laughed delightedly. "Didn't think so," she said. "I've given it up since I've been anchored to this ridiculous chair on wheels. But the pastor insists on dropping by regularly to provide what I'm sure he thinks of as 'spiritual solace.' Dreadful man. Archy, I called for two reasons. First, I want to thank you for the lovely flowers you sent."

"A very small token of my gratitude for a marvelous luncheon."

"Well, it was very thoughtful of you. The second thing is a request. Horace has gone to his club for an afternoon of golf that will take hours. I'd dearly love to have a chat with you—just the two of us—and I wondered if it might be possible for you to come visit for an hour or so."

"Of course," I said promptly, figuring I could return home in time for our Sunday dinner—an early afternoon feast usually followed by a major nap by all the McNallys. "I'll be there in half an hour, Mrs. Whitcomb."

"Sarah," she said. "You *must* call me Sarah. I'll have Jason chill a bottle of this year's Fleurie Beaujolais. Will that do?"

"I'll be there in twenty minutes, Sarah," I vowed, and her giggle had a girlish quality.

I hurriedly pulled on informal duds and bounced downstairs. I paused at the kitchen to see what Ursi and Jamie were preparing. I began to salivate, for they were working on quarters of glazed duckling to be served with a cider sauce.

"Don't you dare serve dinner without me," I warned them. "Be back in an hour. And would you put out some of that cranberry relish, please."

I was at the Whitcombs' palazzo in slightly more than twenty minutes, but the trip seemed to take much less time because I was dreaming about Amazonian contraltos and glazed ducklings. I admit my mind doesn't always work in lucid ways—but neither does yours.

The arthritic Jason met me at the door and slowly—oh, so slowly!—conducted me to the terrace where Mrs. Whitcomb was seated in her wheelchair at a shaded table covered with a jazzy abstract-patterned cloth. An ice bucket, complete with uncorked bottle, was set nearby, and my hostess's glass was half full—or half empty.

She gave me a winsome smile and turned up her face. "Kissy," she commanded, and I leaned to buss her cheek.

She was wearing her usual turban, in an indigo denim this time, and another of her voluminous, filmy gowns that stirred occasionally in a breeze coming off the lake. I took the chair opposite her. Jason, swaddling the dripping bottle in a napkin, added to Mrs. Whitcomb's glass and then filled mine. He departed and I sipped the nectar.

"How do you like it?" Sarah asked.

"Heaven," I pronounced.

"Well, you did go to church this morning," she said mischievously, and I realized again this woman might be ill but her wit hadn't dulled.

"Archy," she said, "tell me something: Are all men idiots?"

I considered that query very, very carefully while savoring another taste of the young Beaujolais. "Perhaps 'idiots' is too harsh a condemnation, Sarah," I said. "But I agree that most men are limited."

"Limited," she repeated. "Yes. Exactly. I knew I could depend on you."

Then she was silent, staring out over the water. It was a thousand-yard stare, and I knew she was not seeing lake, shore, or tacking sailboats.

"I shouldn't bother you with my problems," she said finally.

"If not me—whom? If not now—when?" I tried to say it lightly and was rewarded with a wan smile as she turned to face me.

"All right," she said. "Archy, I love my husband dearly, and I love my son dearly. The two are so unlike—really from different planets—but up to about six months ago they had a—what's it called? A modus something."

"Modus vivendi?" I suggested.

"That's it! They had a sort of unspoken compromise. A live-and-let-live thing. They accepted and loved each other, I believe, even if their lifestyles are so opposite. Horace is a very stiff-necked man. He has his standards."

"I am familiar with the type," I murmured, thinking of my liege.

"Oliver is a hell-for-leather boy. Always has been. And yet the two of them managed to coexist. Horace took Oliver into the business and he's performed brilliantly. Of course there have been disagreements, I can't deny that, but nothing serious. Until, as I said, about six months ago when their relationship became cold and nasty. Their trivial arguments have become rancorous. Spiteful. Sometimes they say things to each other that frighten me. Archy, I'm not asking for your sympathy or pity, but I know I'll be gone soon and I want my son and his father to be close and cherish one another when I'm no longer here to serve as umpire or referee or whatever you want to call it."

She stared at me: a very resolute stare. I had the impression I was listening to this doomed woman's last will and testament.

"Sarah," I said softly and reached across the table to clasp her hand, "I'm sure this is a very real problem that's troubling you. But it's such a personal family matter. How can I possibly help?"

"I know my son is a charming rascal," she said. "But I refuse to believe he could do anything seriously wrong. Nothing unethical or illegal or anything like that. He just *couldn't.* He's my son and I know he's incapable of evil. And yet his father is now treating him with what I can only call suspicion and contempt, as if Oliver might be committing some horrible crime. That's just absurd!"

Her distress was obvious. Hers were not merely the fretful complaints of a dying woman; she was deeply concerned and sharp enough to sense that what was occurring between husband and son was a preliminary tremor that might presage a destructive quake.

"Archy," she said quietly, and our conversation became a whispered dialogue on a drowsy, sunlit midday, "I understand you do investigations for your father's firm."

"Yes, Sarah," I said just as lazily, "that's true."

"I'd like to employ you," she said, looking at me directly. "At whatever rate you name. To see if you can discover what is happening between Horace and Oliver. Neither will talk to me about it; they treat me like a brainless invalid, which I definitely am not! Since both are unwilling to answer my questions, I want you to find out what's going on. I don't expect you to make recommendations on how their quarrel may be resolved; that's my job. But I can't begin until I know the cause. I need information. Will you try to provide it? Our arrangement will be known only to us."

I finished the bottle into her glass and mine, knowing as I poured that I was about to do something exceedingly foolish. But I really had no choice, did I?

"I shall do as you ask, Sarah," I said. "With the understanding it will be an attempt with no guarantee of success. And I want to hear no more mention of rate, charges, or billing. This is a small service for a beautiful woman I love."

Her smile was radiant as she lifted her worn face to me. "Kissy," she said, and so I did.

I drove home in a contemplative mood, musing on the promise I had just made to that wounded woman. Naturally I believed the conflict between Whitcomb *pére et fils* was rooted in the financial matter my father and I had discussed: Oliver wanted to create a national chain of funeral homes as rapidly as possible; his father thought it a loony idea not worth discussing. I had mentioned nothing of this to Sarah, of course, respecting client confidentiality.

At that moment I really thought I had two discreet inquiries in progress: investigations into the exceptional profits of the Whitcomb Funeral Homes and into the enmity between the president and the chief executive officer.

Exactly what do people mean when they speak of "a pretty kettle of fish"? I've never seen one—have you? This entire Whitcomb affair was rapidly becoming an ugly kettle of fish.

Fortunately I arrived home in time for the glazed duckling.

With cranberry relish.

16

I started phoning Binky Watrous early Sunday evening, called every half hour, and eventually found the lad at home shortly after 10:30 P.M.

"Archy," he said, "if you value our friendship, make this brief. I am flogged, utterly flogged, and if I don't get some shut-eye I doubt if I shall live to see the sun rise over the yardarm tomorrow."

"Binky, old sod, what have you been up to?"

"We flew to Ocala early this morning."

"Who is 'we'—or who are 'we,' whichever is grammatically correct."

"Me, Mitzi, Oliver, Ernie Gorton, and some other people whose names fortunately escape me."

"You *flew* to Ocala?"

"We did. On a private jet that belonged to someone."

"And why did you fly to Ocala?"

"Oliver wanted to look at a horse."

"He could have stayed in Boca and looked at a poodle."

"You don't understand, Archy. He's thinking of buying this horse."

"Ah," I said. "And did he?"

"He was impressed. It's a two-year-old with good bloodlines. It was a nice horse. I fed it a carrot. And then we partied. At the home of the guy who owns the horse and then on the flight back to Palm Beach. I can state definitely that the grape and the grain are not a marriage made in heaven. Good night, sleep tight, and don't let the bedbugs bite."

"Wait a minute," I said hurriedly. "I expect to see you in my office at ten o'clock tomorrow morning."

His moan was piteous. "Could we make that noon, Archy?" he pleaded. "You want me up to speed, don't you? And I figure twelve hours' sleep will do it."

I agreed to noon on Monday, but I wasn't certain sleep would bring Binky Watrous up to speed. A frontal lobotomy might do the trick.

As I expected, he didn't show up at noon on Monday, but by one o'-clock we were heading south. We took my Miata since I didn't feel Binky was in any condition to navigate even a Flexible Flyer. He had the look of a man brought low by excess. Even the bags under his eyes had bags, and his natural pallor exhibited a greenish tinge that suggested mal de mer. But I was not displeased with his appearance; it fitted the scenario I had devised.

"Where are we going?" he croaked. "And why?"

"We are driving to Broward to see a doctor."

"To cure me?" he said hopefully.

"No, Binky, not to cure you. Only a vow of lifelong abstemiousness might do that. This particular doctor has signed an immoderate number of death certificates submitted to Whitcomb Funeral Homes. And all his allegedly defunct patients have been shipped elsewhere for burial."

"Beautiful. I don't suppose he has much chance of being voted Physician of the Year. What's his name?"

"Omar K. Pflug."

"Impossible."

"Certainly improbable," I agreed. "Although I once heard of a professor of anatomy named Lancelot Tush. Now here's the script I have planned for our visit to Dr. Pflug. You are to play the starring role."

I explained the scam I had devised. Binky was to claim to be a visiting tourist who had arrived from New Jersey with his elderly father only two days ago. They were staying at a nearby motel and the father, who had a long history of heart problems, had unfortunately passed away. Since there had been no physician in attendance, Binky was ignorant of how he might obtain an official death certificate that would enable him to ship his father's remains home to the family plot in Metuchen. The people at the motel had recommended he consult Dr. Pflug.

Binky listened as we sped southward on Federal Highway. It was a so-so day: a lot of greasy clouds with occasional flashes of sunlight. The breeze was right out of a sauna and smelled of sulfur. We drove through one sprinkle of rain but it didn't last long.

"Archy," Binky said, "why are we doing this?"

"To test the bona fides of Dr. Pflug. We are dangling bait to see if he bites. You are to tell him that money is of no importance; your only concern is to get your deceased father home to his final resting place as quickly as possible. All you want from the doctor is a signed death certificate and the recommendation of a funeral home that can handle the details. Think you can play the part of a bereaved son?"

"Of course I can," he said, perking up. "I'll do it just as you told me. No problem."

It took some scouting to find the office of Dr. Omar K. Pflug, and both Binky and I were startled by its location. It occupied the rearmost unit of a grungy strip mall on Copans Road, and I would not care to shop there after nightfall (or even at high noon) unless accompanied by a heavily armed platoon of Army Rangers or Navy Seals.

We didn't stop immediately but made a short tour of the neighborhood until we found a rather decrepit motel, the name and address of which could be used in our planned deception. We then returned to Dr. Pflug's office, parked, and marched up to the door.

I halted Binky for a moment. "Remember," I instructed, "you are a grieving son whose beloved father has just departed for realms where the woodbine twineth. You are racked with grief. If you can manage to stifle a sob or wipe away a tear, it would help."

"Trust me," he said. "I can handle it. I'm a great actor. I once impersonated the Shah of Iran at the Pierre in New York."

"Did it work?" I asked.

"Nope," he said cheerfully.

We pushed in, ignoring a large, hand-lettered sign that declared "By

Appointment Only." The waiting room was definitely not designed to soothe nervous patients. The furniture seemed to have been hastily constructed of unpainted plywood except for two chairs and a couch of dented tubular steel upholstered in an acidic green plastic that made my molars ache. I found the wallpaper of screaming parrots especially loathsome.

There was a young woman lounging behind a make-shift desk. She was painting her fingernails a violent crimson, and although dressed in a nurse's whites she was totally unlike any nurse I had ever seen. Her cap was perched atop a pile of orangy hair and her jacket was carelessly (or deliberately) unbuttoned to hint at the bounties within.

I heard Binky gasp and thought it no more than his usual reaction to any charlotte russe of legal age. I found the lady comely enough but considered her sharp features a mite off-putting.

"Yes, gentlemen," she said, looking up with a vacant smile. "What can I do for you?"

I waited for Binky to demonstrate his claimed histrionic ability.

"My pop died," he blurted.

I could have strangled the sap. He had, I realized, all the thespian talents of Popeye, and my hopes for a successful investigation of Dr. Pflug went into deep six.

But the nurse didn't seem discombobulated. "Sorry to hear that, sir," she said chirpily. "But if your father passed, there's not much we can do for you. I mean, it's too late to consult a doctor, isn't it?"

"It's a private matter," I said hastily. "Could we talk to the doctor? It'll only take a few minutes."

She stared at me, obviously debating whether or not to give us an immediate heave-ho.

"I'll see if the doctor is available," she said finally, rose, and sashayed into an inner office. A googly-eyed Binky watched her go.

"Imbecile!" I hissed at him, but he paid no attention.

In a moment we heard a sudden shout of male laughter from within, followed by what I can only describe as a torrent of giggles, male and female. We waited patiently and eventually the nurse emerged adjusting her starched cap, which was hanging rakishly over one ear.

"The doctor will see you now," she said primly.

We entered an inner office which had all the warm ambience of a subway loo. There were a few medical machines in white enameled cases. I could not identify them, although one might have been a cardiograph. The most striking furnishing was a life-size skeleton of plastic, held upright on a metal support that seemed to have sagged, for Mr. Bones appeared to be dancing a jig.

The man seated behind the bare desk had a head that looked like a huge matzo ball: totally hairless, and the face was soft, doughy and dimpled. But it was the eyes that caught my attention. His gaze wavered and never stopped: up and down, left and right, directly at us and then sliding away. He looked as if he was trying to follow the path of a housefly.

This man, I immediately concluded, was stoned out of his gourd. I couldn't guess his drug of choice, but I had no doubt he was gone and drifting.

"Dr. Pflug?" I inquired.

It took him a beat or two to remember who he was. "I am Dr. Omar K. Pflug," he said at last, smiling with triumph. "And who are you?"

Binky launched into his spiel, and to my delighted surprise he delivered it in earnest tones just as he had been coached: His elderly father had died suddenly and a death certificate was needed as well as the name of a funeral home that would facilitate shipping the deceased to a family plot in Metuchen, New Jersey.

Dr. Pflug tried hard to concentrate on Binky's tale of woe.

"Your father?" he asked.

"Yes, sir."

"Croaked?"

"A few hours ago."

"Where is the corpus now?"

Binky explained the body lay in a nearby motel suite. It had been the motel owners who suggested we consult Dr. Pflug.

That flickering glance swung to me. "And who might you be?" he said, not much interested.

"A close friend of the family," I answered. "Eager to provide any assistance I can."

"Air-conditioned?" he said.

"Pardon?" Binky said, totally bewildered.

"Where the deceased presently resides."

"Oh yes," I assured him. "The motel suite is very chilly."

"Good," he said. "Then he'll keep awhile. I'll be very busy this afternoon. At the beck and call of my dear patients, you know. Perhaps I can make it in an hour," he added vaguely. "Maybe two or three. Give me the address. Meet me there and I'll make it official."

"We'll get a signed death certificate?" I pressed.

"Why not?" he said. "If he's as dead as you say. And I suggest Whitcomb Funeral Homes. Lovely people. Very efficient. Very understanding. Write down the name and address of the motel. And the room number where the departed lies at rest."

I took out my gold Mont Blanc but there was a moment of embarrassment because he had nothing to write on, not a single scrap of paper, not even a prescription pad. Finally he dug into the wastebasket beneath his desk and came up with a *Daily Racing Form.* I scribbled the name and address of the motel on the margin of the front page.

"What time, doctor?" Binky asked.

Pflug's flickering stare settled on him again. "Time?" he said. "For what?"

"When we can meet at the motel," I explained slowly. "And you can sign the death certificate."

That unfocused gaze shifted to me and he floated away. "Surely that's not necessary," he said and began to yawn, great jaw-cracking yawns. He shook his head and the flesh on his fat face waggled. "If you say he's gone, he's gone. I don't take credit cards. Or out-of-state checks."

Binky was completely confused, but I knew where the doctor was coming from and I was delighted. Druggie or not, he had been suckered.

"How much, doctor?" I asked him.

"A thousand," he said, squinting at the ceiling.

"We'll be back here with the cash in an hour," I lied. "And to pick up the death certificate. Thank you for your kind cooperation, doctor."

"Thank you, doctor," Binky said humbly.

"Twenties and fifties," Pflug said, glaring at that droopy skeleton. "Jacksons and Grants."

We left, never having shaken his hand, and moved out to the waiting room. The nurse had finished lacquering her nails and was talking animatedly on the phone. She flipped a hand at us as we departed. "Ta-ta!" she sang out.

We stood alongside the Miata in the parking area.

"Got him!" I said exultantly. "The guy is a dyed-in-the-wool wrongo. Strictly a doc-for-rent. Binky, I despaired of you at first, but then you performed brilliantly. I congratulate you."

"She shook me at the start," he said. "The nurse."

"Yes, I saw you making goo-goo eyes at her. But she's not that attractive."

He looked at me with a shaky grin. "Archy, you don't understand. She's Ernest Gorton's carrottop. His date at the wild party Mitzi and Oliver had at their place after his parents' reception. Oliver went upstairs with her later."

"Ah-ha," I said. "The plot curdles."

17

We stopped at a Deerfield joint for an enormous platter of barbecued ribs and a carboy of beer. While enjoying an hour of unalloyed gluttony we discussed which addiction it was that caused Dr. Pflug to act in such an irrational manner. Binky thought it might be cocaine. I thought it might be the nurse.

On the drive back to Palm Beach I gave Binky his next assignment.

"Look, gramps," I said, "you acquitted yourself with distinction this afternoon, and as a natural progression in your on-the-job training I think it's time you take on an independent inquiry with no assistance from yours truly."

"You want me to interrogate the nurse?" he said eagerly. "Force a confession?"

"No," I said sternly, "I do not want you to cozen Ms. Carrottop at all, except possibly to learn her name, which may prove useful in the future. What I want you to do is run a trace on Dr. Omar K. Pflug. Is he licensed to practice in the State of Florida? What are his antecedents? Where is he from, and has he ever been disbarred elsewhere? What was his education, and where did he receive his medical training? Any malpractice suits against him? Any criminal record? Where does he live? Is he married? In other words, I need a complete dossier on that reprehensible quack."

"Archy," he said plaintively, "how do I find out all that?"

"Ask questions," I told him. "You and the Duchess have a family physician, do you not?"

"Oh sure. Old Doc Fellows. He's a bit of a codger but a nice man. Every time I have a checkup he gives me a Tootsie Roll."

"He knows you," I said. "Start with him. Tell him a friend of yours wants to investigate the legitimacy of a new doctor he's thinking of consulting. Ask your family physician how this imaginary friend should go about it. What State licensing boards to phone, what professional organizations to contact, how he can get a report on the new doctor's medical education and competence."

"I guess I can do all that," Binky said doubtfully. "But isn't there an easier way to handle it?"

"No," I said, "there isn't."

There was, of course, but I didn't want to tell a beginner national agencies could provide all the poop required in twenty-four hours—for the payment of a substantial fee.

I was not being mean or trying to create unnecessary labor for my freshman student. I merely wanted him to learn the nitty-gritty of investigation before he discovered how modern technology has rendered obsolete the role of the literary PI. Computers have replaced Lew Archer, the Continental Op, and their brethren. And the Compaq DeskPro/M Pentium doesn't drink bourbon.

We separated in the garage of the McNally Building. Binky chugged away in his bruised Cabriolet, and I went upstairs to my office, dreaming that the chore I had off-loaded onto my lieutenant would keep him out of my tousled locks for at least a week.

I found on my desk a plump FEDEX envelope from the agency I had faxed, requesting financial reports on the principals involved in the Whitcomb ragout. I lugged the bundle down to the garage, tossed it into the Miata, and headed for home, sweet home. It was then twilightish and what started as a so-so day had definitely become melancholy. It wasn't raining, but the pewter sky looked ready to weep at any moment. I decided against an ocean swim and instead went directly to my dormitory and flopped onto my bed for a short snooze. First a balding spot and now an afternoon nap! What was happening to the debonair, vigorous A. McNally we all know and love? Was I becoming a young geezer? Perish forbid!

Morale had been rejuvenated by the time I awoke. I showered, pulled on casual duds, and galloped downstairs in time for the family cocktail hour. That went well and a dinner of broiled Maine lobster went even better. The noble crustacean was nestled on a couch of Ursi Olson's special risotto with just enough saffron to banish my blahs completely. I returned to my desk ready to labor, convinced I would unravel the Whitcomb tangle *tout de suite,* my temporary attack of alopecia would disappear, and I might become the Peter Pan of Palm Beach.

Fortunately, the dossiers I had received were succinct, resembling computer printouts in their use of abbreviations. I mean, they weren't novellas—just precis of the information requested, factual and exact to the penny.

I started with the reports on the four Whitcomb department heads, in charge of purchasing, maintenance, personnel, and merchandising (including public relations). Their records were brief and I went through them swiftly.

All four (three men and one woman) were earning generous salaries, and their annual expenditures and investments seemed commensurate with their income and net worth. There were no suggestions of wild profligacies, although one gentleman, the maintenance supervisor, had made a great number of recent purchases from L. L. Bean. I couldn't understand what need a South Florida resident would have for heavy wool mackinaws and fleece-lined boots. Then I noted his age; he was sixty-four and nudging retirement. I reckoned he was planning to spend his remaining semesters in the Maine woods or thereabouts.

When I turned to the dossiers on the chief directors of the three Whitcomb Funeral Homes, it was a nag of a different hue. Each of the trio (all men) was also earning a more than adequate salary, but their current net worth seemed excessive when linked to annual income.

It didn't take long to discover that the good fortunes of all three were of recent vintage, like the past six months. The bank deposits of the first had increased appreciably. The second had made a large cash down payment on a million-dollar Boca Raton town house. And the third had purchased a Lexus, a customized hot tub, not one but four gold coin Corum wristwatches, and similar costly doodads.

I stared at those records in amazement. Where on earth was their loot coming from? The funeral director who was banking his cash was acting prudently, if not cautiously, but the other two were plunging and taking on heavy debt as if their newfound income was just going to go on and on.

I put this puzzle aside for the moment and turned to the balance sheets of the individuals who interested me most: Horace Whitcomb, son Oliver, and Sunny Fogarty. But before I could focus my gimlet-eye on their journals, my phone pealed and the caller was one of the objects of my curiosity—and possibly the object of my affection.

"I trust I am not disturbing you, Archy," Sunny Fogarty said formally.

"You trust correctly," I assured her.

"I now have information I believe is significant. I think you will be interested. Could we get together? Not tonight of course; it's too late. But I was hoping you'd be free tomorrow evening."

"Never free," I said loftily. "There's always a price to pay. But yes, I'll be available tomorrow evening. What time and where?"

She hesitated half a mo. "Could you come over to my place at nine o'clock?"

"Sounds fine to me."

"I'll expect you then," she said crisply and hung up.

I sat staring stupidly at the dead phone. It had not been the warm, intimate conversation of a female and a male who had recently shared one of life's sublime gifts. I wondered if she now regretted our joust. It was a discomfiting thought, and I resolutely cast it from my mind—with as much success as one might ignore a hangnail.

I took up the reports on the three principals.

Horace Whitcomb wasn't yet a decamillionaire but inching close. In addition to his handsome salary, he was also drawing a hefty annual bonus. Total income, I figured, more than covered his basic living costs. And he had wisely invested in a large portfolio of tax-exempt municipal bonds, the income of which, in the form of dividends and capital gains, he promptly reinvested, obviously believing in what Wall Street likes to call "the miracle of compounding."

Our client's personal ledger showed a heavy outlay for medical expenses which, considering his wife's condition, was understandable. I had a vague feeling that his periodic cash withdrawals, in various sums ranging from five hundred to five thousand dollars, seemed excessive. But they could be explained by the upkeep on that palazzo he had inherited as well as the purchase of his museum-quality ship models.

All in all, I found nothing in Horace's management of his wealth that ran up red flags and set bells ringing.

I began scanning the analysis of son Oliver's financial health. I must confess I expected to find the heir to Whitcomb Funeral Homes in deep doo-doo. From what I had learned about his lifestyle, I had assumed he'd be in hock up to his nostrils with a balance sheet revealing wild and careless expenditures that had him teetering on the edge of personal bankruptcy.

I couldn't have been wronger—or more wrong, whichever Mr. Webster prefers.

Oliver had a net worth in the neighborhood of three million—which is a pleasant neighborhood if you're thinking of moving. Yes, he had liabilities—mortgages, loans, and such—but they amounted to less than twenty percent of his assets: no reason for panic. And while he seemed to be a free-spending bloke with a taste for big-ticket items, he was quite capable of paying his bills from Whitcomb salary and bonus plus investment income.

I won't say I was shocked, but I was certainly surprised. He proved not to be the profligate I had anticipated. In fact, I thought he was managing his money remarkably well: no splurging on real estate in the Australian outback or on ostrich farms in Texas. I mean, the lad appeared to be a semiconservative investor with a keen appreciation of the risk-benefit ratio.

I had obviously misjudged him. He was not the pot-smoking resident of hippiedom I had imagined. Instead, his balance sheet presented a portrait of a knowledgeable businessman. It was a puzzle.

I put his record aside, took up the dossier of Sunny Fogarty, and encountered another puzzle.

That perplexing lady had never exactly talked a poor mouth, but she had emphasized how important her job and salary were to her, how horrendous the expenses were of keeping her mother in a nursing home, and had generally given me the impression that the legitimate prosperity of Whitcomb's was her sole concern.

But her ledger painted a somewhat different picture. I don't wish to imply she was loaded. She was far from that, but she was also far from hurting. Her salary and annual bonus from her employer easily covered her expenditures with enough left over to build a small but profitable portfolio of Treasury notes and bonds.

There were a few things in her report that baffled me—or rather things that were *not* included. Her new car was listed under her assets, as was her condominium. But there was no mention of a loan on the former or a mortgage on the latter. In addition, Sunny's credit card charges for new clothes, accessories, and jewelry were practically nonexistent. Yet I knew how smartly she dressed, and not cheaply, I assure you.

I stacked all the credit accounts, bound them with a thick rubber band, and slid the whole pile into the bottom drawer of my battered desk. Then I spent a half hour ruminating on everything I had just read.

I admit I felt like a voyeuristic CPA, but what I had done—although it may seem to you a shameful invasion of privacy—was necessary if I was to discover what offenses were occurring that threatened our client's well-being. I now had no doubt there was frigging in the rigging at the Whitcomb Funeral Homes, but as to what crimes were being committed, by whom and for what purpose, I hadn't the slightest.

I would love to be able to tell you that at this point, almost halfway through my narrative, I began to get an idea of what was going on. Unhappily, I didn't have a glimmer. I was as befuddled as I had been the first evening the investigation began.

But from long experience I have learned how to deal with befuddlement. You disrobe, take a hot shower, don a silk robe, light a cigarette, and enjoy a small nightcap while listening to a tape of Sinatra singing "One for My Baby . . ." Then you go to bed.

Your befuddlement remains, but you just don't care. You sleep well and dream of a holiday weekend at Veronica Lake.

18

Occasionally I have been accused—unjustly, I aver—of devoting entirely too much wordage in these accounts to rhapsodic delineation of meals I have enjoyed. It is true that I believe good food is the second-greatest pleasure life has to offer. It is also true there is a hand-lettered and framed inscription hanging on the wall of my study that declares: "Nutritious Ain't Delicious!"

But I assumed everyone feels the way I do, and it comes as something of a stun to learn I have calorie-conscious readers who count grams of fat and the sodium content of their daily nutriments—and probably prefer a nibble of tofu to a peanut butter and jelly sandwich on Wonder bread.

It is out of respect for the convictions of these demented few that I shall limit the description of my luncheon with Oliver Whitcomb at Renato's on Tuesday to a single comment: The salmon parisienne was heavenly. I don't wish to titillate anyone's taste buds by extolling the splendor of the brandy Alexanders we drank as dessert. You must seek your own heaven; I found mine.

Of more significance to this magnum opus is the conversation that took place during our feast. Oliver showed up clad in black suit, white shirt, black tie—quite a contrast to my glad rags.

"I have an important funeral to supervise this afternoon," he explained.

I thought it curious phraseology. I mean, *all* funerals are important—are they not?—and especially to the star.

He wasted little time on small talk: nothing about the weather, sports, or the inflated cost of a good bagel.

"I'm really excited about our expansion to the Naples area," he said. "I figure if our business—or any business—isn't growing, then it's falling behind. Don't you agree?"

"Perhaps," I said cautiously. "But there can be dangers in too-rapid expansion. It's meant taps for a lot of healthy companies."

He waved my warning aside. "We'll be able to afford it out of current profits," he said confidently. "They're increasing enormously. And opening on Florida's west coast will be only the first step in establishing the nationwide chain I see as our future. I have a plan all worked out, and believe me, it makes sense."

Then he was silent as our food was served, and I had an opportunity to observe him more closely. He had inherited his father's patrician handsomeness, but Horace's features had a certain craggy strength while son Oliver's face was softer. I don't wish to imply it was weak, but there was a discernible fleshiness testifying to a good life that included much rare roast beef and fortified wines.

"Y'see," he continued, "the mom-and-pops are finished. Bigness is the name of the game. Look at how the giant discount chains have put so many local stores out of business."

There was no doubting his seriousness. It was obviously a subject to which he had given a lot of thought. What amazed me was that I now saw no evidence of that easy charm he had exhibited at our previous encounters. It made me wonder if that genial warmth was not a natural attribute but a role he played to win what he sought.

That might be true, I reckoned, unless his present performance as an earnest, intent businessman was the façade and he really was the lightweight charmboy I had presumed him to be. People are endlessly fascinating, are they not? I mean, even the dullest are Chinese puzzles. Sometimes they can be solved—but not always.

"I owe it to my father," he went on solemnly. "As well as my grandfather. They built the family business with a lot of hard work and by taking risks to expand. I want to do the same thing."

He paused and looked at me expectantly, as if waiting for praise.

"Mmm," I said, finishing my salmon.

"It's doable," he said with conviction. "I want to establish a national network of brand-name funeral homes, either company-owned or franchises. I've met with some very smart moneymen, we've crunched numbers endlessly, and everyone believes we can swing it."

My plate was now empty. His was not but he seemed to have little interest in those wonderful viands. I was now convinced he had prepared a business presentation for me, a script, possibly even rehearsed, all to persuade me, to win my acquiescence. It was a selling job he was doing, and doing well. But why he needed my approval I could not have said.

That was when he ordered the brandy Alexanders and continued his spiel.

"The brokers I have selected worked out a three-part program. The first requires start-up or up-front money for fees to get this thing rolling. Those funds will be provided by Whitcomb's current cash flow without the need of a bank loan. The second step will be a private placement of stock to interested investors. And the third move will be a public offering of stock, probably initially listed on the NASDAQ exchange. How does that sound to you?"

"It appears you have gone into this very thoroughly," I said diplomatically.

"I have," he said, slapping a palm down on the tabletop for emphasis. "But there is one rub. A fly in the ointment, so to speak. As I'm sure you know, Whitcomb's is a privately held corporation. Shares are owned by my mother, father, myself, and small amounts by longtime employees under a profit-sharing plan. But what I hope to accomplish means going public: selling a portion of the company on a stock exchange. My father is dead set against it. He wants the business to remain strictly within the family. I've tried to explain to him that a public offering doesn't mean we'll lose control; we'll still hold a majority of voting shares. But he's a stubborn man."

Oliver shook his head sorrowfully and finished his dessert. He drew a deep breath, and I anticipated the "hook": the final closing of his eloquent and well-reasoned sales pitch.

"What I'm hoping you might do," he said carefully, "is help me out. I'm sure my father will discuss my project with your father. It would be dad's way to ask his attorney for advice. I'd like to think I could depend on your understanding and cooperation if your father brings up the subject."

I gave him a rueful smile. "My father rarely asks my opinion on legal counsel he gives to clients."

"I know," Oliver said, "but he *might*. And if he does, I'd like to think you're in my corner."

He said no more while he called for a check, paid the bill with plastic, and we moved outside. I thanked him for a splendid luncheon, but I don't think he was listening.

"By the way," he said, not looking at me, "when it comes time for our private placement—shares of stock sold to a limited number of investors—I'll be happy to put your name on our preferred list. After we go public you could make a mint."

"Thank you," I said, trying to keep any trace of sarcasm out of my voice. "That's very kind of you."

We shook hands and he departed for the "important funeral" he was to supervise. I stood there a moment realizing I had just been the object of an attempted bribe. I wasn't insulted. Amused really, because I knew what little effect I could have on the decisions of Horace Whitcomb or my papa.

Oliver's pitch to me, I decided, revealed a woeful ignorance of my influence, which was practically nil. Either he was misinformed or he had become aware of my investigation into Whitcomb's recent unexplained prosperity and was essaying a measure of damage control.

Whatever his motive, I had learned he was a very determined chap, much deeper than I had originally thought. And that he was intensely ambitious I now had no doubt whatsoever. But as we all know, ambition is a two-edged sword.

I drove away with the conviction that I had just lunched with a three-dimensional man, not the cartoon of a lint-headed, high-living prodigal I had first believed him to be. And what bewildered me most about his chameleonic personality was his marriage to Mitzi, that panther. Was it love that drove him to such an unlikely union or could it have been a deliberate desire to offend his conservative father and by so doing declare his independence?

An intriguing enigma—and I loved it.

If you've devoured previous tales of my adventures, I'm sure you're aware that occasionally I dabble in stocks. Nothing enormous, I assure you; just a hundred shares here and a hundred there. *Pour le sport,* you might say. I mean, I don't go to Las Vegas, and everyone knows Wall Street is the biggest casino in the world.

My broker is a jolly chap of Chinese ancestry named Wang Lo. I've tried to convince him that if he expects to succeed as a stockbroker he should change his name to Wang Hi, but he won't hear of it. He's a popular member of the Pelican Club, and it was he who taught me how to bolt tequila straight with a lick of salt and a bite of fresh lime.

I'm sure my account is Wang's tiniest, but he's unfailingly polite and willing to spend time shooting the breeze even if it means no commissions for him. Anyway, when I arrived back at my office I phoned him and, after an exchange of pleasantries and genial insults, I requested his advice.

I outlined Oliver Whitcomb's business plan, without mentioning any names of course. I merely told Wang an acquaintance of mine was trying to get a new project moving and wanted me to invest. Should I or shouldn't I?

"That three-step plan is fairly conventional," Wang told me. "A lot of new companies get started that way. Some make it, some don't. Very chancy, but there's always the possibility of a new McDonald's or a new Xerox. This pal of yours—is he asking for up-front money?"

"No, he says he can manage that himself. He's just asking if I'd be interested in the private offering."

"Well, that sounds a little better, Archy; the risk is somewhat reduced. If he's got his start-up funds, it shows he's probably not peddling emu ranches or rhinestone mines. I really can't tell you what to do unless I know more about it. It's not another new chain of pizza joints, is it?"

"No, Wang, it's a chain of noodle palaces."

"Hey," he said, "I might put a few bucks into that myself. But only if they promise to serve curried rice stick noodles, my favorite."

"I'll tell him that," I promised, and we hung up laughing.

About all I had learned from that consultation was that Oliver Whitcomb had a viable business plan and was apparently not running an out-and-out swindle. I'm no financial wizard, but I could see that what Oliver termed "a rub, a fly in the ointment"—id est, his father's objections—might doom the project before it got off the ground.

Just to make certain, I phoned Mrs. Trelawney and asked if our honcho was present and could grant me an audience of no more than five minutes.

"Oh Archy," she said, "I doubt that; he's so busy."

"Inspecting his briefs again, is he? Be a luv and ask, will you?"

She came back on the line and told me I could have five minutes, no more.

I went leaping up the back stairs to poppa's office and found him seated at his antique rolltop desk reviewing a humongous stack of legal documents.

"Yes, yes, Archy," he said irritably, "what is it now?"

"Sir," I said, "something curious has come up concerning the Whitcomb Funeral Homes investigation, and I need to know who actually owns the business. I presume Horace Whitcomb holds a controlling majority of the stock."

He stared at me. "This is important to the successful conclusion of your inquiry?"

"Yes, father, it is."

He paused a moment, then drew a deep breath. "In that case I shall reveal that you presume incorrectly. The majority of shares are held by Mrs. Sarah Whitcomb."

I was astonished. "How can that be?"

"Very easily," he said testily. "The shares were legally transferred to his wife's name by Horace Whitcomb for tax purposes. Of course her shares are always voted as her husband recommends since she has little knowledge of or interest in the business affairs of their privately held corporation."

"I see," I said, beginning to get a glimpse of what was going on. "Thank you for the information."

He thawed briefly. "Making any progress, Archy?" he asked.

"Yes, sir. A little."

He nodded. "Keep at it," he commanded and went back to his bumf.

I returned to my office just long enough to pick up my panama and then set off for home. I decided an ocean swim was needed to soothe the day's rigors I had endured, to say nothing of restoring me to fighting trim for my meeting that evening with Sunny Fogarty.

My slow wallow had the desired effect, and the family cocktail hour followed by a light dinner of veal marsala completed my rejuvenation. I dashed upstairs to make entries in my journal concerning recent events. I was about to close up shop and prepare for my tête-à-tête with Ms. Fogarty when a phone call stopped me.

"Archy," Sunny said, "I'm glad I caught you before you left. Could we make it ten o'clock instead of nine?"

"Of course," I said manfully. "No problem. But would you prefer another night?"

"No, no," she said hurriedly. "I want to see you tonight. It's important. But a neighbor asked to stop by for a while to ask me about her investments, and I couldn't very well refuse. I hope our meeting an hour later won't inconvenience you."

"Not at all," I said. "I'll be there."

"Thank you, Archy," she said gratefully.

I hung up absolutely certain the female neighbor seeking investment advice was a fabrication. Sunny's voice had taken on the deeper, more solemn and intent tone prevaricators use, thinking it will convince the listener of their honesty and sincerity.

I had no doubt the lady was lying.

19

I make no claims to possess ESP and I trust you don't either. But have you ever entered a room and had the definite impression it was recently occupied by a visitor now departed?

That was the feeling I had when Sunny Fogarty led me into her condo. She had told me she expected the visit of a female neighbor, but

I had a distinct notion that her guest had been male. Later that night, when I analyzed my reaction, I realized there were rational reasons for it: the down cushion of an armchair was still deeply depressed and, although I am no supernose, I did detect an ever-so-faint odor of cigar smoke plus another scent difficult to identify. My best guess was that I had sniffed a man's rather spicy cologne.

Naturally I made no mention of my suspicions to Sunny. She had welcomed me graciously and almost immediately supplied me with a tot of iced vodka, for which I was thankful.

She was dressed smartly, as usual, wearing a loose charmeuse T-shirt and silk jeans dyed to resemble denim. I thought the latter amusing. Similar to people who install gold bathroom fixtures but insist they must be tarnished. There are such odd creatures, you know.

"Sorry for the delay, Archy," she said. "But I really couldn't help it."

"No problem," I assured her again. "You're looking mighty perky this evening, Sunny."

"Am I?" she said, genuinely surprised. "Thank you. I wish I felt perky, but I don't. The deeper we get into this mess, the more depressed I become. And frightened."

"Frightened? How so?"

"Because I know now that someone is trying to destroy Whitcomb or at least use the funeral homes in a criminal scheme. Archy, in effect I am the chief financial officer and feel I have a fiduciary duty to make certain our business is conducted in a legal and ethical manner. And I find this matter a cause for grave concern."

I think I successfully hid my amazement. I mean, that rather pompous speech was so obviously rehearsed she lacked only a promptbook. I merely nodded encouragingly.

"As you know," she continued, "I've been checking the invoices of the airlines which handle Whitcomb's out-of-state shipments, trying to discover the names and addresses of the consignees."

"The information missing from your files."

"*Stolen* from my files," she said angrily. "As you discovered, most of those shipments went to New York, Boston, and Chicago. At LaGuardia in New York, practically all of the caskets were picked up by the Cleo Hauling Service."

I looked at her, puzzled. "Sunny, isn't that a bit unusual, to deliver human remains to a hauling service?"

She was drinking an amber liquid with bubbles. I guessed it might be ginger ale or something similar. Now she took a great gulp of it as if she needed whatever strength it might give her. "Unusual?" she repeated. "Archy, it's practically unheard of. The coffins are customarily picked up by local funeral homes or cemeteries. Sometimes by relatives or churches when a service is to be held. But by a hauling company? That's just ridiculous! Would you like another drink?"

"I think I need one," I said, holding out my empty glass.

"You will," she said. "The worst is yet to come. I'll have one, too. I've had enough diet cream soda for one night."

She returned with our drinks, and I noticed mine was larger this time, and it turned out to be gustier. But hers was the same size and, I hoped, of the same toughness. I mean, I did not believe Sunny was trying to paralyze me.

She seated herself on the couch close to me. She continued: "It's definite that the majority of shipments going to LaGuardia in New York were consigned to the Cleo Hauling Service. Now would you care to guess who picked up most of Whitcomb's shipments to Logan in Boston and O'Hare in Chicago?"

I groaned. "Don't tell me it was the Cleo Hauling Service."

"You've got it," she said, and we stared at each other. "Archy, what on earth is going on?" she burst out. There was fury in her voice and, I thought, an undertone of fear.

"We'll find out," I promised, "and bring it to a crashing halt. I'm as convinced as you that there's a nefarious plot afoot aimed at your employer and our client."

She gazed away, looking at nothing. "If I let anything bad happen to the company I'd never forgive myself. Never! Horace Whitcomb has been so good to me. He's helped me so much. He's given me a chance to be happy."

"Like a father, is he?" I said casually. It was perhaps an intrusive thing to say, but as you well know, I'm a nosy chap.

She turned to look at me directly. "A father?" she said. "I wouldn't know. My real father deserted my mother and me when I was three years old."

"Oh," I said, an admittedly vacuous comment. "Well, I think Horace Whitcomb is a splendid gentleman."

"Yes," she said, "he is that. And I can't have him hurt. I simply won't stand for it."

Suddenly she had become too heavily emotional. She was falsifying again, just as she had when Binky and I first visited. After that encounter the would-be Hercule Poirot of Palm Beach had declared the lady was scamming us—or trying to. I thought his judgment was accurate.

I believed she was sincere in her professed loyalty to Whitcomb, but I still sensed she was not revealing all she knew. That troubled me. Not because I suspected she might be involved in the caper—whatever it was—but because what she was holding back might enable me to write "Finis" to this case a lot sooner. Now I had to spend time and the racking of my poor, deprived brain in an effort to tweak out the mystery she kept hidden.

"Something bothering you, Archy?" Sunny asked.

"Pardon?" I said. "Oh no. Just woolgathering." And then, because I have a talent for improv, I forged ahead. "I was thinking of your comment that Horace Whitcomb had given you the *chance* to be happy. That was well said. The Declaration of Independence lists 'the pursuit of happiness' as one of our unalienable rights. What a wonderful phrase! 'Pursuit' is the key word. I suspect Tom Jefferson used it ironically or at least slyly, meaning to imply that the chase after happiness is more important than its capture."

Sunny smiled and took my hand. "Let's go see if we can capture it," she said. We finished our drinks and off we went to the tourney.

I won't label Sunny Fogarty as Rubenesque, but she was abundant and all the more stirring for it. Her body was vital, overwhelming. I hung on for dear life and, in addition to my pleasure, had the added delight of being a survivor.

But I must admit that despite our yelps of bliss I could not rid myself of an aggravating unease that there was a dichotomy in her motives and in her actions. Just as during our first tumble, I had the antsy feeling that she was a Byzantine woman, very complex, and quite capable of giving mouth-to-mouth resuscitation without becoming emotionally involved.

I sensed there was a deep and muffled part of her that she would never surrender, ever, to anyone.

But I cannot deny it was a joyous evening. For me at least. And before I departed, Sunny clutched me in a hot, almost frantic, embrace, and I began to believe she was a woman torn.

I promised I would investigate the Cleo Hauling Service and report the results to her ASAP. She gave me a brave smile and walked me to the door, clutching my hand tightly as if she feared to let me go. No doubt about it; she was a riddle, a troubling riddle.

I was home shortly after midnight with absolutely no desire to jot notes in my journal, smoke a coffin nail, listen to music, or have a nightcap, no matter how tiny. In truth, the McNally carcass was totally drained, wrung out, and hung up to dry. All I sought was blessed sleep, hoping the morn would bring roses back to my cheeks.

I had a delayed breakfast on Wednesday morning, having enjoyed a few extra hours of catalepsy. I found Jamie Olson alone in the kitchen, puffing on his ancient briar, which had a cracked stem bound with a Band-Aid. He was also nursing a mug of coffee, and I had no doubt he had added a dollop of aquavit to give him the push to face the rigors of another day.

Jamie offered to scramble a brace of eggs for me, but I settled for an OJ, a bran muffin, and black decaf. Very abstemious and totally unsatisfying. Why do all healthy meals remind me of wallpaper paste?

I sat across from Jamie and thought it a propitious time to start redeeming the promise I had given Mrs. Sarah Whitcomb: to discover the reason for the enmity between her husband and son.

"Jamie," I said, "do you know Jason, houseman for the Horace Whitcombs?"

"Yep," he said. "One year younger than God. Got the arthritis."

"I noticed. Nice man?"

"Jase? The best. Him and me have a belt together now and then."

I was about to observe that "He and I" would have served even better but restrained that pedantic impulse.

"There seems to be a quarrel between Horace and his son Oliver. The next time you have a belt with Jason you might inquire as to the cause."

Jamie considered that a moment, staring at his fuming pipe. "Couldn't ask straight out," he said finally.

"Of course not," I said hastily. "Didn't expect you to. But you might hint around. Gently, you know. Tell him you've heard gossip. Something like that. He may tell you something he wouldn't reveal to me."

"Yep," he said. "Jase don't blab when it comes to his family. But I can buy him a Bushmills. That's his favorite, and it would be a treat for him."

I took a twenty from my wallet and slid it across the table. "Buy him two Bushmills," I said, "and see if he'll loosen up about Horace and Oliver."

"With two Bushmills in him," Jamie said mournfully, "he'll tell me again about Peaches and Daddy Browning."

I was preparing to depart when the phone rang and I picked up in the kitchen.

"The McNally residence," I said, figuring it was probably a call for mother.

"Archy?" Binky Watrous said. "Why aren't you in your office?"

"Because I'm here," I explained. "What's on your mind, Binky?—if you'll forgive a slight exaggeration."

"How about buying a fellow lunch?" he asked eagerly.

"And what fellow do you suggest?"

"Come on, Archy," he said. "You don't pay me a salary, and the least you can do is feed me for all my hard work. I've got a lot of neat stuff to tell you. Besides, the Duchess has canceled my credit cards. Archy, I'm *starving!*"

"All right," I relented. "Meet you at the Pelican Club around twelve-thirty."

"Can't we go somewhere tonier?" he said plaintively. "And more expensive."

"No," I told him.

I drove to the McNally Building, went directly to my office, and got on the horn. I phoned Operator Assistance in New York, Boston, and Chicago. I called vehicle license and registration bureaus, trade associations, and even chambers of commerce. And by noon I had my answer.

Or rather I had no answer. None of the sources I contacted had any record—past, present, or applied for—of the Cleo Hauling Service. Apparently it did not exist.

I can't say I was shocked. After all, it would be a fairly simple scam to finagle. One truck for each of the three aforementioned cities, the trucks purchased secondhand or stolen. Ditto for the license plates and registration. No insolvable difficulties. Then you painted whatever you wished on the truck sides, added a phony address, and you were in business.

But *what* business?

20

Leroy Pettibone, our esteemed chef at the Pelican Club, occasionally grew bored with preparing his special cheeseburgers or seafood salads for luncheon. Then he switched to what he called a Deli Delite: a hot corned-beef sandwich on sour rye with a heap of coleslaw spiked with coarsely ground black pepper, and a plate of kosher dill spears. Leroy had also discovered a hot mustard made in Detroit, of all places, that made your eyes water.

The Deli Delite was not the equal of masterworks from the Stage or Carnegie in Manhattan of course—but then what is? But it was as yummy as anything of the genre I had tasted in South Florida.

And that's what Binky Watrous and I had for lunch, with enough cold beer to keep our palates from charring.

"All right, Binky," I said as we scarfed, "what's the neat stuff you said you had to tell me?"

"About this Dr. Omar K. Pflug," he said, mumbling through a mouthful of corned beef. "He was kicked out of New York and New Jersey. And now he's working in Florida. Also, he's a druggie."

"Why was he kicked out of New York and New Jersey? Was his license to practice revoked or was he just accused and is under investigation? And for what? Has he been licensed to work in Florida?"

"Well, those are just minor details, aren't they? I mean, the guy is obviously a wrongo."

"Binky, did you check with your family physician or contact professional associations and the state licensing board as I suggested?"

"Well, ah, no," he said, taking a chomp of a pickle. "I thought there really wasn't much point in going through all that folderol. So I just asked Mitzi Whitcomb and she told me."

I tried to repress a groan and didn't quite succeed. I looked at him, saw a brain sculpted solely of cottage cheese, and wondered if I had suddenly become a victim of synesthesia.

He must have sensed my outrage, for he immediately became defensive. "You can depend on what Mitzi told me," he said. "Absolutely!"

I took that *cum grano salis*. With a heap of *salis,* if the truth be known.

"Binky," I said, "did it ever occur to you the lady may be lying?"

He was astonished. "Why should she do that?"

I sighed. "People usually lie for reasons of self-interest of which you wot not."

"Well, Mitzi wouldn't lie to me."

"Oh? Give me a because."

"Because she's in love with me."

"She told you that?"

"Not exactly. But she let me paint her toenails."

This surreal conversation, I realized, was getting me precisely nowhere.

I asked, "Did Mitzi Whitcomb reveal any other nuggets of information?"

He pondered a moment, pale brow furrowed, a shred of coleslaw hanging from his chops. Then he brightened. "Sure she did! The carrottop, the nurse you saw in Pflug's office—well, she's no nurse. She's not exactly a hooker, but she's sort of a call girl and uses the doctor's place as a home base."

"Some home," I said. "Some base. Did Mitzi tell you her name?"

"Rhoda. Mitzi didn't know her last name."

"Is Ernest Gorton managing her?"

"I don't understand."

"To put it crudely, is Gorton her pimp? Providing customers?"

"Oh," he said, and I think he actually blushed. "I don't know anything about that."

I finished my second beer and sat back. The Deli Delite had more than adequately compensated for that wretched bran muffin I had for breakfast.

"All right, let's assume Mitzi Whitcomb's information is accurate. Then what we've got is a rogue doctor willing to sign fake death certificates, presumably to finance his drug addiction. He also shares working quarters with a call girl who may or may not be the girlfriend and/or employee of Ernest Gorton, a Miami hustler who claims to be in the import-export trade. Is that how you see it?"

"See what?" Binky said.

There was no point in screaming at the pinhead. He was a good-hearted chap, no doubt of that, but his thought processes were so sluggish as to be almost immobile.

"Binky," I said gently, "discreet inquiries demand the ability to deal with complexities and complications. You must be able to endure total confusion temporarily with the faith that eventually you will be able to bring order out of chaos. You follow?"

"Oh sure," he said. "Hey, let's have a kirsch at the bar. Just to cut the grease, you know."

Later we were in the parking area when, emboldened by the cherry brandy, Binky said eagerly, "What's my next assignment, kemo sabe?"

"If you are to play Tonto to my Lone Ranger," I told him, "you must demonstrate energy and inspiration. I suggest you investigate Rhoda, the faux nurse. Discover her last name and home address. Determine whether she is Ernest Gorton's inamorata or merely his employee. And what is her relationship to Oliver Whitcomb."

He was completely flummoxed. "How do I do all that?"

"Use your imagination," I advised. "Perhaps you might start by asking Rhoda for a date. Take her home to have dinner with the Duchess."

He blanched and began to tremble. "Oh golly," he said, "I couldn't do that. You're joking, aren't you, Archy? Tell me you're joking."

"I'm joking," I assured him. "How you do it is up to you. Just do it."

"I wonder if she'd enjoy birdcalls," he said thoughtfully.

"I'm sure she would," I said. "Try a cockatoo."

I apologize for that one.

I drove back to the McNally Building asking whatever gods may be why I had been saddled with a disciple who was such an utter goof. It wasn't that Binky was incapable of reasoning, but his gears had slipped a bit, just enough so his thinking was slightly skewed. I mean, he was the kind of numbskull who, informed that a friend had choked to death on a fish bone, was likely to inquire, "Broiled or sautéed?"

I arrived at my office to find a message that Mr. Horace Whitcomb had phoned and requested I return his call. The number given was Whitcomb Funeral Homes' headquarters in West Palm Beach, and I had to navigate through the queries of receptionist and private secretary before their chieftain came on the line.

"I hope I'm not disturbing you, Archy," he said.

"Not at all," I said. "How are you, sir?"

"I'm well, thank you," he said, his voice at once stiff and hollow. "But Sarah is back in the hospital."

"I'm sorry to hear that, Mr. Whitcomb."

"Well, it's only for more of those damnable tests, and I hope she'll be home by the weekend. But she's somewhat depressed, as you can imagine. She asked if I'd call and see if you have time to pay her a short visit. Just for a few moments, you know. I think it would cheer her immensely."

"Of course I'll visit," I said. "Immediately if hospital rules permit."

"You'll have no problem," he said. "Sarah is in a private suite." He gave me the hospital name and address. "Thank you so very much, Archy," he said huskily. "I know my wife will be delighted to see you."

Errands of mercy do not come easily to yrs. truly, and I find hospital visits particularly difficult. In fact, I *loathe* hospitals. Most of them look like fortresses or warehouses, and then there's that deplorable hospital odor. No matter how much wild cherry spray they use, one still imagines an underlying scent of sickness and sheet-covered bodies on gurneys.

And also, of course, there's your own behavior to sadden you: the stretched, mirthless grin and a complete inability to keep the conversation casual and comforting. How Florence Nightingale and Walt Whitman did it I shall never understand.

But off I went to visit the hospitalized Sarah Whitcomb. Naturally I could not arrive empty-handed, but I decided against flowers; she was sure to have plenty of those. I stopped at a gift shop and found a windup music box. There was a tiny porcelain lady in a formal gown on top and she twirled as you heard a plinked "I Could Have Danced All Night." Kitsch? It was, but I hoped Sarah would find it as amusing and evocative as I did.

I guessed Horace Whitcomb was paying horrendous daily rates for that private two-room hospital unit, but my first impression was that I had entered a motel suite. An upscale motel, to be sure, but there was still the hard, impersonal look: everything gleaming, everything of assembly-line sleekness including framed floral prints bolted to the walls and an excess of vinyl and Formica.

The bedroom was a little better, a little softer, and Mrs. Whitcomb lay in a bed covered with gaily patterned sheets I was certain she had brought from home. She was lying still, her skull now covered with a blue medical cap. Her head was turned and she was staring out the window at the endless sky.

"Sarah," I said softly.

Slowly—oh, so slowly—she moved to face me and her bright smile was almost enough to cause me to lose my cool and blubber.

"Archy!" she said. "What a sweetheart you are to come visit an old, decrepit lady like me."

"Neither old nor decrepit," I said. "Madonna wanted me for the afternoon, but I told her I had a better offer."

Her eyes squinched with merriment but her laugh seemed to cause pain. "Kissy," she said.

I leaned to kiss her cheek and then pulled up a small armchair covered with a trompe l'oeil fabric depicting the Colosseum. Just what I needed.

"Getting along, are you?" I asked. It was the best I could do; I was acutely uncomfortable.

"Getting along," she said. "Right now I'm very drowsy. I think they've given me something. If I fall asleep while we're talking, I hope you'll understand."

"Of course," I said. "But before you snooze, here's a little nothing I brought for you."

I unwrapped the music box, wound it up, and set the porcelain dancer twirling.

Sarah's reaction was unexpected. Tears came to her eyes and she reached out a quavery hand.

"It's beautiful," she breathed. "Just beautiful. Thank you so very, very much. But how did you know?"

"Know what, dear?"

"When I was a young girl I loved ballroom dancing. I even entered contests and won prizes. In those days it was all waltzes, the fox trot, the two-step, and if you were very daring, the tango. Thank you again, Archy. It's the loveliest present anyone has ever given me."

"I admit I cherish the tune," I said. "I like songs with a melody. But that's hardly a weakness, is it?"

"If it is," she said, "it's one more ailment to add to my long, long list."

She seemed to be fading, her voice dimming. I had to crane to hear what she was saying.

"Oliver tells me the two of you had lunch."

"We did indeed," I said. "A splendid luncheon."

"Oliver likes you," she said and looked at me awaiting the expected response: "And I like Oliver."

When I cannot lie I prefer to finesse. To be perfectly honest (well, no one is *perfect*), I didn't much like Oliver Whitcomb. So I merely murmured, "That's very kind of him," and Sarah accepted that.

"What I asked you to do," she said with some effort, "and what you promised to do, was to investigate the hostility between my husband and my son. Have you discovered anything?"

"Nothing conclusive," I told her. "I think it may be just a generational conflict. Each man has his own standards. And I know I don't have to tell you how far and how fast the world has moved in the past fifty years. Sarah, it may be just the difference in their ages that causes their disagreements."

She looked at me a long time in silence and then her eyes closed. I thought she might have fallen asleep but she hadn't.

"Archy," she said faintly, "I think you are an intelligent and sensitive man."

"Thank you," I said. "I wish I could agree."

She waved that away with a flap of a palsied hand. "But I think there's more to the situation between Horace and Oliver than a difference in their age. Something else is going on that's tearing them apart. I sense it. Archy, I love my son, love him more than anything else in this world. I can't stand the thought of him being hurt, and especially by his father. I am telling you these things because you're not one of the family and because I trust your judgment and discretion. I know I don't have much time left and I want you to be witness to this: If I ever have to choose between my husband and my son, God forbid, I will side with my son. Do you understand what I'm saying?"

What she had said had been spoken in tones of such sad finality that I knew she had given the problem much anguished thought and had come to her decision with sorrow and regret.

"I understand, ma'am," I said gravely.

"But I still hope that with your help I can bring them together again. You will try, won't you, Archy?"

"I'll try," I promised again.

"I'm falling asleep now," she whispered. "I can feel it coming on."

"I'll leave," I said, rising. "Sarah, be well and may all your dreams come true."

"Thank you," she said in a tattered voice. "Play the music box again for me."

I departed to the tinkly notes of "I Could Have Danced All Night."

21

It had been a shaking experience, not only to visit a doomed woman but to be plunged into the midst of what was obviously a familial crisis. So it was curious—as odd to me as it must seem to you—that during my drive back to the McNally mini-estate on Ocean Boulevard I could not concentrate on the Whitcombs' travails but only on how they might mirror my own relations with my parents.

I arrived home, slid the Miata into our three-car garage, and went looking for mother. I found her in our little greenhouse talking to her begonias, and she looked fetching in a flowered apron that swathed her from neck to knee.

I followed her about as she watered her darlings, pinching off a dried leaf here and there, and told her of my visit to Mrs. Sarah Whitcomb in the hospital.

"That was very sweet of you, Archy," momsy said approvingly. "I do hope you brought her a get-well gift."

"I did indeed," I said and described the music box.

Mother was delighted and said she'd surely visit Sarah or at least phone to gossip awhile. I said I was certain Mrs. Whitcomb would welcome a call.

All this chitchat was stalling on my part, you understand. What I really wanted to do was ask mother, if circumstances demanded a choice of her sympathy, love, and understanding between her husband and her son, which of us would she choose? You can see how deeply I had been affected by Sarah Whitcomb's dilemma.

But I could not bring myself to ask the question. It would be an excruciating decision for her to make, I knew, but even worse I felt that even posing that louche query was an impertinent invasion of her privacy.

And so, after a time, I wandered away, none the wiser but reflecting how often children (myself included) regard their mother and father simply as parents and rarely make an effort to consider them as individuals or give a thought to their secret lives, what they had sought, won, lost.

I went upstairs to my digs still pondering the infernal complexities of family ties. I had told Mrs. Whitcomb I suspected the hostility between her husband and son might be a generational conflict. I did believe that was part of it but not the total answer.

Now, preparing for my daily ocean swim, I brooded about my relationship with my own father. There was certainly a generational factor at work there, but more a difference than a conflict. I mean, he wore balbriggan underwear and wingtips. I wore silk briefs and tasseled suede loafers. Big deal.

I knew I would never be as erudite as he, and in turn he was not as streetwise as I. There had been and would be disagreements between us of course—how could there not be?—but never dark looks, clenched fists, and muttered imprecations.

Not once had we treated one another with less than civility, however formal, and there's much to be said for it. And for a bemused love never verbally expressed but which was real and enduring. That I knew.

After my saltwater dip, the family cocktail hour, and dinner (shrimp and scallops sautéed with capers, roasted peppers and sundried tomatoes) I waddled upstairs with some effort and set to work bringing my journal current on the strange affair of the Whitcomb Funeral Homes. There was much to record, but none of my scribblings yielded a clue as to what was going on. All I had was an account of disparate facts and fancies that revealed no pattern or even a wild surmise.

I interrupted my labors to phone Connie Garcia, that paragon I had been neglecting shamefully. She was in a chipper mood and we gibbered for almost half an hour, exchanging tidbits of gossip and scurrilous opinions of close friends and local political muck-a-mucks.

"By the way," Connie said, "about an hour before you called, one of my spies reported she spotted your pal Binky Watrous wining and dining an orange-haired judy at a Lauderdale McDonald's."

"How does one wine another at a McDonald's?" I asked, reasonably enough.

"Just a figure of speech, doll. Anyway, my informant says she was all over Binky like a wet sheet."

"He was probably imitating a lovesick whippoorwill."

"No doubt," Connie said. "Just thought you'd be interested."

"Oh, I am. Mildly. Give you a call on Friday, Connie. Maybe we can tear a herring over the weekend."

"Let's," she said. "Before all the snowbirds arrive and we can't get a table."

We disconnected and I hung up thinking Binky Watrous, the wannabe Inspector Javert, was taking my advice to heart and displaying energy and inspiration. I was sure the orange-haired judy was Rhoda, Ernest Gorton's carrottop, but I doubted if birdcalls and a Big Mac would be sufficient to entice startling disclosures.

I finished my journalistic chores, skipped a nightcap and final ciggie, and went directly to bed. It wasn't that I was physically weary but the McNally neurons were churning and I sought sleep to deliver me from all the bedeviling puzzles encountered during the day. I hoped I might awake the following morn with an apocalyptic inspiration that would solve the Whitcomb case, reveal the whereabouts of Atlantis, and explain why our laundry always withholds one of my socks.

Such was not the case of course. I awoke Thursday morning, peered out my window, and saw a world swaddled in murk. I mean, the fog was so thick you couldn't see a foot in front of your face—which made things difficult for podiatrists.

Even worse, the weather mirrored my inner gloom. Sleep had brought no grand revelations; I was still mired in perplexity. Can you wonder why I was in such a grumpy mood and so silent at breakfast with my parents that mother inquired solicitously if I was coming down with something?

"Nothing serious," I assured her. "Just a galloping case of frustration."

"A lot of that going around these days," father remarked, which was his version of Wildean wit.

I arrived at the McNally Building about an hour later, having tooled the Miata slowly through the swirling mist. I sulked in my office and wondered what to do next. Felo-de-se was one possibility, but I rejected it.

I was saved from a fatal attack of the megrims by a phone call from Sgt. Al Rogoff.

"How're you doing, buddy?" he asked.

"Surviving," I told him. "Barely. And you?"

"Lousy. This miserable fog. We've had more crashes than I can count. Mostly fender-benders but a few bloody messes. Listen, when can you and I get together?"

"You have information about Ernest Gorton?" I said, suddenly on the qui vive.

"Some," he admitted. "And some questions for you. I should be home by four o'clock. How about dropping over to my chateau around then?"

"I'll be there," I promised.

I arrived at his mobile home later that afternoon, bearing a cold six-pack of Molson ale. He put out a bowl of honey-roasted cashews and we settled in. Al's place always reminds me of a slightly tatty's men's club: lots of oak furniture, worn leather, and a total disregard of the trendy and uncomfortable. It made you want to kick off your shoes, and I did.

We sipped a little ale, popped a few cashews, talked lazily of this and that. Then the sergeant got down to business.

"About Ernest Gorton," he started. "You told me a client thinks this guy is clipping him and that's why you wanted a trace. Was that the truth?"

"No," I said.

"Didn't figure it was," Rogoff said equably. "You lie even when you don't have to—just to keep in practice."

"That's what Connie Garcia keeps telling me."

"She's right. Okay, sonny boy, let's have it: what's your interest in Ernest Gorton?"

"It's a long story."

"We have a six-pack; take your time."

I told him about the Whitcomb Funeral Homes investigation. Not everything of course. I said nothing about the conflict between Horace and Oliver, the anguish being endured by Sarah Whitcomb, or my uneasiness about the role Sunny Fogarty was playing. Al had no need to know. But I did give him the bare bones, including Oliver's close friendship with Ernest Gorton and the activities of Dr. Omar K.

Pflug and Rhoda, who was no more a nurse than I was a nuclear physicist.

I finished speaking. The sergeant opened another ale, took a deep draft, and looked at me reflectively.

"Beautiful," he said. "I just love these swamps you drag me into. Nothing as simple as a post office massacre or a terrorist plot to blow up City Hall. You only get involved in the wheels-within-wheels cases."

"That's not fair," I protested. "When this thing was first brought to our attention, both my father and I thought it was nothing. Now we both think it's for real."

"Yeah," he conceded. "It does sound like something is going down."

"That seems plausible to me."

Rogoff's smile was cold. "Let me tell you about Monsieur Gorton. From what I heard from my Miami pals, this guy has megabucks. They say he's got green eyes: all he sees is money. He's into everything rancid you can think of. Drugs, money laundering, ripoffs of high-priced labels, prostitution, guns. Is that enough for you? If not, how about this one: He's also suspected of killing horses."

"Of *what!?*"

"Rich no-goodniks who own a valuable Thoroughbred, trotter, or jumper that's not performing up to snuff want the animal put down so they can collect the insurance. Gorton has the rep of providing experts who can make the slaughter look like an accident."

I gulped. "That's nice," I said.

"Oh yeah," Al said. "Sweet people."

I recalled what Binky had told me about Oliver and Gorton flying to Ocala to inspect a horse. But I related nothing of that to Rogoff. It might have been an innocent trip. Maybe.

"He is one active villain," the sergeant continued. "And the kicker is that he's never done time. Archy, the man is no dummy. He's got layers of management, and if his soldiers or sub-bosses have to take a fall, he provides money for their defense and takes care of their families while they're inside. Loyalty up and loyalty down. I mean, the guy's got a tight organization. It's not as big as the Mafia or the Colombian drug cartels—although he's worked with both of them—but his outfit is lean and mean. He's been busted a hundred times and always walks away singing 'Who Cares?' "

"A charmed life," I observed.

"Yeah," Al said. "But what the hell, it's rumored he has local pols on the pad. Now here he is palsy-walsy with the chief executive officer of a chain of funeral homes that's shipping north a lot of dead people from Florida. What's going on?"

"He's getting rid of his victims?" I suggested.

Rogoff thought about that a moment. "Maybe," he said.

"Illegal immigrants? He's charging for airlifting them north in caskets? No, scratch that. They'd probably never survive in sealed containers packed into an airliner's cargo bay."

We looked at each other and both of us shrugged.

"Two problems," Rogoff said. "One: What is Ernie boy doing? And two: Why is Oliver Whitcomb apparently cooperating? Blackmail?"

"Perhaps," I said, but I didn't think so. I was beginning to get a glimmer of Oliver's motives, but I didn't want to mention it to Al; he'd be convinced I had played too many games without a helmet.

I stayed for an additional hour. We each had another ale and wolfed cashews while we reviewed again all the known facts and discussed possible scenarios that might account for them. Our conclusions. Zero, zip, and zilch.

I drove home in a weighty mood. I believed I knew Oliver's reason for cultivating a friendship with such a scurvy knave as Ernest Gorton, but I shared Sgt. Rogoff's bewilderment as to what exactly those two wiseguys were doing.

Later, of course, I realized what Rogoff had told me about Ernest Gorton that afternoon contained sufficient clues to solve the mystery. But at the time neither the sergeant nor I was perspicacious enough to see it.

I blame it on good ale and honey-roasted cashews.

22

It had been a curiously condensed day—Rogoff had given me a great deal to ponder—but it wasn't over yet. I was in my belfry, preparing to descend for the family cocktail hour, when my phone began ringing. For some peculiar reason I thought it a particularly insistent clangor and was briefly tempted to ignore it. But who can resist a ringing phone? I picked up.

"Oliver Whitcomb, Archy," he said, positively burbling with bonhomie. "How you doing, fella?"

"Very well, thank you," I said. "And you?"

"Got the world on a string," he said breezily. "Listen, Mitzi and I just decided to have a spur-of-the-moment minibash tonight. Nothing fancy. Very informal. Very casual. Come as you are. We'll have a few drinks and laugh it up. You're cordially invited. Can you make it?"

I didn't hesitate. "Sure I can. Thanks for the invitation."

"Great! Anytime after nine o'clock. Binky Watrous promised to show up. You have our address? If not, we're in the Boca book."

"I'll find you."

We hung up and I decided Oliver was making a determined effort to be friendly. My ego is not emaciated, as you well know, but I could not believe he sought my palship simply because of my sterling character or aftershave lotion. The lad was eager for my attendance at his "minibash," but for what reason I could not then have said. Four hours later I knew.

All of which explains why, at about nine-twenty that evening, I pulled into the white graveled courtyard of the Whitcomb mansion in Boca Raton. There were already a dozen parked cars but the one that caught my eye, other than Binky's moldering Cabriolet, was a custom-made silver Cadillac stretch limousine. That thing was so long it should have been articulated with a separate driver to operate the wheels of the rear section.

A thug in chauffeur's garb was leaning against the front fender, smoking a cigarette and staring at the heavens. Trying to locate Cassiopeia, no doubt. His uniform was shiny silver to match the car's finish.

I strolled over. "Quite a yacht," I observed.

He looked at me without interest. Brutish chap. "Yeah," he said.

"How on earth do you turn a corner?" I asked.

"It ain't easy."

I made a guess: "Ernest Gorton's car?"

"You got it," he said, flicked his cigarette butt away, and yawned in my face. Mr. Congeniality.

I entered the tessellated front door, disappointed that I wasn't greeted by a periwigged flunky in knee breeches. As a matter of fact, I wasn't greeted by anyone but heard a cackle of talk and laughter coming from a chamber at the end of a marble-floored entrance hall. As Binky had told me, everything in this polished dwelling seemed to be constructed of mirrors, stainless steel, white leather, and tinted glass. Obviously "brown furniture" was anathema to the younger Whitcombs.

I entered a crowded living room with a wet bar along one wall with enough bottles on display to grace a luxe hotel. Few guests paused quaffing to inspect the newcomer, but Oliver came bustling forward to shake my hand heartily and give me a welcoming grin.

"Great you could make it," he said. "Just great! What do you think of our place?"

"Impressive," I said.

"You don't think it's too architectural, too stark?"

"Not at all," I lied. "If it ain't baroque, don't fix it."

His laugh was almost a roar and he clapped me on the shoulder. "You've got a great sense of humor, Archy," he enthused. "Great! Listen, I'm not going to introduce you to all these fun people. Just mingle and introduce yourself. The bar is open for business, but you'll have to mix your own poison. Live it up!"

He was trying too hard.

He drifted away and I headed for the pharmacy wondering if I was a fun person, qualified to mingle with this pot-smoking assembly most of whom looked ten years younger and a hundred years more with-it than I. I was certain they could identify all the current rock stars, which I couldn't. But I consoled myself with the thought that not one of them could name America's greatest war song, which I could. In case you're wondering, it's a 1918 classic entitled "Would You Rather Be a Colonel with an Eagle on Your Shoulder or a Private with a Chicken on Your Knee?"

I mixed a very mild vodka and water at the bar, reckoning it was going to be a long night. Then I turned to inspect the other guests. I spotted Binky Watrous in one corner sitting on the lap of Mitzi Whitcomb. Yes, *he* was sitting on *her* lap. I don't believe Sherlock Holmes ever did that with Irene Adler.

In another corner I saw Ernest Gorton looking as rumpled as he had the first time we met. He was wearing an undoubtedly costly three-piece suit of black silk, Italian cut, but it was so wrinkled I could only conclude he slept fully clothed. He had one meaty arm about the bare shoulders of the orangy-haired young woman I had last seen in the office of Dr. Omar K. Pflug—Rhoda, the carrottop, wearing a tight sheath of silver sequins, to match Gorton's stretch limo, I supposed. The man had an incredible lust for color coordination.

Following the host's instructions, I circulated assiduously, introduced myself, and met a great number of people I devoutly hoped I would never meet again. I suffer from *snobisme,* as you may have guessed, and I found the Whitcombs' guests agonizingly superficial. Conversation? Complete piffle, concerned mostly with holidays taken or planned, new *in* restaurants in Palm Beach County, the latest local political scandal, which movie heroes were gay, and the possibility of curing impotence by acupuncture. I shan't go into details about *that.*

And so I had another drink, or two, simply to endure until I could make a decent departure. Binky had vanished with Mitzi Whitcomb before I had a chance to speak to him. I wasn't even certain he was aware of my appearance. He had the glassy look he gets when he's addled by unrequited love or a surfeit of beef Stroganoff.

But Ernest Gorton was mindful of my presence.

"Glad to see you, Archy boy!" he shouted, clamping one of those fleshy arms about my waist. "Having fun?"

"A plenitude," I assured him.

"Love the way you talk," he marveled. "Just love it! Hey, you got time for a private confab?"

"Of course."

He looked around the living room. More invitees had arrived, the decibels were rising. In addition, despite the air conditioning, the atmosphere had become fuggy with the smell of burning grass. Oliver's friends, I concluded, definitely did not smoke cigarettes from packs labeled with the Surgeon General's warnings.

What truly surprised me was the expression of distaste on Gorton's phiz as he inspected the scene. If Al Rogoff's information was accurate, these fun people were Ernie Boy's customers. But there was no mistaking the contempt in his glower.

"Let's get out of this circus," he said. "We'll talk in my buggy."

He led the way outside to the Cadillac limousine. Some buggy! The glittery chauffeur was still leaning against a fender.

"Take a walk, Jake," Gorton said gruffly. The bruiser nodded and moved away.

We entered the wheeled cathedral. You don't crouch or slide into a car like that; you step in reverently, resisting an urge to cross yourself. We sat in the back, and I noted a little refrigerator, a little bar, a little TV set, a little cellular phone and fax machine. If that car had a little Port-o-John you could have lived there comfortably and never emerged.

"I got some Martell cognac here," Ernest said. "Okay by you?"

"Excellent."

He poured our drinks into outsized crystal snifters. Good cognac should be as much inhaled as tasted, and one ounce is a gentleman's tot. But he must have poured at least three ounces into each glass, and I had visions of enrolling for the 12 Steps the very next day.

"Have I got this right?" Gorton said abruptly. "Your father is an attorney but doesn't do litigation. You started out to be a lawyer but got kicked out of school. You're single and live with your parents. You drink but you're no doper. You do investigations for your father's firm. How'm I doing?"

"You're correct," I acknowledged, realizing he had gone to some trouble to learn my record. But I supposed that was one reason for his success. He was careful and he was thorough: a man of many talents, most of them feculent, and an overwhelming greed.

"I got a proposition for you," he said. He paused to give me an arctic grin. "An offer you can't refuse. I got this business in Miami. Import-export, like I told you. I got some good lawyers, courtroom guys, who know how to protect my interests. But my business is getting so big I need a sharp operator, someone who knows the laws but at the same time knows how to ask the right questions. I mean, I'm into a lot of things, this and that, and I'm always getting these business projects thrown at me. They all require an investment of capital on my part. You know? Now what I need is someone who's got the know-how to evaluate these deals. Do they have a profit potential or are they just scams? I think you're the man to handle the job."

He paused and we both continued to sip our brandies. I was listening attentively to his pitch. Oh, he was good! If he was a legitimate businessman his spiel would have made sense to me. But I knew he was proposing a no-show job. An experienced hustler with his background would never depend on someone else to make his investment choices.

"It's very kind of you to make the offer, Ernie," I said.

"I like you," he continued, tapping my knee. "I genuinely and sincerely like you. Of course you'd have to move to Miami. But that's no problem, is it? I have points in a couple of lush condos and I could fix you up with a flashy pad. What I'm talking about is a salary of fifty grand a year. Under the table if that's the way you want it. How does that grab you?"

"Tempting," I said. I looked down at my glass and saw to my horror it was almost empty. If I were required to take a Breathalyzer test at that moment, I'm sure a siren would wail, bells ring, and the U.S. Marine Band would launch into "Stars and Stripes Forever."

"Well?" Gorton asked. "How do you feel about it?"

"A generous proposal," I told him. "But surely you don't expect an immediate answer. It's an important decision and I want to give it a lot of thought."

He patted my knee again. "That's another thing I like about you, Archy. Most of the guys who work for me got sushi between their ears, but you know how to *think*."

"Thank you," I said humbly. I know how to do humble.

"How much time?" he said. "I need help and I can't wait forever."

"A month tops," I told him.

"Make it two weeks," he said, the demon bargainer.

"All right," I agreed. "I'll let you know within two weeks."

We finished our cognacs and, with some effort, heaved ourselves from those cushioned thrones and exited.

"Coming back to the party?" Gorton asked.

"I don't think so," I said. "You've given me a great deal to consider. I better go home and get started."

He nodded. "I'll be in touch," he said and stalked back to the Whitcomb Museum of Modern Schlock and all those fun people.

I drove home slowly and cautiously. Despite the Brobdingnagian brandy I had consumed, the McNally gray matter (it's really a Ralph Lauren plaid) was surprisingly lucid and functioning. My conclusions?

Misconceptions: I had originally tagged Ernest Gorton as a two-bit grifter. I now saw him as a criminal Machiavelli and definitely not a man to be trifled with. I had also erred in assuming he and Oliver

Whitcomb were equal partners and equally culpable in whatever their mischievous enterprise might be. But I now judged Gorton to be the leader and instigator.

I had no evidence of that—it was all supposition—but I thought it logical and believable. Of one thing I was absolutely certain: Ernest Gorton was aware of my discreet inquiry and was attempting to buy me off. He had first tried to bribe me with a case of wine, probably to test the level of my venality. Rejected, he had then upped the ante with an offer of fifty thousand a year. I could not help but suspect the Oliver Whitcombs' "spur-of-the-moment minibash" had been organized at Gorton's urging (or command) simply to give him an opportunity to subvert me.

I wondered how he had learned of my investigation. Binky Watrous may have revealed too much to Mitzi Whitcomb while romancing that lubricious lady. He might have boasted of his role as my assistant. That peabrain trusted everyone. He had never recognized the existence of evil in the world. Since he was nice, he assumed the entire human population of the planet was also nice. I'm sure he'd condemn an ax murderer of nothing more than bad manners.

But if Binky had not queered our game, there was another way Ernest Gorton may have become aware of an investigation into his activities. I was convinced other personnel of the Whitcomb Funeral Homes—especially those three nouveau riche directors—were deeply involved in the plot. Oliver could hardly organize and conduct a scheme of such magnitude without inside assistance. And perhaps his fellow conspirators had noted Sunny Fogarty's digging into records of Whitcomb's out-of-state shipments of human remains.

It was even possible, I reflected gloomily, that my visits to Sunny's condo had been observed. Jeepers, her apartment (including the bedroom? Gulp!) may have been bugged, and the efficient and painstaking Ernest Gorton knew exactly what was going on. I waggled my head angrily at such fears; I was becoming as paranoid as father and I initially thought Ms. Fogarty to be.

Before I fell asleep that night I was assailed by yet another fear. If I continued to resist Ernest's bribes and blandishments—as I fully intended to—what might be his final solution to end my prying? I didn't care to dwell on that. I don't have Binky's Pollyannaish philosophy; I did not think Mr. Gorton was a nice man.

23

Friday was bloomy. The fog and overcast had blown away, and an azure sky looked as if it had been through a wash-and-dry cycle. More important, my anxieties of the night before were banished by sunshine; the customary McNally buoyancy was working its wonders and I was ready for a fight or a frolic.

I awoke in time to breakfast with my parents, and what a treat it was! The previous evening we had feasted on a roasted Butterball turkey and on Friday morning Ursi Olson started using leftovers by serving creamed turkey on biscuits. Scrumptious! And a little dab of mild salsa instead of cranberry sauce didn't hurt.

Invigorated by the matutinal bracer I drove to the office singing another of my favorite songs: "It's a Sin to Tell a Lie." Loved the tune; totally disagreed with the lyrics. I was no sooner at my desk than Connie Garcia called.

"Archy," she wailed, "we can't have dinner this weekend."

"Oh? Got a better offer, have you? Kevin Costner?"

"You silly," she said. "One of my Miami cousins was in an accident. Her car was totaled and she's in the hospital with broken bones and God knows what else."

"Ah, what a shame," I said. "Can I drive you down?"

"You're sweet to offer, but I wouldn't think of it. I'm taking an afternoon flight."

"Then how about lunch?" I suggested. "You better have something before you start out."

"Well . . . okay," she said. "But I'm so shook I probably won't be able to eat. It's Gloria—the girl who got hurt—and you know she's my favorite cousin. We're practically like sisters."

"Tell me about it at lunch," I urged. "The Pelican at noon?"

"Thank you, Archy," she said, and I could hear she was close to tears. A very emotional woman, our Connie.

I parked my mocs atop the desk and fell to brooding about the Whitcomb case. Well, perhaps brooding is a bit excessive; what I actually did was review everything I knew and everything I surmised about that strange affair. I tried to make sense of what was happening, but none of the scenarios I devised sounded the clarion call. I could not find any coherence in all those incongruous facts and fancies.

There was one fact I did not have. I also had no idea whether or not it might prove significant. Probably not. But while conducting a discreet inquiry I like to collect as many snippets of skinny as possible, even if most of them prove to be the drossiest of dross.

I could have obtained the information I sought by calling Sunny Fogarty. But because of my suspicion that rogues were at work in the hushed environs of the Whitcomb Funeral Homes I thought it prudent not to phone her office.

And so I spent half an hour calling Air Cargo Services at three national carriers. At the end of this chore, having been shunted from one department to another, I had an answer to my query. Human remains in a coffin, properly gift-wrapped for air shipment, weigh approximately four hundred lbs.—an interesting factoid that will enable you to enliven conversation at the next cocktail party you attend.

I was preparing to depart for luncheon with Connie when I was delayed by a phone call.

"Al Rogoff," he said brusquely. "Can you make lunch at twelve-thirty?"

"No, I cannot," I told him. "I have a prior engagement."

"Who with—one of your tootsies? Cancel it."

"I do not have a date with a tootsie," I said indignantly. "And I refuse to cancel."

"All right, all right," he said. "Don't get your *cojones* in an uproar. Suppose we come over to your office at two o'clock."

"*We?*" I asked. "Al, are you suddenly using the royal plural pronoun—or may I expect a visit from two or more persons?"

"Two of us."

"And who will be the other visitor?"

"You'll find out," he said and hung up.

It was such a weird conversation I wondered if Rogoff wasn't already out to lunch.

Connie was seated at the bar when I arrived at the Pelican Club. She was gazing mournfully into a glass of Evian and definitely drooping. I gave her a hug, a cheek kiss, and hustled her to our favorite table in the dining area.

Priscilla came bopping over, took one look at Connie, and said, "What's wrong, honey?"

My paramour gave her a brave smile. "Family troubles, Pris. My favorite cousin got smashed up in a car accident in Miami. I'm flying down to see her this afternoon."

"Aw, that's rough," Pris said, instantly solicitous. "I hope she comes out of it okay. Listen, I think you better have a stiff wallop and then some solid food."

"Me, too," I said.

"You!" she scoffed. "You need a stiff wallop like Missouri needs another flood. How about vodka-rocks first and then a big platter of Buffalo chicken wings with Cajun-style rice and maybe a beer to put out the fire."

"Excellent medicine," I told her. "Thank you, nurse. And don't forget the Rolaids for dessert."

Connie was eager to talk during that luncheon and I was content to listen. She told me more about her extensive family than I had heard before. Most of her relatives were Marielitos and were succeeding admirably in their new homeland. For instance, Gloria, the injured cousin, managed a boutique, and her father had opened a Cuban art gallery.

Listening to Connie chatter on about parents, grandparents, uncles, aunts, cousins, and all their progeny, I began to comprehend part of the attraction this woman has to me. Perhaps the major part.

She is physically alluring—but so was Mrs. Agnes Snodgrass, my homeroom teacher in the sixth grade. She has inexhaustible brio—but so did Eve Arden. She has wit and sensitivity—but so did a dozen other women with whom I had briefly consorted.

I think my abiding affection for Connie is due to her ordinariness. I don't mean that as a put-down, of course, for she is a lady of quality, feisty and passionate. The ordinariness I refer to is the life she lives. You must understand that most of the women I dallied with, or who dallied with me, were encountered during the course of my discreet inquiries. More often than not they had lives of noisy desperation.

When I begin to believe that *all* women are like that, Consuela Garcia offers a healthy dose of normality. Quite simply, she restores me to sanity. Her world consists of the basics: family, job, friends—and me. You may find normality a bore; I found it a blessing. In fact, in the treacherous and sometimes violent world in which I moved, my attachment to Connie may well have been my salvation.

Professor McNally's next lecture on Psychopathology in Intergender Relationships will be held on Tuesday at Radclyffe Hall.

By the time we finished lunch, Connie's spirits had been elevated if not restored to their usual vertiginous heights. I had lent a willing ear to her nonstop monologue, but I cannot claim credit for her recovery. I think it was the Cajun rice that did the trick.

We parted outside. Connie held me close, looked at me sternly, and said, "I may be gone for a few days or a week. You'll behave, won't you?"

"Don't I always?"

"No," she said.

We paid mutual lip service and she promised to call me from Miami. Then she was gone. I watched her drive away. I had a sudden, mercifully brief attack of guilt and contrition. Don't ask me why.

I was a few minutes late getting back to the McNally Building and looked into the reception area to see if my visitors had arrived. They had. Sgt. Al Rogoff, in uniform, was seated next to a tall chap in civvies who was wearing sunglasses so dark they were practically opaque. Both men looked grim.

I made a brief apology for my tardiness and led them up to my model office—model in the sense of being a miniature, *not* an ideal. The three of us squeezed in and Rogoff introduced his companion: Special Agent Griffin Kling from the FBI office in Miami. He was built like a pencil and looked as if he had once been an artiste of the slam dunk. He took off those menacing specs before he shook my hand. I wished he had left them on; his eyes were pale and hard.

I got him seated in the swivel chair behind my desk. Al took the folding steel chair reserved for visitors. I stood.

Kling wasted no time. "Two nights ago," he started, "I was having a few belts with a friend of mine who's with Metro-Dade homicide. He told me he had received a query from Sergeant Rogoff here regarding Ernest Gorton. The reason my pal mentioned it was because he knows of my interest in Gorton. That creep's been Number One on my personal Most Wanted list for more than five years. I know he's into everything rotten, but I've never been able to nail him. On top of that, about a year ago I was running an informant, a nice young kid who got racked up on a minor drug rap. We turned him and he was paying his dues until he got smoked. Gorton ordered the kill—I'm sure of it—but I couldn't pin it on him. That slime has become a real—" He paused helplessly. "What's it called when you can't get something out of your mind?"

"An idée fixe?" I suggested.

"Is that what it is?" the FBI agent said. "Well, I got it. I want to see Gorton put down so bad I can taste it. So when I heard Palm Beach was asking questions about this shark, I drove up here hoping to find out something I can use. But Rogoff says it's not official business and not something he can tell me. He claims it's your baby and if you want to give me what you've got, it's okay with him, but he can't without your say-so. How about it?"

I was grateful for Al's discretion. He had acted honorably, knowing what his uncooperative attitude might cost him.

My first reaction was to refuse to reveal anything about the Whitcomb affair to the FBI. But then I realized those shipments of coffins across state lines might possibly have shattered federal laws. In addition, it would do no harm to have a colleague in the Miami area, Gorton's home territory.

I was silent for such a long time the Special Agent became impatient.

"Do you know exactly what Gorton is doing in this neck of the woods?" he demanded.

"Not exactly," I admitted. "But I'd wager it's something illegal."

"You'd *wager?*" Kling said, blinking.

"That's the way Archy talks," Rogoff advised him. "You'll get used to it."

"How about a quid pro quo?" I asked the FBI man. "I'll tell you what I know if you'll promise to keep Sergeant Rogoff and me promptly informed of any developments resulting from my information."

He rose to his feet and extended a hand to shake mine once more. "Done," he said and sat down again.

I told him what I had previously related to the sergeant: the unexplained increase in Whitcomb's income, those puzzling out-of-state shipments to the same consignee in New York, Boston, and Chicago:

the Cleo Hauling Service. I also mentioned Ernest Gorton's close relationship with Oliver Whitcomb, CEO of the funeral homes.

As before, I said nothing of the equivocal roles being played by Sunny Fogarty, Horace, and Sarah Whitcomb. But I still had the feeling the drama being enacted there had a peripheral but perhaps meaningful connection to the criminal activities at the mortuaries.

"That's all you've got?" Griffin Kling said when I finished my recital.

He had taken no notes but, staring into his stony eyes (an easy trick if you concentrate your gaze on the bridge of the nose between the eyes), I knew he had missed nothing and would forget nothing.

"It's all I have," I assured him.

He nodded—but I was certain he didn't believe me. He was a hard man and wouldn't testify the sun would rise tomorrow until he saw it.

"All right," he said. "There are a few things I can do immediately. I'll contact our offices in New York, Boston, and Chicago and request they trace ownership of the Cleo Hauling Service. And if they can spare the manpower—excuse me, the personpower—I'll ask them to tail the Cleo trucks when they pick up coffins at the airports."

"I'm betting those trucks aren't delivering to funeral homes or cemeteries," Rogoff put in.

"I'm betting the same thing," Kling agreed. "But all that out-of-town stuff is going to take time. Meanwhile there's something I can do. Gorton's front is a legit import-export company. Mostly he brings in wood furniture from South America. The business seems to be clean. It better be; we've persuaded the IRS to do an audit every year. Anyway, Gorton has a warehouse out near the airport where he keeps his furniture inventory until it's sold and trucked out. I think I'll request twenty-four-hour surveillance on that place, either by a stakeout or concealed TV cameras. How does that sound?"

"Makes sense," Al said.

"Has the warehouse ever been searched?" I asked.

The agent's smile was as cold as his eyes. "Twice," he said. "By me. I thought he might be bringing in drugs in hollowed-out parts of the furniture. I struck out; the furniture was just that; nothing hidden in holes, panels, or anywhere else. Now I figure the vermin isn't a smuggler; he's buying his stuff directly from the cartels, cash on delivery in Miami."

"Are drugs his main source of income?" I said.

"Only a part of it. I'm convinced he's into guns, brand-name ripoffs, money laundering, and maybe even counterfeiting. Lately there's been a flood of the queer in South Florida. I tell you this Gorton is a world-class nasty and he's going to take a fall if I have to chill him myself."

There was no mistaking the triple-distilled venom in his voice. Rogoff and I traded a quick glance. We both knew how unpredictable and potentially dangerous a lawman can be when obsessed by a private vendetta.

Special Agent Griffin Kling apparently realized he had said too much. He rose abruptly and donned his black sunglasses. "I'll be in touch," he said crisply. "I'll keep you up to speed on what's happening in Miami, and I hope you'll let me know of any developments up here."

"Of course," I said.

There was another round of hand-shaking and the two men departed. I reclaimed my swivel chair and stared down at my desk blotter where, I saw, Kling's nervous fingers had ripped every match from a book and then had shredded the cover into jagged strips. Obviously a stressed man and I wondered if I had made an error of judgment in welcoming his assistance.

Doesn't W.S. say something about having a long spoon when you eat with the devil? I must look it up.

24

What a delightful Friday evening that was! Because nothing happened to roil the McNally equanimity. Father stirred up a pitcher of excellent gin martinis at the family cocktail hour and Ursi Olson served *cervelli con uova* for dinner. That's calves' brains with eggs, and if you haven't tried it, don't knock it.

I went up to my hidey-hole, played a cassette of Sinatra's "Duets," smoked an English Oval, sipped a very small marc, worked on my journals in a desultory fashion, and suddenly realized I was happy. That always comes as something of a shock, does it not? I mean, you have problems, troubles, frustrations, and then you realize how gossamer they are and you're content to be breathing. Of course it may have been the calves' brains, Sinatra, or the brandy that brought on my euphoria, but whatever the cause I welcomed it.

Connie Garcia phoned around nine o'clock to tell me her cousin's condition had stabilized and doctors were hoping for a complete recovery. Good news. My belle amour said she'd probably remain in Miami for three or four days, and when she returned she definitely expected an orgy à deux, both gustatory and physically frolicsome. I gave her a verbal contract.

And so to bed. Not forgetting to spread my arms wide to the ceiling and murmur, "Thank you, God." That's as serviceable a form of prayer as any, innit?

Saturday turned out to be an equine of a different complexion, and I was rudely wrenched back to the demands and insecurities of reality. I slept late and awoke with vague hopes of a lazy, laid-back weekend. Maybe some tennis, a round of golf, a game of poker, perhaps a gimlet or two or three. Look, Mr. Holmes had his cocaine and I have my Sterling vodka. Which of us is to be more severely censured?

I bounced downstairs to a deserted kitchen. Father, I reckoned, was on his way to his club for 18 holes with a foursome that had been playing together for so many years I swear they now communicated solely with grunts. Mother and Ursi were probably out shopping for provisions.

I had a jolt of Clamato, toasted a muffin I slathered with peach preserve, and boiled up a pot of instant black. I was on my second dose of caffeine when Jamie Olson came wandering in and planted himself down across the table from me. He was smoking his pungent old briar and in self-defense I lighted my first cigarette of the day.

"Got a raccoon," he reported glumly. "Pried the lid off the trash can. Made a nice mess."

"I thought the new can we bought was supposed to be raccoon-proof."

"Supposed to be," he said. "Wasn't. Them animals are smart buggers. Could work a combination lock, I have no doubt. Any coffee left?"

"Maybe a cup," I said. "Help yourself."

We sat awhile in silence, sipping and smoking.

"Jason," he said finally. "The Whitcombs' man. We hoisted a few together yesterday afternoon."

"Good," I said. "Learn anything?"

"Some. Like I told you, Jase is no blabbermouth when it comes to his family. But he admitted things are rough these days between father and son."

"Did he give any reason for their *casus belli?*"

"Their what?"

"Conflict. The reason for their dissension."

"I think it's money."

"That's odd," I said. "Both Horace and Oliver are loaded."

"Uh-huh," Jamie said. He was quiet a long time and I waited patiently. There was no point in trying to hurry our houseman; he had his own pace, more an amble than a stride.

"Want me to guess?" he asked finally.

"By all means."

"It's Mrs. Whitcomb. From what Jason said, she's fading. He doesn't think she's going to make it. Mebbe—I'm guessing now—she's got more cash than husband or son. And that's what the squabble's about. Who inherits."

I looked at him, astonished. "Jamie," I said, "you're a genius."

"Just guessing," he said. "Told you that."

We said no more on the subject. We cleaned up the kitchen and then I raced upstairs to flip through my professional diary, wanting to verify a vague memory. I found it: Father had told me that for tax reasons, Horace had transferred a majority of shares to his wife.

Jamie had been almost right. Sarah didn't have more cash than husband or son, but she held controlling interest in the Whitcomb Funeral Homes. That was the cause of the antagonism: Who would end up a lion and who a lamb?

You may think it inexcusably crass and unfeeling for husband and son to be concerned with inheritance while wife and mother is expiring in a motel-like hospital suite. If you feel that way, you have had little exposure to the basic motivations of human behavior. They are not depraved, y'know; they are simply *human.*

I phoned Sunny Fogarty, hoping to find her at home on a gorgeous Saturday morning.

"Archy!" she said. "I was just thinking about you."

"Thank you," I said. "And I, you. Sunny, I'd like to see you briefly as soon as possible. I have a few questions."

Short silence. "But not on the phone?" she said. No dummy she.

"Correct. And not at your home or mine. You know Mizner Park in Boca?"

"Of course."

"There's a bookstore. Liberties. Do you think you could be browsing at noon?"

Pause again. "Is it important?"

"It is."

"Then I'll manage," she said. "Archy, you're being very mysterious."

"I'm being very paranoid," I told her. "I'll explain when I see you. I'd love to ask you to lunch, but I don't think it would be wise. We'll chat a few moments and then go our separate ways."

Third pause. "All right, Archy," she said. "I trust you."

That was comforting. And somewhat daunting.

I had pulled on casual and rather raddled duds that morning, but now, preparing for a clandestine rendezvous at a smart bookstore, I decided something spiffier was called for. If you think me inordinately vain, you're quite right. I donned an aqua polo shirt of Sea Island cotton, slacks of go-to-hell fuchsia, and a jacket of properly faded madras. No socks. The loafers were cordovans with floppy tassels—which drive mein papa right up the wall.

It really was a splendiferous day and all during that exhilarating drive south to Boca I lustily sang "Enjoy Yourself—It's Later Than You Think," which pretty well sums up my basic philosophy.

I found Sunny Fogarty standing before the cookbook section at Liberties. She was leafing through a volume on soufflés. I joined her and selected a treatise entitled *Wild Game Stews*. That tells you something about us, does it not?

We stood shoulder to shoulder and conversed in hushed tones.

"What's this all about, Archy?" she said tensely.

Speaking rapidly, I gave her a succinct account of Ernest Gorton's apparent involvement in illicit activities at Whitcomb Funeral Homes and what I interpreted as his attempted bribery to convince me to end or soft-pedal my investigation.

"He's aware of my inquiries," I told Sunny. "No doubt about it. And I think his information originated from within your office."

She nodded. "I've suspected someone has been listening in on my calls. I know positively my personal files have been searched. And our computer records have been tampered with."

"The villains are probably aware of your suspicions and investigation. What concerns me is that I fear they also know you have requested assistance from McNally and Son. They may even have observed my visits to your home. I don't wish to alarm you unnecessarily, but you may be under surveillance and perhaps your apartment has been bugged."

Her face grew increasingly grim. "Yes," she said, "that's possible."

"I think it best you use a pay phone whenever you wish to contact me," I went on. "I really shouldn't have called you at home this morning, but I had no choice. That's why I selected a public place for our meeting and suggested we forgo luncheon just in case you might have been followed."

She accepted these dire warnings with admirable stoicism, and I saw again what a strong woman she was. I didn't want to add to her strain by relating what I had learned from FBI Special Agent Griffin Kling about the nasty proclivities of Ernest Gorton. After all, Sunny had no need to know; she had quite enough on her plate at the moment.

"Archy," she said in a toneless voice, "you said on the phone you had questions."

"I do. Two of them. First, have you heard anything recently about the condition of Mrs. Sarah Whitcomb?"

"Not good," she said, her face suddenly frozen. "Mr. Horace told me the doctors give him no hope. First they talked about years, then it was months, then weeks; it spread so swiftly. Now I'm afraid it's days."

"Dreadful," I said. "A lovely woman."

"Yes," she said. "She's been good to me, so understanding when my own mother became ill. I'll never forget her kindness."

"How is Mr. Horace taking it?"

"He's trying to cope. But he's hurting."

"And Oliver?"

"I wouldn't know about him," she said curtly. "What's your second question?"

"Financial. Does Whitcomb hold a large cash reserve?"

She looked at me. "What an odd thing to ask. Will it help your inquiry?"

"I can't swear it will, but it might."

"I shouldn't reveal our balance sheet," she said. "After all, we are not a public company. But I'll take the chance. As I told you, Archy, I trust you. Up to about six months ago our cash balance was nothing extraordinary. About average for the past several years. Then those out-of-state shipments suddenly ballooned, and so did our cash reserve. I put most of it in three- and six-month Treasury bills. I can't give you an exact figure, but it's considerable. Is that what you wanted to know?"

"It is," I said, "and I thank you."

We replaced our books on the shelves and smiled quizzically at each other.

"Archy," she said, "what you told me about people possibly being aware of our, uh, connection and my apartment being bugged, I guess that means you shouldn't come over again."

"I'm afraid that's what it means," I agreed. "Until we bring order out of chaos."

She sighed. "I'll miss you, Archy," she said.

Was I imagining it or did I detect a note of relief in her voice? I decided I would never understand this enigmatic woman.

Sunny departed first and I watched her go, thinking what a stalwart figure she cut. I waited a few moments, then wandered out into the midday sunshine. I toured Mizner Park and found a German restaurant I hadn't known existed.

After inspecting the menu posted in the window and being panged by hunger—my customary state—I popped inside for a platter of plump potato pancakes with hot sauerkraut. There are those who like a spicy ketchup on their latkes; I prefer apple sauce. I also had a stein of an excellent chilled lager.

I headed homeward reflecting that after my Teutonic snack I was in no condition for tennis, golf, or any other physical activity more vigorous than a game of jackstraws.

But the McNally aptitude for creative delusions had not been impaired and Sunny Fogarty's answers to my two questions began to form the spine of a theory explicating Oliver Whitcomb's role in what was happening at the funeral homes. I still didn't know exactly *what* was happening but had no doubt that, to paraphrase Woollcott, it was immoral, illegal, and fattening—to Whitcomb's bank account.

I spent the remainder of Saturday afternoon sharpening my solution to one part of the Whitcomb puzzle. A rereading of the jotted notes in my journal persuaded me that, as I had remarked hopefully to Sunny, order was beginning to emerge from chaos.

I must admit right now that my elegant scenario turned out to be wrong. Not totally wrong, mind you, but half-wrong. In my defense I can only plead guilty of making a case from insufficient evidence.

Well, what the hell, Columbus thought he had landed at Calcutta.

25

I accompanied my parents to church on Sunday morning. This rare event, I confess, was not due to a sudden upsurge of religiosity. Actually I was hoping for another glimpse of that Amazonian contralto in the choir. Sad to say, she was not present.

Could she be ill? If so I would have been happy to hasten to her bedside with a jar of calf's-foot jelly or a crystal decanter of chicken soup. But of course I didn't know her name or address.

I mention this ridiculous incident merely to illustrate my addiction to fantasies that sometimes engross me. Fortunately, few of them are ever realized.

I returned home in a grumpy mood and immediately began making phone calls hoping to arrange some action on the courts, links, or even around a poker table. But all the pals I contacted had already made Sunday plans; I was odd man out, an unwonted and disturbing role.

Finally, in desperation, I phoned Binky Watrous. He sounded as if he had just undergone several hours of CPR.

"Binky," I said, "why are you breathing like that?"

"I'm fortunate to be breathing at all," he said hollowly. "Archy, when I signed on I had no idea the job would entail so much wear and tear on the old carcass."

"Let me guess: You partied last night with Mitzi and Oliver Whitcomb."

"With them and a gaggle of other fruitcakes. It was a traveling party: here, there, and everywhere. I think at one time we might have been in Fort Pierce, but I can't be sure. Those people skitter around like characters from that Christmas ballet, 'The Ballbreaker.' "

"Binky," I said gently, "it's called 'The Nutcracker.' "

"Oh," he said. "Well . . . whatever. Archy, you know what I need right now?"

"A new head?"

"It would help, but before I have a transplant I'd like a very big, very strong, very peppery Bloody Mary."

"So mix one."

"I can't. The Duchess decided I've been imbibing too much and she's put our liquor supply under lock and key. Guess who's got the key. Not me. And the saloons aren't open yet. Archy, if you have a soupçon of charity in your heart, help me!"

I sighed. "All right, Binky. Drive over and I'll give you an injection."

"I can't drive over."

"Why not?"

"I don't have a car."

"You didn't total it?"

"No, but I left it somewhere."

"Binky, where did you leave your car?"

"I can't remember, but I'm sure it'll come to me after I take my medicine."

"If you don't have a car, how did you get home last night—or this morning?"

"Someone must have delivered me."

"Who delivered you?"

"I don't remember."

"Binky," I said, "everyone knows that before you are allowed to become a private eye you are required to take and pass a peculiarity test. You have just qualified. Hang on, old buddy. I'm on my way."

I went into the kitchen and hurriedly prepared a quart thermos of iced Bloody Marys. I remembered to take two plastic cups and set out for the Duchess's rather grungy residence on South County Road. Binky was waiting for me outside, slowly to-ing and fro-ing with hands thrust deep in trouser pockets, his head hanging low. The poor lad did appear to be one short step away from rigor mortis.

"You have my plasma?" he croaked.

I nodded.

"Not here, not here," he said hastily. "The Duchess is probably watching from her window and cackling at my torment. Let's vamoose."

I had no desire to chauffeur this shattered hulk to the McNally home even for the purpose of resuscitation. Nor did I wish to park on the beach where a gendarme might become outraged at the sight of a desperate young man swilling from a quart thermos. So we ended up in the vacant parking area of the Pelican Club, which had not yet opened for business.

I poured Binky a cup of Bloody Mary and he gulped greedily.

"More!" he gasped.

"In a few moments," I said sternly. "If you are willing to overindulge you must be ready to accept the consequences."

"What was I to do?" he demanded, enlivened by the stimulant (it was the horseradish that did it). "I couldn't sit there like a lunkhead, could I, when everyone else was swigging or smoking. By the way, her name is Starlight; I remember that."

"Whose name is Starlight?"

"Ernie Gorton's carrottop, Rhoda Starlight."

"You're jesting."

"Well, her real name is Rhoda Flembaugh, she told me, but Rhoda Starlight is her stage name."

"Uh-huh," I said. "And what stages has the lady graced lately?"

"Mostly tabletops in nudie clubs," Binky said, staring longingly at the open thermos. "But she says she's not doing that scene anymore. Claims she's self-employed."

I poured him another cup and one for myself. I felt I needed it and deserved it. Actually, I was pleased with Binky's report. Despite his intemperate roistering he had managed to collect a few nuggets that might prove to be meaningful.

"But I don't think so," he said, sipping his second drink slowly with beamy satisfaction.

"Don't think what, Binky?"

"That Rhoda is self-employed."

"Oh? And what makes you think that?"

"She spent a lot of time chatting up some of the more exciting birds at the party. I got the feeling she might be recruiting."

"Recruiting?"

"You know. Luring them into a life of ill repute."

I didn't laugh or even smile. I'm proud of that. I said, "Binky, do you suppose she works for Ernest Gorton? That she's his CEO in a call girl ring operating in this area?"

He looked down into his empty plastic cup. "I guess it's possible," he said finally. "Archy, I really don't like these people. They're not top drawer."

"No," I agreed, "they're not."

We shared the watery remains of the Bloody Marys and then I drove him home.

"What I'm going to do," he declared, "is get into bed and sleep nonstop for forty-eight hours."

"A wise decision," I told him.

We pulled into his driveway, and there was his battered MB Cabriolet. Binky whimpered with delight, hastened to his heap, and patted the dented hood.

"Hiya, baby," he crooned. "Did you come home to daddy?"

Disgusting.

I accomplished nothing of importance during the remainder of that day. I futzed around my quarters, read the newspapers, leafed through a few mags, smoked two cigs, listened to a Hoagy Carmichael tape, dined with my parents (we had roasted salmon with a basil sauce), returned to my mini-suite and took an hour's nap, rose to shower, watched the last half of a Dolphins game, attended the family cocktail hour, supped with my parents (we had spaghetti bolognese), returned upstairs and listened to a cassette of Ella Fitzgerald singing Cole Porter, picked up my journal and put it aside, croaked out a chorus of "Just One of Those Things," and decided I had done enough work for one day.

Exciting, huh? Have your eyes glazed over?

I have detailed that litany of ho-hum activities to prove my life is not all harum-scarum adventures, brief moments of violent action, and the pursuit of loves, both requited and un-. I mean, I do have periods of soporific ennui. The only reason I mention it is that I hope it may give us something in common. Surely you've had times with nothing better to do than count the walls.

Sleep came swiftly, which was a blessing because my dreams were rather racy—improbable but racy.

A phone call awakened me on Monday morning.

"H'lo," I mumbled.

"Aw," Al Rogoff said, "I bet I woke you up. And it's only eight-thirty. I'm frightfully chagrined. Can you ever forgive me?"

"No," I said. "What's it doing outside?"

"The sun is shining, birds are twittering, God's in His heaven and all's right with the world. Satisfied?"

"Sounds good. I may eventually arise. And what is the reason for this reveille?"

"I got a call from that FBI guy Griffin Kling. He's keeping his part of the bargain. He says his offices in New York, Boston, and Chicago traced the registration of trucks owned by the Cleo Hauling Service. It didn't take them long—but why should it? They probably made one phone call. Anyway they got a name. Didn't you tell me there was a fake nurse working out of the office of that flaky doctor?"

"That's right."

"The name you gave me was Rhoda. Got a last name?"

"I do now. Her stage name is Rhoda Starlight. Apparently her real name is Rhoda Flembaugh."

Sgt. Rogoff whooped with delight. "Kling says the Cleo trucks are registered in the name of Rhoda Flembaugh. How do you like that?"

"Love it," I said. "Just love it."

"What's the connection between this Rhoda and Ernest Gorton?"

"Very close," I told him. "I think she's his madam running a call girl ring in this area. She's been observed recruiting."

"Yeah? Observed by whom?"

"Binky Watrous."

"That's like saying she was observed by Daffy Duck. But she and Gorton are definitely connected?"

"Definitely."

"I'll call Kling and give him the good news. That guy is sweating to cut off Gorton's family jewels. He's still working on who eventually gets those coffins Whitcomb is shipping out. Keep in touch."

He hung up and I swung out of bed yawning, pleased with the way the day had started. It seemed to me we were webbing Ernest Gorton. I had little doubt we could snare that villain and he would plea-bargain by betraying Oliver Whitcomb and his cohorts. Gorton knew all the tricks of survival in his corrupt milieu.

I drove to the McNally Building musing on the role of Griffin Kling in this affair. The FBI agent struck me as a very odd chap indeed. I admire Sgt. Al Rogoff as an estimable law enforcement officer, and one of the reasons is that he never lets his emotions and prejudices influence his professional judgment.

But I sensed Kling was a man haunted by furies. Somehow he had settled on Ernest Gorton as a symbol of everything wrong in the world. If he could bring Gorton down, it would mean not only the end of a single criminal career but would be a blow against the forces of evil and a victory for decency, cherry pie, and white socks.

I arrived at my office to find a message requesting I phone Horace Whitcomb at home. I hesitated a moment, wondering if I should first inform my father. But then I decided to call and discover why Mr. Whitcomb was phoning the drudge of McNally & Son.

"Archy," he said, "I apologize for bothering you."

"No bother at all, sir."

"Oliver is with his mother at the moment and I'm at home. I'll go to the hospital at noon after Oliver leaves."

Of course it was possible Sarah was allowed only one visitor at a time. It was also possible that husband and son, or both, had no desire to meet at the bedside of the stricken woman.

"Could you come over for a short time?" Horace asked, and I detected a note close to desperation in his voice. "I hate to burden you with my problems, but I really need to talk to someone personally involved."

Moi? Personally involved? That was enough to send a frisson jittering along the McNally spinal cord.

"Of course, sir," I said. "I can be there in twenty minutes."

"Thank you," he said, and I thought he sounded weepy.

It took a bit more than twenty minutes, for traffic was horrendous that morning. But eventually Mr. Horace and I were seated on his terrace, gazing out at the sun-sequined lake and brunching on coffee and mini-croissants with lemon butter.

"And how is Mrs. Sarah feeling?" I inquired.

He tried to control his distress but failed; his eyes brimmed. "She's dying," he said, and my hope for a felicitous day went into deep six.

26

I had no idea what to say; I'm not good at commiseration. But it was not compassion he was seeking.

"I have a confession to make," he said, looking at me steadily now, patrician features sagging with a mixture of sorrow and shame. "It concerns the illegal activities taking place at the Whitcomb Funeral Homes."

"Sir," I said, and it was my turn to be desperate, "don't you think it would be wiser to discuss this matter with my father? He is, after all, your attorney. I have no legal standing whatsoever."

He gave me a gelid smile. "Your father is completely trustworthy, I know, but he can be a rather intimidating man."

I could not disagree with that.

"Besides," he went on, "you have been the one conducting the investigation Sunny Fogarty requested."

Curiously, I was not unduly shocked by the revelation that he was aware of her initial consultation with McNally & Son and my resulting discreet inquiry.

I told Mr. Horace as much. "It seemed incredible to me," I said, "that Sunny should recognize something illicit was going on and you not know of it. But she insisted the suspicion of wrongdoing was solely hers, you hadn't a glimmer and were not to be informed of my nosing about."

He sighed. "Please don't blame Sunny. She was merely following my instructions faithfully, as she always has. Of course I knew something unethical and probably illegal was going on. It's *my* business, Archy, as it was my father's and grandfather's. I know it was well as I know my collection of ship models. If the placement of a potted palm is changed in any of our homes I notice it at once. What I'm trying to say is that Whitcomb Funeral Homes are my life. You may think it odd that mortuaries can constitute a full and rewarding existence, but they do. I have nothing for which to apologize."

"Sir," I said, "if you suspected skulduggery was going on, why on earth didn't you conduct a quiet internal investigation and then, if your suspicions proved valid, call in the police?"

He looked away from me, gazing somberly over the spangled lake. "Archy," he said, "I love my wife. I love Sarah with a devotion so deep and so intense that sometimes I wonder if I shall be able to carry on after she's gone. God damn it!" he shouted suddenly. "Why couldn't I have become ill instead of her? It's not right! It's not fair!" Slowly he calmed. "I do not tell you this to ask for your sympathy or pity but to explain why I acted the way I did. As much as I love Sarah, so does she love our son. I don't mean to imply she loves me the less, but Oliver is and always has been precious to her. We tried to have more babies but didn't succeed, and so my wife lavished all her maternal love on our only child."

I could guess what was coming but wanted to hear him say it. I knew it would resolve some of the riddles that had been gnawing at me.

"And then," he said, turning to look at me directly again, "I became aware of our unexpected increase of income during the past six months. I asked Sunny Fogarty to look into it. We agreed something very troubling was going on."

"The huge number of out-of-state shipments?" I suggested.

He nodded.

"You might have told me from the start," I said. "Instead, Sunny tried to make me believe it was my discovery."

"I apologize for that," he said. "It was a scurvy thing to do but had to be done. Because it became obvious to Sunny and me that the chicanery taking place could not succeed without the active participation of our three chief funeral directors and my son, who is supposed to oversee the day-to-day operations of the entire business."

"Why didn't you confront Oliver and demand an explanation?"

"I couldn't!" he cried. "Don't you see it was impossible? My wife became ill about five years ago and her condition has steadily worsened. She has accepted that with more fortitude and grace than you or I could muster, I assure you. Could I go to that terminally ill woman and tell her our son was probably a thief and I was turning him over to the police? Could I really do that? Tell her the child she loved so very much was a criminal?"

I lowered my head. "A horrible dilemma," I murmured.

"Yes," he said. "Horrible. I could not devastate my wife's final days, nor could I allow Oliver to continue his depredations against an honorable business that's been in the family for three generations. I talked it over with Sunny Fogarty, and we decided our only option was to proceed against Oliver with an outside investigation in which I apparently played no part. It would be an inquiry by McNally and Son, our attorneys, and whatever was uncovered would be strictly a legal matter. Then I could assure Sarah I would do everything I could to aid our son's defense. It wasn't much of a solution to my problem, was it, but I saw no other choice."

"I can't think of anything else you might have done, Mr. Whitcomb. Booting Oliver out of the company would have destroyed your relationship with your wife. I should tell you she is aware of the hostility between you and Oliver. But she has no idea of the cause of the conflict. I doubt, from what you tell me, she could ever be convinced her son capable of criminal behavior."

"Thank God for that," he said fervently. "If it's possible to die happy—and I'm not sure it is—it's what I wish for my wife: that she may quietly and peacefully slip away without pain and with her love for me and her son intact. She deserves nothing less."

We were silent for a few moments. I had no hint of what he was thinking, but I was brooding on the infernal complexities of living: enduring disappointments and tragedies, coping with problems and challenges, seeing ambitions thwarted and hopes deferred—just spending your ration of days doing your damndest to hang on to your sanity.

Mr. Horace straightened up in his chair, squared his shoulders, and took a deep breath. I could not interpret his expression; sadness and resolve were mixed.

"Archy," he said, "what I've told you this morning has been a sort of preamble to what I must say now. Sunny Fogarty has kept me informed on the progress of your investigation. I gather that Ernest Gorton is involved in what's going on."

"It certainly appears so."

"He sounds like a loathsome character."

"He is that, sir."

"My son's close friend," he said bitterly. "Sunny also told me you believe this Gorton knows of your investigation and has attempted to buy you off."

I nodded.

"If Gorton is aware of your relationship with Sunny, do you believe she is personally at risk?"

I hesitated a beat or two. "I think her double-checking of your files and computer records is known to the perpetrators. I think it probable her office calls are monitored and her home phone may be bugged. Yes, I believe she is under close observation, but whether or not her safety is threatened, I simply cannot say."

"Can you swear it's impossible?"

"No, sir, I can't swear that."

"Then it is possible?"

"Yes," I said softly. "Considering what's at stake and Ernest Gorton's reputation, I must admit it's possible."

"That's what I feared," he said tonelessly. "And it's why I ask you now to end your investigation immediately. Sunny and I will end our inquiries as well."

I was astounded. "Mr. Whitcomb," I burst out, "you can't do that!"

"I can," he said, "and I will. You are an employee of the legal firm that represents Whitcomb Funeral Homes, are you not? I intend to write your father requesting your inquiry be ended. If it is not, I shall terminate our association with McNally and Son."

I glared at him furiously. "You realize that such a course of action will in all probability allow what is apparently a crime in progress to continue."

"I know that."

"And the suspected criminals, possibly including your son, may then succeed in utterly destroying what you have described to me as an honorable business that has been in your family for three generations."

"I know that also. But the personal safety of Sunny Fogarty, a devoted employee, takes precedence. If her life is at risk—and you admit it is possible—I'd rather surrender than see her harmed."

My fury slowly cooled to admiration. He had obviously wrestled with this quandary for many sleepless hours and had come to the only decision he could live with. It was a high-minded decision. It was also an impossible decision.

"Sorry, Mr. Whitcomb," I said, "it can't be done."

His face grew stony. "And why not?" he demanded.

"For two reasons, sir. First of all, you refer to me as an employee of

McNally and Son. I am that and it pleases me. But regardless of your relationship with our firm, I shall continue my inquiries no matter what."

"Even if your father orders you to stop?"

"Even if he does. But I doubt if that will ever come to pass. He knows me better than you do, Mr. Whitcomb. And you don't know my father either. Yes, he can be an intimidating man, but he is also an extremely upright man. Never in a million years would he order me to end a criminal investigation. And I have absolutely no intention of doing so, whether as an employee of McNally and Son or as a private snoop. I have my standards, sir, just as you have yours."

He was silent, staring at me.

"You may or may not believe what I have just said," I continued. "But now let me give you the second reason why your proposed cancellation of the investigation is out of the question. This is information Sunny Fogarty did not relay to you because I didn't tell her."

I then related the involvement in the affair by Sgt. Al Rogoff of the Palm Beach Police Department and Special Agent Griffin Kling of the Federal Bureau of Investigation.

"Both men are experienced law enforcement officers," I told Mr. Horace, "and no way are you going to persuade them to end their digging. Agent Kling in particular is positively ferocious in his intent to end the criminal career of Ernest Gorton. Kling is a driven man, and I assure you any plea to end his crusade will be ignored."

Mr. Whitcomb drained his coffee, and when he replaced his cup it clattered on the saucer.

"I suppose you think me a fool," he said dully.

"No, sir," I said, "I don't think that. But events have been set in motion and they have an inexorable momentum you cannot stop. Until the matter is concluded—successfully, let us hope—Sunny Fogarty must take her chances, and so must you, I, Oliver, Ernest Gorton, and everyone else even remotely connected. We are all pawns, Mr. Whitcomb."

"Yes," he said with a twisted smile, "aren't we? And especially Sarah."

I didn't know what he meant by that and didn't ask.

Unexpectedly he yawned, stretching his arms wide, and I realized my guess of sleepless hours of worrying had not been amiss.

"I started the whole thing," he said ruefully. "Told Sunny Fogarty to look into it. And now see what's happened: my son a deceiver, Sunny's safety at risk, my business threatened, the FBI involved. I have been hoisted by my own petard."

"I don't think that expression particularly apt, sir," I told him. "It implies self-destruction, and you're far from that."

"Perhaps," he said, not really believing it. "What do you propose to do now?"

"Continue what I have been doing. Sniff about, ask questions, listen to what people say and observe what they do, wait for things to happen. And sometimes give them a nudge."

"It's an art," he said. "What you do."

"Not quite," I said. "More of a craft."

Silence again, a long silence while he scrabbled at crumbs on the tablecloth. "My God," he said in a low voice, "we do manage to mess things up, don't we?"

I feared he was losing his nerve and it alarmed me. "Sometimes it seems so, Mr. Whitcomb," I said, "but one never knows, do one? I mean, think of those lads who fought the men-of-war in your collection."

That brightened him. "Yes," he said, "you're right. Have you ever heard the apocryphal story of what happened when John Paul Jones was battling the *Serapis* from the bridge of the *Bonhomme Richard?* His ship was riddled, on fire, sinking, decks awash with the blood of dead and dying sailors. Jones was called upon to surrender and shouted back, 'I have not yet begun to fight!' A Marine marksman high in the rigging looked down at the destruction below and said, 'There's always one son of a bitch who never gets the word.' "

We both laughed and I hoped he would be that son of a bitch, though naturally I didn't mention it. I thanked him for the morning's refreshment, we shook hands, and I departed. I drove slowly back to the McNally Building, thinking that for all his candor, his revelations and confessions, he had not yet told me the complete truth. The man was concealing something that troubled him mightily. I was convinced of it, but what that secret could be I had no idea. I had the dizzy notion it was the key word in a perplexing crossword puzzle. Ferret it out and everything would become clear: solved and elegant. Or so I thought.

I descended into our underground garage, parked, and hopped from the Miata. Herb, our security guard, came lumbering over, his big dog-leg holster flapping against his thigh.

"Hey, Mr. McNally," he said, "you got a visitor. A lady."

"Banzai!" I said. "Where is she—in the reception room?"

"Nah," he said, jerking a thumb. "Over there."

I turned to look. A new white Honda Accord. Very nice. I started toward it and the driver's window came purring down. I leaned and peered within. There was no mistaking that tangerine hair: Ms. Rhoda Starlight/Flembaugh.

"Hi there!" she said brightly.

27

"Treat a harlot like a lady and a lady like a harlot." Who said that? I have no idea, although it sounds like the Earl of Chesterfield advising his son. But I resolved to follow this counsel, so when Rhoda gave me a Cheshire cat grin and patted the seat beside her, I obediently circled the car, entered, and immediately became aware of the scent she was wearing. Stirring. One might even say invigorating—and I do say it.

"Arky," she said. "I can call you Arky, can't I?"

"If it pleases you. Actually my name is Archy."

"Of course. Archy. We met once before, didn't we?"

"We did indeed. Briefly. In Dr. Pflug's office."

"Oh, *him*," she said disdainfully. "Ernie calls him El Jerko. Isn't that funny?"

"Hilarious," I said.

"Well, I shook that turkey," she went on. "I'm self-employed now. My own business."

"Good for you."

She dug into a bulging wallet, extracted a business card, and handed it to me. The engraved legend was simplicity itself: "Rhoda. Physical Therapy for Discerning Gentlemen." This was followed by a phone number and, wonderful to behold, a fax number. No address.

"Are you a discerning gentleman?" she asked.

"I try," I said modestly. "I don't always succeed."

She laughed and clamped a warm hand on my knee. "Ernie has told me so much about you I just knew we had to become better friends. Are you busy this afternoon?"

"Unfortunately I am. An appointment with my trichologist for the repair of a small tonsure."

"Golly," she said, distressed. "Does it hurt?"

"The pain is excruciating," I said, "especially when the wind is from the east."

"Then how about tonight?" she inquired. "You could come to my place or I could come to yours. No charge. It'll be a freebie."

"Rhoda," I said, "you are an extremely attractive young lady and your beauty is exceeded only by your generosity. But there is something you should know: I am engaged to be married to a woman I have known for several years. I love her dearly and have sworn to her my undying devotion and absolute faithfulness."

The hand on my knee didn't relax. "She doesn't have to know, Arky."

"Archy. But I'll know, won't I, and it will make me feel like a cur."

"You must love her very much."

"I do, I do!" I cried, and if I could have wiped a tear from my eye or stifled a small sob I would. I have no shame—as you well know. "Rhoda, she means the world to me and I could not live with the thought of betraying our love. Have you ever felt that way?"

The warm hand was withdrawn from my knee. "No," she said sorrowfully, "but I've dreamed of it. Some guy who would really turn me on and we'd make it together. I mean, I'd cook and clean for him and everything. But you're right; if I found out he was cheating on me it would spoil the whole deal."

"Of course it would. I knew you'd understand how I feel."

"Yeah," she said, "I can see where you're coming from. I hope you make it. Right now my life's the pits."

I felt a momentary twinge of guilt at the way I was misleading this poor, brainless lass—but I really had no choice, did I?

I opened the passenger door and prepared to withdraw.

"Rhoda," I said, "I hope you find the true love you're seeking and start a new life."

"You really believe that could happen?" she said hopefully.

"Of course it could," I assured her. "You must think positively."

"What does that mean?"

"Be confident that better times are coming."

"Yeah," she said determinedly. "I've got to keep thinking better times are coming. Thanks, Arky."

I stood there and watched the white Honda Accord exit from the garage. I felt dreadful. I had tried to be a bucker-upper, but if I had given her a lift I knew it would be brief. Her life had fallen into a cast-iron mold and it would take a sledge to smash it.

Of one thing I had no doubt: Rhoda's unexpected visit and invitation had been ordered by Ernest Gorton. Her offer of a "freebie" was his Ultimate Bribe. The way his mind worked simply amazed me. He had decided his offer of a no-show job at a handsome stipend might be rejected. If money didn't work, sex was another option. And if that failed, I was certain he would resort to a threat of physical violence.

I began to appreciate Mr. Horace Whitcomb's fear of Sunny Fogarty being endangered. And I found myself sharing Special Agent Griffin Kling's fury at this brute's machinations. Ordinarily I am a "live-and-let-live" sort of bloke, but Ernest Gorton's evil designs caused me to question the latter half of that philosophy.

I hadn't totally prevaricated during my surreal chat with the car-rottop. It was true I had an appointment with Herman Pincus, my tonsorial artiste, that afternoon. And it was a delight when he showed me, with the aid of two mirrors, that the bald spot on my bean was now boasting the fuzz of a hirsute peach.

I endured another hot oil massage, and Herman assured me it would not be long before my luxuriant locks were restored to their pristine glory. What a relief! You think me guilty of vanity? Of course I am. And so are you. Self-love is the only enduring passion. C'mon, admit it.

I returned to my office and found a message requesting I phone Al Rogoff instanter.

"Progress report," the sergeant said briskly. "I told Kling about Rhoda Flembaugh, Gorton's floozy, and he couldn't have been happier. He just called me. He ran a trace and she's got a record. Nothing heavy. Loitering for the purpose, lewd and lascivious behavior, and swell stuff like that. Anyway, Kling is going to pay her a visit and ask how come a nice girl like her is the registrant of trucks in New York, Boston, and Chicago used to haul stiffs."

"I hope Special Agent Kling is a discerning gentleman," I said.

"You hope *what?*"

I told him of my recent tête-à-tête with Rhoda. Al chuffed with laughter.

"That tootsie is something else," he marveled. "No charge to you, huh? You think Gorton put her up to it?"

"Of course he did. The scoundrel is determined to find my weakness and exploit it."

"He'd do better to offer you a mauve velvet fez."

"True," I admitted. "It might succeed. Let me know how Kling makes out with Madame Pompadour."

I had no desire for lunch that day, having pigged out with Mr. Whitcomb. But I thought a period of quiescence was in order after a hyperemotional morning during which I felt like a shuttlecock being batted about by people playing a game with no rules. Something tall and cold at the Pelican Club would restore the McNally aplomb, I reckoned—but it was not to be.

I was starting from my office when the accursed phone rang and I stared at it with loathing. I was briefly tempted to depart and let it shrill its heart out to an empty room. But then I dreamed it might be the White House beseeching my advice on how to handle the latest crisis in the Udmurt Republic. Or, better yet, it might be the Amazonian contralto from the church choir who had tracked me down and wished to become better acquainted. It was neither of course. The caller was Oliver Whitcomb.

"Archy!" he said, all false joviality. "Can we have a drink together?"

"When?" I asked.

"Now," he said. "The sooner the better."

"I was just heading for the Pelican Club," I told him. "Do you know it?"

A pause. "Yes," he said. "All right, if you insist."

I had suggested, not insisted, but I was in no mood to truckle. And so, half an hour later, Oliver and I were seated at a table in the almost deserted bar area of the Pelican. I had a depressing premonition the travails of my day had not yet ended and I was to be treated to another dose of someone else's angst. I wondered idly what it might cost to rent a confessional wherein I could ply my trade.

We had ordered gin and tonics, and Oliver gulped his greedily. I am proud to say I sipped genteelly—and frequently. Whatever was troubling the lad kept him silent a few moments, giving me the opportunity

to eyeball his attire. He obviously had no "important funeral" sched-
uled, for he wore the threads of a Neapolitan toff. I have a fondness
for rather assertive duds, as you well know, but Oliver's costume
looked as if it had been created by a designer hooked on Crayolas.

"I visited mother in the hospital this morning," he said moodily.

"Oh?" I said. "And how is she feeling?"

He shook his head. "Not good. I wanted to have a heart-to-heart,
but it was a no-go. She was hallucinating. Kept talking about ballroom dancing. Old stuff. I couldn't get through to her."

"A sad situation," I said—the most neutral comment I could devise
at the moment.

Then his talk became so pizzicato it went beyond desperation and
entered the realm of franticness.

"It's the will, y'see. Mother's will. She holds controlling interest in
the business. Naturally I expect to inherit her shares." He stopped
sputtering and looked at me expectantly.

"Naturally," I murmured.

"But I've got to *know,*" he rattled on. "After all, it's my future, isn't
it? I just assumed . . . But now I'm worried. So much depends . . . Have
you seen mother's will?"

"No."

"Do you know what's in it?"

"No."

"I called your father. He said he can't release that information. Suggested I ask mother. But the woman can't talk sense. She's at death's
door."

Death's door. A grisly cliché. Unless, of course, it's a revolving door.

"Archy, could you ask your father? About my mother's will."

"I could," I said stonily, "but it would do no good whatsoever. He'd
never tell me and he'd be horrified by my asking."

"Yes? Well, how about this . . . There must be a copy in your office
files. Could you sneak a peek? I need to make sure I inherit. There's a
lot riding on this, Archy."

"Oliver, have you asked your father? He probably knows."

His laugh was harsh. "My father and I are not simpatico these days.
Archy, will you do it for me? Take a quick look just to confirm I'm in-
heriting. I can't tell you how important it is to me."

If I were a courageous, stand-up chap I would have delivered a stern
"No!" immediately. But he was in such an agitated state I feared that

if I rejected his appeal he would launch himself across the table and go for my jugular with his incisors.

"I'll see what I can do," I said weakly.

"Good man!" he said, almost weeping with gratitude. "Good man! Do this for me and there's a nice piece of change in it for you."

We drained our glasses, shook hands, and departed. One drink. That's all we had. I swear.

I drove slowly home, pondering what Oliver had just unwittingly revealed about the motivation for his association with Ernest Gorton. The plot was becoming clear to me, as I'm certain it is to you.

I had time for a swim that afternoon prior to the family cocktail hour. It was during my languid wallow that I began laughing and succeeded in choking on a mouthful of the Atlantic Ocean. The reason for my mirth? In one day I had been promised a "freebie" by Rhoda Flembaugh and "a nice piece of change" by Oliver Whitcomb. My position as Chief of Discreet Inquiries at McNally & Son was suddenly offering an abundance of fringe benefits.

Dinner that evening was something that might tweak your salivary glands: mahimahi sautéed with fresh herbs, tomatoes, garlic, and olive oil so virginal I was certain it had taken a vow of chastity. Profiteroles for dessert. I restrained myself and had only four.

"On a diet, Archy?" father inquired. Sometimes the pater's sarcasm can nip.

I scuttled to my lodgment after dinner and set to work. I had been neglecting my journal shamefully and had a great deal to record since the last entry. I worked steadily and conscientiously, for I am not just another pretty face; when duty calls, McNally is ready to click heels and salute.

I was briefly interrupted by a call from Connie Garcia in Miami. She said she expected to return in a day or two, and it was welcome news; I missed that lady.

"Behaving yourself, laddie?" she asked.

"Don't I always?"

"No," she said. "I'll get a complete report on your activities from my spies when I come back."

"There's nothing to report," I protested. "The naughtiest thing I've done since you left was watching *The Sound of Music* on TV."

"Liar, liar, pants on fire!" she scoffed and hung up.

I went back to my scribbling, labored determinedly, and finished shortly after eleven o'clock. I poured a marc, lighted a cigarette and began reviewing the entire account of the Whitcomb affair.

The role Oliver was playing now seemed evident to me, as was the hostility between son and father. The mysteries remaining concerned the curious behavior of Horace Whitcomb and Sunny Fogarty. And, of course, puzzle numero uno was the out-of-state shipments of coffins going to a hauling service obviously owned by Ernest Gorton even if he had taken the precaution of registering his trucks in the name of the tarty Rhoda.

I wrestled with that enigma through one more brandy and one more cigarette. I experienced no grand epiphany. Finally I gave up, disrobed, and went to bed. I hoped to dream of Gene Tierney but Maria Ouspenskaya showed up instead. Oh well, it could have been Hoot Gibson.

28

"I think the Duchess hates me," Binky Watrous said gloomily.

"Nonsense," I said, although I wasn't so sure. "It seems to me she's been the soul of forbearance. Got you out of that scrape with the belly dancer in Tulsa, didn't she?"

"Well, yes, but she makes me eat oatmeal for breakfast. I detest oatmeal and she knows it. But she insists. Says it'll build strong bones. Who on earth wants strong bones? Not me. I mean, what can you *do* with them? Got a cigarette?"

I shoved my pack across the desk. It was Tuesday morning and when I had arrived at the McNally Building I found Binky grumping about, obviously in need of a kind word. I took him to my office and offered what cheer I could.

"Still partying with Mitzi and Oliver?" I asked him.

That quickened him. "Mostly with Mitzi," he reported. "Oliver isn't around much these days. Apparently his mother is extremely ill and also Mitzi says he's got all these big deals cooking. And talking about deals, one of Whitcomb's pals wants me to put some money in a new product he's bringing out."

"Oh? What is it?"

"A cognac lollipop. A sure winner, don't you think?"

"Absolutely," I said. "Are you going to invest?"

"Come on, Archy, you know I have a bad case of the flats. But if I had a few bucks I'd certainly plunge on the cognac lollipop. It can't miss. I don't suppose you'd—"

"No," I interrupted, "I would not. All my cash is tied up in a gerbil ranch. Binky, has Mitzi ever said anything about Oliver's relationship with his father?"

He thought a moment. At least I believe he was thinking. It was hard to tell with Binky. He might have been dozing.

"Yes," he said finally. "Once she remarked that Oliver was the apple of his mother's eye and the lemon of his father's. That's not bad, is it, Archy?"

"No, not bad."

He snapped his fingers. "Something else. I almost forgot. There was a small party at the Whitcombs' last night. Well, it wasn't really a party. More like a gathering. Maybe six or seven people. Oliver wasn't there, but Ernie Gorton showed up. Stayed a few hours. Very friendly. Talked to everyone."

"Uh-huh. Was Rhoda present?"

"No, she didn't show up. Mitzi says Rhoda has her own business now. She even has a fax machine."

"Will wonders never cease?"

"Anyway, after everyone left, Mitzi and I were alone and she told me Gorton had offered her a job."

I roused. "What kind of a job?"

"She didn't tell me, but she said the salary was stupendous. That was her word: stupendous."

"Binky, did you get the feeling Mitzi was interested in working for Ernest Gorton?"

"Oh yes. Definitely. She was charged. She said Gorton has deep pockets. Deeper than her husband's."

"That I can believe," I said. "And then what happened?"

He looked at me, puzzled. "When?"

"When you and Mitzi were alone in the Whitcombs' home and she told you about Gorton's job offer."

"Oh. Well, then we went skinny-dipping. No, that's not strictly accurate. She did, in the pool behind their house, but I didn't. To tell you the truth, I had consumed a number of brandy stingers and feared if I entered the pool, clothed or unclothed, I would immediately sink to the bottom without the strength to rise."

"You must eat your oatmeal," I admonished. "So what did you do?"

"Just lolled on a lounge and watched her. There was a full moon and I had a terrible desire to howl. Mitzi really is an excitement, Archy. If I was loaded I'd plead with her to dump Oliver and share a glorious future with me."

"Very poetic," I said. "But the lady has a bottom-line mentality?"

"What a bottom," he said dreamily. "What a line. Archy, tell me something honestly. Do you think I've been doing okay in the discreet inquiry business?"

"Your efforts have exceeded my expectations," I assured him—a valid statement since my expectations had been nil.

He left my office a much jauntier lad than when he entered. You may think it was a silly conversation, but amidst all that dross I spotted a few sparklers confirming my theory about Oliver Whitcomb's activities and a few that were to prove of some significance in solving the riddle of Ernest Gorton's despicable schemes.

The brief encounter with Binky elevated the McNally spirits and I was in a hemidemisemi ebullient mood, thinking the day was starting out splendidly, when everything turned drear. It began with a phone call from Sgt. Al Rogoff.

"I'm at home," he said. "Kling is here. Can you come over?"

His numb voice alarmed me. "Something wrong, Al?"

"Yeah. The Lauderdale cops fished a floater from the Intracoastal last night. Rhoda Flembaugh. Shot once through the back of the head. An assassination."

I closed my eyes. I tasted dust. "All right," I said faintly. "I'll be right there."

I drove slowly and carefully. (I always do that after hearing of a sudden, violent death.) When I arrived at Rogoff's I found the two officers seated at the round oak table working on mugs of black coffee. I was offered a cup but politely declined. I know how Al makes coffee: boil a pan of water, throw in a handful of coarsely ground beans, let the mixture boil until it's the color of tar. The taste? "Battery acid" springs immediately to mind.

"Tell Kling about your meeting with Flembaugh yesterday," the sergeant said. "I've already told him, but maybe you can add something."

The FBI man turned those black sunglasses to me, and obediently I recited everything I could recall of my conversation with Rhoda. I added that I was convinced Gorton had sicced her on me in an effort to halt my investigation into his connection with the Whitcomb Funeral Homes.

"I hope the fact that I rejected her advances had nothing to do with her demise," I said—anxiously, I admit.

The Special Agent spoke for the first time since I had entered. He had not granted me even a "Hello" or a "Hi."

"No," he said, "don't blame yourself. I triggered the kill. What I figure happened was this: Rogoff told me the trucks of the Cleo Hauling Service were registered to Gorton's playmate. Late yesterday I looked her up and tossed a few hardballs. I got nothing from her. A squirrelly broad but smart enough to keep her mouth shut. We're checking the phone logs, but I'm guessing the moment I was out of her place she called Gorton and told him the Feds had been around asking about his trucks. He didn't like that and so he had her put down just to make sure she'd never spill."

"He did it?" I asked.

"Not personally," Kling said. "This is one careful shtarker. He doesn't do the heavy work himself. He knows plenty of crazy dopers who'll pop someone for fifty bucks. Meanwhile he's miles away when it happens."

"When did it happen?" I asked.

"We're waiting for the ME's estimate. Probably around midnight, give or take."

"Then you're right," I said. "Gorton was miles away. At a party at Oliver Whitcomb's home in Boca."

I told them what Binky Watrous had reported: Gorton had showed up, acted in a friendly manner, talked to several people.

The FBI man sighed and removed his cheaters. His pale eyes looked infinitely weary. "Oh sure," he said. "Setting up an alibi. That bastard doesn't miss a trick."

"Something else happened at the party," I said. "I may be imagining this but it makes a nasty kind of sense."

I related what Binky had told me of Gorton's job offer to Mitzi Whitcomb at a "stupendous" salary.

"If Gorton knew Rhoda Flembaugh was being taken out," I argued, "he'd need a replacement, wouldn't he? Someone to run his call girl ring in the Palm Beach area. Who better than Mitzi? She has a lot of moneyed contacts, many of them druggies. And Oliver, her husband, can't object because Gorton has him by the short hairs."

The two officers looked at each other.

"It listens," Al Rogoff said.

Kling nodded. "I'll buy it," he said. "I like it because it's the way Gorton operates. He's a businessman, an entrepreneur, one hell of a manager. He's always planning, looking ahead, figuring angles and percentages. If he had gone legit he'd be a zillionaire today. Instead, he's dead meat. He doesn't know it yet but that's what he is—dead meat."

Once again I was shocked by the venom in his voice. I think even Al Rogoff was made uncomfortable by his intensity. If Kling had obviously been a religious fanatic I would have assumed he considered himself God's surrogate on earth. But in the absence of that motive I could only guess his passion sprang from professional hubris.

I must admit the man frightened me. I don't wish to imply he was irrational, a raving maniac, or anything like that. But he was suffering from a monomania so condensed it was consuming him. I was happy not to be the subject of his rabid vengefulness and wondered if Ernest Gorton knew he was the target of such an implacable nemesis.

I asked him if he had learned the identity of the final consignees to whom the Cleo Hauling Service was delivering all those caskets.

He donned his dark sunglasses again and paused a long moment. I think he was considering how much to reveal.

"Preliminary stuff," he said finally. "There was one drop at a Boston funeral home reported to have mob connections. Another delivery was made to a private home in Westchester County in New York. The owner is a wheeler-dealer with a lot of loot in offshore banks. We're still working it, but so far there's no pattern."

"Where do we go from here?" Rogoff said.

"Since the Flembaugh woman got whacked," Kling said, "we've put twenty-four-hour surveillance on Gorton's warehouse. The phones there and in his home and office have been hung. But I don't expect anything from that. The guy loves to use pay phones—and never the same one twice. A dummy he ain't. You want a prediction?"

Rogoff and I looked at him.

"Why not," Al said. "I even believe horoscopes."

"In the next two or three days the body of a young doper will be found in the Miami-Lauderdale area. Either he'll have his throat cut or maybe a slug through the ear. The local cops will have no suspects and no motive."

"But you will?" I said.

"Sure," Kling said, almost cheerfully. "The corpse will be the guy who popped Rhoda Flembaugh. That'll be Gorton's work—cutting his link with her killer. I told you he's a smart piece of dreck, didn't I?"

There didn't seem anything more to be said, and after a few moments I departed even more depressed than when I had arrived. I gloomed we were all spinning our wheels while Gorton went his merry way, doing exactly what he had set out to do. In other words, we were playing a reactive role but that vile blackguard was calling the shots—literally and figuratively.

In such a despondent mood I really had no choice but to drive directly to the Pelican Club, hoping to convert the McNally spirits from the torpid to the fizzy.

I lunched alone at the bar. Priscilla brought me an excellent salad of shrimp and chicken with a few chunks of pepperoni tossed in to give it a kick. I also had toasted bagel chips and a few glasses of our house wine, a chardonnay that always reminded me of Fred Allen's quip about the Italian winemaker who was fired for sitting down on the job.

Lunch consumed, I discovered to my dismay that I had not yet achieved the verve I sought, and I knew the cause: I could not forget the cruel extinction of bubbleheaded Rhoda. A great brain she was not, but I didn't believe there was malice in her. She was simply trying to survive and didn't succeed. I could only hope she had been totally unaware of her impending doom and had gone to her death laughing.

Musing on her sad fate, I went out to the parking area and discovered all four tires of my fire-engine-red Miata had been slashed. My poor baby was settled down on the tarmac like an exhausted bunny. It took only a sec for my bewilderment to become outrage. Then I may have uttered a mild expletive sotto voce.

I was examining the damage when a scuzzy gink strolled over, hands thrust into the pockets of a polyester leisure suit I thought had been declared illegal in the 1960s. He had a coffin-shaped face and eyes that looked like rusted minié balls. I had never seen him before and devoutly hoped I would never see him again.

"Took a hit, huh?" he said.

I nodded.

"Funny they should pick your heap out of all the cars parked here."

"Yes," I said. "Funny."

"Maybe someone's sending you a message," he said with a ghastly smile. "Think about it."

He stalked away and swung aboard a black Harley that looked as big and menacing as a dreadnought. I watched him roar out of the parking lot. He wasn't wearing a helmet and I wished him only the best—an uncontrollable skid, for instance.

29

I shall not bore you with a detailed account of my activities during the following afternoon hours; you might snooze. Suffice to say I returned to the Pelican Club and started feeding quarters into the public phone. I called a towing service, my garage in West Palm, a retailer of tires, a car rental agency, my insurance agent, and Sgt. Al Rogoff, who was incommunicable.

All I can tell you is that I functioned in a practical manner and shortly after five o'clock that evening was heading homeward behind the wheel of a white Acura Legend. It was okay, but driving a closed car gave me a mild attack of claustrophobia after years spent in a top-down convertible with the wind uncombing my hair and the Florida sun giving nourishment to all those hungry squamous cells on my beak hoping to become malignant.

I pulled into the graveled turnaround of the McNally faux Tudor yurt just as my father had garaged his Lexus and was heading for the back door, toting a bulging briefcase. He paused to watch me park and crawl out of the Acura. He gave me a bemused glance.

"Changing your religion, Archy?" he asked.

"Not by choice," I said grumpily. "Sir, can you give me some time tonight after dinner?"

"Regarding what?"

"The Whitcomb investigation."

One of those tangled eyebrows slowly lifted. "Is that why you're driving this vehicle?"

"Yes, sir, the two are connected. Tangentially."

"Very well. I'll see you in my study after dinner. Please try to make it short. I brought work home with me. Interesting case. Concerns an estate on conditional limitation. Do you know what that is?"

"No, sir."

"Nor do I—exactly. Nor apparently does anyone—exactly. That's what makes it interesting."

Which explains why, at about eight-thirty that evening, I was seated in the squire's study, occupying a leather club chair facing his magisterial desk. He didn't offer a postprandial glass of port or jigger of brandy and I was just as happy because I wanted to exhibit absolute lucidity—as likely a prospect as my becoming world champion of the clean and jerk.

Ordinarily I do not give the boss progress reports during the course of my discreet inquiries. He is only interested in the final results. Also, I suspect, he would rather not know the details of my modi operandi, fearing they might be an affront to his hidebound code of ethics—which, of course, they would be.

But there had been developments in the Whitcomb case of which he should be made cognizant since they involved legal problems he might be called upon to solve. Speaking rapidly, I delivered a précis of what had recently occurred, including my meetings with Horace and Oliver Whitcomb. *Mon père* listened to my recital without interrupting, but when I had concluded he began pelting me with questions.

"Horace Whitcomb was aware of our investigation from the start?"

"Yes, sir. He is an alert businessman with a sharp eye for details. It was he who first noticed the inexplicable revenue increase and asked Sunny Fogarty to request our assistance since he didn't wish to distress his dying wife by a showdown with their son."

"And in the event of his mother's death, Oliver hopes to inherit a controlling interest in Whitcomb Funeral Homes?"

"I believe that's his hope, father. It's the reason why he's been building up their cash reserves, so he can start his expansion program the moment he becomes the majority shareholder."

The sire looked at me strangely. I can only describe his expression as one of grim and sour amusement. I had the oddest notion he was about to reveal something that might turn the Whitcomb inquiry upside down. But apparently he thought better of it and returned to his interrogation.

"And in his effort to increase Whitcomb's cash balance, Oliver struck a deal with this gangster Gorton?"

"That's the way I see it, sir."

"An illegal activity?"

"Undoubtedly."

"You feel Gorton is responsible for what happened to your car?"

"I'm sure of it. He ordered the kneecapping of the Miata. It was a message to me to end my prying or risk a more violent response."

"I don't like it," father growled. "I don't like it one bit. But Sergeant Rogoff and the FBI agent are in pursuit of Gorton. Is that correct?"

"Yes, sir."

"Good. It's their job. Archy, I strongly urge you to cease and desist from any further inquiries into the schemes of Ernest Gorton. Is that understood?"

"Father, I can't cease and desist. I'm already involved and can hardly send Gorton a letter of resignation. In addition, Sunny Fogarty is in danger. I could not endure seeing her suffer the same fate as Rhoda Flembaugh. I simply cannot wash my hands of the whole affair and stroll away."

I knew the pater was concerned for my personal safety and I appreciated that. But if he had his ethical code, I had mine. No way was I about to give up this chase. Succumb to the crude threats of a wannabe Alphonse Capone? I think not.

The guv didn't argue, knowing it would be fruitless. He said, "Do you have any idea of the exact nature of Gorton's role in this matter? Why all those caskets are being shipped north?"

"No, sir. No idea whatsoever. At the moment."

"Getting rid of the victims of gang killings?"

"Possibly. I'm hoping the FBI investigation will give us a clearer picture of what's going on."

"During your last conversation with Horace Whitcomb," he said, switching gears on me, "did he agree our inquiry was to continue?"

"He did. After I convinced him it was impossible to terminate it as he had requested."

"Good. Keep a careful record of your billable hours, Archy."

And on that happy commercial note we parted.

I trudged upstairs to my third-floor cage reflecting I had not been entirely forthcoming with the author of my existence. It was true, as I told father, I thought Oliver Whitcomb had made a devilish bargain with Ernest Gorton in order to further Oliver's dream of creating the McDonald's of mortuaries.

But I suspected there might be another reason for their partnership: Gorton was a dependable source of all those "controlled substances" people stuffed up their schnozzles or injected into their bloodstreams. I did not believe Oliver was hooked, but I suspected many of his moneyed chums were. And it was those same stoned pals our hero wanted to keep happily dazed, for he was depending on them to help finance his grandiose plans.

But that was speculation and I could be totally wrong. I have been totally wrong before—as when I assured Binky Watrous he would suffer no ill effects from eating a dozen fried grasshoppers.

I knew I should work on my journal, bringing that magnum opus current, but the prospect of scribbling for an hour was a downer. I yearned for a more challenging activity, something that would set the McNally corpuscles boogying and enliven what had really been a dismal day.

And so, when my phone rang, I pounced upon it, hoping it might be Consuela Garcia announcing her return. In truth I missed my fractious fräulein. But it was not Connie; it was Sunny Fogarty.

"Archy," she said in a hushed voice as if afraid of being overheard, "I'm calling from a public pay phone. I'd like to talk to you tonight. Is there any safe place we can meet?"

I thought swiftly. I can do that, y'know. Not habitually but occasionally.

"Suppose I pick you up in half an hour," I suggested.

A pause. "But if I'm under observation," she said, "won't they recognize your car?"

"I'm not driving the fire engine tonight," I said blithely. "I have a white four-door Acura. No one in his or her right mind would ever link it with A. McNally, the registered playboy and bon vivant. Wait in the lobby of your condo. I pull up, you pop out and pop in, and off we go. It'll work."

"You're sure?" she said doubtfully.

"Can't miss," I said with more confidence than I felt.

"All right," she said. "I wouldn't ask you to do this if it wasn't important to me."

"Thirty minutes," I repeated. "White Acura sedan." And I hung up before she raised more objections. The lady seemed spooked, and I didn't blame her a bit. I had no desire for another encounter with that knife-wielding gent in the polyester leisure suit.

It went beautifully. Sunny was waiting, scurried to the Acura, and away we sped. I glanced in the rearview and saw no signs of pursuit. Certainly not a black Harley. That was comforting.

"Why don't we just drive down the coast and back," I proposed. "I have a full tank. Well, I don't but the car does, and I think we'll be more secure on wheels and in motion rather than holing up at some public place. Is that acceptable?"

"Fine, Archy," she said, putting a hand lightly on my arm. "It'll give us a chance to talk in private."

"You told me it was important."

"It is," she said. "To me."

Not another word was uttered while I headed for A1A and turned south. It was a so-so evening: scudding clouds, high humidity, a gusty breeze smelling of geriatric fish. It was the sort of dreary weather that would make a knight want to curl up with a good book—or one of the pages.

We were closing in on Manalapan when she finally spoke.

"Archy," she said, almost whispering, "I want to apologize."

"Oh? For what?"

"Mr. Horace told me he informed you that he knew of your investigation from the start. I'm sorry I misled you and your father."

"Perfectly understandable and forgivable," I assured her. "You were merely following the instruction of your employer."

"Yes, and he had a good reason for acting as he did. He didn't want his dying wife to learn he had discovered their son might be engaged in a criminal conspiracy. Mrs. Sarah loves Oliver so much."

"I cannot quarrel with Mr. Whitcomb's motive," I said. "I'm sure he did what he thought was best. But he set in motion an investigation that can't be stopped."

"He said the local police and the FBI are now involved."

"That's correct."

"Archy, do you think Oliver will go to jail?"

"It's quite possible, Sunny. As well as the other Whitcomb employees who are accomplices in the scheme."

"But what *is* the scheme?" she cried despairingly.

"We're working on it" was all I could tell her.

"You may think it an awful thing for me to say," she went on, "but I hope Mrs. Sarah won't live to hear her son has been imprisoned."

"Not so awful. A very sensitive and empathic hope. What is her condition?"

"Not good," she said gloomily. "The doctor says it's probably a matter of days. She's going, Archy."

My desire for an activity to enliven a dismal day was thwarted. I should have stayed home, I decided, and worked on my journal. This conversation was definitely spirit-dashing time.

We were almost down to Delray when I pulled into a turnaround and parked for a few moments. I did this because Sunny had started weeping, quietly and steadily, and it seemed unfeeling to continue driving while she was so distraught.

"And if that isn't enough," she said between muffled sobs, "my own mother is fading, and I don't know how long she has. Archy, everything is just falling apart. Everyone I love seems to be dying and I've never been so shaken and miserable in my life. I just feel my world is ending."

Then she turned suddenly to embrace me. Not passionately, of course; she was seeking solace and who could blame her. She buried her face betwixt my neck and shoulder, making little snuffling sounds like a child who's fallen and is hurting.

"Sunny," I said, hugging her firmly, "you're going through a bad time. But you're a very strong woman and I know, I *know* you'll survive intact. Are you familiar with Lincoln's philosophy, appropriate to all times and situations? 'This, too, shall pass away.' It may sound cold and hardhearted in your present state but do keep it in mind. I think you'll be surprised at what consolation it offers."

After a few moments we shared a chaste kiss, disengaged, and returned to Palm Beach. Sunny's head remained on my shoulder during that silent drive home, and occasionally she touched my arm or shoulder, as if she wanted to make certain I was there, to make contact with the living.

It had been a harrowing evening and I trust you'll be muy simpatico when you hear that, arriving back in my belfry, I immediately poured a double brandy and flopped down behind my desk to sip and recover from that wounding conversation.

I discovered that, in my cowardly way, I didn't even want to *think* about my talk with Sunny Fogarty. And so I donned earphones and listened to a snippet of tape: Gertrude Lawrence singing the yearning "Someday I'll Find You." I played it not once, not twice, but thrice.

I finally went to bed in a deliciously melancholic mood, reflecting that Mr. Lincoln may have been correct.

But the memory lingers on, does it not?

30

We now arrive at a section of this narrative which I find, regretfully, somewhat embarrassing to pen. It concerns how I discovered the exact nature of Ernest Gorton's flagrantly wicked scheme.

I wish with all my myocardium I could claim my discovery was the result of deucedly clever deductive reasoning—akin to Mr. Holmes solving a case by noting a dog *didn't* bark. But I'm sure you respect me as a chap of absolute veracity, scrupulous and exact, not given to embroidering the facts. And so I must be truthful about what happened. I fear you'll find it ridiculous—and it *was* ridiculous.

It began on Wednesday morning when, as usual, I overslept. Upon awakening I immediately phoned my West Palm garage and was overjoyed to learn the Miata was re-tired, back in fighting trim, and could be reclaimed at my convenience. Good news indeed.

I breakfasted alone: a frugal meal of cranberry juice, black coffee, and a croissant sandwich of liverwurst, jack cheese, tomato, a slice of red onion, and just a wee bit of a macho mustard. Invigorating.

I was heading for the garage when mother came trotting from our little greenhouse. She was clad in Bermuda shorts and one of my cast-off T-shirts. Over this costume she wore a soil-soiled apron, as so many pistil-whipped gardeners do, and I knew she had been digging into or perhaps transplanting one or more of her precious begonias. We exchanged a morning kiss.

"Archy," she accused, "did you have onions for breakfast?"

"Not me," I protested. "It must be that new Polish mouthwash I've been using."

"Listen, darling," she said, "do you think you might get over to West Palm Beach sometime today?"

"That's where I'm heading right now, luv. To get my car out of hock."

"Would you do me a favor?"

"I'd go to hell fa ya," I said, "or Philadelphia."

She giggled delightedly. "That's cute. What's it from, Archy?"

"Beats me," I admitted. "One of those oddments rattling around my cavernous cranium. A song lyric, I think."

(Dear Reader: If you happen to know the source of that quote, please drop me a line. Much obliged.)

"Well, here's what happened," momsy went on. "I ordered some hanging scented begonia bulbs from a garden supply house. I specifically and definitely asked for the apricot basket but they sent the lemon which I already have. I want to return their package and request what I ordered or a refund. I have it all packed up and addressed. Could you take it to that mailing place in West Palm and send it out by UPS?"

"Of course I can and shall," I averred. "Give me the package and I'll be on my way."

An innocuous incident, was it not? Merely the incorrect delivery of lemon-scented begonia bulbs when apricot had been ordered. Who could have guessed that trivial business would lead to the solution of the Crime of the Century? Certainly not A. McNally, the demon detective who once again learned the importance of chance and accident.

It took me an hour or so to return my rental, bribe an attendant to give me a lift to my garage, and ransom the Miata. I paid for everything with plastic and kept a record of the extravagant cash tips I distributed. Papa might be interested in billable hours; I was just as interested in my next monthly expense account.

Then I set out for the mailing emporium to send mother's begonia bulbs on their way. I'm sure you have similar handy and useful services in your neighborhood. They pack and address shipments of all shapes and sizes, and send them off via United Parcel Service, Federal Express, Airborne Express, or whichever carrier you request. Of course one pays extra for this convenience, but it's well worth it to have the paperwork professionally prepared.

The mailing outlet was crowded when I arrived, and I wondered how the U.S. Postal Service could hope to compete with express shippers offering speedy delivery, sometimes overnight, of everything from a legal-sized envelope to a leather hippopotamus hassock swaddled in bubblewrap and encased in a carton that looked large enough to contain a Wurlitzer.

I sent off the mater's package by UPS, received a receipt for same, and wandered outside musing on the scene within and imagining what would have happened to our nation's commerce if we were still enamored of the Pony Express. I was climbing into my rejuvenated Miata when it hit me.

I cannot declare it was a stroke of genius or claim my sudden revelation gave me the urge to yelp with joy and execute a grand jeté, toes atwirl. My first reaction was a desire to smite my forehead sharply with an open palm, devastated by chagrin that I had been such a brainless ass I hadn't grasped it before. "It" being Ernest Gorton's odious machinations.

Instead of driving to my office in the McNally Building, I returned home, for there was work to be done to verify my sudden enlightenment. I cannot describe my mood as one of exhilaration. Grim would be closer to the bone—and admittedly a smidgen of humiliation at not having solved the puzzle sooner.

I climbed directly to my oubliette and, donning my reading specs, began poring through my journal, that scrawled compendium of the frivolous and the meaningful. What I sought, y'see, was evidence to lend credence to my theory. No, strike that. It was *not* merely a theory; it was a conviction, a certainty, not an opinion but a faith.

I found evidence aplenty to convince me I had lucked onto Ernest Gorton's crafty design. And you know, I found myself feeling a grudging admiration for the scoundrel. He had created a criminal enterprise at once simple, almost foolproof, and exceedingly profitable. It required boldness on his part, of course, but it was now obvious he was a man of unlimited audacity.

I jotted a page of brief notes: facts to substantiate my analysis of Mr. Gorton's illicit activities. Then I sat back and pondered what to do next. I knew my hypothesis must be brought to the attention of Sgt. Al Rogoff and Special Agent Griffin Kling—after all, the Gorton investigation was their baby—but I wasn't certain how to announce my discovery and which law enforcement officer should be the first informed. Cops are more protective of their territory than wolverines.

So, as is my wont, I dithered. And a very pleasant dithering it was, lackadaisical and pleasurable. Have you noticed I've made no mention of lunch? I had none. Skipped it completely by deliberate choice. Naturally I was famished, but I had recently noted the waistbands of my slacks were shrinking at an alarming rate, and I decided it was time to take a keen interest in my caloric intake.

I returned from a leisurely ocean swim to dress for the family cocktail hour and dinner. That night Ursi Olson served sautéed chicken breasts with grapes and grilled veggies. Dessert was cheesecake with a fresh blueberry sauce. I had two portions of everything—but then I had omitted lunch, hadn't I?

Despite that holiday afternoon and evening I had not ceased wrestling with the problem of what my wisest next move should be. By the time I retired to my digs after the cheesecake I had made my choice and phoned Sgt. Al Rogoff. I determined he should be present when I revealed my brainstorm. I might never be associated with Special Agent Kling again, but Al's continuing friendship and assistance were too valuable to cut him out of the loop.

I found him at home and he wasn't too happy at being disturbed by my phone call.

"Now what?" he demanded.

"What," I said, "is a complete, logical, and irrefutable explanation of Ernest Gorton's criminal involvement with the Whitcomb Funeral Homes."

"Yeah?" Al said, his voice sharpening. "You got a bright idea?"

"More than a bright idea," I told him. "It's the trut', the whole trut', and nothing but the trut'. Can you persuade Kling to drive up tomorrow? I shall disclose all to both of you then."

"Can't you tell me now?"

"No," I said. "I don't chew my cabbage twice."

"What an elegant expression," he said. "I must remember to use it— maybe in the next century. All right, I'll give Kling a call and get back to you. I hope you're not shucking me on this, because if you are, it's the end of the road for us, buddy."

"Not the end," I assured him, "but a new, more glorious era of a close and more trusting relationship."

"Bleep you," he said and hung up.

He phoned back in about forty-five minutes. "Okay," he said, "it's set. It took some fast talking, but Kling finally agreed to drive up tomorrow morning. Where do you want to meet?"

"Hadn't thought of it," I confessed. "Any suggestions?"

"Kling doesn't like restaurants. He thinks the salt shaker may be bugged. How about my chateau again? At noon."

"Fine," I said. "If you feel like it, order up some pizza and beer, McNally and Son will pick up the tab."

"Of course," he said. "Naturally."

We now fast-forward to noon on Thursday. Nothing unusual happened in the interim except that I awoke in time to breakfast with my parents (we had smoked salmon and scrambled eggs) and I arrived at my office at the traditional 9:00 A.M., shocking all the fellow employees I encountered and occasioning a few snide comments.

I worked dutifully at listing the billable hours father had requested and recording my own out-of-pocket costs. They would eventually appear on my monthly expense account, which was now beginning to rival the gross national product of Sri Lanka.

I arrived at Chez Rogoff just as the delivery lad was departing, and by the time I parked and entered Al's snug and pleasantly scruffy mobile home, he was setting out three medium-sized pizzas: meatball, pepperoni, and anchovy. He also provided Coors Light in frosted glass mugs: a welcome touch.

On this occasion Special Agent Griffin Kling rose to greet me and shake my hand. It was similar to receiving a benediction from the Grand Lama, even if he neglected to remove his semiopaque sunglasses. The three of us immediately began devouring hot pizza and swilling chilled brew. I could not resist casting a furtive glance or two at Kling. Have you ever seen anyone chomping a slice of meatball pizza while wearing black specs? An unsettling sight.

Curiously it was he who offered the first revelation.

"We have Gorton's warehouse under twenty-four-hour surveillance," he told us. "Last night around midnight a semi pulls up and starts unloading. The sign on the truck says it's from the Cleo Hauling Service of New York. We got all this on videotape. Okay? So then they start unloading the truck, carrying the cargo inside the warehouse. You know what? Caskets. All colors, plain, fancy, whatever. They had to be empty because two men were handling each one easily. No fork-lifts. Maybe twenty coffins. The truck was unloaded and took off. Now what do you suppose was going on?"

I laughed. "Easy," I said. "Mr. Gorton is such a shrewd money-grubber he was having the empties returned."

Rogoff looked at me. "What the hell are you talking about, Archy?" he demanded.

I took the page of notes from my jacket pocket, spread it alongside my pizza plate, and began my presentation.

"Al, you told me Gorton isn't tied to the Mafia or the Colombian drug cartels but he's worked deals with both. He knows how they operate, he knows their problems, and he figured a way to make them an offer they couldn't refuse.

"What he did was set up a service for the air-lifting of drugs, guns, and money to distribution centers in New York, Boston, and Chicago. How is contraband ordinarily transported within the forty-eight contiguous states? By courier, car, van, truck, or small planes. But all those are easy targets for arrest and seizure. Individuals and trucks can be stopped and searched. Ditto private cars. And small planes need certification and are supposed to file flight plans.

"But our hero came up with a scam that couldn't miss. The deceased are shipped out of Florida at an enormous annual rate. Each casket is crated or placed in a carton clearly labeled 'Human Remains. Handle with Extreme Care.' Who's going to open a package like that to verify the contents?

"The dear departed depart from Florida in the cargo holds of legitimate airlines. The coffin, crate, and corpse weigh about four hundred pounds. Gorton learns all this from Oliver Whitcomb, who's in need of ready cash. Ernest realizes immediately that those caskets can be filled with guns, drugs, or laundered money, providing he doesn't exceed the usual weight by too much.

"Hey, maybe he was offering his customers flight insurance. If the plane crashed, the airline would have to pay, wouldn't it? But that's just smoke on my part. I think the way the scheme worked was this:

"Gorton makes a deal with Oliver Whitcomb. The original caskets are purchased through Whitcomb Funeral Homes. They're loaded with the goodies in Gorton's warehouse. Then they're trucked at night to one of Whitcomb's three mortuaries. The director in charge, working alone or maybe with a helper on the pad, crates the casket for out-of-state shipment.

"The phony death certificate is supplied by that zonked-out Dr. Omar Pflug. The paperwork and shipping invoices are prepared by the crooked funeral directors. Gorton pays for death certificate, coffin, crating, cost of the airlift, and probably a bonus. What does he care? He's making a lush profit from his clients, who are happy to pay mucho dinero for guaranteed overnight delivery.

"Ernest Gorton is operating a Coffin Air Express. The CAE. How does that sound?"

Special Agent Griffin Kling finished a slice of anchovy pizza and wiped his lips carefully with a paper napkin. He stood, turned his back to us, leaned to look out one of the small windows.

"You got it," he said tonelessly. And then he kept repeating obsessively, "You got it. You got it. You got it."

31

He finally quieted but still didn't turn to face us. Rogoff looked at me curiously.

"How did you happen to come up with that one, Archy?" he asked.

"Genius," I said.

"Luck," he said.

"A bit of both," I admitted. "The question now is, where do we go from here?"

Then Kling turned. I don't believe he had been listening to my exchange with Al.

"It fits," the FBI man said. "Our offices up north have checked out maybe a half dozen of the places that took deliveries from the Cleo Hauling Service. They're all no-goodniks. Funeral homes with bent-nose connections. Guys with records of security frauds. One hustler suspected of supplying guns to terrorists of all stripes. So when you tell me Gorton is running a ratty air express from South Florida, I'll buy it."

I was about to repeat my question of what happens next, but Kling would not be interrupted.

"The thing to do," he said, "is bust that warehouse."

I glanced at Rogoff and I swear he gave me a quick wink. I had the feeling we were both thinking the same thing.

"Sir," I said to Special Agent Kling, doing my humble bit, "I wouldn't presume to tell you how to conduct a criminal investigation—I'm the rankest of rank amateurs—but wouldn't it be better to seize the loaded caskets after they've been picked up by the Cleo Hauling Service at LaGuardia, Logan, and O'Hare? Then you'll have evidence of interstate shipment of contraband. It's even possible you may find Gorton's fingerprints on one or more of the coffins."

"Nah," Kling said decisively. "A waste of time. I smell blood. We'll raid the warehouse as soon as possible—maybe tonight if I can get the go-ahead. I hope Gorton will be there," he added with savage joy. "But even if we don't collar him and his soldiers actually loading the caskets, we'll pull in everyone in sight. Then we'll go looking for those funeral directors and that Oliver Whitcomb. We'll lean on them and I guarantee at least one of those bozos is going to cut a deal and talk. We might even be able to pin Gorton for snuffing Rhoda Flembaugh. This is the chance I've been waiting for. Listen, I've got to run. I want to get back to Miami and get the show on the road. I'll let you know how we make out. Thanks for the feed."

Then he was gone. Rogoff and I were left with a few cold crusts from the demolished pizzas. But the supply of beer hadn't been exhausted and we each had another mugful, slumping down and relaxing. Kling's presence was daunting; no doubt about it. The man was so perpetually intense it made my fillings ache.

"I don't like it," Rogoff remarked.

"The raid on the warehouse?" I said. "I don't either. The cart before the horse and all that sort of thing. He's not building a case methodically and logically; he's the proverbial fool rushing in where angels fear to tread."

"My, oh my," Al said. "We're full of folk wisdom today, aren't we?"

"Touché," I said. "But I didn't hear you making any objections while he was here."

"C'mon, Archy, think straight. I'm a Palm Beach copper who's supposed to warn guys who go jogging without a shirt. You want me to tell the FBI how to run a major case? They'd label me a redneck sheriff and put me on their shit list."

"But you don't approve of the raid on the warehouse, do you?"

The sergeant shook his head dolefully. "Kling has other options but he's so hyper about Gorton he's got to go for the muscle. I'm betting that bust will prove Murphy's Law in spades."

I drove away from Rogoff's assembly-line hacienda reflecting that his foreboding mirrored my own. I have confessed to you on several occasions in the past that I am a lad devoted to the frivolous and trivial. I simply refuse to take anything seriously. I have absolutely no absolute beliefs—other than grated ginger is wonderful on fresh oysters.

And so I found Griffin Kling's zealotry disturbing. I am willing to admit that fanatics have accomplished much of value in the history of the higher primates. Artists, for instance, and poets, composers, architects and such—monomaniacs all—have created wondrous things. But a distressing number of the obsessionally driven have engendered wars, inquisitions, pogroms, and general nastiness that prevent an international chorus of "On the Good Ship Lollipop."

Exhausted by such sober meditation, I decided the McNally spirits required a goose, and so I used my cellular phone to call Binky Watrous, that *homme moyen sensuel.* (Short translation: a goofball.) Surprisingly he was at home and eager to chat.

"Golly, I'm glad you called," he said. "Listen, Archy, do you think I should grow a beard?"

"*Can* you?" I asked.

"Of course I can," he said, offended. "It might take some time, but I'm sure I could do it if I set my mind to it."

"I'm on my way to the Pelican Club," I informed him—a sudden decision. "Why don't you meet me there for a spot of R and R, and we can discuss your plans to cultivate facial foliage."

"You're on," he said enthusiastically. "The Duchess wants me to accompany her to a flügelhorn recital, but I shall tell her the demands of my job-training come first. Righto?"

"Righteo," I said, topping him.

Within the hour we were seated at a table in the bar area of the Pelican. I thought it wise to continue drinking beer, and Binky ordered a mild spritzer with a peppered Russian vodka as a chaser. Nutsy.

"I guess you heard about Rhoda Flembaugh getting murdered," he said mournfully.

"Yes, I heard."

"It rocked me. I mean, she was a wild one, Archy, but really quite nice. I was wondering if I should go to the gendarmes and tell them I knew Rhoda and we had shared a Big Mac or two. Do you think I should?"

"No," I said firmly. "Keep out of it, Binky. The police have a good idea of who ordered her killing, and your personal relations with the victim will hold no interest for them whatsoever. And speaking of your many and varied intimacies, are you seeing much of Mitzi Whitcomb these days?"

"Not really. I suspect she may be giving me the old heave-ho. I mean, the Whitcombs are still running their open house and I drop by frequently, but I think Mitzi is too busy working for Ernie Gorton to pay much attention to her most devoted admirer. Namely, me."

"Oh? What sort of work is she doing for Gorton?"

"I'm not sure but now there seems to be an amazing number of yummy young lasses lolling around the premises and just as many older guys wearing gold chains, silk suits, and face-lifts. I think Mitzi may be running a dating service. You know—introducing lonely singles to each other."

A *dating* service? What a goober my aide-de-camp was!

"That's possible," I said. "Or Mitzi could be selling subscriptions to the *Kama Sutra Gazette*."

"Oh? What's that?"

"A new magazine. Profusely illustrated. Very *in*. Does Oliver attend these soirées?"

"Some," Binky said. "Not always, but occasionally. He's drinking an awful lot these days, Archy. I don't think he enjoys the idea of his wife working for Gorton."

"Uh-huh. And does dear old Ernie put in an appearance?"

"Well, he's been there every night I've dropped by. He doesn't stay long. Just pops in, says hello to everyone, has a private chat with Mitzi, and pops out. What do you suppose is going on, Archy?"

"Infamy," I said.

He finished his wine spritzer and started on the chaser.

"Binky," I said, "when we started our semi-professional association you more or less agreed to follow all my suggestions, instruction, and orders without question."

"Well, I have, haven't I?"

"You have indeed and I commend you for it. I now have another and probably final command. I want you to sever your relationship with Mitzi and Oliver Whitcomb, with Ernest Gorton, and all their snorting pals. You are not to visit the Whitcomb maison again or attempt in any way, shape, or form to contact the residents or guests thereof. In other words, Binky, cease and desist."

He was astonished. "You mean I can't even enjoy a jolly gibber with Mitzi on the phone?"

"I don't want you to even *dream* about her," I said sternly. "Momentous events have been set in motion, and I fear the Whitcombs, Gorton, and their coterie are quite likely to have their hilarity squelched and their lifestyle dampened by stalwarts of the law. Why, they may even be shackled and dragged off to durance vile. And this cataclysm may occur within a few days or a week at the most."

"What's going on?" he said indignantly. "You must tell me what's happening."

"I would if I could," I assured him, "but I have been sworn to secrecy. It involves plans by agencies and officials at the highest levels of the U.S. government."

"Gosh," he said, suitably impressed.

"What I definitely do not want," I continued, "is to have you caught in the wreckage and perhaps charged with misdeeds of which I know you are totally innocent. I'm sure the Duchess would be as horrified as I."

He became even paler, if such a thing were possible. "Oh no," he said hoarsely. "No, no, no. We can't have it. She's already threatening to cut my allowance. Insists I economize. I'm already buying underwear made in Hong Kong. What more does she expect?"

"Then you agree to end immediately all connection with Mitzi, Oliver, and their circle?"

"I agree," he said sadly and looked longingly at his empty glasses.

I felt he had endured enough of a shock to earn a refill and so I fetched him another spritzer and vodka from the bar.

Binky sipped his fresh drink appreciatively and then said, "You know, Archy, what you do—these discreet inquiries and all—it's for real, isn't it? I mean it's not all giggles."

"Of course it's real. Sometimes people get badly hurt. Sometimes people get killed."

"The trouble is," he said with abashment, "it's fascinating, isn't it? All the raw emotion and that sort of thing. I don't mind telling you it's a new world for me. I never realized people lived like that. Oh, I know there's plenty of mean things going on, but I supposed all the evil was committed by thugs in leather jackets and baseball caps. Now I find upper-drawer citizens with big bucks and mansions can be just as slimy as your average mugger. It comes as a bit of a shock."

I knew what he was trying to say. "You're such a tyke, Binky," I told him. "Frequently the people I investigate are moneyed, well educated, charming, and utter rotters. Class really has nothing to do with it. Net worth and beluga for breakfast do not prevent ignobility. Have you had your fill of discreet inquiries?"

"Oh no!" he said determinedly. "It may be an acquired taste, but as I said, it's fascinating. You're not going to fire me, are you, Archy?"

"How can I fire you when I didn't hire you?"

"No, but you let me help. And I did assist, didn't I? I admit I have a great deal to learn, but I'm certain my performance will improve as I gain experience. Can't I continue my on-the-job training for a while?"

As usual I temporized. I wasn't certain I wanted a geeky Dr. Watson walking up my heels but Binky was correct: he *had* contributed to the Whitcomb case.

"Let me think about it," I said. "When our current investigation is closed we can talk about it further. What will be the reaction of the Duchess if you keep working without pay?"

"She'll be delighted to get me out of the house," he said, "but not half as happy as I to be absent from that mausoleum. You've never been inside, have you, Archy?"

I thought a moment. "I don't believe I ever have."

"Then you're obviously not aware that every upholstered chair is equipped with an antimacassar crocheted by the Duchess."

"You jest."

"Not so," he said darkly. "About once a month, when she's not home, I swipe one of those disgusting rags and toss it into a distant trash can. It's driving her right up the wall. The Case of the Disappearing Antimacassars."

He cackled insanely and I feared he might be paddling a leaky canoe. The lad was a trial, I could not deny it, but neither could I ignore my very real affection for him, as one might have for a mentally disadvantaged brother whose main (and possibly sole) talent was birdcalls.

"Binky," I said, "about this beard you're thinking of growing."

"Oh yes!" he said, bright with anticipation. "What do you think?"

"I don't wish to be brutally frank," I said, "but let me be brutally frank. The growth presently on your upper lip which you claim to be a mustache is so fair, so almost colorless that it can hardly be seen in full sunshine. I fear a beard may exhibit the same gossamer quality."

"I could dye it," he suggested.

"And risk having it drip down your shirtfront when it rains? No, m'boy, I don't think a beard would suit you."

"Actually," he said, "I was hoping it might make me look more, you know, mature. I mean, you and I are about the same age but you look so much older than I do."

"Thank you very much," I said.

The remainder of our conversation was so absurd I'm ashamed to detail it here. Suffice to say I left Binky that afternoon with the horrifying realization I had just been chittering with a cartoon character from Boob McNutt.

32   .

The mood of that day had as many zigs and zags as the tail of an affrighted Halloween cat. And there was more to come.

I returned home and saw a swampy ocean in such turmoil I immediately decided to eschew my daily swim. Instead I ascended to my eighth heaven and recorded the day's events in my journal. I also had time for a sweet nap before preparing for the family cocktail hour.

But when I descended to the second-floor sitting room I found only mother present. She was seated in a wicker armchair and dabbing at her brimming eyes with a square of cambric.

"What is it, dear?" I said fearfully.

She looked up at me, her face wracked. "Mrs. Sarah Whitcomb passed away this afternoon."

"Oh," I said, feeling I had been punched in the heart. "Ah, the poor woman."

"Father called and said he's going to the hospital to see if he can assist the family. He doesn't know how long he'll be gone and suggested we start dinner rather than wait for him."

"Does he want me to join him?"

"He said nothing about it."

"Then I certainly shan't intrude. Her death was expected, mother, but it still comes as a blow. She was a brave lady."

"Yes. Very brave. Might we have a drink now, Archy?"

"Or two," I said. "Much needed."

I did the honors and stirred the martinis as I knew my father would—to the traditional recipe: a 3-to-1 mixture of 80-proof dry gin and dry vermouth. Not astringent enough for my taste but it was what my parents enjoyed and I had no desire to challenge their preference.

Nothing more was said until we both had consumed almost all of our first libation. I don't believe it enlivened us but it helped dull the pain.

"Archy," mother said, "do you remember the Whitcombs' party we all went to, the first big affair of the season?"

"Of course I remember."

"Well, I was talking to Sarah for a few moments. Just the two of us. And suddenly she asked me if you and father get along together. Wasn't that an odd thing to say?"

"Very odd."

"Naturally I told her that you and father get along very well, that you're quite close. And she gave me the saddest look and said, 'You're very fortunate.' I've remembered it because it was such a puzzling thing. Don't you think?"

"Yes," I said and rose to top off our glasses. We finished the dividend and started downstairs to dinner.

"I didn't know her very well," mother said. "She wasn't an intimate friend, you know, but I did admire her. I had the feeling she was an unhappy woman—and not only because of her illness. But she always had a smile. That's important, isn't it, Archy?"

"It surely is."

"Now you're going to tell me there's a song lyric that says it better."

"Of course," I affirmed and sang, "Smile, though your heart is breaking . . ."

"Yes," mother said, gripping my arm tightly. "That was Mrs. Sarah Whitcomb."

I think we both felt lost at the dining table without the presence of my father. He really was captain of our ship, and for all his foibles and cantankerousness we depended on him to chart our course. Moms and I were halfway through the crabmeat appetizer when we heard the sounds of the Lexus arriving and being garaged neatly and swiftly. A moment later the lord of the manor came striding in. His expression revealed nothing. He leaned down to kiss mother's cheek.

"Glad you started," he said to us. "I'll wash up and be down in a moment."

Well, it was more than a moment and I suspected he might have detoured to the sideboard in the sitting room for a quick wallop. Eventually he appeared, took his place at the head of the table, gobbled the crabmeat, and caught up with us while we were working on slices of beef tenderloin with purple Belgian bell peppers in a red wine sauce.

"How did it go, father?" the mater asked timidly.

He gave her a brief glare. He detests her addressing him as "father" although he frequently addresses her as "mother." Do you understand that? I don't.

"As well as could be expected," he replied to her question. "Arrangements were made. We'll all attend the funeral service. Burial will be private."

"Was Oliver present?" I asked him.

"Yes," he said, not looking at me but concentrating on his beef. "This sauce is excellent. Oliver was there but his wife was not. I thought that exceedingly strange. Archy, I'd like to see you in my study after dinner."

"Yes, sir," I said.

After dessert (apple tart with cinnamon ice cream) mother went upstairs to write the McNallys' letter of condolence to Mr. Horace Whitcomb. I followed father into his study. He closed the door firmly and went directly to the marble-topped sideboard. He poured each of us a snifter of cognac—not his best but good enough. He motioned me to a club chair and took his throne behind the massive desk. I thought his visage was now uncommonly grim.

"I didn't wish to mention this at dinner," he said, "because I feared it would upset your mother. But the scene at the hospital this afternoon was dreadful, simply dreadful. Horace and his son got into a shouting match that became so rancorous I feared it might result in physical combat. I was able to separate them and keep them apart, but the atmosphere remained one of vicious spite. Meanwhile the deceased was being prepared for transfer to a Whitcomb funeral home. The whole thing was unseemly, Archy, most unseemly."

"I concur," I said. "What was their argument about?"

"Horace accused his son of being unfeeling, inattentive, and cruel during Mrs. Sarah's illness. Oliver blamed his father for his infrequent visits, claiming Horace was guilty of deliberate malice in thwarting his plans for expansion. Both were almost incoherent in their fury. Extremely unpleasant." He said this wrathfully as if the bad manners of others were a personal affront.

"Deplorable," I murmured and sipped my brandy.

"Their conflict leads me to believe your investigation may be more decisive than you and I anticipated. Have there been any recent developments?"

"Yes, sir," I said. "The whole thing is unraveling."

I brought him up to speed on what had happened and was about to occur. He interrupted only once, when I described Ernest Gorton's stratagem of airlifting contraband up north in caskets within cartons labeled "Human Remains."

"Clever," father remarked, and I thought I detected a small smile of wry amusement.

"Very," I agreed and went on to detail the plan of FBI Special Agent Griffin Kling to raid the Gorton warehouse and, if evidence discovered warranted it, to arrest Oliver Whitcomb and others involved in the plot.

I concluded and there was silence for a mo. Then the old man rose to replenish our snifters. That was an indication of his perturbation. Ordinarily he would have asked me to play the butler.

"You obviously believe Oliver Whitcomb is guilty," he said when he was once again seated upright in his high-backed swivel chair.

"I do believe that," I said firmly.

"And his motive?"

"Oliver had grandiose plans for expanding the Whitcomb Funeral Homes into a nationwide chain, plans to which his father was bitterly opposed. Oliver knew his mother held a controlling interest, and he also knew she was mortally ill and he assumed he would inherit her shares since he was an only child and well aware of her devotion to him. So he decided to take action to realize his ambitions even before her demise. His first step was to build up the cash reserves of the Whitcomb Funeral Homes to have sufficient funds to cover initial expenses. He then intended to make a private offering of stock prior to the time he could go public and have Whitcomb shares listed. He believed when that happened he would become an overnight multimillionaire. The scenario has been used before, father, and sometimes it's succeeded."

"And sometimes, usually, it's been a disaster. But there was no way Oliver's game plan could possibly have succeeded."

"Oh?" I said. "Why is that?"

He rose abruptly from his chair and began to pace back and forth behind his desk, hands thrust into trouser pockets. His head was lowered, but I caught sight of his expression and thought he looked unutterably sad.

"If your hypothesis is correct, Archy," he said, "and I believe it may very well be, Oliver's aspirations were doomed from the start. You say he assumed he would inherit his mother's shares upon her death?"

"Yes, sir, I think he assumed that. Although recently he became rather antsy about it and attempted to bribe me to determine exactly what was in Sarah's will."

My father made a noise that sounded suspiciously like a snort. "He was correct to become, as you say, antsy." He stopped his pacing to face me with a bleak smile. "Oliver was basing his future prosperity on an assumption. When it comes to inheritance, Archy, assumption can result in disappointment, if not despair. I can now reveal something to you I thought unethical to reveal while Mrs. Sarah Whitcomb was still alive. I believe I've already informed you that for tax reasons Horace Whitcomb transferred a controlling interest in the company to his wife. I had a hand in the drawing up of that conveyance and made certain it was clearly stated that if Sarah should predecease her husband, her shares would revert to him. So as things stand now, Horace holds the majority of voting shares in Whitcomb Funeral Homes."

I don't believe my mandible sagged but I'm certain an ordinary bloke would have been rendered speechless, a condition completely foreign to my nature.

"Father," I said, my voice sounding strangled even to me, "what you've just told me means that Oliver's criminal conspiracy with Ernest Gorton could not possibly profit Oliver, that he took horrendous risks for no reason whatsoever and now must pay a serious penalty for his rashness."

"It would appear so," the squire said in his lawyerly way.

If I was startled by *mon père*'s revelation I could imagine what Oliver Whitcomb's reaction would be when he learned he had wagered his future on the turn of a roulette wheel which didn't include his number. I thought he'd do more than mutter, "Drat!"

"With your permission, sir," I said, not giving a reason for my request (knowing he'd guess it), "I'd like to bring this information to the attention of Sergeant Rogoff and Agent Kling."

Prescott McNally, Esq., fell into his mulling mood, one of those lengthy silences during which he carried on a slow mental inquiry, debating all the pros and cons of my suggestion. He goes through the same process when trying to decide if the flavor of a baked potato would be enhanced by a soupçon of pressed caviar.

"Yes, Archy," he said finally, "you have my permission to inform the authorities of Oliver's current status anent his inheritance—specifically the absence thereof."

"Thank you, father," I said, wondering if, in *his* will, he had bequeathed me his fondness for prolixity.

I left his study, trotted upstairs to my sanctum and immediately phoned Sgt. Al Rogoff. He wasn't at home but I found him at headquarters.

"What are you doing in the office at this hour?" I asked.

"Paperwork," he said briefly.

"I don't think so," I told him. "You know Kling's raid is going down tonight and you want to stick close to your direct phone or telex or computer network or whatever you defenders of the public weal are using these days, just so you can keep track of what's happening. Do you plan to sleep at your desk tonight?"

"I might," he said, and his tense tone warned me I better lay off the chivying.

"Al," I said, "there's something you should know, and if you have the opportunity I hope you'll relay it to Griffin Kling. I have my father's permission to reveal this."

I told him of Oliver Whitcomb's disastrous error in assuming he would inherit his mother's shares in the Whitcomb Funeral Homes. Instead, the controlling interest would revert to his father.

"If Oliver is arrested," I went on, "or even hauled in for questioning, I thought the revelation that his brief career as a master criminal has been a gold medal no-brainer and he never had a tinker's damn of achieving the result he anticipated—well, it might embitter him to the extent that in his angry frustration he'll be willing, if not eager, to implicate the other miscreants in the plot."

"Jeez," Rogoff said, "you're beginning to talk just like your father. But you're also a foxy lad. I catch what you're trying to say and it might work. If I get a chance to talk to Kling I'll tell him what you said. He'll need all the ammunition he can get. Archy, that Oliver—what a putz he turned out to be. I mean, he had a good job and a good future, a hot-to-trot wife, money in the bank, and a Boca mansion. But he wanted more, takes a stupid risk and goes for broke. What's with morons like that?"

"He's a man in a hurry," I said, giving him an instant analysis. "He's never learned to slow down, look around, and take time to smell the garlic."

"Yeah," Al said, "I know what you mean."

33

I knew I should hitch up my pantaloons and labor at bringing my professional diary up-to-the-minute. But it had been such a chaotic day, I found the prospect of even an hour's donkeywork positively repellent. All I wanted to do was sit quietly, adopt a thousand-yard stare, and breathe through my mouth.

I was saved from that repugnant lassitude when Consuela Garcia phoned. My inamorata had returned!

I find it difficult to explain why the sound of her dear, familiar voice and the knowledge that she was once again a part of my daily existence energized and invigorated me. She really was a refuge of sanity and normalcy in a world that had lately seemed to me unbearably scuzzy.

We must have jabbered for almost an hour, and other than her cousin's improving health I don't believe our conversation included a single topic of importance. But chitchat can be pleasurable, y'know. I mean, it's not necessary that every dialogue be concerned with the International Monetary Fund or the endangered state of the Ozark big-eared bat.

Connie wanted to have dinner at the Pelican Club on Friday night and I happily agreed.

"Been behaving yourself, son?" she asked.

"I have been living an exemplary life," I declared, and I had—recently.

"I haven't had time to check with my tattlers but I shall, and I hope you're telling the truth."

"Connie, would I like to you?"

Her laugh was so hollow it echoed. "See you tomorrow night, sweet," she said. "I warn you I might get mildly potted—I'm so happy to be back."

"In that case, suppose I pick you up around sevenish. Then you won't have to drive."

"Good thinking. You'll be the designated driver and I'll be the designated drinker."

"Um," I said.

After that bracing interlude I went to bed and descended into a deep and satisfying slumber.

It lasted until I was awakened by the persistent ringing of my bedside phone. I squinted to see the time: almost 4:30 A.M., and I knew it would be bad news. Who but Death calls at that hour?

"Rogoff," he said harshly. "Griffin Kling bought it."

It took a moment for my sleep-fuddled brain to comprehend. "He's dead?" I said stupidly.

"Him and another FBI agent. Two wounded. One perp out and three bleeding. That's the latest tally I got. Sounds like the O.K. Corral."

"Was Gorton there?"

"No mention of him. Archy, it was what you'd call a monumental balls-up. They're still trying to sort things out."

"Al," I said, "what are you going to do now? Hang around? Go home?"

"I guess I'll head for bed," he said dully. "I've had it for one night."

"Stop by," I urged. "I'll put on some coffee, maybe mix up an early breakfast. Okay?"

"Yeah, sure," he said gratefully. "I can use it. I'm shook. I didn't particularly like the guy, did you?"

"No," I said.

"But I respected him," Rogoff insisted. "He was a lawman. So am I. It's hard to take."

"I can understand that."

"No, you can't," the sergeant said. "I'll be there in half an hour or so."

I pulled on jeans and T-shirt and went padding downstairs barefoot. I glanced out the kitchen window and saw the sky had a dull, leaden, predawn look.

I put water on to boil and rummaged through the fridge for vittles Rogoff might enjoy. I selected eggs, a few slices of salami, an onion, and red bell pepper. I had started preparing a quasi western omelette when father entered the kitchen. I was happy to see he was wearing a seersucker robe I had given him on his last birthday.

He looked at me inquiringly. "Suffering from malnutrition?" he asked, and even after being roused from sleep he had the ability to hoist aloft one hirsute eyebrow.

"For Rogoff," I explained and told him of Al's report on the shoot-out at Gorton's warehouse in Miami.

"And the sergeant is coming here?"

"Yes, father. He's had a bad night. I think he's in need of sustenance."

"Of course. Do you mind if I remain and hear what he has to say?"

Typical Prescott McNally: couching a command as a request.

Al's timing was most felicitous. The omelette was beginning to crisp around the edges when his pickup pulled into our graveled turnaround. I slid a few slices of sour rye into the toaster as Rogoff came clumping in and shook hands with my father. He looked beat.

He washed his hands at the kitchen sink, removed his gun belt, and joined us at the table. Father and I didn't have anything but watched as he attacked his omelette, buttered toast, and steaming black coffee. He ate avidly as if he had consumed nothing but a single graham cracker in the past twenty-four hours. Not bloody likely.

"Good grub," he said to me. "Do you cater wedding receptions?"

"Sure," I said. "Also proms and bar mitzvahs. Al, I told father about that calamitous raid on Gorton's warehouse. Anything new since you phoned me?"

"Yeah," he said. "The chase is on for Gorton, Oliver Whitcomb, the three funeral directors and their stooges. That's why I've got to get back to headquarters instead of going home. Two of those directors live in the Palm Beach area. We're supposed to liaise with the FBI trackers when they get up here."

"They intend to arrest Oliver Whitcomb?" father asked.

"Yes, sir. I don't know if they have a warrant but with two agents dead they're in no mood to observe the legal technicalities. Besides, they have probable cause coming out their ears."

Hizzoner made a tch-tch sound. "This will cause Horace Whitcomb considerable pain. Naturally, sergeant, I shall say nothing to him about Oliver's predicament. He'll learn of the arrest soon enough. And then I expect he'll contact me to recommend an experienced criminal defense attorney to represent his son."

I looked at him in astonishment. "Father, Horace is well aware of what Oliver has been doing. After all, Horace initiated the inquiry that eventually ended Oliver's short criminal career. Are you suggesting that Horace will now aid his son?"

The old man stared at me sternly. "Of course. In any way he can. Oliver's illicit behavior has nothing to do with it. Horace Whitcomb is an honorable man, and this is family."

"Blood is thicker than water," Rogoff put in. "But not thicker than this coffee," he added, pouring himself another cup.

The idea of Horace helping defend his wayward son was incomprehensible to me, even though the senior didn't think it extraordinary at all. Perhaps I'll understand it when, if ever, I become a paterfamilias.

"Al," I said, "about Ernest Gorton—where are they searching for him?"

"They're looking for him here, there, everywhere. And I'll bet a million they'll never find him."

"Oh?" father said, interested. "Why not?"

"Look, counselor," the sergeant said, "this guy is a slime, granted, but a smart slime. Always one step ahead of the law and his competitors. Now don't tell me a shrewd apple like him wouldn't have a failsafe plan in case things got hairy—which they have."

"How would he manage it?" I asked.

"Set up a residence and fake identity in some pipsqueak country that doesn't have an extradition treaty with the U.S. But I can't see Gorton spending the rest of his life in a jungle hut or beach shack. He's a guy who needs action. My guess is that he's got a beautiful villa and fake papers in some South American country. He changes his name and maybe even has plastic surgery. All this is going to cost plenty in bribes to local pols, but that's no different from how he was operating in Miami. And he can afford it. So now he's a new man and can get back in the rackets again, in the country where he's living and in international trade in drugs, guns, money laundering, prostitution, and so forth. Believe me, we haven't heard the last of Ernest Gorton, no matter what his new name might be."

"A depressing prospect," my father remarked.

"Yeah," Rogoff said with a snarly laugh, "ain't it. Listen, I've got to get back to the salt mines. If anything important comes up I'll let you know. Thanks for the feed; it was just what I needed."

Then he buckled on his gun belt and was gone. Father helped me clean up the kitchen.

"Sir," I said, "if Oliver Whitcomb and the others are indicted and brought to trial, as they may well be, do you think I'll be called upon to testify?"

"I doubt it very much, Archy," he said, doing a good but not perfect job of hiding his amusement. "After all, what evidence do you have to offer?"

I reflected on that and acknowledged he was exactly right, as usual. I had no hard evidence to offer. Just guesses, suppositions, unsubstantiated hypotheses.

I returned to my interrupted slumber in a mood far from gruntled. It was an injury to my amour propre to realize that in the Whitcomb affair I had been a small cog on a large wheel. But even the absence of a single cog can freeze motion, can it not?

I awoke a little after 10:00 A.M. on Friday, feeling not at all refreshed and yearning for a few more hours of Zs. Before showering and shaving I sat on the edge of my bed and made a few phone calls—the first to Al Rogoff. He sounded uncommonly brisk for a man who had been conscious and functioning through a sleepless night.

"Well?" I demanded.

"We got 'em all," he reported. "Including Oliver Whitcomb. His father's been informed."

"What about Mitzi, his wife?"

"Picked her up, too."

"And Gorton?"

"Like I told you—he's long gone. Talk to you later." And he hung up.

My second call was to Binky Watrous. I obviously woke him up, which pleased me.

"What's happening?" he said groggily.

"Lots," I said. "The authorities have found Judge Crater, Amelia Earhart, Jimmy Hoffa, and have identified Jack the Ripper and the mountebank who wrote Shakespeare's sonnets."

"You're kidding."

"Have I ever? Listen, Binky, I don't think this will happen, but if any chaps with badges come around asking questions about the Whitcomb case, claim you know naught of the matter. This is a firm command."

Short silence. "You mean you want me to lie and tell them I'm totally ignorant?"

What a cue! "It's scarcely a lie, old boy," I said and disconnected.

My third call was to Sunny Fogarty's office. I was told she was not available. I then phoned her condo and let it ring seven times before giving up. Isn't it strange that one usually knows when no one is home? The ringing has an empty sound. I know it's ridiculous, but I'm sure you've had the same experience.

I went through my usual morning ablutions and dressed in a natty manner, hoping it might elevate my spirits. I donned an artfully wrinkled sky-blue linen sport jacket (no shoulder pads, of course), slacks of rust-colored covert, and suede loafers in a sort of tealish shade. The ensemble, I decided, was striking without being bizarre. I was certain my father would have a contrary opinion.

After a scanty breakfast (Oh, black coffee, and two croissants with heather honey) I drove directly to the McNally Building wondering if at that moment Ernest Gorton was flying to his hideaway abroad. Wherever he was heading I reckoned he was traveling first class. Sgt. Rogoff keeps assuring me it is gross stupidity to believe that in this world virtue is always rewarded and vice punished. Sad to say, he is probably correct.

I phoned my father when I arrived at my office and was pleasantly surprised to be put through immediately. I relayed Rogoff's most recent information.

"Thank you, Archy," he said formally, "but I am already aware of Oliver's arrest. Horace Whitcomb called a short time ago to tell me the news. He is coming over to discuss legal representation for his son."

"How did he sound?"

"Resigned, I would say, as if he had expected such an outcome to the inquiry he instigated."

"Father, what do you think will happen to Oliver and his accomplices?"

"I imagine there will be plea bargaining, but I fear Oliver and the others will serve prison sentences of various durations. I do not believe they will get off lightly. Two special agents of the FBI have been killed; the authorities will not be in the mood to be merciful."

"A sad situation," I said.

"It is," he agreed, "and I am glad McNally and Son will no longer be playing an active role in the affair. You will cease all your inquiries immediately." Thus ordained His Majesty.

"Yes, sir," I said, resisting a terrible desire to drop a curtsy.

34

Not quite, pappy. There was still a bit of unfinished business, a little tidying up to do before my record of the Whitcomb case could be closed. But before I could call her again, she phoned me.

"This is Sunny Fogarty, Archy," she said, sounding tearful.

"I tried calling you earlier, Sunny, but couldn't get through."

"I was with Mr. Horace," she said. "He's had a bad morning. I suppose you've heard what's happened."

"Yes, I heard."

"Archy, I'm home now. Is there any chance of your coming over?"

"Of course," I said. "Shall I bring us some lunch?"

"Oh no," she said. "Thank you but no. I'm really not hungry. But I do want to see you."

"I'll leave at once," I told her, hoping I might have the courage to ask her a direct and perhaps an insolent question. But if she answered honestly it would relieve an irritation that had bothered me from the start, a nagging as persistent as a vagrant lash on the eyeball or a fleck of lettuce snagged in one's bicuspid.

I think the way Sunny Fogarty dressed was part of the contradiction that puzzled me. A dichotomy, one might say—and I do say it. If it is true clothes make the man, clothes *are* the woman.

She met me at the door of her condo wearing a severely tailored pantsuit of black gabardine. But the jacket was unbuttoned to reveal a ruffled white silk blouse also unbuttoned in a manner I found disturbingly seductive. She ushered me to the couch in the living room and tried a brave smile.

"Quite a morning," she said.

"I can imagine."

"Archy, I'm having a chardonnay, but I suspect you might prefer something stronger."

"You suspect correctly," I said boldly, needing resolution to ask my impertinent question.

"Will vodka on the rocks do?" she asked.

"Splendidly," I said, and a few moments later she brought me a beaker of iced elixir that would have transformed a mild-mannered lemur into King Kong.

"How is Mr. Horace taking all this?" I said.

"Remarkably well. He has the funeral of Mrs. Sarah to arrange and now he must do what he can for Oliver. Plus reorganizing the funeral homes and hiring new directors and assistants. But he's a strong man and he's coping."

"I'm sure he's depending on you for assistance," I said. Crafty me—leading into the rude query I was determined to make.

"I'm doing what I can to help," she said evenly, "and so are all the other employees not involved in that dreadful business."

She rose from the armchair, removed her jacket, and joined me on the couch. It could have been an entirely innocent maneuver, I agree, but one never knows, do one? She sat quite close and looked at me directly.

"Archy," she said, "I asked you to come over because I have an apology to make."

"Sunny," I protested, "you've already apologized. You admitted you and Mr. Horace were aware of Oliver's shenanigans before you asked McNally and Son for a discreet inquiry."

"No, no," she said with a small smile of rue. "This is *another* apology. A personal apology."

She placed a soft hand on my arm and answered the question that had been bedeviling me.

"I want to explain why I went to such lengths to protect Horace and why I may have misled you in the process. I even withheld things I knew and made you discover them yourself. It was all because I didn't want Horace to be hurt. You see, dear, he and I have been intimate for, oh, perhaps five years, ever since his wife became ill."

She paused and looked at me as if awaiting an expression of shock. But I was not shocked. Would you have been? I think not.

"Oh," I said, my suspicion confirmed. After all, there was the expensive condo, the new car she drove, those frequent payments for clothes and jewelry in her credit dossier. The lady was obviously living beyond her means, and the unexplained prosperity of others is always sufficient to ignite my penchant for nosiness.

"You mean a lot to me, Archy," she continued, "and it is important to me that you know why we did what we did. Horace's wife was dying. My mother is totally out of it and hasn't long to go. That's what brought us together. Can you understand it?"

"Not quite," I said, taking a deep swallow of my chilled plasma. "I must confess I'm an absolute klutz when it comes to grasping all the subtleties of he-she relations."

"It was grief, Archy," she said intently. "Like two people huddling together in a bomb shelter, comforting each other against the death outside. Of course we bedded; I won't deny it. But it was not passion; it was a sharing of sorrow—and fear."

"That's heavy," I said.

Sunny nodded. "I know but it's true. There was guilt, of course—there had to be guilt because his wife was still alive."

"Do you suppose she knew?"

"I believe she did. I like to think she approved—or at least accepted it with equanimity. She was a marvelous woman, Archy."

"She was indeed."

"Horace tried to compensate for his conduct by giving me gifts. It really wasn't necessary. I told him that but he insisted. Somehow it helped him deal with his guilt. Men are so strange. As for my guilt, I could endure it because I knew it was temporary; it couldn't last. The bombs were falling closer and closer. I think I need another drink. Are you ready?"

"Good Lord, no!"

She returned with a refilled wine glass and seated herself close beside me again.

"Two questions, Sunny," I said, "and I'd love to know the answers. There was once a Polish king known as Boleslaw the Bashful and I expect I shall go down in history as Coleslaw the Curious. First of all, did you grant me the pleasure of your bed just to ensure my continued cooperation in the investigation?"

She clamped my arm again, tightly this time. "Oh no!" she said hotly. "Don't even *think* such a thing. I simply wanted us to enjoy. I wanted it to be purely physical, mindless, and fun. I wanted to surrender completely and for a brief, wonderful time forget all my problems and share joy instead of sorrow. Did I succeed?"

"Of course you did," I lied valiantly and have never uttered a more meritorious falsehood. "And now I must ask my second question: Will you marry Horace Whitcomb?"

Her grip on my arm slackened and she looked at me sadly. "You still don't understand, do you? Of course I won't marry Horace. It wasn't a mad, crazy love affair, a lust neither of us could resist. All we had was shared grief. And after that is gone, we have nothing."

This woman was too deep for me by far.

"Surely you have plans for the future, Sunny."

"Oh yes," she said determinedly. "I intend to stay with Whitcomb Funeral Homes until we have it functioning normally again. Then I'll leave and find another job. When my mother passes away I might move elsewhere. California perhaps."

"Mr. Horace will urge you to stay," I told her.

"He already has. But I want to put all this in the past and start a new life. Does that sound foolish?"

"Not at all. Romantic, but not foolish. What exactly are you seeking, dear?"

"I can't explain," she said. "I'm not sure myself."

I didn't believe that. She was a woman of secrets to the last.

There didn't seem much more to be said. Our final parting, a light embrace and kiss, was more bro-sis than he-she.

"Let's keep in touch," she said.

"By all means," I said.

Kindred liars.

I departed and aimed the Miata toward home and emotional security. I suffered one brief pang of remembrance: a vital woman, strong and zesty in bed.

I found my thoughts returning to what Sunny Fogarty had revealed of her relationship with Horace Whitcomb, described by my father as an honorable man. I believed Sunny had told me the truth—or at least what was valid for her. But I found her story so singular, so alien to my experience, that I could scarcely accept it.

And so, hewing to folk wisdom—"A boy's best friend is his mother"—I sought out Mrs. Madelaine McNally after I garaged my tumbril. I found her in our greenhouse.

"Mrs. M.," I said, "I'd like to take advantage of your superior acumen and ask help in solving an enigma that puzzles me."

She paused, brass watering can in hand, and looked at me inquiringly. "What is it, Archy?"

"Do you think it possible a man and a woman might form a close relationship—an intimate relationship, in fact—simply because both are suffering great sorrow in their personal lives?"

She didn't hesitate a moment. "Of course it's possible," she said promptly. "Grief does bring people together, you know. They cling to one another."

"Mother, I always thought passionate twosomes were based on physical attraction and shared interest in such things as opera, Bugs Bunny cartoons, ballet, and smoked provolone sandwiches on pumpernickel."

"Oh, Archy, people link up for so many reasons, and sadness is certainly one of them. Misery loves company just as happiness does."

I pondered that for a moment. "You're saying the motives for intimacy are many and varied?"

"Very many and very varied."

This was a fresh perception to me and I could not let it go. "Could a shared prejudice or hatred or bigotry be the motive for a man and woman cleaving to each other?"

"Of course," mother said matter-of-factly. "Even nasty people fall in love, Archy."

"I guess," I said gloomily, wishing I knew more than I did. But I consoled myself with the thought that Mr. Einstein probably had the same vain hope.

"Have I answered your question, dear?" she asked, not at all dismayed by the lesson she had taught me in the realpolitiks of love.

"You have indeed," I assured her, "and I thank you for it. By the way, I won't be able to join you and father for cocktails and dinner. Connie has returned from Miami and we're going out for a night on the town."

"That's nice, darling," she said brightly. "Have a wonderful time."

"I fully intend to give it my best shot," I vowed, kissed her velvety cheek, and left her asking a Merry Christmas begonia why it was drooping in such a shameful fashion.

The sea was paved that afternoon, but I was in no mood for a dunk. Nor did I have any desire to scribble in my journal and close out my account of the Whitcomb case. Instead, I lay on my bed fully clothed, stared at the ceiling, and suffered a severe case of weltschmerz.

I am not often depressed, being cheerful by nature, but recent events had brought me low. I was discomposed by so many people dancing about as if Walpurgisnacht would go on forever.

I suddenly realized what would cure my jimjams. I rose and called Connie Garcia, phoning her at the estate of Lady Cynthia Horowitz. I figured Connie had gone to work immediately to make up for all her absent days.

"Lady Horowitz's residence," she said crisply. "Consuela Garcia speaking."

"Archibald McNally speaking," I said just as snappily. "Is it on for tonight, hon?"

"You betcha," she said. "You pick me up at seven and off we go to the Pelican Club."

"Do me a favor, will you, Connie. I'd like to wear a dinner jacket. Will you get gussied up?"

Shocked silence. Then: "You want to wear a dinner jacket to the Pelican?"

"Yep."

"You'll be tarred, feathered, and ridden out of town on a rail."

"I don't care. It's something I must do. Will you humor me?"

"Say 'Please.' "

"Please."

"Say 'Please with sugar on it.' "

I groaned. "Please with sugar on it."

"Okay," she giggled. "I'll get all dolled up. It'll give me a chance to wear a neat coat dress I bought in Miami. It's white silk and makes me look like a vanilla Popsicle."

"Yummy," I said. "See you at seven."

Then I disrobed and went back to bed smiling for a much needed nap. If the Whitcomb affair had an almost operatic intensity, I was determined that evening would be as innocent and memorable as a pop tune. I don't know the lyrics of *La donna è mobile* but I can sing every word of "It Had to Be You."

35

When attending a formal affair in South Florida's clammy clime, I usually don a white dinner jacket, soft-collared shirt, and a tie and cummerbund of a modest maroon or even a sedate tartan. But not that evening.

I unzipped a garment bag to extract my black tropical worsted dinner jacket and trousers. The jacket had black satin lapels, the trousers black satin stripes, but the costume was really as conservative as a shroud. I also laid out a starched shirt, wing collar, onyx studs and cuff links.

I knew exactly what I was doing. The Whitcomb case had been such a raw and vulgar affair that I needed a healthy dose of convention to restore my emotional balance. My traditional uniform was one small step in recovering the comfort of custom. I have neither the gall nor the desire to deny the past.

Showered, shaved, and scented, I dressed in my formal attire, prized my feet into patent leather shoes, and descended to the kitchen. I moved rather stiffly, I admit, as if I were wearing a suit of armor and feared I might creak.

Mrs. Olson was preparing dinner and turned as I entered.

"Oh my, Mr. Archy," she said, awed, "you look so handsome!"

"Thank you, Ursi," I said, preening. "Do you think perhaps I need a boutonniere?"

She pursed her lips and regarded my costume thoughtfully. "Possibly," she said. "Something to add a bit of color to the black and white. But we have no fresh flowers available other than your mother's begonias, and they won't do."

"No," I said, "definitely not."

"I do have some fresh parsley available," she offered. "Do you think a sprig of that would help?"

"Just the thing!" I cried happily, and a few moments later I had a small bundle of that marvelous herb pinned to my lapel.

I had a hazy hope of how I wanted that evening to progress and end. And so I entered the pantry and searched the shelves bearing the McNally liquor supply. (The costly vintage wines are stored in a locked, temperature-controlled cabinet in my father's study.) I found what I sought: a bottle of Korbel brut. I slid it with two crystal champagne flutes onto the lowest shelf of our refrigerator.

Then I set out to rendezvous with the vanilla Popsicle.

Yikes! but Connie looked super, all slithery in white silk and with the excited, prideful look women get when they know they're splendidly dressed. Her long black hair was down and gleaming. The only jewelry she wore was the diamond tennis bracelet I had given her. What a glittery manacle it was!

I embraced her gently, not wishing to crush her coat dress.

"Welcome home, darling," I said. "I missed you."

"Did you?" she said eagerly. "Did you really?"

"Scouts' honor. I pined away while you were gone. Lost pounds and pounds."

She pulled away to inspect me. "I don't think so. Archy, you look spiffy, but what's that in your buttonhole?"

"Parsley."

"I hope you're kidding."

"I am not. It is a sprig of fresh parsley. It is decorative and should our dinner contain a gross amount of garlic, we can nibble on it to sweeten our breath."

She hugged my arm. "Nutty as ever," she said happily. "Let's go."

If Connie feared our finery would be greeted with raucous scorn by the raffish Friday night roisterers at the Pelican Club, she totally misjudged their reaction. Most of the lads and lasses beginning a bibulous weekend were clad in funky denim, leather, and T-shirts bearing legends ranging from the indelicate to the scabrous.

But when we entered, the chatter and laughter ceased as heads swiveled in our direction. Then many of our pals leaped to their feet and treated us to a vigorous round of applause interspersed with such cries of approval as "Oh, wow!" and "The baddest!"

Connie and I bowed graciously in all directions—royalty acknowledging their worshipful underlings. Then we paraded to the dining area where we claimed our favorite corner table. Priscilla came moseying forward to bring us down to earth.

"Going to a masquerade?" she inquired.

"None of your sass," I said sternly. "We merely decided the joint needed a touch of class."

"Gee," she said, "I wish you had warned me; I'd have put on clean overalls. Naturally you'll want champagne cocktails to start."

"Naturally," Connie said.

"I'll have to serve them on paper napkins," Pris apologized. "All our lace doilies are in the laundry. I'm sure you swells will understand."

"Of course," I said loftily. "Noblesse oblige."

You would think, wouldn't you, that in view of our splendiferous attire we might dine on pheasant under glass or perhaps a roasted capon stuffed with minced hundred-dollar bills. But the Pelican Club was unable to provide such amenities, and Chef Leroy's special that night was pot roast with a fresh horseradish sauce so good it made one weep—literally.

Connie was at her magpie best during dinner, regaling me with trivia about her trip to Miami, the recovery of her injured cousin, the trials and tribulations of her multitudinous relatives.

Earlier in this account I suggested my attraction to this woman was due to her providing an island of normalcy in the sometimes violent sea I was called upon to navigate. I imagine some of you faithful readers must have shaken your heads sagely and thought, "That Archy! Just another example of his dissembling. He likes Connie because she's a dishy broad."

Well, yes, that was certainly part of it. But as mother has instructed me, intimacy is rarely simple. What human bonds are? Sgt. Al Rogoff once told me of a case he handled in which a woman bludgeoned her husband with a cinder block while he slept. Her reason? "He snored," she told the cops. But surely that was only one motive in a long, festering record of grievances.

We had shared a single dessert—a wickedly rich raspberry shortcake drizzled with Chambord—and were lazing over double espressos when Connie asked me what I had been doing during her absence.

"This and that," I said.

"I'll bet it was the Whitcomb case," she said. "It's been in all the papers and on TV every night. I'm sure you were mixed up in it because you asked me weeks ago about Oliver and Mitzi."

"I was involved," I admitted. "Up to my dewlaps. But there's little I can add to what you've already heard or read. It was a mess, Connie. Listen, do you know what I'd like to do now?"

"Yes," she said.

I laughed. "Later," I said. "There will be a short station break. Stay tuned."

We drove back to the McNally mansion manqué. It was a glorious night, almost completely cloudless with a wispy breeze from the northwest. The moon wasn't full, of course—that would have been too much—but there was enough showing to remind me of Guy Kibbee. It was a loverly stage set that convinced me I'd live forever.

I retrieved the chilled bottle of Korbel from the fridge and popped the cork. Carrying the bubbly and two glasses, I conducted Connie down the rickety wooden staircase to the beach. She asked nary a question nor made any objection. I led and she followed. What a sweetness!

She was wearing no hose and had only to kick off her suede sandals. But I had to pry off my patent leathers and peel away knee-high socks. I rolled up my trouser cuffs and we left all our footgear in the moon shadow of a palm. Before we started our stroll I poured each of us a glass of champagne. We linked arms before sipping. Cutesy? I suppose. But there was no one to see but God and I hoped He approved.

We ambled down to the water's edge where mild waves came lapping in. The ocean was still calm and it seemed layered with a pathway of aluminum foil leading to the rising moon.

"Oh," Connie said, staring out at the glistening sea and breathing deeply. She tilted her face up to the night sky. "Look at all those tennis bracelets!"

"Exactly," I said.

We wandered southward through warm froth that rarely doused our calves. The packed sand was cool and provided easy strolling. We saw the lights of fishing boats and the blaze of a passing cruise ship. Once we heard the melodious call of a seabird neither of us could identify.

"Binky Watrous should be here," I remarked.

"Bite your tongue," Connie advised.

We paused occasionally while I refilled our glasses.

You may think this barefoot ramble along a moonlit beach by a formally dressed couple sipping champers was a schmaltzy thing to do. But schmaltz is in the eye of the beholder—and you've never read a more disgusting figure of speech if you happen to know the original meaning of the word.

It was a fantasy and I was aware of it. After experiencing the crudity of the Whitcomb case I wanted to recapture the laughing elegance of a world I never knew and perhaps never existed: the clever, self-mocking era of Noel Coward songs, Fitzgerald novels, Broadway musicals, and William Powell movies. I was trying to recreate a madly joyous time I imagined.

"A penny for your thoughts," Connie said, "and not one cent more."

"I was thinking about dreams," I told her. "And how they shape our lives."

Then I described some of the dreamers I had met during the Whitcomb investigation:

Mrs. Sarah: Dying while listening to a tinkly music box.

Oliver: Driven by a fierce ambition to prove himself a money-spinner nonpareil.

Ernest Gorton: He of the green eyes with limitless greed and a vision of limitless wealth.

Mitzi Whitcomb: She saw a constantly expanding universe of young studs and giggles.

Griffin Kling: A man nurtured by a vengeful rage that eventually destroyed him.

Rhoda Flembaugh: She yearned only for a chance to change her luck.

I said nothing of Horace Whitcomb and Sunny Fogarty. But they too had their illusions.

Dreamers all.

Connie listened intently to my brief recital and suddenly shivered. "Archy," she said, "I'm getting chilly."

I set bottle and glass in the sand, took off my dinner jacket, and draped it about her shoulders. She looked enchanting.

"Let's go back," I said.

"Let's hurry," she said.

We turned and skipped along the strand under the spangled sky, silvered by moonlight, and hearing the sea's soft susurrus. We held hands and sang "You'd Be So Nice to Come Home To."

We had reclaimed our footwear and were preparing to board the Miata when Ms. Consuela Garcia declared, "I know what I want to do now, Archy. You?"

"I concur," I said.

"Then let's do it," she said.

And so we did.

McNally's Puzzle

1

She slapped my face.

I have mentioned in previous accounts of my adventures that I am an absolute klutz when dealing with a weeping woman. I am even klutzier (if there is such a word) in coping with a person of the female extraction who commits an act of physical aggression upon the carcass of Archy McNally, bon vivant, dilettantish detective, and the only man in the Town of Palm Beach who owns a T-shirt bearing a portrait of Sophie Tucker. (She once hefted her voluminous breasts and said, "Hitler should have such tonsils.")

But forgive these digressions and allow me to return to the problem of being the victim of a lady's wrath: to wit, a sharp blow to my mandible. I mean, what was a gentleman to do?

1. Grit one's molars and stiffen one's upper lip in silence?
2. Return the slap while muttering a mild oath?
3. Bow politely and say, "I deserved that"?

Actually, the third choice would have been the most fitting but I was too startled by the sudden attack to make any reasonable response. Let me explain:

Her first name was Laura and her last name is of no consequence to this narrative. She and her wealthy husband of three years had recently finalized what was described as an "amicable divorce"—if there is such an animal, which I doubt.

Laura received a humongous cash settlement. Her ex-hubby retained possession of their Palm Beach mansion with all its rather atrocious furnishings and, of course, his personal property, including a famous collection of sports memorabilia. It had occasionally been exhibited in local museums which could not snare a traveling Monet show and had to be content with a display of ancient gutta-percha golf balls and a stained leather helmet once worn by Bronko Nagurski.

The star of the collection was a 1910 Sweet Caporal cigarette card bearing a likeness of Honus Wagner, famed shortstop of the Pittsburgh Pirates. It was believed only thirty-six of these rare baseball cards still existed, and one recently sold at auction for $450,000.

You can imagine the husband's fury and despair when, shortly after his divorced wife decamped, he discovered his beloved Honus Wagner card had decamped as well. But he had no proof his ex had filched his most valuable curio. And so, rather than create a foofaraw with the local gendarmes, he brought the problem to his attorneys, McNally & Son.

My father, Prescott McNally, is the lawyer. I, Archibald McNally, am the son. I do not hold a legal degree due to a minor contretemps resulting in my being excommunicated from Yale Law. But I direct a small department (personnel: one) devoted to Discreet Inquiries. I do investigations for clients who would prefer to have potentially embarrassing matters handled with quiet circumspection instead of seeing them made public and possibly detailed in a supermarket tabloid next to an article entitled "I Am Pregnant with Elvis's Love Child!"

It took only a bit of nosing about to discover the lady was a member of the tennis club to which I belong—although my dues are frequently in arrears. Soon thereafter we were confronting each other across the net. I am not an accomplished tennist, although I do have a ferocious backhand, and it didn't take long to discover Laura was a calm and cool expert. To put it bluntly, she creamed me.

An after-set gin and tonic led to my inviting her to a luncheon and eventually a dinner. Working my wicked wiles, I capped a week of gastronomic seduction with a feast at the Chesterfield (rack of lamb and then a Grand Marnier soufflé). Replete and giggling, we returned to her quarters in a West Palm condo rental. By this time we were sufficiently simpatico that I do not believe either of us doubted how the evening would end.

And so it did. In my own defense I can only plead I was as much seductee as seducer. I mean this was an inexorable progression betwixt a frisky lass and an even friskier lad. What was one to do? Kismet.

But I did not neglect my motive for engineering this joyous occasion. And when the lady scampered into the bathroom after our frolic I scampered to the chest of drawers in her bedroom. And there, under a stack of perfumed undies, I found the stolid portrait of Honus Wagner, his baseball card sealed in plastic. I slipped it into my wallet, delighted with such a triumphant night.

But then, as I was dressing, she came trotting out, naked as a needle, and went directly to her store of flimsies. She discovered my theft almost immediately. She stalked over to me and I fancied even her satiny bosom was suffused with indignation—if not fury.

That was when she slapped my face.

After recovering from my initial shock, I launched into an earnest and detailed explanation. It was not actually larceny, I pointed out; I was merely recovering property illegally removed from the possession of the rightful owner. And as an employee of her ex-husband's attorney it was my duty to reclaim that which was undeniably his. Besides, I argued, my act of pilferage had been to her advantage since it would prevent her ex from filing a complaint of her alleged crime with the polizia.

I prided myself on speaking sincerely and eloquently. As readers of my previous discreet inquiries are aware, I am rarely at a loss for words. Glib, one might even say. Laura was obviously impressed, listening to my persuasive discourse in silence. When I concluded she drew a deep breath. Lovely sight.

"I guess you're right," she said. "But I want you to know I didn't intend to sell the stupid thing or profit from it in any way."

"Then why did you take it?"

"I just wanted to teach him a lesson," she said.

I shall never, never, *never* understand the gentle sex.

It was pushing midnight when I tooled my red Miata back to the ersatz Tudor manse on Ocean Boulevard housing the McNally family. It was the first week of November and it would be pure twaddle to describe the night as crisp. The weather in South Florida is rarely crisp, tending more toward the soggy, but I must report the sea breeze that

Friday night was definitely breathable and the cloudless sky looked as if it had been decorated by Tiffany & Co.

Lights were out and no one was astir when I arrived home. I garaged my chariot and toed the stairs as quietly as I could to my mini-suite on the third and topmost floor. I disrobed and bought myself one minuscule marc and a final English Oval before retiring. It had been a somewhat stressful evening and I must confess I was plagued by a small tweak of shame. My successful gambit for recovering the Honus Wagner baseball card had not been strictly honorable, had it? Caddish, one might even say.

I occasionally suffer an attack of the guilts and have found the best cure is a good night's sleep, when a mambo with Morpheus dilutes crass behavior to impish mischief. And so it happened once again, for I awoke the following morning with a clear head, a pure conscience, and only a slight twinge in the lower jaw to remind me of Laura's energetic slap the previous evening. She had been entitled, I acknowledged, and decided I was fortunate that in addition to her tennis prowess she was not also a master of kung fu.

I roused in time to breakfast with my parents in the dining room. Our Scandinavian staff, Ursi and Jamie Olson, had whipped up a marvelous country feast of eggs scrambled with onions, ham steaks, fried grits, hush puppies, and coffee laced with enough chicory to afflict us all with a chorus of borborygmus.

"Goodness," my mother, Madelaine, said, "it *is* peppy, isn't it? Just the one cup for me."

My father was dressed for his customary Saturday golf game with the same cronies he had been playing with as long as I could recall. They were known as the Fearless Foursome at his club for they had once insisted on completing the back nine while a category three hurricane was raging.

Prescott McNally, Esq., wore his usual golfing uniform: white linen plus fours and argyle hose. This attire might have appeared ridiculous on a man of lesser dignity but pops, with his grizzled eyebrows and guardsman's mustache, carried it off with casual aplomb, as if he might be heading for a round at St. Andrews.

"Archy," he said as we left the dining room, both of us still rumbling dully from our gaseous breakfast, "a moment of your time, please."

We paused in the hallway outside the door of his first-floor study.

"The baseball card?" he inquired.

"Recovered," I said. "It'll be on your desk Monday morning."

"Excellent," he said. "Any unexpected difficulty or expense?"

"No, father. The lady was most cooperative."

He looked at me and raised one jungly eyebrow, a trick I've never been able to master. But he asked no questions. The pater prefers not to learn the details of my discreet inquiries. I do believe he fears such knowledge might result in his disbarment. He may be right.

"I'm happy the matter has been concluded satisfactorily," he said in his stodgy manner. "Then you have nothing on your plate at the moment?"

"No, sir. My platter is clean."

"Good. Do you know Hiram Gottschalk?"

"He's on our client list, is he not?"

"He is."

"I've never met Mr. Gottschalk personally but I have a nodding acquaintance with his son, Peter. He's a member of the Pelican Club."

"Is he?" father said. "And what is your reaction to him?"

I chose my words carefully. "I find him somewhat undisciplined," I said.

"So Mr. Gottschalk has led me to believe. He is a widower, you know, and in addition to his son he has grown twin daughters, presently vacationing in Europe. Are you also acquainted with them?"

"No, sir."

"Apparently they're due to return shortly, and perhaps you'll have the opportunity to meet them."

"Perhaps," I said. "Father, doesn't Mr. Gottschalk own that store in West Palm that sells birds?"

"Parrots," the sire said. "The shop is called Parrots Unlimited. That's the only species he handles."

"No auks?" I asked. "No emus or kiwis?"

He was startled. "Archy, you seem remarkably well informed about exotic birds."

"Not really," I said. "The names I mentioned are frequently used in crossword puzzles."

"Oh," he said. "Well, in any event, Mr. Gottschalk came in to consult me. We have been discussing for some time his plan to set up a private foundation. He is a wealthy man. Not from his parrot store, I assure you. But he has inherited a considerable sum, the greater part from his deceased wife, and we have been exploring options that might legally diminish his estate tax. But yesterday Mr. Gottschalk didn't wish to talk about taxes. He asked if I could recommend a private investigator to look into a matter that's troubling him. I told him of your employment as our house specialist in discreet inquiries. He seemed happy to hear of it and requested your assistance."

"Ready, willing, and able, sir," I said, resisting a momentary urge to genuflect. "What's his problem?"

Father paused a beat or two. Then: "He fears someone is trying to kill him."

"Surely not a maniacal macaw," I said.

Mon père glared at me. He does not appreciate my feeble attempts at humor at the expense of clients of McNally & Son. He feels they deserve respect since they put barbecued duck on the McNally table. I do respect them, I really do. But modicum is the word for it since many of our moneyed customers whose problems I deal with turn out to have a touch of sleaze.

"I suggest you visit Mr. Gottschalk on Monday," the boss continued. "I should warn you he is, ah, slightly eccentric."

"Oh?" I said. "In what way?" I remembered the old saw: "The poor are crazy; the rich are eccentric."

"In various ways," he said vaguely. "I'll leave it to you to make your own judgment. It's possible his fears are completely groundless, but I feel it's a matter deserving investigation. There's no point in his going to the police, of course. He has received no written or phone threats. No attempts have been made on his life. It's just a feeling he has. The police could do nothing with that, and rightly so. But please look into it, Archy."

"Of course," I said. "Monday morning."

He nodded and departed for his golf game. I went upstairs to change my duds for what I hoped would be an active and rewarding weekend during which I planned to play the role of a Palm Beach layabout: a bibulous lunch with Binky Watrous, an ocean swim, dinner with Consuela Garcia at the Pelican Club on Saturday night, golf on Sunday, perhaps a visit to Wellington polo in the afternoon. Good food. Good drinks. Jokes and laughter.

I record this trivia to convince you I do not spend *all* my time outwitting villains and righting wrongs. There is a gloomy Hungarian saying, something to the effect that before you have a chance to look around, the picnic is over. I have no intention of ignoring the picnic, ants and all. Not that I am given to excess. "Moderation in all things," Terence advised. (He wrote, of course, before the invention of the vodka gimlet.)

After a raucous session of poker with three pals on Sunday night (I won the princely sum of $3.49), I returned home early in the ayem and had a curious and rather unsettling experience.

I was in a beamish mood, a bit tiddly, and as I pulled in to the area fronting our three-car garage I saw in the headlight glare an enormous black bird stalking slowly across the gravel. Lordy but he was huge, and for one wild moment I thought I had spotted the last pterodactyl on earth.

It was a crow of course and not at all spooked by finding himself in the limelight. He turned his jetty head and gave me what I can only describe as a don't-mess-with-me look. Then he resumed his deliberate walk.

There was something disconcerting, almost ominous in the insolent parade of that funereal fowl. I watched him until he vanished into shadows as dark as he and my élan disappeared with him. I cannot say I felt menaced but I was slightly unnerved by the brief glimpse of that feathered phantom. He seemed so sure of himself, y'see, and totally indifferent to everything but his own desires.

If I wished to anthropomorphize I'd have said the bird personified evil. That's a mite much, you say? I'd be inclined to agree but Mr. Thomas Campbell was soon to be proved correct when he penned:

"Coming events cast their shadows before."

2

I overslept on Monday, reverting to my usual sluggardly habit. I finally hoisted myself from the pillows, showered and shaved. I dressed with something less than my usual éclat since I intended to meet with Mr. Hiram Gottschalk and wished to convey the impression of a sobersided investigator, a trustworthy representative of McNally & Son. Hey, I even wore socks.

I breakfasted alone in the kitchen and limited myself to only one croissant sandwich of salami and smoked Muenster. Then I set out for the McNally Building on Royal Palm Way. I distinctly recall having selected from my large collection of headgear a Monticristi panama I had recently bought. The purchase of that marvelous hat had put a severe dent in my checking account and I had the original black ribbon band replaced with one of snakeskin. Raffish, doncha think?

I left the baseball card with Mrs. Trelawney, my father's private secretary, and then went down to my own office. It is as commodious as a vertical coffin, and I do believe I have been sentenced to such a windowless cell by *mein papa* so he might never be accused of nepotism. I, of course, thought it prima facie evidence of parental abuse.

I looked up the number of Parrots Unlimited in the West Palm directory and phoned. A woman answered, I identified myself and asked to speak to Mr. Hiram Gottschalk. He came on the line a moment later. His voice was dry and twangy.

"You Prescott McNally's son?" he demanded. "Archibald McNally?"

"That's correct, sir."

"Call you Archy?"

"Of course," I said.

"Call me Hi," he said. "Hate the name Hiram. Makes me sound like a Nebraska farmer."

"Oh, I don't know," I said. "Hiram Walker and I are old friends."

He picked up on it immediately. "Say, you sound like a sharp kid. Want to see me, do you?"

"Yes, sir. At your convenience."

"Right now suits me fine," he said. "Come on over."

"On my way," I told him, and hung up, warning myself to be careful in greeting Mr. Gottschalk. "Hi, Hi" just wouldn't do, would it?

I found Parrots Unlimited with little trouble. It was on Hibiscus Street out west toward Cooley Stadium. I discovered a legal parking space about two blocks away and strolled back, grateful for my panama because the November sun thought it was still July.

The store was larger than I had anticipated and appeared to be well maintained. There were no live birds behind the plate glass windows as one might expect of a pet shop, but there was an attractive display of framed color photos of macaws, lovebirds, cockatoos, parakeets, and one magnificently feathered Edward's Fig-Parrot. There was also a printed sign: "BOARDING AND GROOMING AVAILABLE AT REASONABLE RATES." And a hand-scrawled notice: "Part-time assistant wanted. Inquire within."

I opened the door and entered, fearing I would be greeted with a cacophony of squawks and an odor that might loosen my fillings. Nothing of the sort existed. The interior was clean and uncluttered, the cool air smelled faintly of a wild cherry deodorizer, and rather than indignant screeches, all I heard was a subdued peep now and then, leading me to wonder if a wee bit of Valium might not be added to the daily diet of that multicolored aviary.

Just inside the door a large, pure-white parrot was perched on a well-pecked branch of soft wood. It was uncaged and untied. I paused to stare at it and the fowl turned its head to stare back. It had beady, red-tinged eyes, reminding me of my own after I have inhaled three brandy stingers.

I was approached by a salesperson, a plump, attractive young lady who was less parrot than robin redbreast.

"May I help you, sir?" she chirped.

(It always depresses me to be addressed as "sir" by a nubile lass. I dread the day when it may become "pop.")

"This bird," I said, gesturing toward the unfettered white parrot. "Why doesn't it fly away?"

"His wings have been clipped," she explained. "It's a completely painless procedure."

I found that hard to believe. I know I'd suffer if my wings were clipped.

"My name is Archy McNally," I told her. "I have an appointment with Mr. Gottschalk. Would you be kind enough to tell him I've arrived."

"Just a moment, please, sir," she said, and left.

I wandered about examining the extraordinary selection of parrots being offered for sale, some in individual cages but many in communal enclosures where they seemed to exist placidly together. There were also racks of bird feed, grooming aids, books, cages, perches, and toys. It was truly a psittacine supermarket, with one glassed-in corner apparently devoted to the grooming and treatment of birds with the sniffles.

The perky clerk soon returned to conduct me to Mr. Hiram Gottschalk's private office at the rear of the store. It was a smallish chamber with steel furniture and a computer installation on a separate table. The only item rarely found in commercial offices was a large, ornate cage on a stand. Within was a single parrot of a gray-blue color. It turned its head to watch me warily as I entered.

Our client was a short, stringy man sporting a nattily trimmed salt-and-pepper Vandyke. I guessed his age at about seventy, give or take, but his features were so taut I imagined additional years would wreak little damage to that tight visage. His eyes were hazel and alert. Exceedingly alert. A sharp customer, I reckoned.

We introduced ourselves and shook hands. His clasp was dry and firm. He saw me glance at the caged parrot behind his desk.

"Name is Ralph," Mr. Gottschalk said. "Give him a hello."

"Hello, Ralph," I said pleasantly.

"Go to hell," the bird said.

I glared at him and he glared right back.

"Did you teach him that?" I asked Hiram.

"Not me," he said. "Unsociable critter. No manners at all. Pull up a chair."

I sat alongside his desk, trying not to look at Ralph, who continued to eye me balefully.

"Tell me something, Hi," I said. "Do parrots mimic human speech naturally or must they be taught?"

"Generally," he said, "they require endless repetition. Audiotapes help. But then, occasionally, they'll surprise you by repeating something they've heard only once."

"A word or phrase? Something simple?"

"Not always," he said. "Here's a story for you. . . . A few years ago a very proper matron came in with a blue-fronted Amazon. Nothing wrong with the bird—it was gorgeously colored—but she had purchased it from a seafaring man in Key West, and apparently he had thought it a great joke to teach the female parrot to say, 'I'm a whore.'

"Naturally the new owner was much disturbed and asked if there was any way to rid her pet of this distressing habit. I told her it was doubtful but by a curious coincidence we were boarding two macaws belonging to a man of God who was then on a religious retreat in

Scranton. The minister's two birds were extremely devout and spent all their time reciting prayers they had obviously learned from their owner.

"I suggested to the matron that her profane bird be placed in the same cage with the two pious macaws, where she might learn to temper her language. The matron eagerly agreed, and that's what we did.

"The moment the three birds were joined, the female blue-fronted Amazon screeched, 'I'm a whore, I'm a whore.' And you know, one of the macaws turned to the other and said, 'Glory be, Charley, our prayers are answered.' "

Mr. Gottschalk stared at me, absolutely po-faced. "Isn't that a fascinating story?" he asked.

"Remarkable," I said, just as solemnly. "Quite remarkable. And did the three parrots live happily ever after—an avicultural *ménage à trois,* so to speak?"

"Something like that," he said, and we nodded thoughtfully at each other.

"Got a lot of parrot stories," he went on. "Things you might find hard to believe. They're very intelligent birds. Some can imitate a dog barking or a faucet dripping. Many researchers think they're smarter than chimps or dolphins. I've known budgerigars who could recite nursery rhymes or indecent limericks. My daughters are in Europe right now—they'll be home in a few days—and they wrote me how amazed they were to find parrots who spoke French, Italian, or Spanish. What's amazing about that? The birds will imitate the sounds they're taught. I once heard of a lorikeet who could mimic a police siren. But enough about parrots. That's not why you came to see me, is it, Archy."

"No, sir," I said. "My father tells me you feel your life is in danger."

"Not just feel it," he said decisively. "I *know* it. No threatening letters or phone calls, you understand, but several things I don't like."

"Such as?"

"My dear wife departed this vale of tears three years ago. I kept a framed photograph of us on my bedside table. It was taken at an outdoor cafe on the Cap d'Antibes. We were both young then, laughing, holding our wineglasses up to the camera. A lovely photo. I cherished it. The last thing I saw before sleep and the first thing I looked for in the morning. About a month ago I returned home to find the glass shattered and the photograph slashed to ribbons."

I drew a deep breath. "Ugly," I said.

He nodded. "A week later I opened my closet door to find a mass card taped to the inside. You're familiar with mass cards?"

"Yes, sir."

"You Catholic?"

"No, sir."

"Well, I am. Not a good one, I fear, but once tried, never denied. In any event, the name of the deceased on the mass card was mine."

I winced. My father had warned me our client was "slightly eccentric," and after his ridiculous anecdote about the devout macaws I had begun to suspect he might be a total goober. But now, listening to the disturbing events he related, I became convinced he was an intelligent man despite his quirky sense of humor. I believed he was troubled and telling me the truth. I mean, who but a professional novelist could dream up such bizarre incidents as the slashed photograph and the taped mass card?

"One final thing," Mr. Gottschalk said. "When we bought our house my wife very definitely forbade me to bring in any parrots. She thought they were dirty, selfish, and cantankerous—and indeed some of them are. She finally allowed me one male mynah, only because its coloring matched her decorative scheme for our Florida room."

"Surely mynahs are not parrots."

"Of course not," he said crossly. "Members of the starling family. But I love all birds and mynahs are lovable, this one especially so. His name was Dicky and he was beautiful. Extremely intelligent. Mynahs are superior to parrots in mimicking human speech, you know. Dicky could faultlessly recite the first verse of 'Battle Hymn of the Republic.' In addition, he had a delightfully apologetic manner. If he soiled his cage, upset his water, or made a mess of his feeding cup, he'd duck his head and cry, 'Dicky did it.' He said it so often it became a family joke, and if any of us had a minor mishap—spilled a glass of wine or broke a plate—we'd say, 'Dicky did it.' What a wonderful bird! My wife loved him. I thought we all did."

He paused. I said nothing, dreading the finale of his tale.

"Last week I went down for breakfast," he said, trying to keep his voice steady and not succeeding. "Didn't hear Dicky chirping as he usually did early in the morning. Went into the Florida room to take a look. The door of his cage was open. He was lying dead. Someone had wrung his neck."

We were both silent a long moment, wrenched. I couldn't look at Mr. Gottschalk but gazed up at Ralph behind his desk. The bird appeared to be sleeping.

"Sir," I said finally, "I don't wish to come to any premature conclusion from what you've related but it seems obvious to me—as I'm sure it is to you—that these acts of what I can only term terrorism could not have been committed by an outsider. The culprit must be a member of your household."

"Yes," he said, his voice muted with an ineffable sadness. "I'm aware of that. It hurts."

3

He had obviously been brooding on the matter, for he had prepared a list of all the family members and staff of his home, their names and relationship to him or their duties. I glanced at it briefly.

"A good beginning, Hi," I said, "but I'll really need to meet these people without their knowing of my assignment. Can you suggest how that might be done?"

He pondered a moment, then brightened. "My daughters are returning from Europe tomorrow. We're planning a welcome-home party on Wednesday night. Family, friends, and neighbors. Open bar and buffet dinner. Very informal. No starch at all. Begins around six or so and runs till whenever. Why don't you show up simply as a guest, a representative of my counselors-at-law."

"Excellent suggestion," I said. "I'll be delighted to attend. Have you also invited the employees of your store?"

He paused to look at me curiously. "I haven't," he admitted. "Do you think I should?"

"How many workers do you have?"

"Four full-timers. The manager, Ricardo Chrisling, and three clerks. And we're trying to find a part-timer for scut work."

"Invite them all," I advised. "I want to meet everyone you deal with on a daily basis. In addition, you'll score brownie points as a kindly employer."

He gave me a wry-crisp smile. "I was right; you *are* a sharp lad. All right, I'll ask them."

I pocketed his list and rose to leave. We shook hands again. This time I thought his clasp was weaker, as if the recital of dreadful events recently endured had enfeebled him.

"Give Ralph a good-bye," he said.

"Good-bye, Ralph," I said, knowing what was coming.

The bird opened its eyes. "Go to hell," it said.

And on that cheery note I departed.

There were several customers in the store and I waited until the young lady I had first encountered completed the sale of a bag of cuttlebone to a scrawny, bespectacled teenager who looked as if he might also profit from an occasional snack of calcium.

"Hello again," I said, giving her the 100-watt smile I term my Supercharmer, since I feared she was too innocent to withstand the power of my Jumbocharmer (150 watts).

"Hello yourself," she said brightly. "Arnold McIntosh, isn't it?"

How soon they forget! "Archy McNally," I repeated clearly. "Now you know my name but I don't know yours."

"Bridget," she said. "Bridget Houlihan."

"Mellifluous!" I said admiringly. "Comes trippingly off the tongue. Bridget, I see you have a notice in the window advertising for a part-time assistant. I have a friend who might be interested. If he decides to come in, may I give him your name? Perhaps you could then direct him to the proper person for an interview and questions about his competence."

"Oh, sure," she said. "Tell him to ask for me and I'll take care of him."

"Thank you so much," I said. "Have a grand day."

"I mean to," she said pertly. What a delightful bubble she was!

I exited into the sunshine and boarded the Miata. But before starting up I buzzed Binky Watrous on my cellular phone.

"Save me!" he cried piteously.

"Save you?" I said. "From what?"

"The Duchess wants me to accompany her to a charity luncheon followed by a two-hour film on the mating habits of emperor penguins. Apparently the males incubate the eggs by balancing them on their feet."

"I wish you hadn't told me that," I said. "I really didn't want to know. Listen, old boy, tell the Duchess you've received an emergency call concerning your on-the-job training to become the Nick Charles of Palm Beach. It's of vital importance you meet with me immediately to discuss a case of criminal conspiracy threatening the very existence of Western Civilization."

"Gotcha," he said happily. "Where and when?"

"Pelican in half an hour. I'll be at the bar."

"Of course," he said. "Naturally."

The Pelican Club is a private home-away-from-home for many of the glossier thirty-somethings of the Palm Beaches. It is located in a decrepit freestanding building out near the airport and offers a bar area, dining room, dartboard alley, and all one could wish for in the way of raucous fellowship, generous drinks, and a menu that disgusts cholesterolphobes.

As one of the founding members, I can testify we were close to bankruptcy when we had the great good fortune to put the fate of our club in the capable hands of the Pettibones, a family of color. Simon, the patriarch, became club manager and bartender. His wife, Jas (for Jasmine), was our den mother who saw to housekeeping chores, preserved limited order on unruly weekend nights, and was capable of gently ejecting members whose conduct exceeded her generous standard of decorum. Daughter Priscilla served as waitress and son Leroy as chef.

Under the aegis of the Pettibones the Pelican Club had flourished and its fame had spread. We now had a long list of wannabes (m. and f.) eager to wear on their jackets the club escutcheon: a pelican rampant on a field of dead mullet. It had certainly become my favorite watering hole in South Florida, and if my monthly tabs were shocking I consoled myself with the reminder that I conducted more business there for McNally & Son than I did in my emaciated office. Thus I could rightfully claim a goodly portion of my expenditures for beer and cheeseburgers on my expense account. Our treasurer, Raymond Gelding, frequently disagreed—but we all know what treasurers are like, don't we.

It wasn't quite noon and the club was deserted when I removed my panama, swung aboard a barstool, and relaxed in the dim, cool interior that always smelled faintly and delightfully of Grand Marnier.

"Mr. McNally," Simon Pettibone greeted me, "I haven't seen you in a long time."

"I know," I said. "It must be almost forty-eight hours. Mr. Pettibone, it is unexpectedly warm and steamy out there—a theme park called Sauna World—and I am in dire need of something tall, frigid, and refreshing. Suggestions?"

"You know," he said, "last night a young lady asked for a Tom Collins. Haven't mixed one of those in years. She seemed to enjoy it. Like to try one?"

"The ticket!" I cried. "I knew I could depend on you. Please make sure the ice is cold."

"I'll try," he said, not changing expression. Mr. Pettibone and I have an understanding.

He really is an expert mixologist and I watched with admiration as he constructed my Tom Collins and added the fruit.

"No straw," I warned.

"Wouldn't think of it," he said.

I sipped and rolled my eyes. "Elixir," I said. "Mr. Pettibone, are you familiar with a member named Peter Gottschalk?"

"I am," he said shortly.

"My father asked my opinion of him and I said I thought he was rather undisciplined. Do you think I was being unduly censorious?"

"No," he said. "On target. He's a wild one. Jas has booted him out a few times. Not for intoxication, mind you. He doesn't drink all that much. But occasionally he starts talking in a loud, irritating voice. Practically shouting. Butts in where he's not wanted. Becomes a real nuisance."

"What does he shout about?"

"Nonsense. Crazy stuff. No rhyme or reason. He just goes off. No control."

"Could it be physiological?" I asked. "Mental?"

"Could be," Mr. Pettibone said. "One minute he's nice as pie and then suddenly he's raving. Maybe it's a brain thing and a pill could straighten him out."

"Maybe," I said. But at that moment Binky Watrous came scuttling in and I was faced with the case of another man with a brain problem. Binky lacked one. He and a female companion had once been arrested for playing hopscotch in the Louvre.

He slapped my shoulder and slid onto an adjoining stool. "I'll have a fresh cantaloupe piña colada," he declared.

Mr. Pettibone and I glanced at each other. "Sorry, Mr. Watrous," he said. "No fresh cantaloupe available today."

"No?" my pal said. "What a shame. In that case I'll have a double Cutty Sark."

Typical Binky. The would-be Philo Vance was a complete goof.

I ordered a refill and we carried our drinks to the dining room before the luncheon crowd came charging in. We grabbed a corner table for two and Priscilla sauntered over. She was wearing a T-shirt, splotched painter's overalls, and a baseball cap with the visor turned jauntily to one side.

"Well, well," she said. "The Dynamic Duo. Batman and Robin."

"Enough of your sass," I said. "What's Leroy pushing today?"

"Vitamins," she said. "He's on a one-day health kick. A gorgeous seafood salad with fried anchovies."

"That's for me," I said. "Binky?"

"I'm game," he said. "But go easy on the lobster. It gives me a rash."

"Yeah?" Pris said. "Men have the same effect on me."

She bopped away and Binky took a yeomanly gulp of his Scotch. He was a palish lad who looked as if he might shampoo with Clorox. He sported a mustache so wispy one feared for its continued existence in a strong wind. But despite his apparent effeteness—or perhaps because of it—he was an eager and successful lothario, and I hesitated to estimate the limit of his conquests if his mustache had been black and long enough to twirl.

After the accidental death of his parents when he was a toddler, Binky had been raised, educated, and generously supported by a maiden aunt known to Palm Beach society as the Duchess. She was not an actual duchess of course but could have played one on *Masterpiece Theatre*. It was said she had once fired a butler for sneezing in her presence.

The Duchess had heretofore financed Binky's travels, brief romantic liaisons with ladies who sometimes made greedy demands, and his gambling debts. But recently she had brought her largesse to a screeching halt and demanded Binky seek gainful employment. But he had no experience in any practical occupation. His sole talent was birdcalls and there are very few, if any, Help Wanted ads headed "Birdcaller Wanted."

In desperation Binky had approached me with the request I take him on as an unpaid assistant in my Department of Discreet Inquiries for McNally & Son. It was to be on-the-job training and Binky had visions of becoming a successful private investigator. I thought he had as much chance of becoming a successful nuclear physicist, since of all my loopy friends he was the King of Duncedom.

Against my better judgment, and only from a real affection for this twit, I had allowed him to assist me on one case and had been pleasantly surprised to find his contributions of value. I had told him only those details of our client's travails I felt he needed to know, and I'm certain that in his ingenuous way he was totally unaware of the significance of the information he uncovered. But he did help me bring the case to a satisfactory conclusion. I mean he hadn't been an utter disaster and the idea of having a nutty Dr. Watson amused me.

"Binky," I said as we awaited our meal, "a new discreet inquiry has been assigned to me, and I feel I may benefit from your unique skills."

He preened. "Of course I shall be happy to assist you," he said formally. "No chance of a paycheck at the end of the week, is there, old sport?"

"Afraid not," I said regretfully. "The old man wouldn't approve. It must be part of your unpaid apprenticeship."

He sighed. "Better than nothing I suppose. The Duchess has been feeding me a diet of dirty digs lately, asking when I intend to land a job. If I can tell her I'm learning how to become a private eye, even if it's temporarily no-pay, she may stop her grousing."

"Also," I pointed out, "it will provide a perfect excuse for your absences, eliminating the need to accompany the Duchess to charity bashes and those flute recitals you so rightfully dread."

"How true, how true," he said, brightening. "I'm your man."

"You understand, don't you, that I'm to be captain of the ship and you a lowly seaman not allowed to question my judgments."

"Of course," he said. "You lead and I shall faithfully follow. What is it, Archy?"

"There's a bird shop in West Palm. Parrots Unlimited. That's all they sell—parrots. And accessories for their care and feeding. They're looking for a part-time assistant. I want you to apply for the job and do your best to obtain it."

He was horrified. "Surely you jest."

"I do not jest."

"Jiminy crickets, Archy, they'll have me cleaning out the cages."

"That will probably be part of your duties," I admitted.

"I know nothing about parrots."

"But you're—" I started, but caught myself in time. I had been about to say "birdbrained" but changed it to, "You're bird-minded. Your imitations of birdcalls are famous in South Florida. Your mimicking of a loon is especially admired."

My flattery didn't succeed.

"I really wasn't destined for a career of cleaning birdcages," he mourned.

"You'll be paid for your labors," I reminded him. "It won't be much, granted, but it'll be walking-around money. That should make both you and the Duchess happy."

He was wavering but still not wholly committed and so I played my trump card.

"There is a young lady who works there," I mentioned casually. "Quite attractive. You may be interested."

He blinked his pale eyes twice. "Oh?" he said. "A cream puff?"

"A charlotte russe," I assured him. "A mille-feuille. Possibly even baklava."

He sighed. "All right," he said. "I'll do it."

Many people have accused me of being devious. They may be right.

4

Our salads were served and those fried anchovies proved so salty I was forced, forced to order a carafe of the house chardonnay. And dreadful plonk it is, its only virtues being that it's cold and wet.

As we munched our greeneries I offered Binky a few suggestions anent his assignment.

"If you are interviewed by Hiram Gottschalk, the owner," I said, "I advise you to regale him with the recitation of your birdcalls. He is a confessed bird lover and I think your unusual talent may convince him to hire you on the spot."

"Oh sure," Binky said. "I'll give him the cry of the yellow-thighed manakin. That'll impress him. Say, Archy, this is really awful wine. Can't we have a bottle of Piper-Heidsieck?"

"No," I said. "When you arrive at Parrots Unlimited seek out the young lady I mentioned. She'll aid your application for employment. You may mention my name; I've already alerted her to the possibility of your coming in. Her name is Bridget Houlihan."

"Oh?" he said. "Of Irish descent?"

I looked at him. "Possibly," I said. "Or perhaps Estonian. Binky, if you are hired—and I'm confident you will be—I want you to lavish all your multitudinous charms on the other employees. Learn their names, details of their private lives, observe personal habits, note relationships with fellow workers, including the manager, and especially sound out how they feel about their employer, Hiram Gottschalk."

"In other words, you want me to snoop."

"Exactly."

"That'll be fun," he said happily. "I enjoy snooping, don't you, Archy?"

"I prefer to consider it unobtrusive investigation," I said stiffly. "But yes, snooping is what I require of you. I should also mention Mr. Gottschalk's twin daughters are returning from a European trip tomorrow and will be feted at an informal welcome-home bash at the Gottschalk residence on Wednesday evening. Employees will be invited, so if all goes well I may see you there."

"Hey," he said, brightening, "this case is beginning to sound like one continuous round of merriment."

I didn't believe it would be but didn't wish to disabuse my eager helot. We finished lunch and, feeling contrite about that blah chardonnay, I treated him to a Rémy Martin at the bar. He finished his pony in two gulps—Binky is definitely not an accomplished sipper—and he departed in a blithe mood, vowing to apply for part-time employment at Parrots Unlimited as soon as he had enjoyed a postprandial nap.

I drove directly home in no mood to return to my claustrophobic office, which I always imagined had originally been designed as a loo for pygmies. What a delight it was to reenter my air-conditioned aerie where every prospect pleased and only I was vile. I shucked off those fuddy-duddy threads I had donned to impress Mr. Gottschalk, lighted my first English Oval of the day, and got on the horn.

My first call was to Consuela Garcia, the young lady with whom I am intimate when she is not accusing me of real or fancied infidelities. Connie would, I knew, be hard at work as a social secretary to Lady

Cynthia Horowitz, one of the wealthiest chatelaines of Palm Beach. Lady Cynthia has six ex-husbands, mayhap a PB record, and at least six hundred enemies she zealously enrages with her acidic wit and political clout. I am thankful she considers me a friend.

Connie was happy to take a moment off from organizing a reception Lady Cynthia was planning for a visiting Zimbabwean griot.

We gibbered a few moments about such vital topics as Connie's new recipe for spicy sautéed trout and a curious dream I had a few nights previously involving Irene Dunne, Akim Tamiroff, and a Ferris wheel.

"Listen, dear," I said, "I have a problem."

"The dream?"

"No, it concerns a chap named Peter Gottschalk. You know him?"

"Do I ever!" she said. "He's always hitting on me at the Pelican. A real dingbat."

"So I understand. You know I chair the Membership Committee, and we've had several complaints about his acting in an irrational way. We could throw him overboard of course and let him founder, but that seems cruel. Besides, he might sue. Simon Pettibone thinks it may be a mental disability and the poor boy needs professional help. Are you acquainted with his parents?"

"No, but I've met his twin sisters."

"Have you now," I said.

The reason for my subterfuge is obvious, is it not? If I had started candidly by asking, "Do you know the Gottschalk daughters?" Connie would immediately assume I was casting covetous eyes on one or both and demand to know the reason for my interest. I hadn't lied, you understand, just dissembled. I'm rather crafty at that.

"What kind of females are they?" I asked casually. "I mean, do you think they're sympathetic and understanding? Would they be willing to urge their brother to seek help for his crazy behavior?"

"I don't know," Connie said doubtfully. "Sometimes they act like a couple of ding-a-lings themselves. Maybe it runs in the family."

"Maybe," I agreed. "Well, it wouldn't do any harm to attempt to enlist their assistance. I'd hate to chuck Peter Gottschalk from the Pelican Club simply for not acting in a reasonable manner."

"That's right, kiddo," Connie said. "Set that requirement and you'll be the first to go." She hung up giggling.

I hadn't learned much, had I? But that's the way I work most of my cases: a slow, patient accretion of facts, observations, opinions, surmises, and sometimes apparently inconsequential details such as grammar, dress, and knowledge of how to eat an artichoke.

My second phone call was to Lolly Spindrift, who writes a gossip column for one of our local gazettes. Lol and I have had a profitable quid pro quo relationship for several years. Occasionally I feed him choice tidbits of skinny about my current cases (without compromising client confidentiality) and in return Lol gives me tasty morsels from his consummate knowledge of the high jinks and low jinks of Palm Beach residents.

"You swine!" he shrieked. "Hast thou forsaken me? Things have been so dull! My stable of tattletales seems to be infected with an epidemic of discretion. A horror! I have to struggle—*struggle,* darling!—to fill each day's report. Tell me you have something juicy for dear old Lol."

"Nothing exciting," I admitted, "but it may be worth a line or two if you promise not to mention his name. Call him the scion of a wealthy Palm Beach family. He's about to be booted out of an exclusive private club for improper behavior."

"Name of scion?" Lol demanded. "Name of exclusive private club?"

"Peter Gottschalk," I said. "The Pelican Club."

He sighed. "Peter is a world-class nitwit and the Pelican is about as exclusive as Diners Club. Look, sweetie, this scoop you're offering doesn't quite rival the sinking of the *Titanic.*"

"I know, Lol, but I hoped it might be worth an item."

"Only because I have nothing better. Now what do you want?"

"Do you have anything on the Gottschalk daughters?"

"Oh-ho," he said, and I heard the sudden interest in his voice. "Do I detect a preoccupation with the Gottschalk family? Something going on there, luv?"

"Possibly," I said. "If so, you'll be the first to know."

"I better be. The daughters are Judith and Julia. Identical twins. Two wildebeests. Not as fruity as their brother but almost. Maybe it runs in the family." (Cf. Connie's remark.)

"Unrestrained, one might say?"

"One might," he agreed. "They're very attractive, ducky, which may tickle your id, but they're not my species, as you well know. The girls are remarkable look-alikes. Their favorite caper is to date the same man, separately and alternately, without revealing their deception. The poor stud thinks he's bedding Judith. He might be. Or it might be Julia. They're practically indistinguishable and think gulling their lovers is the funniest hoax in the world."

"Surely they don't dress alike."

"Oh no, they don't carry their twinship that far."

"Ever married? Either or both?"

"Not to my knowledge. Only to each other."

"Thank you, Lol," I said gratefully. "You've been much help, as usual. I'll stay in touch."

"Do that," he warned. "Or I may be forced to publish an entire column on the romantic peccadilloes of Archibald McNally."

"Perish the thought."

"I shall," he said. "Temporarily."

Although interested by what I had learned, I called a halt to sherlocking for the remainder of the afternoon. I tugged on cerise Speedo swimming trunks, added a terry Donald Duck cover-up and leather sandals, grabbed a towel, and went down to the sea for my daily dunk.

I did the usual two miles, south and back, flogging my flaccid muscles into action. Truthfully it was more of a wallow than a swim but I finished with a great sense of accomplishment, hoping *mens sana in corpore sano* really applied to me but with a lurking suspicion I flunked the *sano* part.

I returned to my den, showered away salt water and sand, and dressed casually in time to attend the family cocktail hour. This is not an hour of course, more like thirty minutes when the McNally tribe traditionally gathers in our second-floor sitting room for a pitcher of gin martinis mixed by the lord of the manor. After one wallop—and occasionally a small dividend—we all troop downstairs for dinner.

Dinner that night was sautéed yellowtail snapper with potato patties Ursi Olson had made with a few tablespoons of sherry. Good for Ursi! Dessert was a chocolate cheesecake. Ursi hadn't made that; it was store-bought. It was excellent but so rich I could feel my arteries slowly hardening. I could scarcely finish a second slice.

Back in my digs I kicked off my mocs and donned reading glasses. Yes, despite my tender age, I do need specs for close-up work. I never wear them in public of course since they make me look like a cybernetic nerd and would utterly destroy my sedulously cultivated image of a cavalier, a dashing combination of D'Artagnan and Bugs Bunny.

I sat at my arthritic desk and started a fresh page in my journal. This is a professional diary in which I keep notes of my discreet inquiries. I am not yet a resident of la-la land, you understand, but now and then I do forget things and find a scribbled record an invaluable aid.

I wrote rapidly in my crabbed hieroglyphics, which even I sometimes have trouble deciphering. I started with my father's alert: Hiram Gottschalk feared for his life. Then I added everything that had happened since: my visit to Parrots Unlimited, interview with the client, enlisting of Binky Watrous, and what I had learned from Simon Pettibone, Connie Garcia, and Lolly Spindrift.

Finally I dug out the list Mr. Gottschalk had given me of members of his household: family and staff. I was copying their names when one caused me to pause. His housekeeper and apparently mistress of the Gottschalk ménage was Yvonne Chrisling.

I distinctly recalled Hiram telling me the name of the manager of Parrots Unlimited. It was Ricardo Chrisling, an uncommon surname. I had to assume Yvonne and Ricardo were related. Wife and husband? Sister and brother? Mother and son? I found it intriguing and determined to seek a solution at the Gottschalk welcome-home party on Wednesday night.

It was close to eleven o'clock when I completed my labors and I was pouring myself a small marc as a reward when my phone rang. The caller was Sgt. Al Rogoff of the Palm Beach Police Department. Al and I have joined forces on several cases in the past. He provides me with official assistance when he can and I act as his dragoman to the arcane complexities of Palm Beach society.

Our relationship is, I truly believe, one of genuine friendship. But it does not lack on occasion a certain competitiveness. I mean when we're cooperating on an investigation the sergeant doesn't tell me all he knows, or guesses, and I return the favor. But that just adds a little cayenne to the stew, does it not?

"How's it going, old buddy?" he asked.

"Swimmingly," I replied. "And you?"

"Existing. The last squeal I had was an old dame boosting avocados from a local supermarket. Pretty exciting, huh? You working anything?"

"Nothing important. Dribs and drabs."

"Oh sure," he said. "Because if you were on something heavy you'd tell me about it, wouldn't you?"

"Of course."

"When shrimp fly," he said. "All right, I'm just checking in. If anything intriguing—your word, not mine—comes up, give me a shout. I'm bored out of my gourd."

"Aren't we all?" I said, and we disconnected. It wasn't time to bring Al into the Gottschalk inquiry. Not yet it wasn't and I hoped it never would be. But I was troubled by—what? Not a premonition—I rarely have those—but by a nagging unease caused by the three frightful accidents that had befallen Hiram Gottschalk. I did not take them lightly.

I like to go to sleep in a merry mood and so that night before retiring I listened to a recording of Tiny Tim singing "Tip-Toe thru the Tulips with Me."

It helped.

5

I awoke the next morning knowing exactly what I intended to do. This was a rarity since I usually regain consciousness in a semibefuddled state, not quite knowing where I am or even who I am. I recall awakening one morning with the firm conviction that I was Oscar Homolka. I am not, of course, and never have been.

What I intended to do requires a smidgen of explanation.

A few years previously Sgt. Al Rogoff had introduced me to Dr. Gussie Pearlberg, a psychiatrist who had her home and office in Lantana. Dr. Pearlberg did not specialize in forensic psychiatry but on several occasions had provided local police departments with tentative psychological profiles of serial thieves, rapists, and killers. Her predictions had, in most cases, proved remarkably prescient.

She was a wonderful woman, eighty at least although she would only admit to being "of a certain age." It was said she had been psychoanalyzed by Dr. Sigmund F. himself but I cannot vouch for that. She had outlived two husbands and three children but her grandchildren and great-grandchildren were her joy. She had absolutely no intention of retiring, and why on earth should she, since her mind was twice as nimble as shrinks half her age.

After making her acquaintance I had mentioned her acumen to my father and several times he had recommended her to clients or the relatives and friends of clients in need of psychiatric counseling, always with satisfactory results. The woman really was a blessing and it was she I intended to consult as soon as possible. Not in regard to my own shortcomings, I assure you; they're incurable.

I called her office at ten o'clock and, as usual, she answered the phone herself.

"Dr. Pearlberg," she said in her raspy voice. She has, I regret to report, a two-pack-a-day habit.

"Dr. Gussie," I said, "this is Archy McNally."

"Bubeleh!" she cried. "You have been neglecting me shamefully, you naughty boy."

"I have," I admitted, "and I apologize. How is your health, dear?"

"I am alive," she said, "and so my health is excellent. And you? Your family?"

"All in the pink," I assured her. "Doctor, when may I see you?"

"Personal?"

"Not me," I protested. "I'm the most normal and well-adjusted of men."

She coughed a laugh. "Let's just say you've come to terms with your madness. So it's professional?"

"Yes. One of my discreet inquiries. To be billed to McNally and Son. Can you fit me in?"

"I have a cancellation this morning at noon. You can make it?"

"Of course I can and shall with great pleasure. The couch won't be necessary."

She laughed again in her rattly voice. "Don't be so sure, bubeleh. Remember: The older the violin, the sweeter the music."

I had plenty of time to stop at a gourmet bakery and buy a pound of raspberry rugalach, which I knew Dr. Gussie dearly loved. Then I pointed the Miata's nose southward. It was a day designed for convertibles, for the sky was unblemished and a ten-knot breeze smelled faintly of salt. I don't remember singing but if I did, it was probably "It's a Most Unusual Day." Or it might have been "I've Got a Lovely Bunch of Coconuts."

The psychiatrist's office in Lantana always reminded me of the New York aphorism: "If I had my life to live over again, I'd like to live it over a delicatessen." Not that Dr. Pearlberg worked over a deli, but her second-floor office was atop an antique shop. Rather fitting, wouldn't you say, since they were both dealing with the past.

In fact, her office might have been furnished by her downstairs neighbor. It was all flocked wallpaper, dusty velvet drapes, lumpy brown furniture, and a couch covered with what appeared to be crackled black horsehide. Dim diplomas hung on the walls and there were chipped plaster busts of Freud, Beethoven, and one I could not identify but which looked unaccountably like Zero Mostel.

The entire chamber resembled a photo of a Viennese psychiatrist's consulting room of the 1920s. Adding to this illusion was the light, for no matter what time of day I visited, the office seemed suffused with a sepia tone, everything gently faded. That room deserved to be preserved in an album, the way things were in the bygone.

"Bubeleh!" Dr. Pearlberg said, and, as was her wont, kissed the tip of a forefinger and pressed it against my cheek. "What a delight to see you again. How handsome you look!"

I proffered the box of pastries. She ripped it open immediately and popped one into her mouth, groaning with contentment. "Thank you, thank you, thank you," she said. "What a treat for a relic like me."

"Nonsense," I said. "Dr. Gussie, you're getting younger as I get older. Do you think that's fair?"

"What a scamp you are," she said, "fooling a fat bobbeh. Now sit down and light a cigarette so I can have one."

I did as she directed. I sat in a sagging armchair alongside her elephantine desk. We both lighted up, blowing plumes of smoke toward the stained ceiling.

"So?" she said. "What's the problem?"

"A client, who shall be nameless, thinks his life is being threatened. I believe his fear is justified."

I then described the three untoward acts to which Hiram Gottschalk had been subjected: the slashed photo, the mass card, the strangled bird. Dr. Pearlberg listened to my recital intently. She finished her cigarette and lighted another from the butt of the first.

She was a squatty woman, almost as broad as she was tall. Pillowy face. Her wig was a virulent orange and she did have a hazy but discernible mustache, neither of which bothered her or anyone else who knew and admired her. She may have looked like a granny but she had a mental prowess that made the rest of us feel like village idiots.

When I had concluded, she said, "I don't like it."

"Nor do I," I said, and told her that although I had only started my investigation I had come to a preliminary conclusion: The threat against our client came from a member of his staff or his family.

"The family," she repeated, her harsh voice a mixture of scorn and sadness. "Always the family."

"Doctor," I said, "regarding the three incidents I have described, can you discern any pattern?"

"Perhaps," she said. "Usually in cases of this nature there is a progression from the subtle to the obvious. An acceleration of disturbed passion. The slashing of the photograph of the client and his deceased wife appears to be an attempt to destroy a happy memory, demolish a remembered relationship. The posting of the mass card with the client's name I interpret as a warning he is in danger if he does not mend his ways. The third act, the killing of his beloved bird, escalates the pressure. This, the bird strangler is saying, will be your fate if you persist in doing what you are now doing."

I sighed. "Not a happy prospect," I said. "In effect you're saying the client's death may be the only option left to his enemy."

"Yes, Archy," she said. "That is what I feel. The client has received no written or phoned threats?"

"No. None."

"Then there is little the police can do."

"But what can *I* do?" I said desperately.

"Do what you do best," she advised. "Pry. Meet everyone he's connected with. Ask questions. Get to know them all. Then come back and we'll talk again. This troubles me."

"Yes," I said. "Me, too."

I rose to depart but she grasped my arm, stared with those lucid hazel eyes.

"Sonny, you haven't asked the most interesting thing."

I was startled. "Oh? What is it?"

"Is the psychopath responsible for these acts of aggression a man or a woman?"

I looked into those knowing eyes. "Which do you think, Dr. Gussie?"

"Either," she said. "Or both."

And I had to be content with that Delphic utterance.

I drove home in a mood somewhat less than gruntled. Dr. Pearlberg had told me little more than I had already suspected but her reaction to Mr. Gottschalk's predicament had raised my anxiety level. And I was grateful for her suggestion that the perpetrator might possibly be female. I am such a romantic cove I usually leap to the conclusion that practicers of viciousness are limited solely to the masculine sex. Alas, dear reader, 'tis not so. Consider the career of the charming lady who made lampshades of human skin during the Holocaust.

Ursi was puttering about the kitchen when I arrived. She was preparing a bouillabaisse for our dinner and if you could have bottled that fragrance your fortune would be made. Call it Eau d'Poisson and every trendsetter in the world would put dabs behind the earlobes.

She interrupted her labors long enough to construct a towering Dagwood for me. Thick slices of sour rye served as bookends, and the literature within included slices of smoked turkey, beefsteak tomato, and Bermuda onion: all with a healthy dollop of Ursi's homemade mayo containing a jolt of Dijon mustard. I carried this masterpiece up to my suite, silently giving thanks to John Montagu, 4th Earl of Sandwich. I also lugged two bottles of chilled Dos Equis.

I was seated at my desk, devouring my delayed lunch with eye-rolling rapture, when the damn phone shrilled. I was tempted to let it ring itself to smithereens, but then I imagined it could be an invitation to a social affair during which I might meet the current Girl of My Dreams who bore a remarkable resemblance to Theda Bara. No such luck. The caller was Binky Watrous.

"Archy," he said excitedly, "I got the job at Parrots Unlimited!"

"Delighted to hear it," I said, munching away.

"They hired me around noon and I started work immediately!"

"Excellent. And how are you getting along?"

"Wonderfully!"

"Meet everyone?"

"Uh-huh. Archy," he added soulfully, "I'm in love."

"Oh?" I said. "Which parrot?"

"No, no. It's Bridget Houlihan."

"Ah," I said. "The Hibernian crumpet. Fancy her, do you?"

"She's such a marvelous female," he enthused. "Sweet and charming. And talented. She plays the tambourine."

"Binky," I said, "I'm not sure one can *play* a tambourine. Don't you just shake it or bang it? I mean Brahms never wrote a lullaby for tambourine, did he?"

"Oh, you can play it," he said with great certainty. "Bridget and I are thinking of getting up an act. I'll do my birdcalls while she accompanies me on her tambourine."

I hastily finished my first beer. For some unexplainable reason I recalled the comment of a Hollywood wit who remarked on the natural affinity between Rin-Tin-Tin and Helen Twelvetrees. In my relationship with Binky I seemed to be playing the actress. But I resolutely put this nuttiness from my mind.

"What about the other employees?" I asked him.

"There are two clerks in addition to Bridget. Young kids. Boy and girl. Tony Sutcliffe and Emma Gompertz. I think they may have a thing going."

"Cohabiting?" I suggested.

"What does that mean?"

"Living together."

"Like me and the Duchess?"

"Not quite. Living together as husband and wife."

"Oh," he said. "Well, yes, they may be cohabiting. Did you ever cohabit, Archy?"

"No," I said.

"I did," he said. "Once. For a weekend in Glasgow."

"What on earth were you doing in Glasgow?"

"Cohabiting. And drinking Glenlivet."

"Binky," I said, sighing, "can we get back to business? What about the manager?"

"Ricardo Chrisling? A very slick character."

"Slick? In what sense? Slippery?"

"Oh no, I wouldn't say that. More like sleek—you know? Hair carefully brushed and shining. Silk suit and all that. Might even have a manicure."

"Handsome?"

"I suppose impressionable dolls might think so. I find him a bit on the gigoloish side."

"Smooth?" I suggested.

"Very smooth," Binky said. "Exceedingly smooth."

I asked him if employees had been invited to attend the party welcoming home Mr. Gottschalk's twin daughters.

"We have indeed," he said happily. "Even I, the most recent and lowliest of the peons. You'll be there?"

"Wouldn't miss it," I assured him. "Don't get hammered, Binky. Behave yourself."

"So I shall, old boy," he vowed. "I'll be the very soul of decorum. By the way, while I was being interviewed by the owner he told me the most amazing story about two macaws who prayed all the time. It seems this woman had bought—"

"Stop right there," I said. "He told me the same tale."

"Do you believe it, Archy?"

"Of course. Indubitably."

"I do too," he said. "It just proves what incredible creatures birds are. Equal or superior in intelligence to many humans."

"How right you are," I agreed. "Keep up the good work, Binky. See you at the bash tomorrow night."

We hung up and I hastened to add the names Tony Sutcliffe and Emma Gompertz to my journal before I forgot them. I doubted if this young couple had any connection with the threats against Hiram Gottschalk. But one never knows, do one?

Then I finished my lunch and because the radio and TV had warned about riptides I skipped my ocean swim that afternoon. I took a nap instead and slept fitfully, troubled by wild images: a black crow stalking into the shadows, a strangled mynah, a beady-eyed parrot condemning me to Hades.

I blamed the nightmarish snooze on the smoked turkey in my luncheon sandwich. All those damnable fowl seemed determined to make my life miserable. My discomfiture, I decided, was definitely for the birds.

6

Mr. Gottschalk had told me this party was to be informal, without swank, and so I dressed accordingly. I had recently purchased a lightweight wool sport jacket in a houndstooth check of olive, gold, and blue. Sounds rather citified, does it not? Dullsville in fact. But it had suede buttonholes. It's the details that seduce me.

I perked up my subdued jacket with a pink Lacoste and slacks of a lemonade shade. Plus loafers in a hellish vermilion. No socks. When I inspected the complete ensemble in the bathroom door mirror I decided the effect was twee but not too. The stodgy jacket marked me as a man of substance but the accoutrements proved I was capable of frivolity. Oh lordy, how we deceive ourselves.

The client's home was located in an upscale neighborhood of Palm Beach which appeared to be a small territory inhabited solely by fanatic horticulturists. I mean, I have never in my life seen such a profusion of tropical foliage. It was like driving through a South Florida rain forest, and if I had heard the chattering of monkeys and the snorting of wild boars I wouldn't have been a bit surprised.

The Gottschalk manse was quite a sight. It had been built, I judged, in the 1930s as a Mediterranean-style villa. More recently, additions had been made that were more Lake Okeechobee than Mediterranean. There were two wings, a guest house, an enlarged garage. The original edifice had also been embellished with bays, turrets, a widow's walk, and a tall, battered cupola which seemed to have no reason for existence other than providing a comfort station for migrating fowl.

It was an eccentric dwelling and, I thought, probably suited the owner just fine.

There were several cars already parked in the slated driveway. One of the vehicles, I noted, was Binky Watrous's dinged 1970 Mercedes-Benz 280 SE cabriolet. Trust my loopy Dr. Watson to be early when free booze and tasty viands were available.

I entered into a brightly lighted interior, a circus of bustle, loud talk, hefty laughter, and the recorded voice of Tony Bennett singing "It Don't Mean a Thing." I was somewhat taken aback by this jollity only because I was privy to the grave problems of the host. The dichotomy was disturbing and I decided my wisest course was to dull my unease with a dram or two of suitably diluted ethanol at the earliest possible moment.

I had those two drams during a chaotic party. But my libations were minuscule—infinitesimal one might even say—and I assure you the McNally mental faculties were not hazed. I smiled, conversed, joked, and followed Dr. Gussie Pearlberg's instructions to pry, ask questions, get to know them all.

It was a kaleidoscopic evening and I shall not attempt to give it a linear or temporal sequence.

I was standing at their modest bar, adding a bit of aqua to my 80-

proof, when I felt a light touch on my shoulder. I turned to face a smiling woman, mature, stalwart, and not much shorter than I. She was quite dark: tanned complexion, jetty hair, black eyebrows that looked as if they had been squeezed from tubes.

"Good evening!" she said in a hearty contralto voice. "I'm Yvonne Chrisling, Mr. Gottschalk's housekeeper. And you?"

"Archy McNally, representing McNally and Son, attorneys-at-law. I'm the Son."

"Of course," she said, offering a hand. "So nice of you to come."

"So nice of you to invite me." Her handclasp was dry and surprisingly strong. "You have a lovely home, and it appears to be a joyous party."

She laughed. "Well, thank you. The occasion is to welcome the girls home from Europe. As for our home, I'm afraid it may seem somewhat, ah . . ."

"Disheveled?" I suggested.

She laughed again, a throaty sound. "Exactly. You do have a way with words, Mr. McNally."

"Archy," I said. "And may I call you Yvonne?"

"Of course. Everyone does."

"Now that we have a first-name relationship, may I ask a personal question?"

Her face didn't freeze but I did detect a sudden wariness. "Ask away," she said.

"I know the manager of Parrots Unlimited is Ricardo Chrisling. Your son?"

"Stepson," she said rather stiffly. "By my husband who is now deceased. Do enjoy yourself, Archy, and don't forget the buffet. We don't want you going home hungry."

She gave me a nothing smile and moved away. She was wearing a very chaste long black skirt and severely tailored jacket. Her costume reminded me of a uniform: something a keeper in an institution might wear. *"Und* you *vill* obey orders!" Silly, I admit, but that was my impression.

Wandering about, glass in hand, I found Binky Watrous and Bridget Houlihan seated close together on a tattered velvet love seat. They were gazing into each other's eyes with a look so moony I wanted to kick both of them in the shins.

"Hi, kids," I said, and they looked up, startled.

"Oh," Binky said finally. "Hello, Archy. Have you met Bridget?"

"I have indeed," I said. "Good evening, Bridget."

"The same," she said dreamily, not releasing Binky's paw. "Honey, do the call of the cuckoo again."

I hastily departed.

I found the host putting another LP on his player and was happy he had not switched to CDs, which are too electronically perfect for me. I cherish those scratches and squawks of old vinyls. Mr. Gottschalk was about to place the needle on an original cast recording of *Guys and Dolls*.

"Excellent choice, sir." I said.

He looked up. "Hello, Archy. Glad you could make it. Enjoying yourself?"

"Immeasurably."

"Like old recordings, do you?"

"Very much."

He paused to stare dimly into the distance. "I do too. And so did my dear wife. On our tenth anniversary she gave me an ancient shellac of Caruso signing 'Vesti la giubba.' "

"What a treasure!" I said. "Do you still have it?"

He gave me a queer look. "I don't know what happened to it. I'll try to find it."

The record started and I listened happily to "Fugue for Tinhorns." He lowered the volume and turned to me. "Have you met my daughters?"

"Not yet. How shall I tell them apart?"

"Very difficult. But one of them has a mole, a small, black mole."

"Oh?" I said. "Which one—Judith or Julia?"

He grinned mischievously. "I'm not allowed to tell."

"Well, where is this small, black mole located?"

His grin broadened and he tugged at his Vandyke. "You're an investigator, aren't you?" he said. "Investigate and find out."

What an aging satyr he was!

The buffet was really nothing extraordinary: a spiral-cut ham, cocktail franks in pastry cozies, chilled shrimp, crudités, cheese of no particular distinction, onion rolls a bit on the spongy side, and, for dessert, petits fours I suspected had been stamped out in a robotized Taiwan factory.

There was, however, one dish I sampled and found blindly delicious. Cold cubes of *something* in a yummy sauce. At first I thought it might be filet mignon, but it lacked the meat's texture. I ate more, entranced by the flavor and subtle aftertaste. Finally, determined to identify this wonder, I found my way into the Gottschalks' kitchen.

There I met a plumpish couple identified in Hiram's list of his staff as Mr. Got Lee, chef, and his wife, Mei, who apparently functioned as a maid of all work. They were wearing matching skullcaps of linen decorated with beads and sequins, and I've never encountered more scrutable Orientals in my life. Both giggled continually; they either enjoyed high spirits or had been hitting a gallon jug of rice wine.

I introduced myself and we all shook hands enthusiastically.

"Ver' happy," Got said in a lilting voice.

"Ver' ver' happy," Mei said, topping him.

"My pleasure," I assured them. "You have prepared a marvelous party."

They both bowed and I was treated to another chorus of "ver' happy's" interspersed with giggles.

"Tell me," I said, "what is that excellent cold dish in a spicy sauce? It tastes somewhat like broiled steak but I'm sure it's not. What on earth is it?"

More giggles and a lengthy explanation in English so strangled I could scarcely follow it. The treat turned out to be thick chunks of portobello mushrooms grilled with seasoning, cooled, and then marinated in lots of swell stuff for an hour and served chilled.

"Well, it's wonderful," I told them, and they beamed. "You enjoy working here, do you?"

The beams faded and they looked at each other.

"Ver' happy," Got said.

"Ver' ver' happy," Mei said.

But the lilt was gone from their voices. The giggles had vanished. They were not, I decided, quite as scrutable as I had first thought.

I was heading for the bar to refill my empty glass, since the contents had unaccountably evaporated. Ahead of me was a trig young man pouring himself a pony of Frangelico.

"Wise choice," I remarked.

He turned to look at me. "I think so," he said, with emphasis on the "I."

"Archy McNally," I said, proffering a hand. "I represent McNally and Son, Mr. Gottschalk's attorneys."

"Oh?" he said, and gave me a brief, rather limp handshake. "I'm Ricardo Chrisling. I manage Parrots Unlimited."

I had already guessed since he was everything Binky Watrous had described: handsome, sleek, possibly "gigoloish." Binky had been accurate but he had not caught the lad's finickiness: every shining hair in place, a shave I could never hope to equal, the three points of his jacket pocket handkerchief as precise and sharp as sword points. I wondered if the soles of his shoes were polished and the laces ironed.

I must confess my description of Ricardo Chrisling might be tainted by envy. He was, after all, about ten years younger than I and closely resembled Rodolfo Alfonzo Rafaelo Pierre Filibert Guglielmi di Valentina d'Antonguolla, a/k/a Rudolph Valentino. I mean he was a *beautiful* man, features crisp and evocative. He really should have been out in Hollywood filming *The Return of the Sheik* instead of futzing around with parrots.

"Nice party," I observed.

"Isn't it?" he said rather coldly. I didn't think he was much interested in me. And why should he be? I wasn't a female. "Meeting everyone?" he said casually.

"Gradually," I said. "I haven't yet come upon the guests of honor."

"The twins?" he said. "You will. They're not shy."

I didn't know how to interpret that. "How does one tell them apart?" I asked.

"One doesn't," he said, gave me a bloodless smile, and moved away.

He left me with the feeling he considered me a harmless duffer of no importance. That suited me. I didn't want anyone in that household to suspect I was a keen-eyed beagle tracking a miscreant threatening the life of the lord of the manor.

There were other guests in addition to Mr. Gottschalk's immediate entourage. There must have been twenty or thirty—friends, neighbors, business acquaintances—and I found them an odd but pleasant lot, all eating and drinking up a storm.

I met Yvonne Chrisling's masseuse, the Got Lees' greengrocer, a morose Peruvian who was apparently a parrot wholesaler, and one shy chap, barely articulate, who appeared awed by his surroundings. He finally admitted he mowed Mr. Gottschalk's lawn and this was the first time he had been inside the house. We had a drink together and got along famously because this seemingly inarticulate fellow could sing "Super-cali-fragil-istic-expi-ali-docious." I can't even pronounce it.

I also introduced myself to the young clerks from Parrots Unlimited—Emma Gompertz and Tony Sutcliffe—the twosome Binky Watrous reported had a "thing" going and might possibly be cohabiting. They appeared to be an innocuous couple, agreeable and polite, but really not much aware of anyone but each other. Their behavior—hand holding and dreamy stares—was remarkably akin to Binky's conduct with Bridget Houlihan.

Romance was rife that night, positively *rife*.

I finally spotted the twins, Judith and Julia Gottschalk. I then experienced a moment of panic, fearing I was suffering an attack of double vision.

Nothing of the sort of course. They were simply twins but so alike one could only marvel at their oneness. They were, I guessed, in their early thirties. Both had deep brown eyes and brown hair with russet glints, cut quite short. They were dressed differently, one in a silk pantsuit, the other in short leather skirt and fringed buckskin jacket. I suspected they shared a common wardrobe; their physical proportions seemed identical.

They were chatting animatedly with each other and I wondered if twins ever became weary of their mirror images. They certainly didn't seem bored at the moment, for they laughed frequently, occasionally leaned close to whisper, and once shook hands as if sealing a private pact. I thought them enormously attractive young ladies and hastened to join them.

"Welcome home!" I said heartily, giving them my Jumbocharmer smile for I felt they were mature enough to withstand it.

"Thank you," they said in unison, and Pantsuit asked, "And who might you be?"

"I might be Ivan the Terrible," I said, "but I am not. My name is Archy McNally, and I work for your father's attorneys."

"You're a lawyer?"

"Not quite. More of a para-paralegal. And you are . . . ?"

"Judith," she said. "I think." She turned to her twin. "Am I Judith, darling?"

"I thought you were this morning," Leather Skirt said. "But now I'm not so sure. You may be Julia."

"Which would make you Judith."

"I suppose. But I can't be certain. I don't *feel* like Judith."

Both looked at me with wide-eyed innocence. I realized this was a routine that amused them greatly and they used frequently to befuddle new acquaintances. They obviously had inherited their father's quirky sense of humor.

"I think I have a solution to this difficult problem," I said. "Suppose I address each of you as Mike. Won't that make things a lot simpler?"

Both clapped their hands delightedly and gave me elfin grins.

"Well done," Pantsuit said.

"Good show," Leather Skirt said. "I love the idea of us both being Mike."

Their voices were identical in pitch and timbre.

Pantsuit stared at me reflectively. "Archy McNally," she repeated. "We've heard that name before. Are you a member of the Pelican Club?"

"I am indeed."

"Peter has mentioned you. We've never been there, have we, Mike?"

"Never, Mike," her sibling said. "Take us there to lunch, Archy."

"I'll be delighted. When?"

"Tomorrow. Is twelve-thirty okay?"

"Twelve-thirty is perfect."

"How should we dress?" Leather Skirt asked.

"Informally. Laid-back. Funky. Whatever."

"That's cool," Pantsuit said.

"You know how to find it?"

"We'll ask Peter. Thank you for the invite, Archy."

Mike #1 leaned forward suddenly to kiss me briefly on the lips. Her buss was sweet and tangy as a Vidalia onion. Ah-ha! Now, I reckoned, I'd be able to tell them apart. But then Mike #2 duplicated her sister's action. Her kiss was sweet and tangy as a Vidalia onion.

Archibald McNally, the master criminologist, flummoxed again.

7

Guests began leaving an hour before midnight. I looked about for Binky Watrous and his Celtic knish but they had already departed. I decided it was time to make my adieus and sought the host to thank him for a pleasant evening. But Hiram was nowhere to be found and so I delivered my farewell to Yvonne Chrisling.

She was in a more relaxed mood than at our initial meeting. At least her handclasp was warm and she seemed reluctant to release me.

"Thank you so much," I said. "It was a lovely party."

"It was sweet of you to come," she said. "I'm glad you had a good time and I hope you'll visit again. Did you meet the twins?"

"I surely did."

"And what did you think of them, Archy?"

"Very personable," I said carefully.

She gave me a cryptic smile. "They're not as scatterbrained as many people think. Quite the contrary."

Then she turned away to exchange good-byes with other guests, giving me no opportunity to ask what she meant by her last oblique comment.

I exited into a sultry night, the air close and redolent of all that gross vegetation. I found my Miata and there, lolling in the passenger's bucket, feet up on the dash, was Peter Gottschalk. He was smoking something acrid and I hoped it might be tobacco.

"Good evening," I said as calmly as I could. I do not appreciate my pride and joy being occupied without my permission, especially by irrational acquaintances.

He patted the door. "Nice heap," he said.

"It is," I agreed. "And now I intend to drive it home. By myself. Alone."

It didn't register. I wasn't certain he heard what I said.

"How was the party?" he asked.

"Very enjoyable."

"Bloody bore," he contradicted me. "I cut out fast. All those phonies."

I was standing alongside the passenger door wondering if I would be forced to drag him out by the scruff. But his last denouncement intrigued me.

"Phonies?" I repeated. "You're referring to the guests?"

His laugh was more of a snort. "I don't even *know* all those stupid guests. I'm talking about the family and staff. Hypocrites, every one of them."

"Surely not your father."

"Him, too," he said bitterly. "Maybe the worst. They think I don't know what's going on. I know damned well what's going on." He suddenly straightened and flicked away the butt of his cigarette. "Hey, let's you and me make a night of it. We'll go to the Pelican first for a couple of whacks and then take it from there."

"Some other time," I told him. "I'm getting audited by the IRS in the morning so I better get a good night's sleep."

I was afraid he might flare but he accepted the rejection equably. I suspected he was accustomed to rejection.

He climbed out of the car and stood on the slated driveway, swaying gently. He was a thin, almost gaunt chap with hollow cheeks, sunken eyes. His hair was a mess and it was obvious he hadn't shaved for at least two days. But he was decently dressed in denim jeans and jacket. A cleaner T-shirt would have helped, but you did not expect to find him sleeping in a cardboard carton under a bridge. I mean he was reasonably presentable if you didn't gaze too intently into those stricken eyes.

"Now I feel great," he declared. "Just great."

"Glad to hear it," I said.

"Maybe I'll cop the old man's car and make a run to the Pelican Club myself."

"Don't you have your own wheels?" I asked.

"Nah. They grounded me. And took away my license," he added.

I wanted to warn him, but what was the use? He'd never listen to me. I doubted if he'd listen to anyone.

"See you around," he said lightly, and went dancing off into the darkness.

I drove home slowly in a weighty mood. The evening had left me with a jumble of impressions. It resembled one of those Picasso paintings in which all the figures seem to have six limbs and three eyes. And you view them frontally and in profile simultaneously. A puzzlement.

It was still relatively early when I arrived at my very own mini-abode. I could have spent an hour or so recording the evening's events in my journal but I needed to sort out a plethora of reactions and try to find significance in what I had seen and heard. I disrobed and treated myself to a small marc and an English Oval to aid my ruminations.

After thirty minutes of heavy-duty brooding the only preliminary conclusion I arrived at was that when it came to dysfunctional families the Gottschalks were candidates for world-class ranking. It was a hypothesis given confirmation when my phone rang shortly before I retired.

"Archy?" the caller asked, and I recognized Hiram Gottschalk's dry, twangy voice.

"Yes, Hi," I said. "I tried to find you to offer thanks for a delightful evening but I couldn't locate you."

"You know that Caruso record I told you about. The one my dear wife gave me on our tenth anniversary."

"Yes, sir, I remember. The old shellac of Enrico singing 'Vesti la guibba.' "

"After I mentioned it to you I was bothered because I couldn't remember where I had put it. So I went searching. I finally found it about ten minutes ago. Someone smashed it. Now it's just junk."

"I'm sorry," I said softly.

"That record meant a lot to me. A gift from the woman I loved."

"I understand, Hi," I said. "Would you like me to come over now and we'll talk about it?"

"No, no," he said. "Thank you but that won't be necessary. I just thought you should know."

"Of course. Hi, I don't wish to be an alarmist but you should be prepared to find yourself a victim of similar acts of terrorism or viciousness before I can discover who is responsible."

"You think you can find out?"

"Absolutely," I said stoutly. There are some situations demanding unbridled confidence with all dubiety ignored. This was one of them.

"Thank you, Archy," he said gratefully. "You make me feel a lot better."

I went to bed that night wondering if the future would prove me Sir Galahad or Sir Schlemiel.

By the time I clumped downstairs on Thursday morning my parents had long since breakfasted. I found Jamie Olson sitting alone in the kitchen. He was sucking on his old briar (the stem wound with a Band-Aid) and clutching a mug of black coffee I was certain he had enlivened with a jolt of aquavit. His chaps were definitely fallen.

"What's wrong, Jamie?" I inquired.

"That damned raccoon again," he said indignantly. "Got the lids off both trash cans. Made a mess. I'm going to catch up with that beast one of these days and give him what for. You want some breakfast, Mr. Archy?"

"I'll make it. Anything left over?"

"A cold kipper."

"Sounds good to me. I'll toast a muffin and slide it in with a bit of mayo. Enough hot coffee?"

"Plenty."

I had a glass of V8 Picante, prepared my kipper sandwich, and poured a cup of inky caffeine. I sat across the table from our houseman.

"Jamie," I said, "ever hear of the Gottschalk family?"

The Olsons, our staff of two, are part of a loose confederacy of butlers, maids, chefs, housekeepers, valets, and servants of all species who minister to the needs of the wealthier residents of the Palm Beaches. Experience had taught me that this serving but by no means servile class knew a great many intimate details about the private lives of their employers. It was information they would never divulge except, occasionally, to others in their profession when a good laugh was wanted.

"Gottschalk?" Jamie repeated. "Nope. Never heard of them."

"They have a live-in Oriental couple, Got and Mei Lee, chef and maid. Do you know anyone who might be acquainted?"

He relighted his charred pipe. My father also smokes a pipe. His tobacco is fragrant. Jamie's is not.

"Mebbe," he said finally. "I know Eddie Wong, a nice fellow. He buttles for old Mrs. Carrey in West Palm. You want I should ask Eddie if he knows—what's their names?"

"Got and Mei Lee. Yes, please ask him. I'd like to know if the Gottschalks have a happy home. And if not, why not."

Jamie nodded. "I'll ask."

Before I left for the office I slipped him a tenner. Pop would be outraged, I knew, since the Olsons were more than adequately recompensed for keeping the McNally ship on an even keel. But I didn't feel their salaries included Jamie's personal assistance to yrs. truly in my discreet inquiries. Hence my pourboire for his efforts above and beyond the call of duty.

I had two messages awaiting me when I arrived at my cul-de-sac in the McNally Building. I answered Sgt. Al Rogoff's call first.

"Heavens to Betsy," he said. "You're at work so early? Why, it's scarcely eleven o'clock."

"I do work at home, you know," I replied haughtily. "Sometimes with great concentration for long hours."

"You also sleep at home. Sometimes with great concentration for long hours. But enough of this idle chitchat. You know a guy named Peter Gottschalk?"

I hesitated for a beat, then: "Yes, I know Peter. Distantly. He's a member of the Pelican Club."

"That figures. Is he off-the-wall?"

"I really couldn't say. From what I've heard, he's been known to act occasionally in an outré fashion."

"Outré," Rogoff repeated. "Love the way you talk."

"Why are you asking about Peter Gottschalk?"

"Because early this morning, about two or three, he outréd his father's car into an abutment on an overpass out west."

"Holy moly. Anyone hurt?"

"Nah. He didn't hit anyone. Just plowed into the concrete doing about fifty. All he got were a few bruises and scratches. God protects fools and drunks—which makes you doubly blessed."

"What about the car?"

"Totaled. A new Cadillac Eldorado. His blood test showed alcohol a little above the legal limit. Nothing definite on drugs. Maybe he just fell asleep."

"Maybe," I said, not believing it for a minute.

"Uh-huh. Archy, the guy doesn't have any suicidal tendencies, does he?"

I swallowed. Sgt. Rogoff is no dummy. Trust him to come up with an explanation for Peter's accident that matched my own.

"Not to my knowledge, Al," I said faintly.

"Well, his license has been pulled but he didn't hurt anyone and his father isn't preferring charges, so we're squashing the whole thing. But I think the kid needs help."

"Could be," I said cautiously, and that was the end of our conversation.

I sat there a moment, shuddering to think of what might have happened but didn't. I wondered just how long Peter Gottschalk could go his mindless way depending on God's mercy. Not too long, I reckoned. Ask any gambler and he'll tell you there's one sure thing about luck: it always changes.

Since I'm firmly convinced life is half tragedy and half farce, I decided I needed a bit of the farcical and so I answered the second message. It was from Binky Watrous, my very own harlequin.

"Why aren't you at work?" I demanded.

"Because I clean cages only four days a week," he explained. "Hey, Archy, I like that job."

"And the fringe benefits, no doubt. Super party last night, wasn't it?"

"I guess. Bridget enjoyed it."

"Oh-oh," I said. "Do I detect a slight note of discord?"

"Well, that's why I called. Bridget wants to get married."

"To whom?"

"To me," Binky said gloomily.

"Congratulations."

"Archy, I don't know what to do and I need your advice. I am smitten but do you think a man can be satisfied with one woman?"

"At a time?" I said. "Surely."

"No, no. I mean one woman, the same woman, forever and ever."

"Ah, now you're entering the realm of philosophy—if not cosmology."

"I suppose," he said. "I was never much good at that sort of thing."

"Think about it, Binky," I advised, "before you come to any decision." I knew full well that urging this dweeb to think was similar to cheering on a three-toed sloth in a decathlon. "First of all you must consider if you are financially able to provide for a wife and perhaps eventually a family on the income from tidying up parrot cages."

"Yes," he said, "that is a problem, isn't it? I don't know how the Duchess would react to my getting hitched. She might even turn off the cash faucet. That would hurt. I've got to rack the old brain about this, Archy."

"Do that," I said. "But don't forget the only reason you're working at Parrots Unlimited is to assist me in a discreet inquiry."

"What?" he said. "Oh. Sure. I remember."

"For the nonce, I'd like you to concentrate your snooping on Ricardo Chrisling. That handsome lad interests me. See if you can find out where he lives and with whom, if anyone. Does he have a consenting adult companion, or does he play the field? Any unusual habits or predilections? I want you to provide a complete dossier on Ricardo. I suspect he may be more than just another pretty face. Find out."

"Listen, Archy," my henchman said distractedly, "do you think it's really necessary I marry Bridget? I mean, couldn't we, you know, uh, what's that word?"

"Cohabit?" I suggested.

"Yes!" he said eagerly. "Couldn't we cohabitize?"

I groaned and hung up. If I were a cat Binky would be a hair ball.

8

I had dressed with special care that morning, preparing for my luncheon with the Gottschalk sisters. I hoped they might be impressed by careless elegance, so in addition to a silver-gray jacket of Ultrasuede, black silk slacks, and a faded blue denim shirt I sported an ascot in a

Pucci print and used a four-in-hand as a belt, à la Fred Astaire. No socks of course.

I had suggested the twins dress informally and so they did: one in a rumpled suit of white sailcloth, the other in a magenta leotard under a gauzy blouse and open skirt. They looked smart enough but I had the impression they were dressing down and their garments had been adapted from street styles by frightfully pricey French designers. They were wearing trendy costumes as foreign to their taste and nature as the sari.

The arrival of these two lovely look-alikes at the Pelican Club occasioned startled reactions from members in the bar area. Even Priscilla in the dining room was so surprised by the entry of doubles she tempered her sassy impudence and treated us with solicitous politesse. I imagined the sisters were accustomed to the stir their appearance caused and took it casually as their due.

I wish I could describe our luncheon in lip-smacking detail but I confess my remembrances are vague. My recollections are hazy since all my attention was concentrated on how they looked, what they said, and trying to follow Dr. Gussie Pearlberg's injunction to pry and ask questions.

Mike #1 swung about to examine our surroundings. "Rather grotty, don't you think?" she asked her sibling.

"Yes but comfortably so," Mike #2 replied, and they both gave me pixieish grins.

They surely must have noted my discomfiture, for I truly believe the Pelican to be the ne plus ultra of all private clubs in the Palm Beach area. Grotty, yes. Raffish, undoubtedly. Unconventionally stylish, true. But where else could I leap upon a table late Saturday night and attempt to sing "Volare"?

"Archy," one of the sisters said, "this game has gone on long enough and we've decided to come clean with you. I'm Julia."

She was wearing the sailcloth suit.

"And I'm Judith," the other said.

She was wearing the magenta leotard.

They both looked at me as if expecting gratitude.

I dimly recall we were drinking Kir Royales at the time. And I definitely remember their stares of wide-eyed innocence. I didn't totally believe them or totally disbelieve them. I was willing to suspend judgment since I had an ace in the hole or rather—from what Hiram Gottschalk had revealed—a mole in the hole.

"Julia and Judith," I repeated, nodding to each in turn. "Yes, that does simplify things, and I thank you for your confidence in me. I swear I won't tell a soul."

"Tell them what?" Julia asked.

"Which of you is which."

"And how could you possibly do that?" Judith asked.

This was, I believe, my first indication that I was not dealing with bubbleheads and that these two females had more than lint between their ears.

I sighed. "You have a point," I admitted. "Which means every time the three of us meet you must identify yourselves again. What a drag! Couldn't one of you agree to a small tattoo? Perhaps the symbol of pi engraved on one earlobe."

They stared at each other, then stared at me.

"Are you completely insane?" Judith demanded.

"He is," Julia said. "Absolutely bonkers."

I believe at the moment we were working on an enormous seafood salad and demolishing a bottle of sauvignon blanc.

"Happy to be home from Europe?" I asked. "Or devastated?"

"We had a marvelous time," Julia said. "But we're glad to be back. Aren't we, Judy?"

"Oh yes. Definitely. Daddy needs us."

It was at that exact point the tenor of our conversation changed. Up to then it had been breezy silliness, a lighthearted exchange of nonsense. But Judith's comment, "Daddy needs us," signaled a switch of gears. I began to wonder if this luncheon had been requested with a motive other than to examine the flora and fauna of the Pelican Club.

"I'm sure your father was happy to see you return safely," I said, deciding to let them reveal what they obviously intended with no urging from yrs. truly.

It came out with a rush.

Julia: "He worries us."

Judith: "He's acting so strangely."

Julia: "He thinks his personal possessions have been stolen when he's probably just misplaced them."

Judith: "He's convinced there's some kind of a crazy plot against him."

Julia: "But he's not senile."

Judith: "Oh no, nothing like that. Just these absurd notions."

Then they looked at me as if I might be Dr. Kildare ready to deliver an instant and perceptive diagnosis.

"You feel all his fears are delusions?" I asked.

"Oh, absolutely," Julia said.

"No doubt about it," Judith added.

"It could be quite innocent, you know," I said. "Your father is getting along in years and many older people suffer from short-term memory loss. But he seems to be functioning admirably as an efficient and successful businessman. Surely you don't think he needs professional help."

"Oh no," Judith said.

"Definitely no," Julia said. "He's not that bad. Yet. But because you represent his attorney we thought you should be told of how irrationally he's been acting lately."

"Oh yes," Judith said. "Quite irrational."

"Could you give me some specifics?"

"He thinks someone in the house destroyed an old photograph of him and mother."

"And most recently he claims someone broke an ancient phonograph record he treasured."

"I admit they don't sound like much," Judith said, "but they worry us."

"And he thinks someone killed our mynah," Julia put in. "Poor Dicky died a natural death but daddy won't admit it."

"I see," I said, although I really didn't. Not then.

"Well anyway," Judith said with a brave smile, "we thought you should know."

"About the way he's been acting," Julia said. "So you might tell your father."

"I'll certainly do that," I promised, and thanked them for their revelation. They seemed satisfied they had accomplished what they had set out to do.

"If he does any more nutty things we'll let you know," Judith said.

"By all means do," I told them. "His actions may be a temporary aberration or may be an indication of a much more serious psy-chopathological condition." I said this with a straight face. Is there no limit to my dissembling?

The sisters looked at me with admiration. I had obviously reacted in the manner they had wished.

We finished luncheon and moved to the bar, where I introduced them to Mr. Simon Pettibone. If he was awed by meeting such comely twins it didn't interfere with his preparation of three excellent vodka stingers, enjoyed by one and all.

I then accompanied them out to the parking lot. They were driving a new pearlescent-blue Mercedes-Benz SL500 coupe. I looked at it in amazement.

"This incredible sloop is yours?" I asked, my founded being dumbed.

"It's ours," Julia said lightly. "We like to travel first-class."

"Nothing but the best," Judith said just as gaily.

I was the target of two identical kisses and then they were on their way. I watched them depart, trying to analyze my reaction. Willie S. came to my aid as he so often does. He wrote: "Double, double, toil and trouble . . ."

I drove directly home. The McNally nous was astir and I was eager to bring my professional diary up to date. A great many things had oc-curred since the last entry and I knew it would take an afternoon of scribbling to record events, conversations, impressions, and conjec-tures. Surprisingly, the anticipation of this donkeywork didn't daunt me.

I worked determinedly for more than three hours, skipping my usual ocean swim. I finished my journalism in time to shower, change my duds, and join my parents for the family cocktail hour.

Father seemed in an expansive mood and I deemed it an opportune moment to bring up again a request I had made several times. The McNally household once had an additional member: a magnificent and noble-hearted golden retriever. Max had gone to the Great Ken-nel in the Sky but his doghouse still existed alongside mother's potting shed.

Since his demise I had suggested the McNally mini-estate would be enlivened by the patter of canine feet, but the only reaction I could ex-tract from the Don was, "I'll think about it." Over martinis that evening I repeated my plea and added that a smart hound might assist

Jamie Olson in locating the whereabouts of the rapacious raccoon raiding our trash cans.

"All right," father said unexpectedly. "Find a dog you like but don't buy until mother and I get a look at it."

"Yes, sir," I said happily. "I'll find a winner."

"Not a Chihuahua, Archy," mother said firmly. "They always look so *naked.*"

"Definitely not a Chihuahua," I promised.

Dinner that evening was far from haute cuisine but nonetheless enjoyable. We had a down-home feast of grilled turkey franks, baked beans with brown sugar, and heaps of sauerkraut tinted with cumin. Cold ale, of course. Nothing fancy but lordy it was delicious. Ursi Olson provided warmed frankfurter rolls and a mustard from hell. You had to be there.

I plodded groggily upstairs after dinner and began reviewing the notes I had jotted on the Gottschalk inquiry. My reading resulted in no epiphanies but did indicate three areas I felt deserved continued and intensified investigation. To wit:

1. Why was such a handsome and apparently sophisticated chap as Ricardo Chrisling utterly without duende and working in a parrot emporium? And what was his personal relationship with his stepmother, the redoubtable Yvonne, housekeeper of the Gottschalk ménage?

2. Why were the twins, Julia and Judith, so intent on convincing me of the growing looniness of their father? Were they correct, or did they have a veiled motive I wot not of?

3. Was Peter Gottschalk so mentally and/or emotionally disturbed that he might be the perpetrator of all the acts of terrorism threatening his father?

I was musing on these puzzles and a few minor ones—such as why Binky Watrous thought Johann Sebastian Bach was a dark German beer—when the ringing of the phone roused me from my reveries.

"Not one but *two!*" Consuela Garcia said accusingly.

Well, of course I knew she'd find out eventually—but so soon! I knew it hadn't been Priscilla who tattled—she doesn't blab—so it was probably one of Connie's many informants who was present at the Pelican Club during my trialogue with the Gottschalk twins.

"Connie," I said sternly (I can do stern), "those ladies are the daughters of one of McNally and Son's most valued clients. They requested a meeting to discuss personal family matters which I cannot and shall not reveal. But I assure you it was strictly a business conference."

"Including champagne cocktails, wine, and a stop at the bar afterward," she said darkly.

"I tried to be an accommodating host."

"Did you accommodate one by going home with her later? Or making plans for a cozy evening of three?"

"That is an unjust suggestion," I said hotly. "You are accusing me of behavior of which I am totally innocent."

"But you're thinking about it, buster," she said. "Aren't you?"

It infuriated me because, of course, it was true.

"I resent your unreasonable suspicions," I said, "and I refuse to endure them. I think you owe me an apology."

"It'll be a cold day in Key West when I apologize for thinking you're cheating on me or planning it."

"Your delusions are your problem. My conscience is clear."

"Like the Miami River," she said. "Don't call me; I'll call you—which may be *never!*" She hung up.

I replaced the phone with a quavery hand. Connie and I had engaged in many squabbles in the past, most of them concerning my real or imagined infidelities. But none had the virulence of our latest controversy, and it left me shaken.

It was such a complex enigma. I was honest in claiming I had not misbehaved with one or both of the Gottschalk twins and had no firm plans to do so. Connie was correct in divining that I had lust in my heart. But if males can be punished for their illicit fantasies, there aren't enough prisons in the world to hold us all.

When I went to bed that night I punched the pillow angrily several times. It wasn't my light-o'-love Consuela Garcia I was striking. It was an ineffectual attack against sardonic, implacable destiny. Men are men and women are women, and never the twain shall meet.

Who said that? I did.

9

I wish I could write Friday morn dawned bright and clear. Actually it dawned dull and murky with a sky resembling a sodden bath mat. The kind of day designed to convince one of the utter hopelessness of rising and facing life's demands.

But when duty's bugle sounds the charge, McNally is not found skulking. I resolutely completed the usual morning drill and arrived at my office less than an hour late after stopping at our cafeteria for a container of black coffee and two glazed doughnuts. My abstemious breakfast at home (one skimpy scone) hadn't dulled a hunger I feared might be the first indication of serious malnutrition.

I lighted an English Oval for added nourishment and phoned Lolly Spindrift.

"Lolly," I told him, "let me be perfectly frank."

He giggled. "Darling, I've known two Franks in my life and neither was perfect, believe me."

"Then let me be perfectly honest," I said. "I need to tap your inexhaustible reservoir of inside skinny but at the moment I have nothing to offer in return."

"The story of my life," he said, sighing. "All right, luv, what do you need?"

"Do you have anything on a dazzling bloke named Ricardo Chrisling?"

Brief pause. "No, I—wait half a mo. The name rings a distant bell. I know I don't have him in my personal file but let me dig into the paper's database."

I sipped my coffee, nibbled a doughnut, puffed my ciggie, and tried to relax while Lol made his computer search.

"Got him!" he said triumphantly. "Which proves the Spindrift total recall is not weakening. Probably due to those memory pills I pop every morning."

"Memory pills? What are they called?"

"I forget. Anyway, about a year ago there was an imbroglio at one of our local boîtes. A private party of six South American gents. Voices were raised, fists were brandished, and eventually a pistol was drawn and fired several times. When the police arrived one of the *sudamericanos* was dead, thoroughly riddled. Our reporter asked an investigating officer how the deceased had perished. 'From an excess of holes,' the cop said. Isn't that delightful? All the other partyers were questioned. One of them was your boy, Ricardo Chrisling. But apparently he wasn't held or charged—just questioned. That's all I've got."

"Thanks, Lolly," I said. "I owe you one."

"Keep it firmly in mind," he advised. "You know what happens to people who stiff me, don't you? I reveal their innermost secrets in print."

"Makes me shudder. I shall eventually pay my debt. I am, after all, a man of honor."

"Hah!" was all he said.

I hung up with the conviction I had been correct in deciding Monsieur Chrisling deserved intensive investigation. Not that attendance at a private party resulting in a homicide condemned him, but it did make one question the traits of his friends and associates. I have been present at many, many parties, as I'm sure you have, at which the waving of a pistol and the resulting ventilation of one of the guests would be considered bad form. I mean it's just not done, is it?

Part of my interest in Ricardo Chrisling, I reckoned, came from an innocent faith common to us all that beautiful people, women and men, possess natures as felicitous as their physical attractiveness. It always comes as a shock, does it not, when these gorgeous folk turn out to be wicked wretches.

In any event, I imagined that while Hiram Gottschalk was a client of McNally & Son, it was possible Ricardo Chrisling was a client of Skull & Duggery.

I was still musing on the role Ricardo might or might not be playing in the program of threats against Hiram when I received a phone call from Yvonne Chrisling. It made me wonder if it was mere coincidence or if I was being played as the schnook du jour by a gang of slyboots for reasons of which I was totally ignorant.

"Archy," she said in her brisk contralto, "Mr. Gottschalk and Ricardo are flying up to Orlando to attend a convention of exotic bird dealers. The twins are going to a charity dinner and one simply can't depend on Peter. So I fear I must dine alone, which always depresses me. I was hoping it might be possible for you to join me tonight. Short notice, I admit, but if you can make it I'd love to see you again."

"Delighted," I said without hesitation. "What time?"

"Seven-thirty?"

"I'll be there. Not formal I trust."

"No," she said, laughing, "definitely not formal. Thank you for responding to the plea of a lonely old lady."

We disconnected. Responding to the plea of a lonely old lady? And I am Richard Coeur de Lion. The Gottschalk party proved Yvonne had a plenitude of friends and neighbors she might have called in to assuage her alleged loneliness. But she had selected *moi*. Even my gargantuan ego could not accept that. It wasn't my ineluctable charm, tousled locks, or Obsession cologne that inspired her invitation; Madam Machiavelli had a dark motive for wishing to feed my face.

Doodle was flapping at the Chez Gottschalk.

I spent the next hour scanning ads in the Yellow Pages and phoning kennels and pet shops requesting information on how I might acquire a canine of pleasing disposition but with an inborn prejudice against marauding raccoons. I discovered I could purchase any breed, ranging from Afghan to Rottweiler, which met my requirements. And all, I was told, were purebreds possessing AKC diplomas.

Finally it occurred to me a purebred wasn't absolutely necessary. I mean I'm not a purebred. Are you? So then I called a few charity pounds offering stray, lost, and cast-off dogs for adoption. They weren't selling their boarders but asking for a contribution. They assured me the would-be adoptees were healthy, with all the proper inoculations. I selected one particular shelter to visit only because the young lady who answered my queries sounded exactly like Jean Arthur.

The pound, a mile or two west of I-95, turned out to be a reasonably clean establishment devoted only to finding homes for vagrant dogs; no cats, rabbits, monkeys, snakes, or gerbils need apply. The husky-voiced lady I had spoken to on the phone turned out to be a bit older than I had anticipated but quite attractive in a healthy outdoorsy way. She had a bronzy suntan (her nose was peeling) and wore a rumpled khaki safari suit: jacket and shorts. Her bare legs were muscled and magnificent. We investigators are trained to observe such things.

She introduced herself as June August—which made me hope her middle name might be July. We got along famously. She led me down row after row of cages, all mercifully shielded from sun and rain, and pointed out the fenced area where her tenants were taken for a run or a frolic. There was a lot of barking, yapping, and howling going on but the decibel rate didn't seem to disturb June.

"Where have they all come from?" I asked her.

"Some are runaways," she said. "Or just lost. Some were deserted by owners who relocated. A few are brought in by young couples who can't handle a big dog anymore because they have a new baby. Sometimes they're dropped off by old people who are going into a hospital or nursing home. They cry. It's very sad. Listen, my partner is off today and I want to stay close to the phone. Why don't you just look about and see if you can find the hound of your dreams."

She flashed me a toothy smile and strode back to the ramshackle office. I did as she suggested and wandered down the rows of cages inspecting the inhabitants. I reckoned there were few purebreds present, if any, but all the mutts seemed in good health, with clear eyes and glossy coats.

As I came close I was occasionally snarled or growled at, but most of the dogs reacted as if they were delighted to see me. They jumped up against their cage doors yipping or, once or twice, whimpering piteously. I interpreted this behavior as the "Take me! Take me!" syndrome you've probably noticed if you ever looked at a pack of eager puppies in a pet shop window.

There was one fellow who caught my eye. He wasn't making any noise but as I passed slowly by he grinned at me. You think animals can't grin? Nonsense. Dogs grin, cats grin, dolphins grin, and as for chimps—gold medal grinners.

I completed a tour of the occupied cages and returned for another look at the peaceable one. He was still sitting on his haunches, apparently content with the world and his fate. I looked at him and he looked at me. A mixed breed, no doubt about it, but I thought he might have a lot of Jack Russell in him. Definitely a terrier type, with dark brown ears and head, white muzzle, chest, and legs, and dark brown patches on his short-haired back suggesting a map of the British Isles.

"Good afternoon, sir," I said to him politely. "Enjoying life, are you?"

He yawned.

I was still marveling at his aplomb when June August came up and laughed. "You found Hobo, did you?" she said.

"Is that his name—Hobo?"

"That's what we call him. State troopers picked him up trotting north along I-ninety-five."

"Probably heading for the Westminster Kennel Club show in New York. No one advertised his loss or distributed fliers?"

"Not to our knowledge, and we always check those things."

"How old do you guess him to be?"

"The vet we use estimates two to three years. Not a pup but not full-grown either. The vet says he probably won't get much taller or longer but he'll fill out through the chest and shoulders."

"Fixed?" I asked.

"Oh yes, he's been neutered."

"No wonder he looks so content. Would you object if I asked you to let him out so I may see how he moves?"

"Not at all. We'll take him to the run."

She began to unlatch the cage door, and I said, "Won't you need a collar and leash?"

"Nah," she said. "Not for Hobo. He's a perfect gentleman."

Cage opened, the dog jumped down onto the ground and enjoyed a slow, languorous stretch. June and I headed for the fenced exercise enclosure and he came along. He didn't precede us or follow but trotted alongside as an equal. I thought he moved smoothly with no sign of an infirmity. His head was up and his trot was almost a bounce. A very pert hound.

Once inside the fence, he paused to look up at the leaden sky, apparently decided it was of no interest—which it wasn't—and began to wander about sniffing at the sand and at spots where other dogs had marked their territory. He moved nimbly and once, startled by the appearance of a small chameleon, he leaped suddenly sideways, then returned to paw at the intruder a few times until it scuttled away.

He gave us a glance over his shoulder and then began running as if to prove what he could do. I mean he really raced around the interior of the corral, flat out, ears back and legs pumping. What a display of speed that was! He skidded to an abrupt stop and resumed his placid sniffing, not at all winded by his exultant dash. He halted at a far corner of the run.

"Call him," June August suggested.

"Hobo!" I yelled. "Here boy!"

I held up a hand; he looked and trotted over to us immediately. I leaned down. He nosed my fingers and allowed me to fondle his ears. He seemed to like it. I know I did.

"Did you train him to do that?" I asked June. "To come when called."

"Nope," she said. "He caught on from the start or maybe he had been trained by a previous owner. Whatever, he's one brainy dog."

"I agree," I said. "I'm going to make you an offer you can't refuse. I can't take Hobo at the moment because the final decision rests with my parents. I'll persuade them to come out here as soon as possible and take a look at him. I'll give you twenty dollars now as a sort of option. You keep Hobo until a final decision is made. If he's rejected, you keep the twenty. If he's accepted we'll make an additional hundred-dollar contribution to your organization. Done?"

"You've got it," she said happily. "Come back to the office and let me fill out some papers. I have to ask questions about your ability to care for one of our orphans."

Hobo was returned to his cage with no obvious objection on his part. June and I repaired to her disordered office, where I handed over my business card and a double-sawbuck. I also provided the names of two references and described the McNally property: a few partially wooded acres on Ocean Boulevard in Palm Beach.

"With a doghouse already on the premises," I added. "It's a comfortable condo formerly occupied by a golden retriever we owned who passed away from the ravages of old age. But his home still exists and is large enough to shelter Hobo, I assure you."

"Sounds wonderful," she said, sighing. "I do hope your parents like Hobo."

"What's not to like?" I said. "The kid's a charmer."

Before I departed I returned to Hobo's cage to take another look. He was still awake, sitting placidly, observing the world and thinking dog thoughts. We stared at each other a moment, and you may think me a complete nut but I swear he winked at me. He did, he really did.

What a rascal!

10

I decided to drive home rather than return to the office. After all, it was Friday afternoon, not a period when any self-respecting entrepreneur initiates new projects or even furthers the old. It is a time for exhaling and contemplating a weekend of relaxation, entertainment, wassail—whatever turns you on.

But en route I was suddenly stricken by a fearsome hunger, a craving for calories that could not be denied. I stopped at the first fast-food factory I encountered, parked, and rushed inside. I ordered their half-pound hamburger, medium rare. A mistake. It was touted on the menu as being made of one hundred percent top-grade ground beef. After one bite I was convinced it was one hundred percent top-grade minced galoshes.

I ate less than half of this abomination, tried a few spears of greasy french fries, took one sip of an acidic cola, and then fled. I continued my journey homeward in a surly mood. I realized my taste buds had taken a terrible whumping that day and I could only hope the dinner offered by Yvonne Chrisling would restore the McNally palate to its customary vigor.

It seemed to me a leisurely ocean swim might help dispel the morning's gustatory longueurs, and I was donning beach duds when Binky Watrous phoned from Parrots Unlimited. He was in exuberant spirits.

"Ricardo and Mr. Gottschalk have gone to a bird show in Orlando," he explained. "So today I'm selling along with Bridget and Tony and Emma. I've already flogged a macaw, three parakeets, and a peach-fronted lovebird. Isn't that fantastic!"

"Excellent," I said. "This could become a lifelong career for you, Binky."

"Well, I'm not sure," he said cautiously. "When Ricardo returns I'll be cleaning cages again. I don't much dig that guy, Archy. He has all the charisma of Grant's Tomb."

"Well put," I told him. "My sentiments exactly."

"Listen, the reason I called is that Tony and Emma are having an

after-dinner open house Saturday night. It turned out they are living together and they're having this informal party. BYOB. Bridget and I
plan to be there and I asked if I might invite you and they said of
course, the more the merrier. Would you like to attend?"

"Sure," I said. "Sounds like fun."

"Maybe you could bring Connie."

"I don't think so. She and I are not communicating."

"Oh?" he said. "A tiff?"

"The mother of all tiffs."

"It'll pass," he said breezily. "Now grab a pen and I'll give you the
address. Anytime after eight o'clock tomorrow night. Archy, bring a
good vodka, will you? At the moment I seem to be tapped out."

I jotted down the information. Binky went back to extolling the
merits of budgies and I went to immerse myself in the Atlantic Ocean.
My slow swim had the desired effect: it calmed me, soothed me, and
convinced me that one day I might learn to write haiku or play the bag-
pipes.

At the cocktail hour that evening I informed my parents I would not
be joining them for dinner since I had accepted an invitation to dine
with Ms. Yvonne Chrisling, housekeeper for Mr. Hiram Gottschalk.

"That's nice, Archy," mother said.

Father gave me a swift glance but said nothing.

I then described my visit to the animal shelter that morning and
how I had selected a dog which, with their approval, I felt would make
a happy addition to our household.

"Pedigreed?" father asked.

"No, sir. A mixed breed; he has no papers. Terrier type. I'd guess he's
part Jack Russell. Brown and white. Very trim. Very attractive. Strong
and fast."

"What's his name?" mother said.

"Hobo," I replied, and waited for one of the pater's hirsute eyebrows to elevate. It did.

"Ah," he said. "An aristocrat."

"Please," I urged, "take a look at him. I think you'll be as impressed
as I am."

"He doesn't chase birds, does he?" mom asked anxiously.

"He won't if we tell him not to," I assured her. "This is a very intelligent canine; he knows which side his kibbles are buttered on."

The senior McNallys looked at each other. "We could go out Sunday morning after church," mother offered. "Will there be someone there on a Sunday?"

"I'm sure there will be," I said, "but I'll phone to make sure."

We waited for our liege to announce his decision.

"Very well," he said, after a short spell of mulling. "We'll take a look at Hobo."

I drained my martini. "Thank you, sir," I said. "I think you'll be pleased with him."

He gave me a wry smile and uttered something I never in a million years would have expected him to say. "But will he be pleased with us?" he asked.

I bade my parents an enjoyable evening and a good night's sleep. I then set out for the Gottschalk home, stopping at a liquor store along the way to splurge on a bottle of Duckhorn Vineyards merlot. I figured if dinner turned out to be indifferent, or worse, a choice wine would ease my anguish.

Yvonne met me at the door with an air kiss and a warm handclasp. She was wearing silk hostess pajamas in a cantaloupe hue, quite striking on a woman with her darkish coloring. Her dangling earrings were a primitive creation of beads and stones. Her hair was drawn tightly back and fastened with a silver barrette also in a native design. The total effect was somewhat assertive. She seemed more chatelaine than housekeeper.

I proffered my gift of wine. She thanked me and inspected the label with interest. "Will it go with Oriental food?" she asked.

"It will go with *anything*," I assured her. "Except possibly chili dogs and sauerkraut."

"I think we can do better than that," she said, laughing. "Come along."

She preceded me, tittupping into the dining room where one corner of the long table had been set for two. Lighted candles flickered in frosted hurricane lamps. I discerned a faint odor of an exotic incense— but this being South Florida, it might have been roach spray.

"I thought we'd start with a little hot sake," Yvonne said. "Not too much; it's powerful stuff. Just enough to wake up our appetites. You approve?"

"Sounds wonderful," I said manfully, even though my appetite is always on the *qui vive* and I would have preferred something icy and astringent.

I don't know if Yvonne had a floor buzzer or if the maid had been lurking, but Mei Lee suddenly appeared bearing a black lacquer tray that held a small pot and two wee vessels no larger than eyecups.

"Good evening, Mei," I said, smiling at her.

"Ver' ver' happy," she said, giggling.

She poured us tiny tots of the warmed sake and padded away. We sampled and Yvonne looked at me inquiringly.

"Excellent," I said—only a slight exaggeration. "But not something I'd care to drink all evening if I hope to remain vertical."

"Oh, no," she said. "Just an aperitif. We'll have your wine with dinner. Archy, I can't tell you how grateful I am you could join me. With everyone gone for the evening I'd have been forced to endure a lonely meal—very depressing. Thank you so much."

I thought she was laying it on with a trowel, but perhaps she was sincere. Perhaps. But there was no doubt she was playing the gracious hostess and I couldn't fault her for that.

"My pleasure," I told her. "Will Mr. Gottschalk and Ricardo be gone long?"

"They'll be back tomorrow afternoon. It's really a buying trip. All the bird wholesalers show what they have to offer and retail stores like Parrots Unlimited make their selections."

"Are you interested in parrots?" I asked her.

"Not much," she admitted, and gave me a bent smile. "I prefer chickens, ducks, capons, quail, and pheasants. Roasted of course."

"Of course," I agreed. "You and I think much alike."

"I know we do," she said, so firmly that my original impression of this woman was confirmed: she was Ms. Resolute. I suspected even her whims were inviolable.

I wish I could describe the dinner served that evening in precise detail but I cannot since all the dishes were foreign to me. I had to depend on Yvonne to tell me what we were eating. To the best of my recollection this was the menu:

Seaweed rolls with black mushrooms, green onions, and minced baked ham in a paste of chicken breast, dry sherry, and other disremembered ingredients.

Eight-treasure winter melon soup with lean pork, crabmeat, and shrimp.

Spicy chilled noodles.

Steamed ginger chicken with mandarin pancakes.

Crispy nut pockets with pitted dates, roasted peanuts, and honey.

A pot of steaming tea was available but both Yvonne and I went for the merlot.

I enjoyed that meal, I think, but I was more perplexed than delighted. I had never eaten such food before and so I could not judge whether it was excellently or poorly prepared. I could identify such seasonings as ginger, fennel, and cinnamon. But when Yvonne casually mentioned star anise, lotus seeds, and fuzzy melon, she lost me.

Our exotic dinner completed, we moved to a comfortable corner of the blowzy living room. Yvonne brought out snifters of Armagnac, which was exactly what I needed to relax my uvula. We sat close together on the tattered velvet love seat.

"A remarkable feast," I said to her. "And I thank you."

"You enjoyed it?" she asked, and I thought her glance was mischievous.

"It was different," I admitted. "Something I've never had before and I'm still trying to sort out my reactions. At least it makes me question if a meat-and-potatoes diet is not dreadfully limiting."

"It is," she said decisively. "I wish Mr. Gottschalk would learn that. Got Lee rarely gets a chance to practice his art. He really is an excellent chef, you know, but Hiram insists on red meat and perhaps a baked potato slathered with sour cream and chives. I hate to think of what it's doing to his arteries."

I smiled but said nothing. If Mr. Gottschalk, at his age, preferred a broiled sirloin to stir-fried veggies it was surely his choice to make and should be respected.

"But he simply won't listen to me," she continued, staring into space. "Even though he's aware of the unhealthy effects of his favorite foods." She paused to turn her head and look at me directly, unblinking. "But then he's been behaving so strangely lately."

She stopped and waited for my response. I didn't say, "Ah-*ha!*" aloud of course, nor did I even *think,* Ah-*ha!* But mommy didn't raise her son to be an idiot and I knew very well we had now arrived at the nub of the evening; to wit, why I had been invited for dinner à deux.

"Behaving strangely?" I repeated. "How so?"

"He has these wild ideas," she said. "Delusions really. He misplaces things and believes someone in the house has stolen them. He breaks things accidentally and accuses others of their destruction. Our mynah,

Dicky, died a natural death but Hiram is convinced the bird was killed. Archy, I'm telling you these things only because you represent Mr. Gottschalk's attorney and I felt you should be aware of his increasing . . . his increasing . . ."

I suspected she wanted to say craziness but thought better of it. "Irrational behavior?" I suggested.

"Yes," she said gratefully. "Exactly. His increasing irrational behavior."

"Do you believe he needs professional help? A psychotherapist perhaps or even a psychiatrist?"

"I don't know," she said, frowning. "I really don't. But his conduct troubles me. Sometimes I fear he is not all there, if you know what I mean. Archy, I hope you'll repeat what I've told you only to your father. After all, he is Mr. Gottschalk's attorney and I think he should be made aware of his client's condition."

"Of course," I said. "I shall certainly inform him."

Then, having accomplished what she had obviously planned, she relaxed. We spent a pleasant final half hour chattering about saloon singers of the past we had both heard, live or on recordings: Tommy Lyman, Helen Morgan, Nellie Lutcher, and many others long gone but not forgotten.

Finally, my Mickey Mouse watch edging toward eleven, I rose to take my leave and thank her again for her hospitality.

"And you won't forget to tell your father?" she said. "About Hiram."

"I won't forget," I promised. "Father should know of this unhappy development."

"Good boy," she said, patting my cheek, and I wondered if the moment I left she would hasten to her record of pupils' deportment and paste a small gold star next to the name of A. McNally.

But teacher relented at the door to grasp me close and bestow a firm if brief smooch on my lips. "Thank you so much for the wine," she breathed. "And just for being here. You made my evening, darling."

If she was acting she deserved a tin Oscar at least.

11

One of Sgt. Al Rogoff's favorite jokes, oft repeated, is: "Last night I slept like a baby; I woke up crying every two hours." My slumber on Friday night wasn't quite as disturbed but it was fitful enough. I simply could not relax but kept flopping about like a beached mackerel.

It wasn't all those spicy viands I had consumed that were causing my distress; it was a mental malaise I could not identify. I had a vague feeling of unease, as if vile plots were astir at the Gottschalk manse I was powerless to foil. I had a disheartening suspicion I was being used, manipulated, for what purpose I could not imagine.

Finally, the dark at my window just beginning to gray, I sank into a deep sleep, mercifully dreamless. When I awoke and glanced at my bedside clock it was pushing ten-thirty. I had all the symptoms of a racking hangover, which was outrageous since my alcoholic intake the previous evening had been if not minimal then certainly restrained.

It required a shave and a long hot shower followed by a cold rinse to restore the McNally carcass to any semblance of normalcy. I pulled on my usual Saturday morning costume of T-shirt, jeans, and loafers. But before descending for a late breakfast I remembered to phone the dog shelter to ask if someone would be in attendance on Sunday. I was assured they'd be open and would welcome visitors.

I found Jamie Olson in the kitchen brewing a fresh pot of coffee: a welcome sight. I poured myself a tall glass of chilled tomato juice into which I stirred a bit of horseradish. I also toasted two big slices of Ursi's homemade sour rye. Those I smeared with cream cheese allegedly flavored with smoked salmon although I couldn't taste it. Then Jamie and I sat at the enameled kitchen table, sipping cautiously at our steaming coffee mugs.

I told him about Hobo and how my parents had agreed to take a look at him on Sunday after church.

"A terrier?" Jamie said.

"Sort of. A mixed breed but mostly terrier. He looks to be strong and I've seen him run. He's fast."

"Uh-huh. Male?"

"Yes. Short coat."

"Been fixed?"

"Yes."

"How old?"

"Two or three years. Around three."

"He might tree that raccoon."

"I think there's a good chance," I said, "if you urge him on. He's one smart hound."

"We'll see," Jamie said. "Some terriers can be hell on wheels. Others just whimper and go hide."

"Hobo won't whimper," I told him. "He's got too much pride."

"Mebbe," Jamie said, and lighted up his old, pungent briar. And I had my first cigarette of the day in self-defense.

We smoked awhile in silence. Jamie is a taciturn man; he considers small talk a waste of time. So I refrained from commenting on the weather or the high cost of haircuts.

Finally he said, "Those staffers you asked about."

It took a mo to get my brain into gear. The effect of sleep deprivation, no doubt. "Got and Mei Lee, chef and maid for Hiram Gottschalk?"

"Yep," Jamie said. "I asked my friend Eddie Wong about them." He paused.

"And?" I said.

"They're closemouthed, that lot. But Eddie says Got and Mei are looking for a new spot."

"Oh? They want to leave the Gottschalks?"

"Eddie says so."

"Did he say why?"

"Nope. Just they want to go. If Eddie knows why, he ain't saying. But he made a face."

"Thanks for your help, Jamie."

"Not much," he said. "But when people don't want to talk they won't."

A truism if ever I heard one. But Jamie had provided another small piece of the puzzle bedeviling me. I washed up my breakfast things, stacked them in the countertop drainer to dry, and returned upstairs to my dorm. I confess I had a fleeting thought a short nap would be welcome, but I determinedly discarded such a disgraceful notion and continued to function.

For the remainder of the morning I scribbled in my journal, not only noting recent events and intelligence but posing questions to myself which I am certain you are also asking as you follow this chronicle. Nothing at the moment made a great deal of sense. But as I explained to Binky Watrous on one occasion, enduring a temporary mishmash is a challenge to an investigator's patience, determination, and acumen. The reaction was vintage Binky.

"What?" he said.

It was about one p.m. when I finished my grunt work, much too late to call pals for a round of golf, a set of tennis, or any other energetic activity. Besides, I was in no mood or physical condition for strenuous exertion except a jolly game of jacks or a rollicking session of mumblety-peg.

I changed into jazzier threads, including a sport jacket of black and white awning stripes. My father once unkindly remarked it made me look like a fugitive from a chain gang. I didn't dare mention that his sport jackets seemed designed for wear at memorial services for President Millard Fillmore.

I set out for the Pelican Club, my spirits already beginning to ascend. I anticipated a quiet, soothing hour or more, perhaps exchanging philosophical profundities with Mr. Simon Pettibone. I would imbibe an exhilarating alcoholic concoction or two. I might even enjoy one of Leroy's special burgers with a slice of red onion atop. Suddenly life was once again worth living and I found myself singing "I Don't Want to Set the World on Fire." As I recalled, the rest of the lyric went, "I just want to start a flame in your heart." Can gangsta rap compete with that?

The Pelican was almost deserted, as I knew it would be on a pleasant Saturday afternoon. The golden lads and lasses would be cavorting on the courts, links, beach, or mayhap just swinging idly in a hammock for two.

I stopped at the bar to exchange greetings with our club manager.

"Something to wet the whistle, Mr. McNally?" he inquired.

I considered. "Perhaps I'll move to the dining room and have a spot of lunch. I'll see what Leroy is pushing and ask Priscilla to bring me a fitting beverage to sluice it down."

He leaned across the bar and beckoned me close. "Peter Gottschalk is back there," he warned in a low voice. "By himself."

"Ah," I said. "What condition?"

"Sober but quiet. Very quiet. I'd say depressed."

"Tell you what," I said. "Mix me a stiff vodka gimlet now, please, and I'll have a gulp of Dutch courage before I join him. Perhaps I'll cheer him up."

"Or perhaps he'll depress you."

"A distinct possibility," I admitted.

I took a swig of the sturdy gimlet and headed for the dining area. Peter was seated alone at a corner table. There was a half-empty pilsner of beer before him, a basket of salted pretzels, and a saucer of mustard. He was staring moodily at this feast and didn't look up until I spoke.

"H'lo, Peter," I said, trying to sound chirrupy.

"Oh," he said. "Yeah. Hi, Archy."

"May I join you?"

"If you like. I should warn you I'm lousy company."

"I'll take my chances," I said, and slid into the chair facing him.

"I goofed," he said suddenly. "I guess you heard."

"No, I heard nothing," I lied. "How did you goof?"

"Totaled the old man's car. The night of the party."

"Were you hurt?"

"Scratches and bruises. Nothing serious. I was zonked. But things are hairy at home. I'm staying away as much as I can."

"Well, as they say in Alaska, be it ever so humble there's no place like Nome."

He looked at me. "Have you ever been in Alaska?"

"No."

"Then how do you know they say it?"

"Peter," I said gently, "I never intend my nonsense to be taken literally."

"You're right," he said unexpectedly. "Things have been happening to me lately. Losing my sense of humor is one of them. I don't know what's going on."

I feared prying into his personal angst. "May I share your pretzels?" I asked.

"Sure. Help yourself."

I dunked one in the dish of steroidal mustard. "What was your father's reaction?" I inquired.

"Well, he didn't kick me out or anything like that. I guess he was just disappointed in me. It's okay. I'm disappointed in him."

I hadn't the slightest idea what he meant by that and I don't believe he did either.

He took a swallow of his beer. "I've got to do something," he declared.

Now I was curious. "Do what?"

"Something. Anything. Everyone else in that zoo has a plan. I mean they know what they want and they're going for it. That's my problem: I don't know what I want. You never met my mother, did you?"

"No, I didn't."

"A beautiful woman. I loved her so much. When she died everything fell apart. You know what I'm saying? It all went bad."

I was trying to keep up but this conversation was becoming increasingly incomprehensible. "The family?" I ventured.

"Down the tube," he said portentously. "Kaput. Rack and ruin."

"Your father—" I started, but his rancid laugh cut me off.

"A puppet!" he cried. "That's what I call him—the puppet. I hate my father."

He said this with such despairing venom I wanted to reach out and pat his shoulder. Then, to my astonishment, his mood abruptly changed. A complete flip-flop.

He grinned at me and laughed aloud. "Hey," he said, almost burbling, "let's you and me go have some fun. How about Fort Liquordale or Miami? Find some action. Meet a few kindred souls, preferably female. What say?"

"Some other time," I said with an arctic smile. "I'm on the hook for a family do this evening. Two tables of bridge. Very dull but I promised to take a hand."

"Too bad for you," he said with a foolish smirk. "Then I'm off to explore this great wide, wonderful world we live in."

He jerked to his feet, gave me a floppy wave, and rushed out. I sat there, exhausted by the tension of dealing with such a disordered personality. I ate two more pretzels dipped in mustard and finished my gimlet. Priscilla came over and looked at me sympathetically.

"He's a holy terror, isn't he?" she said.

I nodded.

"He didn't sign his tab."

"I'll pick it up."

"Would you like something, Archy? A burger? Salad?"

"No, thanks," I said. "I seem to have lost my appetite."

"Who wouldn't?" she said. "I feel so sorry for the guy. He's just out of it."

I returned to the bar.

"How did you make out with Gottschalk?" Mr. Pettibone asked.

"Rough going."

He nodded. "I have an old uncle—my mother's brother. Lord, he must be pushing the century mark. He's still got most of his marbles. Most but not all. I visit him and sometimes he says crazy things. Truly insane. I never know whether to correct him and maybe set him off, yelling and screaming, or just go along with what he says to keep him peaceable and happy in his nuttiness. It's a problem. You know what I mean?"

"I know exactly what you mean and it is a problem. I don't know the answer. But Peter is a young man. Too young to give up on."

"Maybe," Mr. Pettibone said. "But I guess that's not for you or me to say. If he can be fixed it'll take more than a smile and a stroke."

I would have liked to continue our conversation but a quartet of members came barging in, two couples dressed in tennis whites. They rushed the bar, boisterous and apparently delighted with their present and with nary a doubt of their future. I envied them. I finished my wallop while our mixologist was creating four different esoteric drinks, all of which seemed to require an inordinate amount of fresh pineapple, maraschino cherries, celery, or key limes.

I drove home in a subdued state, the meeting with Peter Gottschalk having put an effective kibosh on my temporary euphoria. The yearning for a nap returned in full force and I now saw no reason to resist it. I had a miserable night's sleep to repair, and perhaps an hour or so of Z's would recharge the McNally neurons and enable me to extract a few nuggets of significance from all that puzzling palaver with the junior Gottschalk.

Why on earth would a son think his father a puppet? I considered my own sire a master puppeteer.

12

On Saturday evening I enjoyed a pleasant cocktail hour and dinner with my parents which helped restore my dilapidated esprit. It had not been my customary lollygagging weekend and I set out for the party being hosted by Tony Sutcliffe and Emma Gompertz hoping the informal bash would completely rejuvenate my usual stratospheric gusto.

(Connie Garcia hadn't phoned but I determinedly ignored that disappointment. My Brobdingnagian ego simply would not allow me to make the initial rapprochement. Please do not remind me that pride is the first of the seven deadly sins.)

The two clerks of Parrots Unlimited lived in a cramped one-bedroom condo in West Palm. I had stopped en route to pick up a liter of Sterling vodka as urged by my lunatic Dr. Watson, and by the time I arrived the party was already flaming. It was a bit of a shocker to realize the other celebrants were at least ten years younger than Binky and I. But the gulf between twenty-somethings and thirty-somethings didn't seem to discombobulate my aide-de-camp. And why should it, since his mental age is teen-something?

A card table covered with a bedsheet (mercifully clean) served as a sideboard. There was one large platter of Ritz crackers and cubes of process cheese slowly turning green. Understandably no one appeared interested in this nosh; the stacks of plastic cups and gallon jugs of wine, all with screw tops, were the attraction.

I don't mean to be snooty in this description of Emma and Tony's party. Obviously their income and that of their friends was limited. But they were sharing laughter and companionship and if the wine was a vintage of last Tuesday—so what? In my salad days I attended and hosted many similar revelries and no one ever thought of objecting when the cab or zin was served in Smucker's jelly jars.

Binky grabbed my bottle of Sterling like a cookie addict who had endured a week without his daily Pepperidge Farm fix. He found ice somewhere and came back with plastic cups of chilled and scantily watered vodka for me, Bridget Houlihan, and himself.

"I'm teaching Bridget to appreciate the glories of eighty-proof," he informed me.

"It tastes like medicine," she said with a shudder after one small sip.

"It *is* medicine," I agreed. "But need not be inhaled or injected. I have found it an effective disinfectant for small wounds as well as an excellent gargle for a raspy throat."

She looked at me doubtfully and I wandered away. I moved through the gabbling throng (it seemed like a throng only because the apartment was so cramped) and found host and hostess. I thanked them for their hospitality and assured them it was a marvelous party. They glowed although I doubted if they recalled who I was. Their memories might have been dulled by the volume of hard rock thundering from two speakers large as coffins.

I decided to have one more tincture of Sterling and then split. But when I went searching for the vodka bottle I saw Ricardo Chrisling standing alone, gripping a plastic cup of red wine. Well, he wasn't alone of course—one couldn't be in that mob—but he was withdrawn, solitary, with a fixed smile that struck me as remote if not supercilious. I moved through the crowd to his side.

He was wearing Armani, naturally, beautifully tailored. The man's immaculacy amazed me. Didn't he ever drop a button or stain a cuff? He was so *complete*. I was absolutely certain he had hairs removed regularly from ears and nostrils.

"Ah," he said. "Archy McNally."

I was pleased he remembered my name. "In the flesh," I said, "sort of. Good to see you again, Ricardo. How was the Orlando trip?"

If he was shocked by my knowledge of his activities he didn't show it. He flipped a hand back and forth. "So-so," he said. "We bought the usual. Nothing very extraordinary except for a magnificent pair of varied lorikeets. Are you interested in parrots?"

"No," I said, and he gave me his glacial smile.

"I promised the kids I'd put in an appearance," he said. "I have and now I'm ready to leave. Are you staying?"

"Actually I was going to have one more small swallow and then cut out."

He looked at me speculatively. "Why don't you have your swallow at my place?" he suggested. "Something better than jug wine. This really isn't my scene."

I accepted his invitation gladly. The unending jackhammering of hard rock was flossing my ears and I yearned for a spell of quiet. We stole away and I am certain our departure wasn't noticed. Certainly not by my fruitcake assistant who was entertaining a fascinated audience with his repertoire of birdcalls, including that of the Slovenian grebe.

I would have imagined a lad as frigidly elegant as Ricardo would be driving something sinuous, foreign, and frightfully expensive. A Lamborghini Diablo? But no, his personal transportation was a white four-door Ford Explorer. Room enough for a troop of tots or cargo—lots of cargo. It was a nice enough vehicle, mind you, but I thought it an odd choice for a man who wore Armani (black label) and favored French cuffs on his silk shirts.

I began to have second thoughts about Ricardo Chrisling. My first impressions are usually accurate—but not always. I once tabbed a chap to be a complete schlub and he later turned out to be a bloomin' genius.

It wasn't only the car Ricardo was driving that made me begin to doubt my incipient evaluation of his character and personality. There was an added factor: the links on those French cuffs were miniature dice. Costly, I'm sure, but more Las Vegas than Paris, wouldn't you say?

I followed Ricardo's truck to a neighborhood not far from where the wine party was still blasting away. But this was an upscale area of West Palm, a quiet section of private homes and low-rise condos, all nicely landscaped with trim lawns and a restrained selection of dwarf palms. It was not an enclave of the *rich* rich, but just as obviously the residents were not financially disadvantaged, if you will forgive my use of the politically correct gibberish *au courant* these days.

Ricardo's dwelling was on the second floor of a modest three-story building. He had not one, not two, but three locks on his front door, and I waited patiently while he found the proper keys.

"Security problems?" I asked.

"No," he said shortly. "And I want to keep it that way."

He flipped on a bright table lamp and I looked about. His one-bedroom condo was high-ceilinged and airy. Now I must give you my first impressions, again after warning they have occasionally proved faulty in the past.

The apartment looked like a model room displayed in a South Florida furniture store. The mirrored wall, the colors, furnishings, lighting—everything was pleasant enough but so pristine and spotless it was difficult to believe the place was actually inhabited.

That was my first reaction. The second was a conviction the condo had been decorated by a woman. The feminine aura of pastels was the tip-off: all those soft shades of aqua, lavender, and the palest of pinks and yellows. I mean the room was totally lacking in vigor. It seemed to have been created with colored chalks.

Of course a female interior decorator may have been hired to create that tinted meringue. Or perhaps Chrisling had purchased or leased the condo fully furnished and never bothered altering it to conform to his personal taste. But it was definitely a womanly apartment, not quite fluffy but so . . . so *delicate* I wondered if Ricardo, even when alone, closed the door of the bathroom when he used it.

I go to such lengths to describe his living quarters because they puzzled me. I simply could not believe a man dwelt there comfortably. *Suffocating!* That's the word I've been seeking.

De gustibus non est disputandum. And if you think that means there is no accounting for tastes you're right on. And who wrote it? Our old friend Monsieur Anon.

"Do you like brandy?" Ricardo asked suddenly.

"Very much," I said.

"Ever have Presidente? It's Mexican."

"No, I've never tried it but I'm willing."

"Nice flavor," he said. "I think you'll like it. I'll get us a glass. I'd appreciate it if you didn't smoke."

He disappeared and I sank into a plumpish upholstered armchair. A mistake. I sank and sank, wondering how I'd ever get out of the damned thing without the aid of a block and tackle.

He returned with the brandy in stemmed liqueur glasses rather than snifters. But that was all right; I can rough it. He handed me a tiny tot and waited until I took an experimental sip.

"Well?" he asked.

"Excellent," I pronounced. "Flavorful, as you said."

"You don't find it a bit sweetish?"

"A bit," I admitted. "But not overwhelming."

"An acquired taste," he said. "Very popular south of the border."

"You've been to Mexico?"

"I have friends there," he replied, which didn't exactly answer my question.

He moved away from me to a couch covered with unspotted periwinkle velvet. He didn't sit but leaned back against one of the armrests. It put him at a higher altitude than I. I was entrapped by that quicksand armchair and so he towered. I recognized it as a common ploy of business executives. If you sit or stand at a higher elevation than your visitor you automatically reduce him or her to an inferior.

"I wanted to get out of that madhouse," he said abruptly. "Also, I wanted to talk to you in private."

"Oh?" I said, and took another sip of Presidente. It was emboldening.

"Let's see if I've got this straight," he said, speaking rapidly now. "Your father is Hiram Gottschalk's attorney. And you are your father's assistant. Correct?"

"More or less," I said. "But I am not a lawyer. If this concerns a legal matter I suggest you speak to my father."

"No," he said firmly. "It hasn't come to that. Yet. But I think you should know Hiram has been acting crazy lately."

"Acting crazy? In what way?"

"He thinks someone has a grudge against him. Smashing his phonograph records, slashing an old photograph, even strangling Dicky, the mynah he owned. It's all a crock of course. Strictly in his mind. What's left of it."

"Is he becoming senile? Alzheimer's perhaps?"

Chrisling shrugged. "Who knows? But the trip he and I just made to Orlando was hard to take. I mean he just wasn't talking sense. Even the wholesalers noticed it. A few of them asked if he was sick."

I was silent. Ricardo took a gulp of brandy that drained his glass.

"His son," he said. "Peter. Have you met him?"

I nodded.

"Then you know he's off-the-wall." His laugh was harsh. "Maybe it runs in the family. Anyway, I thought you might want to let your father know how Hiram's been acting."

"Yes, of course," I said, and finished my own Presidente. "He should be informed." I struggled from the armchair's embrace and stood. "Thank you for the transfusion. I better be on my way." I realized he had nothing more to say to me. He had accomplished his purpose.

"Wait a sec," he said, and left. He reappeared a moment later bearing an unopened bottle of Presidente brandy. "For you," he said with his tight smile. "Enjoy it."

"Thank you," I said, startled. "It's very generous of you."

"My pleasure," he said, but I didn't think it was.

I drove home slowly. It was a reasonable hour, not yet midnight, and I was reasonably sober. And so I was capable of totting up what I had heard the last few days.

1. The twins, Judith and Julia, had told me of their father's nuttiness.
2. Yvonne Chrisling, housekeeper, had told me of Hiram's conduct.
3. And now Ricardo had told me of his employer's erratic behavior.

A chorus of harpies.

There were, I decided, two possibilities. One: Judith, Julia, Yvonne, and Ricardo were joined in a conspiracy to convince me—and through me, my father—that Hiram Gottschalk had gone off the deep end and his mental capabilities were no longer to be trusted.

But if it was a conspiracy, what could be their shared motive? And if such a motive existed I could not believe the members of the cabal would have decided to attempt to enlist my support not once, not twice, but thrice. That, I was certain they would recognize, would be overkill. These were not stupid people.

The other possibility, I had to acknowledge, was that each separately, without knowledge of the others, was speaking the truth, and Hiram Gottschalk had flipped his wig. My father had warned me from the outset the client was eccentric. Perhaps what *mein papa* saw as eccentricity was or had evolved into something approaching lunacy.

My wisest course of action, I concluded, was to have a personal meeting with Hiram as soon as possible. After all, we had only met twice. A one-on-one interview would help me judge his mental condition. If I thought him normal, even if idiosyncratic, I would suspect a vile plot existed involving his children and employees. If he exhibited obvious symptoms of paranoia, then I would certainly suggest to my father that Mr. Gottschalk be urged to consult Dr. Gussie Pearlberg.

Having untied the knot of my doubts and insecurities, I regained the safety and comfort of my own snug den with a feeling of relief. My cave was, I admitted, somewhat grungy compared to Chrisling's immaculate apartment. But my sanctuary is *me,* completely mine, and I grin every time I walk in.

Before I retired I opened the Presidente brandy Ricardo had given me and had a taste. It was nice enough but lacked the punch of marc. But then what doesn't?

I fell asleep wondering why he had gifted me a bottle. I didn't think he was a Greek but I could not forget Virgil's warning.

13

My parents went to church on Sunday morning, as usual. And, as usual, I did not accompany them. I attended only when my sins become unendurable—a rare occurrence since I customarily find virtuous reasons for misdeeds, as I'm sure you do as well.

They returned and we all piled into mother's nicely restored 1949 Ford station wagon, familiarly known as the Woody. It really is a charming antique, fully operable, with a V-8 engine and side panels and tailgate of finely grained wood.

Father drove since he has an absurd notion that I am a speed demon. I am not, of course, and even if I were I can't see a '49 Ford wagon competing in the Daytona 500, can you? Mother insisted we bring along the collar and leash formerly the property of Max. I agreed because I didn't wish to cause dissension, although I knew Max's collar would go about Hobo's neck at least twice.

June August greeted us at the dog shelter and I introduced her. I think my parents were favorably impressed and I'm sure she was, since they were still wearing their Sunday-go-to-meeting uniforms, the picture of puritan rectitude. We all repaired to the cage harboring Hobo and stood in a semicircle observing him.

He was curled into a ball, sleeping soundly. But becoming aware he had an audience, he opened one eye, examined us, then rose to his feet, yawned, stretched, and pressed his nose against the door of his cage.

"Hiya, Hobo," I said. "Have a nice snooze? I've brought some friends to meet you. Could we have him outside, please, Miss August?"

She opened the door; he immediately jumped to the ground, had another luxurious stretch, and then looked at us more closely. And you know, the villain picked out the one of his four visitors who would determine his fate. Tail wagging, he sidled up to mother and gave her an affectionate ankle rub.

"Why, Hobo," she said, obviously enchanted, "you *are* a friendly pooch, aren't you?"

She leaned to scratch the top of his head and tweak his ears. He writhed with content. That kid must have studied method acting. I looked at father. *Both* his hairy eyebrows were hoisting aloft. He knew Hobo had conquered.

"Would you like to see him run?" June August asked.

"I don't think that will be necessary," I said, and looked to my parents for approval. They nodded and we all returned to the office to sign papers and ransom Hobo.

Twenty minutes later we were on the way home. As I had guessed, there was no need for collar and leash. Hobo bounded readily into the Woody and sat rather grandly between mother and me, making no fuss but viewing the passing scene with calm curiosity. I think father was amused.

"Not a very excitable beast, is he?" he said.

"No, sir," I agreed. "But deep. Definitely deep."

We arrived at the McNally manse and alighted. Hobo leaped down, shook himself, and looked around at his new surroundings. Ursi and Jamie Olson came from the kitchen to join us and examine the latest addition to our household.

"What a cute doggie!" Ursi said.

"Um," said Jamie.

The five of us were standing there, staring at the terrier, when suddenly he took off. I mean his acceleration was incredible. One moment he was still, the next he was a brown-and-white blur. He raced away from us, ears laid back, tail horizontal, and dashed into the wooded portion of our mini-estate.

He reappeared, circled the garage at full speed, and disappeared again. We caught glimpses of him darting through the underbrush, charging around the entire McNally domain, apparently never pausing to take a sniff.

"He's not running away, is he?" mother asked anxiously.

"Of course not," I said, praying my faith in Hobo would be justified.

Finally the scoundrel came skidding to a stop in front of us. He flopped onto his side, panting mightily, tail thumping. I think we were all astonished and puzzled by his behavior.

"Now why did he do that?" Ursi wondered.

Father pressed a knuckle to his bristly mustache, probably to hide a smile. "I suspect he may have been celebrating," he said.

I think it occurred simultaneously to all of us that we had made no preparations to feed and water our adoptee. It was decided a wooden bowl of water would be temporarily provided along with leftovers from our Sunday dinner and supper. Hobo would not suffer from malnutrition for one day, and mother and Ursi promised to go shopping for him on the morrow. They planned to purchase everything a healthy hound might desire: a supply of food, bowls, brush, comb, flea-and-tick spray, and perhaps a rawhide bone to exercise his molars.

"And some treats," mama said happily. "Little biscuits and nibbles. Things like that."

"But no gumdrops," I warned.

She stared at me. "Archy," she said, "I never know when you're joking."

"All the time, darling," I said, and hugged her.

My parents and Ursi went indoors. Jamie and I introduced Hobo to his new condo, beckoning him forward to examine the doghouse formerly occupied by Max. The strange dwelling didn't spook him at all and I was convinced the kid was fearless. He poked his head through the doorway, looked around a moment, then slowly entered. I leaned down to see what he was doing. Just sniffing, inspecting the premises he had inherited. Then he came bouncing out, tail wagging.

We took him on a tour of the McNally domain and he followed along happily, occasionally frisking ahead. He explored the garage, potting shed, and greenhouse. Apparently he found nothing to which to object. We have a low stone wall bordering Ocean Boulevard and he could have leaped it easily. I pointed to the traffic speeding by and said, "No! No!" as sharply as I could. I hoped he understood he was not to venture onto the highway to chase cars.

We returned to the main house and I left him in Jamie's care. The two seemed to have formed an instant rapport, and I wondered how long it would be before Hobo was smoking a pipe and drinking aquavit.

I went up to my snuggery to relax before dinner. I was happy the adoption of Hobo had been glitchless. I hadn't mentioned it but I did hope the others would not attempt to teach tricks to our new family member. I mean it's quite sensible to train a dog to obey simple commands such as Stay, Heel, and Sit. Even Fetch. But when it comes to such things as Shake Hands and Play Dead, I object. It's an insult to a dog's dignity, making him exhibit his total serfdom. If your boss commanded you to lie down and roll over, what would be your reaction? Exactly.

Dinner was short ribs of beef, which everyone agreed was a fortuitous choice. The bones, rinsed free of a delightful red wine sauce, would keep Hobo content for the remainder of the day. I even added a single small macaroon just to convince him he had arrived at a canine Ritz.

I postponed the usual après–Sunday dinner nap to add a few lines to my journal describing the curious conversation with Ricardo Chrisling the previous evening. I also jotted a separate note to remind myself to call Mr. Hiram Gottschalk the first thing Monday morning to set up a meeting.

I finished those minor chores and was about to collapse onto the mattress for a few hundred welcome winks when my phone destroyed that hope. Ah-ha! I thought. Connie Garcia is calling to apologize for her unseemly behavior. Not quite.

"Archy McNally?" A sultry female voice.

"I am indeed. And you?"

"Judith Gottschalk."

A short, shocked pause. Then I said, "Judith! How nice to hear from you."

"I got your number from daddy. I hope you don't mind."

"Not at all."

"Listen, you live on the beach, don't you?"

"Practically in the sea."

"It's such a gorgeous day I'd love to take a dip."

"Of course," I said bravely. "And Julia?"

"She's got the sniffles or something. Maybe the flu. She plans to spend the day in bed."

"What a shame," I said, resisting the urge to ask, "With whom?"

"Could I pop over for an hour or so? Just long enough to get wet."

"Come along," I said, not terribly enthused at the prospect.

"Got any bubbly?" she asked in a tone implying that if I didn't I was a hopeless dolt.

"I think I might be able to find a bottle," I said, a bit miffed by her peremptory demand.

"Do try," she said. "See you in thirty minutes or so."

She hung up and I sighed. But then I reflected that an afternoon with one of the twins might prove more productive than entertaining both at the same time. Encouraged, I went downstairs to the pantry, found a bottle of Korbel brut, an excellent wine, and popped it into the freezer for a quick chill along with two plastic cups. Then I climbed up to my aerie again.

I changed to swimming trunks imprinted with portraits of the Pink Panther and added a cover-up of aubergine terry. I slid my feet into flip-flops and picked up a beach towel.

I flip-flopped downstairs and waited at the kitchen door until I saw the blue M-B come charging into our driveway, skidding to a halt with a scattering of gravel. Judith Gottschalk alighted, then leaned back inside to retrieve a beach bag and an enormous pagoda-shaped hat of fawny linen. She was wearing a gauzy cover-up beneath which the eagle-eyed McNally discerned the world's tiniest bikini, in a calico pattern. If my father had observed her arrival from his study window I reckoned his eyebrows had ascended to his hairline.

I plucked the Korbel and plastic cups from the freezer and went out to greet her. She gave me an air kiss and then examined my offering.

"But it's *domestic*," she said in a snippety tone approaching outrage.

I refused to be offended by her pettishness. I glanced at the label. "Jumping Jehoshaphat, so it is!" I exclaimed with shocked chagrin. "I could have sworn I selected a bottle of an '83 Krug. Well, it's chilled, so I'm afraid we'll have to make do. Shall we go to the beach?"

She pouted. I don't think she was accustomed to having her desires thwarted—or even diluted. The Gottschalk twins, I decided, were enamored of the lush life and expected it as their due.

We went down to the strand and scouted three locations before Judith approved of a spot to spread my beach towel. I saw no difference in any of the places; sand is sand is sand. But that's a characteristic of pooh-bahs and would-be pooh-bahs. Observe their behavior in a restaurant; they will *never* accept the first table offered by the maître d'.

Finally we were settled, I opened the bottle of champers, and we each had a cupful. At least she had the grace to murmur, "Very nice." Then we went down to the sea, which proved a mite chilly but still held just enough summer warmth to be more invigorating than uncomfortable.

Judith was not a swimmer; that was obvious. She was more of a dunker, careful not to get her hair wet. She was also a bobber. You've seen them I'm sure. They stand in waist-high water and bob up and down, occasionally slapping their shoulders and upper arms vigorously.

I did nothing but get my knees wet while I watched Judith cavort. I was, I admit, a bit put out by her behavior and kept my distance. Not exactly Miss Congeniality, was she? She finally emerged from the briny and strigiled water from her torso and legs with her palms.

"That was divine," she said.

I was happy she approved of the Atlantic Ocean.

She strolled ahead of me back to our spread. I studied her lilting walk in the minuscule bikini plastered to tanned and glistening hide. Poetry in motion? Yes indeed. But whether it was a sonnet or a limerick I could not have said.

We drank more Korbel and she opened her beach bag to extract a package of rice cakes. She offered me one and I politely took a bite.

"Good?" she asked.

"Appetizing," I responded, thinking it was about as tasty as I imagined a coprolite would be.

She lay on her back, stretched out like a gleaming starfish. She placed her hat over face and head. I lay propped on my side examining her attractive carcass with more than prurient interest. I found it: a small black mole, no larger than an aspirin tablet, nestled low on the left side of her flat abdomen. I restrained myself and didn't shout, "Eureka!" or even, "Hoover!" But I believed I had solved one small equation: Mole equaled Judith.

"So, Archy," she said, voice muffled by her hat, "what have you been up to?"

"This and that," I said, and then revealed something I hoped might provoke a reaction. "I had a drink with Ricardo Chrisling last night."

"Whatever for?" she said, disdain curdling her voice. "The man is a viper, definitely a viper." Pause. Then: "I hope you won't tell him I said so."

"Not me," I assured her. "Discretion is my stock-in-trade."

She removed her hat and donned mirrored sunglasses to look at me. At least I think she was looking at me. With those specs it was hard to tell.

"Archy," she said, "did you talk to your father? About what my sister and I told you—how crazy daddy has been acting lately."

"I haven't had a chance to inform him as yet," I confessed. "But I fully intend to."

"You absolutely must," she said firmly. "We cannot let it go on and maybe get worse."

That had an ominous tone but I made no reply. Shortly thereafter she announced she wished to leave, and so we did. A very perplexing few hours. I mean I really didn't understand the reason for Judith's unexpected visit. It may have been quite innocent; she merely yearned for a brief ocean dunk. I did not think so.

That night before retiring I was still puzzling over our short encounter. Two things gradually surfaced from the bowl of Grape Nuts I call my brain.

First: Judith had referred with obvious malevolence to Ricardo Chrisling as a viper. It would certainly suggest the twins were not joined with Ricardo in some adroit plot against Hiram Gottschalk. Coconspirators rarely malign each other, do they?

Second: Was it really Judith Gottschalk with whom I had spent a not very exciting afternoon? Judith with the abdominal mole. She had said Julia was home with the sniffles. But could I have been deluded and was it actually Julia I had watched bobbing in the sea? Julia with the mole.

It was a crossword puzzle with no clues.

14

I may have set a personal record for oversleeping on Monday morning. By the time my dreams of Rita Hayworth had evaporated and I awoke, it was nudging ten o'clock and I muttered a mild oath. I staggered to the window and peered out. A gummy day with a ponderous iron sky pressing down and all the palm fronds hanging limply. I seriously considered returning to Rita for another hour.

But there was work to be done, Western Civilization to be saved, and so I went through my usual morning routine, still somewhat somnolent. I was tugging on a lovat polo shirt that seemed distressingly snug, when my phone pealed. I glared at it, wondering what fool would call at such an outrageous hour. The fool was my father.

"Archy?" The tone was cold.

"Yes, sir," I said, expecting he would demand to know why I had not yet appeared at my place of employment.

"Hiram Gottschalk was killed last night," he said, speaking rapidly. "Sergeant Rogoff informed me a few moments ago. He says it is clearly a case of homicide. He will be contacting you later. I want you to tell him everything you know about our late client's fear for his life and whatever you may have discovered in your discreet inquiry. Is that understood?"

"Yes, father," I said faintly, and he hung up abruptly.

I just stood there, trembling. My drowsiness had vanished to be replaced by a sadness so intense I could scarcely endure it. And guilt of course. If I had worked harder, if I had moved faster, if . . . if . . . if . . . But I had failed and the man was dead.

I collapsed at my desk. I could not bring myself to make a journal note of my failure. Instead I read and reread the note I had scrawled to myself to set up a meeting with Hiram Gottschalk as soon as possible. I was about to destroy that punishing reminder but then propped it up against my rack of reference books. I wanted to view it continually. "Vengeance is mine; I will repay, saith the Lord."

"You better believe it," I saith aloud.

I knew it would be useless to call Sgt. Rogoff. He was probably at the crime scene and would phone when he had completed the details of opening a homicide investigation. I could think of nothing I might do at the moment but mourn. I surrendered to that, had a tasteless breakfast, and drove slowly through a sticky morning to my cubicle in the McNally Building on Royal Palm Way.

I wondered, not for the first time, if I was temperamentally suited for my chosen profession. Perhaps I should open a small haberdashery or seek employment as a waiter in a restaurant with enough chic to offer Grand Marnier soufflé. "Hello! My name is Archy and I shall be your serving person this evening." Any job would do in which violent death was not routine. I am essentially a peaceable chap with, I admit, a dollop of timidity.

I smoked much too much that morning, remembering Mr. Hiram Gottschalk, recalling our brief conversations, and realizing how much I liked him, really *liked* him. He was capricious, no doubt about it, but there was no malice in him and whatever his sins I did not believe they deserved murder. I hoped Sgt. Rogoff would phone and suggest we get together to exchange information. But my only call came from Binky Watrous, who sounded as shaky as I felt.

"Archy," he said, almost wailing, "did you hear what happened?"

"Yes, I heard."

"It's terrible," he lamented. "Just terrible. He was a *nice* man, Archy."

"I know. Where are you calling from, Binky?"

"The store. We're closed for business of course. But we're all here. The birds have to be fed and the cages cleaned. But it's all so sad. The girls are crying. I feel like joining them. Do you ever cry, Archy?"

"Only at weddings."

"Listen, Ricardo called and told us to close up early. I guess he's in command now. So we're going to lock up and go out to lunch together. Do you want to come along?"

"Thank you, no, Binky. I'm waiting for a phone call."

"Archy, when you told me to get a job at Parrots Unlimited you said it was part of a discreet inquiry. Does Hiram's murder have anything to do with it?"

"Possibly," I said cautiously. "I won't know until I learn more about what happened."

"Then you'll tell me, won't you? I mean I am your lackey, cleaning out cages and all that, so I have a right to know."

"Of course you do," I agreed. "And so you shall. Now get off the line like a good lad and maybe the call I'm awaiting will come through."

He hung up but my phone didn't ring again that morning. I packed it in around one o'clock and went home for lunch. I was in no mood for the conviviality of the Pelican Club. It seemed to me indecent to seek companionship as a quick fix for my melancholia. *Mirabile dictu,* I found a cure on the grounds of the McNally duchy.

I dismounted from the Miata and heard the fast scrabble of claws on gravel. I turned to look and Hobo came racing around the corner of the garage. He skidded to a halt in front of me, panting, and jumped up to put paws on my knees. He seemed happy and he made me happy. What did he know of failure and murder most foul? He was just glad to see me and I blessed him, leaning to stroke his ears and scratch his hindquarters, which made him squirm with delight.

"Hobo," I told him, "you are a canine Samaritan and I thank you."

Jamie Olson came ambling up, gripping his old briar. His creased features wrinkled even more as he gave me a gap-toothed grin.

"That's some beast," he said.

I looked at him. "Don't tell me Hobo found the raccoon."

"Yep."

"Tree him?"

"Nope. Didn't give him a chance. Tell you what, that hound is swift. Set out after the critter. You should have heard Hobo snarl. Scared the daylights out of Mr. Raccoon. He went skedaddling south with Hobo right behind him. I finally whistled the dog back and he came. But I figure that raccoon is in Broward County by now and still running flat out."

I gave Hobo an extra helping of pats. "Well done, sir," I told him. "Keep up the good work."

I went into the house, my sunken spirits somewhat elevated by the tale of Hobo's hunting prowess. Ursi was working in the kitchen and offered to prepare a lunch but I respectfully declined. My appetite was blunted—a *very* rare occurrence, I assure you, and indicative of how deeply I had been affected by the news of Hiram Gottschalk's murder.

Up in my hidey-hole I reviewed all the notes I had made on what I was now fancifully terming the Puzzle of the Patricidal Parrot. I chose the adjective because I was convinced the birdman had been topped by a close relative. But a desperate search of my journal revealed nothing of significance. Just bits and pieces, dribs and drabs.

I existed in a mindless stupor for a half hour or so. I was thinking but it was a chaotic process, skipping from this to that: Ricardo Chrisling's taste in interior decor to Judith Gottschalk's mole, Peter Gottschalk's irrationality to Yvonne Chrisling's dictatorial manner. I mean the McNally cerebrum was in a tizzy with a surfeit of stimuli, whirling like a bloody carousel with the brass ring continually out of reach.

I was saved from total mental collapse by a phone call, finally, from Sgt. Al Rogoff. He was obviously in no mood for idle chatter.

"You going to be home for a while?" he demanded.

"The rest of the day as far as I know."

"Suppose I come over now. Okay?"

"Sure. Hungry?"

"I could use a sandwich and a beer."

"You've got it," I said. "How does it look, Al?"

"The Gottschalk kill? Pretty it ain't. See you soon."

I went down to the kitchen. Ursi had finished her chores and was gone; I played the short-order chef. I made Al two sandwiches, both with luncheon meat: sliced chicken breast with tomato and mayo, and salami with pickle relish. Even preparing this sumptuous repast didn't perk my appetite and I feared I might never wish to eat again. That put me in a better mood; absurdity always does.

Al pulled up outside in his pickup truck. It's not that he couldn't commandeer an official squad car but he has a nice sensibility about how Palm Beach residents feel about having a police vehicle parked in their driveway. Neighbors ask questions or gossip. I couldn't care less, of course, but I appreciated his discretion.

He came lumbering into the kitchen, took off his sagging gun belt, and slumped at the table. He looked more weary than grim and we did nothing but nod to each other. I popped two cans of chilled Coors and gave him one with the sandwiches. I gripped the other as I took a chair facing him.

"Rough morning?" I said.

"Not a barrel of laughs," he said. "Thanks for the feed. You make these sandwiches?"

"I washed my hands first."

"I hope so. Your father says Gottschalk thought someone was after him. Right?"

"Correct."

"Why didn't he come to us?"

"Come on, Al," I said. "Get real. He had received no threatening letters or phone calls. Would you have done anything?"

He picked up the chicken sandwich. "You're right," he admitted. "Until he got snuffed. Now we got to do something. Did you believe him?"

I flipped a palm back and forth. "Maybe yes, maybe no. Here's why he was spooked . . ."

I related what Hiram had told me: the slashed photograph, mass card, dead mynah, shattered phonograph record. Al listened closely while chomping through his first sandwich and picking up the second. I brought him another beer.

"You think he was telling you the truth?" he asked.

"I thought so at first," I replied. "What reason would he have to lie? But then I began talking to his children and employees, and they told me he'd been losing his marbles, had delusions of persecution. They implied senility."

Rogoff stopped scarfing and drinking to stare at me. "Did you ask them if he had been acting nutty, or did they volunteer the information?"

"They volunteered," I said. "They may have been right."

"Do you believe that?"

"No," I said.

"Me neither," he agreed, and started on his salami sandwich and second beer.

"I think they were trying to convince me Hiram was non compos mentis," I said. "They wanted me to tell my father his client's judgment was not to be trusted."

"And why do you suppose they wanted you to do that?"

" 'Ay, there's the rub,' " I said. "Hamlet's soliloquy."

"Thank you so much, Professor," he said. "I learn a lot when I talk to you. It takes weeks of hard work to forget it."

"Al, it couldn't have been an intruder, could it?"

"A masked villain who breaks in, kills, and escapes without stealing anything? I don't think so. But some moron tried to make it look like that. A pane of glass in the patio door was broken and the door was wide open."

"So?"

"All the broken glass was on the outside."

"Beautiful," I said. "Either a moron, as you said, or a murderer so emotionally disturbed by what he had done that he wasn't thinking straight."

"Or she wasn't," Rogoff said, finishing his beer.

"You think it might have been a woman?"

"Possibly."

"Al, you haven't yet told me how Hiram Gottschalk died."

"According to the doc, the victim was probably snuffed while he slept."

"But *how*? Shot, stabbed, strangled, smothered?"

"You don't want to know."

"I *do* want to know," I said angrily. "I want you to tell me."

"He was stabbed through both eyes with a long, slender blade, something like an ice pick, probably a thin stiletto."

I groaned. "I wish you hadn't told me." I found myself involuntarily pressing palms to my own eyes, to make certain they were still there.

"Archy, don't repeat what I just told you: the stabbing of the eyes. We're holding out on that, just telling the media he was knifed to death. We keep a few details back to check fake and real confessions."

"I know," I said. "I shan't repeat it to anyone, I assure you. It's not something I'd care to mention casually at a Tupperware party. Al, I know you've only started your investigation but I'm sure you've met all the whirlybirds involved. Any first impressions?"

"Yeah," he said. "How do you tell the difference between the twins?"

"You don't," I told him. "Think of them as one woman. But what I want to know is if you have any initial feeling or instinct about who might be responsible for Hiram's quietus."

"You know," he said, "I've decided you talk the way you do because it helps soften the world's nastiness. You can't face crude reality, can you?"

"I can face it," I said defensively, "but would prefer not to. You haven't answered my question. Who is your number one suspect at the moment?"

He sighed. "It's got to be the son, Peter Gottschalk. The guy is such a wacko. I mean we're talking world-class kookiness. He's capable of shoving a shiv into his father's eyes while the old man slept."

"But why?"

The sergeant shrugged. "Maybe just for the fun of it. I don't know whether or not the kid is a druggie—we'll find out—but he sure acts like one. So he's got to be tops on my hit parade. That doesn't mean I'm going to stop looking at the others. Where were they last night? What time did they go to sleep? Did they hear anything? See anything? The usual drill."

He rose, buckled on his gun belt, looked at me. I was still nursing my first beer.

"You going to keep digging?" he demanded.

"You want me to?" I asked him. "Or do you want me off?"

He considered a moment. "Keep nosing," he said finally. "They might tell you things they won't tell me. And I know you'll report anything you learn."

"Of course," I assured him.

"Of course," he repeated.

We smiled at each other.

15

I know you'll be delighted to learn I regained my appetite on Monday evening. Well, of course it had to happen because Ursi served beef stew Provençale with fettuccine, and what man, woman, child, or werewolf could resist that? Oh, how I gorged! But remember, I had ingested scarcely a morsel all day. It is foolish (and painful) to deny the body's demands.

Dessert, mercifully, was a simple lime sorbet. By the time I waddled from the dining room I had decided that life, despite its eternal frustrations, was indeed worth living. The guv stopped me in the hallway.

"You talked to Sergeant Rogoff?" he asked. "About Hiram Gottschalk's murder."

"Yes, sir. I told him what little I had learned. He wants me to keep nosing about."

The sire nodded approvingly. "Good," he said. "Do it."

And that was the extent of our conversation. I went upstairs to my journal, wanting to find a factoid I dimly recalled. I found it: a scrap of conversation with Peter Gottschalk at the Pelican Club. "I hate my father," he had said.

But now, with Peter being Al Rogoff's chief suspect in a heinous killing, the son's emotional comment took on an added resonance. I debated informing the sergeant but decided not to *pro tempore*. One impulsive utterance was hardly evidence of murderous intent, was it? Was it?

Disturbed about where my duty lay, I deserted my quarters, went downstairs and outside. I wandered over to the doghouse. Awakened by my approach, Hobo emerged slowly, yawning, tail wagging feebly.

"Sorry to disturb your slumber, old man," I said, and leaned down to peer within his shelter.

There was now a square of old carpeting on the ground, and he had been provided with plastic dishes holding food and water. There was also a rawhide bone and a toy that looked like a stuffed cat and already showed signs of enthusiastic gnawing.

"All the comforts of home," I told him. "You've got it made, Hobo."

I sat down on the patch of lawn about his mansion. He came close and curled up alongside. He rested his head on my knee and looked up at me. I am trying very hard not to anthropomorphize too much but I swear that animal knew or sensed I was troubled. His look and manner were concerned and sympathetic. Ridiculous? Possibly.

I stroked him steadily and absently, scratching his ears and head, smoothing his coat down to his tail. He allowed me, although I suspected he might have preferred snoozing within his castle. I don't know why but caressing the dog was marvelous therapy. I suppose I might have achieved the same result with a cat, gerbil, hippopotamus—or even, I thought suddenly, a mynah who responded to all approaches by repeating, "Dicky did it."

I finally arose, gave Hobo a final pat, and returned to the house. I paused at the kitchen door and looked back. He was standing at the entrance to his dwelling, watching me. To make certain I'm safe inside, I fancied, and then recognized it was so loony that if I kept it up I'd soon be inviting him in to join me for luncheon at the Pelican Club.

Up in my den again, I treated myself to an English Oval and a marc, parked my feet on the desk, and surrendered to the gruesome puzzle biting at me since I spoke to Sgt. Rogoff. Hiram Gottschalk had been stabbed through the eyes. Wouldn't your average, run-of-the-mill assassin, anxious to complete the dirty deed and escape, knife a sleeping victim in the heart, or at least the chest, once or many times? But no, the killer had deliberately pierced the eyes. And through those orbs of seeing into the brain. Why?

Obvious, was it not? A deranged slayer sought to make Hiram Gottschalk permanently sightless. He had seen too much, and so he had to perish. I could come to no other conclusion. Could you?

But that judgment solved little. It merely engendered more questions. What had Hiram seen—or what was he seeing? Why did his witnessing have to be abruptly terminated in such a vicious manner? In my brief conversations with the man, I had thought him mildly eccentric but hardly the possessor of dark secrets so ominous they demanded his death. Someone thought otherwise.

I went to bed that night still pondering what Hiram might have viewed that caused his demise. The result of my mulling? Nada.

Connie Garcia didn't phone.

Tuesday might as well have been called Bluesday. Not the weather—that was sprightly enough—but I was feeling far from gruntled. The perplexities of the Gottschalk affair were nagging, of course, and Connie's intransigence was infuriating. Her refusal to make the slightest effort toward a rapprochement was a blow to the McNally ego. After all, who had taught her the complete lyrics of "May the Bird of Paradise Fly Up Your Nose"? *Moi!* And cold rejection was my reward. Maddening!

A breakfast of scones with apricot preserves helped but I was still in a tetchy mood when I drove to work. I decided my megrims could only be vanquished by resolute action. I would make phone calls, ask stern questions and demand answers, pry relentlessly, and by the end of the day I would have Hiram's killer by the heels.

It didn't happen. I found myself slumped at my desk, counting the walls (four) and wondering what to do next. There's a German word for my condition: *verdutzt.* The Yiddish version is *fartootst.* Both mean confused, bewildered. At the moment A. McNally was definitely fartootst. Plussed I was non.

My brain was saved from a total scatter by a phone call from Julia Gottschalk. At least she claimed to be Julia. The voices of the twin sisters were so alike I could not be certain but took the caller at her word.

"Julia," I started, "I want to express my—"

"Yes, yes," she said somewhat testily, cutting my condolences short. "I know how you must feel. We all feel the same way. Archy, I'd like to see you as soon as possible."

"Oh? Sniffles better?"

"What?"

"Your sister said you were indisposed. Cold, flu, or whatever."

"Oh that," she said blithely. "It went away. When can we meet?"

"Lunch?" I suggested.

"No can do," she said promptly. "Judith and I must go shopping. Something suitable to wear at the funeral, you know."

"Of course," I said, amazed at the priorities of Hiram's loving female offspring.

"Around three o'clock," she said firmly. "The bar at the Cafe L'Europe. We'll have some nice shampoo and a cracker or two."

"I'll be there."

"See you then," she said lightly, and disconnected.

I sat staring at the dead phone. Hardly the wail of a grieving daughter, was it? "Shampoo and a cracker or two." Was that her idea of a wake for her murdered father? I wondered if Mr. Gottschalk had been fully aware of the character of his progeny. Parents sometimes do have a tendency to view their kiddies through glasses so rose-colored they're practically opaque. My mother, for instance, firmly believes me to be sterling. Father, on the other hand, is convinced I am tarnished brass.

I was still musing on that curious exchange with Julia Gottschalk when I received another equally puzzling call.

"Archy?" she said. "This is Yvonne Chrisling."

"Oh, Yvonne. Please let me express my condolences for your loss. He was a fine gentleman and I shall miss him, as I'm sure you all will."

"Of course," she said. "And I thank you for your sympathy. The sooner they find the fiend who did it, the better. It was an ugly, despicable crime, and I haven't stopped crying yet."

She didn't sound as if she was weeping, or had been, but perhaps she had herself under control. No surprise there.

"Archy," she said, "the last time we spoke we discussed how

strangely Hiram had been acting recently. Did you tell your father about that?"

"No, I did not. I didn't have the opportunity."

"Good," she said. "Because it's all meaningless now, isn't it?"

"Quite right."

"That's a relief," she said, and I thought it was to her—a relief. "There's no point in bringing it up since the man has passed. Well, I must ring off. Things are in an uproar, as you can imagine, with the police, reporters, television crews, planning for the funeral, and so forth. The children have been of no help whatsoever. But I do want to see you again as soon as things settle down."

"If there's anything I can do to help, please let me know."

"I'll do that," she said warmly. "I know you represent Hiram's attorney but I think of you more as a friend. A close friend."

"Thank you, Yvonne," I said, thinking, Close friend? Since when?

"Ta-ta," she said, and hung up.

It was the final "Ta-ta" I found particularly distasteful. I mean it was so frivolous. The woman's employer had been brutally slain, stabbed to death through the eyes, and she said, "Ta-ta."

Suddenly I realized if I had failed to take action that morning as I intended, action had come to me. I had received two communications and though neither was apparently of earthshaking importance, both were what I call nuzzles: little nudges by which fig leaves are raised ever so slightly and nakedness can be glimpsed. My lady callers had intrigued me, not with revelations but with teasing hints of hidden treasures. And both, I reckoned gleefully, had me pegged as a simp. I thought that was just dandy.

I was beginning to regain a measure of the usual McNally esprit when I received my third call of the morning. It was from Binky Watrous but had no deflationary effect.

"Hi, Archy," he said brightly. "I'm at home."

"Bully!" I said. "Whose?"

Short silence. Binky, as I'm sure you're aware, is not too swift. "Why, I'm at *my* home," he said finally. "I don't work on Tuesdays. Archy, did you know there are more than eighty-six hundred species of birds?"

"Heavens to Betsy!" I exclaimed. "Would you wait half a mo while I make a note of that."

Another short silence. He was actually pausing to enable me to jot a record of his disclosure. What a dweeb!

"And how many species of parrots do you estimate are in existence?" I asked seriously, keeping my prank alive.

"Oodles," he said. "Just oodles."

It was fun diddling Binky but I felt it had gone on long enough. "And this information on the variety of our feathered friends is the reason for your call?"

"I thought you'd be interested," he said somewhat aggrievedly. "It might help our discreet inquiry, mightn't it?"

"A remote possibility."

"Actually," he blathered on, "there's another reason. I phoned Bridget Houlihan at Parrots Unlimited. Just to chat, you know. We've become close."

"Glad to hear it."

"*Very* close," he said in a tone so smarmy his shins would have been endangered had he been within kicking distance. "We've been working on our act where Bridget plays the tambourine accompanying my birdcalls. We thought we might try it out at nursing homes. Bring a little jollity to the oldsters. What do you think, Archy?"

My first reaction was to cry, "Have you no mercy?" But I restrained myself. "A generous impulse," I said.

"Anyway, Bridget told me this morning Ricardo Chrisling had two visitors. Ricardo has moved into Mr. Gottschalk's private office and the poor man isn't even buried yet. Also, Ricardo told the clerks to put Ralph, Hiram's personal parrot, up for sale. That seems rather unfeeling, doesn't it, Archy?"

"You're right, Binky; it does."

"Well, Ricardo had these two visitors, apparently friends or business acquaintances. He gave them a tour through the store and then took them into his office and closed the door—something Hiram never did. Bridget said she didn't like the looks of the two strangers."

"Oh? Why not?"

"Too much flash. That's Bridget's word—flash. Shiny silk suits and lots of gold jewelry. Also, they spoke a foreign language with Ricardo. Emma Gompertz thought it was Spanish but Tony Sutcliffe said it was Portuguese."

"Esperanto?" I suggested. "Or perhaps pig Latin."

"Bridget said that after the visitors left, Ricardo called the staff together and told them he planned to increase the variety of parrots offered for sale, concentrating on rarer, more expensive birds. He said he would give them instructions on their care and feeding. That guy is really taking over, Archy. Can he do that?"

"I don't know the ins and outs of the situation, Binky. I don't know who inherits Parrots Unlimited. I presume it's one of the assets left to his children. If that's true and they want Ricardo to continue managing the store, then he can do whatever he pleases providing it's lawful."

"I guess," he said. "But Bridget doesn't like it and neither do Emma and Tony. They're all upset."

"Change affects some people that way."

"So you think it's okay?"

"I didn't say that. As political pundits like to predict, time will tell. You're working at the store tomorrow?"

"Yep. Nine to five."

"Keep asking questions," I instructed. "You're doing fine."

"I am?" he said happily. "Archy, when can I go on salary as your paid assistant?"

"Time will tell," I told him. "Meanwhile, consider your fringe benefits. You met Bridget Houlihan, didn't you?"

"Oh yes," he said soulfully. "My very own mavournik."

"Your *what?*"

"Mavournik. You know—a lovely Irish missy."

"Binky," I said gently, "the word you seek is mavourneen."

"Whatever," he said dreamily.

I gave up.

16

I had a slow and solitary luncheon at the Pelican Club during which I indulged in some heavy ratiocination. Oh yes, I am capable of that occasionally even though you may think me just another pretty face. I came to no startling conclusions, mainly because I had so little to go on. But I was convinced Mr. Gottschalk had been put down by a member of his household. And I was certain mischief had been afoot prior to his demise and might well be continuing even after the poor man met his quietus.

Al Rogoff had told me there are two main motives for homicide: sex and money. In this case I suspected money took precedence since it was difficult to imagine the elderly Hiram was the victim of a crime of sexual passion. But one never knows, do one?

I arrived at the Cafe L'Europe on the dot, figuring I'd have a twenty- or thirty-minute wait before Julia Gottschalk appeared, fashionably late. But she was already present, sitting at the bar and sipping a flute of a vintage champagne while nibbling a bit of toast heaped with sturgeon roe. My expense account took a sudden liftoff.

I paused a moment before making my presence known. The grieving daughter of a slain father was wearing a ruby velvet jumpsuit belted with a flowered Hermès scarf. She also flaunted white leather boots and a necklace of multihued Lucite chunks in cages of gold wire. Not exactly sackcloth and ashes, was it?

She turned to greet me. "Hi, Archy," she said with one of the twins' elfish grins. "I started without you."

"So I see," I said, and motioned to the barkeep to provide me with a duplicate of her mini-banquet. "I'm glad to see you're bearing up under the sorrow of your father's death."

I tried to keep the sardonicism from my voice and apparently I succeeded for she said, "Well, things have been in a tizzy but life must go on, mustn't it?"

"Indeed it must," I agreed.

"I think it's hit Peter more than Judith and me. The boy is lost, won't talk to anyone, keeps mumbling nonsense and drinking far too much."

"Ah," I said. "Pity."

"But that's not why I wanted to talk to you. Do you remember when we told you how strangely daddy had been acting before he died?"

"Yes, I remember."

"Did you tell your father what we said?"

"No, I did not. Didn't have the opportunity."

"Good," she said, and her relief was evident. "Because it's unimportant now, isn't it?"

"Of course."

"So we can just forget about the whole thing—right?"

"Right," I affirmed.

"Good," she said again, much assuaged. She motioned and we finished the bottle of bubbly with another spoonful of fish eggs on toast points.

"One other thing," she said, nibbling thoughtfully. "Do you know what's in father's will, Archy?"

I was startled. "Of course not. How on earth would I know something like that, Julia?"

"You're sure?"

"Cross my heart and hope to die. I'm certain you'll learn the details shortly. Probably within a week or so. Why don't you phone my father and ask?"

"We could but we don't want to seem pushy."

It was difficult to refrain from hooting. Pushy? Yes, I would say the twins suffered from a severe case of chronic pushiness, wouldn't you?

Moments later she finished her costly snack and grabbed up her blue leather Louis Vuitton shoulder bag. I received a small cheek kiss. Then she was gone. I was left wondering what her purpose had been in scheduling our brief meeting. Wondering if she really was Julia and not Judith, knowing there was no way of knowing unless she unzipped the jumpsuit and proved she possessed no small abdominal mole.

And wondering, as I examined the tab presented to me, how I could convince Raymond Gelding, treasurer of McNally & Son, that vintage Krug and beluga caviar were a legitimate business expense.

The perplexities of that day had not yet ended. I was in my lair after dinner, scribbling in my journal while listening to a tape of Louis Armstrong playing such wonders as "Anybody Here Want to Try My Cabbage?" and "I'm a Ding Dong Daddy (from Dumas)," when my phone rang. I grabbed it up eagerly, hoping it might be Connie Garcia calling with a wailing apology—which would make me a ding dong daddy from Palm Beach.

It wasn't Connie. It was Ricardo Chrisling.

"Hope I'm not disturbing you," he said in a tone implying he couldn't care less if he was.

"Not at all," I said. "I was saddened to hear of Mr. Gottschalk's death. Dreadful business."

"Yes," he said. "We're all stunned. Trying to function, you know, but still shaken. A fine gentleman."

"He was," I agreed.

"Archy, the last time we met I happened to mention how crazily Hiram had been acting recently. Really batty. Did you report what I said to your father?"

"No, I did not."

"Glad to hear it," he said, his voice warmer now. "Because with the old man gone it's of no importance, is it? I mean, what's that expression of speaking nothing bad of the departed?"

" *'De mortuis nil nisi bonum.'* Freely translated: 'Say nothing but good of the dead.' "

"Exactly," he said. "We'll let it go at that—okay?"

"Sure."

"Hey, have you tried that Mexican brandy I gave you?"

"I have indeed. Very nice."

"Ready for another bottle?"

"Good lord, no! I have plenty left."

"Well, I have a case of the stuff, so whenever you're ready just give me a shout. Listen, Archy, I like you and hope we can get together for dinner some night."

"Sounds good to me," I said, hoping I effectively cloaked my astonishment.

"Y'see," he went on, very solemnly, "since Hiram was killed I've been doing a lot of deep thinking. Realizing how short life is and how we should get as much enjoyment as we can while we can."

Now I was doubly astonished. Suddenly he had become one of those grinches who saw life as a terminal illness. Very philosophical. But his superficial maunderings did not square with my impressions of the man. I did not believe him capable of "deep thinking." I suspected he was governed more by physical appetites than by moral principles or reasoned enlightenment.

I could be wrong of course. I have been wrong in the past. For instance, I once assured Connie I was quite capable of consuming two enormous bowls of fried calamari and an entire bottle of Barolo without suffering any ill effects. Fortunately we had exited to the restaurant's parking area before I was stricken. I shan't describe it. Surely you've heard of Krakatoa.

I entered the details of my conversation with Ricardo in my journal—with the fey fancy that God might keep a similar record of us all—and then sat back to review the day's findings.

I started with my nutsy chat with Binky Watrous. Disregarding his moony comments about his Erin-go-bragh poppet, I found his report of some interest. Ricardo now seemed to be the honcho of Parrots Unlimited and was entertaining flashy visitors and speaking a foreign language. In addition, the inventory of birds was apparently to be enlarged by the addition of rare and more costly parrots.

What all that signified, if anything, I hadn't the slightest and put the whole matter on hold.

My exchanges with Yvonne Chrisling, Julia representing the twins, and Ricardo were something else again. All three parties had been intent on convincing me of Hiram Gottschalk's increasing irrationality prior to his murder, requesting I report their revelations to my father. And then, after Hiram's death, all three had been just as eager to confirm I had not repeated their comments to his attorney.

Their actions seemed incomprehensible. But I knew they were not stupid people. Venal perhaps, but not stupid. I mean they were obviously following plans that seemed logical to them. But I could not even guess what their motives might be. I reckoned it had to be greed: a hunger for a healthy share of the deceased's estate.

But whether greed was sufficient reason for his brutal murder I could not say. I doubted it since all concerned were living very well indeed while Hiram was alive. But then again one must never forget the first dictum of accumulating wealth: Enough is never enough.

I went to the sheets that night with a very curious thought: Was I dealing with corrupt people? Corruption exists in a variety of modes of course, ranging from the depredations of Attila the Hun to stealing towels from a hotel. But I sensed the malignity in the Gottschalk household was not as flippant as the latter. After all, a man had been viciously put to death and someone in his entourage had committed the dirty deed. It bespoke of infamy that frightened me.

Why can't we all be nice and love one another? And why can't we all have wings and thus eliminate department store escalators?

I awoke on Wednesday morning in time to breakfast with my parents—and that turned out to be a mistake. Not because of the vittles, you understand. Who could object to mini-waffles with clover honey? Not me. But it was father's mood that dulled the matutinal meal.

He was not surly—he's never that—but he was definitely grumpy, and his sour humor put the kibosh on what should have been a pleasant morning assembly of the McNally clan. The reason for his peevishness was explained when he stopped me in the hallway as we exited from the dining room.

"Sergeant Rogoff called early this morning," he said. "While I was dressing." His tone was indignant, implying a gentleman should never be interrupted in the process of donning his balbriggan underwear. "Apparently yesterday evening Peter Gottschalk did not appear for dinner. The maid was sent to his chamber and discovered him lying on the floor in what was allegedly a comatose condition. The paramedics were summoned and Peter was taken to a hospital. There it was reportedly determined he was suffering from an overdose of barbiturates and alcohol."

He paused. I disregarded his lawyerly "apparently, allegedly, reportedly."

"An attempted suicide?" I asked, my heart shrinking.

"It may be so," the squire said in his magisterial voice. "I suggest you contact Sergeant Rogoff as soon as feasible. Try to learn more details of this distressing matter, the boy's present physical condition, and so forth."

"Yes, sir," I said. And speaking as unemotionally as he, I added, "I'll attend to it at once."

"Good," he said, then mentioned almost absently, "If the son dies it will complicate the settlement of Hiram Gottschalk's estate."

Please don't think my father was oblivious to the human tragedy possibly involved here. But he was not a man much given to an outward display of his feelings. An attorney specializing in wills and estate planning accepts the inevitability of illness, decrepitude, and mortality sooner than most of us and so, as a measure of self-preservation, learns to control his personal reactions. Usually it works. Not always.

I waited until m'lord had departed in his black Lexus. Then I went into his study, sat in his chair, behind his desk, feeling as usual like a pretender to the throne. I phoned Al Rogoff at headquarters but his line was busy. I lighted a cigarette and waited patiently, resisting a desire to sneak a nip of papa's best cognac. Early in the morning for a wee bit of the old nasty, I admit, but I was spooked by the news of Peter Gottschalk.

I finally got through to the sergeant.

"Your father tell you?" he demanded.

"Yes. How is Peter doing?"

"He'll survive. Listen, it's not so easy to croak on pills and vodka. Takes a load of both to do the trick."

"Did he leave a note?"

"No, but that doesn't mean anything. Sometimes they do, sometimes they don't."

"But you're convinced it was a suicide attempt?"

"What else? Another piece of evidence."

"Evidence of what, Al?"

"C'mon, Archy, what've you got between your ears—succotash? The kid ices his father and then tries to end his own life because of guilt."

"Is that how you see it?"

"What other motive for suicide could he have?"

"How about grief?" I said. "Ever think of that?"

Rogoff sighed. "You're a doozy, you are. You remind me of the federal judge riding along a country road with a friend. The pal says, 'Look at that herd of sheep. They've just been sheared.' And the judge says, 'They appear to have been sheared on this side.' That's you—always questioning the obvious."

"Al, you're evidently a devotee of Occam's razor."

"Of *what?*"

"Look it up. Where is Peter Gottschalk now—still in the hospital?"

"No, he's been released. He's probably home. I don't have enough on him for an arrest—yet."

"Would you object if I visited him?"

Long silence. Then: "I can't officially say no. But why do you want to visit him?"

"I really don't know," I confessed. "Just to talk I guess. It can't do any harm, Al."

"I suppose not. You'll tell me what he says?"

"It depends," I said.

"Yeah," he said disgustedly, "I figured that. Thank you for your kind cooperation."

17

It was apparent Sgt. Rogoff believed Peter was his father's murderer. Al is rarely wrong in his professional judgments but in this case I thought he was. I simply could not see that poor, disturbed lad as a stiletto-wielding patricide. A weirdo *ja*; a killer *nein*. But I had to admit the son's attempted suicide could be interpreted as an indication of his culpability.

I went back to the desk and phoned Dr. Gussie Pearlberg. Luckily I caught her between clients and we were able to exchange affectionate greetings.

"Dr. Gussie," I said, "I am in Dire Straits, a narrow body of turbulent water between Total Confusion and Utter Despair." I was awarded a croaky laugh. "Is it at all possible you might see me sometime today?"

"Only on my lunch hour, bubeleh," she said. "If you are willing to sit and watch an old lady stuff her fat face, I can see you at one o'clock."

"Wonderful," I said. "I'll be there. Please, may I bring you lunch?"

"No, no," she protested. "Every day I have delivered a nice chopped chicken liver sandwich, a nice kosher dill, a hot tea with lemon, and a nice prune Danish. Listen, sonny, you'll have lunch before you come to see me?"

"Of course."

"Maybe a tuna fish salad with a glass of milk," she suggested.

"That would be nice," I agreed. Never!

I set out for the Gottschalk home wondering if I should bring Peter a get-well gift. But what on earth do you give a would-be suicide? Flowers? Bonbons? A bottle of vodka was obviously out of the question. And so I arrived empty-handed, dubious about this errand of mercy and what it might accomplish.

I was greeted at the door by Mei Lee but before we had time to exchange salutations she was brushed aside by Yvonne Chrisling, whose stern, almost outraged manner softened when she recognized me.

"Oh, I'm so glad it's you, Archy," she said. "The reporters have been driving us crazy."

"I can imagine," I said, and followed her inside. I thought the interior of the Gottschalk manse seemed even more disordered than I recalled from my previous visits.

"How are you coping, Yvonne?" I asked.

"We're surviving," she said with an imitation of a brave smile. "Things are in a horrible stew at the moment but I'm sure everything will soon straighten out."

"Of course," I said, which I didn't believe for a minute. "I was hoping to see Peter. Is he home?"

"He's here," she admitted. "I suppose you heard what he did—or tried to do. I'm not certain he's in any condition to receive visitors."

"Please try," I urged. "I promise not to upset him or stay too long."

She bit her lower lip and I doubted Peter's physical condition was her main concern. I was suddenly convinced she wanted him kept incommunicado for reasons I wot not of.

"Wait here," she commanded.

I waited for what seemed to me an unreasonably long time. Finally she reappeared and conducted me to a second-floor bedroom.

"He's awake," she reported, "but not quite coherent. Don't believe everything he tells you."

I nodded. Yvonne leaned forward to give me a brief cheek kiss and a frozen smile. I thought that was okay. But then she did something so astounding I hesitate to repeat it, fearing you may believe I'm making it up. She goosed me. It's the truth. I swear it. Then, after her astonishing assault, she stalked away without looking back, leaving me with my flabber totally gasted and wondering if I had strayed into a loony bin.

I had expected to find a wan invalid lying motionless in bed under a sheet, staring vacantly at the ceiling. Instead I found Peter wearing jeans and a T-shirt, bopping around the room barefoot, snapping his fingers to the best of acid jazz thundering from an enormous speaker. He had the courtesy to turn down the volume when I entered.

"Hiya, Archy," he said with a feral grin. "Thanks for stopping by."

"How are you feeling, Peter?" I asked. It was the best I could do.

"Just great," he said blithely. "I can't do anything right, can I? The problem was I had too much vodka, got so drunk I forgot to gulp enough pills. Next time I'll know better."

This discussion of the mechanics of self-destruction alarmed me. "I hope there won't be any next time."

He shrugged. "Not at the moment," he said, and continued to jive about the room, still snapping his fingers. He seemed more gaunt than ever, eyes sunk deeper, his entire face a portrait of young desolation. Yet he was obviously in a hyperactive mood; even those recessed eyes were bright and glittering.

"Peter," I said, "ever think of taking a trip? Get away from it all for a while. Maybe a European jaunt. Just as your sisters did. South of France and all that. Change of scene. Meet new people."

He stopped dancing to stare at me. "Great idea," he said. "I'll do it. Change my way of living—right? And if that ain't enough I'll even change the way I strut my stuff. But not yet. I've got to see this through first."

"See what through? The settlement of your father's estate? The solution of his murder?"

He wasn't offended by my rude questions. "Everything," he said, nodding, "I know a lot now and can find out the rest."

"Peter, you're talking in riddles."

He laughed so hard he lapsed into a fit of coughing. But gradually he calmed and wiped his mouth with the back of a hand.

"They think I don't know," he said, the savage grin returning. "They think I'm too loopy to know. But I *do* know. The catbird seat. Isn't that what it's called? Sure. I'm in the catbird seat."

I knew further prying would be useless. This conversation had skidded into dementia. But there was something I had to ask.

"Peter," I said, "you're not in any danger, are you?"

"Nothing I can't handle," he said, and then barked a laugh. "Except from myself."

"If you need any help," I told him, "physical assistance or just a listening ear, I'm available. Any hour."

It wasn't a majestic statement of sympathy, I admit, but it devastated him. He began weeping with great heaving sobs, palms to his face, his entire body trembling with anguish. I had absolutely no idea of how to deal with that and so, following my cowardly instincts, I made a hasty departure. So much for my errand of mercy.

I didn't regain any measure of emotional equilibrium until I was seated at the bar of the Pelican Club, frantically gulping a Sterling on the rocks with a smidgen of aqua. Can you blame me? I had just been wantonly mauled by a beetle-browed dominatrix and had witnessed a vastly troubled lad reduced to the weeps by a simple offer of support. It was enough to drive a man to drink—and so it did.

I remained at the bar, hailed Priscilla, and asked her to bring me a gargantuan cheeseburger with side orders of peppered slaw and Leroy's thick garlic potato chips.

"On a diet?" she said, and when I didn't deign to retort to her impertinence she asked, "Still seeing Connie?"

I flipped a hand back and forth.

"Oh-oh," Pris said. "Trouble in paradise. She was in the other day and wanted to know if I had seen you. I figured there was a problem. It's your fault."

"How dare you!" I cried indignantly.

"You're a man, aren't you? *Ipso facto.* Is that the right expression?"

"It is a legal term," I admitted. "But it doesn't apply in this particular case."

"Hah!" she said, and went to fetch my cholesterol à la carte.

By the time I pointed the Miata southward toward Lantana and the office of Dr. Gussie Pearlberg I was in a chipper mood. All those yummy calories had restored the McNally sangfroid, and no one is sanger or froider than yrs. truly.

A short time later I was slumped in the lumpy armchair alongside Dr. Gussie's bulky desk. I marveled at how this accomplished woman adroitly managed a chopped chicken liver sandwich, kosher dill, container of hot tea, and prune Danish while smoking a filter-tipped cigarette and listening to my concerns.

Actually it was she who ignited our conversation.

"Sonny," she said, "the last time you were here you spoke about a client who feared his life was in danger. He had been the victim of several nasty acts of psychological terrorism. Was he the man who was recently murdered? The owner of the parrot store?"

"Yes," I said. "Hiram Gottschalk. How did you know?"

"I didn't *know,* but I read about it in the papers, heard about it on the radio and television, and I feared it might be your client. I am so sorry."

"Not half as sorry as I. If I had moved faster . . ." My voice trailed away.

"Don't blame yourself, bubeleh," she advised. "Investigations take time; we both know that. Some of mine have been going on for ten years with no resolution. No, there is no reason for you to feel guilty. Some things are inevitable; we simply cannot forestall them. The news reports said only that he was stabbed to death while asleep. Stabbed where? In the heart? Or slashed? How many wounds?"

I drew a deep breath and decided to break my promise to Sgt. Rogoff. "He was stabbed through the eyes with a long stiletto-type weapon."

She seemed more excited than outraged. "The eyes! Now that *is* significant. Indicative. Definitely indicative."

"Of what?" I asked.

She ignored my question. "Who is handling the case?"

"Sergeant Al Rogoff. You know him of course."

"Of course. A good professional policeman with all the talents, experience, and limitations of the breed. Does he have a suspect?"

I trusted her discretion completely. She could be drawn and quartered and never betray a confidence.

"Al does have a suspect," I told her. "The murdered man's son, Peter Gottschalk."

"Oh?" she said, starting another cigarette. "Tell me about him."

I told her everything I knew about Peter Gottschalk: physical description, wild mood swings, laughter and tears, recklessness and accidents, occasional incoherence, attempted suicide and his casual mention of trying it again. And his puzzling remarks about hidden plots within the Gottschalk household, things no one suspected he knew.

Although she didn't interrupt, Dr. Gussie's expression grew increasingly pained during my recital. It may have been the prune Danish but I doubted it.

I finished and asked, "What do you think?"

She stirred, shifting her weight irritably. "It would be unprofessional to venture an opinion without examining the subject personally, Archy; you know that."

"Of course."

"And naturally I would never offer my conclusions in a court of law without many interviews with this Peter Gottschalk."

"Understood, Dr. Gussie. I am merely asking for a snap judgment, *entre nous.*"

She sighed. "Sonny, what you have just told me is almost a classical clinical analysis of bipolar affective disorder. You probably know it as manic-depression. I don't like to term it a psychosis though many professionals do. I prefer to call it a mental illness. Its main characteristic is wild mood swings between elation and despair. From your description, I would guess Peter Gottschalk is a manic-depressive."

"Do they commit suicide or try to?"

"If I told you how many," she said sadly, "you wouldn't believe. But only because their condition is not recognized and they go without treatment."

"What *is* the treatment?"

"Mainly medication. Sometimes neuroleptics. For a long time lithium was the only thing available. But now there are more and better drugs which don't have the side effects of lithium."

"You haven't used the word cure, Dr. Gussie."

"No, and I won't. All we can do at this time is treat the symptoms."

"You mean a manic-depressive must continue to take medication for the remainder of his or her life?"

"Yes, and must be monitored regularly to make certain the results are satisfactory or if the dosage should be altered or another drug substituted."

There was something additional I had to know. "You said suicide is common amongst untreated manic-depressives. Are they also prone to violence?"

"Frequently."

"Homicide?"

She stared at me. "That I cannot tell you because I just don't know. I have seen no studies of murders supposedly committed by manic-depressives."

"But you think it possible they might kill while in a manic or depressed state?"

"Oh, bubeleh, we're talking about people. Human beings. *Anything* is possible."

I knew what must be done but didn't have the courage to volunteer. "Can you suggest a way Peter might be helped?"

She saw through my cowardice at once and gave me a gentle smile. "You know what you must do, sonny. Convince him he must consult me or any other psychiatrist as soon as possible. And I mean *immediately.* If my off-the-cuff diagnosis is correct and he is suffering from bipolar disorder, he is in very great danger every day he goes without treatment."

I groaned. "How do I tell Peter he is mentally ill and needs professional assistance? He's liable to deck me."

"Possibly," she agreed calmly. "He may react with hostility. Or he may simply deny there is anything wrong with him. Or he may surprise you and agree he needs help. Whatever his reaction, you'll have done what you *must* do. The final decision is his."

"All right," I said mournfully. "I'll get through it somehow."

She rose to pat my cheek. "Of course you will," she said. "And you will succeed. You are a very charming, persuasive young man. If I were fifty years younger I would be writing you a billet-doux every day."

"Billy, do?" I said innocently. "But my name is Archy."

"Out!" she said, pointing to the door.

18

Despite the final lighthearted fillip, my conversation with Dr. Gussie left me in a subdued mood. The old chops were definitely in free fall, and a return to my cramped cul-de-sac in the McNally Building was not to be suffered. I needed a spot of alfresco brooding. How does one go about telling a chap he's around the bend? He's liable to reply, "So's your old man," or some other cutting remark, and that would be the end of that.

Dejected by this and other conundrums of the Gottschalk affair, I drove home, pulled in to our graveled turnaround, and alighted from my barouche. My spirits ascended instanter for Hobo came dashing to me. Clamped in his jaws was a short length of what appeared to be a sawed-off broom handle. He dropped the stick at my feet and looked up expectantly.

I laughed. Listen, it was his game, not mine; I hadn't taught him Fetch or any other silly trick. But I picked up his baton and gave it a good toss. He whirled and raced after it. A moment later he came trotting back with the prize clenched in his teeth, dropped it and waited.

We continued our sport for about five minutes and I tired before he did. I think he was disappointed when I stroked his head, told him what a splendid retriever he was, and left him to find other entertainment. I went inside feeling upbucked after my short session with the frolicsome Hobo. He had a gift of conveying joy.

We all have our wonts, do we not, and one of mine is to dither when faced with a difficult decision. I was tempted to delay a confrontation with Peter Gottschalk to another day. Perhaps to the next century when, with luck, I might be dead. But that I realized was an ignoble snivel and so, as the Reverend Spooner might say, I lirded my groins and phoned the Gottschalk residence.

"Hello?" a wary female answered. I thought I recognized the voice of Julia or Judith.

"Hello," I said. "Archy McNally here. Julia?"

"Judith."

"Uh-huh," I said. "How are you enduring?"

"Such a drag," she said. "We'll be happy when it's all over. Julia and I decided we need R and R in Italy to recover. We love Milan. Ever been there?"

"Afraid not."

"Divine boutiques. All the latest."

"I'm sure," I said. "Actually I called to speak with Peter. Is he available?"

"No, he took off."

"Took off?" I said, astonished. "But I spoke with him this morning. I mean he's recovering from an attempted suicide, isn't he. But he's gone? Where?"

"Who knows?" she said. "He's perpetually out to lunch. That young man really should be put away. Thanks for calling, Archy."

She hung up abruptly, leaving me to stare at the silent phone and try to understand her blithe indifference. After all, Peter was her brother, a member of the family. One might expect his condition to be of more concern than Milanese boutiques. I was beginning to get antsy about the Gottschalk twins. Disturbing conduct on their part, wouldn't you say?

I did my afternoon swim in a sea that was chilly but not painfully so. I attended the family cocktail hour, during which nothing was mentioned about the death of Hiram Gottschalk. Mother said Hobo had padded into her potting shed, curled up in a patch of sunlight, and snoozed for almost an hour, waking occasionally to make certain she was still there.

"He's such a dear doggie," she said. "I talk to him and I really think he understands. Do you talk to him, Archy?"

"Frequently," I said. "Although I can't fully agree with his opinion of the International Monetary Fund."

I do believe my father snorted.

Dinner that evening was lamb shanks—one of my thousand favorite dishes. I would have preferred mint jelly but Ursi served it with a ginger sauce. No complaints. Dessert was fresh strawberries drizzled with crème de menthe. A red zin to sluice it all down. Sometimes I imagine my arteries must resemble Federal Highway during the morning rush hour.

I retired to my third-floor digs intending to spend a quiet night adding to my record of the Gottschalk case. Then I might treat myself to a marc and listen to Ella Fitzgerald sing, "Lover, Come Back to Me," and wonder how Connie Garcia could possibly be so cruel as not to phone me. Had I completely misjudged her? Was she totally heartless?

But the revelations and surprises of that confusing day had not yet ended. I received a phone call from my loyal but mentally disadvantaged henchman, Binky Watrous. And even before he spoke I thought I heard the brittle clinking of a tambourine in the background.

"Archy?" he said. "Is this Archy?"

"No," I said, "this is Horace Walpole, author of 'Mysterious Mother' and other wildly popular fictions. Binky, what's *with* you? Of course this is Archy and are you boiled and why do I hear the sound of a tambourine?"

"I am *not* boiled," he said indignantly. "And I am calling from Bridget Houlihan's apartment where we are rehearsing our first appearance at a nursing home in Riviera Beach."

"Excellent," I said. "And that's why you called—to announce your theatrical debut?"

"Not exactly. Archy, something happened at Parrots Unlimited I think you should know about. Discreet inquiry stuff."

"Oh? What happened?"

"Well, you met Tony Sutcliffe, the senior salesclerk there. He knows more about parrots than any of us."

"Of course I met Tony and his companion, Emma Gompertz."

"Sure. Well, ever since Hiram died and Ricardo Chrisling took over, we've been getting some rare and high-priced birds."

"I know, Binky. You told me."

"It seemed to bother Tony. The parrots looked nice to me. Healthy and very pretty. Anyway, this afternoon Tony went into the private office to talk to Ricardo. The door was closed. I don't know what went on. But about fifteen minutes later Tony came out. Archy, he was as white as an umbrella cockatoo and obviously shook. 'I've been sacked,' he told us. That's all he'd say. He began to pack up his personal stuff and Emma started crying. 'Then I'm going too,' she said, and the two of them marched out. Doesn't that boggle the mind?"

"It does indeed," I said. "Did Ricardo offer any explanation?"

"About an hour later. He said Tony and Emma had resigned for personal reasons and he would hire replacements. Meanwhile he asked Bridget and me to cope as best we could until the new people came aboard. It's all so strange. Don't you think it's strange, Archy?"

"Definitely," I said. "Did Tony resent Ricardo becoming the mikado?"

"Well, they never were exactly buddy-buddy but I think it was more than just jealousy. I don't know why Tony got canned and Bridget can't guess either. I mean he knew an awful lot about parrots. But he suddenly got bounced."

"Binky," I said, "you have Tony's phone number, don't you?"

"Of course. Somewhere. And if I can't find it, Bridget is sure to have it. She's very organized. She even makes shopping lists."

"Amazing," I said. "Why don't you give Tony a call and tell him I'd like to buy him lunch. To commiserate on his sacking. You're included of course."

"That would be a decent thing to do," he agreed. "I'll give Tony a buzz and get back to you. Know something, Archy?"

"Know what?"

"I don't think everything is kosher at Parrots Unlimited. I suspect there's hanky-panky going on."

"You may be right."

"I think I'm developing a real talent as an investigator, don't you, Archy? I mean I'm learning how it's done."

"And how is it done?"

"You suspect *everyone*."

"A good beginning," I assured him. "And as a fledgling detective, what is your guess as to the nature of the wickedness transpiring at Parrots Unlimited?"

He paused a moment, then said portentously, "It is my considered opinion that Ricardo Chrisling is running a white slave ring."

"Uh-huh," I said. "Or perhaps counterfeiting food stamps. Call me after you talk to Tony."

What a twit!

No Ella or marc for me that night. I just sat there, neurons atingle, trying to make sense of what Binky had just revealed and wondering if the goings-on at Parrots Unlimited had anything to do with the murder of its late proprietor. I thought there might be a connection, however tenuous, but could not imagine what it might be.

Now we shall fast-forward a few days in this report on *l'affaire* Gottschalk, for nothing of significance happened in the interim. Actually, things of some importance did occur but were negatives, only meaningful by their absence, which, I confess, I hadn't the wit to recognize.

For instance, Thursday and Friday passed uneventfully, and it was Friday night before I recalled I hadn't heard from Binky anent the luncheon with the dismissed Tony Sutcliffe. Nor had I been able to contact Peter Gottschalk to arrange a meeting during which I would attempt to convince him he was semibonkers and required professional help.

It was a leaden two days and the fact that Connie Garcia didn't phone only increased my angst to the point where I considered I might be happier in a monastery. One with a library including the complete recordings of Bessie Smith. More to my taste than Gregorian chants.

I finally came alert on Saturday morning, which was a puzzle because it was a chill, drizzly day designed for lolling in bed. But no, I felt an ineluctable urge to *do*. I decided some—any—action, no matter how unproductive, was necessary to retain my professional standing as a practitioner of discreet inquiries. And so, about noonish, I phoned Parrots Unlimited.

I recognized Bridget Houlihan's chirpy voice. "Parrots Unlimited," she said. "How may I help you?"

"Polly want a cracker," I said. "Bridget, please forgive a stupid jape. This is Archy McNally. How *are* you?"

"Oh, Archy," she said, "Binky and I are so rushed. Ricardo promised to hire two more people but no one's showed up yet. I guess you heard about Tony and Emma leaving."

"I heard and that's why I'm calling. Binky promised to set up a lunch with Tony but nothing has happened."

"I know," she said, "and it's very odd. We've been calling Tony and Emma two or three times a day and no one answers. And none of their friends have been able to contact them. They just seem to have disappeared."

"A holiday?" I suggested. "A vacation after Tony got canned?"

"Maybe," she said doubtfully. "But wouldn't you think they'd tell someone where they were going and for how long?"

She sounded worried.

"I'm sure they'll turn up eventually," I told her. "I presume Binky is busy at the moment."

"Oh yes. He's selling lovebirds to newlyweds."

"Very fitting," I said approvingly. "Tell me, Bridget, how did your act go at the Riviera Beach nursing home?"

"Oh, it was a great success," she said enthusiastically. "They laughed so hard."

"I can imagine."

"And everyone applauded and cheered."

"A standing ovation, eh?"

"Well, not exactly, since most of them were in wheelchairs. But they want us to come back again. 'Better than Valium,' one old man said."

"Wonderful. Tell Binky I called, will you, Bridget, and if you hear from Tony and Emma please let me know."

I hung up troubled by what she had told me of the former clerks at Parrots Unlimited. It did seem exceedingly strange a young, gregarious couple would simply take off without telling anyone of their plans. Even if they were stressed by their sudden unemployment they would surely discuss their predicament and options with friends.

I pulled on a liverish nylon golf jacket and my puce beret and went down to the second-floor sitting room where mother was seated at her spindly desk penning chatty letters to her enormous network of correspondents.

"Moms," I said, "may I borrow your wagon? I have an errand to run, it's weeping out, and I hate to put the lid on my chariot."

"Of course, dear," she said. "I think it has enough gas but don't trust that gauge. Are you dressed warmly enough?"

"Absolutely," I assured her. "I'm even wearing socks." And I swooped to kiss her velvety cheek before taking off.

Mother's ancient wood-bodied station wagon is a balky beast. But on that Saturday morning it behaved splendidly, carrying me safely to West Palm Beach. I took along my cellular phone in case I couldn't find Tony Sutcliffe's home and had to call Binky or Bridget to direct me to the cramped condo where the wine-and-cheese orgy had been held.

19

Memory served and I found the place: a rather scuzzy three-tier edifice of chipped plaster, sun-bleached shingles, and with a dismal lawn that appeared to have been cropped by a bulimic goat.

There was a human-type goat propped against the outside door-frame when I climbed out of the wagon. He was wearing a shabby denim jacket atop splotched painter's overalls and was mouthing a toothpick apparently surgically attached to his lower lip. He seemed engrossed by the lowering sky and didn't give me a glance as I approached.

"Good morning, sir," I said.

How slowly he focused on me. His eyes were so pallid I was tempted to break into a chorus of "Jeepers Creepers."

"Yo," he said tonelessly.

"I'm looking for the manager or super," I told him. "Is such a person available?"

"Me," he said.

I was reminded of Jamie Olson. The two of them would be worthy adversaries in a monosyllabicity contest.

"I'm a friend of Tony Sutcliffe," I said. "Do you know if he's home?"

"Nope."

"Could you tell me the number of his apartment?"

"In the lobby."

"Have you seen him about recently?"

Those washed-out eyes stared at me. I sighed, took out my wallet, extracted a fiver, and offered it. An eager claw snatched it away.

"Not for two, three days," he said, toothpick bobbing.

"I'll see if he's in," I said. He didn't much care and returned to inspecting the firmament.

The handwritten register showed Emma Gompertz and Tony Sutcliffe as residents of apartment 2-B. I pressed the intercom bell. Several times. No response. I tried the inner door. Locked. I was ready to return to the taciturn super when the door was jerked open from within.

The lady about to exit was a bit long in the tooth and dressed flamboyantly. She was startled by my presence.

"Hi," she said tentatively.

"Hi," I replied, thinking her lashes were so heavily loaded with mascara she really should have been accompanied by a Seeing Eye dog.

"You live here?" she inquired.

"No, ma'am, I do not. Just visiting."

"Pity," she said. "Have a nice day."

"You, too," I said. "Have a good one."

"I do," she said, "but I don't get much chance to use it." She winked at me and went merrily on her way.

Then I was inside, recalling the route from my previous visit. Up a grungy stairway to 2-B. I leaned on the bell button. No answer or sounds from within. I rapped the door sharply. Several times. Nothing. I tried the doorknob. It turned easily and I stepped warily inside.

"Hello," I called. "Anyone home?"

No reply.

I closed the door quietly behind me and looked about. Deserted. I went through living room, bedroom, bathroom. All vacant. I even peered into closets and glanced behind the shower curtain at the bathtub. I returned to the kitchen.

The wooden table had been set for two. Dinner had obviously been suddenly interrupted. Plates held half-eaten portions of congealed lasagna. Glasses were stained with dried dregs of red wine, only small puddles of liquid remaining. Cockroaches and one humongous palmetto bug were busy. Not a pleasant sight. And the scent was not something you'd care to dab behind your earlobes.

The only indication of what might have occurred was a single chair tipped over and lying on the floor on its back. I could see no other signs of possible violence. The entire scene said so little but implied so much. Very disturbing. Especially the empty silence.

I left the apartment, closed the door softly behind me, returned to my parked wagon. The super was nowhere to be seen. I used my cellular phone to call Sgt. Al Rogoff at headquarters. He wasn't available, they said, and refused to tell me his whereabouts. I tried him at his home.

"Yeah?" he said.

"Archy McNally."

"Call me on Monday. I'm not working till then."

"Sure you are," I said. "You never stop working. What are you doing right now?"

"If you must know," he said, "I just picked up my laundry and I'm folding my shorts. Satisfied?"

"I'm in West Palm," I said. "Not too far from your place. You could be here in ten minutes."

"Why should I be there in ten minutes?"

"It concerns the Gottschalk homicide," I told him. "It may be something or it may be nothing, but you should see it."

"Why?"

"It would take too long to explain on the phone. Al, please do me a personal favor and get over here."

"The last time I did you a personal favor I almost got iced."

"You're stymied on the Gottschalk case, aren't you?"

"We're making progress," he said.

"Don't gull me," I said. "You're stuck and so am I. This could be a break."

"It better be," he said, "or you get promoted to the top of my S-list. What's the address?"

It was almost twenty minutes before Al's pickup came wheeling in to park alongside my wagon. Meanwhile the overalled super had reappeared and taken up his station next to the outside door. He stared at me with a definitely jaundiced glint. Maybe he suspected I was a cat burglar. Maybe he was hoping for another five. Who knew—or cared?

Rogoff came trundling over to me. He was wearing faded denim jeans and jacket and juicing up a fresh cigar. He was not in an amiable mood. "All right," he said, "let's have it."

I gave him the background, speaking rapidly. Tony Sutcliffe and Emma Gompertz. Former clerks at Parrots Unlimited, owned by the defunct Hiram Gottschalk. Tony's apparent altercation with Ricardo Chrisling, the new honcho. Tony's firing and the resignation of Emma. Their recent disappearance with no mention of their plans to friends.

"So I tried to make contact," I finished. "I think you should see their place."

"Anyone file a missing persons report?" he asked brusquely.

"Not to my knowledge."

"They have any close relatives?"

"I don't know."

"There's a lot you don't know, isn't there, sonny boy? Let's go take a look. What's the apartment number?"

"Two-B."

We marched up to the super. Rogoff displayed his ID.

"Sergeant Al Rogoff," he said. "PBPD. I want to take a look at apartment two-B."

The schlub stared coldly at him. "You got a search warrant?" he demanded.

"No," Al said, "I haven't *got* a search warrant. You *got* an operating sprinkler system? You *got* working smoke alarms? You *got* emergency exits clearly marked and lighted? You *got* garbage cans tightly lidded? You *got* rodents and vermin on the premises? I don't have a search warrant. How much you *got?*"

The super turned wordlessly and unlocked the inner door for us. We tramped up to the second floor.

"You're a rough man," I told Al.

"When I have to be," he said. "What did you touch in this joint?"

"Nothing. Except for the doorknobs."

Then we were inside 2-B. I stood stock-still while the sergeant went prowling. I knew he wouldn't miss the half-eaten meal on the kitchen table, the overturned chair. He came back to me a few minutes later. I could not decipher his expression.

"Wait for me downstairs," he commanded. "I'm going to toss the place."

"Hey," I said angrily, "why do I have to go? I gave you this. Can't I help you search?"

"No," he said stonily. "What I'm going to do is illegal. I don't need an eyewitness."

"Don't you trust me?"

"Dummy!" he said scathingly. "Not only am I covering my own ass but I'm covering yours. What if that goof in overalls files a complaint? Then I'm up for internal investigation. You get called to give testimony as a material witness. Probably under oath. Is that what you want?"

"I'll wait for you downstairs," I said hastily.

I sat in the wagon to escape the drizzle and chain-smoked two cigarettes, something I rarely do. Eventually Rogoff came out carrying a small brown paper bag. His chewed cigar was still cold but when he climbed in next to me he lighted up. I lowered the window.

"Anything?" I asked him.

"Some personal letters," he said curtly. "Names and addresses of people who seem to be relatives."

"Anything else?" I persisted.

"You ever hear of the Fish and Wildlife Service?"

"Of course. It's part of the Department of the Interior."

"Gee, Professor, you know everything," the sergeant said. "Well, they have a Division of Law Enforcement. This Tony Sutcliffe had some correspondence with them."

"About what?"

"I don't know exactly," Al said blandly. "I'll go over it when I have the time and see if it means anything."

He was stiffing me of course but that was okay; there were things I hadn't told him. It's the way we work together: a curious mixture of cooperation and rivalry. I know it sounds stupid but it's effective. Usually.

"What about Emma and Tony?" I asked him.

"If no one files a missing persons report, there's not much I can do officially."

"And unofficially?"

"Ask around. Contact the relatives. Talk to neighbors."

We were silent, neither of us wanting to allude to our primal fear. Finally I had to ask.

"Do you think they left voluntarily?"

"No."

"Someone barged in and grabbed them in the middle of their lasagna dinner?"

"Could be."

"Are they still alive?"

He glared at me. "What kind of a sappy question is that? How the hell should I know?"

"What's your guess?"

He stared out at the melancholy sky. "I think they're gone," he said in a low voice, leaving me to wonder if he meant Tony and Emma had simply been abducted for whatever reason, or were now dead. I didn't dare to keep pressing because I didn't want to know, didn't want my own dread to be confirmed.

We parted without further palaver. Al climbed into his pickup and headed out. I finally got the wagon rolling after some asthmatic engine coughs which caused me to suffer a mild panic attack. On the trip homeward I could not help but recall Hamlet's lament: "The time is out of joint; O cursed spite, that ever I was born to set it right!"

I do tend to drivel occasionally, do I not?

You will have noted, I trust, it was latish in the afternoon and I had not yet lunched. This was deliberate on my part for the waistbands of my trousers had become so constrictive of late I feared friends might soon be addressing me as "Porky."

My dreams of an abstemious diet went glimmering when I returned home. The weather was so inclement an ocean swim was not to be attempted and so I had no choice but to eat. The kitchen being temporarily deserted, I hurriedly constructed a sandwich of heroic proportions: two thick slices of pumpernickel clamping a deck of baked ham, a slice of sharp cheddar, another of red onion, another of beefsteak tomato, the whole painted lovingly with horseradish sauce.

I carried this magnum opus with a cold bottle of Heineken up to my den and settled down to feed my face and reflect on the developments of that frustrating day.

As I gorged I became convinced the disappearance of the two former clerks of Parrots Unlimited did indeed have a bearing on the murder of Hiram Gottschalk. The connection was unknowable at the moment but I felt a relation did exist and required some heavy sniffing about.

To do that, I realized, I would to some extent have to depend on the investigative talents of Binky Watrous—which was somewhat similar to a man with a broken leg leaning on a rubber cane. But Binky was capable of making observations and reporting odd or unusual occurrences, and I reckoned his raw data was necessary if I was to arrive at any intelligent analysis of what had happened and was happening in this baffling puzzle.

In addition to giving Binky fresh instructions—couched in the form of a pep talk since the lad needed constant reassurance he was a reincarnation of Hercule Poirot—I intended to dig into the role of the Fish and Wildlife Service. Sgt. Rogoff had mentioned that the missing Tony Sutcliffe had corresponded with that agency. Al's remark had been so casual I was certain the matter was more important than his offhand manner implied. The sergeant plays his cards very, very close to his vest. And so do I—if I wear a vest. Will a shocking-pink Izod golf shirt do?

The sandwich and the brew worked their way and I was suddenly overcome by the need of a nap. Not a long one, you understand, but a brief, intense slumber to give my wearied gray matter (it's really a Black Watch tartan) a chance to regain its customary zip.

But before I drifted off I had a strange epiphany. Because parrots seemed to play an important part in this affair, I had come to visualize the Gottschalk ménage as an aviary, a cageful of exotic and brilliantly colored birds. Suddenly my fancy was revised and I imaged it as a zoo crowded with ugly and rapacious beasts.

A curious vision certainly but mental pabulum all the same.

20

By Sunday morning the skies had cleared—and I wished I could say that for my thoughts. I was in such a distracted mood I accompanied my parents to church: something, I regretfully admit, I rarely do. The sermon was based on the scriptural dictum "The meek shall inherit the earth." How true, how true, and keep it in mind the next time you're mugged.

We returned home and went our separate ways. Father retired to his study to continue devouring *The New York Times*. Mother hurried to the greenhouse to commune with her begonias. And I went searching for Hobo. I finally found him—or rather he found me. He came trotting out of our small patch of woods and paused for a yawn and a long stretch. I had obviously interrupted a noonday nap but he showed no resentment and greeted my presence with an ankle rub.

I had learned from experience the activity he enjoyed most was what I can only term roughhousing. I crouched before him and we engaged in mock combat. He attacked with snarls and growls, jaws open. I defended myself by cuffing him, pushing him violently away, sometimes even flopping him onto his back.

He never bit me of course but delighted in giving my bare hand or wrist a good gumming. We continued this boisterous play until we both had to pause, panting. Then we went for a short walk about the grounds, Hobo padding contentedly at my heels. Finally I peered into his dwelling to make certain his water dish was filled and bade him a fond farewell, urging him to continue his nap.

I retreated to my own doghouse and shucked off my churchy duds, donning a new cotton robe I had recently bought. Well, it was really a nightshirt and the reason for its purchase was that the back was printed with a photograph of Laurel and Hardy trying to push a piano up a hill. I could relate to that.

I then settled down at my desk, blissfully mindless, and began to browse through the Sunday edition of one of our local newspapers. I found no mention whatsoever of the murder of Hiram Gottschalk, from which I could only conclude the police had made no progress. At least they had the decency not to issue the usual claptrap statement: "The homicide is being actively investigated and important developments are expected shortly."

I flipped the pages to Lolly Spindrift's gossip column. His breezy comments on the deeds and misdeeds of Palm Beach County's *haute monde* are always good for a laugh, or at least an amused smile, but there was one item I found more intriguing than risible. It stated:

"What oh-so-handsome manager of a popular bird supermarket in West Palm is setting new records in the man-about-town sweepstakes, leaving many a female heart atwitter? A word of caution to this lothario's conquests: You haven't got a chance. He may be a gorgeous hunk, ladies, but his heart belongs elsewhere."

I read the item twice. I was certain he was referring to Ricardo Chrisling. But his characterization of Ricardo as a lothario was surprising. I had no idea the lad had so active an avocation. Even more puzzling was Lolly's final remark: ". . . his heart belongs elsewhere." What on earth was the blabmeister hinting? That Ricardo was gay? I doubted it but Monsieur Spindrift would be the first to know. I preferred to believe Lol was implying Ricardo had a one-and-only of the female persuasion.

Another enigma to be unraveled and I knew it might require a champagne lunch to persuade the gossipmonger to reveal more of what he knew or had heard of the passions of Ricardo Chrisling.

The remainder of the day was uneventful except for the dessert Ursi Olson served at dinner. It was zabaglione: whipped cream, brandy, marsala, strawberries, and thin shavings of chocolate.

O cholesterol, where is thy sting?

I started the new week ready for derring-do and hopeful that before the day ended I might accomplish much, perhaps even positively identifying the Man in the Iron Mask. But I began with a more mundane challenge than that.

I must start by telling you McNally & Son, like most legal firms, is computerized. All our attorneys and paralegals have access to databases able to provide almost instant references to laws, judgments, and precedents that would take hours to find in the stacks of lawbooks now mildewing on office shelves.

Everyone at McNally & Son has a PC on his or her desk except for my father and myself. He doesn't need one; clerks do his donkeywork. I don't have one because I am a computer illiterate. In fact, I am a technophobe and have trouble changing a lightbulb without assistance.

Our house cyberflake—every company has at least one—is a dreamy-eyed bloke name Judd Wilkins. He looks more like a 1960s hippie than a 1990s digital nerd, for he wears a long blond pigtail cinched with a butterfly paper clip and sports two earrings in one ear.

Father endures Judd's eccentric appearance and dress (stonewashed jeans and a sequined monkey jacket) because the lad is a certified genius when it comes to the information superhighway, byways, lanes, and trails. I mean he knows everything there is to know about computers, printers, modems, networks, and how they all interface. Is that the correct word?

Anyway, Judd is carried on our employee roll as a paralegal but he is really our interpreter of the Brave New World of Bytes, capable of solving any glitches occurring in our electronic equipment. It is generally known he spends most of his spare time seated before his personal computer in his tiny condo exchanging important messages with strangers ten thousand miles away—messages like, "How's your weather?" I believe Judd is convinced if the Messiah ever returns it will be via Microsoft.

I approached him with a request for info on the Fish and Wildlife Service and particularly their Division of Law Enforcement.

"Government agency?" he asked.

"That's right. Department of the Interior."

"No problem. What do you want to know?"

"What laws are being enforced. What are the penalties if the laws are broken. Prison sentences? Dollar amounts of losses and fines after convictions—if they're available. Number of investigators assigned. The areas most active in criminal activities, whatever they may be. I'm starting from scratch on this. I need anything and everything."

"No problem," he said. "You want names? Addresses?"

"Sure," I told him. "Especially the bad guys."

"They can run but they can't hide," he said. "When do you need this stuff?"

"A week," I said. "Sooner if possible."

"No problem," he said, turned to his keyboard, and began typing.

I left him, wishing I could say "No problem" to every task confronting me.

Back in my very own tomb I phoned Parrots Unlimited and was answered by a male voice I could not identify. I thought I detected a slight foreign accent—Spanish? Portuguese? Icelandic?—but I could not be certain.

"May I speak to Mr. Watrous, please," I said politely.

"He's busy," he said gruffly. "To what does this concern about?"

Beautiful syntax, no?

"I purchased a parrot from him recently," I said, "and the poor bird appears to be molting at a ferocious rate."

"Yeah?" he said. "Okay, hang on; I'll get him."

A moment later Binky picked up. " 'Lo?" he said warily.

"Greetings, son," I said cheerily. "Archy here."

"Shh," he said.

"What do you mean shh?" I said indignantly. "I'm not exactly screaming you know."

"People are lurking," he said darkly.

"Ah. New employees?"

"A married couple. Youngish. Definitely not upper drawer. They lurk."

"Surely they know something about parrots."

"Mucho. Did you know that parrots can die of the fumes from an overheated nonstick frying pan?"

"Why, no," I said, "I don't know that and shall do my very best to forget it. These new people—hostile, would you say?"

"Well, maybe not hostile but, uh, watchful."

"Mistrustful?"

"That's the word, Archy," he said gratefully. "Bridget and I are thinking of deserting the ship."

"Binky, don't do that," I said hastily. "I'm depending on you."

"You are?"

"Absolutely. This is a very important discreet inquiry and you're playing a major role. I want you to observe everything happening at Parrots Unlimited and give me the benefit of your wise perceptions. You've done such a splendid job so far as an investigator and it's of vital importance you continue."

"Well," he said, his voice oozing hubris, "I guess I can stick it out for a while."

"Good man," I said. "Watch, listen, and report. By the way, how are you and Bridget coming along with your theatrical career?"

"A success!" he cried. "We've been invited to perform in three more nursing homes. Our reputation is spreading."

"I can imagine," I said. "Tell me, Binky, do you have a name for your act?"

"Oh yes," he said, preening. "We call ourselves The Busy B's. Bridget and Binky. Get it?"

"I do," I said. "Unfortunately."

I hung up congratulating myself on my fortitude. The Monday tasks I had set were humming along briskly and I resolutely continued. I phoned Lolly Spindrift at his newspaper and found him in an uncharacteristically downbeat mood.

"What's wrong, pal?" I asked.

"Another funeral," he said dully. "I don't know how many more of these I can take. Two this month. About twenty during the past year."

"Close friends?"

"All of them. Not fun, sweetie."

"What time is the funeral?"

"Twelve-thirty."

"Lol, I'm heading for the Pelican Club. I'm not suggesting lunch but why don't you meet me at the bar for a cognac. It will help see you through."

"Yes," he said immediately. "I can use it."

Half an hour later Spindrift and I were seated at the Pelican mahogany. He was working on a double Rémy Martin and I was sipping a tall g&t. Lolly is a small, birdlike chap who usually flashes a chirpy wit. But now he looked wrung out and pinned up to dry. It was obvious sorrow had brought him low; he seemed shrunken and his face was so wrenched I reckoned he was trying hard not to weep.

We drank in silence for a while because I am not very good in the sympathy department. I mean I can feel it and ordinarily I'm glib, but when I try to commiserate it comes out so soppy I can't believe the words are mine.

Finally Lolly perked up and asked, "Why did you phone me, luv?"

"It's not important. It can wait."

"No, no; tell me. Get my mind off the temptation to take a long walk on a short pier."

"The item you wrote yesterday about the bird store manager . . . Ricardo Chrisling, right?"

"Uh-huh. I figured you'd pick up on it since you asked me about him a week or so ago."

"Sparking about is he?"

"Definitely. Hither, thither, and yon–ish. And very successfully from what I hear. He's a handsome devil."

"Your last comment, '. . . his heart belongs elsewhere.' What did you mean by that? He's gay?"

Lol gave me a wan smile. "Wish he was. No, I think the lad is straight. I keep picking up these hints he has a grand passion."

"What kind of hints?"

"Nothing much really. Weekly orders from a florist delivered to his apartment. Late-night comings and goings, also at his place. A diamond choker bought on Worth Avenue. Things like that, all indicating he may be smitten. No solid evidence, Archy, but you know if I waited for definite proof I'd have to close up shop and get in another line of business. Listen, dear, I've got to dash to the funeral. Can't be late, you know. You'll be on time for mine, won't you?"

I nodded, not trusting myself to speak.

"Thanks for the jolt. Just what I needed. I'll get through it now without blubbering. Keep in touch."

"You betcha," I said.

"And now you owe me one," he said, regaining his sauce.

"Acknowledged," I said.

We shook hands. I don't know why but I was glad we did. Then he departed, squaring his narrow shoulders and lifting his chin. Challenging life—and death.

21

The dining area was jammed with the luncheon crowd and so I remained at the bar. The next time Priscilla appeared to pick up an order of drinks I asked her to victual me in situ. "Something light," I told her.

"Like what?" she said. "A double cheeseburger with home fries?"

I sighed. "It's so hard to get good help these days. Try again but not quite so calorific."

"How about a crock of onion soup and a grilled chicken sandwich?"

"Perfect. By the way," I added faux casually, "have you seen Connie around lately?"

"Ask me no questions and I'll tell you no lies."

"What a brilliant bon mot," I said. "Original?"

"Keep it up, buster," she said, "and there'll be more in your soup than onions." Then she looked at me pityingly. "When are you two going to sign a truce?"

"I'm willing," I said. "Tell her that."

"*You* tell her that, Romeo," she said, and chasséd away.

I was consuming my spartan lunch and reviewing my brief conversation with Lolly Spindrift when a sly thought slid into the McNally cranium. If Ricardo Chrisling actually had an unknown inamorata—and Lol is usually on target when ferreting out private affairs of the heart—could it possibly be Julia Gottschalk, or Judith, or perhaps both, the moled and the moleless? Hey, why not? They were not blood relatives; the twins were attractive ladies; he was a "handsome devil." What a *ménage à trois* that would be!

I was amused by the idea until sobered by a second thought. If such a relationship existed, it might hold the motive for the slaying of Hiram Gottschalk. Three conspirators linked by passion, greed, and amorality. A fanciful plot? Of course. But completely illogical? I didn't think so.

I was in a gouty mood when I finished my solitary lunch. Although I had been active that morning I had the painful notion I was spinning my wheels—or even slowly in reverse. All my initiatives seemed to result in more questions than answers. At the moment I could think of nothing to do but plod on and I am not by nature a plodder, fancying myself more Captain Ahab than Bartleby.

I called the Gottschalk home from the pay phone at the Pelican Club. Mei Lee answered and, after identifying myself and inquiring as to her health ("Ver' happy"), I asked to speak to Peter. It was at least three minutes before he came on the line.

"Hullo?" he said in a voice so hollow it seemed to reverberate.

"Hi, Peter," I said with all the cheer I could muster. "Archy McNally. How're you doing?"

"Surviving," he said. "I think. Why are you calling?"

Good question. I had no good answer.

"I have nothing to do," I said lightly, "and thought we might waste some time together. Gorgeous day."

"I got no wheels," he said. "I'm a prisoner."

"Why don't I pick you up," I suggested. "Take a drive. Go somewhere. Even a prisoner is entitled to fresh air occasionally."

"Yeah," he said dispiritedly. "Go where?"

"How about my place?" I said, the best I could come up with. "I've been to your home but you've never been to mine."

"I don't know. I'm in a lousy mood. Down."

"Give me a chance," I urged. "Maybe I can bring you up. You like dogs?"

"Dogs? They're okay I guess. We never had one. Just birds."

"Well, my family has a new pooch. A real character. You've got to meet him."

He wasn't wildly enthusiastic. "If you say so. You'll come by?"

"Sure. Half hour or so."

"Got anything to drink at your place?"

"Of course," I said. In for a penny, in for a pound.

"I haven't showered or shaved in two days," he reported in his sunken voice. "Do I have to clean up?"

"Nah," I said. "Come as you are." I sounded giggly even to myself but he made no response, just hung up and left me wondering exactly what I was doing—and why.

He was waiting for me when I pulled in to the Gottschalks' slated driveway and he was as cruddy as he had warned: unshaven, hair a snarl, jeans and T-shirt wrinkled and soiled. And he exuded an effluvium I don't wish to describe in detail since you may be reading this after having recently dined. I shall only say I was happy I was driving an open car and wished for a more vigorous breeze.

He was singularly uncommunicative during our trip to the McNally manse, answering questions with monosyllables and offering no comments of his own. He seemed oblivious to his surroundings, staring straight ahead with unseeing eyes. I thought him lost in a dark world where only he existed, in pain and confusion.

When I parked on our turnaround he made no effort to get out of the Miata, just sat there looking about with those dulled eyes. I could discern no reactions whatsoever.

"You live here?" he said.

"I do indeed," I told him. "The house is Tudor manqué but comfortable."

"Nice," he said—his first expression of an opinion. It gave me hope.

"Suppose I get us some refreshment," I offered. "Gin and tonics?"

"Vodka," he said flatly. "Just vodka."

I went into the kitchen, hoping he'd still be present when I returned. I built both of us heavily watered vodkas on the rocks and brought them outside. He was standing alongside the car, hanging on to the opened door as if he feared if he relaxed his grip he might collapse. I handed him a drink and he took a gulp, closing his eyes.

"Nice," he said again. "Yvonne won't give me anything. She's locked up our liquor supply. Bitch!"

His virulence shocked me.

"And all the others!" he added just as venomously.

I didn't know how to respond to such hostility—except to change the subject. "How about taking a stroll about the grounds?" I said. "Then I'll show you the house."

"No," he said.

A stalemate was avoided when Hobo came trotting around the corner of the garage and padded up to us, tail wagging.

"This is Hobo," I said. "The latest addition to the McNally household."

I reached down to stroke the dog's head. He moved to Gottschalk, took one sniff, and turned away. I didn't blame him.

"Does he bite?" Peter asked.

"Hasn't yet," I said cheerfully.

"How about another drink?" he said, holding out his emptied tumbler. "No water this time."

This strained encounter, I realized, was getting precisely nowhere, and if he continued to drink it could only deteriorate further.

"Peter," I said, "may I speak to you as a Dutch uncle?"

"A what?"

"Talk bluntly," I said impatiently. "The hard truth. I think you're ill."

He swiveled his head sharply to stare at me.

"You've got a brain," I said, ready now to tell him what I had to. "For your own sake, man, use it. You know you're not acting normally. Wild mood swings. Periods of euphoria alternating with fits of awful depression when you think suicide is the only way out. And sudden violent urges. You're out of control and you know it."

He made a choky sound, face contorted. He dropped his tumbler onto the gravel. It shattered. Then he reached for me, hands clawing. I didn't know whether he intended to throttle me, rip the tongue from my head, or merely cuff me until my fillings loosened.

But he never accomplished his attack. Hobo had been lying at our feet, curled up but awake and watchful. When Peter made his threatening move the dog bounced upright and stood braced, legs stiff. His fangs were bared and basso profundo growls came rumbling from his throat.

Peter dropped his arms immediately. He slumped and slowly, slowly slipped onto the gravel and broken glass. He sat bent over, legs outstretched, head lowered to his chest.

I knelt beside him, fearing to touch.

"Peter?" I said.

"Sure," he said in a voice so faint I could hardly make it out. "I'm sick. I know it."

Perhaps I should have been saddened by this muttered admission but I was elated. I hoped it was the first step toward recovery or at least amelioration of his condition. He finally raised his head and I helped him to his feet and propped him against the side of the car. His face was bleached and he clasped his hands in a futile effort to conceal his tremors.

"Vodka?" he croaked hopefully.

"No," I said firmly, "not from me. Peter, I'm not going to tell you what ails you is no worse than an ingrown toenail. You and I realize it's more serious than that. But help is available if you're willing to accept it. I know a wonderful doctor, an older woman, who's had a lot of success treating illnesses like yours. She's a marvelous diagnostician—and honest; if she feels she cannot aid you she'll recommend someone who can. Will you go see her?"

He nodded.

"Good man," I said. "I'm going to give you her name, address, and phone number. Then it's up to you. I've done all I can. It's your life we're talking about. You understand?"

He nodded again. "Get in the car," I commanded, "before Hobo decides to gnaw on your shin."

I carried my empty glass back to the kitchen and took a moment to jot Dr. Gussie Pearlberg's name, address, and phone number on a scrap torn from a brown paper bag. I went back outside to find Peter seated in the Miata, the door latched. I handed him the scrawled information. He didn't glance at it, just grasped it tightly.

"Tell her I recommended you see her," I advised.

"You really think she can help me?" he said.

"Guaranteed," I said, deciding it was a moment requiring positivism.

"Lord," he breathed: possibly the world's shortest prayer.

I drove him home. He was silent and so was I, fearing any additional advice might turn him off. For instance, I wanted to tell him to lay off the booze and funny cigarettes, but I figured I had played the guru enough for one day.

I exited the car when we arrived at his place, thinking he might need assistance in walking. But he navigated steadily enough, still gripping the scrap of paper I had given him.

"You'll call her?" I asked.

"Sure," he said. "Soon as I get inside."

"I'm not going to ask for a promise or any nonsense like that," I said. "It's your decision."

He took a deep breath. "Thank you," he said. It came out tentatively, almost like a foreign phrase, as if he had never before said, "Thank you."

He went indoors. I returned to my steed and was about to vault into the saddle when the blue M-B coupe came purring into the driveway. I waited and watched as the twins popped out. Both were clad in outfits I deemed outlandish. I had never seen such a surfeit of vinyl, gauze, leather, and fur. Their costumes may have been fashionable but style was lacking.

They came bopping up to me, laughing, each brandishing a corked bottle of Mumm Cordon Rouge. Affixed to the neck of each bottle was a purple orchid, now slightly wilted.

"Look what we've got," one shouted happily.

"A private trunk show," the other chortled. "And bottles of bubbly were the favors. Isn't that fabulous?"

"It is indeed," I agreed. "I know you'll treasure them unopened as mementos for years to come. And to whom, pray, am I speaking? Mike One and Mike Two just won't cut the mustard anymore."

"I'm Judith," one of them claimed.

"Ah, yes," I said, remembering the abdominal mole revealed by her bikini during our brief session on the beach. "And so," I said to the other, "by process of elimination you must be Julia."

"I was the last time I looked," she said, and the two dissolved in a burst of senseless giggles.

"Got to run," Judith said. "Have some bubbles and prepare for the evening's festivities. A charity bash, isn't it, Julia?"

"Something," her sister said. "Somewhere. Hoity-toity I suspect. We must remember to wear panties."

They had another fit of the tee-hees and I thought they were a bit old for this schoolgirlish behavior. I didn't think they were tiddly—but one never knows, do one?

They paused long enough for each to give me a swift peck on the cheek. Then they scampered up to the doorway, flourishing their bottles. I hoped they would not share their bounty with their brother.

But that wasn't the only thing to disconcert me. When they turned away I noted the twin who identified herself as Julia had a small black mole on the back of her left shoulder. There was no mistaking it. She was wearing a strapless cocktail dress, all froufrou, and the mole was obvious.

So both sisters had a mole, identical in size, shape, and color. Significant? Of course not! I laughed with delight because it was a final example of Hiram Gottschalk's quirky sense of humor. "One of them has a mole," he had told me, to pique my interest and set in motion an inquiry that would have amused him.

What an eccentric he was! He may have had faults that led to his death but no one with his taste for harmless mischief should be murdered. That's stupid, isn't it? I know it is but it's the way I feel.

22

The moment I arrived home I went into the pantry to fetch a dustpan. I returned to our driveway, crouched and began picking shards of Peter's broken glass from the gravel. I didn't want Hobo cutting his pads. The hero himself emerged from his house and came wandering over to watch me at work.

"I want to thank you for your efforts on my behalf," I told him. "You behaved admirably."

His tail thumped once: sufficient acknowledgment.

I smoothed the gravel, dumped the glass into one of our trash cans, and went back inside. I judged it too late for an ocean swim and so I spent the remainder of the afternoon detailing the day's activities in my journal. I labored diligently and paused only to join my parents for the family cocktail hour.

After dinner I returned to my desk and completed my scribbling. I sat back and realized I was in a melancholy mood. Definitely an attack of the mopes. I realized it had nothing to do with the Gottschalk case. It had to do with a long-haired, bouncy lady who refused to phone and suggest a reconciliation.

And the worst part of it, the absolute *worst*, was that I could not remember what our disagreement was about. Maddening! Connie didn't call and I wouldn't. Of course it was an ego thing; I admit it. I could not endure crawling, supplicating. I was determined to remain upright, stern, and righteous no matter how much suffering it might cause her.

And so I went to bed, suffering.

I awoke the next morning still assailed by the blue devils. I was tempted to stay in bed for the remainder of my worldly existence, to be fed mush by a hired aide who might occasionally change tapes from my collection of Edith Piaf recordings.

Complete lunacy of course, and I knew it was as I hauled myself groaning out of the sack and stumbled back to reality. I staggered through the morning drill and clumped downstairs to the kitchen, where I found Jamie Olson gumming his decrepit briar and nursing a mug of black coffee.

He seemed to be as much a victim of the megrims as I, for all we exchanged was a listless nod. I fixed myself a meager breakfast of cran juice, a toasted (and buttered) onion bagel, and a cup of black jamoke. We sat across the table from each other, and it was a long time before our glum silence was broken.

"Eddie Wong," Jamie said finally.

I looked up. "Who?" I asked.

"Eddie Wong," he repeated. "I asked him about the staff at the Gottschalks' like you wanted."

"Oh yes," I said. "Sure. Got and Mei Lee. Eddie told you they weren't happy there."

"Yep. Eddie called me yesterday. They left. The Lees. Quit."

"Did they? Better jobs?"

"Eddie didn't know. Says they just took off. Packed up their wok and vamoosed."

"No reason?"

Jamie shrugged.

"Have they been replaced?"

"Yep. A family. Man, woman, two young kids. Spanish-speaking, Eddie Wong says. Called 'em furriners."

"Aren't we all?" I said. "Thank you for the info, Jamie."

I finished my scanty breakfast, slipped him the usual pourboire, and set off for the office wondering what significance the change of staff at the Gottschalk home might have. I doubted it was meaningful but I have come to realize even the smallest details sometimes prove important.

I dimly recall a homicide case of many years ago. A husband took his wife to Niagara Falls by train to celebrate a tenth anniversary at the place where they had enjoyed their honeymoon. The wife fell into the river and was swept to her death. A tragic accident, the police decided—until they discovered the husband had purchased one round-trip ticket and one one-way ticket.

Moral: If you're planning murder, don't economize.

By the time I arrived at my orifice (why do I keep spelling it that way?) at the McNally Building, I was beginning to emerge from my funk and hoped I might live to see the turn of the century and perhaps even learn to play the sweet potato. (I have already mastered the kazoo.)

I was lighting my first ciggie of the day when I heard a respectful knock on my locker door. Rare. *Very* rare. Visitors are usually announced and fellow employees ordinarily come barging in, reckoning their work is of more moment to McNally & Son than mine. How right they are.

I opened the door to greet Judd Wilkins. He appeared as loopy as ever, so physically relaxed I wouldn't have been a bit surprised if he suddenly melted into a boneless heap on the floor.

"Hi, Judd," I said. "Come in and make yourself comfortable in my coffin—if such a thing is possible."

"Nah," he said. "This won't take long and I've got to get back to my machinery. One of the partners wants a rundown on autoworkers who have sued because they were fired for excessive flatulence on the assembly line. That's interesting, isn't it?"

"Not very," I said. "And I wish you hadn't mentioned it."

"Anyway," he went on, "what you asked about—the Fish and Wildlife Service and their Division of Law Enforcement—I can't find all their publications on line but they're available in print. Like five pounds of books, pamphlets, laws, regulations, international treaties, and so forth. Is that what you want?"

"Good lord, no!" I said.

"Didn't think so," he said. "I could get it all from other sources but the printout would fill your office."

"A paperback book would fill this office. Any suggestions, Judd?"

"No problem," he said. "We're tied into nets that can provide any info you want—for a price of course. If you could be more specific, tell me exactly what you need, I could query the nets. Even bulletin boards. If the stuff exists I can download it. But I'll need a few words or a phrase—the shorter the better—to get results."

My mind worked at blinding speed. No? Will you accept "quickly"?

"Parrots," I said.

He looked at me with his dreamy eyes. "Parrots?"

"Parrots," I repeated firmly. "Those squawky, ill-tempered birds who befoul their cages, bite friends and strangers, and recite verses by Edgar Guest. Where do these creatures come from? Are there parrot farms? More importantly, is there a trade, possibly illicit, in rare species? Are parrots being smuggled across our borders along with cocaine and counterfeit Calvin Klein underwear? In other words, is jiggery-pokery going on?"

He wasn't at all flummoxed by my outrageous requests. "No problem," he said. "If it's out there, you've got it."

He departed abruptly. I confess his technological skills humbled me. He was not a nerd, definitely not, but a member of a totally new generation with which I had little in common. I suffered a small pang of *Weltschmerz,* wondering when the world had changed and why I hadn't changed along with it.

I had plans for that Tuesday, activities which might possibly help unsnarl some of the tangles of the Gottschalk homicide. For instance, I hoped to persuade my father to reveal to me the details of the decedent's will. I could think of no good reason why *mein papa* would refuse to divulge this information, since the testament would soon be filed for probate and become public knowledge.

I was about to call his office, begging a few moments of his valuable time, when my own phone rang. The caller was Sgt. Al Rogoff.

"I'm coming over," he said without preamble.

"You shall be welcome of course," I said. "But may I inquire as to the purpose of your visit. Is anything wrong?"

"Wrong?" he said with a brittle laugh. "What could possibly go wrong in this best of all possible worlds? You told me that."

"Never," I said. "You're confusing me with Dr. Pangloss."

"Whatever," he said. "See you in twenty minutes or so." And he hung up.

A half hour later he was occupying the one folding steel chair I'm able to offer guests. It's alongside my desk and excruciatingly uncomfortable, especially to one of Rogoff's bulk. He overflows it and every time I see him planted there I expect the steel to buckle at any moment.

He took out his fat little notebook, stuffed with scraps of paper and bound with a thick rubber band. That alerted me. Al rarely makes notes. When he does I know he considers the matter of sufficient import to warrant a written record.

"Emma Gompertz and Anthony Sutcliffe," he said tonelessly. "They've been located."

"That's a relief," I said.

His face was expressionless. "Not really. They're dead. Their bodies were found in the Everglades early this morning. Both had been shot through the back of the head. Assassinations. Both have been positively ID'd."

I closed my eyes. I couldn't speak.

"It came over the wire about two hours ago," the sergeant went on. "I called but the usual jurisdiction squabble is going on. They don't yet know if the bodies were found in Dade or Broward County. Who handles it? Which sheriff's office? Or the state troopers? The FBI has an oar in too. It'll all get straightened out eventually and whoever takes over will trace Sutcliffe and Gompertz back to West Palm Beach. But I want to stay ahead of the curve and offer what I have as soon as possible. You agree?"

I nodded.

"But I need to know more about them. You think their murders might have a connection with the Hiram Gottschalk homicide?"

"I do," I said, my voice sounding to me like a weak croak.

"They worked as clerks in Parrots Unlimited?"

"Correct."

"How did they get along with the late owner?"

"Fine, as far as I know."

"And how did they get along with the new manager, Ricardo Chrisling?"

"Apparently there was enmity there. He fired Tony, and Emma quit in sympathy."

"The two lived together?"

"Yes."

"Married?"

"I doubt it."

"Do you know what the disagreement was about—the hostility between Chrisling and Sutcliffe?"

"No, I don't know, Al." He had asked me if I *knew* and I didn't. If he had asked me what I suspected I would have told him.

"Do you know of anyone else who might have a reason to abduct and kill Gompertz and Sutcliffe?"

"No, I don't," I said angrily. "They were nice, pleasant kids."

"Kids?"

"Anyone younger than I is a kid."

His smile was bleak. "Yeah, me too. What about the relations between the victims and the rest of the Gottschalk tribe: Peter, the twins, the housekeeper?"

"Their relations? I'd judge they were friendly but distant. Gompertz and Sutcliffe were at the party celebrating the twins' return from a European trip. But all the employees of Parrots Unlimited were invited. Nothing special there."

"What was your take on Sutcliffe and Gompertz. Druggies?"

"No. As I told you, they were just two nice, pleasant kids."

"You don't get a bullet in the back of the head for being a nice, pleasant kid."

The sergeant had been making brief notes as I answered his questions. Now he paused and looked up. "How do you know Chrisling fired Tony Sutcliffe?"

"Binky Watrous told me."

Rogoff was astounded. "Binky Watrous? The Village Idiot? How did he know?"

"He works part-time at Parrots Unlimited."

"Watrous *works*? Since when? I thought all he does is chase centerfolds. It's said he won't go out with a woman unless she's got staples in her belly. How come he's got a job at Parrots Unlimited?"

"I finagled it," I admitted. "After Gottschalk claimed his life was threatened, I decided I wanted an undercover operative in the store."

"Binky is an experienced undercover operative all right," Al said. "Under the blanket and under the sheet. Did he come up with anything?"

"He certainly did," I said loyally. "Most of what I've told you during this rigorous interrogation is the result of Binky's observations."

"I wish you had told me he was working there."

"It slipped my mind."

"Sometimes I think your entire mind has slipped. Is he still working at Parrots Unlimited?"

"As far as I know."

"Good. Keep him there. Has he told you anything else you haven't had the decency to reveal to me?"

"Nothing of any importance."

"Let me be the judge of that."

"After Sutcliffe and Gompertz left, Ricardo Chrisling hired a married couple to take their places. Binky doesn't like them."

"Oh? Why not?"

"He says they lurk."

The sergeant sighed. "They lurk," he repeated. "Whenever I get involved in one of your discreet inquiries it turns out to be fruitcake time."

"Al, is it okay if I tell Binky about the murders of Gompertz and Sutcliffe?"

He thought a moment. "I don't see why not," he said finally. "It'll be on the radio and TV tonight and in the papers tomorrow."

"Binky will be devastated," I said. "He and Bridget were pals of Emma and Tony."

"Who's Bridget?"

"Bridget Houlihan, a colleen who also works at Parrots Unlimited. She and Binky have an *in vivo* romance. And they have a theatrical act. Binky does birdcalls while Bridget accompanies him on the tambourine."

Rogoff stared at me, then cast his eyes heavenward. "Why hast thou forsaken me?" he inquired plaintively.

23

My quandary now, while not intractable, was troubling: How was I to inform Binky of the deaths of Tony and Emma? A phone call would have been unfeeling—don't you agree? The distressing news had to be delivered in person. Over lunch? And if so, before or after the food was served? A silly predicament, I admit, but important to me. I finally decided there was no completely satisfying solution to such a trying problem.

I had a vague recollection, possibly mistaken, that Binky had told me he didn't clean birdcages on Tuesdays. But even if true, his work schedule may have been revised by the new manager. In any event I thought it best to phone him first at his home. My call was answered by the Watrous houseman.

"Master Binky is not available at present," he informed me in sepulchral tones. "You may reach him at his office."

I thanked him and hung up much bemused by "his office" and wondering if Binky had convinced the Duchess he had become a tycoon of birdland. I then phoned Parrots Unlimited and found him there.

"Lunch?" I suggested.

"Uh," he said.

"What does that mean—'uh'?"

"Well, we have to ask when we can leave and for how long."

"Oh-oh," I said. "Boot camp?"

"Something like that."

"I'm inviting you and Bridget to lunch. See if you can finagle it. I'll hang on."

It must have taken almost five minutes but eventually he came back on the line.

"All right," he said breathlessly. "Bridget and I can get out together for lunch."

"For how long?"

"Half an hour."

"Beautiful," I said. "Where?"

"There's a pizza joint across the street we go to."

"Fine. What's it called?"

"The Pizza Joint."

"Love it," I said. "Back to basics. Twelve-thirty?"

"Okay," he said hastily, and disconnected. I thought he sounded distraught, and what I had to say at lunch wasn't going to help.

Sadness does not ordinarily play a major role in my life. I mean I am by nature a cheery bloke, always looking for rainbows during drizzles. And the task of conveying bad news is not one I relish. But this was something I had to do, and I had no idea of how to handle it other than blurt out the truth. One can't tenderize death, can one?

So there we were—Bridget, Binky, and your rattled scribe seated at a Formica table awaiting the arrival of our King Kong Special (cheese, eggplant, sausage, anchovies, and button mushrooms), when I told them.

"I'm afraid I am the bearer of bad news," I plunged. "Emma Gompertz and Anthony Sutcliffe are dead. Their bodies were found early this morning in the Everglades. Both had been murdered."

They stared at me. "You're kidding," Binky said with a sick smile.

I was infuriated by his comment, implying I would joke about such a tragedy. Then I realized he was stunned by my disclosure and his reaction was an attempt to deny reality.

"It will be on radio and TV tonight," I went on. "And in the newspapers tomorrow. They were killed by gunshots to the head."

I had expected Bridget to dissolve and Binky to comfort her. I should have known better. It was he who collapsed, hunching over trying to stay a sob. Bridget put an arm about him, hugged him close, kept murmuring, "There, there." What a brave lass she was!

Binky finally regained control and wiped his bleary eyes with a paper napkin. Our King Kong Special arrived at that moment and we said nothing as we began scarfing, gulping beers to sluice down the spiced mélange. I wondered if tragic news increases hunger: a need to eat and postpone mortality. It's a concept much too recondite for me to understand. But why are wakes such an enduring tradition?

"What should we do, Archy?" Bridget said finally. "Quit?"

"Absolutely not," I said firmly. "Continue working at Parrots Unlimited. I'm sure the police will come around asking questions. Answer them honestly."

Binky glanced up. "It's not right," he said stoutly. "It's just not right. Emma and Tony were good people."

"Of course they were," I agreed. "And that's why you and Bridget must be on the qv. Not only to help solve this horrendous crime but to watch your own backs. Be careful. More than that, be cautious. As Dr. Doyle might say, 'Evil is afoot.' "

Bridget looked at me. "You think the murders of Emma and Tony have something to do with the death of Mr. Gottschalk?"

She asked me that, not Binky. She was, I realized, smarter than he. But then who isn't?

"Yes, I believe so," I told her.

"Are Binky and I in danger?"

"Possibly," I said. "Don't take chances. Look about. Lock and bolt doors. And windows. Reject the approach of strangers. Very antisocial but necessary."

"Archy," she said, "will all this be cleared up?"

"Of course it shall," I said heartily. "Just a question of time. And sooner rather than later," I added.

I think I convinced them. Oh, if I had only convinced myself.

On occasion I have been accused of being a devious lad—justifiably I might add. I do have a taste for the Machiavellian and sometimes indulge in such conduct even when not necessary, simply to keep in practice. During the drive back to the McNally Building I concocted a cunning stratagem that might or might not yield results but was certainly worth a try.

The moment I was in my office I got on the horn to Lolly Spindrift. We exchanged rude greetings. Of course I made no reference to the funeral he had attended the previous day.

"Lol," I said, "I owe you one and it's payola time."

"Goody," he said. "What have you got for me?"

"Early this morning the bodies of a young couple were found in the Everglades. Both had been shot to death. I'm sure your news desk has the story by now."

"So why are you telling me?"

"Because the victims were Emma Gompertz and Anthony Sutcliffe, employees of Parrots Unlimited, the West Palm bird store presently managed by Ricardo Chrisling. He was, you'll recall, the subject of your recent item and our more recent conversation."

I heard his sudden intake of breath. "And Parrots Unlimited was formerly owned by Hiram Gottschalk who himself was stabbed to death."

"You've got it," I said.

"You believe there's a connection between the three murders?"

"I do believe."

He sighed. "It's not my cup of oolong, sweetie, but I'll report it to the news desk. They'll be delighted with the local angle. It should earn me some brownie points."

"That's why I called."

"Tell me something, luv: What's your edge on all this?"

"I'm a troublemaker," I told him. "I want to cause trouble for the killer, whoever he, she, or they may be. I want them to know the law is aware something dreadful is going on at Parrots Unlimited."

Spindrift laughed. "What a sneaky chap you are!"

"You have no idea how sneaky I can be when it's called for."

"Then it's part of one of your discreet inquiries, I presume."

"You presume correctly."

"I hope you'll scurry to me with all the gory details when it's over."

"Lolly, you'll be the first to know," I lied cheerfully.

My second call was to my father's office for I was still intent on learning the details of Hiram Gottschalk's will. I was answered by Mrs. Trelawney, pop's antiquated (and raunchy) private secretary. She reported the master had left for a luncheon conference with a commercial client and did not expect to return that afternoon.

After that I had nothing to do but brood, trying to sort out all the ramifications of the Gottschalk puzzle. Meanwhile I smoked two cigarettes and resolved never to light another until Connie called. It was liable to be an effective vow to ensure eternal withdrawal.

Ms. Garcia didn't phone but Dr. Gussie Pearlberg did.

"I can't talk long, dollink," she said briskly. "Busy, busy, busy. But I wanted you to know your friend came in. Peter Gottschalk."

"Not quite a friend," I said cautiously. "More of an acquaintance."

"A very meshuga acquaintance. Poor boy. I now believe I was right: he is manic-depressive. I have sent him to a good man who specializes in such things. This condition can be controlled with proper medication and frequent monitoring. That is the first thing to be done. But also Peter has another problem and this might not be so easy to solve. You understand?"

"A psychiatric problem?" I ventured.

"I cannot discuss it," she said severely. "But after his manic-depression is stabilized he has promised to return to me and talk some more. I think I can help him. I am calling to tell you what I told him. He is not to drink alcohol or use drugs if he expects his condition to improve. I want you to impress that on him. Definitely no alcohol and no drugs."

"Dr. Gussie," I protested, "I see him infrequently. I am not his keeper."

"But you'll do what you can?"

"Of course. I know you can't go into details but could you give me a hint of the nature of Peter's psychiatric problem?"

Her laugh was short and harsh. "Family," she said. "What else?"

That did it. I had heard enough wretchedness for one day and needed a respite from the gloom. I drove home, roughhoused with Hobo for ten minutes, and left him exhausted while I went upstairs to change into swimming togs: Speedo trunks in such a virulent orange I was sure to be spotted by a rescuing helicopter if I collapsed during my two-mile wallow.

The sea was delightfully warm and calm. I vary my swimming techniques: crawl, breaststroke, and backstroke. Of the three I prefer the second because it sounds so nice. I emerged from my dunk with eyes smarting from the salt but feeling much relaxed and happy. I had time for a short nap before dressing for the family cocktail hour.

Dinner that evening was a feast of hors d'oeuvres with no main dish. We had marinated grilled scallops wrapped in bacon, Oriental barbecued chicken wings, and tiny meatballs in a curry sauce. The salad was endives (my favorite) with a raspberry vinaigrette dressing. Father and I had Pouilly-Fumé. It was an okay wine, not great but okay. Mother had her usual glass of sauterne. It was her preference but I thought it similar to drinking Yoo-Hoo with oysters.

I went upstairs to my journal after dinner and spent an hour recording the day's events relating to the murder of Hiram Gottschalk. Finished, I reviewed my notes and decided it was time to question my father. "Beard the lion in his den" isn't quite an apt expression but it comes close.

If you must know the truth (and I presume you *must,*) I find my father a rather intimidating man. It is simply part of his nature and doesn't diminish my love for him. But I confess I approach our one-on-ones with some trepidation, fearing I may say something or do something to convince him his male offspring is a twerp nonpareil.

The door to his study was firmly closed and I overcame my apprehension sufficiently to rap the portal smartly. I heard his "Come in," and entered to find him settled behind his magisterial desk and, as usual, smoking one of his silver-banded James Upshall pipes. Also as usual, there was a glass of port on his desk blotter alongside an open book. I recognized it as a leather-bound volume from his set of Charles

Dickens. From its bulk I guessed it to be *Little Dorrit* and wished him the best of luck.

"Father," I said, "may I speak to you for a moment?"

He nodded but didn't ask me to be seated. It's his way of telling me to keep it brief.

"It concerns my inquiry into the murder of Hiram Gottschalk," I started. "I feel I am making progress, but slowly, and it might help if you would tell me the major beneficiaries in Mr. Gottschalk's will."

He listened to my request gravely. But if I had mentioned I had a hangnail he would have listened just as gravely. Levity was foreign to him. He thought life a very serious matter indeed, and sometimes I wondered if my own frivolousness was a revolt against the pater's sobriety. He was not a dull man, you understand, but lordy he was earnest. What a scoutmaster he would have made! I could picture him demonstrating how to start a fire by rubbing two dry sticks together to a group of tenderfeet all of whom carried Zippo lighters.

"I see no reason to withhold that information," he said finally. "It will soon become a matter of public knowledge. It is an odd testament but as I told you, from the beginning I found Mr. Gottschalk a rather eccentric gentleman. But of course his wishes had to be respected."

"Of course," I said, and waited patiently.

24

"There are a number of minor bequests," he began. "To old friends, employees, distant relatives, and members of his domestic staff. His home with its furnishings is left to Yvonne Chrisling, his housekeeper. The store, Parrots Unlimited, and the not inconsiderable plot of land on which it is located go to Ricardo Chrisling. The remainder of his assets are to be divided into three equal shares to his son Peter and twin daughters Judith and Julia." He paused to give me a chilly smile. "All this after the payment of estate taxes of course."

"Will there be much left after the tax?"

"A great deal," he said briefly. "If his children invest their inheritance wisely it should support them comfortably for the remainder of their lives."

"Sir, you mentioned minor bequests to his domestic staff. His chef and maid, Got and Mei Lee, have recently left the Gottschalk household. Will their leaving affect their legacy?"

"No."

"You also mentioned bequests to his employees. Father, have you listened to the local news on radio or TV tonight?"

"I have not. Why do you ask?"

"The bodies of a young couple, former employees of Parrots Unlimited, were found in the Everglades. Both had been murdered, shot to death at close range in what was apparently an assassination-type slaying."

He stared at me, his expression growing increasingly bleak. "You believe there is a connection between their deaths and the murder of our client?"

"Yes, sir, I believe that—and so does Sergeant Rogoff."

He was silent a few moments while he went into his mulling mode, mentally masticating information received, comparing it to past experience, essaying various explanations and hypotheses, and eventually arriving at his considered judgment. I would never dare attempt to hurry this process. It would be like urging a sphinx to get his rear in gear.

"Archy," he said at long last, "are you suggesting this unfortunate couple may have been slain because they were included in Mr. Gottschalk's will? If so, I believe you are mistaken. Their bequests are five thousand each. People are not murdered for that sum."

"They've been killed for less," I said tartly. "But no, I do not believe they were shot because of their inclusion in our client's will. I doubt if their killers were even aware of it. I think another motive was at work. I cannot even guess what it might be but I have no doubt all three homicides are linked and were committed by or effected by the same person or persons."

(Why, after a few moments of conversation with Prescott McNally, Esq., do I begin to mimic his prolixity?)

"Do you have any leads?" he asked.

"Several but nothing substantive. I believe the key to the puzzle will eventually be found in the store."

He hoisted one bristly eyebrow. "The store? But all they sell are parrots."

"I'm aware of that, father, but Parrots Unlimited seems to be the nexus of all the deviltry going on."

He terminated me abruptly. "Very well," he said. "Keep at it." He picked up his glass of port and I departed.

Being somewhat miffed by his cold dismissal, I treated myself to a brandy after climbing to my chamber. I sat at my battered desk and considered what he had revealed. He had described Mr. Gottschalk's will as "an odd testament" but that was lawyerly opinion. He did not consider what those bequests might signify. He was deliberately an unemotional man because he felt in his profession emotion could not contravene reason.

But emotion was my realm. It really was what I dealt with—all those sealed cans labeled love, hate, revenge, envy, jealousy, spite, fury, and so forth. And so I interpreted our client's bequests as an index of his heart rather than his head. If you wish to call me Old Softy, you're quite welcome.

Leaving his home and its furnishings to Yvonne Chrisling—what did that signify? It was a munificent gift.

Just as generous was his bequest of Parrots Unlimited to Yvonne's stepson, Ricardo. Surely there was a hidden reason for that. The lad was, after all, merely an employee. Or was he more than that?

The division of the major portion of his net worth to his three children seemed straightforward enough. But I had learned from experience the most beautiful Red Delicious apple might prove to be mealy.

Sighing, I propped up my feet and started reading the entire record of the Gottschalk affair from the beginning. And you know, I found a tidbit that enlightened me. I am not pretending to be a Master Sleuth, because I have played fair and square and casually mentioned the item to you previously.

I wouldn't want you to think I'm cheating. Why, you'd never speak to me again.

The following morning did not begin auspiciously. I do possess an electric shaver but I customarily follow my father's traditional practice of using a porcelain mug containing a disk of soap, badger-haired brush, and single-edged safety razor to depilate the lower mandible. It was a fresh blade and I sliced my jaw. A styptic pencil saved me from exsanguination but I trotted downstairs to breakfast looking like a nineteenth-century duelist from the University of Heidelberg.

"Did you cut yourself, Archy?" mother inquired solicitously.

"A mere nick," I assured her.

"Perhaps you stood too close to the razor," father remarked.

I find his attempts at humor somewhat heavy-handed, don't you?

We had a satisfying morning meal (blueberry pancakes with heather honey) and discussed plans for Thanksgiving Day, fast approaching. Mother suggested it would be nice to enable the Olsons to enjoy a private holiday by not requiring Ursi to provide the usual turkey feast. Unexpectedly father concurred, and it was decided the family would gobble a gobbler at a restaurant that had the sense to serve a sauce of whole cranberries rather than an effete jelly.

"You might invite Connie," mother said, beaming. "If she has no other plans I'm sure she'd love to join us and we'd like to have her."

"Yes," I said. "Thank you."

I drove to the office intending to spend a few hours creating my expense account for the month. I cannot compose madrigals and my expertise at heroic couplets is limited but when it comes to expense accounts I am a veritable Jules Verne. Imagination? You wouldn't believe!

I was happily at work, wondering if I might charge McNally & Son for a haircut, when I heard a tentative rap at my office door. I rose to open it and found Judd Wilkins. He was bearing a roll of bumf bound with a low-tech rubber band.

He looked at me with his dreamy eyes. "What happened to your chin?" he asked.

"Attempted suicide," I said.

He accepted that. "Here's the download you wanted," he said, proffering the bundle. "About parrots."

I was astounded. "So soon? I asked for this stuff just yesterday."

He gave me a glance I could only interpret as pitying. "It's not snail mail you know. There may be some late factoids coming in but I think you'll find what you want here."

"Interesting?" I asked.

"I thought so."

"Anything illegal going on?"

"Yep," he said cheerfully.

"Judd, thank you for your fast work. I appreciate it."

"No problem," he said, and was gone.

I put aside my expense account and began reading the information he had gleaned from cyberspace. It required concentration because the printouts contained misspellings, ellipses, and abbreviations foreign to me. I read the entire record twice to get a general feel of the material and then perused it a third time with close attention to those elements I thought might be significant in solving the Gottschalk puzzle.

Up to that point my interest in matters psittacine had been limited. I mean parrots are beautiful birds, no denying it, but I am usually concerned with more weighty subjects—such as whether or not to drizzle vinegar on potato chips. But after studying the computer-generated skinny provided by Judd Wilkins I became fascinated by the fate of those gorgeously feathered creatures and I hope you will be similarly intrigued.

Here is the gist of what I learned:

The U.S. is signatory to the Convention of International Trade in Endangered Species of Wild Fauna and Flora, a mouthful usually mercifully shortened to CITES. Under that agreement more than a hundred nations attempt to regulate transnational commerce in plants and animals threatened or potentially threatened with extinction.

In addition, our federal and state governments maintain lists of endangered species, about a thousand in number. Overseeing all the multitudinous regulations is the Department of Interior's Fish and Wildlife Service, and their Department of Law Enforcement when needed.

It has been estimated that 250,000 parrots are imported annually and legally into the U.S., despite the numbing quantity of permits required. Many of these birds become part of domestic breeding programs by legitimate and licensed parrot farmers.

But there are approximately fifty species of wild parrots whose importation is verboten. And that's where the smugglers take over. Rare and expensive birds are sneaked in from Brazil, Australia, and Africa. Main ports of entry are Miami and Los Angeles. One authority guesses this illicit trade probably exceeds $25 million annually.

The smugglers' methods are gruesome. Fully grown and fledgling parrots are hidden in luggage, stuffed into plastic piping, concealed in furniture and machinery, buried in mounds of grain, even sealed in ventilated cans. The mortality rate is horrendous. There is a tale of a smuggler apprehended at L.A. who was wearing a specially constructed vest of many small pockets each of which contained the egg of an endangered Australian cockatiel.

Allow me a spot of editorializing.

Apparently in our enlightened land there are people willing—nay, eager—to pay any amount for a brilliantly colored wild parrot, the rarer the better—with no interest whatsoever in the exotic bird's antecedents or how it arrived on our shores. It becomes a status symbol, not a pet.

One of Judd's contributors remarked that parrots suffer when taken from the wild, deprived of their mates, and thrust into a cage. Many of the captured birds develop neuroses, adopt self-destructive habits, or become aggressive. They sometimes bite and claw their new owners. Bully!

It really is a depressing record. As I've told you, I have no special fondness for parrots but the cruel trapping, smuggling, and profitable sale of wild and endangered species seem to me a particularly heinous practice. Especially since so many of those birds die shortly after being wrenched from their homes and imprisoned.

It was time for lunch and I fled to the Pelican Club as relieved as a schoolchild anticipating recess. The joint was sparsely occupied and so I was able to sit at the bar and order a gin and bitters from Simon Pettibone. Our estimable bartender and club manager gave me a quizzical look.

"Feeling ginnish this morning, Mr. McNally?" he inquired.

"Feeling bitterish," I replied. He served my drink and I said, "Mr. Pettibone, I know you to be a man of vast erudition and experience. Tell me something: What do you think of birds?"

"Love 'em," he said promptly. "Chickens, ducks, turkeys, all roasted, fried, or broiled. Any which way. I once ate a pigeon and very tasty it was."

"Oh, I concur," I said, "but I framed my question awkwardly. I was not referring to edible species raised for the table. What do you think of birds kept in cages? As pets or sometimes just as interior decoration."

"Ah," he said, suddenly serious, "that's something else again. I don't hold with caging dumb creatures. I've never had a bird as a pet and never will. It's cruel to my way of thinking. Ever see an eagle soar? Now that's something."

"I understand what you're saying but it's a difficult moral choice, isn't it? I mean I enjoy a roasted duck with a nice sauce of wild cherries as much as you. Never give the poor fowl's fate a second thought. But the idea of keeping a bird in a cage turns me off."

He looked at me. "No one keeps a duck in a cage, Mr. McNally."

"I hope not. But I'm thinking about parrots. Especially beautiful and rare parrots taken from the wild and put behind bars."

"No," he said firmly, "I don't hold with that."

"Thank you, Mr. Pettibone," I said gratefully. "I respect your opinion."

Then I lunched alone but, *mirabile dictu,* I cannot recollect what I had. This is astonishing, even shocking to relate for I have almost total recall of past breakfasts, brunches, luncheons, dinners, and late suppers. Why, I distinctly remember an excellent braised oxtail I consumed in 1984.

The reason for this memory lapse, I think, is heavy and insistent pondering as I scarfed. The knowledge that rare birds were captured in the wild, smuggled abroad, and sold to moneyed collectors distressed me. For the moment, I put aside how this illegal trade might possibly affect the homicides I was investigating. I was disturbed by the birdnapping itself.

I have, I suppose, a very limited personal code of moral conduct. To wit: I strive to behave in a manner that gives me pleasure but doesn't harm anyone else. I mean I'm a live-and-let-live bloke. I've never been an -ist of any sort, not sexist, racist, leftist, rightist, idealist, realist, and so forth. Well, on occasion I act as an egoist—but only on occasion.

What my dilemma amounted to was something you may find ridiculous and I admit had a slightly farcical tone. If I objected to the capture and imprisonment of birds for profit, how could I justify my enjoyment of a baked free-range chicken, much more flavorful than the factory-raised variety?

I agreed with Mr. Pettibone that it was okay to feast on domesticated fowl but wrong to ensnare and incarcerate exotic parrots. But they're all birds, aren't they, and where is the moral justification for the difference in their treatment?

Finally I gave up on my mental maunderings. I could find no way out of the maze of imponderables. It was, I decided, a question with no final answer. Similar to the problem of whether brandied apples or broiled oranges go better with a roasted goose.

25

I arrived back at the McNally Building to find on my desk a handwritten note from Yvonne Chrisling. It was an invitation to attend a "joyous tribute" to Hiram Gottschalk to be held that evening beginning at eight p.m. Not to mourn, she wrote, but to remember and celebrate the life of a wonderful man. "I want it to be more like a cheerful wake," she added.

Uh-huh.

She finished with a fanfare: "Archy, I'll be devastated if you don't come. I want so much to see you again!"

Double uh-huh. I wondered again what game the Dragon Lady was playing and determined to present myself in all my sockless glory at the soiree that evening at the Gottschalk manse. It might, I reckoned, prove as educational and entertaining as a visit to a zoo.

I phoned Sgt. Al Rogoff and was put on hold for at least three minutes. He finally came on the line.

"What took you so long?" I asked. "Finishing an anchovy pizza and a can of Sprite?"

"Close but no cigar," he said. "Actually I was beating a suspect with a short length of rubber hose. What's up?"

"That's why I called. Anything happening?"

"Nope. Nothing of any great interest."

"C'mon, Al, you must be doing *something*."

"Just routine. We got an alleged eyewitness who lives in the same condo as Sutcliffe and Gompertz. She claims she saw the two of them leaving at night with two guys she describes as 'goons.' She says the four of them got in a car and drove away."

"Is this eyewitness a middle-aged lady carrying a ton of mascara?"

"You've got it. You know her?"

"Met her briefly during my last visit. She let me in—a stupid thing to do. I thought her a bit loopy."

"That's the word."

"Can she identify the car they used?"

"Says it was white. Isn't that beautiful? How many white cars are there in South Florida—a zillion?"

"Possibly more. Al, does the apparent abduction and murder of Gompertz and Sutcliffe take Peter Gottschalk off the hook for the killing of his father?"

"Well . . . maybe," he admitted grudgingly. "I can't find anything linking him to the Everglades cases. But that's assuming all three homicides are somehow connected."

"You believe it, don't you?"

"Yeah," he said, sighing heavily, "I guess I do. Have you come up with anything?"

"Parrots," I said. "I think parrots may be the key to the whole megillah."

Short silence. "Parrots," he repeated. "Archy, have you ever considered a brain transplant?"

" 'O ye of little faith.' Believe me, parrots hold the answer."

I was hoping he wouldn't say it but he did.

"That's for the birds," he said, laughed, and hung up.

I tried to get back to fiddling with my expense account but found I had lost interest. My creative juices were still flowing but whereas, at lunch, I had put aside the Gottschalk puzzle to ruminate on the moral implications of gnawing a chicken's crispy drumstick, now I postponed my monthly raid on McNally & Son's bottom line to concentrate on the perplexities of my current discreet inquiry.

I went back to fundamentals, the start of everything. It all began with the acts of personal terrorism and vandalism that frightened Hiram: the slashed photograph, the mass card, the strangled mynah, the shattered phonograph record. They were all deliberate acts of cruelty. If I could determine the motive involved I might be able to identify the perpetrator.

Dr. Gussie had said the destroyed photo was an attempt to eliminate Hiram's happy memory. The same could be said of the smashed Caruso recording, a gift from his beloved wife, now long gone. The posted mass card and killing of his favorite bird were more serious: warnings of a possible impending doom. Those explanations made a grisly kind of sense but led precisely nowhere. They yielded no clues as to who might be responsible for inflicting such grievous pain.

Just as puzzling was the manner of his death. It seemed obvious the killer had chosen to stab the hapless victim through the eyes because he had seen too much. In some benighted countries the hand of a convicted thief is lopped off. Mr. Gottschalk's eyes were destroyed and his life taken because his slayer could not endure his continued observation or witnessing of—what?

But again, all that might be an explanation but it was not a solution, was it? I wrestled with the riddles for the remainder of the afternoon, doodling on a pad of scratch paper and finding myself making crude drawings of eyes and birds. I waited for an inspired flash of insight that never arrived. And so I closed up shop and went home wondering if I might be better suited for another profession. Stuffing strudel was one possibility.

During the family cocktail hour at twilight I casually mentioned I was attending a memorial service for Hiram Gottschalk that night. Father paused in his preparation of our martinis.

"Your mother and I were invited," he said stiffly. "But I thought it best we not accept."

"Sir, would you prefer I didn't go?" I asked him.

"No, no," he said. "Represent McNally and Son. And perhaps you may learn something to further your inquiry."

"Perhaps," I said, thinking, Not bloody likely—which proves how mistaken a sleuthhound can be.

After dinner I went upstairs to change. I decided to wear a *suit*. Can you believe it? Yep, my jacket and trousers matched: a black and tan glen plaid in a windowpane design. Classic but jaunty. I lightened the formality further with a knitted sport shirt of Sea Island cotton in hunter green. Cordovan loafers with modest tassels. The final effect, I decided, was assertive without being aggressive.

I must confess my getup was an attempt to trump Ricardo Chrisling's Armani elegance. Didn't someone once say you can cure a man of any folly except vanity?

It was a so-so night hardly worth mentioning, but I shall. The sky was totally overcast, making for a heavy darkness, and what breeze existed came in fits and starts. I was aware of an unusual odor on the air. Not quite fishy. Not quite sewer gas. Brimstone? Nah. That was my imagination galloping amok.

There was a plenitude of cars already parked on the slated driveway of the Gottschalk estate as I drove in. I spotted Binky Watrous's dented antique M-B cabriolet and was happy my gormless aide would be present. I was sliding from my fire engine–red quadriga when Peter Gottschalk came out of nowhere, hand outstretched. He was grinning. Not a drugged grin or a sappy grin. Just a nice natural expression of pleasure.

"Hiya, Archy," he said. "I was hoping you'd show up."

I shook the proffered paw. "Peter, good to see you again. How are things going?"

"Listen," he said, "I've got to thank you for steering me to that shrink."

"Dr. Pearlberg?"

"Yeah. I went to see her. She's something, she is."

"I concur. A marvelous woman."

"Anyway, she sent me to another doc—a *doctor* doc, not a mind bender—and he's got me on medication."

"Any results?"

"Not yet but I feel better knowing I'm getting help. I'm off the booze and the weed and that's a drag. But I can stand it if my brain starts functioning."

"Good for you," I said. "Coming inside?"

"In a while," he said. "Not right now. I just want to walk around and look at things. It's like I'm seeing them for the first time. That's goofy, isn't it?"

"Not so. Very understandable. Peter, what is this shindig all about? A sort of delayed wake?"

"It's supposed to be but it's just a party. My sisters' idea. They love a bash."

"Tell me something: Do you always know which is which?"

"Oh sure. It's easy. Julia wears Chanel Cristalle perfume and Judith uses Must de Cartier."

I laughed. "I had never considered that method of identification. But what if they switch scents?"

He shrugged. "So what? Who cares? They're a couple of airheads anyway. See you later."

Then he was gone. I stayed a moment thinking of the sobriquet he had used to describe his sisters: airheads. It had been my initial impression also, but now I was beginning to think there was another trait the twins shared. It was darker and far less superficial than their fondness for partying.

The front door of the Gottschalk home was wide open. I entered and paused to glance about. Yvonne Chrisling came bustling up to give me a tight *abrazo* and press a warm cheek against mine.

"Archy!" she exclaimed. "I am *sooo* happy you have arrived. What a delight to see you!"

My ego is of the stalwart variety, as you well know, but her effusion startled me. I do like to fancy I am a reincarnation of Ronald Colman, but I could not believe I had captivated this woman to the degree she displayed in speech and manner.

"Come along," she said in her hearty contralto voice, "and let me get you a drink. You prefer vodka, do you not?"

She grasped my arm and led me to a portable bar set up by the caterer handling the affair. She made certain I was supplied with a heavy Sterling on the rocks with a slice of lime. Then she toyed with my left ear.

"Now I must act like a hostess," she said, managing a girlish pout, "but you and I shall have a nice long talk later."

She moved away, leaving me a bit rattled. I had no doubt the lady was coming on to me, as she had before, and I could not guess her motive. That it was not overwhelming passion I was well aware. And I doubted if she even knew of my store of scabrous limericks. So why was she being so *physical?* It could of course be merely a case of chronic flirtatiousness—but I didn't think so.

I stood at the bar watching her stroll slowly through the throng of guests, pausing to chat, patting shoulders, stroking cheeks, clasping hands. She really *was* physical.

I think "dolled up" would be an apt description of her costume: a strapless sheath of shimmering pink pallettes. Her black hair hung in a glossy sheaf. A diamond choker encircled her strong neck. The effect of those glittering rocks against her dark skin was striking.

As she sauntered slowly but purposefully I suddenly realized she was not acting "like a hostess" as she had said, she was playing the role of chatelaine, entertaining in *her* home, greeting *her* guests. Then I knew, *knew* she was aware of her inheritance. This rumpled mansion, its furnishings and grounds, were now all hers. *Hers!* To do with as she willed. No wonder she was chockablock with brio.

I wandered away from the bar searching for Binky. I finally located him seated in a cozy corner holding hands with Bridget Houlihan.

Their heads were close and when I said, "Hello, kids," they looked up vacantly as if I had just interrupted a shared dream.

"Oh," Binky said. "Hi."

"Hi," Bridget said.

"Hi," I added, "and I trust that concludes the 'hi's' for the evening. Having a good time?"

They looked at each other and I wondered if they were fully aware of where they were, so lost they seemed to be in their private world.

"Binky," I said, "have the police come to the store?"

He nodded. "They showed up today. Two detectives."

"Asking questions about Emma and Tony," Bridget said sorrowfully. "We couldn't tell them much."

"Did they talk to Ricardo?"

"He wasn't there," Binky said. "He's away on a business trip."

"Oh?" I said. "Is he here tonight?"

"I haven't seen him," Bridget said. "Have you, lover?" she asked her swain. *Lover?!* Calling Binky Watrous a lover is similar to labeling Caligula an Eagle Scout.

"Haven't seen him," my unpaid helot replied. "He's away a lot."

"The new employees," I said. "The ones replacing Tony and Emma—are they present tonight?"

"They're here but you won't like them," Bridget advised. "Riffraff."

"The riffest of the raffest," Binky added.

I expressed thanks and left. There were more questions I wanted to ask but I felt I was intruding on their twosomeness (I think that's a new word I just coined). I confess I was envious. I wondered where Connie Garcia was at that moment and what she was doing. Stubborn, mulish, obstinate woman! Grrr.

26

I wish I could tell you I had a blast at Hiram Gottschalk's memorial, but I did not. All the other guests, and there were many, seemed to be having a high old time. The decibel count rose as more drinks were consumed, laughter became raucous, and I even witnessed the sight of a middle-aged man putting a fringed lampshade on his head and attempting an imitation of Carmen Miranda. Yes, I actually saw it.

But despite a second vodka I remained subdued if not dejected. A series of events contributed to my angst.

I met the new domestic staff hired to replace Mei and Got Lee. They were an unprepossessing couple with none of the cheery charm of their predecessors. They were obviously foreign-born and I overheard them conversing in a language I could not positively identify although I recognized a few French words. I finally guessed they were speaking Creole, which might explain their wariness. They acted as if an agent from the Immigration Service might tap them on the shoulder at any moment.

Just as off-putting were the man and woman employed to take the place of Tony Sutcliffe and Emma Gompertz at Parrots Unlimited. I introduced myself and found them a singularly surly and uncommunicative couple. They stood stiffly, full glasses gripped tightly. They seemed totally divorced from the revelry around them and, having put in an appearance, were eager to depart as soon as possible.

"How's the parrot business?" I asked the man genially, trying to jolt him into even the merest semblance of casual conversation. I think his name was Martin something.

"You're interested in parrots?" he said, staring at me suspiciously.

It was all I needed—a challenge like that.

"Well, I'm not," I said briskly, "but my dear old grandfather is absolutely dotty about them. Must have at least twenty, give or take, and he's still collecting. They'll probably outlive him—right?"

"Probably," the woman said. I think her name was Felice something.

"He owns some rare birds," I burbled on. "Beautiful specimens. His ninety-second birthday is coming up and I'd like to buy him a special gift. Do you have any unusual parrots in your shop? I mean something he's not likely to have in his attic."

Martin thawed. A little. "I think we can supply a rare and lovely bird," he said. "Expensive of course."

"Of course," I said.

"Stop by the store and I'll show you what's available."

"Great!" I said. "I know it'll make gramps happy."

I gave them an idiotic grin. Did I know what I was doing? No, I did not but it was a gambit worth a try.

I was beginning to think it was time to make a surreptitious departure, when I observed a pas de trois being performed across the thronged living room. My view was frequently obscured by the mingling of guests and I heard nothing of what was being said. The rising volume of gibble-gabble prevented that.

Peter Gottschalk was seated in the center of the tattered velvet love seat. Crowded in were the twins, Julia and Judith, pressing him between them, a slender dun volume held tightly by two garish bookends. There was a bottle of what appeared to be red wine on the cocktail table before them, and each of the three held a full glass.

From my distance it was a scene in mime but I had no doubt what was happening. The sisters urged him to drink. He resisted. They laughed and whispered into his ears. He laughed. They lifted their glasses. A toast. He took a sip. They gulped and nudged him. He drank more. They all laughed.

I didn't know if the twins were fully aware of their brother's condition but I thought their behavior abhorrent. I wanted to push my way through the mob and strike the glass from his hand. But I couldn't do that, could I? People would think me drunk or insane, and the three principals involved would be outraged by my officiousness. And so I did nothing. Just watched, saddened by the sight of the sisters clutching his arms, petting him, keeping his glass filled. I saw it as a kind of corruption.

Then I did leave, sneaking away and hoping my departure was unobserved. No such luck. I was standing alongside the Miata, looking upward and happy to see the sky was clearing—a few stars were winking at me—when Yvonne Chrisling came running to slide an arm about my waist.

"You naughty boy," she said. "Leaving without a good-night kiss."

"I apologize," I said. "I wanted to thank you for an enjoyable evening but you were busy with your guests."

"I wanted everyone to have a happy time," she said in such a simpering tone I was tempted to utter a blasphemy. "Did you have a happy time, Archy?"

"I did indeed," I assured her. "My only regret is your stepson wasn't present. I was looking forward to chatting with him."

"Ah, poor Ricardo," she said. "On a business trip. He works, works, works. He is so determined to make the business a success."

"I'm sure he shall. But I did have a chance to talk with Peter for a few moments. He seems in much better shape." I watched closely for her reaction.

She sighed. "Such a problem, that one. He's going to doctors, you know, for help in curing his depression and stopping the crazy things he does. But I'm afraid he will not do what they say or take his medication. Peter is so weak, so weak. Are you weak, Archy?"

"Only physically, mentally, and emotionally," I told her. "Other than that I am a tower of strength."

She smiled. "May we sit in your car a moment? I need a few moments away from the hullabaloo."

"Of course," I said.

So there we were, side by side in the parked Miata. I do not believe she was using a perfume but I was conscious of her scent, deep and musky. And disturbing I might add. Dim starlight gleamed on bare shoulders. The diamond choker seemed reflected on dark skin. I thought it a bit chill for her costume but she made no complaint. Perhaps she generated her own warmth, an inner furnace never extinguished. (Oh, McNally, you're *such* a poet!)

She turned sideways and took my hand. "Do you think you shall ever marry?" she asked suddenly.

I was startled. "I honestly don't know, Yvonne. How can one possibly predict something like that?"

"Take my advice and don't marry," she said.

"Oh? Why do you say that?"

"You're not the type."

"You mean there's a marrying type of man and natural-born bachelors who smoke a pipe, keep a cat, and sew leather patches on the elbows of their Harris tweed sport jacket?"

She was kind enough to laugh. "Let me tell you something, Archy. It's a secret but I shall reveal it to you. Every smart woman in the world knows if she had been born a man she would never marry."

"What a cynic you are," I said.

"Oh no, but I am realistic. And I know marrying or not marrying is not so important. A piece of paper. What is important is how a man feels about a woman and how she feels about him. You agree?"

"I do," I said with the uneasy feeling this woman knew more about everything than I knew about anything.

She began fondling my right ear. She seemed to have a thing about ears. That's okay. I have a furtive fondness for the backs of female knees. And it is said the Japanese admire an attractive nape. One never knows, do one?

"Age means nothing," Yvonne continued. "And really, physical attractiveness is not, ah, crucial. It's the stirring one feels."

She pressed closer. I began to appreciate how a trapped ferret must feel.

"Also," she said, "it is necessary a man and a woman who are simpatico do not hurt each other. It is very necessary. You wouldn't hurt me, would you, Archy?"

"Of course not," I said staunchly without the slightest idea where this woman was coming from. She was speaking words that made little sense unless she was implying a meaning I could not fathom.

"I know you won't," she said, and I was immediately aware she had switched from "wouldn't" to "won't." "And I won't hurt you. And so," she concluded with a sigh of content, "there is no reason you and I cannot enjoy an intimate relationship and make each other happy."

Then she enveloped me. I can't think of a more fitting verb for I felt engulfed, surrounded, swallowed as she lurched to enfold me in her arms and plaster my mug with wet, passionate kisses. What a scene! Acceptable in a boudoir certainly but in an open car parked on a crowded driveway? I mean, how louche can you get?

I touched her hair cautiously, fearing I might find a nest of snakes. But it was pure gloss. Was I tempted to respond to the bold advances of this intense woman? Of course I was tempted. I am, after all, not whittled of oak. But if my glands were energized the bowl of Cheerios I call my brain sent forth a warning alert.

She wanted something from me, I guessed, and then I reckoned it was possible she was playing the siren because there was something she *didn't* want from me. Her operatic seduction (opera buffa, not grand opera) might be an attempt to persuade me to inaction. She wanted me to cease and desist. It was an intriguing hypothesis.

Rejection without giving offense to the rejectee is a delicate art. I weaseled of course, as is my wont, and explained to Yvonne as gently as I could that while we undoubtedly were kindred spirits, this was neither the time nor the place for continued intimacy. But our moment would arrive, I assured her, when our new and delightful relationship could come to glorious fruition. In other words, I stalled her.

She disengaged far enough to peer into my eyes. "You promise?" she asked huskily.

"I do not take promises lightly," I told her. It was, you may note, a classic example of a dissembler's talent. Not a lie but not a definite pledge, either.

"When?" she persisted.

"As soon as possible," I replied, which gave me plenty of wriggle room. "I'll call you."

"Very soon," she said, and gave me a final kiss. What a wicked tongue she had! "And if you don't, I shall call you. Frequently."

She may not have meant it as a threat but I took it as such. She was not in the habit of being denied. She gave my ear one last tweak, slid from the car, and stalked back to the party. I watched her go, admiring her erect posture and the way she seemed to thrust herself forward. I could not believe she ever had a doubt in her life.

I drove home at a relatively early hour, congratulating myself on escaping from what might have been a sticky situation. I believe I hummed "Does Your Chewing Gum Lose Its Flavor (on the Bedpost Overnight)?" but it could have been Mozart's Violin Concerto No. 3 in G major. Whatever, I found I had recovered from my brief spasm of *Weltschmerz* earlier in the evening. I wasn't exactly chipper, you understand, but in a relaxed, ruminative mood.

I disrobed in my adytum (there's a lovely word; look it up!), sorry my glen plaid suit hadn't had the opportunity to compete with Ricardo Chrisling's Armani. I donned a new pongee robe embroidered with Chinese characters. I had been told by the merchant the calligraphy could be translated as: "May you have a happy life." But I suspected it meant, "Suffer, you miserable schlub," or some other invidious imprecation.

I poured myself a wee marc and settled down behind my desk for a period of pondering before surrendering to the need for eight hours of Z's. I found myself smiling because I recalled my father's comment at the family cocktail hour. He had urged me to attend the Gottschalk party, saying, "Perhaps you may learn something to further your inquiry." I had doubted it but the senior had been proved right again. Was the man never wrong?

I *had* furthered my inquiry at the squirrelly and totally unnecessary "joyous tribute." Nothing momentous, you understand, but bits and pieces which might prove of value. I had met the new employees of Parrots Unlimited and was not impressed. The recently hired domestic staff was even more questionable.

But those meetings were of peripheral interest. There had been two developments of more significant concern. To wit:

I had seen with my own peepers Julia and Judith encouraging, nay urging their brother to swill wine. The sight had disturbed me but I was willing to give them the benefit of the doubt and assume they didn't know he was under a doctor's care.

But then Yvonne Chrisling had revealed she was aware of Peter's condition, and so it was reasonable to assume he had also told his sisters he was on a no-alcohol, no-drugs regimen. Yet they were plying him with the fermented grape. Just high spirits on the part of the twins and not deliberate conduct? I didn't think so. Attributing their behavior solely to their kicky dispositions was enough to dash a balder.

My second observation of note was—you guessed it—the diamond choker worn by Yvonne. You didn't believe I missed it, did you, or forgot the mention of a diamond choker by Lolly Spindrift when he was detailing the evidence he had of Ricardo Chrisling's career of Don Juanism?

There are many diamond chokers in the world of course, most of them in Palm Beach. But still I thought it a mind-tickling coincidence that Ricardo had recently purchased a choker on Worth Avenue and now Yvonne was wearing a gemmy circlet—to smashing effect I might add.

Even assuming the diamond choker purchased by Ricardo was the one worn by Yvonne—so what? It could well have been a present from stepson to stepmother, perhaps to celebrate a birthday or some other family occasion. But it was such a lavish gift I found myself questioning the motive of the giver and what the recipient might have done to deserve such largesse.

I went to bed about an hour later still musing on the horrid murder of Hiram Gottschalk and the two immutable laws of human existence:

1. Life is unfair.
2. It's better to be lucky than smart.

27

I have a vague recollection of Thursday starting as a zingy day. It could not have been the weather, for it was droopy, with heavy rain forecast for the afternoon. I suspect my Joy D'Veeve (a stripper I once met at the Lido in Paris) was due to a solid night's sleep and the fact that I didn't slice myself while shaving.

After breakfast with my parents I emerged into a drizzly world but my élan was not diminished, because Hobo came trotting up for a morning pat. His coat was glistening with moisture but he seemed not at all daunted by the damp. I checked his condo to make certain it was dry and snug.

While I was examining his house Jamie Olson came wandering, gumming his old briar.

"Morning, Mr. Archy," he said.

"Good morning, Jamie. Hobo's been behaving himself, has he?"

"Yep," he said. "The hound amazes me and Ursi. Smarter than most people we know. About a week ago, mebbe two, three in the morning, it was storming hard. Thunder, lightning, everything. Squall woke me up and I heard a scratching at our door over the garage. It was Hobo. He had got flooded out and come up the stairs to our apartment. I let him in, dried him off, spread an old piece of carpet for him. Suited him just fine. Didn't misbehave or anything, if you know what I mean. Next day it cleared and he went outside again and hasn't moved in with us since."

"Knows enough to come in out of the rain," I observed.

"Yep, and he knows a lot of other things he ain't telling. That dog is *deep*."

I drove to work pleased my faith in Hobo had been justified. I was no sooner in my cubicle when a knock on the door announced a visitor. It was Judd Wilkins, our computer whiz.

"I asked the security guard to give me a call when you showed up," he said without a greeting. "Got a minute or two?"

"Sure I do," I said. "Come on in."

This time he sat in the steel chair alongside my desk. I thought I detected a certain tenseness in his manner. His eyes had lost their dreaminess. He seemed distant, as if he were concentrating on solving the puzzle of the Pyramid Inch.

"What's up, Judd?" I asked him.

"We've been hacked," he said.

I had absolutely no idea what he meant. "Hacked?"

"Invaded," he said. "Someone's got into our computers and is rummaging around."

It didn't, at first, seem to me a matter of great concern. Although, as I've mentioned, I'm a computer illiterate, I am aware cyberspace does not provide complete privacy. PCs offer a tempting target for hackers, thieves, competitors, or innocent tyros attempting to expand their keyboard expertise.

"I thought we had a security system," I said.

"Model-T," Judd said. "I've sent a dozen memos saying we've got to upgrade and get state-of-the-art firewalls. No response."

"Doesn't everyone with a computer on his or her desk have a private password?"

He grimaced. "Passwords? Not worth diddly-squat. One of our senior partners—know what his password is?"

"What?"

" 'Password.' That's his personal, private password: 'Password.' "

"Beautiful," I said.

"Your father has a PC. He doesn't work it but his aides do. Want to know his password?"

"Tell me."

" 'McNally.' "

I groaned. "Why didn't he make it 'Open Sesame'? Judd, are you certain we've been tapped?"

"Absolutely. Someone is inside us and searching around."

"How do you know?"

"I just *know*," he said definitely. "Some stuff has been switched, some is out of order or jumbled, tallies of references are out of sync with past records. Look, it's like someone got into your closet and shuffled your suits. You'd know it, wouldn't you?"

Suddenly the import of what he was saying sank in and I was shaken. "Are you telling me a stranger now has access to all our personal files? Wills, contracts, trusts, agreements, litigation, partnerships, the affairs of our clients, even our personnel records and tax returns?"

"Everything," he said.

"Oh lordy," I said. "My father will have a conniption. You want me to break the bad news? Is that why you're here?"

"Part of it," he said. "I want you to tell him what's happened and how we've got to put more muscle in our security. But there's something else."

My morning vivacity, already diminished, now seemed doomed. "Let's have it," I said, expecting the worst. It was.

"I'm guessing now," Judd said, "but there's a good chance I'm on target. We've been computerized for almost five years with no security problems. I kept warning it could happen but all the fuds said who would want to hack a South Florida law firm. Well, now it's happened. I hate to tell you this but I think you're responsible."

"What?" I cried.

"Not you personally. But you asked me to go on line and see what I could get on parrots, especially anything illegal. It couldn't have been more than twenty-four hours after I queried the nets that we got invaded. Like I said, I'm guessing but I think the parrot inquiry brought in the cyberpunk. I could be wrong but I believe I'm right."

We stared at each other, unblinking. I was, I admit, stunned by his disclosure. My first impulse was to phone immediately for a one-way airline ticket to Shanghai. First-class of course. But my cravenness was vanished by the remembrance of a long-ago incident when, not completely sober, I was confronted by a would-be mugger in New Haven. He was wielding a knife that appeared to be just slightly shorter than a scimitar.

I had looked at him sadly, wagged my head, and said, "Somewhere a mother's heart is breaking."

He was so disconcerted by my remark I was able to escape. At full speed I might add.

The recollection of this daring act enabled me to face the current crisis with some aplomb. "All right, Judd," I said. "I shall urge my father as strongly as I can to install more formidable security in our computer system. Now about your belief my inquiry about parrots sparked the break-in—I don't doubt it for a moment."

He suddenly relaxed, slumping in the hellish steel chair, gratified by my response.

"I know little about computers," I continued. "As I'm sure you're fully aware. But is there any way we can discover who is trespassing and sharing our secrets?"

His eyes closed slowly, remained shut for a moment, then popped open again. "It can be done," he said, "but I can't do it. Don't have the software or the know-how. But I'm exchanging E-mail with a guy down in Miami. He's a real tech-head, the nerdiest of the nerds. He works for a computer security outfit and I'll guess he's their house genius. I'm betting he could track our virus to its source."

"Can we hire him?"

"He's out of everything unless it comes in bytes. I mean he knows nothing about free-lance work, contracts, fees, and so forth. But we could hire the company he works for with the understanding their first job is to find who infected us. If they succeed we can promise them the assignment of redesigning our whole setup to beef security. How does it sound?"

"Great," I said. "Let's do it."

"That's a go-ahead?"

I bit the bullet. "Yes," I said. "A definite commitment from McNally and Son. I'll take the responsibility."

His look wasn't doubtful but it was wary. "Your father will go along?"

"I'll convince him," I said with more assurance than I felt.

He departed and I phoned Mrs. Trelawney immediately, fearing if I dallied my resolve would simply ooze away. I asked for an audience with m'lord but she said he was busy with a client. When he was available she would inform him I had called and relay his reaction.

"Tell him it's a matter of life and death," I said.

"Whose life?" she asked. "And whose death?"

"All of us," I said hollowly. "And I kid you not."

I settled back to await her call. I shook an English Oval from the packet but didn't light it. I just fingered it as a satiated infant might fondle a pacifier. The fog I had been in since the death of Hiram Gottschalk was beginning to dissipate. Not whisked away but softly shredding. And what I saw wasn't pretty.

My summons arrived sooner than expected and I climbed the back stairs to my father's sanctum with some trepidation. After all I wouldn't be the first messenger in history executed for bringing bad news.

I found him seated in his swivel chair before his antique rolltop desk. He waved me to a seat on the green leather chesterfield. He seemed in a genial mood.

"Mrs. Trelawney tells me you wish to discuss a matter of life and death," he said with some amusement.

"A slight exaggeration, sir," I said, "but very slight."

I then reported what Judd Wilkins had told me. I left nothing out, including the probability of my inquiry about parrots being the cause of the invasion.

When I finished, he stood and began striding about his office, hands thrust into his trouser pockets. I do not believe a stranger or even a casual acquaintance would have recognized the depth of his wrath. He was a disciplined man, a controlled man, and loath to display his emotions. But he was my father; I knew him as well as he knew me and I saw the signs of his fury: a hardening of the eyes, a grim set to the jaw, a stiffness in his neck. He was riven by anger and doing his best to conceal it.

"What you're telling me," he said tonelessly, "is that a stranger is now privy to all the confidential data of this firm."

"Yes, sir," I said. "Wills, trusts, litigation, contracts—the whole caboodle."

He stopped his pacing to stare at the floor. "The world is too much with me, Archy," he said. "I know less about computers than you do, I'm sure, but the more I read about the digital revolution, the more I am convinced it means the end of privacy. We could have been burglarized before computers, of course. Documents could have been stolen or copied. But now a teenaged desperado fiddling at a keyboard is able to enter and share our very existence: past, present, and future. It is an obscenity."

"I agree, father," I said. "But there is no need to surrender meekly to electronic assaults without fighting back."

I told him I had authorized Judd Wilkins to hire a computer security company with the understanding that if they were able to identify our assailant they would be given a contract to redesign our computer setup with state-of-the-art safeguards.

Since Prescott McNally, Esq., could not confront the information superhighway with any hope of response, he decided to concentrate his rage and frustration on his mild-mannered scion: me.

"You did *what?*" he demanded in a tone I can only describe as glacial.

I repeated my commitment of McNally & Son. I then arose from my slump on the leather couch and stood erect. If we were to have an altercation I had no wish to be in a subservient physical position.

"You had no right to make such an agreement," he said sternly. "The decision was mine to make and you should have obtained my approval before obligating us to an unspecified expense."

"Father," I said, "be reasonable. You want to ensure everything be done that can be done to prevent future break-ins. And I want to do all I can to obtain the name of the person who is so curious about my interest in parrots. The solution to that mystery may possibly lead to the identity of Hiram Gottschalk's killer. It seems to me the expense I approved is justified by the results we hope to obtain."

"It's not the money," he said, still steaming, "it's the principle of the thing."

(*Nota bene:* When people say it's not the money it's the principle, it's the money.)

"Sir," I said, "I do not feel I exceeded my authority. It was important to get things moving as quickly as possible. If I had delayed until I received your permission, what would have been accomplished? Surely you would approve the hiring of computer security experts, would you not?"

"That's not the point," he said testily.

"Then what *is* the point?" I asked, becoming just as heated as he. "That I went over your head? If it disturbs you unendurably you may have my resignation as soon as I can write it out."

He glared at me. "Oh, don't be such an ass," he said grumpily. "All I'm suggesting—*strongly* suggesting—is you consult me in the future before committing McNally and Son to an expensive and problematic course of action."

I had won a small victory but it was not enough. "No, father, I cannot promise that. Situations may arise similar to the present matter when I feel it best to make an instant decision before clearing it with you. Either you trust my judgment or you do not."

He looked at me with what I can only describe as a sardonic smile. "The apple never falls far from the tree," he observed.

And that inanity reminded me of an undergraduate jape I've mentioned before: The turd never falls far from the bird.

"I will not undo what you have done," he pronounced in a frigid voice, turning to his desk. "Now go back to work."

28

I returned to my office in a mood I can only label as festive. I had climbed into the cage with the king of beasts and tamed him—temporarily at least. But then, on further reflection, my coup was moderated. I became conscious my relationship with my father had been subtly altered during our wrangle. It was not a sea change, mind you, but perhaps the beginning of one.

I was about to resume inventing my expense account when Binky Watrous phoned. He seemed joyous, bubbly in fact.

"Binky," I said, "are you calling from Parrots Unlimited?"

"No, boss, I am not," he said with a giggle. "I have been fired. Along with Bridget."

I gulped. "When did this happen?"

"About an hour ago. Ricardo showed up, back from one of his business trips, and gave both of us the old heave-ho."

"Did he offer any reason?"

"Said the business couldn't afford a sales staff of four—which is a crock. The store is doing a booming business. I mean we weren't just standing around. The place was always busy. In fact, Bridget and I are thinking of opening a bird store of our own. Not just parrots, you know, but all kinds of chirpy pets: canaries, mynahs, swans, penguins."

"Swans?" I said, startled. "Penguins? Why not an ostrich or two?"

"Why not?" he said gaily.

"Listen, Binky, how about you and Bridget meeting me for lunch at the club. Around noonish. You can tell me all about your sacking and your plans for the future."

"Ripping idea. We'll celebrate our release from gainful employment."

I hung up puzzled by this new development. It was apparent Ricardo was revamping Parrots Unlimited, as he had every right to do since he was now the manager and, after Mr. Gottschalk's estate was settled, would be the sole owner. I just wondered what plans he had for the psittacine emporium. A discount store? Something like a feathered Kmart?

I finished my expense account and dropped it onto the desk of Raymond Gelding, our treasurer.

"Oh, goody," he said. "Just what I wanted. I haven't read any really exciting fiction lately."

"To quote a former president of our great republic," I said loftily, "I am not a crook."

"And you know what happened to him," Ray said. "But I must admit I admire your chutzpah, Archy. You are the only employee of McNally and Son who has ever attempted to charge the firm for a purchase of Extra-Strength Excedrin."

"A legitimate business expense," I assured him, turning to leave. "Headaches are an occupational hazard."

"What about my ulcer?" he yelled after me.

I arrived at the Pelican Club at precisely the same moment Binky's battered Mercedes came chugging into the parking area. He and Bridget alighted by sliding out the door on the driver's side, the one closed with a loop of twine. The passenger's door was so tightly jammed only a small explosive charge might have opened it—but I doubt it.

I greeted the kids and we all entered the club and went directly to the dining area. Priscilla came sauntering over to take our order. I asked for Kir Royales for the three of us.

Pris winked at Binky. "You've got a live one today," she told him.

"I hope so," he said. "Bridget and I have just been fired."

"Some people have all the luck," she sighed, and went off to fetch our drinks.

I asked Binky for more details of what had happened but there was little he could add to what he had already related. Ricardo Chrisling appeared an hour after the store opened, called Bridget and Binky into his private office, and canned both of them forthwith. He promised each two weeks' severance and requested they leave immediately.

"What was his mood?" I inquired. "His manner?"

Bridget answered. What a charming young woman she was: saucy, energetic, with a brisk wit. She reminded me in many ways of Connie Garcia. You remember Connie, don't you, McNally? Of course you remember, you poltroon!

"Ricardo was an icicle," Bridget said decisively. "All business. Binky and I were just numbers in a ledger. And bad cess to him. He needed us more than we needed him."

"Hear, hear," Binky murmured.

"The new people," I said. "What are their names . . . Martin and Felice? Yes. They know nothing about parrots?"

"They know," she admitted. "But they treat the birds like products. A box of cornflakes. No warmth there, no sympathy. They had no favorites and sometimes they could be mean."

"Plebs," Binky added. "Definitely plebs."

But then our drinks arrived and I raised my glass in a toast. "To your freedom," I said.

They responded most heartily and I was happy to see they were not at all disheartened by their sudden termination. Relieved, as a matter of fact. I wondered if they envisioned a future on the Las Vegas stage as a duet featuring birdcalls with tambourine accompaniment.

If you're interested in matters gustatory, and I presume you are, our lunch was a gargantuan seafood salad served in a wooden bowl large enough to hold a hippo's hip. In addition to the greens, onions, black olives, bell peppers, mushrooms, and radishes, it contained shrimp, crabmeat, lobster, scallops, and a few chunks of pepperoni for the fun of it. Leroy had prepared a creamy lemon-and-dill dressing. Excellent. We had a chilled bottle of Sancerre. Also excellent.

As we gorged on this healthful repast, Bridget and Binky regaled me with the tale of an incident I found diverting and hope you will too even though it has little connection with the discreet inquiry inspiring this narrative.

It concerns a remarkable happening at a nursing home in Stuart where The Busy B's were entertaining the residents. Binky was giving the coo of the mourning dove and Bridget was spanking her tambourine when an oldster lurched from his wheelchair, hobbled to the center of the floor, and began to perform an arthritic jig in time to the "music."

His impromptu dance elicited such an enthusiastic response that Bridget and Binky determined to revise their repertoire and reproduce or suggest dance rhythms in their act. The results were startling they assured me. At subsequent nursing home performances they had geriatrics attempting jigs, clogs, waltzes, polkas, even a slow-motion Charleston.

You may think this activity by the elderly as exciting as group flossing but I find the idea of gaffers and gammers kicking up their heels invigorating. I trust when I am toothless and spavined I will have the spirit to essay a rumba.

During the remainder of the luncheon I queried my guests on the daily routine at Parrots Unlimited: who fed the birds, who was responsible for totaling the day's receipts, how often inventory was taken, etc. Their answers revealed nothing of significance. Several days passed before I realized I hadn't asked the right questions. This is a frequent failing of detectives and suspicious wives.

We finished, left the Pelican Club, and were standing in the parking area when I felt it necessary to warn them again.

"Please," I said, "do be careful. Emma and Tony were fired and I know I needn't remind you what happened to them. Now you have been sacked. Be extra-cautious."

They assured me I had nothing to worry about; they were perfectly capable of ensuring their own safety.

"If any bullyboy attacks us," Bridget said, "I'll bounce my tambourine off his noggin."

"And I shall befuddle him with the hoot of the barn owl," Binky added.

We all laughed and I watched them depart, wondering about the derivation of the phrase "babes in the wood."

I returned to my sepulcher at the McNally Building and found on my desk two messages reporting phone calls taken by our lobby receptionist. My first callback was to Sgt. Al Rogoff. He sounded desperate.

"Anything?" he asked.

"Nada," I said. "Except Binky Watrous just got fired from Parrots Unlimited. There goes my mole."

"A perfect mole. They're blind, aren't they?"

"Not completely but most of them wear bifocals."

"Very funny. Did you get any skinny from Watrous?"

"Not much," I admitted. "But I wanted someone inside. Now I'm stymied. You?"

"The same," he said glumly. "In spades. The only news to report is Peter Gottschalk is back in the hospital."

It wasn't a great shock. I think I had expected it. "When did this happen?" I asked Rogoff.

"Early this morning. A call to nine-one-one. Too much booze, I guess. Not fatal but they're keeping him under observation. What a saphead the lad is."

"But not a killer."

"I guess not," the sergeant said. "But if not him, then who? Listen, Archy, you really think the Gottschalk homicide is connected to the blasting of those kids in the Everglades?"

"I do and thought you did too."

"I did but now I'm beginning to wonder. Everything's getting cold and we're getting nowhere. You know how solution rates go down as time passes. Have you got anything you can throw me? A crumb?"

I paused a moment, wondering if it was worth a gamble. I decided it was, because if it proved out I would benefit and so would the sergeant.

"Want to take a chance, Al?"

"A chance? Right now I'll listen to some Gypsy with a crystal ball. Sure I'll take a chance."

"You told me an eyewitness stated she saw Emma Gompertz and Tony Sutcliffe being hustled into a white car she couldn't identify."

"That's right."

"Show her a color photo of a white four-door Ford Explorer and ask her if it could be the vehicle involved."

"Who owns a white four-door Ford Explorer?" he demanded.

"I'm not going to answer that; I don't want to involve an individual who may be totally innocent. You wanted a crumb, I'm giving you one. Are you going to do it or not?"

"I'll do it," he said, not at all happy. "What choice have I got? There's nothing else. But if this lays a big fat egg, you and I will pretend we never met. Okay?"

"Suits me," I said, and hung up as surly as he.

I could empathize with the sergeant. He was a professional and I was merely a semipro but I shared his frustration. A devious criminal was outbraining us and I believe we both considered it a sneering attack on our investigative skills. Ego, ego, all is ego.

But when Al said, "There's nothing else," he wasn't speaking for me. I did have a few minor scents I hadn't mentioned to him because they were too vaporous.

Item: The hacking of McNally & Son's computer after I had initiated an inquiry about parrots.

Item: A diamond choker worn by Yvonne Chrisling that might or might not be a gift from her stepson.

Item: What seemed to me a deliberate attempt by the Gottschalk twins to intoxicate their brother even though they were aware of his illness.

But what would be gained if I reported such ephemera to Rogoff? I knew his reaction would be: "So what?" He wanted facts, sworn testimony, hard evidence. He wanted to cut knots open with knife or scissors. I had the patience to untangle, picking endlessly. I really had no choice, did I?

My second caller had been Ricardo Chrisling phoning from Parrots Unlimited. The person who answered was abrupt, almost churlish, and I began to question the efficiency of the new staff. But when Ricardo came on the line he couldn't have been more congenial. Señor Charm himself. A definite change from his previous distant manner.

"Sorry I missed you at the to-do last night," he said breezily. "Had to go out of town on business. Good party, was it?"

"Very enjoyable," I lied.

"Listen, Archy, I've been hoping to get together with you for some time now but I've been so busy since Hiram passed I haven't had time to do what I *want* to do. I know this is short notice but could I treat you to dinner tonight? There's a new Mexican restaurant on Dixie Highway. It's called the Alcazar, which is a laugh because it's really a hole-in-the-wall with no more than ten tables. But the food is something special. No tacos, enchiladas, or any other Tex-Mex garbage. This is classic Mexican cuisine and it's really something. Also, they serve the best margaritas in Florida. How does that sound?"

"I'm salivating already."

"Then you can meet me around seven?"

"Sure."

"One drawback: I'll have to cut and run by nine o'clock. Some friends are flying into Miami from South America and I want to be there to meet them. But we'll have time for a nice leisurely dinner. Okay?"

"Of course."

He gave me the address of the Alcazar and hung up before I had a chance to ask if I should wear a sombrero.

It was a strange invitation, was it not? Totally unexpected, and setting a time limit for "a nice leisurely dinner" seemed to me rather infra d.

This lad, I decided, had a strong penchant for things Hispanic. He had given me Mexican brandy, he was taking me to a Mexican restaurant, he was leaving early to meet friends flying in from South America. And suddenly I recalled Lolly Spindrift telling me Ricardo had been involved in an imbroglio at a local boîte. It had been a private party of *sudamericanos*. And there had been violence, someone had been shot. Now wasn't that intriguing?

But how could I condemn Ricardo Chrisling for his friendship with Latinos? Was not Connie Garcia, a Marielito, my very own light-o'-love? Even though she seemed determined to turn off the light.

29

He was right; it *was* a hole-in-the-wall and required a spot of searching. I finally located the Alcazar at the rear of a mini-mall. It appeared to be a narrow establishment with no advertising other than the name in hammered iron script over a weathered oak door. I was only a few moments late but Ricardo was waiting for me at a tiny stand-up bar to the right of the entrance. He shook my hand heartily, a totally unnecessary long-time-no-see grip.

I had given up hope of competing with his Armani elegance and wore my silver-gray Ultrasuede sport jacket with black gabardine slacks. I was happy to see he was just as informally attired, although his terra-cotta jacket and taupe trousers were both in a nubby raw silk. But the man was without a single wrinkle. I had a mad fancy he had his clothes pressed daily—with him in them.

"Glad you could make it, Archy," he said, and made it sound sincere. "Now you must try a margarita—the house specialty."

"I'm willing."

He ordered from a mustachioed bartender and turned back to me. "How was your day?" he asked. He was trying hard to be genial and I appreciated the effort. But I sensed it was exactly that—an effort.

"My day?" I said, and flipped a hand back and forth. "Half and half. Rough and rugged until you called. Then I decided to pack it in. Went home, had a swim in the ocean, took a short and delightful nap, shared a cocktail with my parents, and here I am. Things are looking up."

"This will help," he said as our margaritas were served in glasses large enough to hold a baby coelacanth. I took a sip and he looked at me expectantly.

"Marvelous," I said. "Absolutely top-notch."

He glowed as if he had mixed them himself. Actually they were excellent drinks but couldn't equal Simon Pettibone's margaritas, which were ne plus ultra. I think Mr. Pettibone's secret was the sea salt he used to rim the glass but I may be mistaken. I am occasionally incorrect, you know. As when I persuaded Binky Watrous he could easily consume a platter of fried rattlesnake meat without suffering a gastric disaster. Wrong!

"What do you think of the place?" Ricardo asked.

I looked into the dining area. Definitely small. As he had said, no more than ten tables. It was a stark room with minimal decoration. There was a single bullfight poster on a whitewashed wall. The matador pictured, Belmonte, bore a striking resemblance to Chrisling: haughty, elegant, severe. Both man and poster gave the impression of repressed passion.

"It's a bit spartan," I admitted, recalling the soft luxury of his apartment. "But I like the way the tables are dressed. Fresh flowers are always welcome."

"We may be eating them later," he said. "Served with cilantro."

His wit wasn't dry; it was desiccated.

I shan't attempt to describe our meal in detail since my palate is not discerning enough to identify subtle flavorings. I know we had a remarkable avocado salad with lime juice; mussels with scallions, white wine, and cream; and a main dish of salmon fillets with garlic and chilies. We agreed to skip dessert since we were both surfeited after more than ample portions of those luscious vittles.

Our choices had been spicy but not too hot and the service was admirable. I told Ricardo how much I had enjoyed it and I hoped we might return to try other examples of Mexican haute cuisine. "Next time you'll be my guest," I said.

"Sure," he said. "But if I can't make it and you want to ask someone else, just mention my name to get a table. The Alcazar has become an *in* spot."

I didn't doubt it for by the time we finished, every table was taken and several patrons were waiting at the bar, each gripping one of those huge margaritas. Ricardo and I were draining final glasses of a flinty Mexican sauvignon blanc when he glanced at his Rolex.

"Sorry," he said, "but I've got to run. Listen, Archy, if you'd care to stay and have a brandy at the bar, by all means do. I have an account here and I'll tell the maître d' to put it on my tab."

"That's very kind of you," I said, "but I think I'll leave as well. Thank you for a most enjoyable feast."

We both rose to depart and it was then the tenor of the evening changed. Later it seemed to me to consist of two distinct acts: the dinner and what followed. I had the notion of a curtain being lowered and being raised again on a totally different scene.

A young woman pushed through the throng at the bar and came hurrying to confront us.

"Hi, Dick," she said breathlessly. "You haven't seen Paul tonight, have you?"

I glanced at Ricardo and saw him wince. You may adjudge me a simpleton but at the moment I thought his discomfort came from being addressed as Dick. But why should he be dismayed? Ricardo is another form of Richard, and Dick is a generally accepted diminutive. My name is Archibald but I have no objection to Archy. However I do have an aversion to Arch, which I feel is more adjective than name.

But then his obvious disconcertment may have been due to the lady's physical appearance. She was attractive enough in a Betty Boopish kind of way, but it was more her costume than her looks or manner which might have caused Ricardo's distress. She was clad in a tarty outfit of flaming red leather, jacket and skirt, the latter so short her bare knees were completely revealed, each a perfect image of Herbert Hoover.

"No, Sonia, I haven't seen Paul," Chrisling said stiffly. Then, remembering his manners, he uttered a swift introduction. "Sonia, this is Archy. Archy, Sonia." No last names.

"Hi, Archy," she said brightly.

"Hi, Sonia," I said just as brightly. Did I have a choice?

"I've got to leave right now," Ricardo said, "or I'll never get to the

Lauderdale airport in time to meet my friends. Archy, do me a favor, will you? Treat Sonia to a drink at the bar. And don't forget to put it on my tab."

He fled and I was left with Ms. Miniskirt. "Would you care for a drink?" I asked gamely.

"Why not?" she said. "I already et."

Most of the waiting customers had now been seated and we were able to find room at the zinc-topped bar. Sonia ordered a margarita of course but I asked for a brandy. I was served a Presidente, the same brand Chrisling had given me.

"Have you known Ricardo long?" I asked casually.

"Dick?" she said. "Sure, we're old friends. He's the handsomest guy I've ever met. Don't you think he's handsome?"

"I do indeed," I assured her. "But what about Paul? The man you're looking for." I meant it teasingly but she became suddenly morose.

"My ex," she said darkly. "A real stinker. He's a week late on the alimony check. That's why I'm looking for him. I'll clean his clock. It's not he ain't got the bucks."

"Ah," I said. "He's gainfully employed?"

"Sure he is. A good job. He's a naval architect."

"He designs navels?"

She looked at me. "Boats," she said. "He designs boats."

"Oh," I said.

"Listen, Archy, I've got a great idea. Why don't you buy us a bottle of something somewhere and we'll go back to my place, let down our hair, and tell each other the stories of our lives. Then we'll see what happens. Okay?"

"Oh, I don't think I could do that," I said hastily.

"It doesn't have to be a big bottle," she told me. "A pint will do."

Our conversation was beginning to take on a surreal quality, and if this tootsiesque young lady had suddenly launched into a dance routine from a Busby Berkeley musical I wouldn't have been a bit surprised.

"Sonia," I said earnestly, "I do thank you for your kind invitation but I'm afraid it's impossible tonight."

"You don't like me? I don't turn you on?"

"I *do* like you," I declared, "and you *do* turn me on. But I have an important errand of mercy to perform tonight. My dear old grandmother is in the hospital and she's depending on me to stop by to read the latest financial report on her investment in pork belly futures."

Look, I wasn't going to let her outgoof me. I could be just as mentally anorexic as she.

"What's wrong with your grandmother?"

"I'm afraid it's a terminal case of flagrante delicto."

"Oh lordy, that sounds awful."

"It is. Endless suffering."

"But listen, couldn't you come over to my place after you visit your grandmother? I mean it's just the shank of the evening. I'll wait for you."

She was being awfully persistent and I think it was at that moment I realized this was quite possibly more than a casual pickup. Despite her fey conversation she was intent on her purpose: to lure me to her lair.

"Sonia, I'd love to," I said with what I hoped sounded like a sigh of ineffable regret. "But after I visit grandmama I'm so wrung out emotionally I'm not capable of fun and games. You understand, don't you?"

"I guess," she said.

"But I want to see you again," I said eagerly. "Perhaps we could make it another night. May I ask for your telephone number?"

That seemed to enthuse her. "You betcha," she said, fished in the pocket of her leather jacket, and came out with a tube of lipstick.

Before I was fully aware of what was happening she had grasped my left hand, turned it over, and scrawled her telephone number on my palm in virulent red lip gloss.

"There!" she said triumphantly. "How's that? I have an answering machine. If I'm not in, leave a message."

"I certainly shall," I said feebly.

"Soon?"

"As possible," I said, looking at the number smeared on my palm with loathing. I prayed Brillo and Ajax might do the trick.

She finished her margarita and leaned forward to give me a kiss and a wink. Then she was gone with a creaking of leather. I gulped my brandy hurriedly, fearing she might return.

"Mr. Chrisling has taken care of the bill, sir," the mustachioed bartender said gravely.

I thanked him and handed over a sawbuck gratuity. He gave me a grateful smile I prayed was sincere. At the moment I was desperately in need of unambiguity.

I drove home slowly, thoughts awhirl as usual, and pulled into my slot in our three-car garage. I switched off engine, lights, and just sat there in the darkness. After a moment I heard a gentle scratching, leaned to open the door, and Hobo leaped into the passenger bucket. I think he wanted to lick my schnozz but I wouldn't let him; I'd had enough unsolicited affection for one night. But I did pet him, stroking his head and back. A few minutes later he curled up on the leather seat and closed his eyes. Lucky dog.

I wished I could sleep as easily and instantly as he, but I could not. All the rusty McNally neurons were in overdrive and the ferment was almost painful as I tried to figure out exactly what had happened that night. I strove to think logically—which you may feel is similar to my attempting a fifty-foot pole vault.

I started by assuming Ricardo Chrisling's invitation to dinner was not simply to have a sociable get-together; the man had an ulterior motive. And it had appeared in red leather. I refused to believe Sonia's intrusion was merely a chance encounter. He had arranged it.

Perhaps it was one of those macho things. Here's a willing chick you should meet and you'll have a great time. But I did not think Ricardo capable of such crassness. He was wilier than that.

Putting aside his scheming for the nonce, I concentrated on the conduct of Sonia.

It would be understandable if she, a not so gay divorcée, was lonely and yearned for companionship, even if it lasted no more than one night. Possible but not probable.

Or she was engaged in Murphy's game, one of the oldest cons in the history of scams. A chippie, real or faux, entices a john to her digs with the promise of instant gratification. Once inside her door the victim is confronted by her alleged husband, boyfriend, pimp, or perhaps an armed plug-ugly hired for the occasion. The mark is robbed and forcibly ejected from the premises. Was that Sonia's script? Possible but not probable.

Which brought me back to Ricardo's role in this farrago. If he had written the scenario, planned I was to meet the available lady with the bees' knees, what in the name of Jehoshaphat could be his reason?

I left Hobo snoozing in the Miata and went into the house, up to my hideaway, still puzzled by Ricardo's behavior and wondering if I was not being paranoid. The man had really done nothing suspicious. He had invited me to a splendid dinner. An acquaintance had unexpectedly appeared. So why was I impugning his motives, searching for any evidence of deception?

I was disrobing, preparing to spend an hour or two bringing my journal up to date, when I stopped suddenly. I think I may have grinned. Because a short memory loss was restored and I recalled something Ricardo had said during the evening. I shall not dignify it by calling it a "clue," but I thought it significant.

Surely you know what I'm writing about, don't you? You picked up on it before I did—not so? If not, you must be patient and be assured your temporarily prideful scribe will reveal Ricardo's slip at the proper time.

Stay in touch.

30

Before I retired on Thursday night I laboriously expunged Sonia's lipsticked telephone number from my palm. A bit of scouring powder helped. But first I copied the number into my daybook. As an amateur sleuth I had learned God is in the details. Or is it the Devil who is in the details? I can never remember which.

Regarding the next morning . . .

There is an anecdote about W. C. Fields—or perhaps it was Jimmy Durante—who was called upon to make a daybreak appearance at his movie studio. As he staggered through the dawn's early light he came upon a lofty tree laden with sleeping and nesting birds. Immediately he began kicking the tree and whacking it with his walking stick.

"When I'm up," he shouted, "everybody up!"

I recalled the story after Sgt. Al Rogoff shattered my deep slumber with a phone call at eight o'clock on Friday morning. Ungodly hour.

"When you're up," I grumbled, "everybody up. Have you no mercy?"

"Not me," he said curtly. "I'm working my tail off and I expect the same from you. Listen, I showed a color photo of a white Ford Explorer to the gooney lady who claims she saw Tony Sutcliffe and Emma Gompertz being hustled away. She says yes, she thinks that was the vehicle used. She *thinks* it was but she isn't certain. A defense attorney could easily demolish her testimony but it's good enough for me. Like I told you, I got nothing else. So what was Ricardo Chrisling's car doing there when the ex-employees of Parrots Unlimited were abducted?"

It staggered me for a sec. "I didn't tell you it belonged to Chrisling."

He was indignant. "You think I'm a mutt? After the loopy dame made a tentative identification I checked the cars of everyone connected with this mishmash and came up with Chrisling. You think he's our hero?"

"I just don't know," I said truthfully. "But I'm happy my tip yielded results. Now you owe me one—right?"

"Oh-oh," he said resignedly. "All right, what do you want?"

"I have a telephone number and a woman's first name. I'd like to know if she's got a sheet."

"This is personal? You're looking to romance the lady?"

"Don't get cute, Al. She's a friend of Chrisling."

"In that case I'll go along."

I told him her name was Sonia and, after a moment, I found her number in my professional diary and repeated it to Rogoff.

"I'll let you know," he said.

"When?"

"ASAP. I think the ice is beginning to break."

He hung up and I went back to bed for another thirty minutes of sweet somnolence. I finally did get to work that morning—late but in an energetic mood. I decided Sgt. Rogoff had been correct; the ice pack was cracking. I hadn't grasped the infamous plot earlier because I underestimated the villainy of the people involved. It's a constant fault; I can never acknowledge the power of sheer evil.

I had two phone calls to make. The first was to the Gottschalk home. I was finally put through to one of the twins. Don't ask me which one although she claimed to be Judith. I inquired as to the condition of her brother.

"Oh, Peter's been released from the hospital," she said breezily. "Right now he's on his way to visit some quack. What a twerp he is!"

I thanked her hurriedly and hung up. I had no desire for an extended conversation. I might get suckered into hosting a champagne brunch.

Before I could make my second call I received one—from Yvonne Chrisling. "You naughty boy," she said reprovingly. "You promised to phone and you didn't."

"Yvonne, we spoke only a day or so ago. I really intended to contact you." Liar, liar, pants on fire.

"No matter," she said, suddenly brisk. "I must see you at once. It's very important."

"Lunch?"

"No," she said authoritatively. "Not in public. And not in my home."

My home": I loved it. A few weeks ago it had been Hiram Gottschalk's home. *Sic transit . . .* and so forth.

"Would you care to come to the office?" I suggested.

"No." She was quite decisive. "I might be seen."

I wanted to ask, "By whom?" but didn't.

"If this is to be a confidential meeting," I said, "as you apparently wish, perhaps we might get together at the McNally residence. We can talk inside or during a walk on the beach—whichever you prefer."

She didn't hesitate a mo. "Yes," she said, "that will do. In an hour. You will be there?"

"I shall. You have my address?"

"Of course," she said. "I'm so looking forward to seeing you again, darling."

I am hypersensitive to tones of voice and I thought her last declaration had a wheedling inflection. Curious for a woman of her resolution.

I had time to make my second call before leaving for a tête-à-tête with the Spider Woman. So I phoned Binky Watrous and found him at home in an excitable mood.

"Do you know anything about yellow-shafted flickers?" he demanded.

"Of course," I said. "Some of my best friends are yellow-shafted flickers, several of whom have been incarcerated for exhibiting their proclivity in public."

"Archy," he protested, "they're birds! Woodpeckers. And they attack anything even resembling a tree. They hammer at it with their beaks. I bought a recording of their hammering and I've been practicing imitating it. It's great, even better than calls. Bridget says with her tambourine and my hammering of the yellow-shafted flicker we'll have a classic. A *classic*, Archy!"

I should have replied, "A classic *what?*" But I couldn't rain on his parade; he was so up.

"Binky," I said, "the reason I called was to ask you about Martin and Felice, the recently hired employees of Parrots Unlimited."

"I already told you. Definitely below the salt."

"Useless, are they?"

"Well, they're not bird mavens, for sure, for sure."

"Then what do they *do?*" I persisted. "The man, Martin, for instance. He does feedings, cleans cages, and similar scut work?"

"Never saw him lift a hand. Sold a bird occasionally but he spent most of his time in the boss's office fiddling with the computer."

My heart leaped like an intoxicated gazelle. "Thank you, my son," I said huskily. "Your skinny may prove of inestimable value. Now go back to your hammering and don't blunt your beak."

I hung up in such an ebullient mood I wanted to chortle—if only I knew how to chortle. Things were coming together, wouldn't you agree? But there were surprises to come I hadn't anticipated. The picture puzzle was not quite complete. Stick with me, kid, and you'll be wearing diamonds.

I drove home hastily and waited only ten minutes on our graveled turnaround before Yvonne Chrisling appeared in a new Cadillac DeVille. And I mean *spanking* new. It was a forest green, a color much in vogue at the time, and had such a gleam it looked as if it had just been driven from the showroom. As the Mad. Ave. pundits advise: If you've got it, flaunt it.

She emerged from the yacht wearing stonewashed jeans and a white canvas bush jacket. I realized I had never before seen her dressed so informally. I liked it; she seemed softer, more vulnerable.

But my impression was quickly dispelled. She gave me a dim smile and then looked about at the McNally estate: our ersatz-Tudor main house feathered in ivy, garage, greenhouse, potting shed, and Hobo's abode.

"Very antique, isn't it?" she said sniffishly.

"True," I said, refusing to be riled. "We planned it so."

"Not to my taste," she pronounced, and it was then I became fully aware of what a snarky mood she was in. "Is there anyone about?" she asked abruptly.

"Probably my mother and the staff."

"Then let's go down to the beach."

"Would you care for a drink of something first?"

"No," she said tersely, and I had a premonition this meeting was going to be as much fun as the extraction of an impacted molar.

I conducted her across Ocean Boulevard, down the rickety wooden staircase to the sand. She took up a firmly planted station in the shade of some palms and showed no inclination to move farther.

"A walk?" I suggested. "Perhaps a wade in the water?"

"I don't think so," she said. "I hate the beach and the ocean."

It was too much. "Then what on earth are you doing in South Florida?"

"Circumstances," she said, which told me nothing. "Archy," she went on determinedly, "I need legal advice."

"Whoa!" I said, holding up a palm. "I am not an attorney. I do not have a law degree or license to practice. I think you better consult my father or another qualified lawyer."

"But you know a lot about the law, don't you?"

"Some," I admitted, cautiously forbearing to tell her the story of why I was booted out of Yale Law.

"This isn't for me," she said. "It's for a friend who has a problem."

She looked at me so wide-eyed and sincere I knew she was lying. Besides, everyone in the legal profession has heard the old wheeze from a client: "I have a friend with a legal problem." Hogwash. The attorney knows immediately it's the client's problem.

"What is it, Yvonne?"

"My friend, a woman, has knowledge of a crime. She wasn't involved in any way, shape, or form but she knows who did it. What should she do?"

"Immediately report what she knows to a law enforcement agency," I said promptly. "She is obligated to do so. If not she may find herself in deep, deep trouble. Concealing knowledge of criminal behavior is not a charge to be taken lightly."

Yvonne showed no indication of surprise or shock. I reckoned she already knew what I had told her.

"But it's not so simple," she said, turning her gaze out to sea: a true thousand-yard stare. "First of all, the individual who committed the crime is close to her. Very close. It would pain her to be an informer."

I shook my head. "She has no choice."

"Another factor . . ." Yvonne continued, looking at me directly again. "My friend is afraid of what the reaction might be of the person she accuses."

"Afraid? Of physical retaliation?"

"Yes."

"She can ask for police protection. She can move, change her phone number, take on a new identity. Whatever will ensure her safety."

"But she must tell what she knows?"

"Absolutely."

"She is entirely innocent, you understand, and now she is trapped in this terrible dilemma and she is frightened. You can sympathize with that, can you not?"

"Of course I can, Yvonne."

I had said the right thing, because her manner was suddenly transformed. She melted, became almost flirtatious.

"How happy I am to have asked for your advice, Archy," she said in a lilting voice. "I knew I could depend on you. We are so compatible. We must see more of each other. You agree?"

"Oh yes."

"*Much* more," she chortled. *She* knew how to do it. "And I shall tell my friend everything you have said. Thank you, sweetheart."

She took my hand as I led her back to the parked Cadillac. She couldn't have been more affectionate. Well, she could have been but I resisted, fearing Hobo might be observing us from his kennel. "Thank you again, darling," she caroled just before she drove away. "What a treasure you are!"

I watched her wheeled castle depart, thinking, There goes one very brainy lady. But more of that later. At the moment I was famished and hustled into the kitchen. First things first.

No one was present and I presumed Ursi and perhaps mother were on a shopping expedition to replenish our larder. I opened the fridge and inspected the contents to see what I might use to concoct a modest, nutritious lunch.

A bag of Walla Walla sweet onions caught my eye. When Vidalias are not in season we send for Walla Wallas or Texas sweets. Admirable onions, no doubt, but I still prefer the distinctive flavor of Vidalias. But one must make do and so I constructed a toasted bagel sandwich holding a thick slice of Walla Walla slathered with Dijonnaise. You've never had an onion sandwich? The mother of all sandwiches. Especially when accompanied by an icy bottle of lager.

I ate slowly with much pleasure, resolutely refraining from thinking about my conversation with Yvonne Chrisling. I finished after stoutly rejecting an urge to make and devour a duplicate—and stoutly is the right word. I then phoned the office, spoke to Mrs. Trelawney, and found my father would be absent all afternoon conferring with a client in Lantana. It meant my necessary meeting with him would have to be postponed until the evening. I must admit I was relieved.

I uncapped another bottle of lager, took it upstairs to my atelier, and settled down for a deep think. Yvonne Chrisling . . .

I recognized she had heavy, heavy motives for initiating our chat on the beach. Her ploy of asking legal advice for a friend was a transparent fraud. She was pleading her own case. And unless she considered me a complete dolt—and I trusted she didn't—she knew I identified her as the troubled woman involved.

But why devise such a Byzantine plot to enlist my sympathy?

It took me almost an hour and the second bottle of lager to arrive at what I considered a logical reason. The lady was, in effect, attempting to cop a plea or cut a deal. She realized or sensed the running wolves—in the shape of Sgt. Al Rogoff and yrs. truly—were baying at her sleigh and coming closer.

"Save yourself" was the belief, the faith governing her existence. Now, feeling threatened, she was moving boldly and shrewdly to protect herself. I didn't want to but I had to admire her effort. It is no easy task for anyone to claim innocence, even the guiltless.

I was convinced I had her pinned. It gave me no joy. It would be simplistic to label the people involved as weak. They were not weak. They were strong, venomous characters who had made a cold, reasoned choice of corruption and its rewards.

Saddened by the perfidy existing in one family, I began to reread my entire scribbled record of the affair. And I arrived at what I believed to be a reasonable (and depressing) explanation of all that had occurred in the Gottschalk nest of vipers.

I intend to complete this penny dreadful as quickly as possible. I know you want to go to bed.

31

My father is more gourmand than gourmet and so I was delighted our Friday night dinner was pot roast with potato pancakes—his favorite. I hoped it might put him in a felicitous mood during an interrogation I simply had to make. Sometimes in our Q&A sessions he adopts a prickly you-have-no-need-to-know attitude which makes me want to run away from home.

"Could I have a few moments of your time, sir?" I said as we left the dining room after a dessert of lemon sorbet and pralines.

"And what is your definition of a few moments?" he asked genially enough.

"Ten, perhaps fifteen minutes."

"Concerning what?"

"My inquiry into the death of Hiram Gottschalk."

He nodded and led the way into his study. "A peg of brandy?" he inquired.

"That would be welcome, thank you."

He did the honors, pouring each of us a small snifter. It wasn't his best cognac but I made no complaint. He didn't ask me to be seated and he also remained standing. It was his way of ensuring our meeting would be brief.

"Well?" he said.

"Father, I have been reviewing my notes regarding the Gottschalk case, beginning with the initial assignment. At that time you mentioned you had discussions with him regarding the creation of a foundation in order to reduce his estate tax. Am I right?"

One hairy eyebrow was hoisted aloft. "Archy, I admire the thoroughness of your records. Yes, you are correct. I had several conversations with Mr. Gottschalk concerning the establishment of a non-profit foundation."

"Could you tell me what he had in mind?"

"He was rather vague about it but it seemed he was interested in financing a sort of aviary in which research and breeding would help ensure the continued existence of endangered species of birds, particularly parrots."

"If he had lived long enough to set up such an institution, it would have reduced his net worth?"

"Naturally. And given him the tax advantages of a sizable charitable contribution, I might add."

"If the foundation had been in place prior to his death would it have limited his bequests to his heirs and beneficiaries?"

He pondered a long time, taking two tastes of his cognac. "Perhaps limited is the wrong word," he said finally. "Heirs and beneficiaries would have profited handsomely even if the foundation was in existence. Specific sums would be bequeathed. If the foundation did *not* exist at Mr. Gottschalk's death, as it does not, those bequests will be larger."

"Much larger?" I persisted.

"Appreciably," he said dryly.

"Father, do you know if Mr. Gottschalk informed his heirs and beneficiaries of his intention to establish a charitable foundation?"

I think he was puzzled by my question. "I have no idea. Why don't you ask them, Archy?"

"I doubt if I'd get a straight answer. Will you venture a guess, sir. Did he tell them or didn't he?"

Again he mulled, finishing his brandy. "I'd guess he told them," he said at last. "Our late client was a very outgoing man. Eccentric but trusting. Is that all?"

"A final question. . . . In the event an heir is deemed incompetent for mental or physical disabilities to handle his or her personal and financial affairs, who is appointed guardian?"

"A court of law would make the decision on the heir's incompetency after hearing testimony from physicians and other relevant witnesses. If the heir is adjudged mentally and/or physically unable to handle his or her affairs, I'd say the most likely guardian to be appointed by the court would be the closest family member."

"Or members," I said.

"Or members," he acknowledged.

"Thank you, father," I said, draining my brandy. "Have a pleasant evening."

"I hope to," he said. "Is this disagreeable business winding down, Archy?"

"I believe it is, sir. With good luck."

"Luck?" he repeated. "We make our own luck."

"Not always," I informed him. "Sometimes we benefit from other people's bad luck."

Profound—no? But I wasn't sure what I meant.

I went upstairs full of beans. After what father had told me, I exulted, I had everything. It wasn't long after that—a short session at my desk flipping through my journal did the trick—I realized I had nothing. Oh, I conjured a marvelous hypothesis elucidating all—including the 5th Problem of Hilbert. Watertight, one might even say, and I do say it. But I had no proof, and without what Al Rogoff calls "hard evidence" it was all smoke and mirrors.

What I needed, I concluded disconsolately, was a deus ex machina. And because I live a clean life and have a pure heart it arrived about an hour later in the form of a telephone call from the crusty sergeant himself.

"You're awake?" he said. "And sober?"

"Of course I'm awake and sober," I said. "And working I might add. 'Neither snow, nor rain, nor heat, nor gloom of night stays these couriers from the swift completion of their appointed rounds.' "

"You work for the post office?"

"It's Herodotus, Al."

"Thank you. I won't forget it for at least five minutes. Listen, about the bimbo you asked me to check out."

"Sonia. What's her last name?"

"She's got about six of them. Take your pick."

"She told me her ex-husband is a naval architect."

"The last time we had her in she told us her ex is a brain surgeon. I think he used liposuction on hers."

"You mean she's got a record?"

"Archy, she's a toughie. Many, many charges. Probations without end. And she did six months for loitering."

"Loitering for what?"

"For the purpose of singing hymns, idiot boy. She's a friend of Ricardo Chrisling?"

"Right now," I said, "I think she's more an employee than a friend. Al, where are you calling from?"

"Headquarters, about to leave."

"Have you had dinner?"

"Of course."

"What kind of pizza?"

"Anchovy."

"Then you must be thirsty. How about stopping by my place on your way home."

"Why should I do that?"

"Two cold bottles of Rolling Rock."

"Be there in about thirty minutes," he said.

The half hour gave me time to kick my cerebral cortex into high gear and decide to limit my revelations to Rogoff. There were things he needed to know to further his investigation of three homicides and things concerning only my own discreet inquiry. Admittedly the two intermixed to some extent but I hoped to keep them distinct. Hopeless hope.

I was downstairs when his pickup skidded to a stop with a scattering of gravel. I uncapped two bottles of beer, brought them outside, and clambered into the cab alongside him. He had been smoking a cigar but mercifully laid it to rest in a huge ashtray attached magnetically to the dash. But the atmosphere remained yucky enough to spur me into lighting an English Oval in self-defense.

He took a heavy gulp of his first beer and sighed. "Manna," he said. Then: "What do you want?"

"Al, why do you think I want anything?"

"Why else would you be bribing me with a couple of brews?"

"Well, it's true I need your cooperation but in return I am about to give you a gift beyond compare."

"Yeah? And what might that be?"

"Listen to this. . . ."

I must have talked steadily for at least ten minutes, detailing my certainty that Ricardo Chrisling was the murderer of Hiram Gottschalk and deeply involved in the killings of Emma Gompertz and Anthony Sutcliffe.

1. Chrisling has close ties to Mexican and South American banditos engaged in the smuggling of endangered birds, particularly parrots, into the U.S.
2. He serves as one of several retail dealers selling these expensive birds to collectors.
3. Hiram Gottschalk became aware of what Ricardo was doing and vowed to expose him. And so Hiram was eliminated.
4. Tony Sutcliffe and his companion met the same fate when they accused Chrisling of the prohibited trade in rare species.
5. Ricardo uses the computer setup at Parrots Unlimited to keep track of his purchases, sales, and customers. The same computer was used to query the net on the subject of parrots, and Chrisling became aware of the interest of McNally & Son in the smuggling of the birds.

I paused to light another ciggie as Rogoff started on his second beer.

"I'll buy it," he said unexpectedly. "It ties in with Chrisling's car being used to grab Gompertz and Sutcliffe. And among the papers I took from their apartment were copies of letters written to the Division of Law Enforcement of the Fish and Wildlife Service. They were about the smuggling of birds on the proscribed list, how the smuggling was done, ports of entry, penalties, and so forth. So Sutcliffe must have suspected something rancid was going on at Parrots Unlimited."

"He didn't suspect," I said, "he *knew*. And like the innocent he was, he confronted Ricardo and probably announced his intention of informing the authorities. And so he and Emma got their brains blown out in the Everglades. Pretty?"

The sergeant took a deep breath. "It all listens," he said. "A very neat solution and I believe every word of it. There's only one thing wrong with it; it's all ozone. You know? Not a thing we can take to the state attorney."

"Al, I've got an expert working on the invasion of McNally and Son's computer. We may be able to prove the break-in originated at Parrots Unlimited."

"So what? Chrisling would claim an employee was doing a little unauthorized hacking just for the fun of it, and he'll promise to fire the guy. Then where are we? Archy, we've got no proof of anything—let's face it."

"I've already faced it," I told him. "And there's only one way to resolve this stalemate: entrapment."

"Don't use that word!" Rogoff cried. "It means my pension."

"All right, then let me put it this way: It's a slim chance of snagging Ricardo Chrisling. It's a gamble, I admit, but you're a gambler, aren't you?"

"Would I be a cop if I wasn't?"

"I think 'if I weren't' is the correct usage."

He sighed. "Always the professor. Okay, let's hear your gamble."

"It involves Sonia, the hidebound vixen. From what you've told me about her I'm convinced she's a pro. I'm also convinced Ricardo plotted what was apparently a chance meeting. The man warned me on the phone he'd have to leave early to drive to the Miami airport to greet arriving friends. But at dinner he said he must rush off to meet those friends at the Fort Lauderdale airport. An innocent slip or change of plans? I don't think so. He was lying and he forgot his original lie. A good memory is absolutely essential for successful prevarication. Ask me; I know."

"All right," Al said, "let's assume he set up your meet with the hustler. What was his purpose? To provide you with a night of fun and games? Maybe he even paid her—a little after-dinner gift."

"I doubt it," I said. "Ricardo has more pride than that. I think she was instructed to play Murphy's game, as designed by Chrisling. I was to accompany the lady to her home, full of good food, Mexican brandy, and unutterable longing. At a designated moment one or more yobbos would appear and whisk me off to the Everglades, where I would meet the same fate that befell Gompertz and Sutcliffe."

"Very dramatic," Rogoff said. "But why should Chrisling want to put you down?"

"I told you," I explained patiently. "Ricardo's computer maven had already discovered McNally and Son was investigating the smuggling of parrots. Chrisling may be a villain but he's no fool. He guessed why I was nosing around—to identify the killer of Hiram Gottschalk. And in addition I was now making inquiries about his criminal and very profitable business activities. He's a direct man, Al; murder solves all his difficulties."

The sergeant fished his cold cigar from the ashtray and ignited it again. And so I had to light another cigarette to match him puff for puff, fume for fume.

"Supposing you're on target," he said, "what's your gamble?"

"I want to phone Sonia, make an appointment for tomorrow night. I think she'll leap at the chance because she struck out the last time. She'll inform Chrisling and the original scenario will be resurrected. But you and your stalwarts will be waiting outside. Concealed of course. And when the ruffians march me out for a one-way trip to the Everglades you'll be able to grab them. And Sonia as well."

He turned to stare at me. "You're a complete and total loony," he said. "You know that, don't you?"

"Al, I told you it's a gamble but I think the odds are in our favor. If it works you'll have Sonia and the muscles in custody. You know the hoods will probably have sheets longer than Sonia's. If you lean on them I wager one or more will spill to cop a plea. They'll tell you Ricardo Chrisling was the boss and masterminded the whole schmear."

"And if it doesn't work?"

"You mean Sonia turns out to be merely a hardworking entrepreneur eager to make a buck? I can handle that situation and beat a graceful retreat with my innocence intact. And you and your crew will have lurked a few hours in the darkness with no result. Is that so awful? You've been on unproductive stakeouts before, haven't you?"

He didn't answer immediately. He was silent a long time and I didn't know if his decision would be yea or nay.

"Okay," he said finally. "I'll play your nutty game. Nothing ventured, nothing gained."

"How true, how true," I said. "And a rolling stone gathers no moss."

"Go to hell," he said. "You'll set it up for tomorrow night?"

"If I can," I told him. "I'll let you know as soon as my dalliance with Sonia is confirmed. Where can I reach you tomorrow? Will you be at headquarters?"

"No," he said. "At home. I start a forty-eight at midnight."

"Sorry about that, Al."

He shrugged. "It comes with the territory. Thanks for the beers."

32

I climbed out of his pickup and waited until he pulled away. Then I went upstairs to wonder if what the sergeant had called my "nutty game" had a chance to succeed. It did, I assured myself, it did, it definitely did. And so I phoned Sonia, the femmy fatally in this circus.

I didn't speak to the lady herself but I reported to her answering machine. "Sonia," I said in what I hoped were fervid tones, "this is Archy. We were introduced by Ricardo Chrisling at the Alcazar—remember? I'd like very much to accept your kind invitation to visit you at your home. I'll bring the refreshment. Could we make it at nine o'clock tomorrow? Nine on Saturday night. Please let me know. I hope you'll say yes. It means so much to me."

I concluded by giving my unlisted phone number. It is not something I ordinarily care to do but I had no choice. I hoped she might return my call before noon the next day, when I had a golfing date with a trio of buddies including Binky Watrous. I prayed he wouldn't wear his plaid tam-o'-shanter, which looked like a Spanish omelette flapping about his ears.

I was sound asleep when I was awakened by the insistent shrill of my phone. I roused sufficiently to look at my illuminated bedside clock through bleary eyes. It was almost three a.m. and I feared what ghastly news awaited me. I picked up the phone with a trembling hand.

"Hiya, Archy," she said cheerily. "This is Sonia. I got your message and you're a sweetie to call. Of course I want to see you at nine tomorrow."

"Your address," I said in a sleep-slurred voice. "I don't know where you live. Wait a mo until I locate pen and paper."

She gave me her address and I scrawled it down as best I could.

"Ooh, I can hardly wait until tomorrow night, darling," she cooed. "We'll have such fun. By the way, I like gin."

She hung up and I rolled groaning back into bed, hoping to resume the dream I had been having of rescuing Joan Blondell from a burning building.

When I awoke about eight-thirty on Saturday morning the first thing I did was don my reading specs to make certain my torpid penmanship of the night before was readable. It was; Sonia's address was legible. Then horror struck. I realized she lived only a few doors away from the abode of Consuela Garcia. What a way to start a new day!

I phoned Al Rogoff and informed him my date with Sonia was set for nine p.m. I gave him the address. He grunted. I had the feeling his joy was underwhelming.

Actually it turned out to be a snappy and invigorating Saturday. After a few moments of worried reflection I concluded the chances of Connie spotting me sneaking into the lair of a local Mata Hari were practically nil and I could safely ignore the danger. Also, it was a super day, climatically speaking, and because I'm so attuned to the weather I found it impossible to be gloomy when the sky appeared dry-cleaned and the sun looked like a just minted one-ounce Golden Eagle.

The golf game was a joy. Binky and I were paired and won easily, earning a nice piece of change. Then we all adjourned to the Pelican Club for a raucous lunch of barbecued ribs and suds. After the gorge we played darts and again I won. Custom decreed the victor buy drinks for the losers, so my triumph cost more than my winnings. Silly, isn't it? But I didn't care; I took my luck at golf and darts as a harbinger of more good fortune to come.

The remainder of the day passed swiftly: the lazy, hazy dream of every Palm Beach layabout. I returned home, had a slow, languorous swim in a soup-warm sea, took a sweet nap, dressed, and joined my parents at the cocktail hour. After dinner I changed my duds to a more sportif costume I thought might impress Sonia. Then I set out on the night's venture, wondering if this was the way C. Auguste Dupin got his start.

Sonia had requested gin and my first inclination was to buy the cheapest corrosive available, since if my prediction of what was to happen proved correct we wouldn't be lifting a celebratory glass. But then I reproved myself for such a non-U decision. It indicated a shocking lack of noblesse oblige. And so I bought a bottle of Beefeater and toted that to the island of our very own Circe, who, as we all know, turned men into swine.

I parked a few streets away and wandered back no more fearful than if I were scaling the north face of the Eiger. I looked about warily but saw no signs of skulking miscreants. Nor did I spot Sgt. Rogoff and his army. I could only hope they were present.

I had no problem gaining entrance to Sonia's den. She was listed on the directory as Sonia Smith. Innocent enough. I pressed the button opposite her name, identified myself on the intercom, and was immediately buzzed in. I rode a rather tatty elevator to the sixth floor, walked down a tattier corridor, and was greeted at the opened door of 6-E by the grinning hostess, who promptly gave me a noisy smooch I could have done without.

"It's happy time!" she cried, and yanked me inside, locking, bolting, and chaining the door behind me. I wondered if I'd get time off for good behavior.

I was pulled into a living room decorated in South Florida Renaissance: glass tables supported on driftwood, milky paintings of conch shells, and tinted mirrors. Lots and lots of mirrors. I saw myself reflected from every angle: a depressing sight. Was I really beginning to sprout a dewlap?

Sonia was wearing a stained denim jumpsuit zippered from hither to yon. She looked as if she were ready to change the oil on your Winnebago. She grabbed the brown paper bag from my hands, extracted the bottle to glance at the label.

"Yummy!" she yelped. "My favorite. Now you make yourself at home while I slip into something more comfortable."

She disappeared with the gin, leaving me bemused. "Slip into something more comfortable." How long has it been since you've heard that line? It was a favorite in the movie romances of the 1930s and 1940s, usually murmured by Ann Sheridan. At the moment I would have liked to slip into something more comfortable, like a flak jacket atop a bulletproof vest.

My foreboding proved accurate when Sonia did not reappear but instead two gross creatures, seemingly as broad as they were tall, came lumbering from the rear of the apartment. They planted themselves stolidly and stared at me.

You must believe it when I tell you fright was not my first reaction. Instead I felt a surge of satisfaction at having correctly analyzed the situation and predicted what was likely to occur. But then, as gratification ebbed, terror took over.

"Good evening, gentlemen," I said with a silly laugh.

"Let's go," one of them growled.

"Go where?" I inquired reasonably enough.

"A little trip," the other said.

"Why on earth should I take a trip with you?" I asked. "I have no desire to travel at the moment."

"Here's why, jerko," ruffian #1 said, and withdrew a snub-nosed revolver from his jacket pocket. He pointed the muzzle at me.

"Well, yes," I admitted. "A sufficient invitation. May I bid a fond farewell to Sonia?"

They didn't bother replying. I was marched out of the apartment, both thugs crowding me so closely I was aware of their scent: something like a geriatric flounder. We waited for the elevator.

"If someone's on it," one of the brutes said, "behave yourself. We don't want to hurt innocent people."

"I'm innocent," I observed.

They looked at me.

Fortunately the elevator was empty and we descended to a lobby apparently just as vacant. My escorts prodded me outside and suddenly it seemed we had stepped onto a floodlighted Broadway stage.

Three cars were drawn up in an arc, and as we exited, their headlights went on and I was tempted to ask my abductors if they'd care to join me in a soft-shoe routine, perhaps to the rhythm of "Shuffle Off to Buffalo."

While we stood frozen in the brilliance, two police officers in mufti came from the lobby behind us and stuck weapons into the ribs of my captors. Their arms rose slowly, just floated up.

What amazed me most about this beautifully executed operation was the total absence of speech. I mean there were no shouts of "Freeze!" or "Hands up!" or even "Eat dirt, turkey!" But then Rogoff and his cohorts were professionals. And so were my escorts—professional hoodlums. There was no need for dialogue; everyone knew what was going down.

The two schtarkers were relieved of their guns, cuffed, and hustled separately into two of the parked cars. Headlights were dimmed and the sergeant came strolling toward me, juicing up a fresh cigar. I think he was trying hard not to grin.

"You okay?" he asked.

"Tip-top," I assured him. "Or will be when the tremors in my knees subside. It was nicely done, Al, and I thank you. But why aren't any of these vehicles police cars? They all look like they're privately owned."

"They are," he said. "If I had asked for an official go-ahead on this chancy game the brass would have thought I'd blown a fuse. So I had to recruit a few go-for-broke guys who'd play along just for the fun of it."

Then I realized the career risk he had taken on my behalf and I was grateful. What a fortunate SOB I was. That stands for son of a barrister of course. "I owe you a big one," I told Rogoff.

"Sure you do," he agreed. "Now let's go up and collect the airhead."

"I don't think she'll let us in," I said.

"Why not?" he said. "We're nice people. Sonia Smith—right? I checked the directory earlier today."

He pressed the button and when she answered on the intercom, her voice sounded a mite shaky. "Who is this?" she asked.

"Ma'am, this is Sergeant Al Rogoff of the Palm Beach Police Department. May I have a little conversation with you, please? It won't take long."

"I'm busy at the moment," she said. "Could we make it tomorrow?"

"On the other hand," he said pleasantly, "I could order up a SWAT team and have your door blasted open with a nuclear rocket. Would you prefer that, Sonia?"

Short pause. Then the buzzer sounded and we entered.

"You do have a way about you," I said admiringly.

He shrugged. "What's the point of having a potsy if you can't use it?"

Sonia opened her door with a bright smile that faded when she saw me. Al displayed his ID. She stood aside to let us enter. She was still wearing the denim jumpsuit but defiance had replaced her former élan.

"Is this a bust?" she demanded. "If it is, you got to read me my rights and I ain't saying a word until I talk to my lawyer."

"Nah," Rogoff said, "this is no arrest. I just think it would be to your advantage if you'd come down to headquarters with me and answer a few questions. If you don't want to, I'll have to go through the business of getting a warrant and pulling you in. It's really unnecessary. If you decide to come along you can always change your mind, clam up, and call your lawyer. It's a very small thing, Sonia. We don't suspect you of a supermarket massacre or anything like that. All we want is a little information on a minor matter. You're not being charged with anything. And if you cooperate you get a gold star next to your name on your records. Might help you in the future—right? How about it? Will you help us?"

He was very persuasive and it didn't take her long to decide. "Okay," she said. "Do I have to stay overnight?"

"Maybe," Rogoff admitted.

"Let me get my handbag," she said, and the sergeant followed her into the inner room. He didn't miss a trick.

When they emerged Al was rummaging through her bag. He held aloft a vial of pills. "What's this stuff?" he asked her.

"Aspirin," she said.

"Now they're making purple aspirin?" the sergeant said. "Crazy. Come along, luv. You'll be home again before you know it."

We let her lock up the apartment. We were waiting for the elevator when Sonia looked at me directly. "Archy," she said reproachfully, "I *trusted* you." Al and I were convulsed. Wouldn't you be?

Rogoff escorted her to the remaining car, keeping a firm grip on her arm. I followed and watched her safely installed in the back seat alongside a cop who offered her a stick of Juicy Fruit.

"Al," I said before he climbed behind the wheel, "may I call you tomorrow to find out what you've dragged out of the creeps?"

He finally lighted the cigar he'd been carrying. "Sure. But make it late. It'll be Sunday and things won't go fast. All the lawyers will be playing golf. Hey, it turned out to be a blast, didn't it?"

"A superblast," I assured him. "And thank you again."

"A big one!" he shouted back as he drove away. I thought at first he was referring to the recent action. Then I realized he was reminding me of my vow: "I owe you a big one." I intended to honor it.

Nerves still jangling, I decided a stop at the Pelican Club was called for. I hoped it would be a peaceable retreat where I could sit quietly at the mahogany and down a cognac or two to reduce my level of adrenaline. No such luck. The parking area was crowded and when I peeked inside I saw a boisterous mob of Saturday night revelers. Not for me; I just wasn't in the mood.

About to depart, I was stopped by the sight of the parking lot jammed with all kinds of wheels from sleek BMWs to hunky Harley

Hogs. I called police headquarters on my cellular phone, identified myself, and asked to speak to Sgt. Al Rogoff. It required many minutes and many dollars before he came on the line.

"Now what?" he demanded.

"Al, how did those louts get to Sonia's apartment and how were they going to whisk me away? Did you look around for a vehicle they may have used?"

"You think I'm a Binky?" he said indignantly. "Of course we toured the neighborhood, and found a parked white Ford Explorer registered to Ricardo Chrisling. You like?"

"Very much," I said happily. "The final nail."

He sighed. "Get real, Archy," he advised. "Try thinking like a rat. Ricardo will claim he loaned his car to a friend or it was stolen. It doesn't prove a thing. Well, maybe it's a small piece but not enough to rack him up for murder-one."

"Where will you be tonight?" I asked him.

"Right here. There is going to be an all-night, five-star production with interrogations, lawyers coming and going, endless paperwork, conferences, black coffee, and burgers."

"Sorry about that."

"Sure you are. Now go home, go to sleep, and call me never. Some of us toil and some of us spin. I toil; you spin. Good night. I hope."

He hung up and I drove slowly home, charged by what he had told me of the presence of Ricardo's van at the scene of my escapade. Al seemed to take it lightly; I thought it meaningful. I decided a muscular brandy followed by sleep might provide the answers to all my questions. Or at least supply eight hours of forgetfulness.

But my crystal ball had cracked; the night didn't turn out as I anticipated.

One never knows, do one?

33

I garaged the Miata and noted the lights were on in my father's ground-floor study. It probably meant he was sipping port and doggedly continuing his self-imposed task of reading his way through the entire oeuvre of Chas. Dickens. It pleased me that in a world of senseless greed and gratuitous violence boredom still exerted its peculiar attraction. A somnifacient, I suspect.

Hobo had roused and come to the entrance of his house when I arrived. I gave him a wave and wished him a sweet slumber. He rewarded me with a single tail thump, then lay down with his chin resting between his paws and closed his eyes. I hoped to emulate him shortly— but it was not to be.

I was upstairs preparing an injection of 80-proof plasma when my phone rang. I think I may have repeated aloud Sgt. Rogoff's querulous query: "Now what?"

"Good evening, Archy," Ricardo Chrisling said. "I hope I'm not disturbing you."

"Not at all," I made myself say.

"Something came up and I thought of you immediately. Martin, my assistant, mentioned you were interested in obtaining a rare parrot."

"True," I said. "A gift for my antiquated grandfather who's a demon collector of birds, the rarer the better." (I remembered *my* lies.)

"I've been able to locate a Spix's macaw," he went on. "I don't know if you're familiar with the species but it's an extremely uncommon Brazilian bird. Only thirty-two known to exist. Collectors would love to have one but since we're friends I thought I'd give you first chance. It's a healthy male and very attractive. Dark blue with a gray-blue head. Yellow eyes. Interested?"

"I am indeed," I said, certain the bird he described would be an endangered species.

"I should warn you it's expensive."

"No problem," I assured him.

"What I'd like to do if I may is pop over to your place, show you a color photo, and we can discuss it. Is that convenient?"

"Of course."

"Be there in about twenty minutes," he said. "I think you'll like this bird, Archy." He hung up leaving me excited by the prospect of confirming his illicit trade in parrots on the proscribed list.

Those twenty minutes gave me time to ingest a brawny slug of Presidente brandy. Thus fortified I descended to our driveway and awaited the arrival of Ricardo Chrisling. I cannot to this day believe I never doubted his story about the Spix's macaw. Which only proves,

I suppose, that although I may know the details of the Peloponnesian Wars, when it comes to more quotidian matters I am a complete dope.

He drove up in a new, dark green Cadillac DeVille, and it set an alarm bell chiming softly. The last time I had seen the car it was driven by Yvonne Chrisling. I assumed it was hers. But perhaps he borrowed it. Perhaps not. Perhaps it was his. Perhaps they shared it. At the moment I was flummoxed by an excess of perhapses and hadn't the time to sort them out.

Ricardo alighted, paused, and seemed to spend an inordinate time inspecting the premises, including the lights burning in my father's study and Hobo snoozing in the doorway of his condo. Then he came toward me with a flinty smile, hand outstretched. We shook: one hard, wrenching clasp.

"Archy," he said.

"Ricardo," I said. "I see you have new wheels."

"Not mine," he said. "My mother's."

Note the "My mother's" rather than "My stepmother's."

"Ah," I said, all my perhapses resolved—if I could believe him. "Would you care to come inside? We can have a drink and talk."

He came closer and looked at me strangely. "I tried," he said sadly. "I really tried to be your friend."

Realization arrived. It was slow in coming, I admit, but suddenly there it was: This man was my enemy and intended to harm me.

"You didn't try hard enough," I said just as sadly.

Lordy, he was fast. His hand snaked into his jacket pocket and came out with a bone handle. He pressed a button and a thin, naked blade swung out and clicked into a locked position. He moved a step closer.

Earlier in the evening I had faced a loaded revolver and was frightened. But it couldn't compare to the fear I felt at the sight of that bare, shining sliver of steel. I can't explain it. A gun can wound or kill as surely as a knife but the latter terrorizes more. Don't ask me why.

"The weapon you used to murder Hiram Gottschalk?" I asked, and my voice sounded quavery even to me.

He didn't reply. He was close enough to thrust at my midriff but not so close I wasn't able to knock his arm aside and grapple. For a moment or two we hugged, straining and swaying. Then he put a heel behind one of my knees, pushed violently, and dumped me onto the ground. He leaned over, stiletto poised, and I regretted I hadn't apologized to Consuela Garcia for any real or fancied hurt.

It was at that precise instant Hobo came charging, paws scrabbling at the gravel. He was a smallish terrier but he attacked like a fifty-pound pit bull. Marvelous, wonderful, magnificent dog! And the sounds he was making! Bloodcurdling, ferocious growls, lips drawn back, fangs showing. I do believe he was slavering in anticipation.

He launched himself upon my assailant, apparently with the intent of ripping out his throat. Ricardo gave a shrill cry of fear and stumbled back, raising his arms to protect himself. The knife fell from his grasp. I scrambled to my feet and kicked it away. I watched with satisfaction as Hobo's assault continued. Chrisling had fallen and was churning and writhing on the gravel to avoid those ravening jaws.

Finally I shouted, "Hobo! Enough!"

He stopped his attack but remained astride his recumbent victim and began barking and snarling ferociously. He sounded murderous but made no attempt to bite.

The ruckus was enough to disturb everyone within hearing distance and so it did. My father came to the back door wearing a maroon velvet smoking jacket and carrying one of his James Upshall pipes. He surveyed the scene and uttered a classic line I shall never forget.

"What is the meaning of this?" he demanded.

With a great effort of will I refrained from hysterical laughter. "Father," I said, "I have just been the victim of a knife attack by Ricardo Chrisling. May I request you call nine-one-one and ask them to send police officers as soon as possible. Also, I would appreciate it if you'd phone Sergeant Rogoff—he's presently at headquarters—and tell him what happened."

I thought my voice was steady. Papa wasn't going to outcool me.

He nodded and went back inside. His place was taken by mother clad in nightgown and robe, fluffy mules on her feet. Then came Ursi and Jamie Olson from their apartment over the garage. Jamie was carrying an iron crowbar and I had no doubt he'd use it as a lethal weapon if necessary.

I can only describe the next hour as organized confusion. Two squad cars appeared, followed soon after by Al Rogoff in his pickup. Eventually there were ten of us surrounding Ricardo, who was still lying supine on the gravel, eyes closed. His face was remarkably calm.

No one wanted to touch him. But when Rogoff arrived he hauled Chrisling unceremoniously to his feet. He was searched, handcuffed, and taken away in one of the squads. Meanwhile Hobo had been shooed back to his house and I had recited an abbreviated report of what had occurred at least three times, the last to the sergeant.

He nodded. "You'll have to dictate a statement," he told me.

"Delighted."

He had taken possession of Chrisling's snickersnee and he fiddled with it, levering the slender blade back into the bone handle and then pressing the button to watch the steel spring out and lock into striking position. It looked as skinny as an ice pick.

"Could be," he said, looking at me.

I knew what he meant. "Not could but *is*," I said firmly.

"No proof," he said. "There's got to be a thousand shivs like this in South Florida."

"Anything from Sonia?" I asked him.

"Oh yeah," he said. "She claims Ricardo hired her just to get you up to her place. She didn't know what for—she says. So where does that leave us? The two slobs are letting their lawyers talk for them. Maybe we can cut a deal, maybe not. Anyway, we've got Chrisling for assault with a deadly weapon with intent to commit murder. That's something. He'll do time."

"Not enough," I said angrily.

"You're right," Al agreed. "Not enough. It still leaves me with three open homicides. Archy, please don't call me again tonight. Your life is beginning to resemble *The Perils of Pauline*."

Finally everyone departed. The only reminder of the hullabaloo was Yvonne Chrisling's Cadillac still parked in the center of our turn-around. I looked about and there was Hobo sitting quietly outside his mini-mansion. I went over and looked down at him. He looked up at me.

"You're something you are," I said. "The smartest, spunkiest dog who ever lived." I got down on my knees, leaned close, put a palm on his head. "How can I repay you?" I asked him. "Broiled tournedos with green peppercorn sauce? No? A raw sirloin? No? How about your very own package of Pepperidge Farm Milano cookies?"

He yawned. I laughed and lightly touched my nose to his. Sickeningly sentimental? Of course it was. But I had to restrain myself from hugs and kisses. I owed him a big one, just as I owed Al Rogoff. I was becoming a habitual debtor.

But I could repay my marker to the sergeant and knew how to do it. The night's events—two escapes from an early demise—had given me the confidence of P. T. Barnum and his reliance on flimflam. I went up to my barracks and exchanged my Technicolored threads for a suit of navy tropical worsted. Definitely a somber costume. Almost funereal in fact. Exactly the impression I wished to convey.

I phoned Yvonne Chrisling. It was then shortly before midnight.

"Yvonne," I said in solemn tones, "this is Archy McNally. Please forgive me for calling at such a late hour. I hope I didn't wake you."

"Oh no," she said. "No, no. I've been reading a novel. What is it, Archy? You sound so serious."

"It concerns a serious matter. About an hour ago your stepson attempted to stab me to death."

"What?!"

I repeated my statement. I thought her shock was genuine.

She mewled. "Are you injured?"

"Fortunately not."

"Where is Ricardo now?"

"In police custody."

She sighed. "He is such a hothead; you wouldn't believe. I'll call the authorities first thing in the morning."

"I'm afraid it might be too late. You may be involved. You know what police interrogations are like."

I hoped to spook her with visions of thumbscrews and truncheon blows to the kidneys. Apparently it worked, for her voice became shaky.

"Why should I be involved?"

"Because he used your car to come to my home and assault me. The Cadillac is still parked in our driveway."

"The fool!" she cried wrathfully. "Can you bring it back here and then I'll drive you home."

"No, Yvonne, I cannot do that. The police are presently checking the registration and will want to photograph the car in position to prove it was used in the commission of a vicious crime." All pure fudge of course.

Silence. Then she wailed, "What shall I do, Archy?"

"I suggest I come over to your place now and we discuss the situation. Perhaps we can find a solution to your predicament."

"Oh yes!" she said, instantly relieved. "Come to me immediately, darling."

I hung up grinning. Zorro strikes again!

I had trouble maneuvering the Miata from the garage; Yvonne's phaeton was blocking the way. But I finally slid free and drove slowly to the Gottschalk home, slowly because I needed time to rehearse my role. And if my tardy arrival made the lady anxious, so much the better.

But she was not my first encounter with one of the dramatis personae. I parked, approached the entrance, and found Peter Gottschalk slumped on the top step. He looked up at me.

"Archy!" he said. "Just the man I wanted to see. I was going to phone you but I lost my nerve."

"It doesn't take nerve to call me, Peter," I said. "A whim will do. How are you feeling?"

"I'm getting there. I've been walking the straight and narrow. No booze, no grass. I'm taking my medication and I go twice a week to get monitored."

"Bravo!" I said. "Keep it up."

"Listen, I guess you thought I was bughouse, didn't you?"

"No, I didn't believe that," I told him. "You were seriously ill and acting irrationally."

"I've been doing a lot of heavy thinking lately," he went on, "and now I can see things clearer than I ever saw them before."

"Such as?"

"My dear sisters. They were trying to keep me wacko so they could control my share of pop's estate. Am I right?"

I knew he was but I said nothing.

"At first, when I realized what they were up to, I wanted to kill them. Then I figured they weren't important enough to kill. Just a couple of greedy bubbleheads. The best revenge is to get healthy and let them keep buying junk until they run out of funds."

"Yes," I said. "A wise decision."

"While I'm letting my hair down," he continued, putting a hand over his eyes, and I wondered if it might be to hide his weeping, "I might as well tell you it was me who slashed the photograph of my mother and father. And then I broke the phonograph record she had given him. Because I loved my mother so much, and I didn't like the way he was behaving. I know now what I did was totally goofy."

"You were ill," I consoled him. "Wild mood swings. Did you tape a mass card inside your father's closet door?"

"No, I didn't do that."

"Did you strangle the mynah?"

"Dicky? Not me. I liked that bird."

I nodded and started toward the door but he held up a hand for a final confession.

"I told you I hated my father, Archy. Maybe I did at the time. But I don't hate him now. He was just human, wasn't he? I mean he wasn't a god without sin or without weakness. None of us are."

Except *moi* of course.

"You've got it," I said. "I'm going to call you and we'll have a non-alcoholic lunch and trade X-rated jokes."

He smiled weakly, wiping his eyes. "I'd like that."

I left him there, sitting alone on the steps of what had formerly been his father's home. I hoped he was recovering from his illness, but he seemed so forlorn. His physical condition might be improving but his spirit seemed sodden. I thought I might call Dr. Gussie Pearlberg to ask if there was anything she could do to rejuvenate his *joie de vivre*.

I was grateful for our brief conversation but he had really told me little I hadn't already guessed. I knew his sisters, Julia and Judith, were willing victims of the most common of the seven deadly sins: covetousness. The avaricious twins were quite capable of posting the mass card after they learned of their father's plan to establish a foundation. And for the benefit of parrots! Horrors! He was going to give away their inheritance. It was not to be endured and he had to be warned of the danger of retribution. Stupid? Of course it was. But that's the power of greed.

Most interesting of all were Peter's comments about his father. He had slashed the photograph and shattered the phonograph record, he said, because he loved his deceased mother and didn't like the way his father was behaving. More grist for the McNally mill.

I rang the bell of the Gottschalk home—soon to be the Yvonne Chrisling home—wondering if I might qualify for a Nobel prize awarded for Unprovable Conclusions.

34

She was wearing a khaki pantsuit of military twill. I was surprised it didn't sport epaulets, a name badge, and two rows of campaign ribbons. I mean the lady was dressed in a uniform. Give her a swagger stick and she'd have made a splendid drill instructor at Sandhurst or Parris Island.

She clutched my hands. "Archy!" she exclaimed. "Sweetheart! My savior!"

A bit much wouldn't you say? I disengaged myself and gave her a sad smile. At least I hoped it was a sad smile and not a smirk, for I was in a smirky mood.

There are two things I must tell you from the outset about the conversation to follow in the disordered living room. First, we both remained standing and neither suggested things might go more smoothly if we were seated instead of confronting each other like warring gamecocks.

Second, I was aware she paused a brief instant before answering my questions. Her hesitations didn't last long, just a beat or two, but I reckoned they gave her time to consider her replies. She was too brainy to be a blurter. Every action, every speech was calculated.

"Archy, have you any idea why Ricardo attacked you?"

"Of course, Yvonne. He knew I had discovered he was dealing in endangered and smuggled parrots. Surely you knew of his criminal activities."

"I wasn't sure but I suspected. I know so little about business."

That should have earned her a hearty guffaw. She knew as little about business as she did about breathing. She was a shrewd bottom-line lady.

"He'll be fined and may serve time for parrot smuggling," I went on. "I doubt if you will be accused of involvement in that scheme. Of course it would help if you provide what corroborative evidence you can."

She was puzzled. "But when you phoned tonight you said I might be involved."

"You are," I told her. "But in a much graver matter. Dick will probably be charged with the murder of Hiram Gottschalk and possibly the slaying of Anthony Sutcliffe and Emma Gompertz."

I had used Ricardo's diminutive deliberately in hopes of eliciting a response and I won.

"Dick," she repeated with a small moue of protest. "He hates that nickname. He wants always to be called Ricardo. As for killing Hiram and those other people, it's just nonsense."

"I don't think so," I said. "You came to me not too long ago asking advice for a woman who had knowledge of a crime committed by someone close to her. The woman you described was obviously you. I urged you then to inform the authorities immediately. I now repeat my recommendation, Yvonne. Go to the police at once and make a voluntary statement. Ricardo is in custody and cannot harm you. But faced with a charge of homicide, he may hope to avoid the electric chair by cooperating with the state attorney and implicating you."

"He would never do that!" she cried.

"Wouldn't he?" I said, and we stared at each other.

"Besides," she said, and I thought I detected a note of franticness in her voice, "what proof do they have? They have no proof."

I improvised boldly. "His car was used to transport Gompertz and Sutcliffe to the Everglades where they were slain. The knife he used to attack me tonight is the same weapon he used to stab Mr. Gottschalk through the eyes." I thought my repetition of "used, used, used" would spook her and it did.

"But his motive," she said desperately. "What could possibly have been his motive? Did he think Hiram suspected his connection with parrot smuggling?"

"It may have been part of it," I conceded, "but I doubt it. Mr. Gottschalk was not a suspicious man; he was a naive man. Even more, he was a good man and could not comprehend others might be evil. No, I think Ricardo's motives were more complex."

"More complex?" she repeated. "I don't understand."

"Sure you do. Now I must say things I would prefer not to say but I must. You were intimate with Hiram Gottschalk, were you not? You shared his bed."

She accepted my pronouncement calmly. This woman never ceased to amaze me. But she had no idea of what I had in store for her.

"It is true," she said equably. "Hiram and I were intimate."

"Believe me," I said hastily, "I do not condemn you. I see nothing wrong in your comforting the waning years of a widower. But Ricardo knew what was going on and was jealous, was he not?"

"Ricardo loves me," she said simply. "And he is a very passionate boy."

"And too frequently his passion erupts in violence," I added. "He was furious about your relationship with Mr. Gottschalk—correct? He knew Hiram had eyes for you. He knew Hiram saw you naked in the bed alongside him. The vision enraged him."

She took a deep breath. "I told him he was courting disaster," she said.

"Courting disaster"? Don't you just love it! I wondered what novel she had been reading.

"There was more to it than just jealousy," I said, playing my trump card. "There was also rivalry. For at the same time you were sharing Hiram's bed you were also romping with your stepson."

She slapped my face.

I trust you will recall that was the opening line of this narrative. And now a repetition. I had to wonder if I was becoming the favorite punching bag of the female sex. An unnerving prospect.

"What a despicable thing to say!" Yvonne spat at me. "I told you Ricardo loves me and I love him. But it is an affectionate love. There has never been anything physical between us. You have no reasons for saying such a detestable thing."

No reasons? Well, perhaps no ironclad proof, but indications I found convincing.

Item: The decoration of Ricardo's apartment, which displayed a woman's influence.

Item: The diamond choker purchased by Ricardo and presumably given to Yvonne.

Item: The report in Lolly Spindrift's column of Ricardo's romantic activities being merely a blind to conceal a secret infatuation.

Item: Yvonne's new Cadillac. Who had provided the funds for that bauble?

"There is absolutely nothing sexual between Ricardo and me," she repeated sternly.

"If you say so," I said, a wishy-washy comment if ever I heard one.

I had hoped for a full confession but I was prepared for denial. "Disregarding Ricardo's motives for the moment, consider the facts as they exist. Your stepson is accused of being a murderer. He is presently under arrest and is being questioned. I told you the evidence against him is strong. You don't know what he might say in an effort to lessen his punishment. I urge you to forestall him by making your own statement to the police as soon as possible. Yvonne, save yourself!"

She gave me a look dark and hard enough to stop an attacking hyena. Then she turned from me and began stalking about the room hugging her elbows, head lowered. She was obviously considering her options. I waited patiently, knowing this was make-or-break time. Finally she stopped her pacing and came forward to face me again.

"All right," she said, her voice tense, "here is what happened. . . ."

She had left Hiram's bedroom to return to her own adjoining bedchamber. It was true she and her employer were having an affair but they slept separately. She heard sounds coming from Hiram's room: footfalls, a gasping cry. She hurried back, fearing he might be ill, perhaps suffering a heart attack.

She found her stepson, dripping knife in hand, retreating from the room, leaving behind the body of Hiram Gottschalk, his eyes bloodied.

"I was shocked," Yvonne wailed. "I didn't know what to do."

Ricardo, she claimed, was as distraught as she. He seemed totally disoriented and she was forced to take command even though she was torn between horror at what he had done and her desire to protect a stepson she loved. And so she had helped him to escape from the house. They had, in their agitated state, broken the glass of the patio door, hoping the police would think the murder had been committed by an intruder.

It was, she admitted, a foolish thing to do. Then, after Ricardo had departed, she waited perhaps thirty minutes, weeping, before she called the police and roused the household.

"And that's exactly what happened," she concluded, putting a hand on my arm. "You believe me, don't you, Archy?"

"Of course I believe you," I said. Did I? C'mon, do you take me for a dunce? The lady's story had more holes than a wedge of Emmentaler and the police would spot them as easily as I did.

How had Ricardo gained entrance to the Gottschalk home? There was no reason for him to have a key. Why hadn't the other residents—the twins, Peter, the staff—been awakened by the sounds from Hiram's bedroom Yvonne had described, as well as her conversation with Ricardo? And why hadn't she called 911 immediately in hopes of saving Hiram? How did she know he was dead? She had said nothing of examining the victim's condition.

Oh, her story was not a complete falsehood, you understand, but it was a half-truth. She had put her own spin on reality in an effort to protect herself. It was understandable but would be wasted on Sgt. Rogoff just as it had been on me.

What had actually happened? You know, don't you? Of course you do. The two of them, stepmother and stepson, lovers, were in it together. The crime had been planned. Yvonne had unlocked the front door to allow Ricardo to enter, after making certain Hiram and everyone else in the house was asleep. The murder was perpetrated noiselessly. The smashing of the patio glass was a mistake but a minor one. The killer departed as silently as he had arrived. Yvonne gave him time to get away and then called the police and went into her grief-stricken act.

Their motive? Remember the song "Money, Money" from *Cabaret?* The lyrics state "money makes de vurld go round." And so it does. With Hiram Gottschalk dead Ricardo would inherit a successful business and a convenient outlet for his nefarious activities. Yvonne would have a home of her own and the two of them would live happily ever after. Why did they need the old man?

"May I call Sergeant Al Rogoff now?" I asked her gently. "He's a friend of mine and I'm sure he'll treat you with respect."

She nodded. She wanted respect. I used her phone and eventually was put through to Rogoff.

"You again?" he said, groaning. "You promised no more calls tonight."

"Sergeant," I said formally, "I am with Yvonne Chrisling at the moment. She wishes to come to headquarters and make a voluntary statement."

He picked up on it immediately, realizing the woman was present and listening to me.

"A voluntary statement?" he repeated. "Regarding the Gottschalk homicide?"

"Correct."

"Bring her in," he said, and could not hide the exultancy in his voice. "I shall await your arrival with open arms."

I was about to say, "That's better than with bated breath," but said nothing and hung up. I gave Yvonne a small smile. "Let's go," I said.

I drove her to headquarters in my Miata. We did not speak during the trip. Rogoff and a female officer were waiting for us. Just before Yvonne exited she leaned forward to kiss my ear.

"When this is all over and I am free," she said in a sultry voice, "you and I must spend a wonderful night together. Not so, Archy darling?"

I was tempted to ask, "A down payment on a lifetime of ecstasy?" but again I bit my tongue and said only, "Of course."

Then I turned her over to the cops.

I drove home in a pensive mood, not as eager for sleep as I thought I'd be, considering the hour and the harrowing events of a tumultuous day. When I was safe in my own sanctum, slowly disrobing, I was still pondering the role I had played in bringing to justice the killer or killers of three innocent people. I wished I could have done more but I was satisfied with what had been accomplished. The final solution now rested with Sgt. Rogoff and his colleagues.

They had two prime suspects in custody and I knew how they would proceed. They would interrogate Yvonne and Ricardo separately of course, suggesting to each that her or his partner in crime was talking freely and condemning the other. "Yes, Yvonne, but he says . . ." "Yes, Ricardo, but she says . . ." The two would find their "love" shriveling away as they attempted to save themselves. The same would be true of their legal counselors, who would urge each to shift the guilt as much as possible in order to cut a more advantageous deal. Justice can be messy. But you already knew that, didn't you?

There was one final puzzle in need of a solution: Who strangled Dicky, the mynah? I thought I knew, but had no intention of mentioning it to my father or Al Rogoff. Both would think I had gone completely crackers. But I shall tell you because I hope you may be more understanding and agree, "Yes, it could have happened as you say."

I believed Ricardo killed the bird because of its repeated squawk, "Dicky did it, Dicky did it." Not only was the use of the diminutive an affront to Ricardo's amour-propre, his insistence on the use of his full first name, but "Dicky did it" was also a constant, disturbing reference to the crimes he was committing and those he planned to commit.

It was a theory but I thought it valid. Ricardo's misdeed was senseless. But we all occasionally act in a manner others may find irrational. I myself have been known to add sliced radishes to a bowl of sour cream.

35

Did I sleep in on Sunday morning? Late, later, latest! By the time I awoke, my parents and the Olsons had departed for their churches. I put together a skimpy breakfast: a couple of toasted muffins with slices of sharp Muenster and two mugs of black caffeine. Okay but dull; definitely not animating.

I was still feeling logy and decided I needed a Bloody Mary to get me up to speed. I very rarely drink anything alcoholic before noon but this, I told myself, was a special occasion. A discreet inquiry was being resolved and I deserved a small reward. But the drink didn't get my corpuscles dancing; I was still feeling feeblish when my parents returned.

I cornered my father before he could settle down with his five-pound Sunday newspaper.

"A few moments, sir?" I asked.

He nodded and led the way into his study. He was not, I could tell, in a sunshiny mood.

"What a ridiculous sermon," he said angrily. "Archy, do you really believe 'Ask, and ye shall receive . . .'?"

"It hasn't worked for me," I said, and he laughed. "Father, I want to give you a summary of the investigation into the murder of Mr. Hiram Gottschalk. I'll make it as brief as possible."

I delivered an account of everything that had occurred since my last report. I told him Yvonne and Ricardo Chrisling were presently being held by the police and I strongly suspected they were both guilty of homicide. Ricardo could certainly be convicted for his attack upon me and his involvement in the smuggling and illicit trade in endangered birds.

The pater interrupted. "Have you been able to determine if our security was invaded by the computer at Parrots Unlimited?"

"No, sir, I have not yet heard from Judd Wilkins. But I think it's now moot. I believe the police will ignore the smuggling charge and the felonious assault and go for a murder-one indictment."

He nodded. I expected him to say, "A dreadful affair," but he said, "A dreadful matter." Well, I was close.

"I shall be in touch with the authorities," he stated, "and determine how these arrests, charges, indictments, and so forth may affect the probate of Mr. Gottschalk's last will and testament. Thank you for your assistance, Archy."

He began to shuffle through his *New York Times* and I was dismissed. I went back upstairs and because I had made no golf or tennis dates for the day I set to work completing my journal record of the Gottschalk case, relieved my psittacosis was ended.

I was interrupted only once, by a phone call from Al Rogoff, and marveled he could still be awake and in such a buoyant temper.

"It's going as planned," he reported happily. "Sonia, the two punks, Yvonne, Ricardo—everyone's singing. We really need a choral director. They all want to cut deals."

"Al, do you have enough to convict?"

"I think so. Maybe no one will fry but Yvonne and Ricardo will do hard time. It'll be a while before we decide who takes the heaviest hit. The mills of the law grind slowly."

I sighed. "The correct reference is to 'the mills of God' but I'll accept hard time for those disgustful creatures."

"Yep," he said cheerily. "Me, too. Stay tuned."

Al's call should have lightened my spirits but it did not. And I knew the cause of my depression. When I was lying defenseless on the gravel, Ricardo's dirk at my throat, I did not think, Mother-of-pearl, is this the end of Archy McNally? No, what might have been my last thought was regret I had not made amends for my disagreement with Consuela Garcia, the cause of which was lost in the mists of history.

I did not gird my loins—not knowing exactly how it was done—but I dealt my ego a sharp blow to the solar plexus and summoned up the courage to phone her, unable to endure my despondency another moment.

"Hello?"

"Ms. Garcia?"

"Yes. Who is this?"

"Archibald McNally."

"I don't recognize the name," she said coldly. "What is this in reference to?"

"It is in reference to a poor, miserable wretch calling to express his most abject apologies and plead for your forgiveness."

"Plead," she said, still chilly but thawing.

"I have acted like a complete rotter," I said. And then overcome by the pleasure of confession I added, "An utter scoundrel. There is no reasonable excuse I can make for my execrable conduct. It was folly and all I can do now is ask for mercy. I know you are a kindhearted woman and I pray you will be generous enough to pardon my stupidity and give me another chance to prove my fidelity."

Short silence. Then: "Perhaps. What did you have in mind?"

"I would appreciate the opportunity of apologizing to you in person rather than over the phone. And I feel it should be a meeting à deux, not in a restaurant or at a bar. I would like to come to your apartment as soon as possible. I would also enjoy bringing sufficient provisions for a light but nourishing Sunday dinner."

"Very well," she said. "Come ahead. But I am still very cross with you, Archy."

"As you have every right to be," I assured her, and hung up, mad with delight.

I had neglected to shave that morning but I did so then. I also changed to more informal duds, including a linen shirt of alternating aqua and lavender stripes which I knew Connie admired. During these preparations I thought of playing a tape of Louis Armstrong singing, "I Can't Give You Anything but Love." Then I decided, under the circumstances, the sentiment expressed was just too hokey. So I put on Satchmo's rendition of "I've Got the World on a String." Much better.

Let's see, what else did I do in the following hour? I phoned Leroy Pettibone at the Pelican Club, hoping he would be there preparing the luncheon menu. He was present and I explained my problem: I wanted to buy five pounds of stone crabs but knew local retail fishmongers would not be open on Sunday.

"No problem, Archy," he said. "Our wholesale supplier works on Sunday getting ready for Monday deliveries. I'll give him a call and tell him to take care of you. He'll probably charge you retail price and it wouldn't hurt if you slipped him a few extra bucks."

"I'll give him an additional fin," I promised. "Perfect for a fish dealer."

"I've heard better jokes than that," Leroy said.

"Who hasn't?" I said, and he gave me the address of the supplier.

I went down to the kitchen and found Ursi Olson preparing our Sunday dinner. I told her I would not be able to join my parents and she was disappointed.

"Oh, Mr. Archy," she said, "it's a leg of lamb with fresh thyme."

"One of my favorite legs," I said, "but duty calls and I regret I cannot share the feast. But if there are any leftovers, Ursi, be sure to save them for me. I may be in dire need later tonight."

I rummaged through our pantry and found a bottle of a decent muscadet and a jar of mustard sauce. It was a commercial product and not half as good, I knew, as the homemade but it would do. I packed both wine and sauce in an insulated bag with plenty of ice cubes and was on my way.

I found the fish supplier in West Palm Beach with little trouble and walked into a wild, noisy scene of rubber-aproned workers busily unloading newly caught fish from iced cartons and cutting, scaling, gutting, slicing, filleting, and repacking portions into plastic bags stuffed with ice. I was finally able to find the bearded foreman and identified myself.

"Oh sure," he said. "Leroy's pal. You want five pounds of stone crabs—right? You want them hammered?"

"Please," I said humbly, having no idea whether or not Connie had the tools to break the heavy shells.

So he swatted the thick claws enthusiastically with a wooden mallet on a butcher-block table. Then he bundled the cracked stone crabs into a plastic bag which I added to my insulated carrier. I paid what he asked for and added what I considered a generous tip. He must have thought so too, for he winked at me.

"Have a nice crab," he said.

I wasn't certain how to interpret that but I thanked him and sped directly to Connie's condo.

She opened the door of her apartment wearing brief cutoff jeans and a T-shirt imprinted with a large crimson question mark. No smile. I thought she looked smashing. Her manner was a bit on the frosty side.

But she could not resist the stone crabs with mustard sauce and by the time we finished half the muscadet things were going smoothly, and we had almost fully regained our former mateyness. Connie is not vindictive; she is a jolly woman who'd much rather smile than frown. But she does require continual stroking.

I shall not repeat the details of our conversation that Sunday afternoon—some things are sacred. But when the wine was finished (with enough stone crabs left for a nibble later) she looked at me intently and asked, "Have you been faithful to me, Archy?"

I was tempted to quote Dowson—"I have been faithful to thee, Cynara! in my fashion"—but thought better of it. Instead I said, "I have been true-blue, Connie, and will swear to it on the Boy Scout Handbook."

She gave me a roguish smile and I reached for her.

She didn't slap my face.